W9-CCK-826

Raves for *The Fox*

"In this lively, accessible follow-up to *Inda*, Smith dares to resolve several plot lines, in defiance of fantasy sequel conventions. Smith deftly stage-manages the wide-ranging plots with brisk pacing, spare yet complex characterizations and a narrative that balances sweeping action and uneasy intimacy."
—*Publishers Weekly*

"The achievement of this writer is only getting more remarkable. Here we have nation within nation, layers of history, and a real sense that there are kingdoms and empires on several continents, with complex interactions among them, and wide variation in their cultures. Every group has its own history, its own objectives, its own grievances. And Smith handles the relationships and machinations among them so deftly that you don't realize you're being given a course in politics. Though the international politics is deftly handled, what matters most is that the personal stories are believable and compelling. In the past few months I've started reading more than a dozen fantasy novels or series; I haven't reviewed them here because they were, to put it kindly, a waste of my time, and I didn't bother finishing them. By contrast, I didn't want *The Fox* to end. I savored every paragraph and continued to live in the book for days afterward. I keep thinking that if I write a good enough review, the publisher or author will relent and let me read the next volume early. Like now. Please."
—Orson Scott Card

"Pirates and plotters fill this swashbuckling sequel to *Inda*. This is a middle novel in this series, but it's full of action, adventure and delightful, larger than life characters, and manages a sneakily sudden, uplifting twist at the end that provides a satisfying conclusion despite looming disasters."
—*Locus*

THE FOX

ALSO BY SHERWOOD SMITH:

INDA
THE FOX
KING'S SHIELD

THE FOX

SHERWOOD SMITH

PB SMI
Smith, Sherwood.
The fox /
33292011750142   PA

DAW BOOKS, INC.

DONALD A. WOLLHEIM, FOUNDER
375 Hudson Street, New York, NY 10014
ELIZABETH R. WOLLHEIM
SHEILA E. GILBERT
PUBLISHERS
http://www.dawbooks.com

Copyright © 2007 by Sherwood Smith.
All Rights Reserved.

Cover art by Matt Stawicki.

Book designed by Elizabeth Glover.

DAW Books Collector's No. 1410.

DAW Books Inc. is distributed by Penguin Group (USA).

All characters in the book are fictitious.
Any resemblance to persons living or dead is strictly coincidental.

The scanning, uploading and distribution of this book via the Internet or any
other means without the permission of the publisher is illegal, and punishable by
law. Please purchase only authorized electronic editions, and do not participate
in or encourage the electronic piracy of copyrighted materials. Your support of
the author's rights is appreciated.

First Paperback Printing, July 2008
1 2 3 4 5 6 7 8 9

DAW TRADEMARK REGISTERED
U.S. PAT. AND TM. OFF. AND FOREIGN COUNTRIES
—MARCA REGISTRADA
HECHO EN U.S.A.

PRINTED IN THE U.S.A.

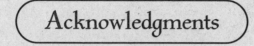

Acknowledgments

With hearty thanks to Elizabeth Bear, Beth Bernobich, Marjorie Ferguson, Danielle Monson, and with a full bow, scrape, and doff of the plumed chapeau to Hallie O'Donovan, Rachel Manija Brown, and Tamara Meatzie for efforts above and beyond. Music: Pandora.com has provided an endless soundtrack.

Last note: those who like appendices (timelines, ship terms, glossary, and historical background, etc.), you can find all these things on my Web page at http://www.sff.net/people/sherwood/inda.html.

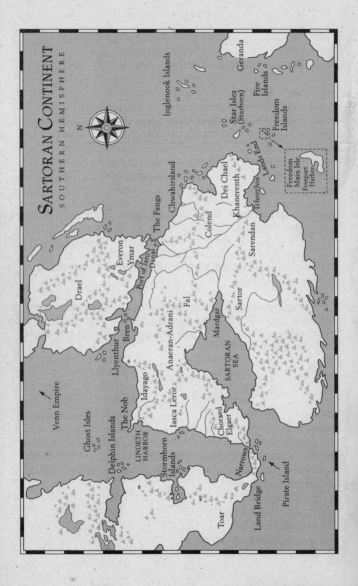

SARTORAN CONTINENT
SOUTHERN HEMISPHERE

N

Venn Empire

Ghost Isles

Delphin Islands

The Nob

Drael

Everon

Ymar

Bren

Llyenthar

Idayago

Inglenook Islands

The Fangs

Danai

Port of

Chwahirsland

Star Isles
(Starborn)

Fire
Islands

Geranda

Dei Chael

Khanerenth

Freedom
Islands

Lands End

Tchorchin

Anaeran-Adrani

Fal

Colend

LINDETH
HARBOR

Stormborn
Islands

Iasca Leror

Mardgar

Sarendan

Freedom
Main Isle

Freeport
Harbor

SARTORAN
SEA

Sartor

Choraed
Elgaer

Narrows

Toar

Land Bridge

Pirate Island

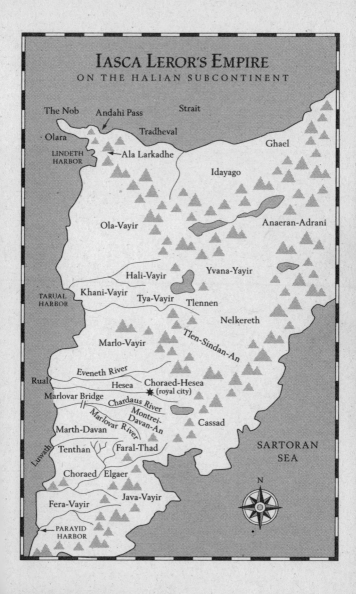

IASCA LEROR'S EMPIRE
ON THE HALIAN SUBCONTINENT

The Nob   Andahi Pass   Strait
· Olara   Tradheval
LINDETH   Ghael
HARBOR   Ala Larkadhe
                      Idayago
                                        Anaeran-Adrani
         Ola-Vayir

      Hali-Vayir   Yvana-Yayir
TARUAL   Khani-Vayir
HARBOR   Tya-Vayir   Tlennen
                                Nelkereth
         Marlo-Vayir
                      Tlen-Sindan-An

      Eveneth River
Rual   Hesea   Choraed-Hesea
Marlovar Bridge   ★ (royal city)
         Chardaus River
              Montrei-
         Marlovar River Davan-An
Marth-Davan   Cassad
   Tenthan   Faral-Thad
                                SARTORAN
   Choraed Elgaer   SEA

   Fera-Vayir   Java-Vayir
                              N
      PARAYID
      HARBOR

PART ONE

Chapter One

IN Sartorias-deles' long history, only once have we seen pirates enjoy the protection of the strongest naval power in the world. The summer of the year 3910, some of the most notorious pirates made increasingly daring raids—such as Gaffer Walic's attack on a trade convoy not two days outside of Khanerenth, which had once possessed the leading pirate-fighting navy in the southern seas.

They won after an extremely hard night of fighting, and thus were more angry than triumphant, more weary than celebrative as they transferred their (few) prisoners and what cargo hadn't been destroyed in the battle.

On Walic's flagship *Coco,* one of the prisoners woke to a crashing headache. When he moved his head, his stomach heaved and bile scalded the back of his throat. He whispered the Waste Spell, and the burn vanished.

He let out a slow, shuddering breath as sweat cooled on his forehead.

The relief lasted three heartbeats. Someone was whispering into his ear. "Wake up, wake up. Inda, listen. You have to wake up."

Marlovan! The language of home.

"Inda. You must act stupid. Gaffer will be calling for you soon. Hear me? Act stupid."

Inda opened his eyes. His headache crashed again. He could barely see. A shaft of slanting sunlight filtering through shrouds outlined in ruddy morning color the contours of sharp-cut cheekbones and jawline, a straight shoulder, an arm. Green eyes. Familiar green eyes.

"Who are you?" he mumbled through bruised lips.

"Fox."

"I know you," Inda observed. Memory images cut through the pain-haze like shards of glass: the fight on the deck of the trade ship he'd been hired to protect, surrounded by the fallen; more and more pirates swarming on board.

Those derisive green eyes—the last thing he saw before being struck unconscious with the hilt of a knife.

Struck, not killed.

And wasn't there an older memory? He could not think.

"We met at my home," Fox whispered in an urgent undervoice. "Before you started the academy. But you must not know me here. Nor use your name. Or Marlovan. Gaffer Walic came after you—you call yourself Inda Elgar, right? He wanted to sell you to the Venn. He thinks you died on the trade ship."

"Gaffer . . . ?" Inda began, but even that hurt.

"Walic. Captain. He wants more hands, but not leaders, understand? Indevan Algara-Vayir is dead. You are not from Iasca Leror. You did not lead the marine defense band."

Inda stared, in far too much pain to catch the sense of that swift run of words. "My band. Some are alive?"

"A handful. Look at me. Listen. We need you," Fox whispered, fighting impatience and desperation.

Walic would be sending someone to fetch them soon. And he was right: above on the captain's deck Walic stirred, his mood of irritation twisting inexorably into anger. He said to his first mate, "Where are my prisoners?"

Footsteps thumped on the captain's deck above; Fox put his lips to Inda's ears, forcing himself to speak distinctly. "We need you. To take this ship."

A command snapped from the gangway forced Inda's awareness outward: he'd been dumped into the waist of the pirate ship.

Fox's breath was warm on his ear. "Remember. No Marlovan or even Iascan. Just Dock Talk. And stupid."

Hands hauled him to his feet. Worms of white-hot agony shot through his arms and his bad wrist; his hands were bound behind his back.

He was pushed toward a ladder and up, the thrusting hand steadying him on the climb.

He shuffled onto the captain's deck. Sunlight struck Inda's eyes like heated needles. He closed his eyes. Mistake. He stumbled over a coiled rope. Guffaws were the first sign of trouble, a sign that the interview with the captain was meant to be entertainment.

"Well now!" Gaffer Walic's voice was a clear tenor, almost as melodic as Tau's. Had Tau survived?

The pirate captain addressed someone in an undertone. Then in Melaeri-accented Sartoran, employing the drawling accents of an aristocrat, he added, "My first mate insists we've uncovered the mastermind behind our late adversaries."

Laughter.

A woman answered in far less refined Sartoran, "No wonder we gutted 'em. Watch! He's gonna trip over the bucket!"

Inda glanced down, realized he wasn't supposed to understand, and so he forced himself to trip over the bucket. Only those long lessons in falling kept him from breaking an arm, but even so the strain when he was yanked to his feet made him bleat in pain.

The captain switched back to Dock Talk. "Well, Fox. You fetched him. What do you say?"

"Stupid as a post, but fights well. Useful as a hand."

Another voice, lower, angry, cut in. "That's the one I saw commanding the action. I know it."

Inda stood with his eyes closed; his stomach lurched.

Fox spoke again, in harsh Dock Talk but with a Marlovan precision to his consonants that chilled Inda's nerves. "He was *relayin'* orders. You was seein' him doin' it, Varodif, through yer glass. But we was seein' the tall, yellow-haired turd speakin' 'em, before he was cut down."

"Yellow-haired turd?" the captain drawled. "Might that be the Marlovan prince we made this entirely too expensive journey to find? Who cut *him* down?" His voice was light, almost sweet, which did not account for the sudden silence, so complete a silence that Inda was for the first time aware of the song of wind through sails, the whine of rope and wood, the *wash-lap-lap* of the sea against the hull.

Yellow-haired turd—the memories flitted like angry bats. Kodl, their leader (though not their commander, hard as he tried), falling. Dun the Carpenter, who had always fought shield arm position at Inda's left trying to protect Inda even with a sword stuck through his chest. Both of them had been yellow-haired.

Dizzy with pain, with guilt and sorrow, Inda opened his eyes again.

The pirates stood in a circle facing the captain, who lounged in an armchair on his deck. The sun shone behind him, a glaring halo outlining the silhouette of a short, burly man.

"I'll find out who, my children," the captain said. "We missed quite a price for him. It comes out of your share if you had a reason, and out of your skin if you were clumsy."

Again the silence, so the captain said, "Stupid will do for us, even if he don't command ships full of warriors. Put him over there with the new recruits. Let's have the next."

Inda was guided to one side, the bindings on his wrists loosened so his numb hands fell useless to his sides. Without having said a word of agreement, Inda became a pirate.

At first it seemed easy.

That changed fast.

From the forward hatchway Rig, one of the marine defense band, was brought up. His hair was matted and sticky with blood, dull red in the bright sun, his face bruised. Two fingers bent in a way that made Inda's guts heave yet again.

"We like," the captain drawled, "the young ones who can be trained, who take orders. Join or die."

Inda tensed. He could not say, *Join! There's a secret plan*— So what could he say?

"Quiet." Fox whispered. "Do. Not. Give. Us. Away."

Inda groaned, his body trembling. A finger-press at his elbow sent white lightning through him, and when he could see again, it was to meet Rig's bleak gaze, a look he would interpret and reinterpret for the rest of his life.

Rig spat on the deck. "You shit-stinking soul-eaters killed my brother—"

That was as far as he got. A pirate ripped a blade across his neck. Inda closed his eyes, but was not spared the sickening sound or the thud when Rig fell to the deck.

Walic sighed. "Why, Nizhac? He would've added splendidly to the meager number reserved for my evening's entertainment."

The pirate pointed at the wad of spit on the deck, and the captain *tsked*. "Too reckless, my friend. Silent, and I like that, but far too reckless. We would have begun by making him lick it up." Inda could see the captain's profile now. The man seemed about forty, fleshy face, hair cut close to his head, a style that looked peculiar to Inda, but was the current aristocratic fashion in Colend. He wore a long brocaded coat embroidered with gold thread that gleamed in the sun, and he sported a huge gold hoop at one ear. "Next."

Inda finally comprehended that he was not the first to join. A few steps away one of his newest recruits trembled, huge shoulders hunched, black hair hanging tangled over a face drawn in misery and shame. He'd joined to save his own life.

Pirates shoved forward three more of Inda's marine defenders. The first two did not look his way but the last stared at him, a white-lipped, narrow-eyed glare of contempt that was all the stronger because it was provoked by fear.

"Well?" the captain asked. "We have much to do. I need crew, and I need entertainment after a night of exertion. Which are you to be?"

They didn't answer. Some of the crew shifted stances, looking seaward or avoiding others' eyes; though Inda thought he was alone in shameful guilt, there were in fact other reluctant pirates who had joined just to stay alive.

"Any others?" Gaffer Walic asked.

"Four," someone called.

Gaffer sighed, waving a hand to and fro. "Bring 'em."

Guiding Thog, Uslar, and Dasta, and half carrying Mutt—who'd suffered a broken ankle in his fall off a mast—was a thin young man whose facial contours released another squealing bat of memory. That sharp chin, the defined cheekbones below a wide flat forehead, the mouth like the upper angle of a triangle revealing prominent front teeth—that rat face had to belong to a Cassad— the former ruling family of Iasca Leror! There couldn't be anyone so like them wandering the world. Inda remembered this face hovering just past Fox's shoulder just before Fox brained him.

The Cassad did not look Inda's way as he led the last of Inda's band behind the three who had refused to join the pirates.

The three the captain had been considering. All tall, muscular, and few as they were, this band of the dead Marlovans had taken far too many of his own crew. He glanced up at the fire damage, the many arrows bristling over his ship. Yes, they were good indeed. "You know you can change your mind," the captain addressed the three.

"I hate pirates," the third said, as he had when first hired by Inda and Kodl. "Fight them, yes. Join them, be damned first."

"Not before we get a night's fun out of hearing you change your mind, over and over," the captain retorted, thinking, *So much for mercy.* He twitched his gaze to small, frail-looking Thog. "Well? Join or die. I hear you're wonderful with a bow. I can use such talent."

The Chwahir girl hated pirates, that much Inda knew about her. He held his breath, waiting for the inevitable, as her black, enigmatic eyes flicked Inda's way. He saw in that glance both accusation and question, a question Inda could not answer: even if it was habit for his band to turn to him for commands, he could no longer command.

But he could beg. "Please." He shaped the word with his puffy lips, not sure if she understood, remembering that cry of hers as Tau pulled her from the wreckage of the mast, *Let me die!* He shaped the word again, *Please*, though he expected her to turn away in scorn.

All she saw was the movement of his bruised lips and the agonized squint of his eyes. Was there meaning in the way he stared at her?

Memory wheeled through her mind, distant as seabirds

against the vast sky. Her heartbeat thrummed in her temples. Pirates, loathed pirates, but not the Brotherhood—and not *them*, the ones she hated even worse than the Brotherhood. She longed to have Jeje there, to hear her sensible voice, and then she remembered Jeje saying one night, *How strange it is that we can't get our own hearts and brains to agree, so why should others agree with us? This wants Tau* (smacking her chest) *but this* (smacking her forehead) *chooses Inda.*

Thog glanced down, straight into Uslar's frightened black eyes. She knew that he, and maybe Mutt, waited for her to choose for them. They were too young, too bewildered, and Mutt too hurt, to do anything but follow her lead. She did not have the right to choose death for them.

She said to Uslar and Mutt, "For now."

"What's that?" the captain drawled. "Speak up."

Thog faced him, squaring her bony shoulders. "I won't shoot at anyone from home."

The captain gave one mirthless guffaw. "The Chwahir runt is the only one with the guts to demand conditions. I don't intend any raids on Chwahirsland anyway, platterface—that's Brotherhood cruising ground these days." He looked up at Dasta. "And you?"

Dasta had understood Inda's single word. If Inda went, there had to be a reason, and even if there weren't, it was better to be with friends. Nothing else in the world made sense anymore. Maybe with friends, life with pirates would be bearable. "I'm in," he said.

"So let's get ready for the fun," the captain said, gesturing toward those who had refused, and every one of the new pirates braced against the anguish of conscience.

But then respite appeared, a sight so unexpected, so astonishing, the newcomers stared. It was a small, round, fair-haired woman wearing what looked like a formal court gown—loops and loops of lace, ribbons, on fabulous brocade—something you never expected to see on a pirate ship. None of them knew the gown was three years out of Colendi fashion, and even in fashion would never have been worn by its dead owner outside, during the day. The jewels around the low-cut neck glittered with painful brightness.

"Coco has a new toy," she said, laughing as she swept aft through hastily deferring pirates. "Pretty-boy says Coco can have him *if* there's no torture of his mates." She pouted, then crooned, "Coco wants her pretty boy."

And there was Tau, following in her wake, clean and dressed in a new shirt and trousers, a bandage around his forehead like a headband, over which his freshly washed golden hair fell loosely, a gleaming hip-length cape fluttering gently in the breeze. The expression on his extraordinarily handsome face was tight with self-mockery.

The captain slapped his knee. "What? Traders carry their own bawdy-boys? Never knew them for merry wights. Well, then, a promise is a promise, my sweet."

A casual flick of his fingers, and three pirates turned on the three who had refused and slit their throats.

Pirates got rid of the bodies, fetched buckets, and sloshed the deck free of blood. And so, without any words of memorial, Inda's mates were gone.

"Clean these up and feed them," Captain Walic said with a weary wave of his hand at his new crew. "Put them in watches. Any extra can go over to the *Sea-King*. They need a top-hand or two. Come, Coco, let's see what your new toy can do for us." He got to his feet and strode down the deck, his crew and the newcomers all motionless around him.

Walic, the startling female, and Tau vanished into the cabin and shut the door.

The pirates turned wearily to repairing damage and restowing the taken cargo.

Inda was still gripped by Fox Montredavan-An, who stared at the captain's door, his mouth tight with distaste.

"Tau was trained in his mother's pleasure house, but he's been with us for years," Inda croaked.

Fox's eyes were a rare shade of green—not the usual hazel mixture of gray and brown and bits of spring green, but an aggressive summer green, glinting with pinpoints of light reflected off the sun-splashed water running alongside the ship. "He's a bawdy-house boy, like Coco was a bawdy-house girl," Fox retorted softly, in Iascan. "He moves like one, he sounds like one, that means he thinks like one. They sell themselves; they'll sell anything."

Inda was too exhausted, hungry, and pain-hazed to argue. Tau was alive, Tcholan, Thog, Dasta, and the two scrubs—Mutt and Uslar—were alive.

Right now that was all that mattered.

Fox's sarcastic expression changed to a narrow-eyed assessment. "Come along. Can't have you dying on your feet."

Inda obeyed, glad to be following someone from home, someone he could trust. His wounds and bruises hurt too much for him to want to talk. Peripherally he noticed things. Outside of the damage that he and his band had done, the ship was clean. Many of the pirates moving about were stiff; others had bandage-wrapped arms, legs, and heads.

Inda was pushed down onto a pile of winter sail that had been brought up to the weather deck so the hold could be restowed. He tried to listen while the pirate with the tinkling chimes braided in his hair barked words at him. But the slamming pain radiating from the lump behind his ear where Fox had struck him had increased to deafening effect.

Larboard watch . . . mizzenmast sails and cut-boom crew . . . rope repair when not tending sail or working the boom . . . front of the fighting when they fought . . . "You listenin', stupid?"

Inda made an effort to concentrate. "Yes."

It took him so long to get that word out, the second mate decided he really was stupid. All the better. He wanted no trouble on his watch. "You newcomers are expendable. If you're good, you live."

His loud laugh rang through Inda's skull.

"If you mind orders, you might even work up to a cut of the loot. Cap'n pays well when you're loyal and don't cross him." Another even louder laugh. "Cross him, and you're entertainment."

Inda closed his eyes when, at last, the harsh voice went away. A cup of soup was pushed into his hands. He drank it, then let the cup fall to his lap. Nothing mattered except one breath, in, out. Another, in, out. For a precious instant the world was content to move around him, leaving him a mote caught in meaningless motion.

It did not last.

"Come on."

He was pulled to his feet. The headache crashed, but not as resoundingly; a soft blanket dropped between him and the worst of the pain. Without surprise or curiosity he recognized the herbal tranquility of expensive green kinthus: a heavy dose.

"We'll begin with repair aloft." Fox lifted a hand toward the mizzenmast as the Cassad closed in behind them.

Inda fumbled at the shrouds. Brisk hands pulled and tugged him until the three of them sat on the masthead, the enormous gaff sail snapping in a long curve below as they began to pull arrows out of the mast.

The kinthus had muted most of the pain by now, but Inda had trouble grasping with his fingers. Not that it mattered. Nothing mattered—an effect of green kinthus, which smothered emotion as well as pain. "I didn't know pirates used kinthus," he observed, as the rat-faced Cassad dropped to his knees beside him, working at an arrow just below the masthead.

Fox uttered a short laugh at the mild inquiry in Inda's face, his heavy-lidded brown eyes. "They don't. You repair yourself, or your mate, or die. It's mine. My mother having taught me something of herbs, and a few healer spells." He spoke in Marlovan again, soothing to Inda's spirit.

"Marlovan," Inda murmured. To Fox's silent companion, "You're a Cassad."

A snort. "Montrei-Vayir. My mother was a Cassad."

Inda squinted, trying to bring into clearer focus that broad, high forehead, cheeks tapering over bones even more sharply cut than Fox's. Thin sun-bleached hair pulled back into a sailor's tail. "You're Barend," Inda said. "Aren't you? Sponge's cousin? He talked a lot about you."

"Sponge?" Fox repeated, brows aslant.

Inda was surprised. "King's second son—"

"I thought his name was Evred."

"We call him Sponge," Barend said, and Inda was again surprised; if he'd found another Marlovan, he knew he would have talked about home all the time. But apparently these two did not. Oh, right. It was Barend's royal ancestors who exiled Fox's royal ancestors. Were they friends? No matter now . . . what mattered was, "When did you see Sponge last? Was he well? Still in the academy, of course—"

"I haven't been home for, oh, three years," Barend said, chuckling under his breath. "Seems like thirty. Been even longer for Fox," Barend added, jerking a thumb toward the redhead before he reached up for another arrow.

"Yes, and you're going to tell us what happened at home," Fox said, leaning forward. "As soon as we lifted the information about a reward for 'Lord Indevan from Iasca Leror, son of the Prince of Choraed Elgaer' we saw to it Gaffer Shitbrain got the bright idea of taking you to sell to the Venn." He yanked free five arrows, one after the other, with surprising strength.

"Then we had to find you," Barend said. "That was some chase." He dumped his arrows onto Inda's lap.

"But we did," Fox said, tossing another arrow down. "And here you are. So now you talk. We still don't know what happened at home to set the Venn on the homeland."

"I don't know either." Inda tentatively felt the scabbed lump behind his ear, then let his hand drop. "Just that there's war in the north. Found out when the Venn stopped our old trader in the strait. Yapped out threats against Marlovans. We lost the trader not long after, so we started the marines."

"That's how we tracked you," Barend said. "You were getting quite a rep."

Inda shook his head slowly. "Tracked you." How many of the marines he'd trained, ate with, slept beside, fought beside, were now dead?

He pressed the heels of his hands against his eyes, as if to press away the memories, but it hurt his face, so he dropped his hands. "I haven't been home since I got sent away. When I was eleven, almost twelve."

Fox's face changed from interest to mockery as he leaned back against the mast for a moment, his long fingers absently tapping out one of the old drum tattoos against the wood. His profile was expressionless, only the narrowing of his eyes betraying his disappointment—and self-mockery.

Barend sighed, knowing that Fox was angry with himself for hoping there would be news about home. For caring.

Barend did care, and he wasn't angry at dashed hopes, just resigned. On his last visit home he'd heard about Inda's dishonor and disappearance, not from his cousin Evred, but from his own mother. Now he realized that the "dishonor" had been thorough, to be expected if his father had anything to do with it—though Barend could not imagine why it had happened. Evred had not made Inda sound like the sort of boy to earn dishonor but more like a hero from the old ballads.

Barend opened his hand toward Fox. "Anyway it was his idea. Pick a likely yellowhead and make sure he died, say that was the Marlovan 'lord' and rescue you. You made it easy, leading us to you with the Marlovan fox yip. Then we saw not one but two tow-heads near you, both of 'em good fighters." He stood up to yank out a couple more arrows.

Fox studied Inda in his filthy shirt and deck trousers, his face bruised, his sun-bleached brown hair tangled with dried blood and sweat. Inda was short, broadening through the shoulders and arms, still knobby in the awkward way of adolescents. Fox calculated rapidly as he worked two arrows free of the spanker gaff. Inda couldn't be more than sixteen.

Whistling tunelessly, he thought back to that battle to take the traders. Good fighter, and—though he'd continue to lie through his teeth, the first mate was right—Inda had also been in command. At sixteen?

Inda was also thinking about the fight, but from the other side. Underneath the soft cloud of kinthus lay the pain of sorrow—he knew that, like wounds sustained during a fight, it only hurt a little now, but later it would be terrible. "My mates," he said hoarsely. "You killed Kodl and Dun."

Fox and Barend heard the emphasis on "you." Barend looked at the arrow in his hand—probably made by one of those mates. "Didn't know they were your mates," he muttered.

Fox jerked his chin over his shoulder. "If it wasn't us, it would have been someone else. Maybe Brotherhood. How many of you would have survived that? Or," he leaned closer, eyes narrowed, "if offered the chance to join Gaffer Walic's merry crew, would they have? Would you, if I hadn't warned you?" He threw his two arrows down onto Inda's lap.

Emotion seeped up through the kinthus. "I don't know," Inda said, staring down at the arrows—the top one made by Dun. He recognized the beautiful smoothing. From the anguish his mind wailed *why?*

Before he could voice it, Fox spoke again. "You probably would have done what we did," Fox said. "Survived. And then, if you heard about someone from home, you would do anything to—" He stopped, unwilling to reveal himself by saying the words *hear about home*.

But Inda, extraordinarily sensitive despite the influence of kinthus, heard it anyway.

To Barend, things were simple: three Marlovans against the rest of the world.

Fox sensed Inda's ambivalence. Time for a deflection. "How did you manage to get a Delf to join your band, anyway? Far as I can see, the Delfin Islanders are as notorious for avoiding outsiders as they are for their clan feuds."

Barend chuckled. "I keep hearing the only time you can get Delfs to agree on one thing is when outsiders try to interfere with 'em. Then they all band together long enough to scrag you."

"Ours was on my first trader," Inda said, thinking sadly of tough, scrawny, bird-nosed Niz. "He went right along with the marine defenders idea when we lost the ship. Since we couldn't get hired in any kingdom port."

Fox flicked a glance Barend's way. "So your father must have gotten his wish—and his war."

Barend snorted, not quite a laugh. "If Iasca Leror really did conquer Idayago, then my father finally became Harskialdna instead of a mere Sierandael."

Sierandael: the Marlovan title for the peacetime Royal Shield Arm, as Harskialdna was the coveted title for wartime Shield Arm.

"Harskialdna," Barend repeated. "What he wanted. He always gets what he wants. Except for me." He grinned.

Inda drew in a slow breath. "Why is the captain called Gaffer?"

Fox sent a look of hatred down toward the deck. "Because he took a ship when he was a mid. Mutiny. You don't want to know what he did to the captain, but it involved a gaff. That's why he only wants stupid hands who can fight. He lives in fear of another mutiny. If you're seen talking to anyone by his favorites and they suspect conspiracy—and they are always looking for conspiracy—you'll get the rope's end, if not a torture party all for you. So guard your tongue waking and sleeping." Fox's teeth showed briefly. His fingers drummed faster. "Let's finish. We've got all the arrows—you can sleep while we plug up the holes. Questions?"

"How did you survive?" Inda asked. "You're not stupid."

Fox grimaced. "The pirates who attacked our warship wanted crew. I was younger than you, but I could fight. I went along to stay alive, then jumped ship when I saw a chance—" He hesitated, then jerked his chin again, a dismissive gesture. "It's a long, boring story, but I ended up on a privateer attacked by Gaffer Walic. I was in even worse shape than you, but I'd killed some dozen of them first. The first mate hammered me from behind with a sword hilt. For a couple of days I couldn't see out of one eye or hear from one ear. It took me a long time to comprehend even simple words. Walic assumed I was stupid but handy in battle, so I lived. We were part of the fleet that burned Barend's trader convoy half a year later."

"Fox recognized my handsome Cassad features," Barend said with a twisted grin.

Fox snorted. "Once you've even seen a drawing of a Cassad—or someone descended from a Cassad" —he jerked a thumb at Barend— "you can always recognize them. I lied my way onto the sorting crew under the second mate. Told Barend to be stupid."

So they wanted to hear about home. They want to band together with other Marlovans.

"How does one be stupid?" Inda's voice was fading.

"By never speaking. By being slow with words when you do have to speak. By serving as the butt of jokes, and pretending you don't realize it. By obeying Walic and the first and second mates, who are his Shield Arms, to use our own terms. And doing it without reaction." The last, uttered in soft tones of such repressed rage, of loathing, tightened the back of Inda's neck.

Fox rose abruptly, picking up the arrows from Inda's lap. Inda returned to what mattered to him most. These were Marlovans. One was Sponge's cousin; the other had been kind to him once. "You said. When you woke me. About taking the ship."

Fox's brows slanted sharply. "That's the thought that has kept me alive these past couple of years. With you, and your followers, and the best of the forced hands, maybe we can do it. There are enough forced hands who hate the Gaffer as much as we do. It's finding the time and place to get together and plan that's the trick."

Inda experienced a tectonic shift in his thoughts as pieces of his fractured worldview settled again into a semblance of a whole. These fellow Marlovans had joined to survive, not to become pirates. They wanted to band together . . . and they wanted— "To go back home," he said out loud, savoring the words. The prospect of happiness, of *meaning*. "And fight the Venn." He got slowly to his feet.

Fox's soft gust of laughter was a lightning strike to Inda's new, fragile sense of purpose, found after five long years hunting for a semblance of one.

"Fight the Venn!" Fox mocked, his sea-green eyes wide with derision. "Fight the *Venn?* We're supposed to act stupid, not *be* stupid. I want this ship for myself." He poked his bundle of arrows into Inda's chest. "And you're going to help me take it."

Chapter Two

THE scout craft *Vixen* sailed through the night, running from pirates.

Fire scorches and bristling arrows in the hull and up the single mast evidenced the ferocity of the fight from which they'd fled.

Jeje sa Jeje, steady at the tiller all night, tried at dawn to sleep. As she lay in her hammock all she saw was the uneven battle, lit at first by fire arrows and torches, then by burning ships. Her orders from Inda were to run to Khanerenth and bring back aid to the marine defenders.

Exhausted as she was, she returned to the deck. The light of day showed that they had sailed into a fog bank, which was good for hiding but not for wind or navigation. But Jeje kept the scout under full sail, watching the slackened mainsail with jaw-locked tension as the worn winter canvas— their summer sail had been ruined by arrow holes—rippled and sagged, belled then sagged again.

Rays of glaring sunlight stabbed through the fog during late afternoon.

The younger of the two Fisher brothers who made up part of her crew had given up trying to pry arrows out of the rail and mast. He had turned his attention to the sun shafts lancing below the surface of the greenish water, illuminating faces, arms, then fins. He looked into Jeje's strained face, and made a praiseworthy—though misguided—attempt to distract her by saying, "Got something to drop over the side?"

He leaned over the rail, miming an overhand throw. A sinuous flick of silvery tail, and the mer vanished below the shifting layer of light.

Jeje felt the urge to kick him overboard, then regretted it. The boys were new hires. This was their first cruise as marines—they hadn't lived with Inda and Tau for five years, ever since they were ship rats, as Jeje had.

Every reminder ripped like a splinter straight into her heart.

The youngest of her crew, Nugget, called from above, her voice like the cry of a bird. "What did you see?"

"Merfolk," the boy yelled back, pointing to the now-empty waters. "Spying on us."

"They're just mers," Nugget scoffed.

"When we were little they used to follow our fish boats. We used to drop rocks we carried special to drive them away. So they wouldn't try to drag us into the deeps."

"They're curious. Not wicked." Jeje had also spent her childhood aboard fishing boats. She kept her voice even, though it was a struggle. "My ma told me only the young ones spy on us. The older ones don't bother with air-breathers."

The boy perched on the rail, his snub nose wrinkled. "But all the songs 't home say they take you down into the deeps if they catch you."

Jeje snorted. "Most songs are a lot of dream-kiting, my granny says."

"So what's true?"

"That they get you only if you go overboard in a storm or you're thrown over by pirates or something."

"So they drown people?"

Jeje shook her head. A cross sea smacked them amidships, dashing up a cool lacework of spray into their faces. That meant another wind change. "I dunno. Nobody ever comes back to say whether they were drowned or taken down and given a tail instead of legs. Me, I don't care. Either way, you lose your life, at least the one you know."

A flicker on the edge of her vision made her blink. A

cold wash of worry snapped her upright, tension pounding in her forehead. "Look there!"

A shaft of sunlight splashed fiery white drops of liquid light over the top of the water, and this time it did not vanish, but broadened slowly. The fog gleamed in the sun as it dissipated. Jeje turned her head up to the masthead, where Nugget had perched precariously since dawn. "See anything?"

"Swirls of fog. It's almost lifting," Nugget called down. "Oh!" she added as a puff of breeze sent the vapors whorling. Thinner . . . thinner . . . another gust of wind, and—

And . . . the sea was clear.

"Nothing anywhere," Nugget shouted joyfully.

Tension released its merciless grip on Jeje's neck, but her jaw still ached and her skull rang. So no one was hiding in the fog with bow drawn, but that left Inda and the others fighting . . . *how* many pirate ships against the two last traders?

"You can come on down now, Nugget, and fix yourself some grub. Watch change!" she yelled.

The older brother popped through the single hatch and leaped onto the deck, pausing only to ruffle Nugget's tangled, butter-colored curls as she scrambled down.

"We're still under orders to fetch help. Take over, same course," Jeje said. "Keep us as taut as can be."

She waited until he'd gripped the humming tiller in its sling—the wind was picking up again, sending them shooting forward over swelling white tops—and she moved forward to where Testhy, the last of her crew, crouched in the shaded coop they jokingly called the forecastle, poring over his charts. All that was visible were his thin, habitually hunched shoulders and his rusty-tinged pale hair, usually braided neatly but now scruffy. Testhy, like Inda, was left over from their early days on the Pim trader, but he'd been in another watch and Jeje didn't know him well.

"Any idea where we are?" she asked, brushing her short dark hair out of her eyes. An image flickered in her mind—she had to look at least as scruffy as Testhy—to be followed within a heartbeat by her usual indifference to such matters.

What was far more important: nobody (except the Venn) dared ever sail more than a day, or perhaps two if you were desperate, away from any coast; navigation was by sun, chart, and landmark.

Testhy frowned over his markers. He needed the steadying influence of indisputable facts before he could trust himself to speak. "Sun's where I wanted it to be, so we're proximate, running north-northwest. If we don't spot any sail who can fix our place, we need a land sighting." He touched the detailed coastline above Lands End.

Jeje looked down at the beautiful chart, hearing Inda's voice, *I don't care if the* Vixen *is always going to be around us, I think they still need maps. Uh, charts.* He'd corrected himself fast, but not before everyone laughed. Maps! Even after five years, he slipped into landrat lingo.

Maps. Her heart constricted as she remembered that terrible fleet of pirates closing on the convoy. *Inda. Tau.* She forced the memory away and bent over the expensive chart. "Sail," she said. "Too much to hope we'll find some independent fleet that might be able to help us."

Testhy stated the obvious in his precise way: "Only ones can rise against big pirate fleets, much less Brotherhood, is the kind of fleet kings put up."

"So it'll have to be Khanerenth's royal fleet," Jeje said uneasily. She hated the thought of dealing with warships. But she was under orders.

Testhy jerked his shoulders up in his characteristic shrug. "They're spread too thin to heed much beyond their own shoreline is what I heard in Freeport Harbor."

"Maybe they'll heed us. Let's grab some rest. While we can."

The cry came from on deck. "Land ahead!"

The sun was sinking beyond the distant rough line of land, outlining it admirably for the navigator. Testhy splashed water on his face, then studied the charts. Pride warmed him when he identified the land as Khanerenth—right outside Tchorchin Harbor.

"Sail ahead! Two, no, three! Big capital ships, from the rigging—hull-down, larbo'bow!"

Nugget scampered past, light as a cat, and leaped up onto the boom to peer out. Testhy and Jeje looked at one another in grim anticipation, then Jeje moved to the tiller to take over. Right now she had the wind, so if needed, she could escape. She reached for her glass.

Sunset fire rimmed the mountains, lighting up the tips of the masts and their sails, moving in stately and precise station. Definitely warships. Pirates rarely moved in exact station.

The ships gradually took shape: first the tall masts, their layers of triangular sails, and then the outline of big navy brigantines with the Khanerenth clover-and-crown on the foresail and pennant of the flagship.

"Signal," Jeje said.

Up jerked the red flags—the worldwide signal for help.

In answer the blue flag then the white flowed up the flagship's tall foremast: the scout craft's chief to report aboard the flagship.

Testhy ducked into the cubby and reappeared, the charts rolled under his arm. "Shall we both go?"

Jeje frowned. Testhy seldom met anyone's eyes—it had been a couple of years, Jeje had realized once, before she discovered his were blue. He was just that way. But his manner was furtive as scraped his two front teeth over his chapped bottom lip.

"All right." She wished, as she had all night, that the crew rotation hadn't put her with Testhy; she longed for Rig, or Dasta, and especially for Thog, daughter of Pirog.

The mental image of Thog's round, flat Chwahir face made her heart squeeze again. She turned away, as if she could physically escape emotional pain, and that made her think of Inda, and the way he used to twitch or jerk to escape what they figured had to be bad memory.

Inda, Thog, Dasta, Rig. Tau. Taken by pirates. Or killed by pirates.

She gripped the tiller.

They guided the *Vixen* around and under the lee of the flagship, smooth as a cygnet.

The sailors on duty aboard the warship watched with interest as the crew of what looked like mostly children loosened sail on the scout. As it drew near, a susurrus of comment passed from the top hands to the deck crew at the sight of the arrow-spiked hull and the merciless scoring of burn marks.

The two who climbed swiftly aboard wore no uniform nor did they dress flash, like pirates. The taller one, a youngish fellow with rusty-pale hair, deferred to the shorter one carrying ship papers: a young woman in plain sailor's smock and summer deck trousers, her face brown, her body boyish in shape—strong shoulders, narrow hips. What kind of fight had they escaped?

Testhy and Jeje politely flicked their foreheads in salute to the captain.

"Who are you and what aid do you seek?" the captain said in Dock Talk.

Jeje hesitated, studying the tall, thin young captain. Hair worn back in a four-strand sailor's queue, a good sign: the politically appointed landsmen captains usually wore their hair in land fashions and were worthless to a man or woman, in Jeje's liberal opinion.

"Jeje sa Jeje, chief of *Vixen,* scout for our current hire, four ships out of Sarendan, Drapers Guild owners, carrying cotton-silk and other cloth goods up to Jabreis. Attacked by pirates."

Heavy brows furrowed. "Brotherhood?"

"No. But it's a big fleet. Three big raffees, one old trysail, at least six schooners, some sloops."

"Tops'l?"

"Blank."

The wind brought a mutter from one of the bowmen in the mizzen-top, "No wonder we seen no one for nigh three days."

The captain glanced over the rail at his two consorts, then at his first lieutenant, who grinned with anticipation. "Sounds very like Gaffer Walic's fleet. For that we'll need reinforcement." He scanned the darkening sky, sniffed the wind. "If we bustle we can catch the tide. Follow us into port."

Jeje and Testhy scrambled back down into the *Vixen* and
followed the navy ships into Tchorchin Harbor. Clouds
tumbled upward in the northeast, sending gusts of wind
slamming into their sails; the tide was making as well. Just
before midnight bells they glided in, the *Vixen* rating that
rarity, a mooring at the wharf, alongside the naval craft.

"You're now chief mate," Jeje said to Loos, the older of
the Fisher brothers.

Nugget waited until Jeje and Testhy reached the shore,
then helped herself to the little pile of coins kept in the
chart cubby and jumped onto the dock.

"Hey," cried the new chief. "Come back! She didn't say
liberty."

"She didn't say no, either. If anything's open I want to
find some cinnamon rolls as good as Rig's. If I do I'll get
enough for all of us," Nugget called back.

Leaving the would-be chief sighing as he thought, *So
much for command.*

Testhy and Jeje followed the first lieutenant, stumbling
with exhaustion and clumsy efforts to regain land balance.
Testhy felt as if the brick promenade leading to the harbormaster's huge, castellated building was moving with a slow
roll, and his knees had gone watery.

Jeje picked up on his tension without knowing the reason, but she was too tired to remark on it as the first spatters of a rainsquall splashed warmly on their faces.

The harbormaster was a tough old woman who reminded Jeje at once of her grandmother on the other end
of the continent. She felt her spirits lift, a relief that vanished as the questioning went on far too long. When did the
atmosphere change? She was only aware of it when the
harbormaster said, "The matter will be dealt with," and dismissed them with a cold-eyed nod.

Testhy had been watching the scribe in the far corner,
who'd signaled something to the harbormaster when Jeje
gave the names of their three marine leaders: Handar
Kodl, Fussef Niz Findl, and Inda Elgar.

Ryala Pim was here, Testhy thought as they followed a
runner to a small anteroom. *Reported us as pirates who
stole her ships, like she said she would.*

They'd scarcely sat down on the worn benches outside the harbormaster's office when, to their surprise, the first lieutenant returned with a furtive air.

He was short, fair, and looked very much younger than he had on deck—Dasta's age, or maybe even Inda's. He jerked a thumb toward the door. "Cap'n sent me to say you better hop."

"What?" Jeje gasped.

The lieutenant's Dock Talk was staccato, hard to follow, as he motioned to Jeje. He snapped open a scrolled order and flicked one finger over the seal at the bottom, which had the faint glitter of magic attesting to its being genuine: a sved. Used all over the maritime world, the term had come to mean truth. "Here's the sved on your people. *Your* name isn't in the arrest-on-sight book. She won't grab you if you hop. Two o' your marine captains and one other fellow are listed. Not the Delf. The main one is that lord."

Jeje looked from one to the other. "Lord?" she asked again, more weakly, because she didn't see question in Testhy's face, but a scowling comprehension.

The lieutenant saw it too, and said to him, "The captain said he heard about your marine band. Good rep on the seas. But you have to understand, the new king wants no trouble with the Venn. That Marlovan lord. Elgar, I think the name was? He's on the capital list for theft of three ships, alongside o' some Iascan fellow, Handar something—"

"Kodl?" Jeje squeaked.

"That was it. And some Toaran with a name that sounded like a snake's hiss."

Testhy did not offer his name.

"Charge made by a shipowner out west—"

"Ryala Pim," Testhy said in a low voice.

"That was the name! Anyway, if we were to rescue them, especially the Marlovan lord, and word got out, and it does when anything happens with those names on the capital lists, the Venn will call us treaty breakers. Nobody can stand against them, especially not us. We're trying to recover from losing half the navy a few years ago, but even back then we wouldn't have been able to stand against them."

"So what you are telling me is that because of this accusation, which is a lie, you have to call Inda and Kodl and the rest of us *pirates?*"

"Cap'n knows you aren't pirates. But not the landsmen. All they know is this Pim is a member of the Shipowners' Guild in good standing—or at least was until our own troubles here, when we had a couple years' break in the records. So we have to take her accusation seriously, and that means treat anyone whose name is on that list like a pirate, yes, until either the name goes off the list, or he's reported dead. If we catch the Marlovan lord in particular and turn him over to the Venn—he being Marlovan, and the Venn are at war with them—it means Venn aid on the seas. We need it." And, at Testhy's white-lipped glare, he added, "It's become a political decision, see?"

Jeje said numbly, "You won't go after those pirates?"

"Can't send a rescue," the lieutenant said, shaking his head. "Only a war fleet. We can't rescue pirates fighting pirates. Especially a big fleet like Gaffer Walic's. It would take most of our navy to find and fight him. Then all pirates on both sides get it." He drew his finger across his neck.

"But your captain knows we're not pirates, we're marines, on a legitimate hire."

"Except the names of your commanders are on the capital list." Voices outside in the hall caused the lieutenant to jerk around. "Look, I gotta run, and you better, too."

"Wait," Jeje said, and the young man looked back warily. "This Gaffer Walic. Does he follow Brotherhood custom? Kill ships?"

He grimaced. "Sometimes. Though word is he's been on the recruit. Building a fleet. He wants into the Brotherhood, which means he has to win a big action. That means taking on good ships and crew." He slipped out and shut the door.

"Then they might be alive. But what's all that about lords?" Jeje asked. She wanted to stomp and smash everything in sight. "That part makes no sense!"

"I'll explain, but not here," Testhy said.

Jeje nodded, heartsick and weary.

Testhy led the way into a narrow stone warren of streets.

Questions surged about in Jeje's head like flotsam on high tide, nothing reassembling into answers.

Rain, sudden and warm, shocked her into awareness of her surroundings. They passed the glowglobe-lit official buildings (many still under construction from the burnings of the last civil war) to the older shops and eateries and doss-houses used by the seagoing trade. It was so late most shops were closed up, but light emanated from a low-roofed sailors' place—the sign bore a crudely painted schooner on the side of a beer mug—at an intersection lit by hanging lanterns.

The stuffy interior smelled of brine, sweat, stale beer, and boiled cabbage, a tang too familiar in every port they'd ever visited to be noticed. Testhy, still shocked at how close he had come to being arrested—or maybe killed, or given over to the Venn—plopped into a chair at a corner table near an open window, where they could see the door and the other patrons, and where they had a second exit; so much of Inda's training had become habit. He thrust trembling fingers through his hair to his scalp, pressing hard as if to hold his head together. *And some Toaran with a name that sounded like a snake's hiss.* His breath chuffed out.

"Talk," Jeje said low-voiced, in Iascan.

Testhy had learned that language over the past five years. "Inda is a Marlovan. Son of a prince. Ryala Pim showed up at Freeport Harbor right after we were on the *Dancy,* remember? About to winter over?"

Jeje nodded. "And you didn't tell any of us?"

"Kodl ordered us not to. Said Inda didn't want anyone to know. Didn't make any difference any way I could see, so I forgot about it. Anyway, she accused us all of being pirates. Wouldn't listen, accused *us* of Leugre's mutiny! Demanded the money for her ships. Then when Inda tried talkin' sved, she spouted all that—even said his real name—and some gabble about how some other Marlovan had accused him of being a coward or killing some other boy or something, where those Marlovans do their war training when they're young. Didn't make any sense. What did make sense was the threat Ryala Pim made: she was

going to report us in every harbor. And then she disappeared—by magic token!" He snapped his fingers. "Like
that!" He scowled. "We saw her signed-sealed sved today.
She musta reported us right here, in this harbor." He
jerked his thumb down at the unswept floor.

Jeje shrugged off the existence of the capital list for a
moment. Inda?

She glared at Testhy, jaw jutted, her brown eyes so wide
he could see the whites all the way around.

"I can't believe Inda is a coward, or whatever it was
those stupid Marlovans said. It's impossible." Her voice
was already low—she sounded like one of the fellows if
you didn't see her speak—but now it was so husky she
seemed to be growling. "But I guess I'm not surprised he's
some sort of lord. He knows too much. I mean about reading and history. You hear about how princes and princesses
get armies of tutors and servants and things. But none of
that matters now. What is important is if the Khanerenth
navy did send ships, they'll kill our friends. Except Inda,
who will be a prisoner given to the Venn."

"That seems to be it."

"Based on the lies Ryala Pim told."

Testhy scratched his head again, tiredness and the flood
of giddy relief after the shock of his near escape making his
mind foggy. No one had bothered to come out of the back
room to wait on them. The few other mariners at the other
plank tables sat drinking or talking in low voices. "Seems
to me that the Venn won't care about the ships. They want
Inda. Rank. Marlovan. It would mean something if the
Venn tell the Marlovans they have him."

"That's politics, all right," Jeje said in disgust. "You know
it as well as I do; Inda's been with us since our rat days, and
he was too small to have fouled the hawses of kings and
land battles and the like. Not on his own. The whole thing
sounds like an excuse for politics of some kind, and it
makes my gut boil!"

"But that's in Iasca Leror, clear on the other side of the
world." Testhy turned up his palms. "It hasn't anything to
do with you or me here and now. Seems to me our first job
is to find a new berth somewhere. New name—at least for

me." *Snake's hiss* . . . He winced. "I don't even know where to start."

"And give them up as dead?" Jeje muttered in that low growl. "You heard what that first mate said. They could be alive. Alive, and forced to act as pirates."

Shock, relief, now anger. "He's a lieutenant. In navies they have ranks." Testhy twisted his lips. "You're still trotting behind Taumad's shadow?"

Resentment made Jeje hot. She struggled against a nasty retort. "No. I'm not. It was Inda I was thinking of. And Tau, too. Mates—they are our mates, all of them. Kodl, who's been a good first mate since we were all rats on the Pim ships—he looked out for us, always. Dasta who never wears a jacket. Dun the carpenter, too, even though he didn't talk much. And the new crew—Rig making us those cinnamon rolls as long as we don't expect him to ever be a baker for real. Thog, always quiet. Ready to work. Wumma and his carvings. Don't *you* feel like they're a–a—" She groped, fingers poking the air. Family wasn't the word. She had that at home. Lovers wasn't right either, though she'd had only one tumble with dear Yan, but that memory would stay secret and precious.

Testhy actually met her eyes for a moment, but in the way his eyelids lowered and his shoulders hitched up, Jeje understood that he didn't believe her about their being mates. Again she felt resentment flare, hotter than fire and as destructive, but she could see in his face, in his hunched posture that he expected to be attacked, and her anger cooled enough for her to say, "You don't need to know what happened to them?"

Testhy dug his fingernail into the rough board of the table. Jeje's straight black brows were quirked, furrowing her high brow—she looked hurt. She was probably the most popular of the entire band outside of Inda, yet she hadn't the least idea of it. Testhy had thought a lot about the strange phenomenon of popularity because he wasn't. People hardly noticed him; it had always been that way.

He shook his head once. "I think I know," he said to the table, so softly she almost couldn't hear him.

"But we don't. And I have to find out."

"Why? What can you do if you do find out they are alive?"

"I can try to—oh, I know it sounds stupid. Like some strut-rump trying to be a hero from a ballad, and maybe I'll end up sunk, or dead, or laughed off the docks. But I know I have to find out. And do something. It's because I know Inda would do it for me, if he'd been on the *Vixen*."

Testhy's brows rose. Then he shook his head. "Maybe for you. You all were mates. Like you said."

"You were, too," she retorted, and when she saw his lips twitch in denial, she said, "you could have been." But as she said it she realized he couldn't have, for whatever reason. She knew his likes and dislikes in food, because you can't share a wardroom without discovering that, but where he went on liberty she had no idea. She'd never thought about it before—hadn't been interested enough to ask.

So she was trying to make him a mate now because she needed one, not because she wanted him as a mate. Regret, sharp and fierce, seized her. Everything had changed, and not because of the pirate attack. Things had changed inside her head.

She said slowly, "Inda would go after you."

Testhy grimaced, then shunted one shoulder up under his ear, a sharp movement. "Maybe. But he's better at fighting. If he lives, he might survive. I wouldn't, not against pirates out at sea, not against the lawful authorities here. *Your* name isn't on that list! Makes sense to find a new berth. Get on with my life."

"No, my name isn't. I guess your way makes sense. But I don't think it's right." As she spoke, she groped mentally toward a new discovery. "I have to find help. Fast, before those navy ships do anything. And if *they* won't help because they think we're pirates, then it's to pirates I will go. Well, privateers."

Testhy sighed. "Privateers don't run rescues."

"Sure they do. If there's a reward."

Testhy stared at her, mouth turned down at the corners.

Jeje's face heated. "All right, so privateers might not help me. But just the same I'm going to sail back to Freedom Islands. Find someone there. Because I sure won't here."

That's it, she thought, *that's it. I'm not just following orders. For the first time it's me who's making the decisions.*

Testhy said, "You will never get the old life back."

Jeje clamped her teeth together. *Is that what I'm doing after all?*

They sat there staring at one another, both realizing the conversation had shifted from "we" to "you" and "I." Shared purpose had vanished like fog between the harbor-master's office and here; they both knew that when they got up from that sticky old table they would part, probably forever. And both felt enough regret to keep talking.

Testhy said, "We have good skills. We're alive. Let's stay that way. Move on." But his sky-blue gaze was again on his calloused hands.

"I have to know for sure. It's right. Even if it's not sensible."

Testhy shook his head, and would not look up.

"Fare you well, then." She got to her feet.

She half expected him to follow, out of habit if nothing else, and she hoped he would, but his fear of pirates was too strong; he watched her go, and then comforted himself by thrusting a hand into his pocket to check the little stash of coins he'd always kept by him, ever since their first cruise. He left, walking away from the docks.

While Nugget and the brothers sat aboard the *Vixen,* munching stale berry pastries that Nugget had bought from a dockside tavern before it closed, Jeje walked alone through the rain back to the dock. She was captain of her own life now; she was giving the orders. There was no pride. Or joy. Or triumph. She felt tired and heartsick and full of questions that had no answer.

Chapter Three

ON a sultry night two weeks later, far to the southeast of Choraed Elgaer, the Sierlaef—heir to the kingdom of Iasca Leror—downed more sweet wine, chilled in high mountain streams and brought down by Runners during the night. It was special wine, imported at great cost, but he drank it like water as he watched two young women dancing a slow, undulating dance completely unlike the girls' dances at home. Instead of the long robes he was used to, these girls wore tight blouses cut low, silky skirts that clung to the body, and sashes made of small bells around their hips that jingled and caught the eye in a way he liked very much. The Sierlaef saw the one with the biggest hips sending him speculative glances from heavy-lidded dark eyes, and he swallowed more wine, trying not to let anticipation heat up into urgency. There was still the after-dinner poetry to get through, and then meeting with that old bore Horseshoe Jaya-Vayir to plan the next day's patrol of the eastern mountains.

Noise from behind brought him to his feet, the wine cup crashing down to the table. The Jarl's heir looked up, puzzled. The Sierlaef frowned toward the side entrance, from where a buzz of excitement spread through the room. Everyone crowded up, staring, turning and talking to those behind, until liegemen in crimson and gold came striding in.

"Shit."

Did the Sierlaef really say that? The teenage heir exchanged a startled glance with his cousin, who would be his future Randael, or Shield Arm.

Neither understood the royal heir, and truth to tell they didn't much like him either. But he was here, seemed to want to stay, so they'd had to drop everything and entertain him for long, weary weeks of waiting for possible attack over the border.

They watched in relief as the Sierlaef began shoving his way past servants bearing more wine and food, toward—

The Harskialdna himself! The boys scrambled to their feet, the musicians paused, the dancers stopped. They could have been invisible now—everyone pushed toward the new arrivals, leaving them alone at the far end of the room. The dark-eyed one who had been hoping for a night with a prince—and the resulting favors—threw down her hand drum and marched off in disgust.

The Sierlaef's attention had shifted to the tall, dark-haired man who stood in the middle of a crowd of men, all deferential to him. His host, the Jarl of Jaya-Vayir, was finishing his formal greeting to the Sierlaef's uncle, the Harskialdna, brother to the king.

The Sierlaef pushed forward, and the men gave way. He practiced the words soundlessly first, making sure his stuttering tongue would not falter; when he reached his uncle he said, "My father sent you?"

Anderle-Harskialdna grinned his wolf grin at everyone, and his voice was too loud, too jovial, as he said, "No, no, Aldren. No alarms, I only carry his greetings on my way to the border to inspect the supply lines."

His uncle—the man who had raised him—was the only person who called him Aldren. To everyone else he wasn't even Aldren-Sierlaef, he was "the Sierlaef."

The Harskialdna still grinned as his words were whispered outward through the crowd, and they all visibly relaxed. Only the Sierlaef recognized the signs of his uncle's anger. The old fear swooped through him, followed hard by anger. He'd had time to think, waiting here these long weeks. Think about how, all the years he was growing up, his uncle had never quite told the truth, only what he wanted believed.

Surely the official Runners would be back by now, with word of Tanrid Algara-Vayir's death. The problem was they inevitably stopped in the royal city first. If so, that meant his uncle knew. And here he was, instead of the Runners.

The Sierlaef's anger cooled into apprehension, then flared again. He knew his uncle would try to interfere with his plan to make his way northwest to Choraed Elgaer, and Tenthen Castle, to claim Joret Dei now that her betrothed, Tanrid Algara-Vayir, was dead. The brat Inda was long gone. There was no one left to marry her to.

I am the future king. It is an honor for her to be chosen by me, the Sierlaef said inside his head, where there was never any stutter. *Aldren-Harvaldar, war king.* Maybe soon; his father near seventy!

The Sierlaef was smiling by the time his uncle had gotten rid of the Jarl, his Randael, their liege men, and Runners of both houses, and they stood alone in the guest chamber set with the best furniture the family had to offer.

"They're reading your father's letter about Tanrid Algara-Vayir right now, so you'd better get out your black sash for the bonfire. Your father ordered bonfires at every Jarl's house, in honor of the death of a commander appointed directly by the king." He watched the heir narrowly, and as he'd feared, the Sierlaef showed no surprise.

"What have you done?" the Harskialdna whispered.

"I?" the Sierlaef snapped, surly and defensive.

"You know what I am talking about. I arrived in the royal city after the Runners from Idayago. Brigands killed Tanrid Algara-Vayir? Who's going to believe that?"

"In Idayagan dress."

The Harskialdna brought his fist down on a hand-carved wingback chair—moved for the first time in two generations to the guest chambers in honor of the royal heir. Not that he'd noticed. He'd grown up with such items all around him.

"If your father orders an investigation, how many Idayagans will die before the truth comes out and he starts ques-

tioning your men? Who won't be able to hide under
kinthus that those brigands were in fact your hires?"

Fear returned. "R–ruh–rr—"

"Runners? My men opened all the messages sent to the
royal city, but they were not alone in that. Did you forget
Sindan? If he figures out something was suspicious, I can't
stop him from reporting to your father. And what then?"

"But Unc—" *Uncle Sindan* the Sieralef almost said,
though he hadn't thought of his father's lifelong mate as
"uncle" for years. "S–Sindan away. At Olara. Made certain."

"How could you possibly forget that he has Runners all
over, spying on everyone, reporting to him and not to me?
There is nothing whatsoever I can do about what he learns.
You *know* he pretends to defer to me, but he reports
straight to your father. Olara," the Harskialdna finished in
disgust. "Aldren, if you haven't learned it, learn it now. He's
got eyes all over the kingdom, and they are loyal only to
him."

And to Father, the Sierlaef thought. *Not to you.*

The Harskialdna sighed, then rubbed his forehead. "I
hope I never have to ride like that again. I did it to save
you. As soon as I heard about the bugle call I knew your
hand lay behind it. What possessed you to have them use
an academy call?"

Relief and triumph both flooded the Sierlaef. He crossed
his arms, grinning. "Planned that. Horn by Tanrid."

"Yes, so they assumed. And grief seems, at least so far, to
keep them from questioning why Tanrid, whose head was
always cool, would be lost enough to blow the academy
war game ride-to-shoot call."

"None of 'em know it. All dragoons. Riders. Either Sala
or Trad Varadhe castles. No academy. Except your Runner."

"Your brother knows it."

"What?"

"Your brother," the Harskialdna's eyes narrowed in
fury, "was there. He was so very much there he arrived at
the end of the attack, barely too late to save Tanrid."

"What? He–he—"

"Was supposed to be building harbor walls, yes," the

Harskialdna said with savage sarcasm. "But he tangled
with some local hustler, had a tiff, and dusted off to cry on
Tanrid's shoulder. A fellow, by the by. D'you think
Tanrid—"

The royal heir flung up a hand and cut him off. His
brother's and Tanrid's sex lives were irrelevant; even in the
extreme unlikelihood that Evred and Tanrid had discovered a sudden mutual passion, Tanrid was dead, and his
passions no longer mattered to anyone. As for the Sierlaef's brother Evred—not seen in years and whom his servants knew better than to mention—the Sierlaef still
envisioned his younger brother as the clumsy, awkward
poetry-spouter of six years ago. He knew his uncle's penchant for worming out secrets, just from curiosity if not to
use them to enforce obedience; this secret, if it even was
one, was already worthless. "Evred said?"

"He hasn't said anything. That I know. He did write off
to the Algara-Vayirs as well as your father, but I saw those
messages. Evred's letter was quite correct. The usual wine-
sauce about Tanrid's valor, plus he added some poetry in
obsolete language, probably as a sop to the women, very
much in your brother's usual style." The Harskialdna
shifted his attack. "So you intended your 'brigands' all to
die?"

The Sierlaef grinned. "Made sure. Expected reward."

"And your assassin? What's to prevent him from talking,
since he saw the reward his party got?"

The Sierlaef laughed, though he endured the familiar
twinge of regret at the necessity of killing his Runner
Vedrid, who was fast and smart. However, there was a
kingdom full of fast, smart fellows who wanted to be Runners to the future king.

King.

"Well?" the Harskialdna demanded, his harshness motivated by a wave of fear that he'd lost control, that he would
be implicated, and what the king would do.

The Sierlaef looked up, angry enough to get out what for
him was a very long speech with a minimum of stutter.
"Thought of that, too. He didn't know the plan. Different
orders. Any 'brigands' left alive, kill them. After, sent him

to Buck Marlo-Vayir. Said meet me there. Sent message,
kill him. Said he'd betrayed me."

"What?" His uncle's voice cracked. "You brought in
someone else?"

The Sierlaef felt the words piling up, and his tongue and
lips already started that hated flutter.

He glared at his uncle. That glare, once considered
sullen, had become frightening in its intensity, expressing
so many years of frustration and rage.

"Y–you. Wanted Buck. As n–next Harskialdna," the
Sierlaef whispered, because whispers sometimes damped
the stutter. He had no idea how sinister it sounded.

The Harskialdna flung out his hands. Anger, confusion,
most of all a sense of lack of control—he hated that more
than anything or anyone in a long list of hatreds—struck
him silent.

Over the years he'd driven a wedge between the heir and
Evred so that they would never ally against him. *He* was to
be the heir's guard and guide and future adviser. From the
beginning Evred had been far too smart, prone to read the
records, just like his father, and then to question. The
Harskialdna had been afraid Evred would be as difficult to
control (for the kingdom's own good) as the king had
turned out to be. The Marlo-Vayir boy had been obedient,
big, strong, handsome, and most of all unquestioning. And
the hints the Harskialdna had carefully dropped about the
possibility of his being promoted to a royal connection in
the future had bound the Marlo-Vayirs to him. But during
the past few years that bond seemed to have eroded.

But he couldn't speak of that. It admitted his own gradual loss of control.

The Sierlaef's thoughts paralleled his uncle's to an astonishing degree, but the days of free communication had
also vanished.

The Sierlaef's mind shifted swiftly from image to image:
Buck Marlo-Vayir in the good old academy days obeying
without question, glad to be one of the elite Sier Danas, the
Companions; Evred reading in two languages when his
older brother couldn't manage one; the promises his uncle
had made that had turned out not to be true.

Well, it was time to make them true. *He* was the future king, not his uncle! Buck had shown a tendency to argue these past few years, so this order concerning Vedrid would be a test. Meanwhile, why not have his own brother as Harskialdna after all? A scholarly, obedient brother who would take care of the boring logistics, like trade and army training and taxes, leaving his older brother full command of the army. That's what Harvaldar meant: *war king*.

The rightness of it helped steady his tongue. "Buck Marlo-Vayir." He enunciated each word hard and distinct. "Will do what he's told." *Or die a traitor's death.*

The Harskialdna stared in horror across the room into the heir's angry eyes and realized he was not addressing a wayward boy. The Sierlaef was a man now, a man who had his own plans, a man who could issue threats—*do what he's told*—and had the kingdom to back him.

The future king had decided he was going to be telling his uncle what to do, not the other way around.

The Sierlaef said, "Father can in–fuh–fuh . . ." He forced himself to slow down, enunciating harshly. "*Vest.* Igate. Our people. All who know are dead. Idayagans. If they die, so? Seal our hold."

The Harskialdna swallowed and then, in a fair attempt to smooth over his capitulation, asked, "So what will you do now?"

The Sierlaef grinned again, and years of pent-up resentment made that grin a nasty sight indeed. "What I want. When I want. How I want." He pointed at his uncle. "You make it happen."

"Vedrid? Executed?" Buck Marlo-Vayir repeated. He was hot and irritable in his gray coat, but an unexpected visit from the royal heir's Runner seemed to require no less.

Nallan, the Sierlaef's Runner captain, was familiar from the days when Buck and the Sierlaef and the rest of the Sier Danas became seniors, putting up their hair as academy horsetails. Nallan had been willing to clean boots and do the horsetails' stable chores on the sly—anything to earn the approval of the next king. And he'd hated any new Runners whom the royal heir liked.

Tall, blond, competent, Nallan was smirking now. He clearly loved conveying these orders from the royal heir.

"Did the Sierlaef say why?"

"Treachery," Nallan said.

"Then it will be done," Buck stated, not asking why a charge of treachery from one of the royal family didn't require a trial. It was obvious that once again the Sierlaef was sidestepping the rules for his own purposes as he'd done many times, though it had never before cost someone's life.

But he's going to be the next king.

Nallan smirked again. "I'm to stay until I see his body."

Fury flared hot and bright; however, Buck had learned during their boyhood academy days not to express anything at all around the heir or his most trusted spy. "Then take your gear down to the Runners' rooms and settle in. I'll give the necessary orders."

He waited until he'd seen Nallan cross the small courtyard to the Runners' space adjacent the barracks; then, he ran down to the arms court, where he found his younger brother Landred—renamed Cherry-Stripe his first week at the academy—busy with the arms master.

Cherry-Stripe was surprised to see Buck dressed formally—best riding boots, his gray war coat buttoned to the high collar, sashed at the waist, the long skirts gathering dust as he crossed the heat-shimmering stones. In *this* weather?

Cherry-Stripe cast a puzzled glance at his brother's tight-lipped, brow-furrowed face. Buck leaned up against a hitching post and crossed his arms, so Cherry-Stripe turned back to the waiting arms master and finished his bout.

When it was done Buck made the old academy "behind the barracks" sign with a briefly turned thumb, so Cherry-Stripe said to the arms master, "I'm going to get something to eat, and then I'll be over to look at the two-year-olds."

The man flicked his fingers to his heart and walked to the other end of the court to observe the off-patrol Riders galloping past a post and hacking at it with swords.

The brothers ran through the drifting dust to an older part of the castle, moldering and mossy, and clambered up

to their favorite perch from which they could watch, unseen, through ancient arrow slits.

"Nallan is here." Buck grimaced in disgust as he undid
the wooden buttons of his coat, eased out of it, and laid it
carefully beside him. Air ruffled over his sweat-damp shirt,
briefly cooling him, and he sighed. "Orders. From *him*.
We're to kill Vedrid on sight."

Cherry-Stripe gasped. "Vedrid? Why?"

"Treachery. Supposedly. Nallan stays until it's done. So
he wants an eyewitness. Can't imagine what Vedrid's done.
Or how to move against him. He being a friend, almost
kin."

"But Vedrid's already here."

"What?"

"Mran told me at breakfast," Cherry-Stripe explained,
referring to his betrothed, little Mran Cassad. Like all the
Cassads she was small and rat-faced. Cherry-Stripe had
grown up with her, and they were allies as well as betrothed. She always knew everything going on in and
around the castle. "Fnor told her. Sheep-house," he added
with a roll of the eyes.

Buck snorted a laugh. He'd forgotten that his own intended wife, Fnor Sindan-An, had begun a hot romance
with Vedrid during the Sierlaef's long stay a couple of
years past. Apparently time and distance hadn't diminished that romance, which wouldn't matter to him one way
or another: Fnor and he had made a pact when they
reached the age of interest that they would not sleep with
one another until they were married, so they'd have something to look forward to. Until then they expected one another to dally with whomever they liked—and get in plenty
of practice.

What was far more serious was the fact that Vedrid was
related to a goodly number of the older Marlo-Vayir armsmen and Runners; there had been several marriages between the liege folk of various Tlen clans and the
Marlo-Vayirs.

"We better go talk to him," Buck stated, picking up his
coat.

They clambered down again, from long habit splitting

off. By mutual consent they avoided their father and uncle. They knew what their father would say, as he always said. *If it's a royal order, you obey. That's the oath you swear. If it's a stupid order and there's trouble someday, at least you kept your end of the oath and the family's honor.* And Uncle Scrapper, Father's Randael—as Cherry-Stripe would one day be Buck's Randael—would silently nod.

Their father had said the same sort of thing a lot over the past ten years. Buck had come to realize Dad had not approved of the Harskialdna's old plan to replace the king's second son with him, but he'd obeyed, because it was his place to obey. Buck sensed his wily old dad was as relieved as he was that the never-explained plan had apparently been forgotten.

One brother grabbed some bread and cheese, while the other ran down to the stable to inspect the horses, saying casually that he and Cherry-Stripe wanted to take a pair out and check their paces.

No one questioned that. Buck slipped inside long enough to give his own Runner a whispered "Keep Nallan busy." Then they were off.

The abandoned shepherd's hut the young people used for assignations lay up beyond the hills that rose like sloping shoulders eastward behind the castle. The grasses were golden tipped from the summer sun and birds chirped as they rode by. Once they saw the grasses move as some animal raced northward, intent on its own affairs.

When they saw the hut, Buck gave a single academy fox yip by way of polite warning. Cherry-Stripe snickered, hoping to catch Fnor looking disheveled and silly; she had gotten frosty of late ever since his mother had taken to staying away for long periods, nursing her own mother far away.

But the two who appeared at the door were fully dressed, she in the summer over-robe and voluminous riding trousers that the women habitually wore, he in his Runner-blue coat. The wry look that Fnor sent the broth-

ers made it clear that whatever they were doing, it wasn't
in bed.

Vedrid looked sick. His face was gaunt, his pale hair
straggly.

The brothers slid off their horses, leaving them ham-
pered only by the quilted saddle pads and reined halters.
The mounts trotted downhill to the delicious grass beside
the stream. Inside, Cherry-Stripe kicked the door shut and
thumped his shoulders against it; Buck dropped onto the
weatherworn feedbox someone had put under the single
window as a makeshift table and leaned back so he could
see the pathway to the castle.

Vedrid said, "Tanrid-Laef Algara-Vayir is dead."

The other three reacted as he expected: Cherry-Stripe
startled, Buck wary, and Fnor pursing her lips, her hands in
her sleeves.

"You'll hear it through the king or the Harskialdna
soon," Vedrid went on. He looked up, his mouth long with
repressed pain. "He's dead, and I think I was part of it."

Buck said, "I got orders from Nallan to kill you. For treason."

Fnor jerked her chin up, her lips parting, but she did not
speak.

"Do it." Vedrid shook his head once, then threw his head
back, and the brothers saw the sheen of unshed tears in his
eyes. "Fnor's spent the morning trying to talk me out of
doing it for you. I'd rather it be by your hand. Then I don't
die a coward in addition to being a traitor."

"Wait. Wait." Cherry-Stripe smacked his hand against
the wooden lintel. He coughed impatiently at the dust he
raised, then demanded, "What happened?"

"What I think, or what I know?"

"Both," the brothers said together. But no one laughed.

Fnor gave Vedrid's arm a gentle tug and he sank down
onto the narrow bunk, with Fnor perched next to him, arm
thrown round his thin shoulders in silent support.

He sighed. "The Sierlaef sent me north, saying he'd discovered a plot against Tanrid-Laef and there was not
enough time to summon the men necessary to stop it. That
the assassins were sent by someone so high he dare not

write any real orders lest it touch off civil war. I thought he meant the Idayagan king, plotting against us. They can't face us in the field, so they plot. That much I had heard from the Harskialdna, so I believed it. The Sierlaef gave me what I know now were false orders, supposedly to cover me against the attention of Idayagan spies. I rode straight north, nearly killing the last three horses."

Buck grimaced and Cherry-Stripe cursed under his breath. Fnor flushed with anger. They all loved horses, sometimes more than people, and they also knew what kind of ride that had to have been.

"I arrived at the castle right before it happened—out in the woods, half a watch's ride away. I didn't know I was too late until I saw Tanrid's body brought in. I was tired, desperately so, but I did not speak to anyone because I thought myself surrounded by spies. I waited until night, sent false orders to the guards, and slit the throats of the two they did capture. Glad to do it, too. Or at least the first one. They were dressed like Idayagans, but when I'd killed the first, the second started cursing me in Marlovan! At first I thought he was dishonoring our tongue, but after he was dead it occurred to me he spoke it too well to be a foreigner."

Buck and Cherry-Stripe exchanged sour glances. Yes, this affair stank of the Sierlaef's above-the-law attitude, all right.

Vedrid gazed sightlessly at the warped wooden walls, rubbing his hands over the worn blue fabric covering his knees. "The Sierlaef told me if I was too late to prevent Tanrid-Laef's death, to come here after I'd finished the assassins and await orders. So I started down south, but slower. I had time to think. They weren't Idayagans hired by their king, not if they spoke Marlovan, so who sent them? And how did the Sierlaef know about this conspiracy anyway? Why didn't he send the army against the conspirators? He could do it and not break the treaty, not if the Idayagans had already broken it with their plot." He looked up at Buck. "If he really wanted to save Tanrid-Laef's life, why did he send only me?"

"So you think the Sierlaef was behind it?" Cherry-Stripe asked, astonished. "Why?"

"Joret Dei, of course," his brother said impatiently. "He wanted Tanrid out of the way because Joret wouldn't dally with anyone but her betrothed."

Cherry-Stripe said, "I thought that was only the hots."

"You never saw him around her."

Fnor shook her head, remembering what she'd seen during her days in the queen's training, when the heir had spied on Joret, had made any excuse to see her, talk to her, no matter how hard she tried to avoid him. "It's more of a craze," she said to Cherry-Stripe. "All the old folk used to laugh, saying how the Montrei-Vayirs were known for life-long crazes back in the old days."

Buck didn't hear her. He looked out the little window, frowning, at the western plains under the bright blue sky, his mind running ahead. "If he issued orders to kill you," he said at last, "it's to shut you up."

Vedrid lowered his head and Fnor hugged him wordlessly against her.

Buck fingered the sun-brassy ends of his long horsetail hanging over his shoulder nearly to his lap. "Treachery. Someone high up. It's all true, though not the way it's meant—just like the Sierlaef. He always bent the rules, and his uncle cheered him on the charge. When we were academy horsetails," he added in a pained voice, "it was fun. We were the kings, the masters never stopped us, the older boys never messed with us. Rules didn't matter, as long as we weren't cowards or thieves. Even the first year guards deferred to us, all on account of *him*. Ever since we got out of the academy, the Sierlaef expects us to be his Sier-Danas, but we aren't. Not even Hawkeye. We all knew he'd one day break rein and give us some crazy orders he'd expect us to obey, like when he sicced us on his brother and the rest of the scrubs. But that was only academy scrags. Now he'll do it for more serious things. It's been like . . . like saddle-galls you can't see, waiting for the next crazy order. You can feel 'em in the horse's gait. Know something's wrong, and going to get wronger."

"Even if it's wrong, he's given you a direct order," Cherry-Stripe pointed out. "You know what Father and Uncle Scrapper would say."

Vedrid stood up, his hands opening and closing. "If it must be done, I'd rather it be by your hand."

Fnor and Cherry-Stripe turned to Buck, tall, strong, handsome, his hair pulled up on the back of his head, making him look older, as the boys all looked once they gained the right to wear horsetails.

He was not used to this kind of thinking. To carry out the heir's direct order was his duty, and also his right, as future Jarl. As the future Harskialdna? No, he no longer believed that would happen—nor did he want it to.

He said, slowly, "I won't do it."

Cherry-Stripe sighed in relief, and though Fnor smiled, she said softly, "But he sent Vedrid *here*. Why not have Nallan shadow him and do it up north?"

Cherry-Stripe pointed a finger at his brother. "Good question. And I think I know the answer. Because of that crazy business about making you Harskialdna over Sponge—uh, Evred." Though they all still called one another by their academy nicknames, somehow the king's second son had lost his.

"I don't think the Sierlaef wants me anymore, not really," Buck muttered. "Hasn't talked to me or sent a Runner in a couple of years."

"Aldren," Fnor began.

Buck grimaced. "Don't call me that!" He hated sharing a birth name with the Sierlaef. But she only did it when she wanted his undivided attention.

"Then you better think," Fnor said, her expression grim. "Does he want you or doesn't he? I know you don't want it, but if he doesn't either . . ."

Buck smacked his hands on his thighs. "It's a test. And what if I don't do it?"

"Up against the wall," Cherry-Stripe said, and then made a horrible face. "No. Worse."

Fnor added, "If he doesn't order you arrested for treachery, you know the Harskialdna will."

Cherry-Stripe's insides cramped with anger and apprehension. He sucked in a slow breath. "So Nallan has to see a body. *His* body. And won't he gloat, too, if he thinks you're gonna be flogged to death as a traitor!"

Buck smacked his hand against the lintel. "He won't if Vedrid never gets here." He turned to the runner. "Where's your horse?"

"Up in the hills back behind."

"Who else at the castle knows you're here?"

"Just Mran. I reached here last night, was too tired to ride farther." Vedrid tipped his head back toward the bed stuffed with old armor-quilting that had shaped the imprint of many young bodies. "Spent the night, and was about to go down to the castle when I saw Mran out running the pups. I think she suspected something was wrong from my manner."

Fnor nodded, smiling briefly. Mran would. She was observant, even for a Cassad, and they were all smart.

Vedrid went on, "She offered to get Fnor, and I didn't want to face your father yet, or rather face his questions, so—" He lifted his hands.

"Good. Perfect," Buck said. He'd been thinking rapidly while Vedrid told his story. "Mran won't make a peep. See, everything's bad if you're here. So it seems to me our way out is if you never *got* here!"

"That's right," Cherry-Stripe said. Then frowned. "So where is he?"

"Ambushed," Fnor said, eyes narrowed.

Buck grinned. "Right. You find your horse, ride back north, and fake an ambush."

"Fake?" Vedrid frowned, perplexed.

"You take off your blues." A finger indicated the Runner's coat with the silver crown over the heart. "Hack it up with your knife. Bleed on it." A slice of a finger across the inner wrist. "Leave it on a Runner road. They'll think you were left dead and either someone else did the old Disappear Spell or wolves ate you."

The Runners had their own paths, cutting short the more general roads that often circled wide, following old land borders.

"And?"

"Then it's up to you. You could vanish, begin another life. We will never snitch," Buck said.

"Or you could find Sponge—ah, Evred. Tell him what happened," Cherry-Stripe suggested.

The lines of torment in Vedrid's face smoothed a little.

Cherry-Stripe rubbed his hands, then put into words the shift of allegiance that would satisfy Vedrid's own honor. "You're dead to the Sierlaef, since he ordered your death himself. Swear a new oath to Evred-Varlaef. Become his man."

Fnor added, "He will need you."

Chapter Four

COCO looked down at Taumad's sleeping profile, bitter-sweet anguish hollowing her heart. Oh, how *beautiful* he was!

She resisted temptation long enough to enjoy the rare sensation, then reached with her forefinger, tracing the high arch of his brows down around his eye, brushing her fingertip along the extravagant curve of his lashes, then down to his lips—severe even in sleep—to his splendid chin and then around his ear to his hair, spread on the pillow. She ruffled her fingers through it, so like combed and shining golden corn silk, warm near his head, cool on the pillow. She would not permit him to braid it.

His eyes opened, clear, appraising, gold as clover honey in the morning light shafting through the stern windows. Gold, real gold, not mere light brown: those flecks of yellow were the luster of sun through honey—or golden coins in candlelight.

"Your wish?" he asked, his voice slightly husky.

She'd had him to herself ever since Walic left to supervise the new attack, but desire kindled again, as if it had been months, and not a watch-bell since their last tangle. "Ooh, my pretty-pretty-pretty," she crooned, running her hands down his smooth, muscled flesh to ruffle the golden hair on his chest.

His breathing stayed steady, his hands still.

He was ready. It was a matter of will, if you knew the way of it. She, who had been trained in the ways of pleasure since sixteen, had recognized another with the same training, and for the first month it had been wonderful to possess this beautiful young man who knew almost as much as she did about what could be done in bed, and for how long . . . but.

She stared down into the waiting face, her thoughts fluttering as helplessly as a moth pinned down by knife points.

She wanted—no, needed—to see him want her as much as she wanted him. How strange! Everyone on the ship wanted her. Gaffer Walic had wanted her so desperately he had offered her anything she asked, anything at all, if she'd leave the House of Spring and come aboard his ship.

She'd had Walic kill hands who didn't show instant obedience or respect—kill them slowly, so she could watch them beg. Taumad showed those things instantly, with the same readiness she'd shown when she was a worker at the House of Spring and not queen of a pirate fleet.

If she commanded him he would beg and plead, but it would be the lessoned scenarios of the pleasure house with no emotion behind it. "I could kill you," she said, to see if he would show fear.

He didn't. He smiled, that glorious sardonic smile with the deep dimples shadowing his enticing mouth. "Then do it."

"You really want to die?"

A shrug. "Someday I have to. Why not by a pretty hand?"

The thought of a knife in her hand, that beautiful skin marred, smote her with deliciously piquant torment. Someday soon he would surely reach for her first, but until then she could possess him whenever she wished. She covered his skin instead with soft kisses and flicks of the tongue. It was time to exert her own skills, to try to please instead of being pleased. That, too, was new and enticing; could she make him lose control?

Tau sensed the change in her mood and spun it out, almost too long, until he saw she was on the edge of anger; he shifted to the attack and sent her into a swoon of bliss.

Sated at last, she flung herself across his chest. He waited until she had slid into boneless slumber, then arose and moved soundlessly into the adjacent chamber. The ship was reasonably steady. He unlatched the carved wooden lid to the captain's fantastically expensive bath, kept clean by magic, the water refreshingly cool. He bathed long enough to rid himself of her favorite scent. Then he dressed, leaving his wet hair hanging down his back, and ran down to the galley, ignoring the stares of resentment—or lust—or a combination of the two.

Uslar was helping the cook with one of his complicated sauces. Captain Walic's food was quite good, the supply maintained by the endless prizes the pirates had been taking; Tau had heard Walic gloat over how long it had been since they'd had to plan a shore raid. Because, of course, Walic never paid for anything: that was one of the first rules of the Brotherhood.

When Uslar saw Tau he reached beneath the prep table and brought out a cloth-wrapped loaf. He handed it to Tau, his dark eyes pained.

Something had happened. Again.

Tau said quietly, "Inda eating? Or was he part of the boarding crew?"

Uslar flicked a glance upward toward the weather deck.

Tau took the food: enough for two. He climbed to the deck, staying out of the way of the hands, and squinted out through the glaring haze rising off the greenish sea. The prize was a long, elegant private two-master, the wood embellished with carving and fresh gilt glinting in the sun; beyond it one of *Coco*'s consorts was a shadowy silhouette, bracketing the capture, aboard whom the crew still fought. Faint cries carried over the water, and the clash of steel. Pale orange flames licked at the great triangle of the mainsail, now hanging uselessly, as a pump crew of pirates aimed a hose upward. Tau tried to pick Inda out of the busy figures aboard, but the glare was too bright, the haze too thick to make out individuals.

A roar of triumph: surrender. Either that or all the defenders were dead. Tau winced, wondering how many more lives had been snuffed from this world's sunlight. He wondered if their ghosts would walk on the Ghost Isles, and if so, how they got there.

Leaving their bodies to be vanished, and their presence as memories in the minds of the living. Tau still grieved over the deaths of those he'd known, shared meals and jokes with, fought side by side against pirates with, against wind and weather with. He strove to imagine Kodl, Niz, Yan, even old Scalis, all drifting along some mysterious island, their forms somewhere between flame and smoke, but the idea of them wandering as ghosts hurt worse. Surely there was no pleasure in the existence of a ghost—no wine, no talk, not even the warmth of a touch.

The regret was not his alone. All the former marine defenders felt it: Thog the least, Inda the most.

Self-loathing had come to grip Inda so strongly that his nights had become a torment of dreams in which the dead lived and fought again, and he was helpless to save them. *I want this ship for myself. And you will help me take it.*

His own survival had become a matter of indifference.

Three times now he'd been sent to the forefront of an attack and each time he'd meant to escape the bitter despair by standing open to a defender's steel. But his defenses were too good for that, too quick, far too habitual. He discovered with no joy or even curiosity that instinct seemed to prod him right before a sneak attack. He'd whip around and there was always a weapon raised, instinct bringing his arm up to meet the attack.

He could control himself well enough not to return any death blows. Because he fought to defend, and not to win, he gave in to the old habit of watching everything around him. He noted who fought to kill because they loved to kill and who fought out of fear, who wanted to live.

Then, no matter how hard he worked, how tired he was, sleep brought those dreams. Not only the dead marines walked through them, but the boys from the academy before he was disgraced and exiled.

Clash, clang! His body responded with the ease of years of drill though his mind was locked inside his skull, living again Dogpiss Noth's death—seeing his hand, dirty under the nails, freckled across the wrist, fingers tense and spread, and Inda reaching, reaching, touching his wrist. But Dogpiss fell away and lay there in the stream, his open eyes reflecting the stars overhead—

"Hold! Sloop's ours," the second mate bawled out in his huge voice, and Inda flung down his sword, his breath whooping, his once-broken wrist throbbing.

Someone thumped his back. "Captain's barge, Stupid."

Of course he wouldn't be part of a prize crew. Walic only permitted new pirates to serve on prize crews one at a time, and never with the mates with whom they came aboard.

He dropped into the barge heaving on the swells and took up an oar, ignoring his swollen wrist except to wish he'd put on a wrist guard—Walic had plenty of gear in the hold, taken off other ships. But Inda had only gotten clothing to replace his ripped, bloodstained clothes. He hadn't taken a wrist guard because he'd intended to die.

Walic glanced over into his exhaustion-dulled face and smiled to himself. *He's good. Fast, strong, skilled. But doesn't take any initiative. The perfect hand. Too perfect. If he lives through a few more battles, we'll test his loyalty a little.* Walic chuckled, mentally tolling the new recruits, wondering who would provide the most entertaining display under his knife and hot iron.

But that brought back the old grievance. Walic stirred with impatience when he thought of the loss of that boy's commanders. If someone as dull-witted as Stupid was so good with steel, his Marlovan commander must have been beyond human excellence. Subsequent questioning had proved that it had taken two full attack groups to bring down the handful of defenders around Stupid—and half of those had been killed. No one at fault, from what he could discover. It had been the hottest fight they'd had in a couple of years, and he'd lost far more hands than he'd taken— though the death toll of the enemy had been correspondingly high.

What he could have done with someone like that if the Venn had refused to give him what he would have demanded as the cost of his prize!

Ah, his plans. Those were more satisfying to think about.

Walic glanced with tired contentment at his new sloop as the oars dipped and pulled, dipped and pulled. Quite a fleet he was building. Now all he needed was another capital ship or two, the recruits to crew them, and he'd be strong enough to make his bid to join the Brotherhood.

He climbed aboard *Coco,* saw that everything was as it ought to be, then stumped down to his cabin for some rest.

The rest of the crew clambered up after him, Inda one of the last. He turned to help boom the boat up and secure it. When he was dismissed, there was Tau, holding food.

"You haven't eaten," Tau observed, speaking as they were alone, everyone busy with tasks.

Inda didn't ask how he knew that. Nor did he argue. He took the braised fish-and-cheese-stuffed bread and bit into it without thought or pleasure, though he was hungry.

"Get hurt?" Tau asked, aware of the Marlovan redhead watching from above. Tau didn't have to see the contempt on the fellow's face—he could feel it, a matter of indifference to him: the only interest he took in either Fox or Rat was how they'd managed to hide their origins from the captain, who was not unobservant. Maybe he didn't hear accents. The two talked in an abrupt, almost comically harsh Dock Talk that might confuse someone not familiar with the tongues of the Iascan coast.

While Tau mulled this over, Inda forced down a few more bites. He glanced furtively around—so did Tau—then Inda said, "Thog and the others are making a set of red sails."

"So?"

Inda looked into Tau's face, saw only question. "That means the captain wants to be invited into the Brotherhood."

"That's a surprise?"

"You knew?"

Tau lifted a shoulder. "First night. One of what my ma calls unpleasantries of the pillow that he revealed."

Inda grimaced, stole a look at Tau's golden eyes, and then asked, "They say he . . . watches. Is that true?"

Tau smiled. "The first sign of human interest in you in two months. You are alive after all!"

"Huh?" Inda blushed, looking very young, despite his scars. "Never mind. Sorry."

Tau laughed without sound. "It's no matter to me. You spend years naked in a pleasure house, just living. What my ma used to call the symbolic boundaries between us that clothing represents become meaningless, the clothing a costume for players. Sex is a commodity you choose to sell or to trade. It can be a game, it's nearly always a drama, or it's a competition between wills—but always, always a commodity. That's why I wanted to leave, and why it's so ironic that I ended up doing it anyway, and for no pay, just the price of my life." *Of your life, too, had you known it,* he thought, but now was not the time to tell Inda that—if ever.

Inda looked up, his brown eyes sober, and even direct, like his old gaze. "I know you did whatever you did to buy our lives."

Tau only pursed his lips, but inside he felt unsettled as he had in the old days, when Inda, probably five years younger, would offer some remark that made it clear he was as observant as Tau was: observant, emotionally as distant as the seabirds overhead, yet not unconcerned.

"I'm glad you can bear it. Him watching," Inda said, looking away.

Tau remembered how recent Inda's own introduction to sex was, but he didn't smile. Just saw that everyone was busy, and no one cared about a conversation between Stupid and Coco's new pet. "I don't know what Walic's habits were before. But he wears a heavy scar down there. Coco was the only one who could bring him up, and it involves, oh, call it watching a seduction using both pain and pleasure."

Inda looked down at his half-eaten sandwich. "You don't have to tell me anything."

"Inda, why don't you eat? Why try to get yourself killed?"

A flickering look, and then away. Inda would not meet his eyes. "Brotherhood," Inda mumbled. "He wants to join the Brotherhood. I've betrayed Thog."

"How is that possible?" Tau asked, forcing his voice to stay low. "Nothing here is your doing. *Nothing*."

"But I haven't done anything to free us, either."

"You will," Tau whispered, leaning closer. "Or I will. Or maybe it will be Thog. We *will* escape this recruiting ground for Norsunder; it's the one thought that keeps me sane."

Inda's color changed, but he didn't speak, and Tau, who thought he'd gained insight into Inda's despair, realized that he'd only penetrated a single layer. More lay underneath—probably having to do with that mystery back in Iasca Leror that Ryala Pim had flung in his teeth, whatever it was that had brought Inda to the Pim ships in the first place.

Tau sensed a shadow at the edge of his field of vision and leaned against the rail. In Dock Talk, "So the prices of the pleasure houses along the north coast are for the toffs. But you get more sex games to choose from. Now, in the south coast—"

Inda's face slackened a heartbeat before a heavy hand smacked his shoulder.

"Talkin' sex, eh?" It was the second mate, who usually had the night watch. He was a big man, a golden hoop of a ship kill at one ear. His long braided hair was decorated with little golden chimes. "You're not so stupid after all, Stupid, goin' to the one that knows."

Inda looked up, his mouth open.

"But it'll be a long cruise before you get on land, or any pay to spend on sex." Haw, haw, and two laughers joined in from behind. Tau felt relieved, then angry at himself. Being up all night was no excuse for not staying alert.

"Uh?" Inda asked, right on cue.

The second mate thought derisively, *This* rockhead was a commander? "It's your snore-watch, Stupid, which you better get. You'll be replacing the standing rigging on the sloop tomorrow, and you better not be asleep at the job." He swaggered away, the chimes in his swinging braids tinkling sweetly.

Inda slouched below. The crew quarters were empty, as

often happened directly after a battle. Walic did not like idle crew. The first mate had taken a party to repair and sail the prize, leaving the low forepeak crew quarters empty. Inda whirled into the modified knife drill that he and Dun had developed out of the precise drills used by the women in the knife style they called Odni back home. Not that he had his knives. Those had been taken before he woke on this soul-sucking ship; he had no idea who had them.

His mind cut free, remembering Dun, a coastal Iascan coming aboard as a carpenter's mate—just happened to know some fighting—boarder-repel drills on the *Pim Ryala* trader—blond like Marlovans but taller than they usually were—who was he really?—last fight, he seemed not only skilled, he fought like the king's Runners at home—defensive fighting—offensive fighting—women kept Odni a secret—

Hadand, his sister, saying *We have to be able to strike once*—the long drills up behind the pleasure house at Freedom Island—Dun never speaking—refinements—dead, dead.

Kodl dead. Like Dogpiss.

As he had since he was eleven years old, when the pain was too great, he shoved it all away, behind the mental wall between the past and the present. A wall that needed to be stronger and higher, to keep grief and pain inside, where it couldn't escape.

Finished, he wiped his face on his sleeve and dropped into his bunk, staring up at the bulkheads, fighting sleep—imagining that wall going up, stone by stone, to hold as long as possible against the invading dreams.

Tau leaned tiredly on the rail, considering Inda's words—those said and those unsaid. He had no duties outside of pleasing the captain's favorite—and the captain—but he had no place to sleep other than in the captain's cabin, either in the bed or on the deck as Walic and Coco chose. The

thought of going down below where those two lay in
summer-sweaty sleep was repellent; they'd demand his attention soon enough if nothing else was going on.

He beat impatiently at his hair, already dry, and tangling
in his elbows, the rigging, and whatever else it could catch
in as it was played with by the wind. He hated wearing it
down. It was a nuisance—no. Concentrate. He'd worn it
down before and thought nothing of it.

The hatred was because it was a constant reminder of
Coco.

He drifted along the rail, watching everyone for a
chance to slip down below unnoticed.

The lookout overhead cried, "Sail ho!"

Out came the glasses, crew at sail and rope, until the
lookout shouted down to the deck, "Black leaf fores'l!"

"That'll be Eflis o' the *Sable,*" someone observed.

"She's dipping sail!"

Comment whisked round the ship: that meant news. Tau
sighed, knowing his duty, and ran back to the cabin as the
captain bellowed, "Reduce sail."

Pirate etiquette, such as it was, mandated that the captain of the smaller ship or fleet came aboard the larger; the
Sable had more ships, but her fleet was mostly fast, small
schooners. Walic had three capital ships—he signaled the
invitation and *Sable* signaled back an acceptance. Either
his captain acknowledged Walic's superior strength or she
had news that she was eager to impart.

When the tall, fair-haired young captain of the *Sable*
swaggered on deck, Tau was in his place, kneeling beside
the pillows in the cabin, fresh coffee in a silver urn. He was
shirtless, his brown skin covered only by his golden cloak
of hair, because Coco liked him to be so. The stunned, hungry first glance of the visiting captain made it clear that she
had originated in lands north of the strait where men as
well as women hid their nipples.

Coco gloated. Sex was not only her skill, but her weapon.

"What news?" Walic asked.

Eflis glanced once more at Tau, then turned her attention away. So Coco had managed to find some queen's lap-

dog. And was brandishing him for some typically twisty reason.

"Ramis One-Eye," she said. "Took out Chaul of the *Wid-owmaker*'s entire fleet, three to six."

Everybody considered that: three ships to six. And those six no mere privateer or haphazard pirates: they were Brotherhood of Blood—victorious in vicious fights.

The stories about Ramis were strange. Threatening even to pirates. He was called a pirate yet so far no one had talked of raids on harbors or navies or traders—always on other pirates. No one knew to whom he owed allegiance.

And there were worse rumors.

Walic drank to hide the thrill of fear that tightened his guts, lowered his cup, and grunted. "*You* saw it? Or is that the usual bloat of fourthhand news?"

"I saw the hulks burning on the horizon. A half day more and we woulda been in it," she replied. "Just off the north end of Chwahirsland."

Walic smirked. As did everyone who wanted to be invited into the Brotherhood fleet, he obsessively learned the names and stations of all the Brotherhood command groups. "That breaks up the last of the eastern arm, then."

Eflis smiled, her light blue eyes quite aware. "It opens a hole in the fleet, you mean."

Walic laughed at the idea that Eflis thought herself competition for him. It was possible she could beat him out, if she managed to pull off a successful raid on a harbor and take the town or defeat a big royal convoy. But she wouldn't, even if her fleet was larger than his. The only capital ships she showed any interest in were Khanerenth navy—and they traveled in packs too large for her ragtag fleet of small craft to attack successfully.

"They say the captains were thrust into Nightland, right on the *Knife*'s deck, before all eyes. Emis Chaul first."

Nightland. The child's euphemism for Norsunder.

Coco snorted. "Did *you* see that?"

"No. But I believe it." Eflis glanced Tau's way again as he knelt at the side of Coco's chair, clad only in cotton trousers, his head bent, his attention on stirring cream and spice into the coffee as Coco ran her fingers through his hair. She hoped Coco would give her a tumble with that beautiful creature, and cast a look Coco's way to see her smirking as she braided a silver chime into those golden locks. He was there for display, then. A power gesture. Eflis snorted softly.

"Why?" Walic asked, not showing how much the idea bothered him. Oh, he knew Norsunder existed, and if you wanted to live forever, you eventually sought it out and bargained—from a strong position.

The stories about those from Norsunder coming after you were rarer, and those stories that always seemed to include soul-eaters. But they were just stories, from centuries ago. It didn't happen *now;* it was all talk.

Coco's thoughts were sailing down a similar wind, he could see. She tinkled a chime on her palm. "Some baby-tender 'saw' it, no doubt. We all heard it often enough when we were little: 'If you're bad, Norsunder will take you and eat your soul.' Except it never actually happens."

Eflis had meant to bargain with firsthand information from witnesses. As she sat there drinking their coffee she decided that she could never stomach Walic lording over her, or even worse, that stupid bawdy-house rat.

So she shrugged. "That's what they said."

Walic laughed, relaxing. Nothing firsthand. There were no real soul-eaters. Death he could deal out and meant to avoid for himself. Some mysterious and inhuman Lord of Norsunder obliterating you from existence and savoring your anguish as your mind disintegrated, now that was terrifying.

But of course it wasn't real.

So he laughed, and prompted Eflis for more gossip—what prizes she'd taken, what harbors she'd visited, and what was said there. Finally he edged up to what he really wanted to know: "Is Boruin now in charge of the entire east, then?"

Eflis shrugged. "I saw her once, at the Fangs. No signal. We hauled off."

Unless Boruin signaled that she wanted to talk, you stayed out of her way.

"Everyone says she's now got the entire east, at least

while Marshig is out west raiding the land of the flying horses."

Coco paused in braiding more of the second mate's chimes into Tau's hair. She wanted Eflis looking Tau's way again, to see what she couldn't have. "Do those Marlovans really have flying horses?"

Eflis only glanced once. "Who cares? They don't fly over water. It's not Marshig who wants a kingdom, it's Boruin Death-Hand."

Walic's breath hissed in, long and slow, as he remembered the only time he'd sailed with Boruin, who wasn't even twenty at the time. A week's hard fighting—sea, then land, then last the palace. Walic had agreed to ally in hopes of an invitation to join the Brotherhood. But Boruin made it clear all their success meant was she and her allies wouldn't attack him on the seas. He had to command his own big win.

She didn't even cut him in on the palace loot, despite his losses; his last night there all the captains in the fleet were bid to the celebration dinner inside the palace. Walic sank into memory: Boruin standing near the huge fire, one boot on the bloody wreck of the toff she'd toyed with—he was still dying—her shadow dark against the opposite wall, reaching up to the ceiling, as she drank and toasted her future. Her pirates—as crazy as she was—shouting after every promise, *Marshig will die!* (roar) *After I get the Brotherhood treasure map out of him!* (roar) *Then we take us a kingdom!* (roar) *It's a palace for every hand!* (roar) *Jewels to bathe in!* (roar) *Bed warmed every night!* (roar) *And then knife 'em in the morning!* (biggest roar)

Eflis broke into the memory with a wry glance. "As well she's gonna sail west to take on Marshig when she's strong enough, eh?"

Walic chuckled. "She's crazy, that one."

They all laughed and Eflis returned to her ship. Coco and Walic returned to their sleep, leaving Tau to take the dishes to the galley.

That done, he climbed the half dozen steps to the weather deck. The air was hot and breathless, with that killing glare that too often presaged bad weather. The way the pirates peered toward the northwest confirmed his instinct that a storm was forming beyond the curve of the world.

The second mate, on duty during the day as the first mate was aboard the prizes, whirled around at the faint, sweet ring of his chimes in Tau's hair. His temper was evil: it was hot out and he was dead tired. When he saw those little braids framing the bawdy-boy's face, his fingers reached for the big knife he always wore in his sash.

Then he dropped his hand. Coco had taken the chimes, so that was that; though he despised the sight of her latest toy, he remembered what happened to her toys when she got tired of them. He laughed, then called for a change of sail: a fractious wind teased at hair and sweaty skin.

Soon they bucked forward, the bow smacking down through the whitecaps beginning to riffle over the surface. All the sails the ship could carry belled out, everything braced up within a snap of danger.

Tau descended to the waist, wishing he could find somewhere to sleep. He leaned a hand against a bulkhead, eyes closed, nearly sliding into sleep as he stood there.

A step within fighting range woke him. A heartbeat later, steely fingers gripped his hair and flung him around.

Though he was meant to sprawl off balance he side-stepped, one hand in a flat-hand block to redirect another blow into the wood and one foot hooking neatly behind his assailant's ankle.

The foot he hooked twisted expertly away, then a forearm slammed Tau back against the bulkhead, catching him below the collarbone.

He shook back his drifting hair. When he saw Fox's considering gaze, Tau dropped his hands and waited.

"Inda taught you to fight with the Odni?" Fox drawled the word "you" with extreme derision.

Behind him stood the other Marlovan, the one the hands called Rat. He was watching down the companionway.

"Who says I fight?" Tau retorted, folding his arms.

Fox stared into Tau's face. It really was an extraordinarily beautiful face, even when sweaty and marked with exhaustion. Extraordinary because wit refined the handsome features. Gave them character.

Fox had not planned past taking the bawdy-boy by surprise, to see if he begged, pleaded, threatened, or offered trade. Not that he wanted it. He wanted proof his loyalties were for sale, along with his attentions.

Tau waited.

"Huh." Fox lifted his arm and laughed as he and Rat walked off.

Chapter Five

JEJE had not expected the sight of Freeport Harbor to hurt.

Being in charge for the first time had kept her busy looking out for pirates during the long trip southeast, watching the charts on her first attempt at navigating entirely on her own, scanning for bad weather, and dealing with the ongoing chores of ship-handling.

They traded watches off and on, two and two, Nugget having to do a mate's share of the work instead of a new deck rat's. She seemed to thrive on the responsibility. She even slept on the masthead, tying herself on, most nights being balmy enough for it not to seem a hardship for an adventure-craving twelve-year-old. Both Jeje and Nugget stayed awake far past their watches, Jeje too full of questions, worries, and ugly images to want sleep, until she was so exhausted she couldn't fight it.

Any sail on the horizon caused them to spill wind and bowse their sail up tight, making them effectively invisible from a distance; the cost of staying unseen added to the sailing time.

Relieved when they finally spotted the familiar hump of Freedom Islands on the southeast horizon, Jeje and Nugget fell asleep not long after, leaving the brothers to beat southward against the steady winds, at last entering the harbor on the morning tide.

The water was smooth, the sky mild with wispy, curved featherings of white as Jeje lifted her glass to scan the harbor. The ache gripped her heart with the strength of regret and grief and worry and remorse. She swept the glass over the familiar octagonal building jutting above the King's Saunter. It was foolish to hope, but she searched for Inda in the colorful crowd on the boardwalk, scrutinized the ships in harbor, and glared at every figure as if agonizing strength of will could force one of those strangers to be Kodl walking up to the cordage shop to see his sweetheart, or Thog drifting about searching the newcomers for Chwahir outcasts.

Willing was as useless as wishing: not a glimpse of any of them.

"Signal! We can moor at the north dock," the oldest boy said.

Jeje lowered the glass. "We get a dock mooring?" she asked, amazed at the unheard of privilege.

Nugget bounced up and down. "That's because of Woof," she said confidently. "My brother won't stick us in the bay."

Jeje lifted a shoulder, repressing a comment that Nugget's brother, who was the harbormaster's chief assistant, had had no problem with the *Vixen* being anchored out in the bay before they left. That they'd now rate a mooring because Woof wanted to see his sister returning from her first voyage made as much sense as anything else did these days.

Nugget waved violently, shrilling false alarm at that distinct pitch recognizable to anyone familiar with the shrieks of young girls: there was Woof himself, moving down the dock more quickly than his customary elegant stride.

He halted at the edge while the *Vixen* was moored. Jeje folded her charts under her arm and clambered up onto the deck, followed by Nugget, who leaped up and dashed to her brother, gaining her land legs in half a heartbeat.

She flung herself onto him, wrapping her gangling legs around him as he hugged her and pressed a kiss into her tangled, salt-grimy hair. "Woofie! There was a pirate attack!"

Woof set her down, his grin tightening to a wince. "I know. Word's coming in from everyone running south." He patted his sister's salt-spiky curls and turned to Jeje. "Walic or Boruin? I can't believe anyone but those two would be strong enough to take your marine defenders."

Jeje forced herself not to start with her own questions. "Walic. According to the harbormaster at Tchorchin. You heard? Who? How?"

Woof sighed, tipping a hand back and forth, then sweeping it down toward the harbor. "Word went out Walic was hunting in the same area your convoy had been last seen, and not long after there was a smoke cloud that carried to the coast when the wind shifted. A couple of privateers in the area saw the smoke and tacked in to investigate."

Look for hulks and scavenge, Jeje translated. It was typical of certain types of privateers.

"Both came in here. Reported your convoy's being stripped and left to burn, but the fire was doused by rain, leaving the wrecks drifting."

"Wrecks?" Jeje whispered. "No survivors?"

Woof shook his head. "Kodl was spotted among the dead. Fangras of the *Blue Star* recognized his body. Dun the Carpenter as well, and Scalis. He and his crew Disappeared them. The rest of the convoy had either been taken or sunk, so we have no idea who lived and who died." He hesitated, then said, "Thank you for getting Nugget away."

Jeje opened her mouth to explain that Nugget hadn't been their first thought. Inda had ordered Jeje away to get aid when Nugget happened to be serving a watch on *Vixen.*

No one is going to ask about Uslar. Who was the same age as Nugget, Jeje thought with that painful heart-twist of grief. Clues she'd missed before coalesced into conviction: Woof's fine clothes, the way he moved, his assumption that his little sister would be first on anyone's mind. He was a toff.

That is, he had been born one. He obviously didn't own any land now and what's more, he worked as hard as anyone.

So she said nothing.

She was not aware of her scowl.

After another hesitation, Woof shifted his gaze away, then said, "Come upstairs, will you? Dhalshev wants to talk to you, if you've a mind."

Jeje waved a hand, again making an effort not to hammer him with questions. *Kodl dead! Dun, too. But they didn't mention Inda or Tau. Everyone knew Tau.*

Her throat hurt and her eyes burned, though she tried fiercely to control her emotions. *I will believe they live until I hear something else.*

Woof led her to the eight-sided tower that served as headquarters for the harbormaster. She had never seen Dhalshev before, though everyone knew who he was. He'd been fleet commander of the Khanerenth navy before the civil war. Though Jeje had little interest in—and no sympathy for—the problems of kings, it was impossible to sail the eastern waters and not hear that Dhalshev's defection had finally brought the old king down and enabled the new one to settle the kingdom.

Woof walked fast, his lips pressed together as though he, too, was deliberately not asking questions. They trotted up the stairs around and around until they reached the weather-beaten balcony outside the octagon, where a couple of staffers were on duty with field glasses, a flag hand standing by the huge trunk of signal flags waiting for her next order. Nugget ran up to these, greeting them all by name, then crowing proudly, with the heartlessness of the young who only glimpsed danger from a distance, "*We* were attacked by *pirates!* They chased us. Even shot a million arrows at us! Fire arrows! But we were *much* too fast!"

Woof led Jeje inside and shut the door. The front half of the octagon had enormous windows overlooking the harbor. The back half, tucked against the hillside, was covered with mural-sized charts. Two of them matched the charts under Jeje's arm; they were just bigger and more detailed, dotted with little colored pins. The third was a huge map of the island with charting and fleet marks along the west coast. The fourth showed the coast of the north continent, which she ignored, turning back to the map of the island.

Before she could study any of those markers Dhalshev spoke from behind her. "What can you tell me?"

Jeje turned. The tall gray-haired man looked like a Fleet Commander, somehow, even though she'd never seen one in her life. It wasn't his size, though he was taller than Kodl had been, or his trim build. It was his attitude of awareness, of command. He reminded her of Inda running war games on their hill up behind the harbor, or standing on the deck of a hire in the middle of a battle, right before Kodl gave up trying to run the defense and Inda took over.

Her hand moved, doffing an invisible hat, as if she had just stepped aboard the deck of his flagship. The severity of Dhalshev's expression eased for a moment as he returned the gesture.

Jeje gave her report in the manner Inda had trained them to use: outcome, general survey, details.

Dhalshev and Woof were impressed with Jeje's succinct descriptions of Walic's vessels, what she'd seen of their tactics. She then repeated her conversation in Tchorchin Harbor. They exchanged a glance, remembering the harbormaster there.

Dhalshev said, "What do you intend to do now?"

Jeje drew in a deep breath, studying Woof's scrupulously blank expression and the harbormaster's grim one. The fact Jeje was up here, where no one but Dhalshev's own people were allowed, testified to the importance of this conversation to him, though as yet she did not know why.

So talk about what you do know, Jeje sa Jeje! As she had with Testhy, she felt that sense of the wind, or the world, changing. "I want to try to rescue them," she said firmly. "If they are still alive."

Woof knuckled his chin during the silence that followed her words. Dhalshev's face didn't alter, and Jeje discovered she'd been holding her breath. She was braced for what? Scoffing? Disbelief? Dhalshev said, "In the old days I could have sent a fleet in the time it took to write the orders. Those days are gone. Khanerenth couldn't send anyone. I didn't leave them enough ships to do more than guard the coast."

A pang of disappointment forced Jeje to realize she'd unconsciously expected him to take her problem as his own, to tell her what to do. Maybe give her the means to do it.

So command yourself, Jeje. What would Inda do? "I need volunteers. Supplies."

The harbormaster lifted his hand toward the south window. "If you go down to Anki's, you'll find a list of those who have been waiting for Kodl's return."

"Those are recruits," Jeje said, fighting back the cloud of questions. "I need supplies, if not ships."

"You won't get a fleet," Dhalshev warned. "Everyone on the island knows that there will be an attack here, that it's only a matter of time. The pirates lost this harbor to me, and they want it back. They no longer have a good base here in the east, and they want the independent trade I've been building up."

So that explained their tension!

Woof put in, "Walic wants Brotherhood alliance. Boruin is already Brotherhood. She wants command of the Brotherhood's eastern arm, which has been up for grabs ever since Captain Ramis of the *Knife* sent the last fleet commander to Nightland."

That name was like a jab. "Is Ramis coming back?"

Dhalshev said grimly, "No idea what his plans are. I only had one conversation with him, and it was the strangest one I have ever had."

"Did you ask him his plans?"

Dhalshev's mouth tightened in a bleak almost-smile. "He answered every question with a question. He exhorted me to treat fairly with trade, which I have done, but that was a promise I'd made before he arrived. Not all of our traders want to keep it."

"Will Boruin and Walic ally, you think?"

"No. They did once, then argued over the division of spoils. Or rather, she denied him his share, he complained about her up and down the coast, and word got back to her. Both know the other will double-cross them in a heartbeat. That's one advantage to us. The other benefit is the massing of the Brotherhood under Marshig the Murderer, out west. It's inevitable that they will be back when the Iascan war is over, whoever wins, but at least that war buys us time."

Jeje scowled at her brown feet on Dhalshev's patterned

tile floor. His distant, convenient war was her family fighting for their homes.

Dhalshev waved a hand toward the window. "You can spend a lifetime resenting the orders of a bad king, but when that king is gone and no one is issuing orders, once the first sense of freedom fades into everyday matters, you'll find that someone or other wants to step into that gap."

Jeje moved to the window. The entirety of the King's Saunter was visible from this vantage: a broad semicircle paved with pale stone, colorful shops vying with banners and brightly painted shutters and awnings to catch the eye of privateers and sailors strolling by in their best shore-going rig. Everyone was armed. The mistress at the Lark Ascendant pleasure house had been open about how much she liked the marines living there, because if there was trouble she expected them to defend her house.

Jeje realized what it meant to have no king or queen ruling from a distance. Whose law prevailed? One could say the harbormaster's, except who was to enforce his law if his fleet was out defending the harbor and someone decided to make other laws?

Jeje swung around, staring at the map of the main island. "You sent all your fleet out to guard the harbor against a pirate attack?"

Dhalshev stepped forward, raising an arm to block his island map, then as abruptly stepped back. "What do you mean?"

Jeje remembered how he'd deflected her on her entry. Ah! "You're not defending the entire island," she said.

Dhalshev said slowly, "I thought I was. But I admit that I have always fought at sea. I know little about land battles. What do you see that I don't?"

Jeje scanned those markers on the mountaintops: a few at the northern and southern ends of the island, heavy along the west above and below the harbor, but nothing on the east. The detailed chart symbols showed tall cliffs on the east, a lethally rocky coast, riptides, and a nasty current. There were even dated red marks for big wrecks. People trained to sea would consider that coast a natural barrier; she remembered Inda saying after the *Toola* attack, *What*

*we've learned is where we think we're strongest—and
loosen our watch—that's where the smart ones will infiltrate.*

Boruin, Walic, all the worst pirates are smart, she thought,
and easily imagined them landing not ships along that
lethal rocky coast, but lots of smaller boats. And climbing
up the cliffs to attack from behind ...

The fog had lifted, the wind was on the beam. Jeje knew
where she was. Hooking her thumbs in her sash and rocking back and forth on her bare feet, she said, "How about
this. You give me supplies. Crew. And I tell you how Inda
would defend your island."

Dhalshev frowned at Woof, who just whistled.

Dhalshev hesitated for five heartbeats—Jeje counted.
Then he said, "Talk."

When she was done, the harbormaster said, "Woltjen,
see that she gets what she needs."

Jeje and Woof left. As soon as the door was shut, Woof
grimaced like a boy. "When he uses my real name, I know
he's ..." Woof waggled his hand beside his head.

Jeje gestured. "Why? It's just something Inda's taught
us. You don't think it's a fair trade?"

Woof shook his head. "You don't realize. I guess that's a
good thing. But if you wanted you could have taken away
the knowledge of the map and used your pirate plan yourself. Taken the island."

Jeje's face and neck burned. She made a noise of disgust
deep in her chest, and then, to get away from the subject,
"Why worry about pirates? Didn't the king you wanted
take over? Can't you go back and be a navy again, especially if they need one?"

Woof leaned against one of the wind-battered lyre carvings that masked the structure supports. "The civil war
happened because the old king thought he was above the
laws. The new king swore to uphold the laws."

"Yah. So?"

Woof shook his head. "You really are a sea rat, aren't
you? If we go back, then we have to submit to the law, see?
And right near the top of the list is what happens to a fleet
commander who takes most of a kingdom's fleet and
leaves the kingdom, though he'd sworn to protect it."

"Even though he did a *good* thing? And *everyone* knows it?" Jeje stopped, hands on hips. On Woof's nod, she threw her hands out wide and snorted her disgust so hard her nose tingled. "That's *just* why I hate kings and politics. It's all fart stinks, and kings are the biggest stinks of all."

Woof laughed. "Come on, let's get busy."

Chapter Six

ONCE before an internal awareness changed the course of Inda's life, though he did not know it at the time: when the twelve-year-old Evred Montrei-Vayir discovered that the ten-year-old Inda Algara-Vayir trusted him unconditionally—without ambition, calculation, or even awareness.

Here is another internal decision that changed Inda's life, and again he was not aware of it at the time: Coco's demand for cinnamon rolls.

The runaway Chwahir boy Uslar was too small to be a pirate; the first mate would have killed him outright had not the cook mentioned needing extra hands. They ate well on the *Coco*. Captain Walic had declared that if Cook wanted extra hands, extra hands he would have, so Uslar and the other boy, Mutt, were assigned to him.

The cook, who was not a bad sort, though he drank heavily (he drank heavily because he was not a bad sort) muttered to Uslar late one night, "If you have somethin' they want, it makes you valuable, see?"

Uslar had taken that advice, offering one morning, when there was extra pastry crust, to make a cinnamon roll the way Rig had taught him. The result was an instant success.

Now, two months afterward, Coco herself came into the galley, her wide skirts brushing the edges of the tiny space. The cook, instantly anxious, set down his mixing spoon.

"Cook." Coco's small mouth downturned. "There wasn't a single cinnamon roll at my breakfast. I thought I gave orders for two every day."

She held up two fingers, and waggled them coyly. Nobody mistook that for a humorous gesture.

"Yes," Cook said, sending an anguished look at his cookmates. "You did, Mistress Coco."

Uslar stood at the chopping board, trying to be invisible. Mutt, perched behind him on a stool so his almost healed ankle took no weight, hunched down. His face blanched, making his freckles stand out.

Uslar watched Coco's profile with the unwavering intensity of the prey when the predator is near; she resembled a pastry: with her little upturned nose and her soft second chin, bits of unconfined doughy flesh jiggling around her otherwise tight dress. She looked young and merry in lamplight, but when she stepped out in strong sun she appeared closer to her age, which was near forty.

"And?" Her voice was strident as she tapped the nails of those two fingers against the breadboard.

Uslar's mouth dried with fear. He'd heard whispers about Coco and her penchant for knives and blood.

"We haven't a walnut on the ship." Cook spread his hands. "Not one o' the prizes we took had any nuts at all, not the smallest walnut, or even an almond. It's the shaved nuts, see, that makes them rools what they are. I tried, but all I got was a tasteless mess, no rool you'd want to eat."

The ribbons on her flounces quivered, but all she said was, "Walnuts, is it? Then we shall have to get some."

And she rustled away. Mutt sighed in relief. Uslar was too frightened to make even that much noise; he watched the Cook's strong right arm stiffen at his side, his left hand flipping backside-up in Coco's direction, the tendons and muscles so taut his fingers trembled. But the next heartbeat the cook was back at his chopping, and so Uslar resumed his steady mixing, around and around and around.

*　　*　　*

Walic sat in his comfortable chair on deck, considering his next move. His mates each wanted something different, which he ordinarily would have ignored except that he liked each of their plans. Which first? Which first?

All three were sweating, the captain's good mood from the night before rapidly evaporating. When Coco bustled up onto the captain's deck, hips swinging, harsh sunlight glaring off the brilliant yellow of her silks, a jet of irritation scorched his temper.

"There are no cinnamon rolls because Cook is out of nuts," she stated with dramatic petulance, ignoring the mates, who backed out of her way.

Walic massaged his jaw. She did not look the least bit appetizing in the strong light. Sweat marred the bodice of her gown, her skirts swept over half the captain's deck as if claiming it for her own, and the brilliants in the embroidery threw out pinpoints of reflection strong enough to bring tears to the eyes. When he regarded her under the shade of his hand, she looked no better: her face and the neckline of her low gown had gone blotchy in the heat and her fat jiggled when she tapped her foot.

The irritation flared into anger. But then she tilted her head, smiled wistfully, and said with a girlish pout, "Coco is so, so sorry, sweeting. It's so horridly hot and Coco was so, so disappointed."

He let out his breath, looking at the small hands clasped meekly under her rounded breasts so cozily squashed into the gown. He thought about unlacing the front of that gown, and what she'd do then, to make the fire run like it had last night, after her imperious demands on her pet.

Best of all, she couldn't see how Prettyboy hated her. Walic chuckled. Coco thought everyone was in love with her. Well, let her think it—it made for more fun in the cabin and it also meant no one was likely to conspire with her. If her new toy ever showed the least sign of real desire for her, it would be his death warrant. There would be no conspiracies aboard his ship.

"Can't have you going without, can we?" He chuckled again when he thought about what he'd do to Prettyboy in front of her if he ever sniffed any hint of mutiny.

"No, love," Coco said, running her fingernails along his jawbone. "No, and you won't go without either. You wait and see what fun Coco and her pretty-pretty cook for you-oo-oo," she crooned, and then left the deck with a last twitch of her hips and a coy over-the-shoulder glance.

No, she couldn't go without walnuts, not Coco, who managed to be amusing even when acting stupid. He considered his mental map of the islands to the north. His first mate wanted them to cruise in *Widowmaker*'s old territory.

The second mate shook his head, muttering: "I can't get it out of my head that Ramis o' the *Knife* is also hereabouts. I say we go south, because the big guild convoys aren't due round Chwahirsland for at least a month—"

"If, by some chance, they avoid Boruin," the first mate pointed out sarcastically.

"They been sending fleets of warships," the second mate retorted.

They had their exchanges choreographed by now; they argued so the captain would not sniff an alliance, which he'd see as conspiracy. They took opposite points of view and never joined against Walic.

The second spat over the rail—not quite in the first's direction. "Captain o' the schooner even said so, before I killt him. And the big Sartoran silk merchants have yet to come north. If we go south and squat on a point off Lands End, we're sure to catch something good from either direction."

"And the Khanerenth navy? They'll be playing cards, no doubt."

Walic liked them to seem on the verge of fighting.

The second mate appealed to Walic, hands open. "We can take 'em, they're spread so thin, long 's they don't have time to pull together."

Walic shook his head. "They've got more scouts than we do, after Stupid and Prettyboy's Marlovan burned so many of ours. Northeast. Inglenook Islands lie there. We've all seen the nut trees growing wild."

The mates flicked their fingers to their foreheads—Walic liked the niceties of naval salutes to captains—and because the captain was watching, First Mate gave Second

Mate a sneer, and Second smirked, rocking on his heels, his hair-chimes jingling. No conspiracy here, captain!

They tacked for five days north by east through fitful seas until they sighted the islands bumping up on the horizon.

The heat had mounted steadily, intensified by the fretful winds that too often died away in the middle of the day, leaving them to wallow and roll, sails sagging, until even the hardiest was feeling sick.

"Everyone wants a squall," Thog whispered to Mutt after she clambered down from helping set staysails once again. "Everyone wants one so much I am afeared they'll knife Sails if she says she feels it coming once more."

The Sails aboard this pirate vessel had been taken off a capital ship years ago, and was quite kind to the young ones, giving Mutt easy chores when Cook didn't want his unpracticed hands in the kitchen. Uslar had been learning from Rig, which meant he was in the kitchen for full watches, making pastry. Cook and Sails made certain that both boys were seen to be useful.

Thog promised herself she would remember that.

They returned to working on the stiff storm-sails, dyed bloodred, that Captain Walic wanted ready for the day he would be invited into the Brotherhood. The red canvas usually upset Thog, but today she refused to think about what she would do that day. Her head ached enough.

"We'll be doing sails, same 's always," Mutt said. "But maybe you won't be pulled up during your off-watch to sew ribbons for *her*."

"That won't change," Thog retorted. She added in Chwahir—which Mutt had begun to understand—"I'll be sewing her ribbons back on her clothes even if a gale blows every sail out to sea."

She and Mutt smothered their laughter.

On deck, the first mate sat under the awning the hands had rigged on the captain's deck, wearing only a vest and a pair of cotton deck trousers, and rapped out orders.

The two mates had been relentless in trimming the ship

instantly to catch the fickle breezes, which meant the hands had spent more than their watches hauling rope and tending sail in the miserable heat.

At sunset the second mate appeared, his hair-chimes faintly ringing as he yawned.

"Who do we send? Feegy wants to go, and that means his cousin. Says he knows nut trees."

The first mate snorted as he propped a broad bare foot on a barrel. "And you believed him? He just wants to get out of the sail-making party."

The other shrugged. "Said it's those lines o' trees out behind the big ruin. Makes sense to me."

Both pirates were sea-bred, and though they knew nuts came from trees, neither of them could tell you which trees made what kind of nuts. Or how you could tell the difference.

The first mate ran his hands over his thinning hair, which was already damp from sweat. "We'll send 'em. They either come back with full baskets or get the rope's end. But I don't think two's enough. Let's send Rat."

"Yes. He knows something about land. Another?"

The second mate rubbed his big jaw, his chimes ringing; the sound irritated the first mate, but he'd learned years ago to keep his mouth shut about it. "One of the new ones? Young ones climb masts faster, makes sense they'd climb trees as fast."

They looked round, making sure Gaffer was still below. Neither spoke about what was foremost in their minds, though no one was in hearing range. Gaffer Walic had been satisfied that the Marlovan wanted up and down the coast had died by accident in the battle, but First Mate—who had been at the head of one of the boarding parties—had conducted his own investigation. Walic wouldn't like that kind of presumption . . . unless it proved to be right.

"Something still crosses my hawse," he said in a whisper. "On how those orders got mixed. 'Twas Fox, near's I can find, who killed that yellow-haired prince."

But Walic liked Fox. He was never seen talking to anyone except maybe Rat, who was quiet and obedient. He fought better than most hands on the ship, and he carried

out the training of newcomers with callous dispatch. They
knew better than to accuse one favored by Walic without
unassailable proof. So either they found the proof or
waited until he fell out of Walic's favor.

Second Mate lowered his voice. "New one, Stupid, stays
away from Fox. Seen that over and over."

The first mate said, "Seen it, too." So that at least removed the fear of conspiracy. Having arrived at a decision,
he sat back, lacing his battle-scarred fingers around a knee.
"Send Stupid with Rat and the cousins. Whoever comes in
with the least amount gets the rope-end, and watch-on-
watch for a week. Meanwhile we use the time to sound that
inlet again. The chart for these islands is rising ten years
old, and the bottom's bound to have changed."

That decided, they turned their attention to the sails as
the wind died, becalming them within sight of their islands.

Next morning before dawn a gust of wind brought the ship
to life as the fiery eye of the sun appeared on the eastern
horizon. Walic's fleet, approaching from the south, carried
more on the tide than by the wind, which was failing again.

Uslar had just woken; reddish beams of light shafted
through the scuttle to highlight the wood grain of the bulkhead inside the stuffy forepeak.

"Uslar! Come see!"

It was Thog, outside the canvas that served as a doorway. The air was already stifling, so Uslar pulled on his
clothes and plunged his head into the bucket. The zing of
magic felt better than the warm water; blinking drops off
his eyelashes, he ran up in time to see sunlight paint the
sides of cliffs. The smell of vegetation had woven into his
dreams during the night, raising his spirits. Now they
soared as he gazed in wide-mouthed astonishment at the
great carvings of winged figures on the sides of the sheer
rock.

Eons of wind and rain had worn the edges from the figures, but the angle of the morning light highlighted the
carvings with shadow, marking the round faces and narrow

eyes on the figures as they sped upward, wings out-stretched, toward the sky.

Round faces, narrow eyes: Chwahir, or not quite Chwahir, for "Chwahir" was the name the ones who stayed on land gave themselves. Those who took to the mountains, never to return, had taken new names, leaving behind only stories handed down through generations until the sense of them was as blurred as the details of those carvings.

Uslar and Thog lingered until a couple of stinging lashes from the rope end sent them scrambling up the mast to help with the sails. Both kept peeking back until the curve of the headland carried the carvings out of sight and all that remained were the ruins of an enormous, round-windowed building cut into the hills behind the cliffs. A plateau extended out from the southwest side, sloping gently away. Groves of trees grew in once-neat rows—peach, apple, pear, plum. On the summit was a far older ruin, made of marble brought from the far north; along its face were carved leaf-shaped arches.

The island was small, southernmost of a string of islands jutting up like a row of monster's teeth. The others were even smaller, mostly vertical rock; this was the only one with ruins and the remains of a plantation. It appeared to be deserted.

The boat was let down on the lee side, and the four nut-seekers clutched their baskets, already glad of the shadow of the ship, early as it was. The cousins were about the same age and height as Inda, but shaped like sticks, with ropy muscles from hard work and harder play. They were brown-skinned, sun-streaked sailor queues bumping against their upper backs; their chief characteristic was faces set in sneers of habitual challenge. The lighter-haired one was mean by intent, the other mean because his cousin's view of the world shaped his own: it had been the first one's idea to run away from their apprenticeships to become pirates.

"Make it fast," an old hand hollered. "There's a storm comin' in. I can smell it."

"You been smelling it for a week, Longtooth," the first mate shouted. "Sure it's not your own stink?"

The sound of laughter seemed both sharp and curiously monotone, like barks in the heavy air.

Inda wiped his palms down his deck trousers and gripped his oars. His head ached behind his eyes; from the way everyone glowered or squinted, they had headaches as well. Neither he nor Barend spoke. The cousins kept up a running conversation as they rowed up an inlet on the high point of the tide, past fingers of land and unseen pools busy with singing frogs, until the flow carried their boat onto the shingle.

The familiar smells of land made Inda uneasy, even though the individual scents were not those of home. The cousins jostled the two others aside to grab the biggest baskets and they ran up the trail, the leader shouting, "If you come near us, I'll bust your face in."

Barend and Inda watched them toil straight up toward those ancient orchards. It was obvious the pirate cousins mistook fruit trees for nut trees, and Inda, who had endured petty bullying from them, had no intention of enlightening them.

Once the cousins were out of sight, Barend and Inda trudged in the other direction, where both had marked a row of tall candle-chestnut trees when the ship came round, their distinctive flowers looking like pale pink candles set at the ends of broad branches. The raucous squawk of crows brought their eyes skyward. Back and forth, back and forth, the crows cawed; then they shot from the topmost branches, swooped down in a black cloud and up again to a new tree, where they called again one to another.

The sight, the sound, cast Inda back into early childhood, watching birds through his bedroom windows, cawing and diving in and out of the huge black oaks beyond the castle walls.

"Reminds me of Ola-Vayir," Barend said. He spoke in Iascan—another internal blow. "They had a big row of trees on the sea side of their castle. Their branches were like this." He laced his fingers. "They call it 'pleached.' I stayed there, if we landed at Lindeth, when I'd come home."

Inda threw back his head. The chestnut trees grew in a curving row adjacent to what was once a road slanting up to the newer ruin. On a southeast-facing slope he spied other trees: the green, shady ingrifole whose nuts, if the summers were long and hot enough, were rich and buttery. The singing frogs could just be heard from this height.

Barend gazed out to the sea, deep green from here, the choppy waves winking with shards of reflected light. Beyond them the *Coco* rode peacefully, consorts farther out, the smaller ships clustered about them. Only *Coco,* as monarch, rode alone.

He breathed deeply of the thick air; there was a metallic tang to it, like a knife that's been run against the whetstone a long time.

"It's good to talk again without being on the watch for Gaffer Shitbrain's spies. But we should talk with purpose. Like, who of your people can we trust to join a mutiny, when we get a chance to plan one?" Barend asked, switching into Marlovan. When Inda did not speak, he ran rapidly through the crew members, describing what he and Fox had decided about each.

Inda ignored him, walking faster as he surveyed the ridge. Closer to the ruins grew walnut trees. Over toward the orchards were two ragged rows of pecan and almond. The cousins would no doubt find those, if they weren't distracted by fruit pits.

Barend finished—and got no response. "Inda?"

"I see at least four kinds of nuts. And I'd love to see those two turds hauling ropes for me," Inda answered in Dock Talk, then turned away.

Reaching the first of the chestnuts, he got to work. Barend sighed and joined him there under the thick trees, grown so close together the two Iascans could not see the sky.

It was a relief to be out of the sun. Both picked and sorted so intently neither was at first aware of the abrupt silence of frogs and crows. But a gust of hot wind—this time they both smelled the hot-metal tang—that sent leaves rattling caused them both to look up at stirring branches. The shadows had vanished; together they dashed away from the trees and looked skyward to see a spreading cloud covering the sun, changing the light around them to a weird green.

Barend whooshed his breath out. "Old Longtooth was right. There's a big one coming. We better find shelter," he said. Then he laughed. "And let the squall shake down the nuts for us."

"You've been at sea too long," Inda retorted, squinting skyward. "A big squall will strip the trees bare and fling the nuts out to sea."

Neither spoke. They worked as fast as they could, no longer choosing the best. They grabbed everything they could reach. By mutual consent Barend labored up the lane of chestnuts and Inda ran along the crumbling wall to the walnuts. Stinging pellets of hail struck him by the time he had his second basket halfway filled. He scanned quickly, ran around the corner to get the ingrifoles, and was nearly knocked down by a blast of cold, wet wind.

Rattle, tok! The wind snatched the top layer of nuts from one basket. He dashed back around the side of the wall, shoved the baskets into a thorn bush, and then, ignoring his torn skin, raced to the trees and picked up as many nuts as he could until his shirt was full. The bushes tossed wildly in the wind that howled around the tumbled stone corners; he yanked the baskets out, dumped in the wind-stolen load, and felt his way along the wall until he reached a doorway. The shocking drop in wind caused him to stumble, nearly falling.

"Over here." Blue lightning lit the air behind Barend.

The wind screamed outside the wall as he made his way across the dusty tiled floor of what had once been a huge refectory.

Lightning flared again, and thunder crashed right overhead, reverberating through the stone. The hot-metal smell intensified. Lightning strike! Barend and Inda grabbed up their baskets and headed farther inside the ruin, where the cracked roof did not admit rivers of dust-clogged water.

A smaller antechamber with archways at the north and south was reasonably dry, though water was trickling in from the northern room. Through the southern arch they could see another small room with round windows giving a view of the sea. The storm was coming out of the north-west, so these southern windows were relatively sheltered. The sea beyond had changed to a dark, threatening gray churning with white tops. Walic's fleet had hauled round to the southeast to ride out the storm in the island's lee; one consort was visible beyond the great jut of the headland, riding with bare poles except for a scrap of reefed sail.

"So, back to our mutiny. Fox wants us gauging every-one's loyalties and fighting ability," Barend said. "We have our ideas on who we might be able to use, like I told you, but we don't know your old mates."

Loyalties. Inda's gut soured, but he said nothing.

Barend sent Inda a quick glance, then set his baskets down. Water leaked from each into the dusty floor as he prowled the perimeter, making certain the cousins were not anywhere within view—or hearing.

When he returned, he tried a third time. "From your old crew, Tcholan knows how to fight, and Fox thinks he'll join us, right enough. Those Chwahir brats and Mutt can shoot, at least. We know that from Fox's drills. They're academy scrub age, they'll do what they're told, won't they? And Fox thinks your bawdy-boy knows how to use his hands. Even though he never comes weather-side for drills. But how much longer he'll last before Coco gets out her knife makes it hard to plan to use him. Do you think he'll join, or does he like his berth?"

Inda had dropped down into the dust in the middle of the room. His head jerked up. "What was that about knives?"

Barend grimaced. "Coco. When she gets tired of her toys, or they make her mad, she carves 'em up. If Walic doesn't suspect 'em of mutiny and carve 'em up first."

Inda sank back, sickened. "I've got to warn Tau."

Barend said, "Oh, I think he knows it. At least he knows how to keep 'em happy. It's been a long while since the two of 'em have had one of their torture parties. Fox," he added, "thought he was a sellout, or another Coco, but he isn't sure. That's why we need to know if he'd join us, or work against us to keep his easy place."

"Easy?" Inda repeated, grimacing.

Barend lifted a shoulder. "Might be easy to him—aside from the knowledge that one mistake and he's knife practice. But all of us live under that threat. Meanwhile he never stands a watch, gets the best food, and all he has to do is pillow-jig with those two—he might even like it, he's certainly good at it, or he'd be dead—and sit on cushions while Coco plays with his hair. Sometimes he twiddles around with some stringed instrument they have down there and sings ballads. The hands yatch about it, but I've noticed the night watch find excuses to be near the scuttles aft to listen when the second mate isn't watching them."

Inda remembered their ship rat days on the trader when Tau and Jeje had sung ballads together—in those days she took the lower part—but then Tau suddenly stopped for no reason that Inda could see, and he'd never sung again.

"Not as tough as laying aloft in sleet at midnight when we're on the chase, so no lights allowed. Two hands have been lost that way since they took me. Good riddance to both." Barend flung up the back of his hand.

Inda stared down at his scraped hands. *Knife practice.* This was far worse than Thog's whispered words about the red sails and Walic's intent to join the Brotherhood. Tau had to know, but he hadn't said anything. No, not true: he had. In his own way. *It's the only thought keeping me sane.*

"He hates his place," Inda muttered, his face tight with conflict. "But you and Fox want to be pirates."

Barend twitched his fingers toward the windows in the south room. Now nothing could be seen but the blue-white flare of lightning on a solid sheet of rain. "What else is there? As pirates, we'd be free. If we do manage to jump ship and land, being Iascan gets us proscribed, maybe jailed. And if someone suspects us of being Marlovan, like as not we'll be handed off to the Venn. *You've* got a price on your head, named personally. And the funny thing is, Fox said, you are named as a *pirate.*"

Inda finally faced Barend, his gaze unnervingly steady, his expression strange. Barend stared back, uncomfortable, until Inda's gaze lifted and went distant. Inda was lost in thought, so lost he didn't see or hear. Like Sponge used to do.

Inda said in just the sort of musing voice Sponge used to use, "Pirates. Were they born wanting to kill, to burn and destroy, or do you think they've all been betrayed when they were small, then? And so they can betray, because ..." He groped in the air with his scratched-up hands. "Because the lessons about honor and duty they yapped at us when we were little aren't true? Or are some born to cheat and lie and steal, no matter how they were raised?"

Barend laughed. Thunder rumbled and wind and rain roared outside. Brown water washed down through cracks in the northern room's farther wall, streamed through the archway, and crossed their shelter to vanish in the southern room. He said, "Nobody else asks questions like that except Sponge. *Do pirates become pirates because they were betrayed or because they're born that way?* I can just see him asking that."

Inda leaned forward, his expression so intent, so altered from the witless blank they'd seen since Inda's capture that Barend stared back, baffled.

"Tell me," Inda said, in a low, swift voice. "About Sponge. Was Hadand there, too?" Longing so sharp it hurt like a knife ripped through him when he thought of his sister— remembered her determination when they sneaked into the throne room before dawn and practiced the Odni knife forms.

But here was one who knew his home: the urge to hide behind the wall was strong, as strong as several years of habit could make it, but he fought to breach the wall, eager—hungry—for a glimpse of those at home.

Barend uttered a foolish laugh, self-conscious under that ferociously unwavering regard. He wished things were like before, when Inda was ignoring him. No. At least Inda talked now. Fox would say that was good for their plans.

He wriggled his toes in the rushing stream, sending spatters of water into the drifts of dust obscuring the ancient tiles. *So talk back.* "It makes me think of the old nursery. I can almost smell it, the summer sage coming in the row of windows." It was easier to talk if he didn't look at those terrible staring eyes. "The beeswax candles with the herbs put in 'em. Here at the table Sponge reads, and I'm at the other end drawing pictures of horses. Hadand writes letters over there, and little Kialen is working one of her embroidery things for the queen. It's all quiet. Then Sponge looks up and out he comes with one of those questions."

Inda smiled for the first time in a thousand years. A weird giddiness seized his mind, and the wall—for the moment—was gone. "And? What happens next?"

Barend shut his eyes. As always, ever since his first ship journey at a young age, it felt good to think about home— when he was far out of the reach of his father's hard hand. "Hadand will drop her pen and ask what Sponge is reading, and if she knows it she'll start a debate, and if she doesn't she'll bear it off and read late into the night when we're supposed to be asleep. I'm quiet unless my mother has said something wise that I can remember and tell to them, and pretend to sound wise. I never did much like reading, not like Sponge. And Kialen will look at them both, but she won't speak either, unless they remember her and ask, and then she'll whisper it to Hadand."

Inda's chuckle was lost in a clap of thunder.

When it had died away, Barend leaned back on his elbows, chin up as he studied the carvings of winged children in the ceiling. "I don't know. I don't see meaning in much, I guess. My mother always used to tell me to behave with honor. But she never said to behave like *him*. Meant, I figured, my father had none. At least in her eyes. I know he thought he had plenty of honor, which was why I never believed there was any such thing. Not if it was whatever *he* had." Barend shifted slightly and opened a hand. "So maybe Hadand has honor, as does Sponge, but what will that mean when the Sierlaef is king? It seems to me the 'honor' of those who have power is really what suits them best."

Inda scowled at the steadily growing rivulet. The water ran clear in the center, carving its way through the dust, an ever-widening stream. The tile below was patterned, highly stylized lettering in some unfamiliar alphabet, cobalt blue and pale gold. "My mother used to have me parsing her copies of Old Sartoran texts, along with Hadand on her home visits. And Joret, my brother's betrothed. And Tdor

She is. Was. Is. My betrothed." Another pang. "One of those texts said, 'Civilization is not made by single great events.' "

Barend waved a dismissive hand. "I remember my mother quoting that one. Thought it was a crack at my father wanting to become Harskialdna and have his war at last."

Inda closed his eyes. He cherished his memory of Tdor's long face, her steady eyes; he heard her voice over the drumming of the rain. "Tdor says civilization is a net, made up of moral choices. Bad ones tear the net."

Barend laughed. "My father is a tearer. Even if thinks he's a maker. And as for Sponge, you could say he's a maker, but Aldren-Sierlaef beat him bloody all the same. And all the adults called it training. The Sierlaef has no honor—no morals—and it was my father who made him that way, while saying all the right things." Barend laughed again. "The king stood by and let it happen because he was too busy with trade, and scrolls, and future plans, but most of all because he'd never believe anything said against his brother. He thinks they have the same honor." He snorted. "The king means it, my father says it. But the king thinks he means it, too. If brotherhood makes you that blind I'm glad I never had a brother."

A stab of light flickered patterns of reflected light up the walls.

"I think the squall is passing," Barend said, rising.

The thunder, rain, and wind were as loud as before; still the two made their way to the refectory, which was awash with water. As they stared out the round windows, rain slanted down to the southeast under a greenish-gray cloud. A spectacular rainbow arched across the blue sky.

"Let's get the nuts," Inda suggested. "And get down to the boat. If it's even there." His mind was streaming again, like the rivulet in the room behind them, clearing out the mud that had clogged his thoughts ever since Walic had taken them. He needed to think; he could do that while they rowed.

The image of Coco, or Walic and his chief mates, as small children who had a father like the Sierandael—no, he had to be Harskialdna now. What might have happened to them to make them the way they were? It did not change what they now did, but it changed, profoundly, how he perceived their motivations, their place in the world.

The stream caught an image of Fox and tumbled on, faster and faster. He remembered hearing about the Jarl of Montredavan-An sitting up in his tower, exiled on his own lands not because of anything he had done, but because a Montrei-Vayir had managed to knife Fox's ancestor in the night and take the kingdom by treachery. The Jarlan had talked about how the Jarl supervised the great horse-stud there in Darchelde, and she talked about history, as had Fox's sister Shen, who had been merry and full of games. He remembered his own distant cousin, Marend Jaya-Vayir, Fox's intended, who was quiet and kind. But now Inda could see how the Jarl of Montredavan-An, who had never been permitted to ride with the other lords—whose family had once been kings—would waste his life away because of a cruel treaty, and Fox, who never went to the academy, had learned the Odni in secret from his mother before they sent him to sea so he wouldn't waste his life, too. Fox's parents wanted the best life for their heir that they could manage around the cruelty of the treaty that bound them to their land for ten generations. *Treaty.* A betrayal by a knife in the night that was later made into law.

Seen that way, becoming a pirate seemed a reasonable plan. Inda felt his way toward comprehension, drawing on half-forgotten vocabulary learned in his mother's study: Fox denied moral certainties not out of cowardice or dishonor but because moral certainties had been stripped away from him by the law upheld by his own countrymen.

Inda could imagine Tdor insisting that moral *choice* was possible. And if enough people made the moral choice, wasn't that as near to creating a moral certainty as anything else in the world? *Tdor will always be a net maker. That I know.*

The two gathered their nuts and started down, meeting the cousins halfway.

The leader snarled, casting a grimace skyward, "Why is it as soul-sucking hot as it was in morning?" Then he glanced down into Barend's and Inda's baskets and gloated. "We got more'n you did." He eyed Barend. "Save ya the rope's end and watch-on-watch if we even 'em up. But you gotta do our night watches for the week."

Barend noted the peach pits among their nuts, and cast a questioning glance Inda's way. Inda just stood staring witlessly at the baskets. Did he even see them?

"Naw," Barend finally said. "We'll take what comes."

The pirate boy snorted, picked up his oars, and the others did as well: the wind had dropped, the air was again breathless and metallic.

Another storm on the way! They pulled hard, Barend hoping Cook looked into the baskets before Varodif started swinging his rope, the cousins muttering about the weather, and Inda thinking, thinking, thinking.

Chapter Seven

FOR some months afterward, Fox Montredavan-An sustained a series of dreams in which he was running over an endless grassy plain, the wind blowing leaves before him. Golden leaves, or maybe they were pieces of gold, or papers with precious words inscribed, which he tried in vain to catch. No matter how fast he ran, they blew ahead of him, dancing on the wind, until they vanished.

He knew what the dreams meant. He could even identify the moment that inspired them.

Before that moment, no one could foresee anything but a watery death. By the time the rowboat made it back to the *Coco* the second squall was upon them, far worse than the first.

Pirates flung lines down to the four whose baskets of nuts, so carefully gathered and hoarded, were all lost when a kelp-veined wave swamped the rowboat. The four smashed against the side of the ship, holding their breath as the cold water first pounded then sucked at them, their hands clenching the ropes with desperate strength. At last the ship heeled and they emerged, bruised and dazed. Violent heaves from the deck brought them aboard, where they stood, stunned and bleeding, until with hard blows of the rope's end the second mate—awake and angry—sent them aloft.

Furling and reefing was all Inda could comprehend. He

clambered up behind the leader of the cousins, who made the mistake of slewing about to look for his lifelong follower; the ship gave a sudden leeward lurch and flung him screaming into the green wave cresting over the bowsprit, never to be seen again.

Inda gripped the ropes, barely hearing the first mate shouting at him from two arm's lengths away. More hands scrambled aloft. Thirty pirates wrested down the raffee-sail—Walic had to keep them in the lee of the island, riding in the teeth of the wind. Another dozen struggled with Walic to hold the helm.

The wind rose, shrieking. The sound everyone feared reverberated up the ship and through their bones: *Crack!* With stately slowness the foretopmast began to fall. The damage party, already holding axes, sprang to cut away ropes before it could drag the ship into capsizing. The ship plunged into the next green wave, flinging the mast into the white water boiling down the deck, dragging several people with it.

Then began the eternity of fighting wind, rain, storm, and tortured wood, until Inda's brain was as numb as his hands and feet, until he could not remember the past as far as morning, or imagine a future beyond this terror.

Then something bright struck his eyes, almost blinding him. He and his mates stared upward, rediscovering the sun; the wind's scream whined down to a moan through the remaining shrouds, and then hauled around to the southeast, diminishing rapidly to occasional drafts of warm, salt-laden soughs to blend with the hiss of the foaming rollers. It was over, and they could look about, dumbstruck in amazement, to survey the damage without knowing where to begin.

Inda's body was deadened with fatigue, but his mind began once more to stream with possibilities, assessing not just damage but sky, sea, crew, the images coming faster.

Almost right . . . almost—

Walic stumped forward, his embroidered coat hanging sodden, the silken fabric squeaking at his every step. Pointing at the second mate, he snapped, "Take a crew and bring us spars off the island!" And to the first mate, "Get that wreckage cleared away, now! If another comes, we will be ready for it." Then he stumped down the shallow steps into the cabin and slammed the door.

Dazed, nearly bludgeoned into imbecility, the crew turned to their tasks. The worst of the wreckage was cleared and the large boat hoisted over the side; the big second mate and his strongest and most trusted forecastlemen began to row through heavy running seas for the shore, axes at their feet, scowls reflexively turned skyward at the smiling blue sky.

From the helm the first mate waved a hand, and silently—too exhausted to speak—most of the rest climbed below, some too tired to eat, wanting only sleep. The duty crew, a bare minimum, leaned tiredly, a few falling asleep right where they stood.

Fox shoved his way to the galley along the walls, hoping that something hot to drink and some biscuits and cheese would diminish his blinding headache. He blinked uncomprehending at the little pots of herbs rolling about the deck that the cook had not been able to stow before the second storm struck, wondering if he should sleep before he ate. Beyond even that decision, he started when Inda's fingers gripped his arm.

Fox ripped free, then stilled as Inda whispered in Marlovan, "It has to be now."

"Now?" Fox repeated, peering upward at the low bulkheads as though he could check the skyline for another storm.

Inda whispered, "Gutless and his strongest followers are on their way to the island. Varodif is aft at the helm, consorts all blown out to sea, captain in the cabin—" He listed in a quick tumble of words where every enemy was. By the time Fox's mind caught up with the idea that Inda meant for them to take the ship now, not in a month, or in half a year, after secret meetings and careful plans and Fox's watchful direction, but *right this moment,* Inda was on his last item. ". . . and the weapons locker broke open under a falling spar. See? No longer matters that Walic has the only key."

Barend appeared at Fox's shoulder, massaging a

wrenched arm. Behind him lurked tall, strong Tcholan and the strange Chwahir girl, her face pale and tense.

Fox stared in disbelief. "But the ship is a wreck!"

Barend rolled his eyes. "So you want to wait for the Gaffer to hand it over in good shape?" he whispered fiercely. "Or when he and his gang are well rested?"

Fox struggled to comprehend. Mutiny. Now. The moment chosen not by him, but it was the right moment. One he'd missed—

He shook his head violently. A mistake. When he could breathe again, he forced his hoarse voice low: "Send the new hands after Walic?"

"Waste. We need 'em." Inda turned his thumb toward the galley. "Just one for Walic. Cook," he said, taking Fox by surprise again. "Worst grudge." Inda flicked a glance past Fox's shoulder. "Thog? You know who's good below, don't you?"

Thog nodded, her work-roughened hands pressed tightly together at her skinny chest. "I knew you would do it." She breathed the words on an exhaled sigh.

Inda said only, "Make it now."

She flitted away and dropped down the hatch to raise those she'd already chosen as allies. Inda and Fox entered the galley, Fox cramming some bread into his mouth, Inda a sentinel at the door, observing everything.

Barend watched him observing everything, except himself amid the flow of people and events. He was the eye of the storm, his voice and hands moving the storm before him, around him. Barend tried to figure out how Inda had transformed within a single watch from the Stupid of before into what he was now.

He was the only one who knew what to do.

Excitement made his hands shake, his knees watery, made him want to pee, made him want to laugh as he scrambled down the ladder to the lower deck. He shook and pinched awake the battered, bewildered hands that he and Fox had long ago chosen and to each bleary face he whispered the words, over and over, *Take the ship. Now. Get a weapon. Wait for my signal. Your target is*—

They crept swiftly, silently, past pirates sunk into ex-

hausted slumber; though equally exhausted, they moved
with the desperation of those who, once committed, know
the risk: they had to win or die.

They flowed like ghosts along the companionway and up
past the cabin, most of them sending furtive glances at the
cabin door, behind which Walic sat in an exhausted haze
waiting for Tau to bring wine as he tried to soothe the still-
terrified Coco.

Fox's head rang. The galley fire had been doused, no hot
drink possible, so he ducked his head into the pure water
in the magic-cleaned bucket, sucking down great gulps.

The headache had fired into molten rock. But he forced
himself to lift his head and leave the galley. The world, his
place in it, seemed strange and unreal as he slipped down
the hatch behind the galley to his bunk. He pulled out his
fighting knives, then dug down into his gear and retrieved
the Sartoran knives he'd captured from Inda—which he'd
intended to hold until he was ready to use Inda in his plans.
Laughing at himself, he ran back to the galley, not even
pausing to tie on his black fighting scarf, though he hated
sweat in his eyes.

He did not hear Inda's low-voiced instructions to the
stunned cook. He slapped Inda's knives into his hands, and
Inda's fingers closed over them, his face distracted, unquestioning. His mind obviously far ahead.

Cook worked his big, fleshy face as though he would
speak, but said nothing. A sheen of tears stood on his lower
eyelids.

"Go," Inda said softly.

The cook grabbed up his biggest chopping knife and
vanished up the aft hatchway.

"Now," Inda said to those crowded along the passage.

The sense of unreality intensified for Fox when his head
cleared the level of the weather deck. His awareness sharpened, taking everyone in.

Sails used her awl to gut Walic's torture expert, sobbing
as she did so; Nizhac tumbled into the hatch past Fox, who
swung out of the way, then lunged up to the deck.

On the companionway Taumad, dressed only in cotton
trousers, his hair flagging in the wind, struck down one

then another of the torturer's mates, handling the boarding cutlass and a vegetable knife with speed, skill, and a lethal grace.

Stamping feet: Fox whirled as Inda led an attack party onto the forecastle. Inda fought with the unerring speed and assurance Fox had seen only once before, when they first attacked Inda's convoy. Inda grinned, a ferocious, white-toothed grin that distorted his face as he chopped his cutlass into a pirate's neck, then—how could he do that?— kicked up behind himself, straight into the crotch of a pirate bringing his blade down toward Inda's neck. He was so fast you had to concentrate to see the individual moves, but every strike was telling, every block effective. With power focused from his planted bare feet through his shoulders Inda drove his blade straight into one of the first mate's biggest followers. Then—again without looking—he kicked out the knee of the one who had smashed that small Chwahir boy down just behind him.

Inda then snapped his knives out, shifting grip from cut to thrust as he jammed them into attackers on either side. The pirate on the left dropped, blood spraying from a ripped throat; the one on the right staggered, gripped his sword with both hands to drive down at the Chwahir boy struggling to rise, but Inda whipped up his blade and took the man right under his chin. He flung the pirate backward, blood gouting. Then Inda twisted, sword raised in a block as a cutlass slashed at the back of his head; he struck the cutlass aside and kept moving, his blade sweeping in a horizontal arc straight into the ribs of one of Walic's best killers.

Inda whirled back without looking at the dying pirate. The fight had spread out. He leaned his hands—still gripping his knives—on his knees as he panted open-mouthed. Paused to wipe the sweat off his face, then he rasped orders in a dry, wheezing voice. Like they'd first seen on the deck of the Sartoran Guild ship. But this time, instead of watching Inda through a glass as he issued a continuous stream of orders, Fox heard the orders spoken in a voice of command.

The sense of watching from the periphery fled when Inda's gaze met Fox's dead on. "Behind!"

Fox whirled. Brought up his knives, one high and vertical, the other low and horizontal, ready for the Leap of the Deer. The first mate's eyes distended with disbelief and rage.

This duel Fox had rehearsed so often in angry night-watches over the past years that it too seemed part of the dream world as his body responded with lightning speed—the Deer-Kick, block, whirl, Snake-Strike, parry, Duck-Snap—strike—spray of blood, ruby gleam in the sun—

The strange sense of unreality vanished when the first mate thumped dead to the deck.

Fox lifted a shaking hand to wipe his eyes. The others were gawking in disbelief at the fallen pirates on the blood-slimed, steaming deck, Inda standing in the midst of them, whooping for breath.

Fox's headache by now had intensified to forge-hot, hammering pain. He struggled to comprehend what had taken place so fast: new crew as well as old obeying Inda, who had changed from the slouching dullard of yesterday into a commander.

The quiet Chwahir girl was the only one moving, Disappearing the dead, one by one. Fox still gripped his knives; his breath hurt in his throat, his tongue felt like a salt-dried sponge. His head pounded as if struck by white-hot steel, but through it seared a shrill keening. Not inside his head. Outside.

He turned his head—it took more effort than it had to fight the first mate—as two of the forced pirates muscled a wildly struggling Coco up onto the deck.

"What about her?" asked a big, scarred deckhand, licking his lips as he flicked his gaze from person to person. "Who gets to snuff her?"

The mutineers sent up a shout, the older ones volunteering to slice her up like she'd done to this or that crewmember, while she whimpered a crazy mix of threats and pleas, her skirts splashed with Walic's blood. Others seemed uncertain, some looking out to sea for Walic's fleet.

Barend strained to spot the second mate on the island, wondering if he'd thought to take a glass.

"Sail ho! Dead astern!"

Eyes turned skyward to the mizzen masthead, then out to sea. Barend swung the glass, squinting into the glare at the triangle nicking the skyline.

"The sloop?"

"Too small—"

"Three fires!" Mutt, who had clambered up to the mizzen shrouds despite his healing ankle, yelled from aloft.

Three fire arrows: the old signal!

"It's Jeje," Inda said to Tau, his brown eyes wide with disbelief.

Tau did not answer. He could not answer, just laughed freely for the first time in what seemed to be years. His sweet, young laugh clawed at Coco's heart, kindling a yearning to kill whoever it was who could make him smile like that.

"Mutt! Send her a return, two and one," Inda called their old covert approach signal up to the masthead, where Mutt caught hold of the backstay with one hand, and leaned out to wave acknowledgment of the order with the other.

"I'll get the bow," Uslar volunteered, running forward.

Some of the mutineers murmured, wondering how Stupid had managed reinforcement without anyone knowing it. Two moved apart with stealthy haste, hoping he hadn't overheard their plot to jump him as soon as he went below so they could take the ship. "Later," one mouthed, pawing the air in a gesture meant to be covert; the other nodded as he sidled away.

Tau, ignored by both, kept staring out to sea.

"I can help you," Coco wailed. "Tell him, Taumad. I can be anything you like. Or send me to Halliff on the *Sea-King*."

Inda looked around. "Brig for now."

His voice was almost lost, as few listened beside Tau and Thog and Inda's own people. As yet, Fox realized, no one quite believed that the ship was theirs, that already a new hierarchy was fast forming, unperceived. Old habit prevailed: without Walic's deadly authority muzzling them, everyone wanted his or her voice heard. Typical of pirates.

"Death! She can pillow jig with Walic on Ghost Island!"

"Let her choose one o' us," the surviving cousin yelled,

looking around for approval. He had switched sides at once, looking somewhat forlorn without his cousin telling him what to do.

"Let the bawdy-boy decide," a top hand yelled from the main masthead, brushing back tendrils of black curls from her kerchief-bound head. The pirate she'd killed hung upside down, one foot caught in block-and-tackle, arms swinging loosely. "If he wants her to die of the thousand cuts, well, I'm for it. I'd be glad to help," she added, showing her teeth.

Silence fell, except for the creaking of wounded timbers and the distant caw of birds returning to the island.

Coco, dazed from the storm and from Walic's sudden death, now felt a surge of hope as she turned to her beautiful Tau, who had so smilingly tended her down below while the worst of the storm raged. She shivered, thinking of his patient fingers and how she had waited for them to touch her tenderly, just once, on their own, and not at her command, or at the captain's. Just once.

She'd convinced herself of his imminent devotion so thoroughly that her main emotion when Cook went after Walic was relief, and pleasure that she no longer had to hide her love. She had so convinced herself that his roleplaying was real that at first she didn't comprehend his words: "Get her out of my sight."

"What?"

She didn't realize it was she who had shrieked until that short, brown-eyed one they all called Stupid waved a hand at her, and hard fingers gripped her arms, forcing her down below, despite her raging commands to stop, watch out for the fabric of her gown, to let her go—that *hurt!*

"The others will be back," Inda said to the crew. "We better be ready. That fight will be tougher than this one was. We had the advantage of surprise, but I don't believe that will be true again."

The second mate! Everyone exchanged glances, while absently wiping at lacerated skin or massaging wrenched limbs.

"Why don't we sail?" someone asked, hoarse with fear.

Inda pointed at the foremast stump. "We need that topmast spar. We'll get it on board, and as soon as we do, attack on signal. Each takes his man," he added. "They'll fight hard, and we can't afford to lose any more crew. Sailing is going to be hard as it is, we'll be on watch and watch, even after I get Dasta back from the *Sea-King*."

If he's alive, Inda thought, meeting Tau's bleak gaze.

"Leave him," Fox said. "That's too risky."

Inda faced Fox, lifting his chin. "I won't leave Dasta." His mouth tightened. "We never abandon crew."

Fox heard an intake of breath from that weird little Chwahir, but she said nothing, just passed by with cleaning equipment and vanished into the captain's cabin.

The rest of the pirates stared at Inda, and Fox could almost hear those simple words repeating in their heads like the echo of a bell down a valley. *We never abandon crew.* It was probably one of his regular rules for the marine defenders. To the pirates, Fox knew, and to Barend, watching from the helm, it was more like a world change. All of the old crew had seen Walic kill his own people on a whim or for fun. And if he decided to make a fast retreat before possible danger from a warship, he had abandoned scouts to whatever might happen without any apparent regret.

Now they faced Inda—not just his own people, but all of them—as unwavering as flowers tracking the sun.

But Inda's attention was not on them. It was on *him*. Inda was waiting for a challenge. Didn't he see he already had command? No, he probably didn't.

Inda wiped at a trickle of blood from his scalp, his face already bruising from either the fight or his smash against the hull during the second storm, or both. He probably had as stupefying a headache as Fox did—

But he'd seen the right moment, and he'd taken command as if he'd planned it for days. Months.

Fox raised a hand, turning the palm up, his expression mocking: *Over to you.*

Inda wiped his face again, then pivoted, his toes squeaking on the deck. "Right now we'd better get ready," he said in a loud voice. "It'll be a bad fight, and we should be as prepared as we can be for another storm."

The crew shuffled, looked around, wiped at sweaty faces.

Most were uncertain, some surly, all exhausted. Inda began with his own people, each being ordered to a task within the doer's ability—and one by one the remaining pirates were given orders. They obeyed, some of them furtive and motivated by fear; others with the eased faces of those for whom order had been restored.

Inda sent Cook, Mutt, and Uslar to pass food and water around. For a short time before getting to work everyone sat where they were, eating and drinking, talking in low voices. A few gazed passively up at the tangle of sails, rigging, and lines, the soft *slap-slap* of the ocean and the clacking blocks soothing. Some fell asleep right there on the deck; the worst wounded were taken below to their hammocks and tended by their mates.

Inda gave the crew a brief rest; then it was time to rise and work again. Those too hurt to climb cleared the deck of the worst of the blood and battle debris; those in better shape gave a hand with readying the block-and-tackle that would be used to raise the spar expected from the second mate and his crew. Inda occasionally asked Barend to run questions or instructions to those belowdecks.

He gave no orders to Fox.

Chapter Eight

A T sunset one of the two big consorts appeared in the cloud-streaked east. It was frapped under the hull by their newly-made red sails to plug a great gash below the waterline, and sailing slowly under a single jury-rigged mast.

The lookout shouted down, "*Sea-King* on the beam!"

The rest of the fleet was still gone, either overcome by the storm or by the storm-supplied opportunity to flee Walic's control.

Barend rowed over to the *Sea-King* with demands from "Captain Walic" for hands, Dasta among them. Captain Halliff, dazed and exhausted, was too afraid of Walic to argue about relinquishing hands, though he needed them. He had far too many of Walic's spies placed in his crew who would be listening, and he feared what Walic would do if he even expressed reluctance. The memory of what had happened to the last consort who tried to leave Walic's fleet kept him strictly obedient; his only reaction as he watched the requested hands climb up the hatch, gear bags over their shoulders, was a tired wish that Walic would take his own spies back instead. Who ever knew what was in Walic's head?

No, he knew. It was inevitable. After a defeat, or a weather disaster, he inevitably cheered up his crew with one of his "entertainments."

So when Barend paused on the rail and looked back to say, "I forgot. Cap'n wants you to sail round to the western side to repair. More timber there, and you can watch the west while we, in turn, repair," Halliff nodded, too weary and relieved to question. If he sailed all the way to the big trees, he wouldn't have to row back to the *Coco* and witness the torture party.

As soon as the rowboat was out of hearing range, Barend explained to the tired, surly hands what had happened. He enjoyed watching their wariness turn to disbelief. And as he described the fight with bloodthirsty pleasure, their faces changed from disbelief to glee—and then to speculation.

All except Dasta, who stared at the damaged pirate flagship. Inda was there. Inda, who had said "We don't abandon crew." As Dasta gazed the sharp lines of the *Coco* were blurred by tears he did not bother to wipe or to hide.

After dark, Jeje and the *Vixen* drifted up on *Coco's* lee. The scout's deck was crowded with tough, experienced privateer hands from Freeport Harbor.

Jeje clambered aboard, square and sturdy, her narrow face alert as she scanned the deck under the lanterns hanging in the rigging. Her new hires climbed up behind her.

Tau saw her expression ease only when she found Inda—blood-covered and filthy as he was.

"I thought Walic might try to hide in the lee of these islands when that storm came up," Jeje said.

Inda crossed his arms. "Aren't you leaving something out?" He smiled.

"Not much." Jeje flushed, and Tau tried to figure out what he'd missed, but he was far too tired. "I couldn't find any help in Khanerenth," Jeje said. "So I took Nugget back to Freeport. She tried to come with me, and Woof ended up locking her in the harbormaster's tower. We could hear her wailing and cursing him as we sailed from the dock."

A soft laugh from those few who knew Nugget was the only reaction.

"These here had been waiting to sign on with our marines. Said they didn't mind fighting a few pirates as practice." She indicated her crew, now standing in a row behind her, some of them staring aghast at the considerable storm wreckage, and then back at Inda's gore-stiff clothes and hair. "All the way north we drilled to sneak on board like they did the *Toola*, and take it at night. Glad our practice was needed," she added, rolling her eyes, but everyone was too tired to laugh at the mild joke.

"Fighting pirates," Inda repeated, scratching his gritty scalp. The smell of dried blood made his stomach lurch, and he hastily lowered his hand; before he did anything else, he'd get the bucket and dunk his head. "Sounds like we were galloping down the same track."

Jeje said, "Huh?"

Inda smiled briefly. "Later. Now, we need 'em," Inda said, indicating the new crew. He lifted his voice so everyone on deck could hear. "The wood party didn't take a glass. I was watching. But they have to have figured it all out by now, which is why we haven't seen them. I think they'll show up at dawn, with the spar so we won't suspect anything, but they'll have plans. We've tonight to drill."

There is nothing, throughout the history of human beings anywhere, like a threat followed by an immediate goal to cohere a disparate horde. Walic's former crew, though some might be uncertain about Inda, knew the second mate. If he won, his retribution would be cruel and lingering.

And so, at dawn, when it fell out exactly as Inda had said, they were ready, both those on deck with weapons hidden carefully in chosen spots, and those hiding, their weapons gripped in sweaty hands.

The second mate and his crew rowed up, towing the spar, and together everyone worked to boom up the great tree trunk that they'd spent a day trimming and smoothing— the mate's eyes moving constantly over the deck. They all knew those darting glances were furtive attempts to locate the first mate or the captain, who had never left the deck unwatched by at least one of them.

He recognized all those in the open. Jeje's new crew were hidden below deck level in the hatches, behind the

door of the cabin, crouched at the binnacle. Jeje and Thog
squatted out of sight on the mastheads, composite bows
from the *Vixen* and spiral-fletched arrows to hand.

Fox and Inda watched him watch. Inda stood at the forecastle haul line, mouth open, and Fox worked with the
party maneuvering the long, heavy spar to the deck.

Tau leaned against the taffrail, the ends of his long, loose
hair brushed by the wind over his relaxed hands. The second mate eyed him, brow furrowed, then shook his head
until his chimes rang.

At the helm Barend saw him squint his way too long and
thought: *He won't ask questions because he wouldn't believe us anyway. He wants to take us by surprise—but first
he wants to figure out who's in command.*

Once the spar was on deck the second mate backed to
the taffrail, raising his ax.

He whistled sharply, then snapped his attention back to
Inda, who no longer had his mouth open; he stood at the
bow where everyone could see him. Gone was the vacant
face, the shambling, purposeless slouch. The mate had had
an entire night to rest and think, was too experienced to
miss the tautness of the fighter poised to fight.

The first mate had been right!

The two pirates who had hidden in the mainchains
leaped over the rail. "That one!" The second mate pointed
his ax at Inda. "*Long* will you linger under my knife," he
vowed in his home language. Then he bared his teeth and
swept the ax around. "Kill them! All except—"

"*Now!*" Inda shouted.

Both sides charged.

The fight was short and vicious, the summer air filled
with the crashing of weapons, screams, shouts.

Spang! Spang! The pair sent after Inda dropped within
five paces of one another, arrows in their chests from Thog
and Jeje on the main masthead.

The mate swooped down, grabbed up a fallen blade, and
hurled himself at Inda, sword in his right hand held behind
his head for a killing downstroke, the ax gripped in his left
fist held out horizontally, ready to either block or attack.

Four bodies intervened: two pirates trying to get at Inda

first, and Fox and Tcholan trying to fend off the huge mate. Tcholan´ barely escaped death, rolling a hair's breadth from decapitation. Fox ducked a slash on his left, risked a glance, and stumbled when a downed pirate kicked viciously at his legs. Fox chunked his knife into the man's chest as he fell. Another pirate loomed, roaring as his blade whooshed downward.

The two pirates bracketed Inda between them.

Fast as a heartbeat Inda slung his cutlass into the chest of the one about to decapitate Fox; his wrists flexed, and knives dropped from his sleeves into both hands.

Those who glanced his way were astounded at the continuous whirl of those blades. Inda seemed to have eyes in the back of his head, for he always knew just where to block and to strike. The two pirates' longer blades fouled one another, and because the two had never been drilled in fighting together, they frustrated one another, neither willing to give ground, the idea of reward for being the one to kill Inda their single thought.

Elsewhere on the deck pirates dropped, several with arrows in them, most with killing wounds, dead before they hit the deck. Inda's two joined them. He backed up, looking for Walic's second mate, who was a few paces away, fighting to get at him. Inda spotted him, leaped forward—and slipped in slick blood. He landed flat on his back, arms outflung, knives clattering to the deck and spinning away in the gore.

The mate leaped toward the forecastle, his chiming braids swinging and steel in each big fist as Inda's feet slithered in the blood without gaining purchase.

But by then Fox had cleared a space around him. He flicked a glance. Cook was just behind him, having finished off a spike-wielding enemy. He summoned Cook with a jerk of his head, and the two moved to either side of the mate.

It took Fox and Cook together to bring him down, fighting to the limits of their dwindling strength, but bring him down they did, until he lay a hacked and bleeding mess on the deck. Fox bent, hands on knees. Cook spun and threw his blood-smeared carving knife into the sea.

*   *   *

After the bodies were gone, they had to finish smoothing
the mast and step it. The sky was full of marching lambkins,
heralding more rain somewhere beyond the curve of the
horizon.

Tau drifted up to Inda where he leaned for a few moments against the taffrail, rewinding a blood-soaked bandage around his upper arm. He said in a private voice, "Coco
keeps offering promises to those who go below. Some of
them have gotten into the drink and want to let her out for
either sex or torture."

Inda sighed. "Will letting her free settle 'em?"

"No. She'll suborn the weakest and start trouble."

Inda looked up, his eyes bloodshot, but his face eased of
the closed-in blankness of the previous weeks. Tau wondered if he would ever find out what had caused the sudden change in Inda.

Inda squinted up, as the men chanted an old sea song,
ropes tentacling out fore and aft. "There. Soon as that mast
is fidded and the shrouds rattled down, we're under way.
So let's get rid of her. We'll give her the rowboat, as all the
others took too much damage, and I want the longboat for
us." Inda fought a jaw-cracking yawn. "Oh. And Tau. If
there are any others you think ought to go in that boat with
her, let me know."

Taumad shaped the word "Fox" but did not speak it.

Barend and Fox climbed up to their old retreat, the foremast head, to bend the new topsail. When they were up on
the masthead together, Barend cast an assessing glance at
Fox, whose sweat-streaked profile was hard as he stepped
onto the footropes either side of the gaff. "Are you going
to turf Inda?" He was too tired for anything but bluntness.

Fox's head turned, a sharp movement.

Barend's head pounded, but he knew everyone else's
head ached the same, if not worse. They kept moving, de-

spite thirst, hunger, and heat. "Command. You used to talk about the heavy mantle of command. You could kill Inda," he said. Hating the question, almost hating Fox. But he had to know—and he would warn Fox if he could. "Inda's fast with his hands, but you're much better. Proved that when we first took them."

Fox was busy seizing the sail to the gaff. One, two, three, he tightened with expert knots, as though he hadn't heard the question. Barend returned to his own task; he worked by sign with the mainmast crew, who were raising the new topping lift for the foremast. He'd only known Fox a couple of years, if you could call this furtive life knowing. But he'd come to understand some of his ways.

They kept working in tandem with the mainmast crew. The pendant was spliced to the end of the boom, an eyebolt hooped to the front, the tackle linked to both, and then let fall, to be belayed to the mast. The sultry breeze was slowly shifting into the east and cooling; the sail hoisted at last, with those below chanting hoarsely. The last of their strength rapidly gave out, leaving them just enough to seek the promised rest.

Fox and Barend were now alone on the masthead.

Fox leaned back against the mast and clasped his hands around one knee, face angled into the rising wind. "I dreamed for years of my mutiny. Taking this ship." He talked fast, a restless stream of words. "But when the time came Inda saw it. I didn't. Then out of nowhere comes that short, dark-browed . . . Jeje, is it? She crossed the ocean just in case Inda needed her. He's what, sixteen, and he's got that kind of loyalty."

Barend frowned at Fox's faint, mocking smile, and said, "Are you going to turf him or not?"

Fox turned his head. His bloodshot eyes looked very green, reminding Barend of Sponge and the Sierlaef. But then the two kingly families had intermarried before the civil war that put one family in inland exile, and the other on the throne.

Fox drawled, "Why do you ask? Would you?"

Barend snorted. "I've spent enough time around kings and brothers of kings and heirs to kings to hate, and I mean really, *really* hate, what your shit-stinking heavy mantle does to people. So, in case I'm not clear, no."

"So . . . what?" Fox gave him a long, sardonic look. "You planning to go after me if I do?"

"Probably," Barend admitted.

His tone made it clear he knew as well as Fox did that he had little chance of success.

"Loyalty." Fox lifted his fingers and flickered them through the air. "Here's the irony. Inda never said anything about wanting command. But today he said to each person, *Do this, or that will happen,* and what he said made sense—built a picture everyone could see—so everyone fell right into line."

Barend opened a hand, too tired even to grunt in agreement.

"Let's pretend I saw the right moment, too. I probably would have taken Walic's place on the captain's deck and rapped out general orders, and they all would have looked at one another, or asked questions, and I would have lost whatever it is that makes followers choose the next leader. Or maybe they would have challenged me. Then either I have to fight what was supposed to be my own crew, and if I win they'd see me as another Walic, and if I lose, I'm dead. Or I'd wish I were dead." He strove to sound detached, but Barend noticed the flexing of his long hands. "So command passed me by and settled itself on his shoulders. At least, today it did. Shall we see what he does with it?" He moved swiftly, as he often did after talking like that, sliding down the backstay before Barend could draw enough breath to answer.

Barend followed him to the deck, leaving the subject up there in the air. He'd gotten as much of an answer as he ever would.

They sailed away from the island, bearing northwest on the strong east wind; within a watch the island was out of sight, though it had taken two wearying days to beat their way up to it. The *Vixen* glided in their lee.

The wind dropped just before midnight, and thin rain came down, a weepy cold sky promising an end to the long summer. Most of the crew was asleep, exhausted after unremitting labor from the time the storm hit them.

The new recruits from Freedom watched sail and wind. Inda's followers bound and gagged Coco and brought her up, lowered the boat by torchlight, and put her over the side, along with two men whom Tau had named to Inda in private, the two whose whispered conversation had been witnessed by the bawdy-boy they despised.

The two men fought until they realized that they were not to be dragged to the cabin for diversion, but set adrift. They'd submitted to binding and gagging. Now both sat in the stern sheets, their eyes wide and manic in the torchlight. When they saw Coco lowered down, her ruffled skirts flagging in the rainy wind, they shifted, their bodies tense.

On Inda's command Jeje had helped Thog store a precious bucket on that boat, one that had enough magic to purify a month's water, plus several dozen of the hard, long-lasting biscuits called rocks, and a jug of cabbage-slurry.

After the boat was boomed off, Inda tossed down a knife, then turned away, not caring who got to it or what they did with it afterward.

As the two hands struggled to capture that knife with their bound hands, Coco wailed, "Taumad! I'll do *anything,* I *love* you!"

She peered up at him through her tears. His river of golden hair gleamed in the ruddy light; she clasped her hands, willing him to say a word. Just one. Gaffer Walic was already a memory, for once she'd gotten over her fascination with the powerful pirate captain he'd never been anything more than convenience. Taumad, born of sunlight and clean water, why did he not love her when she had been so good to him?

He stared down, not speaking, then wrapped that glorious hair round one fist, gripped a sword blade from somewhere, and hacked off his hair in one stroke. The long locks he flung to the wind. They fell on the water, where they drifted, briefly fire-lined, and vanished. Then, making the

first violent gesture she'd ever seen from him, he threw the
sword to thunk, humming, in the mast.

And then he was gone.

"Taumad!"

A noise behind her. She whirled, saw a blood-smeared
hand holding a knife, the face above it grinning.

Chapter Nine

THOG vanished below to finish cleaning the cabin for Inda. It had been her self-appointed task.

Jeje spotted Tau climbing slowly up the foremast. She hesitated—he paused, looked back, and beckoned. So she climbed up and sat beside him on a furled sail. "What happened?" she said, trying not to stare at the short hair drifting into his eyes.

Tau jerked his head, an impatient movement. She pressed her forearms across her middle to squish the hot flare of desire ignited by the sight of those silken strands sliding back over his forehead. She'd fought that battle and won, the prize being his friendship as it had been when they were all children, without the constraints of physical awareness.

"It's been like living in a very bad play that does not come to an end, and if the watchers do not get their money's worth, they will take you apart in pieces."

Jeje was shocked. Tau rarely exaggerated.

He added with more of his old irony, "I had the fool's role, but it's not as if my ma didn't warn me."

Jeje shivered. "What do you mean?" How long ago that last visit to the Halian coast seemed. Tau's mother—the Butterfly, they called her—had welcomed them into her exquisite pleasure house. Jeje remembered the extraordinary woman who stooped, scented with perfumes and glimmering with jewelry, to kiss them; nothing in her house seemed as exquisite as she.

"My ma said if I don't take them they'll take me." He shifted to Iascan, using "take" to mean "take advantage of."

Jeje sighed, remembering what she'd overheard his mother saying, *My darling Taumad is a romantic.* And the words after—*to surround a romantic with greed, passion, the very desire to possess him, is to close his heart and lock it against you*—confusing then, thought about many times since, all of which seemed to add up to one thing: though he might regard her as a friend, Tau would never love Jeje.

She said, "You need to be rich. Only see who you want."

Tau laughed softly, his profile dark against the pale blue of the sail. "Ma told me that once. One of her lessons in human nature, given to me long before I should have heard them. She said that only the rich can afford to love. One of the reasons I ran off—those lessons—but maybe she's right. At least the wealthy can afford to choose."

Jeje pleated her shirt as she thought back. When they were young and free of all desire or expectation he had talked all the time: to her, and Inda, and Dasta, and Yan. Then he had stopped. Now it seemed he could talk again. Though she had won her long struggle with hopeless expectation, she did not want him to go silent and remote again.

But she would always tell him the truth. "Seems to me the danger of being rich is you get courted for your money."

Tau's soft laugh evidenced less humor than self-mockery. "And some are never courted at all."

Jeje held her breath. It was so rare to hear that tone of voice from Tau, soft, full of regret.

She said, low, "You don't have to tell me if the sex was something horrible. Don't think I want to know."

Tau smiled. "Sex is just a game. Coco was taught the same things I was. She knew I was in control, but she liked it that way—at least for a while. It was new for her. I think in her mind her letting me direct the games in the cabin meant I was courting her. Desired her."

"Ew," Jeje said. Thog had whispered Coco's history to

her while they crouched on the masthead waiting for the return of the second mate with the spar.

Tau waved a hand as though flicking away a buzzing insect. "It was between times that was the worst. I was always caught between her expectation and his suspicion, and the chief mates loved telling me in disgusting detail what happened to former favorites when Walic or Coco were crossed."

When she did not respond, he let out his breath in a long sigh. "That's the good side of my upbringing, that I know how to run the game with anyone, even an enemy. But the bad side is . . . I see sex as a game, not a gift."

"Gift?" she repeated, confused.

"I never wanted to sleep with my friends. And you all respected that. Never tried to possess me. Yet ever since Walic captured us I keep thinking about Yan."

Jeje knew what ground they stood on now. "Was different for him. He wanted sex with friends. For him sex was love."

"Had I had more grace, more forbearance, I would have complied," Tau said softly. "A simple enough gift for Yan, who never asked for anything but our friendship."

Yan was gone, and his emotional tangles as well, so Jeje said, "I did."

Tau's head turned, his pupils black, reflecting ruddy flames from the lantern overhead. "What? You slept with him? I thought it was men only for Yan. And, well, I thought you were like me. Not wanting to risk . . . entanglements, as my mother would have put it, with friends," he added.

She felt unsettled that he'd noticed that much of her own preferences. "Pretty much was men only, but we were talking, and drinking, and he told me how he loved—well, all his friends, and, well, it happened. I was glad it did, after."

Tau was silent, then he said, "You are a very good person, Jeje. You know that, don't you?"

She snorted, feeling her face heat up. "Nah. I wanted a pillow jig. And there he was."

Tau laughed, then veered from the personal, as if some inward weathervane sensed a shift in the winds of Jeje's moods. "I take it Testhy showed his backside?"

"Not at once. He was a good mate until we reached Khanerenth. But there were no orders after we had no success asking for help to go against Walic, because . . ." She frowned, wondering who knew about Inda's real identity. She went on in haste, "Anyway, there's a warrant out for Kodl, Inda, and Testhy, sworn by Ryala Pim. Said we're all pirates, and they're the ringleaders. So me and Testhy parted. He got himself hired as purser's mate on a guild trader. Took him only a morning to find a berth."

"Kodl died fighting," Tau said, as soft rain beaded on his face. "And Dun. Either side of Inda. But Rig and the others died on the deck of Walic's ship, refusing to turn pirate."

Jeje shifted. "I didn't think about that. Inda *did?*"

Tau waved a hand to and fro. "I didn't hear what was said, but I caught a glimpse of Fox and Rat talking to him in the waist. As soon as I recognized the language Fox spoke—Marlovan—I kept Coco busy, hoping those two had some kind of mutiny plot. Afterward it turned out I was wrong, but whatever they said must have got Inda to agree to piracy though he might have been too stunned to know what was going on. He was in very bad shape and never talked about it afterward. He might not even remember."

Jeje relaxed inside, a sudden release of tension that caused an uncomfortable flash of insight: even if Tau had told her Inda had jumped up waving his arms to volunteer, she would have found an excuse for him. *And wasn't I right? Didn't I arrive just as he took this ship?* she told herself. *Yes, so what's he going to do with it now he's got it?*

She ignored that question: they would find out soon, wouldn't they? "Lorenda will be glad Kodl died fighting, and not tortured by a damn pirate," she said to Tau, who had been watching her face and had formed a fair idea of the direction of her thoughts. "They know about Walic at Freeport. When I went to see her for cordage she was already wearing a mourning scarf."

Tau turned on her. "Jeje. That's what Inda meant! You didn't come looking for us, you came to *rescue* us."

Jeje's face burned. "Well, I know it was a stupid idea, but I thought maybe we could run that *Toola* ruse."

Tau shook his head. "I'm the stupid one. Though in my defense, I haven't slept for days. You came to the rescue."

She said gruffly, "You thought I was actually going to offer to join up with Walic's gang?"

"I didn't think at all. We'd fought a battle, and then you were there. And Inda acted like he'd known you would come, as if there had never been a question."

Jeje winced at the tremor in his voice.

"I'd about given up believing that there was any meaning to anything for a while, even Inda . . . No. I won't say it, because he obviously did not give up." Tau drew in an unsteady breath.

Jeje glanced at his profile, half obscured by the raggedly cut hair ruffling in the wind and obscuring his eyes. So he too had feared Inda might turn pirate?

Yes or no, the subject was obviously closed. All right. There were plenty of other questions.

She asked one. "Fox and Rat. Marlovans. Those have to be the two with the home accents."

"You heard that, did you?" Tau faced her again, his eyes bright with a sheen of moisture. He dashed his sleeve across his eyes and it was gone. "How much have you learned about Inda?"

Jeje whistled softly as she kicked her feet in the cool, misty wind. "I know he's some kind o' prince, or lord, or whatever. Testhy hopped out with that, after we were refused help in Khanerenth."

"Ah. Rat and Fox know him—they speak Marlovan with him when they think no one is listening or when no one can understand."

"Marlovan," Jeje repeated. "You hear about it, but you never really hear *it,* outside that time the Venn came aboard us on *Ryala.*"

Tau said impatiently, "It's old-fashioned Venn, with Sartoran verb endings. You could probably understand it if you remember Iascan verbs have somewhat similar endings."

Jeje snorted. "Says you, who gets a lingo second time he hears it. Anyway—"

"Jeje. Tau. Come into the cabin."

That was Inda, calling softly.

And now for the big question neither of wants to ask, she thought grimly.

They scrambled down the new foremast and Jeje followed Tau aft into the cabin. Tau's jawline tightened; Jeje heard his breathing change when they walked into a clean-swept cabin.

Tau braced himself. Gone were the bloodstains from Walic's messy death at the hands of the cook; gone too were the furnishings: the big bed, the ornate pillows and hangings, and Coco's carved cedar trunks of gowns and accessories. The cabin seemed larger, empty as it was except for a table dragged in from the wardroom, the bench built under the stern windows, and the swinging lamps overhead. Even the flower rugs were gone, and the deck boards were scrubbed clean, smelling of damp wood.

The only thing left from before was the fantastically expensive wooden tub full of magically pure and warm water built into the cubby off the main room.

Tau cautiously drew a breath but caught a faint whiff of Coco's scent and felt his throat close with disgust. It was so faint it might only be memory, but he crossed behind Inda and sat on the bench, turning his head to breathe the misting rain that wafted in through the open stern windows.

Jeje's gaze swept the room. Tau had gone remote again, his face toward the night sky. Inda had maps and charts spread before him on the table. Lamps swung above, and bent over him was the tall, lean redhead with the Marlovan accent. Near them lounged the thin fellow with a wide forehead and a sharp-cut face that tapered down to a pointed chin, the one they called Rat. Thog lurked under a bulkhead, Uslar and Mutt sitting at her feet.

Jeje joined them, refusing to formulate her fears into words. But she was honest enough to recognize that they were there.

Inda had bathed, his wet hair hanging down his back. On the deck behind his chair he'd laid a long, luxuriously fluffy towel to catch the drips. Inda wore a new shirt someone had given him, with the loose sleeves he preferred, to hide his knives in their sheaths. The neck of the shirt was, as usual, carelessly half-laced.

Jeje glimpsed the bath in the small cabin behind Inda—and goggled at its size. Three people could comfortably sit in that thing!

Inda saw the direction of her glance, and grinned. "I told the crew everyone gets a turn, soon's we're done talking. That should keep 'em from mutiny, at least for a day."

Dasta slipped in; at a gesture from Inda he closed the cabin door and stood against it, arms crossed.

A secret conference? Jeje's heart thumped and she saw in Tau's stillness that he shared the same apprehension.

Inda lit a lamp, leaving the glass top off so the flame was naked. He set it in the middle of the table, on top of his charts, with the deliberation of ritual, then stepped back, the warm golden light showing the contours of his face; in that light his skin was smooth and unscarred.

"I wanted to hold a memorial," he said in a tentative voice so different than what they'd heard on deck that long bloody day and night. The contrast was startling. He bent his head, gazing at the candle as if emotion were an uncertain thing. "Kodl. Dun. Niz—all of them." He glanced over his shoulder, not meeting Fox's or Barend's eyes. "You can join if you want. Add in anyone you missed from your days with Walic."

No one spoke or moved, though Barend shifted; the candle flames glowed, twin flames, in Thog's wide black eyes.

Inda drew in a deep breath—they all heard the hiss—then lifted the candleholder and passed it in a circle, his eyes closed. They didn't hear all the words, for he mumbled, his voice monotone, but he obviously had thought during that long day: he spoke almost without hesitation, naming every one of the dead from their old crew. Missing no one, not even the very new hires.

Then he sat down, head still bent.

For a long, painful moment no one moved—not because they did not want to, but because yet another shock on top of so many was overwhelming.

So Tau rose from the bench, came forward, and spoke to the flame, his voice clear, pitched exactly right, the words sympathetic and appropriate: the only one there who recognized the words of an ancient play was Fox. But he said nothing.

After that it was easier for Inda's old crew. They all spoke, one after another, even the two boys, Uslar whispering, Mutt muttering so low they couldn't hear him, until he stopped, wiped his eyes with his knuckles, then limped back to Thog's side.

Last was Thog, who passed her hands over the candle, then just stood, unspeaking, so still it was obvious to all her testimony was entirely inward.

When she finished, Inda turned Fox's and Barend's way. Fox gestured, palm down; Barend's sharp cheekbones were ridged with red. He stayed where he was.

Inda moved to the door, opened it, and there was the cook, waiting. Inda stood back, waving him in.

The cook paused just outside the door, looking around uneasily.

"Come in, Cook," Inda said. "Or would you rather take back your name? We're here to discuss changes. That could be one."

"M'name is Lorm, Jarad Filic Lorm, if ye want 'em all, but Lorm's good as any, shared wi' m'dad and brother."

"Then Lorm it is. This here is Barend, and you can call me Inda. We're through with Walic's cursed tags." Inda turned to face the redhead, as if an idea had occurred to him. "Are you—"

"Fox will do," said he, in Iascan. "It was a private nickname in the family. Walic got it from me inadvertently, when I was too dazed to think, but I believe it can be maintained."

Inda hesitated, lips parted, and Tau and Jeje saw that Fox's words held meaning for the three Marlovans that bypassed everyone else. Then Inda carefully touched the slash on the side of his jaw, made by an ax wielded by one of the second mate's men. "We're here because I think we'd better understand one another now. Then settle on what comes next, before we get a snooze-watch. When the others wake up they'll be rested enough to start thinking. If we don't have a united force, then we'll be fighting again—on a ship that's going to broach to if we're hit with any more storms."

Fox crossed the cabin, leaned on the opposite wall. "And so?"

Inda sat back. "So tell me what you see us doing." He gestured broadly. "All of you."

Surprise was the main reaction: Tau saw it in quick exchanges of questioning looks, shiftings, a couple of inarticulate mutters.

"I want to fight pirates," Thog stated.

Inda flicked a glance Lorm's way. "You?"

Lorm shook his big head. "I got what I wanted when I slit Gaffer's throat. He—" The man dropped his gaze and shook his head again harder, as if to dislodge unwelcome memories.

Inda put his elbows on the table and his chin in his hands, careful not to touch the red ax slash. "Go on, Lorm."

The cook looked upward, the liquid gathering in his eyes spilling down his furrowed cheeks. "It's just . . . I used to cook for a fine eatery. Sarendan coast. Famed for me sauces. Coco's House was down the street. We used to send meals there for a price." He looked around, then finished in a rush. "Coco joined up with him. Part of her price was me. They crashed in one night. I refused—didn't want to go to sea, much less with pirates—so quick as death Walic killed my wife. My oldest child. Coco laughing. Clapping her hands when they . . . when they . . ." His hand arced out and away, as if he could thrust memory out of his mind.

Tau had drifted unnoticed near the table. "You don't have to go on," he said kindly. "Unless it will help."

Lorm faced him, saw the compassion there, and drew in a shuddering breath. "I told Walic I'd join. So I could at least save the little one. But he killed her anyway, sayin' that now I'd got nothing to come back for. Then he had them mates fire the house. *Her* giggling the whole time."

The others shuffled, made sympathetic murmurs, faces expressive of vicarious anger, all except for Fox, who gazed at him with narrowed eyes.

Fox was unsettled—no, he felt that he'd failed himself, or the cook, or someone. He had traveled so long with this man but had never heard a whisper of that—nor had he thought to ask. In a couple of months Inda had figured it out. Either he or Tau, but it was to Inda that Tau would speak.

"So what do you want to do now?" Inda asked, his hoarse voice cracking on the last word, but no one smiled.

"Walic was right. Nothin' to go back for. I'll cook for you, but willing, now." Lorm's hands trembled, and he longed for a drink to steady them. "And fight, if need be."

"Fair enough. We need you. Barend?"

Fox struggled against anger as well as tiredness, wondering what else was he going to learn that he should have known.

The possibility of taking command now had narrowed to stabbing Inda in the back. Just as Barend had implied up on the yard.

He didn't hear Barend's *I'm with you,* but he already knew where Barend's loyalties would turn. Had turned.

"Fox?"

"I see us going after wealth," Fox stated, smiling. Right now he was, perforce, a follower; if he went after Inda (which he was not inclined to do) he would be alone. And even the bawdy-boy could fight.

So he would follow. But he would never be submissive— or serious. "Wealth and fighting, for sport."

"Jeje?"

A shrug. "Hadn't thought past finding you." She spoke in a gruff voice, eyes lowered, and Inda wondered with an inward pang if she'd come for Tau, and not all of them as he'd thought. No, that wasn't Jeje's way. She would have come even if Tau, and not Testhy, had been on the *Vixen.* There was some other question in her mind but if she wasn't ready to speak, it was useless to press her.

"Tau?"

"I would like a life of quiet ease, of course. What else?"

Quiet ease. Tau was being indirect again, not meeting Inda's eyes.

A deep breath and coldness in his veins. Inda had it: Tau—and probably Jeje, too—expected him to turn pirate. That's probably what they'd been talking about on the mast.

No. Do them justice. They were afraid he would turn pirate. After all, he was here, wasn't he? And again Rig's contempt scorched across his inner eye.

He forced the image away. "Dasta?"

"Stay with you. Whatever you think we should do."

"Me too," Mutt said, from the floor by Thog's feet.

"And me," Tcholan spoke up, from the opposite corner, his Khanerenth accent clear.

"And me," chimed in Uslar.

Despite his intent to keep emotion from decision, their trust seared Inda. Not Fox, of course, standing there lean and still as a knife, his manner wary and sardonic, but the rest, he knew they were waiting for him to choose what they should do.

His fingers drummed lightly on the edge of one of the charts as he counted up his options: they could do anything—sell the ship, part, run, hide. They could even, as Tau seemed to fear, set up as pirates. But Inda knew what Tdor, the net maker, would say to that: *If you don't make the net, you tear it.*

He answered Tdor's steady thirteen-year-old eyes, so clear in his mind: *If I'm not allowed to be a maker, at least I can rid the world of the tearers, can't I?*

He leaned back in his chair. "So who is the worst pirate in the eastern waters, now that Walic is gone?"

"Boruin," Fox and Tau said at once, echoed a moment later by Lorm, who added, gruffly, "Much worse than Walic. She's not only cruel like him, but crazy and strong. Majarian, her mate, is even stronger. He don't plan, he's the muscle. Plans are hers. Walic talked about her a lot, when he had me serving in the cabin."

Fox added, "Walic's mates talked about them as well. It's as C—Lorm says."

"Good," Inda said.

Because he was still sorting things out in his tired, aching head, he missed the flickers of surprise around him. But no one spoke. They watched and waited.

He opened his eyes, knowing he'd decided. Now to sound assured, if he could. "Tau, you're the only one who won't get his wish if you accept my plan."

Accept. All of them heard that word and again, life sustained a change.

"I'm desolated." Tau made an airy gesture, causing laughter, a noise of release more than genuine humor.

Inda lifted his head. "Dasta, any mates you can trust on the *Sea-King?* We could sail back, use Barend's ruse again."

Dasta pursed his lips, then slowly shook his head.

"I don't know. Maybe a few might be right for us. But you can't be sure because Walic had the ship full of spies. We never dared talk much."

"Then they're on their own," Inda said. "And so are we. We have a damaged ship that's slow with an unseasoned mast. We have pirates as well as privateers for a crew. Some we can probably trust, some not. I have a price on my head, no matter why, and the Venn are looking for me. None of us westerners can go home until the blockade is lifted. If that happens in our lifetime."

He paused. They were listening. "Meanwhile, here's Walic's chart. His goal was to join the Brotherhood of Blood. He has all their ships listed, at least the ones usually found in eastern waters, and he's got their last known positions charted. We can keep adding to that, if we like."

"To avoid 'em?" Jeje asked, her straight brows furrowed.

"No." Inda opened his hands.

"To join them?" Fox asked lazily.

"No." Inda did not miss the subtle signs of relief: lowered shoulders, hands loosening, deep breaths.

He went on as though he hadn't noticed. "We have plenty of money in the chests down in the hold. Hire new crew at Freeport, train and test 'em. Training in hand-to-hand fighting, boarding at sea, boarding at anchor, giving chase. Then, when we're ready, we pick something from this list—" He touched Walic's cherished chart with its chalk marks in red for Brotherhood ship positions. "We find something fast and taut. And take it."

"And?" Jeje asked.

"And make ourselves rich by hunting the pirates who have the most of everything—fast ships, gold, costly goods, all of it stolen at the price of blood and death."

Barend whistled. "You mean what I think?"

Inda touched his jaw and winced. "That hurts more than slices usually do. Ax must've been used to hack away at some poison bush." He put his hand down. "If you stay with me, the plan is this," he said not to the people in the cabin, but to Rig glaring back from memory in silent accusation. "We're gonna make our first big strike at Boruin and Majarian, and then we're going to war against the Brotherhood of Blood."

Chapter Ten

"THE Venn and their allies will come by night, soon as the winds change."

Harbormaster Sholf—newly in charge of the harbor at the Nob at the tip of the Olaran peninsula—frowned at the weather-seamed old Delf woman.

Everyone in his new office stared at her. Delfin Islanders looked like birds, ungainly birds, but when they spoke, anyone who had anything to do with the sea listened.

Harbormaster Sholf, who took over after the slaughter of his old uncle when the pirates burned down the Nob, could count the times a Delf had offered information: three times in his fifty years. And this was one of those three rare times.

His staff was appalled. Only Mardric, the tall young man lounging near the doorway, seemed amused.

"So what do we do, stop rebuilding?" asked Sholf's chief scribe, a hard-working young woman who had lost half her family in the pirate attack.

Sholf wanted to say, "Good question," except he couldn't. He had to seem calm and decisive—a leader—because he knew he did not look like one. His uncle had said, *When you're almost always the shortest man in the room, not to mention the stoutest, people tend to look to you for meals, not for decisions.*

"Even if we all fight, we can't win," protested the new

guild master, hitching up his worn sash under his massive belly.

At least he's fatter than me, Sholf thought, distracted by the movement. *If much taller.*

They all had lost people during the killing spree before the pirates looted the city—a day-long orgy of drinking, singing, fighting, and rutting by the light of the fire—then departed on the morning tide, leaving the devastation to be found by those who had survived by hiding in the ancient caves below the southern cliffs.

I will be expected to stand there with a sword in hand if the pirates come again, he thought now. *And die like my uncle.*

There was one alternative, but the others would hate it so much that he had to let them find it on their own or they would argue against it all night.

And so he waited while they suggested everyone hide and brick up the ancient tunnel entrance. No, that's a stupid idea, let's all take to the sea. And what if the Venn are there, behind the pirates, like everyone says they are? We'll fight. We can't fight. Hide. No. Then we may as well give up the city altogether. Some kind of plan? Oh, yes, a plan against *how* many pirates?

It was Mardric, the lounger—leader of the Resistance to the Marlovan conquerors—who spoke up at last, saying unexpectedly, "Tell the Marlovans."

Everyone fell silent.

Mardric chuckled as he fingered back a lock of wavy black hair that had fallen across his brow. "Come now," he chided, waving a hand to and fro. "Would you not like to see pirates take arms against the Marlovans? I know I would."

That caused another hubbub, everyone trying to speak down the others. Yes, watch them get slaughtered. They think they are so superior. How would they measure against pirates? Taken by surprise. Can they be taken by surprise? But it was his chief scribe who gave Mardric a contemptuous toss of the head before saying, "If they fight, it's for us."

Gradually the voices died away, some looking at her, and

she raised her chin and stated more firmly, "They'd be fighting for *us*."

"But that's supposedly in the treaty they forced on us," the guild master pointed out, hitching up his sash again.

"Yes," the scribe said. "Exactly. They did take on the cost of the rebuilding. Just as they promised. So if they take on the pirates . . ." She groped, as if the right words hovered in the air in front of her.

"If they defend our city against the pirates," Sholf said, "then we have accepted their treaty."

"So you've decided?" Mardric asked, inspecting the clean, short nails on one shapely hand.

A few beginning protests, one snort, but most indicated agreement, however reluctant.

Mardric stared across the room, eyes narrowed, then said, "So you expect us to accept their yoke, like obedient oxen?"

Sholf said, "If they keep the treaty, then I think it right that we do, too. Well?" And he turned to the others. "Do I ride down to warn their prince?"

Mardric laughed. "That fool? Save yourself a trip. Send one of their patrol flunkies." He waved toward the window, which was shuttered against listeners despite the still summer air. The resultant stuffiness did not help anyone's temper.

Beyond that window a small contingent of Marlovans patrolled the harbor and the city, under strict orders from their prince not to interfere unless there was violence.

Their prince.

"A fool from whom you never did find out any information," Sholf retorted, and the others laughed.

They all knew the story, for the Marlovan prince (had he really believed he was unknown when he called himself Sponge?) had either from ignorance or arrogance made no pretense of hiding his infatuation with one of Mardric's spies. Dallo, the spy, had been assigned to work his way among the Marlovan forces by whatever means, and unexpectedly attracted their leader himself with no more than a glance. But the very day after the spy declared he had only to snap his fingers and the prince would come to heel and give them whatever aid and information they demanded, the prince had as suddenly departed.

Sholf said, "If you have not noticed—I have—they don't make decisions without his sanction. From everything I hear, young as he is, and foolish as he might have been when he was among us, they abide by his decisions." He paused, and observed shrugs, nods, tipped heads of agreement or at least acceptance. The news coming up the peninsula from all their various contacts seemed to agree.

"Further, unlike his uncle and those his uncle appointed over us—" Their reactions varied, though the impetus was a universal disgust and anger at the cruelties of the Jarl Kepri-Davan and his son and heir. "Unlike *them*, this young prince appears to regard the treaty as binding. So far he has honored their promises in his judgments."

"How can you blind yourself so willfully?" Mardric retorted. "Does it comfort you? Was it so easy to forget Nalma in the vinelands and her friends, much less everything done after?"

A murmur of protest, of uneasiness, rose.

Sholf said, "I have never forgotten Nalma. Or her friends. Or any of the other young women the Marlovan prince has murdered—except I still wonder, after all this time, why have no other names or towns have been named in this murderous rampage? Or why the king of Idayago himself never talked about it when he signed the treaty?"

"You deny that my own brother saw Nalma and the others in that house before they were Disappeared?" Mardric retorted.

"I do not," Sholf answered. "I have heard, vividly, what that house looked like, all that blood. All the more peculiar that no word of other murders has reached me."

"They don't come out of fear, of course," the old woman said, but Sholf heard the question in her voice.

So he said, "We are not going to answer those questions now. What we do have to answer is: what do we do to prepare for imminent attack? Choose, council. Do we stand to the last man or woman, or do we invoke the treaty and let the Marlovans stand in our place?"

Again he paused, again he saw subtle signs of concession.

"If the winds change soon, there will be no time for the back-and-forth of messengers. Are we agreed that if the Marlovan conquerors abide by the treaty and come in force to our defense, we will abide by it, too? However unwillingly?"

They all signified agreement. Mardric last, lounging there with his superior smile; Sholf waited in patient silence until Mardric said, "Aye."

"Then I will leave today and ride down the coast to Ala Larkadhe."

For Evred Montrei-Vayir, second son of the Marlovan king, his first command could be summed up as a frustrating series of travels back and forth along the Andahi Pass to hearings for petty crimes. Again and again he listened to accusations from both sides for crimes petty and not so petty, such as the wholesale burning of cotton fields just so the evil Marlovans would not get the profits.

He knew some of these burnings were the last protests against the harshness of the Kepri-Davans, who had been initially placed by the Harskialdna as the guards of the north end of the Andahi Pass. But that did not explain the bitterness in the eastern portion of Idayago in particular, the sullen, deliberate resistance. Something else was amiss, though as yet he had not discovered what. He knew this: his judgment, however fair, could not satisfy emotional reaction—either his or the Idayagans'—he had to wall away his feelings and strive to find a balance between the treaty stipulations and Marlovan law.

There was another mystery, perhaps connected, perhaps not. He was certain that, despite apparent evidence, the Idayagans had not ambushed and murdered his former commander, Tanrid-Laef Algara-Vayir, brother to his old academy mate Inda.

Hawkeye Yvana-Vayir, arriving as Tanrid's replacement, had brought reports of attacks all the way down to the southern border of Iasca Leror. It was land warfare that they all understood, had been trained to understand. But the enemies now were in ships: pirates sent by the Venn.

As the summer sun slanted more northward each day Harbormaster Sholf traveled down from Olara's mountainous peninsula to Ala Larkadhe.

There seemed to be an order for the troops to pass along everyone who wished to speak to the Marlovan prince, and so Sholf was handed off from patrol to patrol, scout to sentry, until he reached the enormous castle with the weird tower made of ancient snow-white material that was not quite stone. The wind from the mountains brought an almost subliminal hum. Wind harps. Testament to unimaginably different customs as lived by their ancestors.

Tired, thirsty, the harbormaster was conducted to the room the Marlovan prince had taken for his headquarters, the carved, gilded furnishings shoved to the walls and replaced by a massive table littered with papers.

The room was full of men, all facing the young prince whom Sholf recognized from his stay at the Nob last spring: tall, dark red hair pulled high on the back of his head and hanging down between his shoulder blades in the singular style all these warriors affected, watchful hazel eyes below an intelligent brow.

Sholf ignored the other men. His attention stayed on the prince, who stood before a great map covered with indecipherable marks. He wore a gray warrior's coat no different from any of his men's, tight through muscular shoulders and chest, tied at the waist with a knife thrust through the sash, wide-skirted for riding on the world-famous horses.

The young man, scarcely out of boyhood, looked tired and tense, but his manner was as courteous as it had been last spring.

Sholf said in his diffident Iascan, "We have received word from a Delfin Islander, relayed through our fishing fleet. A small fleet of Venn and many pirate allies were seen north of the strait. The Delfin Islanders say as soon as the wind changes the pirates are going to attack the Nob in force once again. They say that if the pirates take it, the Venn this time mean to hold it."

The prince turned to the tall, long-faced man standing farthest from the center of the room—but from where he could observe it in its entirety. He was Captain Sindan, not just the king's own Runner, but Captain of the Runners. Sholf had been told dismissively that Sindan had given up the military command he'd earned to remain a Runner—thus staying in the royal city at the king's side.

Many thought that he'd thus given up influence, but the most far-sighted among Idayagan and Olaran councils had subsequently come to the conclusion that in fact, Sindan had far more influence and therefore more power than any single man, excepting only the king and his brother.

It was he who had written the Idayagan and Olaran treaty.

Sindan did not speak, but some minute change in his expression seemed to reassure Evred.

The prince said, "The treaty does require us to defend these lands."

The middle-aged, grizzled warrior at the prince's other side frowned down at the map. This man had to be the new Jarl, called Dewlap Arveas, sent in to replace the horrible Kepri-Davan.

Arveas said, not hiding his skepticism, "Why attack and hold the end of a peninsula? It's surrounded on three sides by nothing but ocean, and the fourth is solid mountain. They can't possibly mount an invasion with any speed or secrecy along that narrow coast road." He waved his hand in a circle. "No military value."

Sholf said, "I cannot address questions of military value, for we are not military people." He could not keep dryness from his tone, though the Marlovans did not react. "If the pirates destroy us once again and the Venn settle in, they can make of our harbor a port convenient to their long-range plans for your southern coast."

Arveas said, "Ah! Yes. Repair, refit, resupply. But from the sea."

Another young man, with bright yellow hair and a sharp-cut chin like the prince's, made an impatient movement. This had to be Hawkeye Yvana-Vayir, whose mother had been sister to the Marlovan king and who as a youth had fought in the battle that the Idayagans had lost, the price their kingdom. If the rumors were true, he had been one of the older prince's gang who went on a rampage killing unarmed girls.

The young man glanced at his cousin, then back at Sholf. "You want us to come in force to defend you."

Sholf said, "It was in your treaty, signed by your king."

Again silence, but of a different quality. They all felt the weight of decision, measured by the tension in the young prince's face.

Evred could see in Arveas' skeptical raised brows, in Hawkeye's twisted mouth, they did not believe the man.

"Please, make yourself comfortable," Evred responded, signing to one of the guards at the door. "I promise an answer as soon as possible."

Sholf's mouth tightened. "I shall depart on the morrow, answer or no."

Evred couldn't resist asking, "And?"

Sholf turned his way, the lines in his face deep. "We'll try again to defend what's ours."

They all knew how successful the Nob's defense had been the first time.

But he said nothing more, just followed the guard out.

As soon as the door was closed, Evred said, "Well?"

"We don't have enough men as it is," Dewlap Arveas said.

No one had to point out the obvious, which the Marlovans were trying to keep from the people they had conquered. For the first time since they'd taken these lands, no reinforcements would be coming north at the end of the summer. Instead the Harskialdna was reinforcing the Iascan coast. Evred was going to have to make do with what men he had.

Hawkeye glared at the map. "It's got to be a ruse. An obvious one. Look, we take everyone we have way out to the end of that soul-rotted peninsula, then we have to pull men off the harbors in the north to cover us here. It would be easy as damnation for the pirates to attack the northern harbors!"

Dewlap Arveas' voice was husky from years of field

command. "I have to agree. I don't know about ships, but I do know about land. If we strip the three Idayagan harbors of all but token protection so we can cover this side of the Pass, all they'd have to do is send in a couple of rickety boats full of pirates to take those castles. The cost in lives to retake those harbors would be—" Another circle of his hand.

Evred glanced at Captain Sindan, who had, in his customary manner, listened without speaking. He regarded the prince with a steady, patient dark gaze.

But Evred had known him all his life, had grown up calling him Uncle Sindan. He knew his father's Runner, so scrupulous about protocol, would never disagree with the military men unless asked.

His lack of expression was therefore enough of an answer, and Evred knew not just what Sindan wanted, but what his father would want.

"We made a promise," he said. "We must abide by the treaty, therefore we will have to defend the Nob."

When Evred called him back in to hear the decision, Sholf did not express his relief. His feelings about the conquerors were too mixed for that. He said, "Then we had better make haste. Because the winds are changing."

The result was a brutal ride along the rocky peninsula into the teeth of the first storm of the season. The aging harbormaster rode grimly with them, perched on a sturdy pony.

Evred distrusted his instincts more each day they moved northward along the peninsula. It was only this man's anxiousness to get on, despite his own discomfort at the brutal pace, that convinced him the threat was real.

"Judging the actions of the many by those of one is both human and dangerous." He'd read that in one of the records written by an old Sartoran. *But if he speaks the truth, have they judged us by my own actions?*

There was no one to ask.

Chapter Eleven

TWO men stood on a cliff overlooking the Nob, obscured by a sharp-scented shrub dotted with withering yellow trumpet-liss and curtained by a willow. They watched the long columns of Marlovans riding into the Nob, banners snapping in the winds off the sea, helms gleaming, the odd tear-shaped shields hanging aslant from their saddles like the folded wings of a raptor.

Skandar Mardric and his companion, a tall, languid innkeeper named Dalloran—also a spy for the Resistance—shifted their attention to the bareheaded young man at the head of the column riding beside the harbormaster.

"Well, Dallo. There's your little prince again," Mardric said, waving as though granting a gift. "Back with his piss-hairs."

So obvious a statement was unanswerable. Dallo waited.

Mardric gave him a lazy glance that didn't fool Dallo for a heartbeat. "Well? Are you going to go snap your fingers?"

Below the prince, whom Dallo had known only as Sponge, dismounted. He was promptly surrounded by people.

Dallo had come to the conclusion that Prince Evred Montrei-Vayir had not been foolish so much as inexperienced. He'd amended that fast. But Mardric would just scoff. "I still do not know why he left so abruptly," Dallo said instead.

"Tired of your charms?" Mardric asked laughing softly. He paused, taking time to pick a fallen leaf from his black hair and flick it away. "These youths! Like fireflies—one day aglow, the next gone."

"If he tired of my charms," Dallo said, matching Mardric's caustic tone, "I might not get another chance to speak to him, much less snap my fingers."

"So?" Mardric stared down, for once unsmiling. "All you need to do is get close enough to get a knife between his ribs."

Dallo looked up in surprise. "Why? Will they not send another—along with an extra army or two to exact retribution?"

"Rumor has it they don't have an extra army or two," Mardric retorted.

"And that same rumor has it the older son is as bad as the Harskialdna."

"Good," Mardric said, unsmiling. "Then we don't talk the obscenities of peace and cooperation with our enemies. If our people stay angry, we talk about getting our lands back again."

"Hold. There's Nangel." They watched the harbormaster's chief scribe run up the trail from the high street and elbow her way through the men surrounding the prince. "Do you know anything about that?"

"Tathrim of the fisher fleet sent a skimmer in on the morning tide," Mardric said.

Dallo whistled. "Message. Has to be. You know what it was?"

"No." Mardric admitted, "The scribes won't talk to me anymore."

They watched the men below listen to the scribe who spoke swiftly, brushing her hair impatiently off her forehead as the wind played with it. Then the Marlovans began moving fast and orderly as if in a drill.

"Hmm," Mardric said. "Pirates, you think?"

"Let's go find out." They began sliding down a back trail to come around into the city the long way.

*   *   *

Below, one of Evred's Runners came up to his side, and saluted. "The scouts riding on perimeter reported two men on the northeast promontory watching us. No bows."

Evred winced inwardly, remembering—vividly—his personal encounter with the Resistance. "If they aren't an immediate threat, ignore them. We have an attack to prepare for."

The chief scribe had just reported: "A message came in this morning from the fisher fleet." Then she drew a shuddering breath, adding, "East, about two days out. They are here."

"Who?" Evred asked. "Pirates or Venn?"

"Both."

The screamer arrow whirtled through the frigid night air, arcing high from the northeast into the west wind then vanishing over the water.

Evred stood on the rock-and-tree dotted hill above the half-built houses on the harbor's high street. He peered down at the waiting men from the same place the spies had watched his arrival. Here and there around the well-positioned lines of his own forces crouched small groups of old sailors and harbor folk, silhouettes among the tumbled rocks and old hedges and the half-rebuilt foundations of houses. As if a wind soughed through them the men below whispered, briefly, then faced the northeast.

A local below Evred's vantage commented to the man next to him, who, from the rhythmic sheering sound, kept honing a short, heavy sword, "Damned pony boys never believed us."

"Well they sure as Norsunder do this time," was the retort. "Waiting is shit in shoes. I keep needin' to pee, and I say the spell, and nothin' comes out."

They spoke in Olaran, which Evred had learned last year. It was a lot like Idayagan. He gripped his sword hilt, bracing for the attack now closing on the Nob. Sholf had told the truth and Evred had made the right decision but there was no sense of triumph. He thought of the enor-

mous forces gathered by his uncle and brother all along the
western harbors, stretching southward to Elgaer and
below. He was worried about the three northern harbors in
Idayago that he'd stripped of men in order to reinforce Ala
Larkadhe, whose entire force was with him here.

A heel crunched behind Evred, sending pebbles skitter-
ing down the rock face. The sharp smell of pine rose as the
brown matt of needles was tramped underfoot. Evred
turned his head. The silhouette's familiar outline resolved
into Captain Sindan, who said quietly, "I've had two Runners report that the orders to evacuate the coastal harbors
were obeyed, leaving only our own people as defense. The
locals are safely inland, though under enormous protest."
As usual, he seemed to know what Evred was thinking.

Evred grimaced. To Sindan he could risk speaking on
this matter: "Any report of pirate attacks?"

Sindan lifted a shoulder as he peered between the
gnarled, wind-bent tree branches. Strings of clouds drifted
across the sky, low, shadow-gray, and thick, the ocean
black, the intermittent blue starlight making it difficult to
see. Moonlight was increasing slowly; he hoped it would be
enough.

The Olarans shifted, a couple of them asking unanswerable questions of Sholf, who squatted uncomfortably
below Evred, wishing he hadn't eaten those two extra nut-
cakes at dinner. It had seemed a fine idea at the time.

A dozen of his own cronies waited with him, most armed
with building implements, a couple with old cutlasses that
had newly honed edges.

The Marlovans stationed paces away on either side and
above ignored them. They had no semblance of discipline
and would be worthless as allies. But the prince wanted
them to think themselves allies, so no one could order
them out of the way.

The Marlovans watched northward: nothing more than
pinpricks of light on the far horizon, impossible for land
men to interpret.

"Too soon to know," Sindan said. "I'll expect a Runner
in three days at the least."

Sholf sent a look over his shoulder; despite the crowd

around him, he was listening. He got to his feet and raised his glass.

Sindan thought about the locket at his neck and the king's words, written the week before and transferred instantly by magic: *They are coming from the east. Rec'd report from Adranis.* It had been difficult not to reassure Evred, but word had to arrive either by the usual method or through the Olarans. It was the king's will that the existence of the lockets never be revealed.

Out loud he said, "Even if smaller pirate forces have razed the northern ports on their way here, the damage will have been diminished by our foresight. And if we win a great battle here today, it will make next year easier. You know what Adamas Dei wrote about great battles."

Evred's lips quirked, though he did not take his eyes away from the horizon. *It's people's belief that great battles decide something that makes them decisive.* Evred and his father had discussed it until Evred comprehended that battles themselves decided little; it was what people decided about them that gave them meaning. How they were written down for history, how they were regarded as they faded into history. A battle could be regarded differently from either side.

So ... how would this impending battle be viewed if the Marlovans won? Would they cease to be the enemy in the eyes of the locals at last?

Sholf was watching him—the brief pause had become a silence. Evred peered through the darkness, then said, "Twelve, thirteen, fourteen ships. More behind, I think. It's hard to see them—you have to watch where the stars are blocked."

Sholf put his glass to his eye. "I make out twenty-three, not counting the big Venn squares'ls. They'll stand off and fend off any aid to us from seaward."

And watch how we fight, Evred thought, holding out his hand. "May I look?"

A glass was seldom useful for land war as cavalry did not fight on hills, nor could the best spyglass see over trees, hills, shrubs, fences, or dust; Marlovans relied on scouts, both human and canine. Evred peered at a strangely flat-

tened world, the ships large, as if pressed onto a wall carving. He saw no difference between those ships, other than
some were bigger than others and that might itself be an
effect of relative distance. Except the Venn had white sails,
all the others black. No, red.

He handed the glass back, blinking away vertigo.

Flash Arveas appeared, crouching down beside Evred.
His breath was visible in the frigid air. "D'you want to signal it or should Hawkeye?"

Flash was a friend from their academy days, sent by his
father and older brother as reinforcement while they
themselves held the north end of the Pass. Hawkeye
Yvana-Vayir had been one of Evred's brother's inner circle who had bullied the boys on the Sierlaef's orders during their first year at the academy; distrust from those
scrub days lingered, though Flash and Evred tried to pretend otherwise.

"I will," Evred said.

Flash grinned, fist to heart.

Evred mentally dismissed the familiar annoyance with
his uncle for favoring political over military expedience by
sending the wild-riding, hard-drinking cousin Hawkeye as
Tanrid's replacement. He'd ridden north directly after the
funeral fires for the death of his mother from a riding accident on ice. It had not taken five days in Hawkeye's company to see that the reasons Hawkeye would have made a
superlative dragoon-scout captain were same the reasons
he would not command an army well.

Those who knew ships saw the sails loosened to spill wind.

"They're sending boats," Sholf said.

Evred raised his hand. Flash Arveas reappeared. "Shift
the fire teams for close attack." The ships were apparently
not going to come close themselves.

Flash saluted then slid his way down the hillside; cavalry
boots were not made for rock climbing.

"They know we're here," an Olaran said to Sholf, sending a glance up Evred's way.

Evred wanted to say, "Of course they do! Someone in
your own town probably made certain of it." But he kept
silent.

Below, Flash ran the last few steps to where Hawkeye sat on a flat rock above a stream that broke the seawall. Hawkeye figured the main attack would concentrate on these streams where the seawall broke, so here he was, more than ready, his bannermen and bugler behind him. Flash recognized some of the bannermen from their boyhood days at the academy. They were shifting about, keeping their hands busy, some smoothing triangular signal guidons and the big First Wing banner, others running their fingers in short, sharp swipes up and down wooden shafts as they cracked ever more obscene jokes about the pirates and the Venn. Their snickers did not quite hide their nervousness.

Flash jerked his thumb up toward the hill and said to Hawkeye, "Says he'll sound the attack."

Hawkeye did not react to the lack of title or protocol, but beckoned Flash, who followed him to where they couldn't be overheard. Hawkeye's question surprised him: "Can he command?"

Flash's first reaction was resentment. But Hawkeye's tone wasn't derisive as in *He can't possibly command;* it was a genuine question.

Flash rubbed his gloved fingers over his mouth, thinking. Hawkeye had been in the Battle of Ghael Hills. He'd seen action, and so far Flash and Evred hadn't.

So he said, "I think so. He was really good the last year or so at the academy."

Hawkeye let out his breath with a whoosh, looked around, then said, "The other one couldn't."

The other one—the Sierlaef. The battle—Ghael Hills. A real battle. Flash was glad he hadn't returned a sarcastic answer: whatever had happened in their boyhood days, here was the truth.

Flash stared at Hawkeye, frustrated at not being able to see his expression in the dim light. The rising murmur behind them meant the boats were drawing near; it was almost time for battle.

So he said quickly, "He's not like—" *Inda*, he almost said. But they'd stopped using Inda's name with anyone outside their class years ago. Covering that lapse, he whispered, "He's learned from people. Tried his ideas in the games. He's got a cool head."

Although the answer didn't mean much, Hawkeye turned up his thumb in the old academy gesture of agreement as he studied the coastline. He waved Flash back to the hill and returned to his rock.

His job before an attack was to advise. During an attack he was to make certain that Evred's commands were carried out, and if any mass charge was ordered, to lead. He'd also lead his own wing—the First Wing—which was gathered around him now. His stomach tightened; he wished he was on the hill, but would he be able to make sense of everything from there, especially in the dark? His mind raced backward through memory as he watched those boats: he never commanded a war game as the Sierlaef and Buck had always had precedence—maybe he couldn't— *Yes, I know I can lead a fight even if I can't plan one.* Command—lead—boats near the breakers—ready, ready— *Evred, if you don't signal I will—*

Evred stared out at the dark water crammed with bobbing silhouettes. He motioned to the harbormaster. "Are those Venn or pirates?"

"Pirates," the harbormaster stated. "Venn use their oars in a pattern. Them pirates might have drilled Venn landings. If so, we'll see shields come up right as they hit the breakers."

Anyone could see that the best moment to attack the incoming boats was when they were fighting through the rolling breakers. Apparently the Venn drilled to overcome that weakness; they might have trained their allies.

Evred wiped his hands down his battle tunic, then glanced at his bugler. "Ready?"

Four longboats surged up and down, now riding the blue-white waves—

"Prepare arrows." His voice broke, and he cleared his throat so hard it burned.

One sharp blast on the horn, and all up and down the palisade fire teams whipped up their bows. Arrows sparked with flame. Another blast, and the air filled with the rushing sound of arrows flying, pinpoints of glowing gold arcing toward the breakers. Evred cleared his throat again, as softly as possible, against the tickle of oil smoke at the back of his throat. No sneezes—

Some of the pirate silhouettes raised shields, some didn't. Most let out a roar and their shadow-shapes dove into the almost equally dark water, emerging with weapons raised, the edges of their steel glinting in the soft light of the humming canopy of fire arrows. *No Venn training, then. Allies or hirelings?*

"Better get ready." Sindan touched his shoulder, and Evred reached for the wrist guards worked with the Montrei-Vayir crimson and gold that his betrothed, Kialen, had sent him. He knew the thought had been Hadand's as Kialen, poor little soul, would never think of such a thing. He buckled them, pulled his gloves back on, and checked that his sword was loose in its baldric before he slid his left arm into the shield strap. It felt strange to wear a sword instead of carrying it on his saddle.

Reaching the shore, fifty, maybe sixty men leaped out of each longboat, some of them carrying bucket-shrouded lamps, which cast odd jiggling light pools as they ran with a roar for the walls.

"Defense," Evred shouted at the bugler, ashamed at how high, how sharp his voice sounded, as the first men dashed to the wall. Already locals were leaping over, wild, without any discipline. Three fell, hacked viciously by bawling pirates.

The bugler raised his horn. Evred saw his eyes widen, reflecting the torchlight, as he drew in a deep breath. His fingers trembled, but his blast was pure, the racing triplets blood-stirring, and below Hawkeye shouted, "Line!"

Smooth, drilled, assured, the First Wing's dragoons rose in a line, not leaping forward but staying back, holding ground; as the pirates clambered over the wall, the trumpet called the attack, and the dragoons' spear points glinted as they struck. Shouts, screams, guttural moans smothered the rhythmic hiss and thump of the breakers.

Evred clenched his fists, fingers sweaty inside his gloves. For a short time nothing was visible in the fitful torchlight but a mass of struggling figures. Cries and clashes of steel reverberated through the cold air. More torches flared here and there, and fires kindled, painting the skirmish with a ruddy, beating glow. The pirates shouted, then launched forward in groups to break through the line, which held; fewer from each group were thrown back. Most fell.

Some locals, seeing the line hold, joined, to be thrust aside. They pressed too close, hampering the warriors.

One of them yelled something in Olaran. Evred made out the word for boat. Perhaps they were going to launch into the water and . . . do what? He dismissed them from his attention—the locals couldn't be trusted or controlled because no one was in command. They ran to and fro, many of them retreating toward the buildings.

This battle was his to win or lose.

A great shout rose farther along the rocky shore: a breakthrough. "Defense. Second line," Evred said hard, to keep his voice steady. "Third in attack formation."

The bugler sounded the signal for the second line to emerge, and then the three-short-three-long for the third line to reform into wedges.

"South!" the harbormaster cried. "I count five, six boats, coming up from the south side—"

But Evred had been watching.

"Southern fire line," he said to the bugler.

Longboats ghosted in toward the shore, no lights, the sails barely visible. "Arrows," Evred said, and again the fire arrows rained on the boats.

This pirate group was better disciplined. Shields rose overhead as the boats shot in, straight up to the beach, the arrows clattering harmlessly on the shields sounding like a distant hailstorm. Masses of figures, their steel gleaming cold blue in the starlight, swarmed up the beach—

"South lines defense," Evred said, and this time the bugler was too quick.

"What do you see?" Sindan asked.

"The dragoons are holding line . . ." Evred tried to find the words for what he was seeing, then gave up, after a time forgetting that he'd been speaking. The jumble of images was fast, too fast, sometimes meshing into a whole but more often breaking his attention just as he seemed to make sense of what he saw: a scream near the point drew his attention that way. A flare of fire snapped his eyes to the west. Pirates running into a building—the crash and shatter of wood smashing through windows.

A breaker surged up, more boats riding its crest.

"Signal to the third fire line," Evred called to his bugler. He was surprised his voice was hoarse. He wasn't fighting—except his muscles bunched, his insides cramped, sweat ran inside the quilting under his mail coat.

Yip! Yip! Yip! The academy cry flared up, high, harsh, feral. Evred turned his focus downward, saw reflected in the firelight the crimson and gold banner with the big black bar across it: First Wing. Hawkeye's bright yellow head at the lead of a wedge of riders racing along the shore to—ah! Another load of boats, almost out of sight around a bluff.

That meant the scouts were dead. Evred signaled his last line of reinforcements to swarm down the mountainside to ward the flank attack. He could no longer identify specific wings, much less flights. Here and there three-cornered guidons fluttered, some of them jabbed up and down, others waving in a circle.

Guidons—never thought they were worth carrying—night battle—

Fire—reflection—see mass movement in the fire—

Keep order—

He clamped down on galloping thoughts because they were galloping away from the truth: his force was now fully committed and he had lost his grasp on the battle's shape. If indeed he'd ever had it.

A pang of self-loathing burned through him. He said in a hard voice, "Signal command to wing captains."

Two rippling chords of five notes apiece, and it was done, not that Evred could see any change—

Clang! He spun around. Sindan's sword whirled, blocking one, two assailants. Another ran up from behind. In a single much-drilled move Evred gripped his sword, stepped to Sindan's left without fouling his shield, and brought his heavy cavalry sword down on the bobbing enemy before him. Full strength. Full strength for the very first time; excitement drove his arm hard, but his blade did not cleave flesh, it thudded hard against mail and glanced off, causing him to stagger back a step.

But only for a heartbeat. His body, drilled over years, knew what to do. His hand shifted its grip, his arm whipped round into a tight side-cut. The pirate turned his head to see where the hiss came from and for a moment Evred saw a young face, open mouth, dry lips, the gleam of torchlight in open eyes, then his blade chunked into the fellow's neck and stuck. Blood spurted, smelling hot and salty sweet, and Evred yanked the blade free as the pirate fell, hand clutching weakly at his neck, his body spasming helplessly.

Sindan gasped over his shoulder, "Finish him. Don't let them suffer." *Clunk! Clang!* He raised his shield against the ax-blow of an older man who wore jewel-encrusted silks over his battle gear, the stones a red glimmer reflecting the light of the city on fire.

Evred drew his breath, used both hands to drive his blade down, cutting through the fallen pirate's fingers as well as his neck, and the body went limp, the head mostly cut free, but not altogether. The mess, sidelit from the roaring house fires, made Evred reel, pinpoints of light sparkling across his vision.

Step behind. His arms jerked: up came blade, shield ready.

This time it was easier. The pirate wielded an ax, already in its downstroke. Evred's blade snapped upward so fast, so hard, he nearly took the man's arm off. *Thud.* He ripped the blade free to whirl it around from the other side below the fellow's ear, cutting free a dangling golden hoop. *Chunk.* A sound he had never heard in the academy, the sound of steel burying itself in living flesh.

He did not look at the fallen but whirled to scan the area, saw several pirates retreating rapidly back into the dark. Before him stood Sindan, the bugler, and Uncle Anderle's Runner, dark-smeared swords at the ready. What now?

Sindan motioned the others into a protective circle. Oh. Around *him. Yes, I'm in command.*

Evred stumped back up to his old position, his breath

harsh in his throat. His wrists felt like water and he fought to regain control, holding his breath and letting it out in gasps as he looked back and forth, trying to make sense of the battle.

He couldn't get rid of the image of the wide eyes, the severed neck—a howling roar just beyond the fishing dock—a line of dragoons falling back, overcome by a mob of pirates——he looked away—yes! On the other side the ordered ranks of an entire flight—whose? Whose banner was that? Captain Senelayec—

He smacked the bugler on the arm with his sword hilt. "Senelayec to the left, reinforce."

The boy worked his lips then blasted the commands. The notes were not true, but they were loud, and Evred watched Senelayec's men react to their signal. No more than quick shufflings to reform ranks, and then they ran in tight formation to the aid of the dragoons, meeting the mob of pirates head on in an enormous clash of weapons, shields, and shouts.

Senelayec roared a command, the ridings broke into threes and carved their way into the mob, which melted before their onslaught.

Too long! He had watched too long, and jerked his head to the other side so fast he staggered. Two groups running: pirates. Going back to the boats—

In the streets silhouettes surged back and forth. Fires blazed, obscuring the battle on the south shore. Furious yells rang up the palisades: someone had smashed the bottoms of the boats! Locals? "Good thinking," Evred said, realizing he ought to have thought ahead to those boats, as the desperate pirates turned for a last stand.

Fighting on the fish docks. Fighting on the high road—

A screeching rabble chased pirates down toward the new houses, flinging torches at them, catching some on fire.

Evred gazed, desperate, his heartbeat echoing in his ears, the scene changing everywhere he looked. Chaos! No, the battle had broken into running, chasing, turns, stands, surroundings . . .

"Behind us." Sindan.

Evred whirled, his head pounding sickeningly. The intensity of battle had not abated; he scanned the skirmishes—there, holding. There, holding. There, chasing the pirates down to the sea. East falling back—which captains could he send—wait. He didn't need individual signals!

"Reinforce eastern flank," he croaked.

This time the bugler was ready, notes clear and strong.

Disengaged captains looked about, blowing their own signals. Four, five ridings swarmed over the rocky hill. The pirates in the center fought with desperation. Many on the edges slipped away, or tried to, but someone was on the watch for that, too, and dragoons harried the stragglers and brought them down.

To the west and the city now. Those fights seemed to be over. Knots of locals ran from group to group looting bodies, killing wounded. Most of the beached boats were on fire. From the other side of the fishing dock one managed to launch, the oarsmen sparse.

Out in the sea the big ships rode ghostlike, without any visible reaction.

A smear hurt Evred's vision, and he rubbed his eyes with a gloved finger. The smear remained. He looked up, discovered the glow of dawn in the east.

Somber blue light lifted darkness, forming shadows behind dark-soaked mounds. Women moved from group to group, muttering the Disappearance Spell. Sometimes they exclaimed when a still figure did not vanish: one woman silently brought out a knife and finished off a wounded pirate.

"The street! To the water, the street!" someone cried in Olaran.

Evred turned his head. Small fires had joined into a big conflagration: the new buildings along the main street shimmered in a wall of flame.

Chapter Twelve

IT was noon when Evred wearily made his way toward the tents. He threw back his head, trying not to breathe in the stink of smoke and drying blood, and staggered to a stop, distracted by a flock of gulls diving, swooping, arrowing out and then back. *Is that what the morvende call "the cloud-weaving of gulls"? How do people who have lived underground for three thousand years know anything about birds?* he wondered. His eyes burned, hazed with exhaustion, and though twice he'd drunk water brought by Runners, his mouth was parched.

I never saw Dallo, he thought as he limped toward the tents. And, with a faint return of anger born of humiliation, *If he comes at me I'll kill him.*

Crunch: memory of the sound of a sword striking the cartilage of some unknown man's neck. Man? Barely his own age, if even that. He heard his mother's voice, *every man is someone's son,* and grimaced.

Memory brought an intense image of the pleasure he'd had from Dallo, and he did not see the wind-worn stone road as he forced one foot in front of the other. Dallo had given him a good time, had given him a good lesson, and—inadvertently—a good idea. Since the short-lived affair, Evred had used that anonymous gray Rider coat in his pack whenever he wanted the freedom of anonymity. Few Idayagans knew him by sight. When the Marlovans rode in formation people saw the infamous Marlovan riding coats, the weapons, horses, shields, lances, banners, and not individual faces. "Thank you, Dallo." He laughed softly.

There was his crimson and gold pennon before a tent. He pulled off his sweaty gloves and threw them down on a rock. The flap opened, and Flash emerged, filthy, smelling of smoke and sweat. "Sponge? Did you say something?"

"I wish I had a bath," Evred said.

"I put in an ensorcelled bucket, since all the Runners are running." He chuckled hoarsely. "The harbormaster told me to tell you that the bath house down at what remains of Revel Row said they'd hold places for any of our captains, no charge, once they get the place cleaned up."

"Maybe later," Evred said. "For now I'll make do with the wash bucket."

Flash flicked his fingers to his chest and loped back in the direction of the command center, his horsetail swinging.

The bucket was inside. Full of water, cold. Clean smelling. Evred dipped a cup into it and drank, then shut his eyes as he sorted thought and memory. He'd have to meet with his commanders and discuss the battle. Messages would have to be composed for the Runners to take to the king. Those were just the official ones—the Runners would make their own reports. His father would require specifics on the battle and its aftermath, so he had to order the jumble of images, actions, and reactions.

Hawkeye Yvana-Vayir had been wild during the battle, always at the head of the First Wing, his ridings shouting out the counts of those they had killed. But his wildness was that of battle, not that of lack of discipline. He'd responded promptly to the bugle signals. And as the morning light strengthened, he had been diligent in reining in his men. The other captains followed his lead, forcing the fight-crazed warriors to expend their bloodlust on firefighting. And after that the familiar, steadying tasks such as seeing to the horses, counting the wounded and dead in each riding (few Marlovans dead, many locals), and on bearing the severely wounded to where the healers set up a station. Others were sent to gather abandoned weapons and pick up spent arrows.

While some locals were already drunk, running hither

and yon with little apparent purpose—everyone talking at once, here looking at fire damage, there parading loot taken off dead pirates—the Marlovans had been orderly enough under the hard eyes of their captains, who also watched Hawkeye, and in turn Hawkeye watched Evred.

Captain Sindan—still armed and ready for combat—walked silently, a disciplined and tireless shadow at the prince's left shoulder while Evred forced himself to pace the battle site, west to east, then north to south.

On his leaving for his tent, the exhausted Hawkeye and Captain Sindan took up station at the new command center, which was a central spot relatively free of smoke or blood where all Runners could see the crimson and gold banner. Those with light wounds already bandaged had been put to sorting the scavenged weapons, while others were sent to make sweeps for stragglers; the wounded were cared for, and the cook tents sent smoke drifting in wavering plumes to the gray-piled sky.

Order. Or as much as you could have after unnumbered people had been busy killing one another.

Kill.

Chunk. Sword into neck—

The young pirate again. Evred dipped his chain mail into the water, and then laid it aside to be dried and oiled. But what he saw was that face again as his sword half-severed the pirate's neck.

A cramp of nausea at the image of those wide brown eyes, the horrible gasp as his sword struck. What if it had been Inda?

He cut off an exclamation of disgust. Why this needless self-torture? Of course it couldn't be Inda.

But what if he was there?

Impossible.

Yet there was that report about him being a pirate. Evred could not believe Inda would ride against his homeland, but then he thought, *Why not? We betrayed him. I betrayed him.* Evred remembered holding eleven-year-old Inda the night before he vanished, Evred himself just thirteen. Inda had been sick and shivering, shock and misery in his face. *I promised justice, promising what I couldn't grant.*

Damnation. I'm too tired, that must be it. He stripped down to his drawers, unclasped his hair, feeling that welcome instant of release on his scalp, the prickly feeling of his hair falling loose. He rubbed his fingers vigorously over his head, then plunged it into the bucket. Magic buzzed over his skin and teeth and tongue like thousands of insect feet, flicking away the grit and sweat; he yanked up his head, flinging back his hair so it smacked against his back, cold and clean.

A short while later he was as clean as he could manage, and so he pulled on trousers and a shirt, then stood with his hair dripping, staring at his bedroll with longing. So much to do . . .

"Evred-Varlaef."

The voice was so soft he thought he'd imagined it.

"Evred-Varlaef."

He paused, hands halfway to his shirt-laces, which swung free, tangling in the snake-waves of his hair.

A shadow crossed before the tent. He reached for a weapon, then yanked the flap open—and found him himself almost nose to nose with a familiar face, pale hair—Vedrid, his brother's Runner!

Vedrid, who murdered the last two living assassins of Tanrid Algara-Vayir.

Evred tried to get his tired mind to act.

Vedrid cast a glance over his shoulder, then saluted and whispered, "May I enter?"

They looked at one another, the Runner filthy from hard travel and fighting, armed with sword, knives in each boot as well as at his side, but no weapon in hand; Evred dressed only in trousers and shirt, his feet bare. He held a naked knife in his hand, every line of his body evocative of threat.

Vedrid's face was marked with exhaustion under the dirt and smoke grime. His eyes were desperate, his attitude one of pleading, right hand flat against his heart, left empty.

Evred breathed out, his hand with the knife dropping to his side.

Vedrid, studying the younger prince's face, so different from his brother's, said in a tone of amazement, "You do know."

Evred gestured with the knife, a flick that thrust Vedrid's question aside. "What are you doing here?"

"Buck—that is, Aldren-Laef Marlo-Vayir—sent me."

Buck? Cherry-Stripe's older brother? Evred pursed his lips. Now it was his turn to be amazed. "Sit down," he said abruptly.

Vedrid knelt. Evred looked out in both directions. Runners and warriors moved back and forth, all of them with the frowning focus of those who desperately needed rest. In the distance Captain Sindan spoke to a couple of captains.

He shut the flap and dropped down onto his camp bed, arms on his knees, the knife hanging loose from his fingers. "When did you arrive? Does anyone know you are here?"

"Chased you up the coast, arrived here right after you. Then I had to wait to find you alone."

"So you were here for the attack?"

"I joined some of the locals. We set some boats on fire, then ranged the lower streets for looters breaking away from the battle on the hill," Vedrid said. "There were more than you'd believe. And not all pirates."

"Looters." How his head ached! "Talk," Evred said, gesturing with the knife.

Vedrid glanced at the weapon, his hands on his knees. Evred slid the knife back into its sheath and strapped it onto his forearm, listening as Vedrid talked in a quick, low voice; they were both practiced at tent speech.

As Vedrid told the story of his orders from the Sierlaef, and his ride, the night at the castle, his execution of the supposed brigands, and what happened with the Marlo-Vayir brothers, Evred finished lacing up his shirt and binding up his hair. He never interrupted the report, which was orderly and succinct.

And lethally clear.

Just as clear was the inescapable fact that almost any question he asked might lead directly to a parade in the Great Square, and a long, drawn-out execution for treason—of the wrong people.

". . . and so Cherry—ah, Landred-Dal—he said I ought to offer myself to you as sworn man. Which I so do." The color came and went in Vedrid's face.

Evred rubbed his jaw, wishing he could send the man away until he was rested. But no one must find Vedrid here. "I can't," he said. "I do need a Runner I can trust, but it cannot be you."

Vedrid's cheeks blanched, but he bowed his head.

Evred sighed. "Don't you see? If I take on my brother's man, everyone will want to know why."

Vedrid looked up, his eyes narrowing.

Evred said, "I cannot accuse my brother of murder without proof. The wording of his orders to you would be understood to prevent a death, not to cause one. Everything else could be seen as happenstance. If one so desires."

"One": the Harskialdna. He would demand incontrovertible proof; the king would as well: it was his own son, the future king, who would stand accused. But the only proof was safely dead.

Evred said, with even more care, "It was good of the Marlo-Vayir brothers to want to see to your safety." More than that he could not say: they had circumvented a direct order from the heir to the kingdom. None of them seemed to see what that meant.

Evred had assumed the Harskialdna was behind Tanrid's death, but the more he thought about it, the less sense it made. Tanrid was too good and obeyed orders. He was just the sort of captain the Harskialdna would value. Most convincing was the fact that the Harskialdna's Runners had been too persistent with their questions afterward.

Yet more people than he were now suspicious about that death, as evidenced by the Marlo-Vayirs' decision regarding Vedrid. A single act, so far. Made because they were loyal to the kingdom, to what was right, and not to the Sierlaef: yet their action, as his own, could result in their being flogged to death at the post for misprision.

Evred pressed his fingers to his forehead as a new thought struck him: how many people were beginning to see a separation between the Sierlaef's interests and the kingdom's? No possible good could come of that.

So what to do?

If wrong person overheard the wrong words, rumor would engulf the entire kingdom in civil war. It had happened before. War against outsiders was terrible enough, but no one was more vicious than Marlovan fighting Marlovan.

"I will take your oath, but for now, at least, you will no longer be a Runner in blue. You will have to take another guise. With a mission," Evred added, thinking rapidly, as he observed the pain in Vedrid's face. A loyal man, his life ruined. Maybe not, maybe not. "An important one. Desperately so. But it must remain a secret, for the present."

Vedrid looked up, wary.

"No more killing," Evred said, realizing what his brother's secret missions had come to. "I want information only. For justice, but . . . well, one step at a time. Vedrid, if you wish to serve me, I want you to go east, along every harbor, all the way to Chwahirsland, if you must. Go until you find recent news of Indevan-Dal Algara-Vayir, who might be using the name Inda Elgar. And bring it, do not send it, to me. Only to me."

Justice. He'd said the word. And Vedrid remembered that summer. He saluted, fist to heart.

Evred sighed, exhaustion gripping him again. His thoughts turned back to the breathtaking white towers, glistening like fantastic carvings of blue ice, in the city of Ala Larkadhe—city of enchantment—nestled at the base of the Ghaeldraeth Mountains. He'd managed to stay there twice, but not once had he gotten a chance to explore those ancient towers.

"I will winter in Ala Larkadhe, the old Sartoran city just inland of Lindeth. Do you know where it is?"

Vedrid thought, *But Chwahirsland is at least six months away, with winter travel involved,* and then he realized what Evred Varlaef meant. He was planning to stay here in the north for at least a year.

Vedrid struck fist to heart again, not trusting his voice. Justice. Trust. He had begun to wonder if they really existed.

"Then I will take your oath," Evred said, and dug through his gear for coins to equip Vedrid for his mission.

And there, in low voices meant not to be overheard, they swore the words of allegiance.

*   *   *

"The prince has vanished," Dallo said two days later.

"What?" Mardric exclaimed.

"I told you. He's gone. Someone thinks he rode south to Ala Larkadhe, others think he's gone up the Pass."

Mardric cursed under his breath. "But we didn't see any entourage, there were no trumpets or any of that."

Dallo waited.

Mardric looked up, not seeing the smoke-blackened wood, the people moving slowly as they began the monumental task of cleanup and rebuilding.

"The pirates won't be back," he said finally. "So neither will he. I will ride to Lindeth. And watch from there."

Chapter Thirteen

REFLECTION from the pond below their windows sent light rippling up the pale peach wall. Thog and Jeje lay in their beds at Lark Ascendant watching the light patterns. Jeje wished she was in a hammock swinging in a breeze, and then her mind caught up with what her body knew: winter was over at last.

The air was almost *warm,* smelling of fresh-turned soil, of the sea, not of ice. The cold blue light of winter had given way to an inviting pale gold. She knew, without any message, that Inda Elgar moved below, rousting everyone, telling them to pack their dunnage and get it aboard *Cocodu.* The similarities between the name of the smelly marsh weed *cucudu,* and *Coco du,* "Coco gone" in Dock Talk, had been too funny to resist when Inda changed the name of the ship they'd taken from Gaffer Walic.

Their ship.

In, what, six? Five? Say five years, they'd gone from ship rats on a lowly merch to independents with a fast pirate ship with enough gold on it so that Inda could pay the fee to join Freedom Islands' confederation of privateers and independents.

Even better, they rated not just anchorage out in the roads, but a dockside berth. And that, Jeje knew, was in part her doing as she had alerted Commander Dhalshev to

the weakness of the island. Inda had then given the former
admiral advice on its defense.

Inda had said over New Year's Firstday mulled wine that
they didn't just have a good place now, they had the inside
line of communication. Dhalshev was in contact with
nearly every harbormaster in the east, excepting only
Khanerenth, where he'd once been fleet commander.

Dhalshev had also indicated his approval in material
ways, agreeing to Inda's proposal that Inda's people practice with his patrol ships—once they'd been drilled to Fox's
satisfaction. Inda had said, "We get practice in boarding
and taking ships, they get practice in defense."

Meanwhile, Barend had been forcing them outside the
bay on *Cocodu* and *Vixen* to practice fast maneuvering and
sending and reading arrow and flag signals.

Jeje and Thog had reorganized the bow teams. On two
quick signals they either shot together in deadly sheets of
arrows, or in pairs, one pulling and aiming as the other
loosed, so there would be a lethal continuous release.

All the long, bitter winter.

Jeje let out a sigh of satisfaction.

Spring! Every captain who had been longing for spring
would be tramping his or her deck, getting ready to sail on
the tide in search of trade—or perhaps in search of traders
whose flag indicated the wrong government.

Inda, Fox, and Barend had declared the practice drills
over. It was time to launch in search of pirates.

Jeje saw Thog's eyes open. "Wager we'll leave soon?"

"I would not take that wager," Thog said, unsmiling. She
rarely smiled and never laughed. She looked out at the
world through wide-set eyes, her small mouth pressed even
smaller, her shoulders squared, as if every day presented
some kind of unseen battle.

But now she looked . . . rested. "What are you thinking?"

Reflected sunlight gleamed in Thog's black eyes. "The
wind changed during the night. Did you feel it too?"

"I smell it. Light's changed, too." Winter was over,
though these treacherous eastern waters might yet fling a
blast or two at them.

"It is the first time," Thog said in a low, fervent tone,

"that I have not seen Wumma and Rig and Yan walk through this window with the rise of the sun, and go that way." She pointed to the northeast.

Jeje's neck prickled. Northeast. The Ghost Isles lay that way, though far on the other side of the Toaran continent.

Jeje sighed. It was hard to believe that people really saw ghosts. She couldn't ask Thog, who might bristle. Not that she snapped or snarled. She was an odd, prickly hedgehog sort of creature; when she was angry or upset she'd go silent for a week, shoulders hunched as she worked steadily.

Jeje couldn't believe in ghosts as anything but the fanciful things you met in old ballads. Either a living creature had a body, which you could see, or it didn't. Nevertheless people claimed to see them.

This was the first time that it wasn't "people" seeing them, but someone she knew.

She said, "I miss Wumma and the others. I always think of Rig when Uslar makes those delicious cinnamon buns. I wonder if he and Hav would have stayed in Sartor to be bakers if they'd known?"

Thog jerked her head, a gesture like tossing something away. "Spending their lives as bakers was prison to them. They knew the risks. Took them anyway."

She spoke with conviction. Maybe it was true, maybe it wasn't, but Jeje missed them all, even that nasty old Scalis. Most of all she missed Yan.

"I know what to do," she said. "Help Inda shift the last of the gear down. Get it stowed. Look over the *Vixen* one last time. Then tonight we'll go upstairs and get laid. Who knows how long it will be before the next chance?"

Thog's little mouth compressed. "You go upstairs. Not me."

Jeje turned on her elbow. "Are you getting sick?"

Thog blushed, then sat up. "I don't want sex. There is no feeling there." She pressed her hands to her childish chest. *No feeling except hate.*

Jeje frowned. It was hard to believe Thog had at least three years on her. She looked like she was fourteen.

And how old am I now, anyway? Eighteen? Nineteen? I don't think I'm yet twenty. Jeje gave up counting. She grimaced instead. "For me, it's the opposite. I don't want it with anyone but strangers. Then you go your way and he goes his, no trouble following." No risk. It hurt still to remember Yan's trembling, the fumbling explorations, the shared snuffles of laughter, and then the joy. Next day he was dead, cheated out of a good life by an indifferent pirate hand.

"You think I am wrong?" Thog asked softly.

"Naw. I'm just remembering," Jeje admitted. The memory of Yan, and the year before, all those nights and nights of empty yearning after Tau, of spying to see where he was, of sniffing for his scent when she entered a room. Of silent anguish when she knew he'd been with someone else. No, strangers were best. No wager on that! She said with an attempt at cheer, "Well, as Grandma said when Aunt Bibi set up house with the bricklayer's sister after twenty years with my uncle, we're all made different, and that's a fact."

Thog got up and reached for her clothes. "I'm off to the baths. I'll meet you down at the ship. I have a task there."

"But we're done at the ship!"

"I'm going to work on the banner sail." Thog's eyes crinkled in her version of a smile. "Inda has not asked, but I want it finished before we reach cruising waters."

Jeje wondered what extra meaning there was in a golden fox face on a black background. Inda had been very specific about the way it was to be made, with details added by Barend, and that strange, sarcastic red-haired Fox standing by, arms crossed, jabbering in that Marlovan language that they no longer tried to hide.

Fox had taken over as first mate and Barend as sailing master, superseding everyone Inda knew, but they were experienced sailors. Everyone agreed that Barend was the best sailing master for the pirate maneuvering, and Dasta was going to serve as his mate. Barend had the same exacting eye as Kodl—that being the standard for what remained of the old marines. Fox, as the best fighter, had been put in charge of the hand-to-hand fighting drills as well as the boarding practice.

Tau had the bruises to show it.

As she trod down to the dock, Jeje thought over the winter drills and how Fox always singled Tau out and how their matches seemed more like fights. Jeje didn't understand why those two seemed on the verge of killing one another at times, though they never went off and fought a duel. They didn't even complain about the other behind his back. Fox reserved his invective for Tau's presence, and Tau never said anything at all about Fox. But if his name was mentioned, Tau's mild expression turned sardonic—unsettlingly mirroring Fox's own expression.

Inda behaved differently around the Marlovans. His manner changed subtly. This change had been particularly noticeable when he first suggested the fox banner-sail. Barend had laughed and laughed, and Fox had crossed his arms, his smile mordant—similar to their reactions upon hearing the scout craft's name of *Vixen*—but Jeje found nothing funny in the sight of a fox face.

When Dasta entered the supply room that Mistress Lind had given Inda as his office, he found Inda leaning against the table as he named the ships in the harbor to Tau.

Winter was definitely over. Dasta shut out the long litany whose purpose escaped him—he knew who was in harbor, from where, and who had left. Instead, he contemplated his fellow ex-marines, who were all together for the first time since early winter. Between then and now life had been a long succession of hard labors in brutal weather.

His first sign of the differences had been when he reached into his gear bag that morning for his summer vest—regretfully put away months ago (he never wore a shirt)—just to discover it was far too tight across the back, as well as too short.

So he put the vest in the poor box, and, though the weather was still brisk in the shadows, he was wearing his new vest and new drawstring trousers, his favorite summer gear. Best for action.

Inda actually had on a new shirt—one he hadn't made himself. It was not only unstained, it had laces, and they were neatly done up. Inda had never shown any interest in his appearance. The shirt had to be Tau's influence. Either that or Inda, who had last year discovered sex, finally figured out that looking like a scruffy dock rat was not going to attract anyone's eye.

"Then he has enough for defense if he needs to call on them," Tau said. "What surprises me is how he manages to hide his actual numbers."

Tau was the opposite. Dasta wondered as Tau brushed his fingers over the harbor map how Tau always managed to find clothes that looked toff, though they weren't. That is, no lace, silk, or velvet, like Gaffer Walic.

"Especially on an island," Tau said, straightening up, his linen shirt a smooth line from shoulder to thigh instead of sagging or bunched at the sash, like it would be on most people.

"Woof says they are deliberate about it," Inda replied. "You always refer to a force being somewhere other than where you are. And note who goes looking for it."

Dasta was taken aback. He was now as tall as Tau, the oldest of them. When had that happened? And over the past year Inda had stopped looking like a boy. He was only marginally taller, but he'd grown very broad through the chest. Compact and powerful—the awkward boy was gone.

Inda and Tau seemed to become aware of him at the same time and turned his way.

Dasta said, jerking his thumb harborward, "Got it—"

Footsteps behind.

It was only Fox and Barend, the former in black, as always. Barend, like Inda, wore a new cotton-linen shirt tied with a crimson sash and brown deck trousers.

As Dasta resumed his supply report, Tau retreated to the window, where he could watch everyone with no one behind him. Fox took his place as if Tau didn't exist, Barend leaning next to him, running a finger above Inda's chalk marks.

". . . I got the last of the flour paid for, after Lorm inspected it. They'll put it aboard by noon. Promise, with all sorts of wishes for success, every one of them private." Dasta shook his head.

Inda listened as he studied his chart. "What did you tell them?"

Dasta opened his hands. "I told them what we've all been saying. We're setting out to smash those Fire Island rats for last year's trouble. But they all nod and smile. Like this." He nodded slowly, mimicking the exaggerated nod of one who is in on a secret. "Five people this morning up and said, 'Strike a blow against the Brotherhood for me. I lost a cousin when Boruin fired their trader . . . ' or an aunt, or a brother, or a whole village. All Boruin's kills."

Inda frowned. "If I find out who has the big yap—"

Tau laughed. "Inda. This is a harbor. Everyone knows everyone's business. You listen to rumors yourself."

"I don't talk."

"No, but people notice what you listen to. And they've seen you up at the octagon, which few are allowed in. Even if they know nothing about the defense of the island, they do know Dhalshev has the master charts up there."

"But we never talked about my plans. Just the defense drills." Inda absently wiped his chalky fingers on his fine new shirt, then sat back. "Anyway, no one along the Saunter has said a word to me about where we're going or what we're going to do when we get there."

"Don't have to." Tau laughed from his window vantage, the spring light gleaming in the short hair that waved back from his brow. "Whatever you do has become interesting."

Fox felt a spurt of resentment as he always did when Inda listened to Tau.

"I don't see why I'm interesting. Dhalshev talks to a lot of people, and no one knows what's said up in the octagon." Inda rubbed the side of his face. A healing salve had faded the purple scar running from his cheekbone to his jawline to white, but rubbing the scar had become a habit.

"They ask us." Barend grinned. "We all say we're going after the Fire Island pirates. And meanwhile Mutt is at the charthouse buying this chart here, with the latest details of The Fangs at the mouth of the strait, which everyone knows is Boruin of the Brotherhood's cruising station. And we're all either out in the water or else up on the hill behind the Lark's hothouse in the worst weather, drilling until we drop, in order to go up against someone you turfed once already."

"And everyone knows every detail of Boruin Death-Hand's wretched career and that her flagship is a pirate trysail and faster than damnation," Fox drawled. "You don't seem to understand that nothing is more interesting than notoriety."

Inda tossed the chalk on his palm. "Are we notorious? The harbor is full of suspicious 'independents' and priva-teers whose letters of marque are mostly excuses for reprisals."

Tau opened his hands. "We're more interesting."

"Because of our drills?"

"That," Dasta spoke up. "And because not a one of *them* thrashed the likes of Gaffer Walic. That's why half the brats on the island spent the autumn gathering feathers for us, against our return."

Barend added, "And everywhere people want to sign on."

"I thought the feathers was Nugget rousting her friends to work for us," Inda said, grinning. "I've certainly had most of 'em wanting to join us. Eh, doesn't matter." He sat back. "Here's what does. If everyone is blabbing about us, then what we know, the Brotherhood knows."

Dasta pointed at the map. "If you mean Boruin knows you're comin' for her, yeah. If anyone will talk to her."

"Brotherhood spies're everywhere. Even here," Tau said.

"Anything for a price?" Fox asked, sending a derisive glance toward Tau.

Tau gestured, a mocking flourish in semi-salute. "You tell me," he invited.

Fox flicked up the back of his hand.

Tau smiled as he got to his feet. "If we're departing, I want a last meal on dishes that stay put in front of me."

That signaled a general exodus. Tau found Inda next to him, eyes serious. "Is there trouble between you and Fox?"

"Ask him."

"Did," Inda said grimly. "He said to ask you."

Tau laughed.

"Is it a sex thing? Are you rivals? Or is it each other?"

Tau contemplated Inda's earnest face. What to say? *If only it was that simple! He wants you, Inda. But not your prick; he wants your mind, your soul, he wants to be you. And so he resents anyone you listen to except for him.* In some inexplicable way Inda was still twelve years old. It was that boundary he'd built between him and his childhood Tau suspected, simply from what Inda had steadfastly refused to talk about these past five years. Yet it was still with him, as evidenced in his new banner, in the speed with which he'd adopted these two newcomers from his homeland.

In matters of war Inda was the smartest of them all but in matters of the heart, he was still twelve. If Tau spoke those words, Inda would not understand, would become self-conscious in that way peculiar only to Inda. "Just friendly competition," he said, when he saw Inda still waiting for an answer.

"Keep it friendly," Inda retorted, looking at him askance. "We're sailing toward enough trouble without having it on deck."

Chapter Fourteen

"I THINK I see smoke," the lookout shouted from the masthead of the Sarendan warship *Nofa*.

Captain Taz-Enja squinted at the eastern horizon behind the dawn haze. Sea and sky blended into an infinitude of gray shades.

"Sail hai!" the lookout shouted, and the captain reached for his glass in the binnacle. The horizon leaped forward and flattened, but he could make out a tall triangular shape inside the slow whirls of smoky fog.

"...ship on fire?" someone muttered in the tops and was hushed with a hoarsely whispered reminder they were at battle stations.

A sliver of sun imbued the scene with color. Yes. There. The captain made out the faintest smudge of whitish brown as it swirled up into the breeze ruffling the rippling water.

"Raffee!" the lookout yelled next, his voice cracking. "No kingdom banner—a pirate!"

They've got the wind—what wind there is, the captain thought bleakly, but he said only, "Fighting sail."

His lieutenant, who had pounded up to the captain's deck after the lookout's first yell, started issuing a stream of orders to the crew who'd already begun scrambling into place.

As running feet thudded on the deck the captain kept his glass trained on the shadowy shape that glided slowly closer. Tall masts. On the foremast, a sharp-cut triangular mainsail. Square fore-mainsail—definitely a raffee.

And on that topsail . . . something black, with some sort of face. He rubbed the eyeglass on his trouser leg, though the blur was fog, not smeared glass. What was that, a hawk? Eagle? No. Ears—muzzle—ruff—a fox with raptor eyes.

"Isn't that Gaffer Walic's raffee?" the lieutenant murmured at his shoulder, just audible above the clatter and thock of blocks, the whuffle of sails being readied and bow teams ascending to the mastheads.

"Never seen it," the captain answered, not taking his eye from his glass.

"I saw it once. When I was a mid," the lieutenant replied. He, too, had not taken his eye from his own glass. "They outran us. Never forget the cut of that raffee sail. Sharp. Like a royal yacht. Tight rigged, raked masts, like this one." He lowered his glass, his expression bemused. "But they said he always sailed blank. Swore he would until he could join the red sails."

"Admiralty posted notice that he lost it. Last summer," the captain said. "You were on leave. Some other pirate. Get the list, please."

The lieutenant smacked his glass shut and gestured to a waiting boy, who returned with the most recent list issued to all harbormasters.

The captain lowered his glass and took the paper. The light was now strong enough to read the close-written sheet.

The raffee drew nearer. It had the wind, which was so mild the *Nofa* could not possibly outrun it.

Captain Taz-Enja felt the pressure of imminent decision; there was no time to peruse that long list, so he wordlessly handed it to his lieutenant. While the latter pored over the paper, the captain watched the pirate ship, his bow teams crouched above, weapons to hand, the sail crews gathered in silence along the companionway to either side, boarder-repel teams armed and waiting. Everyone waiting for orders.

"Here it is," the lieutenant exclaimed. "Update end of last summer. Walic defeated by one Inda Elgar, pirate, operating out of Freeport now. This same Elgar was posted as a pirate end of oh-nine." He brought the paper close to his nose. "Known under some other western-sounding name, hard to make out in this light. A prince?"

"Prince?" the captain repeated. "What would a prince be doing with Gaffer Walic? If he wants his own ships, why doesn't he send a minion out to buy some?"

The lieutenant flicked the paper with the back of his fingers. "That's what it says here. At least, so it seems. Why do they have to write the side-notes so tiny? Description: blond, brown eyes, short. A boy? Marlovan out of Iasca Leror. Mutiny, took three trading brigs, reward—tagged as wanted by the Venn. Must have been some mutiny to catch *their* eye!"

"All Marlovans and Iascans with any kind of rank get that tag," the captain said low-voiced as the pirate ship drifted closer, its towering triangular sails bellying gently. "A prince would go straight to the capital list as soon as he crossed their border, no matter how law-abiding." Taz-Enja could make out details now: the tops full of bow teams, though they had not stripped to fighting sail. And there was no battle pennant at the fore, though he knew pirates did not always signal their intentions. "There's no brig in sight, only the raffee, and that sloop windward." The captain brought his glass down and rubbed his eyes, blinking rapidly to get his focus back.

"Scout cutter, too," the lieutenant said, swinging his glass. "Approaching! A little girl at the tiller, looks like a mid tending sail. What does that mean?"

Captain Taz-Enja brought his glass back up to his eye. After a moment, "Pirate ruse?" He voiced the worst, though the signs did not add up to an attack: the cutter moved far too fast to be loaded with pirates below its narrow deck.

Still his heartbeat was loud in his ears as he moved from the stern rail to the side, then gestured to the starboard bow crews to take aim. Anyone who could take Gaffer Walic would be clever as well as bold.

The scout craft was clean, beautiful in line, its long sail curved in a smooth, elegant line like the raffee. Typical pirate arrogance. It glided as effortlessly as a swan over the glassy sea. The strengthening light marked out a girl no more than eleven or twelve with a head full of unruly curls. She controlled the tiller. The youth tending the jib sail line appeared unarmed. He put a bare foot up on the rail as he peered up under his hand at the warship.

("Inda, Inda, he's looking at me! He is, he is!" "That's all right, let 'em look. Long as they don't start shooting.")

The captain swept his glass past their lifted faces and studied the raffee. So far it had made no move to close. Its crew was not motionless; though the tops were full of bow teams, he could make out a work party busy aft, repairing what looked like fire damage, and arrows spiked the hull below the mainchains. Near the wheel a tall figure in black lounged, a glass dangling from his hands, a lock of red hair loose from his queue lifting in the weak breeze. As Taz-Enja scrutinized him for any sign of imminent order to attack, the redhead leaned his forearms between the spokes of the wheel, the glass still dangling from loose fingers; he ignored the war ship as he observed his work party.

The pirate ship had been fighting, and recently, too; from the look of things they'd just put out a fire aboard.

The racketing of sailcloth brought his attention back to the little scout craft, which had spilled the wind as it drew alongside.

The captain nodded to his lieutenant, who bawled in Sartoran, then in Dock Talk, "Hail the boat."

("Inda, please let me answer, pleasepleaseplease!" "Go ahead—but not threatening, just official. Remember, Nugget, they might think we're pirates but we're harmless, friendly, *nice* pirates.")

The curly-haired little girl straightened up proudly. "*Vixen* scout craft belonging to *Cocodu* independent, out of Freedom Isles," she shrilled in Khanerenth-accented Sartoran.

Freedom Isles—though the Khanerenth government officially condemned them as pirates, everyone knew who they were and why they were there. And Khanerenth's new royal navy was not gaining friends these days with its recent policy of stop-and-search on every vessel they met—their excuse was they were looking for their own former navy, now condemned as criminals. Some of them interpreted their orders to include the confiscation of "suspected smuggled goods."

"How long out?" the lieutenant shouted.

"Two days," the girl replied promptly.

("Inda, *please* let me hold my knife. Or my bow!" "No, we're supposed to look nonthreatening." "But that boy on the mainmast shrouds stuck his tongue out at me!" "Stick your tongue out back at him, if you want. But no weapons.")

The captain did not see the exchange between his cabin boy and the girl at the tiller in the scout craft. He stared up at the lean pirate vessel, considering. Anyone sailing from Freedom Isles would go straight north through the Starborns, or else west past Prince Sahan Island, and then either swing north or continue on westward toward Sarendan. They'd left Prince Sahan two days ago themselves. So it was plausible they really were just out of Freedom Islands, which meant they were either privateers or independents, because former Fleet Commander Dhalshev had no dealings with real pirates.

Though these sailed an infamous pirate ship. And what about those notes on the capital list?

So far no challenge—no arrows, no flags, no shouting. Yet the big, sinister pirate ship was in arrow range now.

Both captain and lieutenant tensed. Now would be the time for the raffee to haul over and attempt a boarding if it was going to; they were glumly aware they did not have enough wind to evade.

"Stay off," the lieutenant warned, at a look from the captain. "Or we will shoot."

The boy in the scout craft's bow spoke up for the first time. "We're not looking for a fight." His voice was not as high as a boy's. Young man, then. "Just finished one, with the brigantine *Brass Dancer*." His Sartoran was peculiar—both aristocratic and quaintly old-fashioned.

Captain and lieutenant exchanged glances, each seeing his amazement mirrored in the other.

The captain said, "That was the pirate we have been chasing."

"We caught him cruising too close to Freeport Harbor. Took a prize." The young man waved toward the sloop windward of the big pirate—all they could see were its sails.

Captain Taz-Enja called, "There's a reward, a big one, in Sarendan for anyone who captures the *Brass Dancer*. Or Dal Raskan, its captain."

The young man looked like a youth again when he grinned. *Blond, brown eyes, short.* "I'm afraid the ship itself has already sunk. There seems to have been distilled liquor in the captain's cabin, and fire reached it—" He waggled a hand.

His hair wasn't blond, it was brown, though the top layer, especially around his face, was sun-streaked. Maybe he was more blond when the report was made? Anyway he was definitely short. So . . . was this fellow Inda Elgar? No prince in his experience would be seen publicly in bare feet and plain deckhand clothing. But then what prince turned pirate? More to the point, what boy could lead a successful mutiny against the likes of Walic?

"Whiskey? That's Raskan," the lieutenant said, breaking into the captain's thoughts. "Rumor has it he kept a tub of triple-distilled malt whiskey to bathe in, or to treat his crew when they did well, or for use in questioning. No stories agree on what he did with it, but they all said he had it. And you'd be staggering from the fumes if you were in there long."

The boy—Elgar?—said, "What was left alive of their crew was in a longboat, if you want to catch them. In return, have you any news of recent movements of the Brotherhood of Blood, specifically one who calls herself Boruin Death-Hand?"

Taz-Enja studied that upturned face. No hint of what was going on behind those mild brown eyes. He said, "Most of the red sails have gone west. Except for the pirate Boruin Death-Hand, whose cruising station is north at The Fangs."

The mysterious young man—pirate or prince, neither seemed quite to fit—waved a hand in farewell. He turned away to address the child, who made a horrible face at someone aboard his own ship (the captain realized whom when he heard suppressed chuckles behind him). Then the girl gave a self-important little twitch of her shoulders, rubbed her hands, and swung the tiller. The strange young man tightened sail again.

And the entire crew of the *Nofa* watched the long, elegant sail fill as the scout craft picked up speed, crossed the bow of the big raffee, and vanished on the lee.

The black-sided ship slid past, the tops full of pirates in silent, waiting defense teams, the work crew below busy hammering and sawing.

"We will have to report that," the captain commented.

The lieutenant had not been asked his opinion, so strictly speaking he was not supposed to answer with anything but "Yes, captain." But the day had begun so unreal he observed, "Will anyone believe us?"

The captain swung around and watched the pirate ship head toward the horizon as an east wind strengthened with the morning light, the sea now a brilliant green-blue, full of choppy waves. He smacked his glass to and said, "They will if we catch those pirates off the *Brass Dancer*. All sail, straight south." His voice lowering slightly, "Dranon! Did you want to join the pirate?"

His cabin boy appeared, face scarlet. "No, sir."

"Your notion of discipline seems to match theirs."

"She was showing off," Dranon observed to the deck.

"If the worst a pirate ever does is stick her tongue out, the world will be an easier place to live in. You may think about that for the rest of the day at the masthead."

Sigh. "Yes, sir."

Nugget gloated about her exchange with the Sarendan navy cabin boy for the rest of the week, to Uslar's envy and Mutt's disgust.

As the *Cocodu* sailed northwards, Inda mulled over that devastating blue-yellow explosion. He also considered the nature of rumors.

If Boruin knew as much about them as they knew about

her, he had to use what she knew. Or what she thought she knew.

So, what he knew was this:

She had three capital ships, he had one. Her reputation for relentless cruelty gave even some pirates pause. The only people who survived being taken by her were the rich, and she got the maximum ransom by sending with her demands a finger or toe, once an eye, from a duke's daughter who had been too haughty.

She and her first mate Majarian, a runaway murderer, had picked a crew as strong and vicious as they were. Ganan Marshig, Commander of the Brotherhood of Blood, had selected her to cover the east end of their cruising grounds. The rest of the fleet under Marshig sailed west to plunder Iasca Leror under the watchful eyes of the Venn. When they returned, if she still held control, she would be acknowledged leader of the eastern fleet, young as she was.

Inda stood at the rail watching the sea, or pacing around and around on the captain's deck, pounding a fist on rail, binnacle, wheel, rail again as he made his way around and around. When at last he stopped pacing, he looked bemusedly around the deck, addressing the air. "Where does one buy casks of whiskey?"

Thog, busy smoothing arrow shafts, said softly, "Chwahirsland is where you will get the best, whether corn, rye, or malt."

"Then we are going to Chwahirsland first." Inda started his round again, brow knitted.

"He giving up?" one of the new mates asked Dasta.

"No," Dasta said. "He's thinking. You'll see him back among us again when he's got a plan. Now get that deck swept."

The fellow, about Dasta's age, on the sea all his life, applied himself vigorously to his sweeping, keeping to himself his annoyance at having to dodge around Inda's ceaseless barefooted march.

Chapter Fifteen

THE encounters they had along the way were short and sharp, twice driving away cruising pirates, once a Khanerenth warship determined to board them, and last, some fast-moving coastal galleys, fisher folk who turned pirate when it suited them. They fought haphazardly, relying on surprise. Since they were close to shore, Inda had his crew sink their ships, sending them rowing and swimming back to land. Jeje circled round them in the fast *Vixen*, Nugget and Mutt gleefully sending fire arrows into the rowboats' sides.

The new crew discovered that Fox considered these encounters mere practice, so those who'd gotten in the way of weapons when fighting off attempted boardings wrapped their wounds and kept their mouths shut. Fox required them on deck for drill as if nothing had happened.

As they angled in toward the rocky, dangerous coast of Chwahirsland, they captured two vessels off another fleet of pirate galleys: a big, ugly old caravel and a fine little sloop.

This pirate galley fleet had been lying in wait for a convoy of Chwahir merchant craft outside the mouth of a narrow harbor. It made sense to take the sloop darting about between the galleys. It did not make sense to board and carry the round-hulled, top-heavy ancient transport caravel that the pirates had been using to store loot.

But no one said anything, at least to Inda, who walked

back and forth along the companionway, his feet smacking slap, slap, slap on the wet deck as a brief shower passed overhead.

The ship was squared away to Barend's satisfaction and Fox was overseeing boarder-repel practice when Inda stopped his latest circle of the deck, looked around, and said, "Where's the bosun? Carpenter?"

By the time those two emerged on deck, everyone was listening.

Inda said to the bosun, "Is the treasure transferred aboard us?"

"Stowed where it will stiffen us best," replied the bosun, who was scarcely older than Inda.

Inda waved a hand, then turned to the carpenter. "Build me a cut boom on that tub."

"Cut boom?" The carpenter who had replaced Dun and Wumma was an older man, experienced with wood, but not imaginative. He stared aghast at the clumsy ship rolling leeward, his carpenter's mates still cleaning up and repairing after the fight. Then he rubbed his jaw, ambivalent about arguing with the commander.

Everyone stared in varying measures of disgust and distrust at the old trader caravel.

"What?" Barend laughed. He had no difficulty arguing with Inda. "You try booming a pirate's shrouds with that old bucket and it'll fall to splinters. We'd have to reinforce it right down to the keel, and where's the use in that, even if we had a convenient port in which to do it?"

"I want a big, strong-looking cut boom, metal inset all the way to its point, and I want it off the foremast, with enough preventer stays to make it swing easily, and look wicked seen through a glass," Inda said. "I also want the whiskey casks we're going to buy stored on deck as well as below." And, as they looked at him as if he'd boiled his brains, he opened his hands. "It's a ruse."

A ruse! Inda had a plan at last. Word spread through the ship, and all free hands got to it, stripping the bulkheads in the moldy hold to get enough wood to make a foremast cut boom that would overreach even that on the *Cocodu*.

As they sailed on fragrant winds from the islands behind

them, Inda spent long watches in the caravel, which shouldered clumsily through the sea, masts corkscrewing. The rapping and sawing of the carpentry crew went unnoticed as he experimented with whiskey in small wooden mugs, Thog and Uslar and Mutt helping him.

A full mug did not set fire. A half-filled one did, and they had the singed eyebrows to prove it. Something about fire and fumes combined produced those blue explosions of flame. He did not need to know why; he only had to know what would work.

The false cut boom was finished by the time they rounded the juts of the Jessachwa Mountains. Now they were heading for the strait—and though the Brotherhood might be down to one fleet this far east, this area was also controlled by the Venn. No one knew how many of them had gone west and how many remained to patrol the strait.

Two weeks they sailed, tacking steadily, for the winds had shifted into the west. That brought the weather that was best for covert sailing: cold rain and fog mixing with the warm current going northward.

Inda brooded over his charts whenever he was not on deck. Barend drove the sail crews to better speed. And Fox drilled them all until they fell into their hammocks, muscles trembling with fatigue. Drilled them all, including Inda. There were no complaints, not when everyone could see Fox and Inda on the forecastle sparring an entire watch, every day, in all weather.

They saw no one but Chwahir fishers until one morning, the rising sun lit a jagged line of mountains in the south: the western border of Chwahirsland, east of the Fangs.

"Send Jeje's signal," Inda said, coming up on deck.

Mutt and Uslar embarked on a friendly scuffle. Mutt shot off the whirtler, and the boys laughed at the sound as it arced down to cross the *Vixen*'s bow. They now knew why Inda liked signal arrows instead of flags whenever practical. Barend had told them stories about the plains warriors of the west, and Mutt and his friends had begun using horse jargon (or what they imagined to be horse jargon), even though the closest they'd ever been to the animals was dodging them in mainland ports.

Jeje brought the *Vixen* smartly up, the brothers spilling wind as Nugget tossed up the hook. But Inda tossed it back, and boomed down a heavy bundle wrapped in greenish canvas. Then he leaped down onto the *Vixen*'s deck.

"What are you doing?" Dasta called from the foremast.

Inda shouted back, "Scouting. Wake up Fox, tell him he's in command. Put up Walic's red sails and cruise as showy as possible north and south. Circle the Fangs. Poke past every island harbor. No mainland."

Barend appeared at the rail below Dasta, his hair messy from his snooze-watch. "You mean, we're luring 'em out, is that it?" He paused, taken by a huge yawn.

The deck watch saw Inda grin. "Throw down a war banner."

Barend rubbed his eyes. "We don't know where they are."

"Someone will. Let gossip do our work for us."

Barend whistled. "Won't she come after us with a fleet?"

"That's what I'm going to find out," Inda called back.

The *Vixen* skimmed out into the blue morning waters, chasing the last of the night sky into the west.

When the horizon had sunk *Cocodu*'s hull behind them, Inda said to Jeje, "We'll put into the Danai Mainport at night."

Jeje looked at him in surprise. "You think she's there?"

"I think she's looking for us," Inda said. "What I want to find out is what we can expect by way of aid on her side."

Jeje puffed her cheeks out. "You mean the Venn?"

"Did you listen to the reports off those Chwahir fishers? About the Venn, I mean."

Jeje waved a hand. "Complaints. Ships they stopped, searched, levied a toll on. We already knew all that."

"But they also said the Venn don't loot, they don't kill— except those they have declared war against—and they don't interfere with anyone who pays up."

"So what's that got to do with Boruin?" Jeje scowled.

Inda perched on the taffrail, scruffy in his fighting shirt, which was the old, stained, sun-bleached, mended, and washed one he'd taken out of Walic's wardrobe last summer, the sleeves loose enough to hide his wrist sheaths, the laces long gone, revealing his scarred chest. His long vest was worn and creased. He was barefoot, as were they all, his deck trousers worn and bag-kneed, curls escaping from his three-day-old sailor's queue. "Don't you see?" Inda gestured. "If the Venn obey their own rules, how much do they really trust those who don't have any?"

"Using the Brotherhood to do their dirty work doesn't make 'em any cleaner," Jeje said, watching sail and sky.

"What's that?" Nugget popped up from below and pointed at the grubby canvas roll on the deck. She bent, both hands on thighs. "Looks disgusting!" she exclaimed.

"It is disgusting," Inda called back. To Jeje: "Take us away from land. We'll pull in at night." Inda yawned.

"And until then? I take it you want a snooze-watch?"

"No." Inda snorted a laugh. "There's going to be no gossip about us, only what we gather about others. So here's your new sail. We're going to take a nasty little fishing smack in." He jumped off the taffrail and bent to snap open the length of canvas. They stared, appalled, at the patched, filthy sail wrapped around a small chest. "How much paint you got below?"

Nugget gave a gasp of delight. "A ruse! We get our very own ruse!" She looked pleading. "Do I get to rip up my clothes?"

Jeje looked exasperated. "Why waste good cloth?"

Nugget said, "Oh, I'll sew it all up again, but it's not a fun ruse unless we all get to do it." She patted her plain but well-made clothes.

Inda smiled briefly, then said, "Do what you like about your duds, but there will be no gossip about us, understand?"

As Nugget bounced up and down in gleeful anticipation he grunted, lifting the chest to his shoulder; the contents, shifting, made a rich clinking sound. He set it out of the way.

Then Jeje clapped her hands. "Let's get to work!"

And so it was a thoroughly nasty fishing smack that hove up behind the other fishing craft at sunset, jostling for the cheapest anchorage out in Danai Bay. There was no sign of the distinctive curve of the *Vixen*'s clean white mainsail and beautifully cut jibs, or the pale blue sides, the swept deck. This fishing smack looked like so many others that hadn't gotten any catch: nets tangled, overhanging the sides in clumps, sails bunched instead of furled. And what a mainsail! It alone looked disreputable enough to ward off any interest, or to prevent anyone from noticing that the craft, ugly as it was, didn't smell, like so many others did, of old fish and cooking oil. But the smell was pervasive, shared among the other nasty little fishing vessels anchored there. Inda had pronounced the transformed *Vixen* anonymous enough to permit all five of them, plus the chest, to be in the rowboat heading for shore.

"Remember," Inda said, when they were well away from anyone else. "We are fishers from the *Dusty* out of Bren, used to be merch sailors until the embargo and pirate problems docked our ships. That explains our various accents. Other than that, say nothing. Just listen."

Voices carried across the water from other vessels. On one side, a bad day's catch was a fine excuse to get drunk. On the other side, a family fight was in progress, everyone from baby to granny yelling.

Nugget chuckled, her wide eyes reflecting ship lights in pinpoints. "Woof told me that if you ask a question of strangers, someone's sure to want to know why you asked."

"And to want to tell someone else," Jeje said. "If they think they can profit by it."

"Got it." Loos set his back to rowing. "No questions."

"I doubt we'll hear anything," Inda added. "But if there is anything to hear, we'll catch it if we keep moving until midnight. Then meet back here. We're out on the late tide."

Nugget wriggled at the tiller, mentally embroidering her story as she guided them expertly between the other boats. She loved her artfully torn shirt and trousers, held together by bits of fabric sewn into a motley sash.

She yearned to be the most interesting girl in the room. Just once. In Freedom she was just Woof's sister, and though Inda's crew had lots of adventures, she hadn't been on any of them. Here, if she used her old identity, she'd just be another toff without land or estate—a figure of fun, Woof had warned her once. She knew her map. They weren't all that far from Khanerenth, which was just on the other side of Colend. There might even be other exiles here from Khanerenth.

What could be better than a poor orphan, descended from fierce pirates—no, *escaped* from pirates? She was still angry that Woof had kept her from the cruise in search of Gaffer Walic, but why not pretend she'd been there?

She was putting the finishing touches on a fine story as they closed with other rowboats. They all halted as a schooner moved slowly past, and then, bobbing on its wake, they followed in and tied up at the cheap dock, clambering over other boats to get to the ladder. While Inda stood in line to pay the moor attendant, Nugget ran off alone. She, raised in a harbor frequented by independents and privateers—some of them more pirate than not—was dazzled at the idea of a real mainland port.

The brothers had two ideas in mind: good food—that is, food that they chose instead of what the cook served up—and sex. They could listen while enjoying themselves.

Inda hoisted the brass-bound chest onto one shoulder and he and Jeje started up the long road toward the town. Like most port towns, it was built into the sides of the shoreline in a crescent, the scruffier buildings at the far edges. The main difference from pirate harbors was the evidence of a government lying beyond the loom of the land. There were street lamps along the main road and costly magical glowglobes in the expensive section before the big docks where the capital ships slowly rocked on the water, sails neatly furled. Under that light, in pride of place, were moored two great Venn warships with their upward curving prows and crossed yards from which would hang the towers of great square sails.

Jeje and Inda were not the only sailors who studied the complicated rigging required by square sails and wondered how they handled in deep waters during a storm.

A passer-by commented in accented Dock Talk, "Mighty clean, eh? Guess they can keep 'em that way by watching others fight for 'em."

"I say let 'em, if it cuts down Brotherhood some more."

The group laughed as they vanished in the crowd.

"Brotherhood battle?" Jeje whispered, and on Inda's

shrug, "Where are we going?" Jeje turned her thumb up at the box on his shoulder. "What is that, part of your ruse?"

"No. Have to find where the Guild Fleet has its office."

Guild Fleet? There had been talk at Freeport about some of the strait harbors trying to form a Guild Fleet to protect strait shipping from the increased pirate threat, but no one was in command. From what they heard the "fleet" was mainly comprised of old ships and fisher folk stung too many times by the Venn-allied pirates. Nothing that could do much besides travel in huge convoys just as ships had been doing for ages.

She couldn't imagine what Inda would want with such folk, but she said only, "Woof said their sign is stars on blue." She did not add Woof's scathing comment: *Dhalshev says that they do this sort of thing every generation or so, in absence of a strong navy. The guilds won't put up good money unless there's a real fleet commander, and meanwhile no one will agree on a fleet commander from any kingdom but their own, and so they'll limp along until a storm or a squabble scatters 'em again.* Surely Inda would know all that.

Inda said, "I remember."

Jeje followed in silence as Inda turned up one of the streets lit by glowglobes. Sea-related guild signs hung outside of broad building with wide porches. Many were lit, though it was late; shipping guilds mostly operated by tidal flow instead of the sun's arc.

Inda walked down the street, glancing at every shop until he reached one with a row of five stars, for five main shipping guilds, set in a blue banner: the sign of the Guild Fleet.

It was still lit inside. Inda set the chest onto the counter. The musical *chink!* of pure metal brought someone from the back. She popped the last of a sugared pastry into her mouth, dusted her fingers on her skirt, then said somewhat thickly in Dock Talk, "You want?"

"To send this thing west through your guild contacts."

Frown at the chest. "How far west?"

"Iasca Leror, Lindeth Harbor. Shipowner, Ryala Pim."

Jeje scowled at the floor. So Inda had taken over Kodl's debt. She should have expected that.

Narrow, searching glance from the clerk. "You're aware of the embargo."

"I know. Pay extra." Inda brought a heavy little bag from his inner vest pocket. "Figure there's someone going over the mountains, if not by sea. Venn don't control the mountains, last I heard."

"No. But they got allies. However, there's ways to get people through. It can't be that." She pointed to the chest. "Too heavy, too obvious. I hope your shipowner Pim is honest, because this gold will have to be converted to a letter of credit to our guild in Lindeth. She can redeem it there—after she identifies herself with a guild sved."

The clerk rang a tiny bell.

Inda opened a hand, palm up. "She's honest." As young prentices began counting out the coins, which were meticulously recorded on a slate, Inda leaned against the counter and asked casually, "What's this I hear about a recent Brotherhood battle? We don't get much news in the eastern islands."

The woman gave them a thin smile, too humorless to be a smirk. "The red sail fleet took a beating at The Nob, way west, t'other end of the strait. Right before winter."

"Who won?"

"The horse barbarians."

"Venn?"

"Stood off and watched."

"Anything else?"

She rubbed her ear with her quill feather. "All I know. Winter passes snowed in not long after, so that was the last piece of news through, with the last trade caravan. Some recently off ships down the strait said the Brotherhood retaliated all winter long by attacking all up and down the west coast, in spite of the Venn wanting it for themselves. We don't know what's true, or what they won or lost. We only know the horse hordes're too busy at home to come over the mountains and start slaughtering east."

Jeje felt sick, Inda cold and bleak. Neither spoke.

The transaction did not take long. The letter of credit was made out, and below the official language about money and exchange, Inda wrote in clear Iascan script: *The price of three merchant vessels, and cargo, sent by Inda Elgar.* Below that he wrote something else, in letters that went downward, not across. Then he pushed the paper back, the clerk glanced at it, whistled to herself when she saw the ancient letters at the bottom (which she recognized, but couldn't read), sealed it, and they left.

Jeje followed in silence. After they'd reached Freedom Island, Inda had divided up all Walic's treasure equitably, sending off the crew members he didn't want. Jeje suspected that she was seeing the last of Inda's share, as they had not yet divided up the spoils of their last take. So she only said, "What was that you wrote at the end?"

He sighed. "My birth name. There's a price on it. I don't want the local guard after me."

"What were those letters?"

"Old Sartoran."

They reached a tavern, entered, did a slow circuit through the crowd. The air was warm, smelling of ale, wine, food, salt, sweat. Loud voices, punctuated by laughter. Someone sang an old ballad in Sartoran triple-beat chords.

They pushed through the crowd near the drink, near the kitchens, those lounging around the door watching passers-by as they talked and laughed. They eased by—and out.

And on to another one, then a third, then a fourth. After a time she gave up trying to listen and watched Inda watching. And he did watch, constantly. After a time, he said in a low voice, "I make out two languages here. One is derived from Sartoran, but this other one, Mearsias, is completely unrelated."

He didn't speak again until the midnight bell tolled and the crowds along the boardwalk thinned. The night chill increased, and Jeje was glad to reach the boat dock, where a tired trio waited.

As they rowed back, Inda said, "Anyone hear anything?"

"Cursing against the Venn." The younger brother flicked up the back of his hand. "More against that Boruin. They hate her worse'n shit in shoes. In the strait here she hasn't been killing traders outright—that's what she does in the east. Here she levies more on top of the regular Venn ship-toll if she catches you."

"The Brotherhood lost some battle out west last autumn, and the Venn didn't help," Nugget reported with an air of triumph. "I got that at the orphanage, where I also got a free dinner."

"Orphanage?" Jeje asked. "You went to an orphanage?"

"Well, I am an orphan," Nugget stated, her chin coming up. "We were magic-born, see, so we only had our dad, and he got killed in the civil war. My brother told me that until I'm sixteen, if I'm ever stuck on land, I should go to the orphanages. So I did. I learned lots o' things."

"Good work, Nugget," Inda said, clapping her on the shoulder. "What else did you learn?"

"Do you want to hear about the Brotherhood battle?"

"But we—" Jeje began.

Inda nodded. Jeje sat back.

"There wasn't much, except how lots and lots of pirates got killed, and then everyone had to tell pirate stories. But it was way, way out west, and the Venn didn't help them, and the Brotherhood was angry, and so they went not just raiding but looting and burning the lands the Venn want, belonging to those wicked flying-horse people."

In the golden reflection from the open scuttles of a schooner they were passing, Jeje saw Inda's mouth thin.

"That was all. Rest was blabber. Nothing about Boruin."

Inda didn't speak again until they were back on the *Vixen,* riding out on the tidal ebb. The Fisher brothers got the sails up and Nugget, who seemed tireless, took the tiller again. She guided the *Vixen* between the little fishing craft, each with a lantern at bow and stern, and at last directly out to sea. As the wind increased, sending them pitching through the white-crested waves, Nugget pouted.

She wasn't going to tell Inda or Jeje how the girls at the orphanage had scoffed. How dare they not believe her story!

One of these days it would all be real. *Then* she'd show them.

Inda and Jeje sat at the tiny table in her low, cozy cabin, each cradling hot steeped leaf. She said, "You think that was Iasca Leror Nugget mentioned?"

"You heard the Guild woman." Inda looked down into

his cup. Then he put his head back. "Did you sniff any mention of rift between the Brotherhood and the Venn?"

Jeje sighed. "No. I guess I'm not as quick as you at winnowing out facts from blabber. All I got was people gabbling mostly about themselves, gossip about this or that ship, or who was pillow jigging with whom, and so on. People sure are boring when you don't know them."

Inda gave her a brief grin, and then his brows quirked. "About that battle at the Nob. Don't you have people up on the west coast below the Nob?"

"Lindeth." Jeje shook her head. "And if they didn't hear about pirates long before they were sighted and get well away, then I'm a sea lizard. I *won't* worry. So what did you hear that I missed?"

Inda sat back. "Like I said. Sense of sourness between the Venn and Brotherhood. Venn want Brotherhood raids on the coast. To keep our people busy for when they finally do attack. Also, how Boruin is full of strut. They hate her for that as much as for what she's done." He set his empty mug aside and got up. "Let's get this mess cleaned up, shall we?"

Jeje moved up on deck to take down the nets that she had so artfully arranged earlier. Inda always listened, not just when he was scouting. *That's why you'll never be a good captain, Fox,* Jeje thought, frowning at an unoffending net. *You see yourself in the middle of things, and Inda sees himself outside of things, putting them together, like rigging a ship, until everything works smoothly. His problem— if it is a problem—is he thinks he's invisible, and he's not, at least when he fights.*

Chapter Sixteen

THE full moon was faintly visible behind a feathering of clouds when Boruin's lookout shouted, "Sail hai!"

Boruin ran up on deck, caught a whiff of moldy vegetable: leddas oil. Some idiot must have dropped a lamp.

"What and where?" she called up to the foremast.

The lookout yelled, "Big one coming, dead on the starboard beam. Black sail. Maybe red."

Black sail! Boruin's heart hammered with anticipation as she peered over the rail. It was hard as damnation to see color at night. She willed it to be Ramis of the *Knife*. Whoever took him would soon be Marshig's lead captain—and assassin.

The moon slid, round and blue-white, between two fleecy clouds and the lookout above called, "Red sails."

Boruin's temper flashed. She glanced around for someone to take it out on. No one—they were quiet, in place. But she would. Oh, she would. "Brotherhood? Back?" Without sending a messenger-scout or even a signal? She sifted plans of retaliation. So some encroaching shit was using the western war as a ploy to make a grab for her position.

Well, Boruin knew what to do about that.

"An old merch," the lookout responded, and snorted a derisive laugh. "Can't be ours. I see a raffee. Two sloops and a cutter farther back. That raffee's lines look familiar. Got to be Walic's *Coco*."

Delicious. Boruin had been hearing about these fools for the past couple of weeks, cruising about, daring to wear red sails, as if looking for her. What swagger!

"Ru?" Majarian, her first mate, appeared from forward, moonlight glinting on his teeth and the bare steel thrust through his sash. "Haul wind? Signal the consorts?"

"No. They'll figure it out. I want this big old bucket all to myself. Eager, isn't he? You want to bet Elgar is over there, bowsprit up and sharp to get into my basket?"

Majarian laughed.

"Let 'em think we're asleep. Get the bow crews ready. I want them doubled but hiding. And Mawj, put poison on every arrow. Make 'em scream. I want the platter-faces to hear the screams on the mainland and pee in their beds."

Majarian laughed again as he snapped his fingers at the waiting fight team.

Boruin watched the big caravel lumber closer, and yes, they had a cut boom ready to swing out against their rigging while they shot down from that damned high forecastle onto Boruin's low, flush deck. "Come, Elgar, come on. I got my knees spread just for you," she breathed, peering at that high forecastle from behind her mizzenmast. Was that a flicker of movement abaft the mizzen?

She called, low-voiced, up to her lookout, "How many do you see?"

The lookout bent, her hand cupped around her mouth. "They've all gotta be hiding. Only seen one or two darting about aft. Think the helm's tied down."

Then they were coming in to cut her shrouds before boarding. So they'd all be crouched down behind the rail, ready to leap over. Surprise!

I'll surprise you, Elgar, you shit. I'll surprise you every day for a month, until your last surprise is the taste of your own guts.

The caravel lurched up, old masts groaning. Closer, the red sails belling in the moonlight. What conceit! What stupidity! That old merch might be heavy enough to support a cut boom that large, though she doubted it, but it was not nearly fast enough.

Well, let them come—and fail. She looked up, but her

crew was still, waiting on her signal, taking none of the defensive measures that would make it so easy to fend off that rotting tub.

Boruin licked her lips, shedding anger by counting the things she'd do to Elgar with his own weapons. She'd practice for Ramis on him. And then send his ribboned guts to Freeport Harbor as a sign of what they could expect when she sailed south.

Closer . . . closer . . . had to say they were well hidden. Not that that would benefit them any. What kind of dye did they use to give those sails a sheen? Sag—no, there must have been a squall upwind—smell of leddas oil— wait, wait, no, that's whiskey! Reminded her of that old soul-sucker Raskan, and the way he used to get people drunk before he played with them. Were they drunk over there?

Only way you could get courage to face me, hmmm?

The whiff was supplanted by the weirdly sweet scent of pepper-poison from overhead, freshly brought from the heights of Chwahirsland, as her fight crews busily smeared their arrowheads. The Chwahir used it in small doses in drink to keep their warriors warm and awake on long marches; what interested her was that in larger doses it enhanced pain to an exquisite scale.

Expensive—she'd lost four hands while torching the town that had furnished their latest supply—but worth it.

She laughed to herself as she watched her fight crews slither up to the tops in the dark, hidden by her own bellying red sails. All along forward, where the clumsy forecastle was heading, boarders crouched down, grinning fiercely, gripping their weapons.

Wait, wait, wait . . . and . . . "Helm hard over!"

Just before the caravel stole their wind the ships swayed together side by side, that boom swinging uselessly forward of the foremast. She'd made them miss their sweep, the stupid shits! "Fire arrows!"

Hissing fire arrows arced up at the mastheads and down onto the deck where the clustered attackers would be hiding.

No one heard the splashes on the far side of the caravel's

stern as Tau and Fox dove off, then struck out swimming to the lightless longboat following in the caravel's wake.

Both were underwater when the first arrows hit the sails. They saw only pinpoints of ruddy flame sending wavering reflections in the water.

It was Boruin's boarding crew, ready to swing over, who froze in horror as the little licks of flame on the sails whooshed upward in billowing, roiling balls, then blasted outward.

They had soaked the *entire caravel* with oil! A fire ship? You heard of them, but who was reckless or rich enough to actually—

BAVOOM! The explosion, louder than thunder, punched her ears. A flash of blue-yellow light blinded her; tiny stars swam across her vision until she realized she lay flat on the deck as tiny fireballs rained down through her sails and rigging.

She scrambled to her feet. "Helm alee! Helm alee!" Boruin shrieked, but the roar of the flames drowned her voice.

"WATER CREWS!" Majarian bellowed, waving his arms at the flaming bits of sail and rigging and burning blocks that fell. Some of the crew dashed about, desperately stamping on flames; the bow crews flung their longbows to the deck with a clatter, heedless of anyone below, and slid down the stays to the deck.

Just as the longboat full of picked fighters crept up the stern, slipped over the side, and—shrieking a strange, harrowing cry—*Yi-yi-yi!*—took them by surprise.

"Boarders aft!" was the last thing a pirate shouted before Fox nearly decapitated him with a whip-fast backhand slash.

Majarian seized his long boarding sword and Fox closed with him, knives glinting with reflected firelight along his forearms, teeth showing in a manic grin.

Boruin ran to the rail, screaming orders. Boarded! The first time in ten *years* she'd been boarded and here she was, no weapon—

Almost witless with fury she started toward her cabin to fetch a sword when something hot whiffled by her cheek, leaving a burning stench. She jerked her head up and saw in the ruddy light of the burning caravel two net-draped sloops sailing, one fore, one aft, shooting lit arrows.

Behind her new boarders swarmed over the prow, led by a skinny fellow with a face like a rat, a knife between his teeth.

She smacked her glass to her eye, screaming threats at the captain of her second consort—threats overpowered by the roar of the fire. Why wasn't he here at her aid? Because, she saw with incandescing rage, Walic's raffee had penned her consort hard against the burning caravel so it could sail down her consort's length, steel-tipped cut boom ripping the shrouds all down the consort's weather side.

Boruin whirled around, gripping her glass as a weapon. She would kill the first person she saw, didn't matter a damn who it was. There was Mawj, swinging at a tall shit in black who fought with two knives so fast they seemed to be on fire, steel reflecting the caravel's blaze. She grinned, having found her target, and cat-stalked around his black-scarf-tied head, the glass upraised to attack him from behind.

"Are you the captain?" The voice was polite—even pleasant.

She whirled around, staring into a face of astonishing beauty, pale, drifting hair haloed in reddish flame.

She smiled. Such a cultured voice, so beautiful a face—had to be a toff, with their ridiculous rules.

Widening her eyes and holding out her hands, she pouted. "I don't have a weapon. You wouldn't dishonor yourself by attacking a person without a weapon?"

"Yes," the golden vision sighed as he feinted with one knife, and when she swung the glass to ward the blow, he brought up his second knife and ripped it across her throat.

A short time later Dasta brought *Cocodu* alongside the lee-side of Boruin's rake-masted trysail. Inda swung down onto its deck, then pulled his knives free as he cast a quick glance around. The pirates had retreated forward; Fox and

Barend stood at either end of the captain's deck. The two corpses lying in blood pools at their feet had to be Boruin and her mate.

Inda's eyes lingered as he comprehended the restless, shifting pirates yelling curses: anyone could have slit Boruin's throat, but Majarian lay there striped with a hundred thin cuts, black in the firelight. Only one person fought with such skill and savagery when he was angry.

Inda lifted his gaze to Fox, who appeared unarmed. He stood with his feet planted apart, arms crossed, knives turned up along his forearm, grinning a challenge at the pirates.

Defeat in the mind.

"Elgar the Fox," Barend howled, sweeping his cutlass toward Inda, whereupon Boruin's crew threw their weapons down, some raising hands and crying, "We'll join! We'll join!"

Just as they had on the third consort, which had surrendered after the fire ship went up in flame, the *Cocodu* crossing its bow. Inda had sent over Tcholan's fight band to secure it before they'd moved on to the second consort, which was in dangerous proximity to the fire ship.

More than half the crew had been in the tops of that one, some waiting to defend with arrows, most frantically changing sail to keep them from colliding with the fire ship. Their danger from fire had been desperate enough that they had not seen the *Cocodu* raffee ease up on the other side until the first shrieking grate of the cut boom in the shrouds alarmed them, but by then it was too late. Many fell into the sea; the rest had surrendered.

So here Inda was, facing Boruin's crew as they too surrendered.

It was too easy. Pirates might not fight in drilled teams, but they had to have other strategies—

"Same orders as before," he called to Barend. "Take the weapons and shift 'em all to boats. I don't want any of them, I don't care what they offer. If they pull hard they can make it to Chwahirsland and be dealt with there."

Chwahirsland had been Boruin's main cruising ground. It seemed just to Inda.

Pirates started pleading, arguing, bargaining. Inda left them to Barend and Fox and ran forward to check the status of the third consort. He was distracted for a moment by a whiff of burning oil—and was that whiskey? Maybe a result of the explosion.

The dismasted second pirate ship seemed largely empty.

Ah. The third consort—the one that had surrendered as soon as the fire ship went up in flames—seemed to have changed its mind, and it looked like Tcholan's fight band was fully engaged. Clangs and clashes carried over the water. Arcs of arrows gleamed in the firelight from the sloops, but Tcholan's band, divided between two ships, needed reinforcement.

Inda found Barend's signaler on guard at the hatchway. Inda took his bow, pulled a whirtler from the quiver, and shot it over the *Vixen.* He saw the sweet curve of its sail alter, pick up wind.

Tau came up, his hair ruddy gold in the firelight, one of his fine linen sleeves ripped by a sword cut, drying blood on his arm. He tore the rest of his sleeve free and began binding it around his bicep. "What now?"

"Third one—something looks wrong. Let's get some backup to Tcholan." He lifted his voice to be heard on the *Cocodu,* its stern abreast. "Dasta! Helm to Mutt and get your band to the third!"

Fox appeared, jerking his chin to sling sweat from the fringes of his black fighting kerchief. "Well?"

"Hold here," Inda said. "Get 'em over the side." Behind them shouts, curses, pleas rose—some were fighting again. Fox whirled, ran to Barend's aid.

While the *Vixen* neared Inda scanned again. Little boats clustered around the second consort. Uslar was visible on the foredeck motioning to figures climbing down the sides. Uslar? He and Nugget and Thog had been ordered to stay on the *Vixen,* bows in hand to protect Jeje as she threaded through the ships.

Cocodu had drifted forward to stay free of the burning caravel, which was still showering down bits of burning wood and sail.

Vixen glided under the trysail's lee. Inda jumped onto

the *Vixen*'s deck. The brothers were both at their posts, tending sail instantly; Jeje handled the tiller, ignoring blood staining the side of her tunic.

"Where are the Chwahir?" he asked. "And Nugget?"

"Took the gig. Went aboard number two," Jeje said, breathing hard. "Didn't see 'em leave." It hurt to talk, so she decided against saying that the gig had also carried something covered by old sail. Didn't seem relevant.

Inda again caught the pungent rotting garden smell of leddas oil drifting over the water and said, "We'd better get everyone away from the caravel. It may blast again, and we don't have enough people to be putting out fires the wind might start."

Jeje waved to the brothers. One sent up the single whirtler alerting them to a flag signal and the other raised the flag for dispersal.

Jeje clamped her forearm against her ribs as she surveyed the ships. Pirates forced over the sides into the boats—crew tending sail, putting out fires—everyone busy with at least one task, if not two. But why did Thog leave like that and go on board the second pirate ship?

No one to ask: Inda was gone, scrambling up to the deck of the third pirate ship, a raffee-rigged brig with a broad hull that had probably begun its sailing career as a luxury merchant vessel. As he reached the captain's deck there was a splintering sound and the nailed hatchway flew apart in chunks; Tcholan and his band had hastily hammered most of the pirates below before dealing with the hands in the tops who'd dropped down to fight.

Pirates surged up, weapons brandished, surrender forgotten. They vastly outnumbered Tcholan's band and the hottest fighting of the night broke out.

Inda grabbed up a boarding ax and a short staff and led the way into battle. Dasta took up shield arm position at his left.

Hot, ferocious joy suffused Inda as he whirled and struck, blocked, whirled, struck again, fast and deadly, so fast and deadly no one stood long against him.

Again he was subliminally aware of an attack behind him—like a poke inside his skull, warning him. Every time he heeded that inward poke he was just in time to ward off a deathblow.

From the trysail Fox watched Inda through a glass, amazed at the astonishing change that came over Inda in fights to the death. In practice he was formidable, but Fox was better. In combat, Inda fought as if he were two men— as if he had eyes in the back of his head. Before his ceaseless onslaught the press of pirates began to retreat.

And Tcholan's and Dasta's attack bands, small as they were, backed him perfectly. No pirate passed that drilled, lethally effective line. The ones at the back, seeing their mates falling, wavered, some diving overboard.

The defeated pirates were forced down into the longboat. Many of them stared up at Inda, grim, some desperate, but he stood on a barrel, one foot propped on the rail, sword ready. Splashed with other people's gore. No one was willing to try him again.

When the last one tumbled into the longboat the craft was full pirates struggling for space, the railings barely clearing the black water. Inda turned away as the distance between the boat and the ship widened.

"I'll oversee cleanup," Tcholan croaked, fire from the caravel reflecting in his black eyes.

"I'll scout the cabin."

In the captain's cabin Inda found water in an ensorcelled basin and stuck his entire head in, sucked up mouthfuls of water until his nose stung, a cut—unnoticed till now— stinging his temple. A scan of the cabin revealed charts, a log book, a chest of clothing, and, far more to his interest, an entire closet full of arms.

Through the open scuttle came Dasta's voice, "Hai, what's going on?"

"Who gave them orders?"

That was the raspy voice of Sails, once the first sail-mate of Walic's fleet, now second in command in Dasta's attack band as well as *Cocodu*'s first sail-mate.

Inda dashed out, ax in hand. He emerged topside as the longboat reached the middle pirate ship, the one with the fallen foremast and ruined rigging. Smoke and fitful light from the caravel drifting southward made it difficult to make out anything but silhouettes running about on deck.

He dashed to the binnacle and found a glass. The second ship, empty before, was now crammed with pirates—and his own assigned prize crew nowhere in sight. Had the pirates retaken the ship? Wait. There was the prize crew, in the rowboat hooking onto *Cocodu!*

Anger scorched through Inda, smothering the aches and exhaustion as the longboat pirates swarmed up the sides of the second consort, calling greetings to their mates. All around the ship launches and gigs tossed on the sea, some of them swamping. Someone had broken their bottoms with an ax. Aboard the ship laughter and invective echoed over the water.

Between *Vixen* and the consort Thog stood up in the sternsheets of the *Vixen*'s gig. Uslar sat at her feet, Nugget behind, busy wrapping an arrow. The girl handed her arrow to Uslar, who bent briefly over it, then raised a smoldering fire arrow to Thog. She took it and raised her bow. Efficient, swift—and orderly.

Inda rubbed smoke-burned eyes, coughing as his thoughts ran in too many directions. He needed to get reinforcements to the second consort. He needed to understand what the two Chwahir and Nugget were doing in that damned gig.

Thog raised the bow, took aim, and shot.

The glowing arrow landed squarely in the middle of the great foresail, sending curiously blue flame out in swift runnels. As if the sail had been splashed with whiskey. Whiskey?

"Thog?" Inda shouted, running to the rail.

If Thog heard him, she made no sign. The next arrow landed in the middle of the longboat, the only one afloat. The third arrow hit the mainsail, the fourth the mizzen.

For a moment nothing happened.

Then flames flashed up the foresail, blue, sudden, and bright as lightning, and again on the mainsail. A heartbeat later a terrible fireball swelled skyward from the captain's deck, and fire exploded in all directions. Pirates shrieked in terror. Within a dozen heartbeats the entire ship was ablaze. A blast of hot air struck and the sails above Inda thundered.

The light was so intense it reflected off every shocked face on the remaining ships, from Jeje on *Vixen* to Mutt at the helm of *Cocodu,* his mouth open in astonishment.

"Jeje!"

She wrenched the tiller, bringing the *Vixen* alongside.

The screams of the burning pirates dashing wildly about on the deck of the burning ship rose above the roar of the flames. Many dove overboard—where Thog, standing in the gig, shot them one by one.

Inda leaped onto the foredeck of the *Vixen,* white-faced with anger. He gripped the bloody boarding ax. "*Who ordered that? If Fox countered my orders—*"

Thog's gig bumped up against the *Vixen*. She and her two helpers climbed aboard, Nugget pale, her pupils huge in widened eyes as she shrilled, barely audible, "One got Jeje, but I shot him! I shot him right here!" A smack to her chest. "He fell right off the masthead!"

Inda let her stream of words pass through his mind and out as Uslar climbed up behind her, head lowered, expression closed in the way peculiar to Chwahir in times of stress.

Thog crossed the little deck and stood before Inda, stiff and pale.

Thog stated, "It was not Fox, it was I."

Icy needles of horror prickled through Jeje.

"What?" Inda yelled, staring down at her.

Thog trembled, her face lit by the glow of the firestorm she had created. "I ordered Uslar and Nugget to help me spill the oil and the whiskey on the ship," she said distinctly. "I told Tcholan you wanted him on the third consort. I sent the prize crew to the raffee. We brought up the casks of whiskey to the deck, under my direction, and spilled half on the deck and then righted them. Open. So that they would explode. I poured more down the sails, and I went from boat to boat telling pirates to board. I shot the arrows."

"Why?" Inda's tendons stood out as he gripped the ax.

Her voice was low and hoarse, "Because I know the people they slaughtered in my homeland. *I can name them. One by one.*"

Inda gave a groan and flung himself around, staring helplessly at the burning ship. Already the cries were fading; those few who had made it overboard before the fiery blast bobbed about in the water, their faces pale blobs as they waited for either death or rescue. The longboat slid below the surface, briefly glowing orange and then vanishing.

The ship began to sink, smoke billowing up in a thick black column against the slowly lightening sky, the oily, vile burning-meat smell dying away in the freshening wind. *I will be blamed for that,* Inda thought. *Even if I kill Thog, that act will be laid against me wherever people talk about this action.*

A whirtler went up from *Cocodu*. Jeje raised her glass, saw the lookout on *Cocodu*'s foremast pointing to the southeast, where the bleak blue light of predawn smeared the sky.

She jerked her thumb, and Inda turned. Notching the horizon were the slanting black silhouettes of three ships. He looked around for his glass, remembered he'd left it aboard the pirate raffee, and held out his hand. Jeje thumped her glass into it. He raised the glass to his eye. "Jeje, from now on you'll wear armored quilting into battle," he said flatly, sweeping the ships.

"It was just a spent arrow. Only a scrape on the ribs. Hardly noticed."

They both knew she lied; Inda said, "Take it as an order."

"No. That stuff is heavy. I don't want to drown."

"Shit," Inda said, too tired to get angry again. "You won't drown. If you fall overboard, pull the laces and wiggle free." He frowned, wiped the glass on his shirt, tried again.

The ships sprang closer, the exquisite curve of their taut sails clear in the pale blue morning light: Chwahir schooners, flying the best sails in the world.

Sailing to what, attack? Inda turned around to look again at his own fleet and those ships he'd captured, but then Thog stepped to his side. "They are coming to join you," she said, with conviction.

Inda stared at her. "How do you know that?"

Her bony shoulders jerked up and down. "Everyone knows we were going after Boruin. They will have seen the light from the fire ship." Her upper lip curved.

In the distance Fox shouted orders for defense bands to take their places. *Chwahir. Enemy, or not?*

"They will want to fight the Brotherhood," Thog said.

Inda watched the three ships cutting smoothly through the water, heeling over at exactly the same angle as dawn light stippled the waves with touches of gold and the blue smear in the eastern sky warmed to peach.

Inda could imagine his own crew's heated talk. They'd divide sharply for and against Chwahir, they would divide over Thog's fire ship, over who had done what, who would get what. And underneath it all was the question of command.

He saw it so clearly, despite his scorched lungs, aching head, stinging cuts. *It's not a war game, you haywit.*

He dropped his head in his hands. The screams of burning pirates, the six dead from his own crew, his own voice, so easy that day in Walic's cabin, "We're going to fight pirates." And then Tdor's voice again, from when he was eleven, *It's not a war game, you haywit.*

He raised his head, seeing Tdor's face as he had in so many dreams. *Nobody else is fighting pirates. And I know how to fight,* he told that child—because Tdor was always twelve years old in his mind. *Maybe it doesn't make your net, Tdor. But fighting pirates might save it.*

Even now, despite that inward moral struggle, his mind was busy assessing the battle. Pirates had no discipline. They fought hard and viciously, but they got in one another's way, they didn't listen, they stopped to loot. All that was so much a part of pirate life they couldn't see it as weakness. Drill—and a clear chain of command—could beat them.

But he had to establish chain of command. Thog made that plain enough. Not by force. That was the pirate way. Instead, he thought back to his first year at the academy, and the scrub shoeing . . .

He turned his head. "Jeje, bring me to the trysail. Tie

down the prizes, everyone to report to the trysail, which will be my flagship once we clean it up. Call Sails and the armorer. The Chwahir can come aboard if they want to talk. And afterward," he said into her smoke-smeared, stunned face, "we're going to mark our first Brotherhood kill."

The conversation with the Chwahir was brief.

Three captains climbed aboard, all short, round-faced men with wide-set dark eyes and black hair, dressed in loose woolen tunics over narrow trousers belted at the waist. They looked around the deck, from which the dead, but not their blood, had been Disappeared.

The captains' expressions were as blank as Thog's, but Inda sensed approval. One said, "We came to help you against Boruin, but you did not need us. We will join your fleet if you are going to sail against the Brotherhood."

"Not just the Brotherhood," Inda said, putting to words the new sense of direction that had been so tentative. Words made it real—orders to act on. "We need a day or so to clean up and refit. Then we will set sail for Freedom Islands to take on more crew, supplies, and news. And then—"

They waited. Everyone listening waited, and he said it, so it must be true. *Hear me, Rig? Wumma?* "We will sail against Marshig himself."

"We will join you." The Chwahir's expression changed, almost a smile. "As for sail, we can help."

They left. The hands at the oars matched strokes beautifully, taking them back to their ships.

Leaving Inda's crew standing about, everyone exhausted, some stunned, as the morning light strengthened. Fox, Barend, and Dasta had ranged themselves on the lee side of the captain's deck, blood-spattered and filthy, their weapons in hand.

Everyone waiting for orders—for order.

Inda forced himself to lift his voice. "We'll build a bonfire tonight to salute our dead. Armorer? We need a sheet on deck, so we can make a proper fire. But first, we can salute ourselves." They were listening. "We'll wear ruby hoops. Marking red sail kills. I'll go first."

He pulled his sweat-soaked, gore-splashed shirt off, then motioned to Sails, who had brought a needle out. Gold they'd found below, and jewels, the spoils of pleasure yachts: Boruin had had a weakness for gold and glittering stones. On Inda's order, as soon as he'd boarded the trysail, the armorer (who'd begun as a jewelry-making prentice before a pirate attack had forced him into a new life) had gotten busy banging gold into hoop shapes. No time to smooth them, but the roughness of their make would do. To each he'd affixed one of Boruin's hoard of rubies, all beautifully cut.

Now Inda sat on an overturned bucket, pulled his blood-crusted hair back, and winced in anticipation. "How much will it hurt?" he asked plaintively.

Mutt stared at Inda's body with its cuts and scars, blood in his hair, and snickered. The spark of humor spread—as release—as relief, and soon the whole deck laughed.

Sails pinched his earlobe and jabbed the needle through.

"Ow!" Inda yelped.

"Aw, I was fast," Sails chided in her deep voice, and chuckles rippled through the watching crew. "Here's the hoop. Pour whiskey or bristic over it each day."

"Won't ensorcelled water do?" Inda pleaded. "We pour that over wounds—"

"We're pirate-fighting pirates," Tau said, the first to comprehend Inda's plan to bind them together. He had to sustain the moment, and draw them into a band whose shared enemy was the Brotherhood of Blood. "We're tough, and when we get to Freeport, we're going to strut. It has to be firewater." He kneed Inda off his bucket, sat, and flung back his shoulder-length hair. "I'm next."

"Then me!" Mutt yelled. "Me!"

"No, me me me me me me *me!*" Nugget squealed, bouncing up and down.

"No, I'm next," Barend snarled, swatting at Mutt who skipped away, crowing with mirth.

"And I follow you," Fox said, lounging aft, dressed all in black so no blood showed.

They lined up—one, another, then everyone joined.

Inda beckoned to Thog, who stood apart, watching. She turned his way, her small body tense with expectation. In silence they walked into Boruin's cabin. Inda glanced around in distaste; the silk-covered bed was rumpled and smelled of spilled wine. Weapons with jewels and fine carving along hilts and blades lay everywhere, one knife with blood crusted on it, all of them of little worth to someone who had never paid for anything in her life.

Thog's upper lip lifted, this time in unmistakable disgust. "I will clean it," she promised, in Sartoran.

Inda waved a dismissive hand as he stared down into those unblinking black eyes. "Why did you do that, Thog? Didn't you think the Chwahir would give them justice?"

Thog said, "If they made it ashore they would have been flayed in the public square. By those who know how to make it last."

Inda pressed the heels of his hands against his eyes. He was too tired to think; he didn't want this conversation. But instinct prompted him to have it out now.

Thog waited, her hands at her sides.

"I am not going to argue about justice and revenge." Inda lowered his hands, flexing them. "And I'm not the pug to yammer at you about laws when I'm supposed to have broken them at home, when I've got a price on my head in every harbor on the continent. But Thog, if everyone thinks they can ignore my orders for their own purpose, then we really become pirates."

Thog said, "I will not act so again. I knew that Majarian. He's the one who fired our village and all the ones along the province where once I lived. He killed children and laughed while he did it. After that, Boruin took him on as mate. And they came back again. With that crew. That time was more terrible because they knew where everything was, including the roads in. So they guarded them. Which gave them more time for what they did."

Inda expelled his breath. "Are there any more secrets like that you're going to spring on me?"

"No." Thog looked down at the deck, then up, unsmiling as always. "I hate the Brotherhood, though not as much as

I hated Majarian and those he led. To defeat the Brotherhood I will fight when I am told to fight, I will obey orders,
I will not be part of anyone's disobedience. But defeating
them is not a promise I made on my soul. Killing Majarian's crew was." She was trembling.

"Fair enough," Inda said, and tried for lightness. "You
made my fox banner. You should get a chance to fight
under it."

Chapter Seventeen

. . . and under a distinctive device on their foresail, a golden fox on black, he sailed the black-sided pirate trysail they call the Death down to the Freedom Islands where the rebels from Khanerenth have taken up new lives. There he gathered volunteers, and sailed thence to Sartoran waters.

By the time they reached the next station held by the Brotherhood, they had been joined by a fleet of volunteers. And so this mighty fleet sailed west under the leader known only as Elgar the Fox. But he must be your son, Fareas. My own trusted scribe returned from Freeport Harbor with much testimony about him, including the fact that he is the very same son of a prince against whom piracy charges had been laid in the ports north of us here in Sartor. His name is misspelled according to various accents, but it is recognizable as Lord Indevan Algara-Vayir to those who know it.

Here is what you probably did not expect: two with him are widely rumored to be Marlovans, one being a tall redhead with green eyes, known only as Fox—

SHENDAN Montredavan-An—permitted from her ancestral lands for this rare trip by special dispensation from the Cassad family—leaped up. "Is that all it says?" she demanded in a hard voice. "About my brother?"

"Yes," Tdor Marth-Davan said gently.

No one said, *if that even is your brother.*

Shendan ran from the high tower chamber.

The other young women gathered there for Carleas Ndarga's wedding to the Cassad heir listened to Shendan's swift steps on the stone stairs outside, but no one moved. They all knew Shen wanted privacy as much as she hated pity.

Tdor, that day arrived from Choraed Elgaer, had to clear her throat, which had tightened in sympathy. She coughed, then resumed reading.

—and another whose description so matches the Cassad family, he might be the missing Harskialdna's son.

Carleas Ndarga whistled softly. "I do, *do* so hope that's Barend."

"Fareas-Iofre thinks it is. And therefore, if Barend is there, the other really must be Shen's brother, who was aboard the *Cassad* all those years ago, before it was taken by pirates. Anyway, the rest is family news, and so I did not copy it." Tdor laid the paper gently on the fire, thinking, *Inda, it is your eighteenth Name Day. Please be happy.*

Autumn had turned cold and wet, but the round tower at Telyaer, the ancient Cassadas castle, was warm and bright with tapestries made by generations of Cassad women.

There was a contemplative silence, then Shendan Montredavan-An reappeared at the doorway. Her eyes and nose were red, but she was composed again. "Hadand knows?"

Tdor turned her thumb up. "A copy was sent to her."

Joret sat against the window, the silvery sleet outside a dramatic frame for her glossy black hair and downcast blue eyes. She and Tdor had traveled to the wedding together on the princess' insistence. It had also been Fareas-Iofre's suggestion to use the Sierlaef's own excuse, visiting, as the best way to avoid him. There would be no political trouble if Joret simply wasn't in Choraed Elgaer when the king's heir ostensibly arrived to visit, but in reality to stalk Joret.

The two sat in the window seat side by side. Joret's

beauty contrasted with Tdor's ordinary features. Tdor was tall, gaunt, as shapely, she herself had said wryly, as a plank. Her face was long, her ears stuck out in front of her braids, her coloring was uniformly brown. When she wasn't seated next to Joret and thus forced into the disadvantage of contrast, what people saw first was her expression, which was keen, kind, honest. Joret was not in the least vain. She was steady, sober, hard-working, and most liked her (with some exceptions inspired entirely by jealousy), but Tdor was loved by everyone who knew her.

Mran Cassad asked, "Is Fareas-Iofre's sister's testimony to be trusted?"

"Implicitly," Tdor said, and Joret turned both palms up.

Mran leaned forward. "And Indevan's the heir to Choraed Elgaer, now, is he not? Despite the exile?"

"Yes," Tdor whispered. Joret sent a covert look her way. Tdor stared down at her strong, capable hands, her face pensive.

Joret said, drawing attention away from Tdor, "We must find a way to bring Inda back."

Shendan saluted them with a glass of hot mulled wine. There was a merry lilt to her voice that no one had heard since the days of their queens' training, before she found out that her brother Fox's ship had been captured by pirates. "He was never actually accused of anything, am I right? He just vanished."

"Yes," Joret said.

Mran added soberly, "The boys at the academy were told he'd been in disgrace for cheating. For cowardice, even. Though Cherry-Stripe said there hadn't been any evidence. The Harskialdna had believed some story told by Garid Kepri-Davan, the one they called Kepa Tvei until his brother was killed up north."

No one said anything against Garid Kepri-Davan—not because they'd liked him, but because he and his entire family had been killed by angry Idayagans shortly after his father became Jarl of the Andahi Pass. Many of them considered it justice, but they didn't say that, either.

"I can tell you what happened." Tdor took them by surprise.

Many of them had had brothers and cousins in the academy. A few were betrothed to the very first Tvei class in the academy—the second sons who had been pulled in to be trained with the king's second son instead of left at home to be trained by their families. The second sons—Randael, or Shield Arm in Iascan—was supposed to defend the Jarl's lands when he was away either riding the borders or fighting for the king. The Jarl's wife defended the castle itself, with the Randael's wife (Randviar) as her second in command and go-between.

So they all knew *something* had happened that summer six years ago, but not what. None of the boys would talk about it afterward—their own fathers forbade them. The Harskialdna's name was attached to that mystery, which meant it might seem treason to speculate.

"Whipstick Noth told me everything," Tdor went on. "It was his little brother Kendred—they called him Dogpiss because of his yellow hair—who died. Garid Kepri-Davan lied and said that Inda was going to cheat on one of their war games, and the Noth brother tried to stop him. Actually it was the other way around. They got caught by one of the older boys, who smacked Dogpiss. He fell. Broke his head. His neck as well. For which Inda was unfairly blamed."

"What?"

"What?"

"How is that possible?"

Tdor leaned forward. "Here's why nothing was said. Dogpiss Noth apparently was set up by the Sierlaef himself. Dogpiss told Inda just before the accident happened that the heir had cornered him alone. Said they needed something to laugh about. The Noths were known for their practical jokes in those days. Dogpiss loved practical jokes above anything, even above winning the war games. So he was going to pull some prank, only it was against the rules. Inda tried to stop him, so he snuck away and ended up dead. The Harskialdna wouldn't listen to Inda, was going to cane him in front of the entire academy."

The girls made noises of disgust.

"This part I know from Hadand. The king asked Captain

Sindan to make Inda disappear. There was no proof. The Kepri-Davans were making political trouble and the Harskialdna was set against Inda, but apparently the king believed Inda. Yet—because of the lack of proof—could not publicly gainsay his brother."

"And so Inda vanished," Carleas Ndarga said. "Yes, that matches what Rattooth hinted at." She waved toward the window, and the tower beyond, which was where the younger brother of her husband-to-be lived. He'd been part of that initial Tvei class.

Joret said, "Hadand told us Captain Sindan whisked Inda away to sea but no one was to know."

Shen leaned back, waving a hand impatiently. "Except Tanrid is dead, the Kepri-Davans are dead, and the Harskialdna is busy with his war. What can they do if that old scandal comes out again?"

"Nothing, except how would it help Inda any? That poor little boy!" one of the Cassad cousins said, wincing.

"I know a way to help Inda." Mran grinned, her sharp face resembling her aunt Ndara Cassad, wife to the Harskialdna. "We won't talk about the old scandal. Instead, we'll spread the news about Inda's triumphs against pirates, all over the kingdom. Everywhere."

Tdor gripped her hands tightly together. "How?"

Shendan clasped her arms around her knees and laughed, rocking back and forth. "By pen." And she laughed again. "Everyone knows we women are always writing letters, and none of the men bother parsing our codes so boring our letters are!"

"Of course they're boring," said another cousin, this one popular though she did not have the most penetrating mind. She added quite reasonably, "That way nobody knows what we don't want told."

"That's right, Dnar." Carleas Ndarga was tall, quiet, much plainer than Tdor, with her heavy chin and close-set eyes, but she was very smart. All the girls admired her. She leaned over to pat Dnar's hand. "You're absolutely right. This time, you see, we *want* to spread a secret all over."

The conspirators grinned at one another. Their mothers and grandmothers had handed down the simple codes they used: names of dogs and horses and flowers standing for people and places and political issues of importance. When the code did not suffice, convoluted poetry in the Old Sartoran alphabet did.

Shen said to Dnar, "By the time enough letters cross the kingdom no one will ever be able to track where the original news came from. Or how it is spreading! But we must write everyone to make it work, not just our friends. My first letter shall be home to Marend and my mother about Foxy, for I *will* believe it's he, somehow, with Inda. But Dannor Tya-Vayir is second on my list. She'll be bored wild by now, stuck at home with Hawkeye's father, who scares off all her favorites."

"Being unworthy of the soon-to-be wife of a son of a princess," Mran said, watching Carleas stitching grimly away on her betrothed's wedding shirt. She was embroidering it with yellow suns, the old Cassadas symbol, though she was not fond of needlework. "Bored and that means looking for some way to stir up trouble."

Shen observed wryly, "One thing you can trust our old Mudface for is making trouble."

The older girls smiled at the private nickname from their girlhood years. Dannor "Mudface" Tya-Vayir, who was as proud of her fine looks as she was of her lineage, had as a small girl done something so reprehensible that Tdiran, the king's sister, who had married the Jarl of Yvana-Vayir, had once marched her down to the vegetable garden and scrubbed her face in the mud.

Mudface and her equally unpopular brother Horsebutt loathed the Sierlaef twice as much as they loathed the Harskialdna for bypassing their family favorites when he created those new jarlates up north. Not that Horsebutt cared about his father's liegemen; his hatred was personal, going back to their academy days.

"But Dannor won't be at Convocation this year," Mran pointed out. "The Jarl of Yvana-Vayir insists they have the wedding at home, and on New Year's."

"Hadn't heard that." Carleas glanced up from her stitchery. "What's the truth?"

"The king didn't give him permission to have Hawkeye

and Dannor wed in the throne room," Tdor said. "Like the royals. Hadand told us the Harskialdna wrote in the king's name, saying if the Jarl wanted his son to marry at Convocation it could be held in the great hall, like the other Jarls' sons and daughters."

Everyone knew the Jarl of Yvana-Vayir's pretensions were shared passionately by Dannor. It was the single thing they agreed on.

Mran added soberly, "He would not have dared that if Tdiran-Jarlan had still been alive." But Tdiran had died falling from a horse that had slipped on ice and now there was no one who could rein in Yvana-Vayir's ambitions.

Shendan laughed soundlessly. "So no royal wedding for Mudface. Oh, but it's perfect, don't you see? I report it to her as gossip, and we can safely trust her poison pen to spread the news about Inda and thereby raise again the question of why he vanished in first place. She'll have it all over the royal city before Convocation, just to make the Harskialdna—and the Sierlaef—squirm."

"News about pirates never needs a source, not after that battle at the Nob and the pirate retaliations against the coast all year long." Carleas gave her sudden caw of laughter, and flung a pale blond braid impatiently back. "We'll have every city talking about the heir to Choraed Elgaer out in the world fighting pirates—we will not mention the other two. We need proof they really are Savarend—Fox, that is—and Barend, and anyway their situation is not the same. Let's keep the attention on Inda. If everyone's talking about how he is at war against these damn pirates who have been destroying our harbors, well, the boyhood mess—particularly the cowardice accusation—would vanish like fog in the sun. Even the Harskialdna couldn't gainsay his efforts for the kingdom." She smiled over at Joret. "And if your future husband's triumphs are on everyone's lips, the Sierlaef has even less excuse to come seeking you. Finally, if people ask questions about why he vanished, eventually the Harskialdna will be forced to answer."

"Future husband." Joret sent a quick look at Tdor, a look of muted concern.

Shendan, watching, said, "You come stay with us next, Joret." *Dear, practical Tdor. Is she a romantic after all?*

Carleas laughed. "It's a perfect idea, Joret. You have to go next to Darchelde."

Shen added mockingly, "Even the Sierlaef cannot invite himself there without breaking the treaty, and if he tried, watch the Jarls rise up on their hind legs at Convocation, howling, *Why? What was he doing there? Are we to set aside the shackles binding the evil Montredavan-An family to their lands?*"

"The Sierlaef will be furious," Mran said, gloating.

"But not nearly as much as his uncle will be when Inda's name is on everyone's lips," Shendan promised. "We had all better get busy now, because we'll want to get our Runners across the kingdom and back at least once before the heavy snows come. Give that gossip a chance to take root, so it's growing branches and leaves by the turn of the year."

The others laughed. Tdor laughed, too, though it was forced. She felt a pang of grief, though she knew it was foolish. Inda had probably forgotten them all. Six years he'd been gone—years she'd counted off one by one, celebrating his Name Day alone each autumn, or in private with Inda's mother.

He was eighteen now. And though she was half a year away from twenty, sometimes she felt younger than the bossy, self-righteous near-thirteen she'd been when she and Inda had last seen one another.

He hadn't even reached twelve yet, but when he made a typical little boy joke about looking forward to his father's planned skirmish with some local brigands, she'd snapped, *Just remember this plan is not a war game, you haywit.* How many times had she excoriated herself for her pompous, oh-so-superior nagging—the last words they ever said to one another?

She looked at Joret's sky-colored eyes and repressed a sigh. If Inda ever came home, he'd be delighted to find Joret waiting as future wife, as lovely as she was good. And Tdor did like Whipstick, she did, she *did*.

Nevertheless, when her Runner Noren came to her chamber that night to get her orders, she saw in Tdor's puffy eyes and red nose that she had been weeping, all alone.

Chapter Eighteen

AT year's end, high in an ancient tower in Ala Lark-adhe, Evred Varlaef entered his private room to an astonishing—but not new—sight.

On the old stone floor a dark-haired young man no older than he lay motionless, his eyes wide with fear, his hands trembling, as two huge dogs stood over him, saliva dripping from bared fangs, fur raised the length of their spines, ears flat.

Sindan, just arrived, held his sword tip under the young man's neck. "Assassin," he said briefly in Marlovan. And nudged with the toe of his boot the long, wickedly sharp carving knife lying nearby where it had fallen.

The would-be assassin did not understand that language, but from the way his desperate gaze snapped between Sindan, the dogs, and Evred, it was clear he expected the worst.

Evred hunkered down next to him, one hand resting on the nearest dog, whose growls diminished, though he did not move from his guard pose.

"Why are you here?" Evred asked in his accented Idayagan. "What is it you think I have done?"

The man's pupils shrank, revealing a change in emotion, though Evred could not descry what. He did not answer.

Evred swung to his feet and said, "Let him go."

"To try again?" Sindan asked, low-voiced.

Evred waved tiredly. "If not he, then another will come."
He glanced at those trembling hands, so soft on the palms—
no training here. Just desperation. Why? "Let him go."

Sindan snapped his fingers and the dogs sat, though their
ears remained flat against their narrow skulls and both sets
of pale gold eyes watched, unwavering, as the assassin
climbed to his feet, warily turning.

Evred waved a hand toward the door. The man licked
his lips, took a step—another—another—and then came
the swift hiss of running footsteps down the stairs.

Sindan bent to pick up the carving knife. "If you are
going to continue letting them go, you must agree to keep
the dogs with you. I would not have sent them, except that
the night Runner saw a cupboard door open at the back of
the summer larder that he remembered being locked, and
on examination, discovered another passage." He held up
the knife. "This is our own kitchenware. We search every
stranger who enters the gates now. But next time all our
precautions might not be enough."

Evred sighed. "The dogs may stay."

Sindan laid his palm to his heart and vanished through
the door.

Evred forced himself to sit, to pick up a report, and as
snow patted cat's-paws against the windows, he bent his
mind to the neat columns of winter supplies to the newest
outpost, plus the list of promotions to man it.

When his heart had resumed its accustomed measured
tread, he paused, glancing at the bare walls of glistening
white stone smooth as ice.

New Year's Week was soon, which meant Convocation
at home. Evred was glad he was not there, though he
longed to discuss with his father what he had learned about
ruling a new land. He also missed Hadand, but he did not
want to see his uncle or brother—or hear the gossip about
the fact that the heir to the throne was twenty-five yet
there was no mention of a royal wedding.

Evred looked out the window as the wind off the mountains brought the ghost of a sound, so subtle you could not
really hear it, you felt it.

It was a curious resonance, like what music was before

there was melody. Like wind instruments blown by someone who did not pause to breathe: a long, steady hum that
made your thoughts drift down the flow of time . . .

The wind died, and except for the snapping of the fire, silence closed over the room.

He sighed and returned to the letter he'd received that
morning from the Lindeth Runner.

> *To Prince Evred of Iasca Leror, from the Pim fam-*
> *ily. We are returning the recompense you made us for*
> *the loss of three ships and cargo. The sum has been re-*
> *stored by Lord Indevan Algara-Vayir, as is right. By the*
> *hand of Ryala Pim.*

She could have kept it, Evred thought. Her returning it
was honest, but it might not be indicative of good will. He
considered summoning her to find out how she had received the money. Surely Inda was not there in Lindeth,
merely half a morning's ride away?

The idea made him half start out of his chair, even as his
inner voice insisted *impossible, impossible.*

"Evred-Varlaef."

He looked up, relieved by the sight of Nightingale
Toraca's jowly hound-face. Evred had a personal Runner
now, thanks to his academy friend Noddy Toraca. Noddy's
younger brother Branid Toraca—nicknamed Nightingale
when it was discovered that the gap between his front teeth
enabled him to whistle with amazing fluidity—had cried
himself to sleep at age twelve after hearing the story of Dogpiss Noth. He'd wanted nothing more than to train to be a
Runner for Noddy or one of his circle of friends since then.

"Vedrid's here." Nightingale gestured over his shoulder.
"Stashed him in my own room, on account of what you'd
said."

"Anyone else see him?"

Nightingale shook his head. "He stopped in the city at a
tavern and hired a boy to bring up a message to the royal
Runner, and that being me, I went for him, like you told me
to last winter. Everything spoken, nothing on paper."

Had it been a year since Noddy had sent his brother?

Nightingale had appeared with a typical Noddy message—
*If you need another runner, I recommend Nightingale. He
whistles, doesn't sing*—but Evred had since mentally
thanked his old friend over and over. Didn't sing indeed.
Evred's other Runners—he had a staff of ten now—were
competent men, provided by either the king or the
Harskialdna. They would do their duty, but it was to
Nightingale he had slowly begun to tell things that before
he only dared keep in his head. It was Nightingale who
covered for him when he ventured out in anonymous Runner blue to listen, inspect—or visit a pleasure house.

"Bring him up," he said. "Listen. I forgot about New
Year's, but it's on us in two weeks. If you want to go for
home leave, you may. You've been here an entire year."

"Captain Sindan said that royal Runners ought not to
ask for home leave in wartime." Nightingale shrugged, that
same turtle-on-a-fencepost shrug that characterized
Noddy—shoulders up under his ears, arms dangling. "Because you don't get it, either. Anyway, my brother'll be on
duty at the royal city, our sister married away, Dad's in the
south with the Sierlaef, and Mama is staying with my sister,
so there's no one home to visit."

The sudden clash of steel stilled them both for a heartbeat. The sound was cadenced, followed by a shout and then
two more clashes: time for drill. The day watch had begun.

Nightingale left, and Evred frowned down at his letter.
Maybe he should invent a reason to go to Lindeth. It
wasn't very far, but then distance wasn't the problem, it
was the endless political repercussions of his moving
about, necessarily with a suitably large force if he rode as
himself and not anonymously. The assassination attempts
made his danger clear enough.

Captain Sindan's most trusted Runners had reported
that Mardric, the Olaran Resistance leader, had gone to
ground, reappearing in Lindeth to try to organize the disaffected Idayagans there. He might have been behind the
assassination attempts, or there could be any number of
angry Idayagans, determined to strike a blow against the
Evil Enemy.

Evred, on his anonymous rides, had begun hearing some

of the rumors about the evil Marlovans and what they were supposed to have done.

The door opened then closed behind Vedrid, who was almost unrecognizable. He had cut his hair and wore a shapeless tunic belted with weave and a cloak. Idayagan clothing.

"Welcome back," Evred said, his heartbeat speeding up. "Sit down. Do you require something to eat or drink?"

Vedrid shook his head. "I ate."

"Is it difficult to get through the passes?"

"Not this time. I hired out at Bren Harbor as a courier, and there was so much business I had my pick of what to bring here. But it will be, if the Adranis turn against us. The old king died and the new one wants to end the treaties, using the blockade as an excuse."

Evred leaned forward. "Did you find Indevan-Laef?"

"No. That is, I never saw him. But he's not dead. In fact his name has been removed from the capital list. At Guild Fleet headquarters I found out that the original accusation had been rescinded." Vedrid pushed his short, pale hair impatiently back; he hated hair on his forehead and ears. "Rumor says he's a pirate preying on the Brotherhood of Blood under the name of Elgar the Fox."

"A pirate preying on pirates? To fight against them—or to gain influence over them?"

Vedrid spread his hands. "All I know is that pirates who join the Brotherhood to attack and loot us have been given letters of marque by the Venn. They are permitted to resupply in the harbors on the north side of the strait as long as they keep their attacks confined to our coast."

"What proof is there that Indevan-Laef is Elgar the Fox?"

"None outside of Ryala Pim's accusations. But there were rumors of him being a lord, about his liking to use screamer arrows instead of flags for signals. In one place I learned that Elgar's first name is Inda."

Evred felt a cramp in his hand; he was gripping the pen hard. He dropped it on the table and sat back. "Where was he seen most recently?"

"Sartor Sea, hunting the Brotherhood there."

"Sartor Sea." *Then he's coming home.*

A bugle chord echoed off the walls. *Clash! Clang!* Evred paced to the window and glanced out at the sword drill below. Snow whirled into a manic dance; Evred saw Tanrid's face as he died, lips distorted in his effort to speak, how he relaxed only after Evred promised to find Inda. "Indevan-Laef must be given word about the death of his brother. He does not know that he is the heir to Choraed Elgaer."

"You want me to find him and tell him?"

"No, I want you to find him and bring him to me. It is I who must present him to the king. Who can present him to his father with the old problems declared resolved." He frowned. "That reminds me. You are now my sworn man, so my brother can no longer require silence."

Vedrid flicked fingers to heart, his puzzlement plain.

Evred said, "When you took Idayago did my brother ride off on a murder spree? Against girls?"

Vedrid's jaw dropped. In his honest and unhidden bewilderment Evred had his answer, but he listened as Vedrid said, "No! I was with him the entire time—even when we split off before the Ghael Hills battle. Oh." His face changed. "The first ruse."

Evred frowned. "What was that?"

Vedrid said, surprised, "You didn't know? I thought everyone in the royal castle knew—oh. You were still an academy boy, were you not? Perhaps they kept it all from you."

"Tell me now."

"Isn't much to tell, and that little is shameful enough. On the road—this was just before the attack—the Sierlaef and his Sier-Danas were met by young women who invited them back, promised wine and fun." Vedrid made the crude gesture for a romp in bed. "I wasn't there to see or hear it all, you understand—I had tent duty that day—but Tanrid-Laef Algara-Vayir suspected a ruse, so they all sent a man in their place. Wearing House livery."

Evred whistled under his breath. "No wonder we never heard about it."

"I couldn't go, but Nallan and my cousin both wanted to

go. My cousin had night duty, so the Sierlaef sent him."
Vedrid grimaced. "The Sier-Danas hid in the garden. As
Tanrid-Laef had surmised, the assassins came, but by the
time the Sier-Danas had broken in they were heartbeats too
late: the women had drugged the wine, and all our people
were stabbed right there with their pants off. The Sier-Danas
killed everyone in the house. Fired the house in memoriam—
and then, well, we rode south into the Idayagan trap."

"That was all? No other women, ruses, whatever?"

"Not a one. After the battle we rode the rest of the way
inside three perimeters of guards, on orders of the
Harskialdna, who was afraid there'd be another try for the
Sierlaef. There were no more rides alone—ever."

Evred drummed his fingers on the table. "Sometimes I
go out anonymously, and twice I have overheard references to killing sprees across the kingdom, led by the Sierlaef, against unarmed women." He let out his breath as he
sat back. "So that's the truth—yet whom to tell? How to be
believed?"

Vedrid thought over the bitter invective he'd overheard
while traveling in his anonymous clothes. "The Idayagans
want to believe the worst of us," he stated.

"And so they will. I don't know what to do about that—
another thing to consult with my father about when I can
speak with him eye to eye." He shook his head, then said,
"You had better ride before the weather worsens. Nightingale will get you mounted and supply you with funds."

Vedrid struck his chest with his fist and left.

Evred looked at Pim's letter, then cast it into the fire as
the steady clash of steel echoed up the tower walls.

Vedrid felt better than he had for a year. Even telling that
sordid story made him feel better, because Evred listened,
did not threaten. Vedrid had thought his honor gone with
his hair and blue coat, but that was not true. Even anonymous he had honorable purpose because his orders were
honorable.

He felt so much better that he ran down the stairs, his

mind dashing ahead to plan his route, so involved in to-morrow and the succeeding days that he forgot wariness in the now. He leaped down three steps to the landing, turned, and there he was, face-to-face with Hawkeye Yvana-Vayir, whose footsteps he ought to have heard coming up from below.

Hawkeye's mind was also far away. He'd handed off morning drill to Flash Arveas so he could get an early start on his ride home. But first he had to take leave of young Evred, do it all proper.

So when he nearly ran headlong into a tall, blond fellow he frowned in impatience. Short pale hair, Idayagan dress: a civilian. He raised an arm to push the fellow aside, then paused, because he knew that face.

He *knew* that face! He stared into Vedrid's eyes, saw them widen in surprise and then narrow to wariness.

"Why did the Sierlaef make you cut your hair?" he asked.

Vedrid licked his lips, shifted, his gaze lowered—and out came a lie. "So the Idayagans won't recognize me."

Hawkeye, not known for sensitivity, could feel the Runner lying.

Hawkeye suppressed the urge to slam Vedrid against the wall and demand the truth. He'd always liked Vedrid. If he had been Nallan, who'd been nosing around half the summer, watching, listening, smirking at everyone in that bootlicking way the Sier-Danas had all loathed for years, he would have done it. But Nallan—who'd been spying, and everyone knew he was spying, he'd asked so many nosy questions—had never once dressed civ. Always wore Runner blue with the crown over the heart. And here was Vedrid dressed not just civ, but foreign.

Hawkeye gauged the situation, his need to ride, and what he could do. Then he remembered the windowless chamber off the barracks, laughed, and clapped Vedrid on the back.

"Come," he said, knowing that his rank, and Vedrid's habit of obedience, would force the Runner at least that far. "I have not seen you for a long time, nor any of the Sier-Danas save Tlen, who came up during the summer as reinforcement, but you know that. I want the news of everyone else, and you can take our news south when you ride."

His personal armsmen waited at the bottom of the stairs, ready to ride. Both looked at Hawkeye and Vedrid in mute surprise. All he had to do was flick his eyelids up and tilt his head, and they fell in behind. Good fellows, friends since he was a scrub and his father felt he (as the son of a princess) required them for his prestige. They understood one another with a minimum of words.

The four moved down and down, past the weird white stuff (no joins in the stone? Unnatural!) and into the much newer granite barracks.

"Here. Sit," he said, riding hard over Vedrid's polite attempts to extricate himself. "Let me get you some hot drink. I could do with some myself. It's cold as damnation outside."

A nod to the armsmen to keep him there; the moment he was outside the door shut, followed by the thump of shoulders against it. He was chuckling under his breath when he moved to the nook where a magic-made fire, probably a century or more old, burned low and steady under a grating on which the captains kept hot dishes and drinks on the simmer.

He poured out two cups of the mulled wine, then hurried to the cupboard where the interrogators kept the clay pot with the ground-up white kinthus. Hawkeye had thought it strange at first that Evred-Varlaef would insist questioning be done with costly herbs when beating the lies out of these stinking Idayagan sneaks had seemed a far better reminder of who gripped the reins. But Evred had been insistent—and they did get the complete truth. What's more, the locals knew it. The number of false accusations had diminished this past year.

He brought the clay pot to the nook, where he found Jasid Tlen—wet-haired, tired, scruffy from night patrol—ladling some of the lemon soup into a cup. Since it was Tlen, one of the old Sier-Danas, he didn't retreat, but spooned a couple of generous plops of the white kinthus into one of the cups.

Tlen's pale gray eyes took in the claypot and then widened. "What are you doing?"

"Some truth gathering." In a few low-voiced words, Hawkeye told Tlen what had happened.

They both looked around. The hallway was empty, the barracks silent.

Tlen shook his head. "He'll know what you did when it wears off, and what d'you think the Sierlaef's going to say?"

"He's dressed like that, and lying to me. It means there's another damn plot on," Hawkeye stated.

They both glanced upstairs, each considering.

Tlen shook his head. "Not Evred. Not a plotter."

"True. So why did Vedrid lie to me? I'm sure he was lying." Hawkeye stepped closer, so close he could smell the wet wool of Tlen's coat, the mingled scent of horse and human sweat. "I don't know books, and I don't know politics, but I do know men. He was lying."

Tlen frowned in apprehension.

Hawkeye grabbed his arm. "Listen. If the Sierlaef does have a plot going, well, we'd better know about it. Because his not telling us means it stinks like shit in shoes."

Put that way it made perfect sense to Tlen. "Carry on. I'll ride shield." A last spurt of regret. "May 's well not have everyone in the castle walking in on us committing a capital crime."

Interfering with a royal Runner could net you a nasty day at the posts getting your back flayed, but to counterbalance it there was their long experience with the Sierlaef. If he was hatching another plot, something worse than bending the rules so he could chase after someone else's wife-to-be without any invitation from the female in question, they'd better get prepared. An order from him might come, forcing them to obey whether they liked it or not; something or other had happened that way to Buck, though as yet none of the Marlo-Vayirs were talking.

In fact, Buck's not talking was in itself a kind of warning.

Hawkeye carried the cups in, set the drugged one down before Vedrid. There was no choice for him but to drink it.

The kinthus was so strong it made him gasp when he took his first sip. But he blamed himself for not being alert when he nearly ran into the arms of one of the old Sier-Danas. If the knife was to come now, so be it.

Blissful peace dampened his worries and regrets; his mind separated from his body, floating somewhere out of sight. No worries. No problems. No future, just the endless, glittering string of memories stretching out behind him, as remote as stones.

"Why are you dressed civ and with your hair cut?"

"I had to disguise myself."

"Why?"

"So I would not be recognized—"

People under kinthus would tell you everything they knew, but only if you asked the right questions. Hawkeye frowned as Vedrid rambled dreamily about how he'd gone about putting together his disguise, then said, "Tell me everything the Sierlaef ordered you to do—" He ignored the uneasy shiftings of the armsmen. "Especially if it has to do with this here disguise."

That worked. Out came the entire story.

When he got to his assassination of the last two brigands, Hawkeye stopped Vedrid midsentence and brought Tlen in. The heirs and armsmen listened in stunned silence as the faraway voice went on to the Marlo-Vayirs' ruse, meeting Evred-Varlaef after the fight, his words about no proof, his command about Indevan Algara-Vayir.

Inda. Hawkeye felt old guilt stirring because his was the hand that struck down that scrub Dogpiss Noth. He'd meant it to be just a swat to a scrub breaking bounds when he was stuck on guard. But he'd been drinking (liquor supplied by the Sierlaef) and hit too hard; Dogpiss had slipped, and then, well.

Obviously Evred-Varlaef remembered it, too. They'd called it "the summer with no banner," because nobody really understood the scandal that somehow started with Dogpiss' death. Unlike everybody else, Evred seemed to be doing something about it, even if it was six years late. But he was no longer a boy under his brother's thumb, he was a commander in his own right, next in line to become Harskialdna.

Hawkeye only listened to half of Vedrid's subsequent report. The stuff about pirates and Inda was interesting, and later on he'd be impressed that Evred-Varlaef was trying to right an old wrong—this was the sort of behavior he was coming to expect from him—but more important was the implication that Tanrid's death had been caused not by the enemy, but by *the heir to the throne*. And the Sierlaef'd gotten away with it.

Vedrid smiled with wistful regret when he finished, the dreams closing in. His eyes rolled and his head drooped, and then he slid to the floor, his breathing slow. If he had not been young and strong—and deeply motivated by his newfound sense of honor—his mind would have slipped away on that dark tide, leaving the physical realm altogether.

"I think the dose was too strong," Tlen said, scratching his jaw. "Just smelling it is putting me half to sleep."

"Well, then, you take him, stash him somewhere where he won't be seen, let 'm sleep it off, then send 'm on his way."

"What do I tell him?" Tlen rubbed his eyes and yawned.

Neither was used to plotting. Action, now, that was clear. Fighting an enemy you knew was an enemy—that made sense. When the enemy turns out to be wearing your coat, speaking your language—

Hawkeye grimaced. "Tell him it was a loyalty test, and he's a loyal man, right enough, and to carry on with Evred-Varlaef's orders, fast. Give him money. He's not going to blab about what we did, not after all that he told us."

Tlen opened a hand, his manner uneasy.

"I've got to get riding for home," Hawkeye said. "Don't know what the weather will do, and I want one week of freedom before my own wedding." What he was really thinking was, *Wait until my father hears.*

Chapter Nineteen

THE First Day of New Year's Week dawned bitterly cold. The sun arced far in the north, a ball of pale yellow casting long shadows before vanishing altogether behind the ice-topped mountains of the Andahi Pass high above Ala Larkadhe.

Evred-Varlaef rose from the narrow camp bed he'd set in the highest tower room. And while the two scout dogs who'd slept curled up on either side of him stretched, muzzles pointing toward the ceiling, he glanced out the window at the snow-covered city below, then reached for his clothes.

Inda stands on the deck of his flagship, riding huge green-gray waves under the lowering storm clouds that always seem to be just forming at the mouth of the Sartoran Sea.

Fox leans on the rail next to him, glass steadied in both gloved hands, smiling as he counts out the masts nicking the bleak skyline. "We'll strike them in the flank," Inda says.

Fox smiles wider as he lowers the glass, the wind whipping the long silky fringes of his fighting scarf against his shoulder. "Yes. But we have not taken them by surprise. Look. Fighting sail on every one, and all of 'em in offensive wedge. They just need to tack south-southwest."

The wind is against the pirates, but Inda and Fox know it is a fool who trusts the wind. And the pirates know it, too.

As Evred approached the long curving staircase leading down, he listened. There! Underneath the wind keening around the stone towers, that eerie sound again. It was clearest from the towers; from below, it was hard to make out.

The storm winds skimmed over the icy peaks to rake the little city below, shrieking around the lower buildings, worrying at cracks, drumming at windows, making the sound. Evred paused on the tower stairs, listening for that eerie hum, deep and steady below the wail of the wind. He lost his sense of time in that still tower; as most were gone on liberty or watch, a solitary day stretched ahead.

Inda drops down into the Vixen, *mind racing as he watches his forces closing with the pirates.*

All in line—steady on—watch for the signal—

I can set the plan—I can drill and drill and drill, but . . .

Make it real, Fox. Make it real, Dasta—

Glass. Here they come—tight lines? Breaks there . . . and there . . .

"Fox?"

"I see it!"

"Put Death *right through the middle—"*

Evred descended the last steps and shouldered open the iron-reinforced door as the dogs raced past him into the small court. Evred followed, tightening his sash as the wind pounced, needling whatever flesh it could find. The scout dogs sniffed, lifted their legs, let out steaming streams.

Dogpiss. A sudden reminder still hurt.

When the dogs had finished, Evred picked up the waiting wand from its stone shelf, waved it over the yellow stain and the droppings without pausing as he usually did to witness the flicker of magic. He dropped the wand onto the shelf, then hurried with the dogs to the opposite door. They trod through the silent gray stone halls to the mess hall, which was mostly empty; the dogs, well-trained, scampered to the alcove adjacent the kitchen where their food was kept.

Evred glanced skyward. The bells for Convocation were probably ringing right now, bringing the Jarls to the throne room for their yearly oaths.

How many are whispering to one another about my brother's postponed wedding? No, they will only talk behind closed doors.

Where was Aldren-Sierlaef now? Probably still in the south. How long since he'd been home? A year? More? Twenty-five years old, the year heirs were expected to be married, and no word of a royal marriage.

As Evred ate breakfast alone, he considered the reasons his brother must have sent to their father. He had the excuse of war, of defense of the western coast. And the coast still held, though there had been terrible attacks, burnings, looting, according to Sindan's Runners. Sindan had said recently that the pirates had been seen sailing south in a mass.

Evred put his dishes in the bucket and walked out, footsteps loud in the now empty hall. He wondered if it would be better not to listen to the reports.

Inda signals to Jeje. "I'll command from Vixen.*"*
Fast Vixen *under Jeje's steady, sober hands.*
"Use the sloops to transfer reinforcements."
"Bring them up now?"
"Yes, one to a ship—where is my glass?"

*   *   *

Evred looked down, resting his fingertips on the bony head of the scout dog who paced steadily next to him, claws clicking a counter-rhythm to the ring of Evred's heels.

A canopy of arrows like pen scratches against the sky—Jeje's pale grimace—

Jeje takes an arrow in the forearm—Inda yells for bandages. One of her crew dashes up, pulls the arrow out, and binds the arm with his scarf—Jeje insists she stay at the tiller—Inda divides his attention between the bandaging and the scout rounding Death *to bear down on the nearest pirate—*

"Go, Inda! Go! I can steer!"

At midday Evred brought a stack of reports to the mess hall and finished reading them.

When he laid aside the last he tidied the pile, then let his hands drop. Now what? The rest of the day lay heavy as the snow, ahead of him.

All right, then. Time for an inspection.

He buttoned his coat tight, pulled on a knit cap, and walked around the quiet castle, the patient dogs shadowing him, pausing only for sniffing.

Evred listened, observed the changing of the watch. Sentries walked steadily, dark silhouettes against the pewter sky. Stable orderly. Horses dozing in the loose boxes.

He climbed slowly up the ice-white tower stairs.

Smoke drifts off pirate and privateer ships alike; blood washing down from scuppers, a startling red stream, mixed with icy rain from the sudden sleet squall, the noise of weapons, shouts, screams, the creak-and-smash of a lightning-struck mast falling, sending up a column of white water . . .

* * *

Evred paused at a narrow window, watching the drill down below. Clash, stamp, shout—breath clouding—the sounds echoed up the frozen stone walls.

Everything as it should be. He considered that "should be." Ala Larkadhe—poised between Iasca Leror, Olara, and Idayago—now his city.

His? There had been four assassination attempts so far. The castle was riddled with old tunnels and passages. No one had the time to search them all out. So the scout dogs roamed freely, sniffing doors, ears cocked.

Evred smiled down at the one pacing beside him now. He liked their company, though it made extra work for his staff, having to wand halls and corners.

He hoped Hawkeye had made it safely home, then thought of Jasid Tlen, who also wouldn't be either home or at Convocation: he and Senelayec were probably holed up somewhere along the north coast, if the storm had hit on that side of the mountains, until they could finish their patrol to Ghael and back again.

Evred thought about that ride along the northern coast. The way people stopped in the fields and stared, their faces stony. The towns quiet when they entered, the inns closed. Now he knew why—not that that fixed anything.

As he paced downward, he thought, *I can send proclamations of the truth to be read in every city, I can demand witnesses to every supposed murder outside of that one near the Ghael Hills—but will any of it kill the rumors?*

The answer was: not likely. People believed the rumors because they wanted to believe them.

Only in the harbors did they find a semblance of welcome, partly because they helped defend them, but also because harbor people seemed to pay scarce heed to politics, governments, and rumors from the other side of Idayago. Their lives were bound up in tides and ships.

Evred reached the landing. Next would be the ancient archive room, its great, carved double doors closed and locked with some kind of magic that made your fingers ache, like ice held too long, if you touched them.

Inda scans. Jeje aft on the Vixen, *purple wool hat turning this way and that as she leans into the tiller, watching always for signals from Dasta and Fox commanding* Cocodu *and* Death—

Smoke-enveloped ships. Clashes of steel and cries carrying over the icy water . . .

Whistler! Where?

"Inda, that was Tau—from that big trysail—hai! You think that's their flagship?"

Evred rounded the corner—and the archive doors stood open.

He stopped, then took a step backward, wondering if he was seeing another magical defense, something more lethal. All that he'd been able to find out was that the palace, mostly empty since his grandfather brought this area into Iasca Leror fifty years ago, had this unimaginably ancient archive behind carved doors that was not tended by the previous family, but by the morvende.

Morvende! Yet another rumor, a different kind? Stories about the mysterious cave dwellers filled most histories, but Hadand, who had read more ancient history than he, had told him that the most recent records insisted the morvende lived either on Drael or under the mountains near Sartor. None on Halia, and they never interacted with "sunsider" humans.

He took a tentative step, one hand out. The dog sniffed at the threshold, wagged its tail slightly. The animal did not seem to sense danger, but perhaps a dog wouldn't be alert to magical threat.

"Enter."

The voice was soft, low, the word spoken in heavily accented Iascan.

                        *   *   *

*Tau rides the bowsprit of the biggest enemy pirate ship, his
long legs astride the spar, arms loosing another whirtler in
perfect form despite a windstorm of arrows flying all
around him, some of them leaving comet tails of white
smoke . . .*

Evred walked in, his footsteps unnaturally loud on the glistening white flooring. The round room smelled of dust and
ancient paper with a fresh, astringent overlay of steeped
summer herbs. Expected were the shelves and shelves of
very old hand-bound books and ribbon-tied scrolls. Unexpected was the short figure in white, with white hair, who
stood by the fireplace, reaching for a steaming pan.

*Jeje hauls on the tiller, the Fisher brothers haul the sail
around, and the* Vixen *slants in a tight circle. The sail is loosened and the scout slows as it crosses beneath the pirate
bowsprit.*
   *Tau cups his hands around his mouth against the scream
of the wind and the shouting and clanging of steel. He yells
down to Inda, "This is the flagship. They all expect you to
take on the captain. They won't surrender until you fight
him—it's the pirate way."*

A glance out of pale eyes, so pale the color was indetermi-
nate. Evred's astonished gaze moved from detail to detail
as the person—female, he realized, seeing the slight swell
of breasts, the outward curve of hips under the white
robe—poured the steaming water into a bowl made of
deep blue glass. The hands were hands, not twigs, though
the talons were really talons, long, curved, sharp—like dog

or cat claws growing on thin human fingers. He glanced down to see if she had taloned toenails but the robe hid her feet.

The face was a human face. Her thin skin was pale as milk with a faint blue tracery of veins below the smooth surface, her hair fine as cobwebs, so white it was almost blue. Her age was impossible to guess; there were no lines or wrinkles, but then people who lived for untold generations away from wind and sun would not show age as others did.

A stronger scent of pungent herbs pervaded the round chamber.

"So long shut up, this place always makes me sneeze," the morvende said in a singsong-accented Sartoran. "Unless I sweeten the air." She muttered a word, made a gesture, and the doors closed behind Evred. He perceived a faint scintillation on the edge of his vision as a clean breeze ruffled through the room.

"Who are you?" he asked.

"I am she who tends the archives here. It is my charge to examine the records and to recopy any that age has made brittle. It is I who placed protective magic on the doors. You have tried to enter."

He didn't ask how she knew. "Yes."

"Why?"

"When I have time to myself I like to read."

She pressed her hands together. "I know who you are," she said. "You are the grandson of the conqueror who rode through killing those who had lived here for many years. And he descended from those who took this land you call Iasca Leror from the people who lived there."

Evred said nothing.

Her eyes lifted, narrowing in humor for a moment. "No protest? No defense?"

He opened his hands. "It's the truth."

"Yet you yourself have governed with a light hand. You did not even put to death those sent during the leaf-falling season to enter the chambers above to kill you."

"They didn't succeed. The dogs sniffed 'em out, and my guards gave them enough to think about, I believe. As for the ones after—" He opened his hand, making a shooing motion.

"You are flippant."

"Then I will be serious. I've seen enough death. I don't want to see it again unless I cannot avoid it. I know they hate me and my people. I can only try to govern fairly."

She said, "So it seems. Your actions indicate a character made for peaceful pursuit, but you live among warlike people, and war forms your life's task." She paused, and observed with that hint of humor again, "You say naught?"

"I dislike being watched when I cannot see the watchers."

A very slight shrug. "So it must be when you come among others unasked, with steel in your hands. But we will do you no harm. You are even protected when you are in this chamber, and shall be so long as you continue to use your strength to establish peace. I am here to grant you access to this archive, so you can learn what you will of the past."

Intense pleasure flooded Evred. He stepped closer, noticing that her robe was not in fact featureless white cotton, but woven of polished threads in a subtle, complicated pattern that suggested the twining of vines. "What is where?"

"Look about you. The scrolls are the oldest records, for we keep the copies in the same forms as the original document. Do you read the Old Sartoran?"

"With difficulty."

"You will find no translations here. It is the purpose of this archive to maintain what we find exactly as we found it. And to protect it," she added.

"Fair enough," Evred said, looking at the shelf of scrolls. He thought of Hadand's mother, Fareas-Iofre, who Hadand said stinted her own personal stipend, wearing old, much-mended clothes and making do with furnishings that others would hand to servants, so that she could order such records from Sartor, at ruinous expense. "May I copy anything?"

She indicated a desk across the chamber. "There you will find ink, pens, and paper. Our second purpose is to preserve knowledge, and share when we can. And so we recopy the aging scrolls, exactly as the original was written. And make copies of those as needed."

He laid his hand flat to his heart. "I thank you."

She put her hands together and then opened them, palms up, in the ancient gesture of peace. "I come and go during winter's storms. But you will find that the doors are not locked against you. When you are here, I must request that you keep the doors closed behind you."

"What if they need me?"

"You can hear a summons." He knew she would not approve of any reason he might be summoned. "Have you any further questions?"

"Yes, though this one I do not know if you can answer." He hesitated. "That sound. Do you hear it? Under the wind—"

"Ah." Her eyes widened; they were a pale brown, closer to amber. "You hear the wind harps."

"Wind harps? What could that be?"

She looked up, frowning at the shelves as if for guidance, then trod with soundless step to the oldest scrolls. "Do you know about the disirad?"

"Dih-sih-rahd," he repeated. The front-of-the-teeth consonants and singsong vowels, the liquid "r," were Old Sartoran.

She touched the glistening wall, so like ice mixed with silver. "This is disirad, but with all the magical virtue leached out. Some say that these few remains are all that is left of what was once abundant, before the end of Old Sartor. We do not know. But the wind harps on the mountain above this city were an experiment by my people, oh, a thousand years ago. Maybe more, for we do not reckon time exactly as you do, but it was an experiment to imitate the . . . the sound in the spirit, you might say, of the disirad of old."

"It . . . it sang? It is stone, then, and it sang?"

"It was like stone and yet like metal, and it resonated with all living things in the world. Humans used it to good purpose, and then to evil, finding magic to destroy it. That was before Old Sartor died. Since then, these harps were carved. The experiment was deemed a failure, and so the wind harps stand abandoned on the high escarpments to sing their own song until time and wind and weather re-shape them back to silent stone again." She touched old scrolls. "Read more about them here. I shall depart and leave you to it."

He held up a hand, palm up in habitual gesture, not knowing his ancestors had used it to show a hand empty of weapons.

She waited.

"Will you tell me more about you—and the morvende of today? Like where you live, what your lives are like?"

"Perhaps one day," she said, and murmured something under her breath as she made a quick sign.

She vanished, light winking for a moment where she had stood, a soft gust ruffling the air.

Inda shakes the sweat from his eyes, ignoring the struggling figures behind him, at his sides, ignoring the watchers on the captain's deck where he now faces their commander after fighting his way step by bloody step along the entire length of the pirate ship.

Surprise. The arc, the snap of coincidence—this commander who resembles Master Brath of the academy—same shape of head, same square, muscular body, though ten or fifteen years older, and wearing scarlet silk, his hair short and not in a horsetail. Diamonds glinting coldly in the golden hoops at each ear: Brotherhood commander.

The pirates and Inda's own crew alike step back to form a ring on the captain's bloody deck. Inda gives them a fast glance. He senses their anticipation—sees the bloodlust in their grins, their avid eyes, hears it in their shouts, kindling the same hot lust inside him as the man plants his feet wide on his blood-smeared deck, barbed wrist guards on each arm, a heavy straight sword gripped in both hands, white-knuckled, muscles bunching under his sodden silk.

And as the ship rolls and cold rain hisses all around them, turning the blood to pink streams, Inda flicks out his blades, snapping them up his forearms in readiness.

Evred stepped back in surprise, and then, unnerved, he looked around slowly, running his fingers along the shelves of old, carefully rolled scrolls. Selected one at random, and with careful fingers slid loose its ribbon. The heavy rice paper crackled as he unrolled it.

Inda meets the man's eyes. Now the battle has diminished to the two of them, and Inda's enemy is not a fleet of ships, but a gray-eyed man with sweat dripping down his face, assessing Inda the same way Inda assesses him.

The man grunts and swings.

He's good with a straight sword—but his heavy metal is slow, far too slow for the Odni Hawk-Stoop defense. Inda uses the very first block-and-strike he learned so long ago, and drilled in thousands of times since; he whirls inside of the arc of that swinging sword—the captain tries to alter the force of his lunge—the knife is faster.

The captain falls, the thin stream of dark blood from the gap in his throat shredded by the wind.

And as pirates and pirate-fighters alike shout the man lies there at Inda's feet, the gray eyes staring sightlessly at the sky. Like Dogpiss, just like Dogpiss—

Hawkeye Yvana-Vayir pulled on his wedding shirt, regarding with a grimace of distaste the yellow and blue sash lying on his bed.

"If it helps," said his favorite, a merry young potter named Fala, "I did all the stitch-work. It is strange how I can make the prettiest cups, yet I cannot seem to use a needle with any grace."

Hawkeye bent down, touching the somewhat crooked Yvana-Vayir eagle in blue woven between (very) stylized yellow flames, then grinned, pulled Fala to him, and

kissed her. She laughed and flung her arms around his
neck.

"Then I'll wear it with pride," he mumbled into Fala's
hair. He felt a prickle of guilt, then dismissed it. He
wouldn't let himself say anything against his wife once she
was his wife, but in the meantime, he knew that most people hated Dannor, who never made herself pleasant except
to superiors. She was even more arrogant than her brother
Stalgrid, whom he loyally tried never to call Horsebutt,
though he secretly thought the nickname an insult to
horses. At least Stalgrid was at Convocation, and thus far
away. The Tya-Vayir family representative was one-eyed
Cama. Everyone liked Cama. Especially the girls.

Hawkeye kissed Fala again, thinking: *I wish I could
marry you*, but said nothing. It would only grieve them
both. After tonight he would be honor-bound to go to
Dannor's bed first, if she wanted him there. He suspected
she would just out of spite—at least until she found a new
favorite who would put up with her demands.

"Hurry, now," Fala said, nuzzling his shoulder and then
stepping back. "Your father awaits you and Badger in his
chamber. Beaver is down below with your cousin, helping
host."

Hawkeye whistled softly to himself. His journey, slowed
by three smashing storms in a row, had taken full two
weeks. Immediately on his arrival that morning he'd told
his father what he'd learned from Vedrid. His father hadn't
said much. He'd looked shocked, then angry, but Hawkeye
had been too tired and hungry to stay talking.

That his father wanted to talk now, with the hall full of
wedding guests, made his shoulder blades twitch the same
way they did just before an action, and he wondered if it
had been such a good idea to tell his father everything. But
that was duty. He had to do his duty by father and family.
Right?

He sighed on an exhaling breath, "I wish Mother hadn't
ridden out on that ice."

Fala had no idea why he said it, except in the larger context: she wouldn't say anything against anyone in the family, but she knew—everyone knew—that the princess had

been the only one who had any influence over Hawkeye's father.

He kissed Fala one last time, then they left, each in different directions. She back to join the servants in putting the last of the wedding boughs up in the great hall. He to his father's rooms, where he found one of his twin brothers—in spring they'd be seventeen and horsetails—waiting. "Whew," Badger said privately, rolling his eyes.

No time for more. Their father strode in, resplendent in a new formal tunic, the blue eagle and yellow flames all edged in gold. Too much gold, Hawkeye thought uneasily. Gold was reserved for royal houses. Even the Cassads wore their ancient gold as yellow, at least on their banners and House tunics.

"You have done well, my son," the Jarl said, embracing Hawkeye. "You truly are the son of a princess."

Hawkeye grimaced and Badger made a gag-face as their father paced the length of the chamber. All their lives they had been hearing how their quiet, austere mother was a daughter of a line of kings, until the repetition was mere noise. They were cousins to princes, not princes themselves. Hawkeye would one day be a Jarl, and Badger and Beaver his Randaels. They were happy enough with that.

Hawkeye decided his recent year of command—even more than his wedding—gave him the right to speak to his father man to man. "Father, you've always told us that. But the truth is we all believe that being half Yvana-Vayir is as good as being half Montrei-Vayir."

"Better," his father said, in a low, intense voice that caused Hawkeye to step back, this time not daring to turn his brother's way. "Better! You know, for you will be married under the banner down below, that twice in the last two centuries have we married into the royal family. Once with *them*." His chin gestured southward over his shoulder toward the royal city. "And once with the Montredavan-Ans, who were far greater. Only the betrayal of an assassin's knife in the night could bring them down. It was they who made this kingdom what it is. Never forget."

Well, the boys knew that, too, having sung the older war ballads that were little more than lists of heroic names chanted to stirring drumbeats about the Marlovans' triumph over the Iascans when they first came to this land. There was even one song—Hawkeye had discovered when he first went to the academy that no one else seemed to know it—that was all about hawks and foxes and white wolves, but seemed to hint that it was the Montredavan-Ans, and not the Montrei-Vayirs, who'd driven the Venn north the last time they came in force.

He frowned at the drift of his thoughts. Not enough sleep. He forced himself to listen. But what was their father getting at, going on and on about the family's greatness? His eyes were wild, his fingers shook, and he paced about like a caged dog when the wolves ran beyond the walls, howling at the moon.

"You boys are all old enough to hear what happened, long ago, before I married your mother," said the Jarl, thumping his fist to his chest.

It was a family given that what was told one twin would soon be known by the other. Badger grimaced behind his father's back, fanning himself with a hand; Hawkeye opened a hand: *What can we do?*

When the Jarl whirled again and faced them, the two stood side by side, their faces expressionless.

Their father said, "You have seen that the king honors my rank, but not my kinship claim through his sister. Denying you the chance to wed in the throne room is not an isolated insult, it is one in a lifetime of insults. And all of it the Harskialdna's doing."

The brothers resisted the strong impulse to share a grimace of disgust: this was very familiar territory their father was galloping heavily over.

The Jarl paced back and forth. "You did not know, for it was very nearly deemed a dishonor at the time, but when Queen Wisthia came from the Adranis to marry the king, your mother was to go to her brother as part of the treaty. The Adrani prince begged off with a lot of diplomatic flummery, bringing us near war. There were two things that stayed us. One, the trade dispensations—including taking the expense of sending the spell renewal mages—the Adrani king offered as compensation. Two, his heir had never

actually met your mother, so there could be no insult to
her. Their herald told us in a lot a fancy language that he
had marriage ambitions in faraway lands to the east, the
Adrani having no tradition for treaty betrothals. But that
left your mother with no husband, and so she turned her
eye to me."

What he did not tell his sons—not because he lied, but
because he'd come to believe his own romantic vision over
the years—was that she'd been sixteen, and he eighteen.

The truth was this: during his academy days Mad Gallop
Yvana-Vayir had been handsome, reckless, riding with a
style that outshone both royal brothers, bringing him the
hatred of Anderle-Varlaef, the future Harskialdna. The
Princess Tdiran, with a sixteen-year-old's short-lived and
shallow passion, had fallen in lust with a handsome boy
riding so dashingly in the summer games. And he fell in
love with her royal name. His father had died in one of the
northern battles with the old king, so no one could stop
him from arranging for his own betrothed (who'd hated
him more with every passing year as they grew up together) to marry a Khani-Vayir cousin who had not been
assigned a future wife, being intended for service in the
dragoons.

What his sons heard was this: "I loved your mother from
the first moment I saw her in the stands during the summer
games. And she loved me. After I had gained some experience in the north, I returned and found that my own betrothed wanted to marry elsewhere. So I courted Tdiran.
Tlennen was newly king, and he told her the choice was
hers. His brother resisted. Said such a marriage would disturb the balance of power in the kingdom. Tdiran chose
me, but the king's brother—the *Royal Shield Arm*—forced
me to vow I would never captain an army."

The boys were uneasy at the venom in their father's voice
when he spoke the Harskialdna's title in Iascan. Iascan was
the everyday language of peacetime. Marlovan was the
language of war and honor and should be used then.

"So I promised. Only for the good of the kingdom," the
Jarl stated. His eyes narrowed to slits of anger. "And I kept
my word, but I always understood that vow to hold only

while the kingdom was governed well. The good of the kingdom, boys, requires peace within, and war with the enemy. As soon as someone in power reverses that, well, one must review one's vows."

Hawkeye's back twitched again. "What d'you mean, Father?"

"I want you to listen when Evred-Varlaef speaks. Badger! When you and Beaver return to the academy, you listen as well. If there is any talk that the Harskialdna has committed treachery against any Jarl or his people, I need to know."

Hawkeye stared at his father. "Does that mean you'll go to the king? Settle it that way?"

"Yes." The Jarl smiled wide. Wider. Then shook with silent laughter, and while his sons regarded him in puzzlement, he said, "I will go to the king."

Chapter Twenty

THE *Vixen* skimmed up the face of a cold green wave.
Jeje raised her glass to the foresail masthead on
Boruin's low, sharp-prowed trysail, which the crew had de-
bated renaming *Boruin's Death*, or *Majarian's Death*, or
Pirates' Death—a debate Fox summarily shortened to just
Death.

Inda stood on the masthead, one arm crooked around a
humming taut brace, glass to his eye as wind snapped his
clothing and did its best to free his curling hair from the
tight sailor queue thumping his back. She watched him because she rarely saw him smile like that, especially in this
cold winter wind, with the dangerous southern waters rising to mountainous, green-veined swells.

She frowned back at their fleet—colorful devices on pirate foresails, the Chwahir sails blank, and on theirs the
gold fox on black—trying to find the source of that smile.

But Inda was not looking at his fleet, he was enjoying the
exhilaration of riding so high in the wind as the ship cut
through the swells and ran westward, bringing him ever
closer to home. He hadn't felt that exhilaration since the
he was a ten-year-old in the academy, when they galloped
the two-year-olds horses across the open plains.

A storm was coming, as was inevitable at this time of
year. They sped before it, sending water streaming in high-
arching lacework down the sides. The wind slammed into

the taut sails from the starboard beam, sending them heeling dangerously in the growing swell, but fore-and-aft rigged ships with new, beautiful Chwahir sails loved this sort of wind.

He cut a glance down at the deck, pleased with the black knife-shape of the *Death* gliding with menacing elegance through the turbulent waters. Above, new sails the pale cream color of the excellent Chwahir flax described eye-appealing arcs against the gray sky above. Warmth bloomed behind his ribs at the beauty and speed of this ship—faster than the *Vixen* even, in the right wind.

But the cost was a very narrow hold, and that meant more frequent stops; even the other ships carrying extra cargo couldn't keep both themselves and the *Death* supplied for protracted periods at sea.

There in the north lay the jagged purple juts of the passage called the Narrows that wound its way through the Land Bridge, linking two great continents. On the other side, they all knew, the Brotherhood lay in wait. Maybe close, maybe far. But there.

Before then, they had to stop. They were going to risk Pirate Island, supposedly reclaimed from the Brotherhood three years ago by Ramis of the *Knife*. If it had not been retaken by Marshig and the Brotherhood fleet, Inda ought to find news there for the buying.

Inda slid down a backstay, judging the tremendous roll of the ship with habitual ease.

Barend was sailing-master, and though Inda had been learning the finer points of wringing speed out of capricious winds, Barend—trained on capital ships instead of an old trading tub that took great care of their sails—was far more skilled in judging wind, sea, and how much each vessel could bear.

The mood of the crew Inda could gauge, even if he couldn't always express what it was he saw. But he relied on Tau for that. Tau, or Jeje.

Jeje. He winced, his eyes straying to their last subject of disagreement—one of their very few. There was Nestra at the helm, her curly hair blowing, her winter jacket and heavy woolen trousers wind-pressed against her generous curves.

Inda jerked around again before their eyes could meet, and studied the others. The duty watch stared with fixed attention forward as if the exertion of will could pull them into harbor faster.

He'd better get their share of the loot counted out.

The storm had intensified into a gale by the time they sailed under reefed foresails and bare poles into the shelter of the harbor. Almost at once the wind diminished, fouled on the headland. Their vigilance increased, focused no longer on nature but on their fellow humans.

No pirate ships lay in wait, stripped to fighting sail, bow crews in the tops. They made it up the harbor and into the mouth of the river on the height of tidal flood. The storm pounded the other side of the island—here it was bitter and wet as they tied everything down, anchored, and drew lots to find out who got first liberty.

Inda was busy in the cabin, counting out fair shares from their last victory and tying them into the little bags that his new Sails and his mates had sewn together. The clink of coins, a stray current of air bringing the smell of baking biscuits from the galley, flung Inda back to summer in memory, and for a moment he was no longer sitting in the cabin aboard the *Death*, he was standing on the deck as they sailed into Freedom Harbor, the scent of baking biscuits mingled with brine. He breathed it in before saying to Tau, *Are we pirates? I don't feel like one—but there isn't a name for us. Because we're still killing like pirates.*

And Tau said back, his mockery very like Fox's, *I enjoyed killing Boruin. I guess that makes me a pirate. It certainly doesn't make me peace loving.*

We kill in fair fights. She liked killing unarmed civs.

Boruin was unarmed.

Inda retorted, restless—almost angry—*So we're pirates. If news has reached Freedom about Boruin, we'll get lots of volunteers. Will you sort them for me?*

And Tau's mocking voice, later the next day: *Here are two lists. All of them can fight, and they all claim to be inde-*

pendents or privateers. This list I think will follow your orders. This list I don't believe were ever privateers and will revert to pirates in the heat.

And despite the weeks of drill, Tau had been right. During the worst of the battle at the Sartoran Sea, most of his Second List hires reverted to pirate habit, fighting for him or herself, forgetting the drills, ignoring orders.

"It's the pirate way—"

Staring up like Dogpiss—

Inda dug the heels of his hands into his eyes, his elbows knocking into his half-counted piles of coins, which clinked to the table, unnoticed.

"Inda."

Inda pulled away his hands and flexed them, then rubbed his ear where the new hoop still itched.

Barend dropped down onto the other chair, elbows thumping to the table. The coins jingled faintly. "Memory?" Barend asked, the swinging lamp overhead shifting the sharp-edged shadows of his face from one side to the other and back again, the light glowing like blood in the ruby earring dangling below the edge of his crimson knit cap.

Inda had never discussed Dogpiss even with the Marlovans. What would be the point? Those days were long gone. And as for piracy—

"How close we came to losing at the Sartoran Sea," he said; now he understood Tau's mockery. It wasn't Inda he'd mocked, but himself. Tau had to be wrestling with the same question: if they deliberately sought pirates to kill and loot, were they pirates? Because killing was still killing, and taking loot was still taking loot.

Barend studied Inda, saw the familiar closed-in expression and thought back to the battle.

Which they near as damnation lost.

Discipline. Inda was right. You could have great plans, but they weren't any good if you didn't have the discipline to carry them out.

Like when the wind veered against Inda's fleet and the three Chwahir smoothly cut off the two biggest consorts from the pirate flagship with a firestorm of arrows arcing with comet tails of smoke through the squall so that the minor ships had to concentrate on putting out fires instead of supporting their allies. The Chwahir definitely had discipline, though rumor had it they had terrible punishments for small infractions, something Inda was absolutely against. Inda said if people can't follow orders, they get off the ship.

Fox didn't agree, but he didn't disagree. There were no punishment parades on Inda's ships, no floggings . . . but Fox had a way of thrashing people at drill, using only his hands, when he thought they warranted it. So no one gave Fox any trouble.

And nobody wanted to fight with Inda, even at drill: they'd all seen him in action. Fox was his inevitable partner.

Barend remembered Fox and his handpicked assault band leaping down into the launch, racing to the second consort, swarming up the sides straight into battle against superior numbers. And winning.

Barend looked up. "Here's what I know. Our own boys and girls have been a whole lot more serious about drill since then."

Inda opened a hand. With the other he rubbed his ear, remembering how Dasta and some of the others had insisted, before they even cleaned the deck of the captured flagship, that Sails pierce Inda's other ear, acknowledging, pirate fashion, that he was a commander who had beaten another commander.

Even though it had been some weeks since then—each day filled with drills and threatening weather—this ear seemed to itch and burn every time he thought about the Brotherhood. Fighting them *felt* right. They did nothing but loot and kill. But he was doing the same to them.

So the question is do they think what they do is right?

He stared out at the busy harbor without seeing it.

Did Ganan Marshig ever think about right and wrong?

Here's the truth, Inda thought grimly. The Brotherhood lay waiting in the north. For him. And despite all the worries of planning, logistics, questions, he felt that stirring of excitement at the prospect of battle.

"Speaking of boys and girls. Liberty crews waiting,"

Barend said, thumb jerking back. "Want some help finishing here?"

Inda flicked a hand up and they swiftly finished counting out the piles.

"All right," Inda said at last, leaning back. "Anyone who wants to be paid off send in here. Nestra will be last," he added, feeling his neck heat.

Barend gave a nod of unqualified approval. "I guess you know she wouldn't take a night watch if there was sleet," he said. "At least, not since—" Barend flapped his hand vaguely between Inda and the upper deck.

"Since we started hammock dancing," Inda said, the heat creeping up to his ears, which made the one itch even more.

He'd thought he was being so circumspect but everyone knew, and had known, and hadn't said anything, not even Mutt, whose watch she'd refused to serve on. Inda himself had overheard her—the very night after he and Jeje had argued about her—when he opened his scuttle to get some air, and Nestra was right above, stating in a very different voice than the one she used with him, *I don't have to go out in sleet now I've got Elgar by the prick. If you give me trouble, brat, I'll give you more.*

"She's so good with a bow." Barend sat back, arms crossed, grinning. "But she's loud."

"Jeje was the only one who said anything. If you all knew it, why didn't anyone besides Jeje speak up?"

Barend's smile faded. "Because maybe you wanted that. Maybe it was your deal. She warms your bunk, doesn't have to do her share of the work."

"She decided that herself. I didn't see it. At first. Jeje came in to confront me, asked why I was setting up a Coco. I thought she was exaggerating because they don't like each other. I should have known better," Inda admitted.

"So you never saw her as trouble?" Barend asked.

Inda shook his head. "Back in Freeport, first night after she hired on. She came down into the cabin, right here. Midnight. I was at the charts. She had a bottle of wine, and this silky shirt on. No vest. She drank out of the bottle, handed it to me, soon 's I took a pull she ripped off her shirt. Threw the bottle out the window there and then ripped off my shirt." He tipped his head. "Maybe that was the first sign of trouble, but I really thought she was, oh, interested. In *me*. Not in—" He lifted his hand in a circle, indicating the captain's cabin.

Barend whistled. "Now, you know I usually don't think much about sex, unless I'm in port. An indifference I seem to have inherited from my mother. Easy, that way. No problems. But if Nestra'd done that to me, well, Norsunder take the rule."

"She made the fun last all night," Inda said with real regret.

The cabin door opened on Barend's whistle and Fox strode in, his black silk fighting scarf tied around his head for warmth. Strange, how a ruby-set golden hoop at one ear made him look threatening. Even rat-faced Barend, with gold swinging at his ear, looked tough. Inda fingered his ear again and wondered if he alone looked stupid: though he'd scowled into a mirror, looking at the earring, his new shirt, even his scars not two days before, his mental image of himself was still the round-faced eleven-year-old boy who'd glanced every morning into the academy barracks mirror to see if his gray smock was straight before running out to callover.

Fox leaned against a bulkhead. "Problem?"

"No," Inda replied. "But send Nestra in last."

Barend rose. "This I don't want to hear."

"I do," Fox drawled. "Let me be the one to fetch her."

Inda had handed out the second to the last bag when Nestra stamped into the cabin, Fox right behind her, and started yelling. Nestra was a smuggler born and bred and to her it had seemed perfectly acceptable to expect benefits from sleeping with the captain.

Inda waited out her tirade, trying (with little success) not to watch her splendid bosom rising and falling under her silken shirt, and when she was done he said, "Everyone takes a watch."

She stared at him, then snorted. "On some ships it's a fair enough trade—you give your fun to a dull dog, and get some ease in return."

Inda figured at least his face couldn't get any redder. He opened a hand in apology. "Maybe you could have trained me to be a fun dog?"

"Eat shit and die," was her unequivocal response.

Fox offered her bag of coins, his manner a polished insolence much more effective than words. She grabbed it out of his languid fingers and swaggered topside, pausing in the middle of the deck to shrug into her jacket. When she saw Inda emerge from the cabin she yelled back over her shoulder, "Especially when he's the worst lover I've ever had."

Then she stamped to the rail, hips rolling, hoisted her waiting gear to her shoulder, and scrambled down the rope ladder to the liberty boat.

Of course everyone was smirking, or even worse, trying not to smirk as they studied the sea, the sky, the ropes with totally unconvincing attempts at disinterest. Would his face catch on fire? It sure as damnation felt like it!

"That's all right, Elgar," called Gillor, who had been a top-hand on Walic's ship—another forced into piracy. She swung down from the mainmast, where she'd made a last check on the rigging and sails, as she was mainmast captain. She thumped him on the shoulder. "I'm a better hammock dancer than she ever could be. You give me a try."

"How about after we take the Brotherhood," Inda mumbled. Barend was snickering loudly behind him, being no help, damn him. "Go on," he added awkwardly. "Enjoy your liberty."

Gillor stepped close, so close they stood eye to eye. She had black eyes, with long lashes, and a steady gaze. "You don't want any Coco," she breathed, and he felt her breath on his cheek, warm and slightly spicy smelling from mulled wine. "Only we on the old crew knows what that means. You don't want any Coco, and I don't want to be one. But I don't like being an only, see?"

Inda felt his mouth go dry. "Maybe we can talk about it after . . ." He waved a hand, the heat of embarrassment now prickling in his armpits, despite the bitter wind.

With a hearty laugh Gillor flipped back her ribbon-braided black hair and swung down into the first liberty boat, where she promptly got into an insult fight with Nestra. Inda was relieved when they all picked up their oars and the gig started away.

"Nestra will blab our strengths and weaknesses all over the island," Fox said. "Unless you want her stopped." His eyes looked hard as glass in the wintry light.

"No," Inda said. "It's not like the Brotherhood doesn't have spies all over who can count us as fast as she can talk anyway. There's no way our coming is a surprise. Still, I want you two to scour the harbor. Listen to every scrap of news while I set up supplies." He looked down at his hands, then shook his head. Rubies, cold in the winter wind, thunked against his jawbone on either side.

I'm a pirate fighting pirates.

"First thing I want to see to is getting barbs on my wrist guards."

Chapter Twenty-one

THE new harbormaster chuckled in welcome. "Well, here ye are at last." He lifted a gnarled finger and pointed at the ruby on Inda's nearest ear hoop. "Brotherhood ship kills, eh? Ha ha ha! I ain't seen anything so good since Ramis came in here and slammed Sharl the Brainsmasher and his ugly crew through the Black Gate into damnation. What a fight that was! And not a blink of regret, not after them made life so bad here these ten years."

Black Gate. There it was again, a reference to a hole ripping in the air and water and soil of the world, and people being thrust through it into somewhere dark and timeless, to vanish when the hole did. Unbelievable—yet there were too many witnesses to attest to it.

"There are some who sez they want to join you against the Brotherhood, if you'll have them," the harbormaster continued. "Me, I say, talk to Swift first. He's the best of 'em, and knows the rest. You'll find him like as not over at the Dancing Sun, t' other end o' the harbor on the hill. But that's for drinkin' and talkin'—for eating, all the captains prefer Svanith's, down Middle-street, hard against the hill."

Inda thanked him, paid the anchorage fee, and departed.

"They all know who we are," Thog whispered as they started down the rain-washed, flagstoned street lined with storage and supply houses, all low buildings designed to withstand wind.

"They'll be comin' to offer info about Marshig, you watch," promised Lorm the Cook, his watery eyes crinkled in anticipation.

"Then we can compare rumors," Inda said.

Thog huddled in her woolen coat. "We will not know if Brotherhood spies will be offering themselves as allies."

Inda said, "Tau can sort out the possible allies. He always catches something I miss." He turned. "Mutt, go tell Taumad to take up station at the Dancing Sun, will you? I'll meet with him tomorrow. Today is for ordering stores and looking at what's going on in the harbor. I have an idea."

Mutt took off at a run. Inda, Thog, and Lorm emerged from the warehouse street into a broad polygon that opened onto five streets—probably the only five streets on the island. They crossed the polygon and headed up Middle-street, which curved along the base of white chalk cliffs parallel to the shoreline. Thick-walled shops lined both sides, many shut up; in most living spaces above the shops shutters were open and windows ajar for air. Mellow golden light slanted down, stronger than the cold, weak glow of the sun above the northern mountains. Restday's songs and laughter sounded from behind windows and briefly opening doors.

Inda thought of his home, the drums and songs, the wine and bread. A door to an ale shop opened wide as they passed, light and the aromas of dark barley-brew and its drinkers enveloping them; somewhere inside a small boy sang a ballad in Sartoran.

Lorm, the former cook aboard Gaffer Walic's pirate flagship, had been struggling to stay sober since Walic's death. As the warm, spicy air bathed their faces he lifted his chin, his breath hissing in through his teeth. The light outlined his tense profile; beyond, Thog's head was bowed, her blue-black fall of hair curtaining her round, flat Chwahir face, her night-black gaze bent to the rain-slick flagstones below her feet. *I have a family, at least,* Inda thought. *One day I will see them. He will never see his. And neither will Thog.* He drew his jacket tighter against him, though the chill was not on his skin but inside it.

They worked their way down the street to begin the task

of victualing and resupplying, finding business done much like it was in Freeport Harbor: polite and straightforward, as you came to expect when dealing with violent people. Open curiosity, asking questions only after he indicated he was willing to answer them in exchange for news.

As in Freeport everyone seemed to be aware of their business. He heard many variations on words like: "And so you're Elgar the Fox? Wearin' rubies, I see, heh heh! I hope you've got a hundred more rubies waitin' for you on the other side o' the Narrows! Now, what they tell me is this . . ."

When at last they had finished, Lorm—who acted as fleet bosun as well as flagship cook—returned to the dock to supervise the transfer of goods aboard their ships. Inda and Thog walked on to Svanith's Inn at the end of the street; beyond were mere pathways. When they entered the common room went quiet and all eyes turned their way.

Thog ignored the stares. Inda felt the pressure of their interest, their expectation, as he sank down at the table that Jeje had been holding.

Once he felt the gazes withdraw again, and voices rose, resuming conversations, he said, "Any news?"

Jeje made a sour face. "I had Uslar follow Nestra. She went up into the hill behind us to a bow maker, where she started blathering about us."

"Go on." Inda fingered his earring. How did Brotherhood captains manage with itchy ears in a fight? "These're a stupid idea," he muttered. "Wish I'd stayed with one. Better, none."

"Wrong." Jeje pushed her palms toward him. "Tau thinks it was a great idea. They make us look tough. We have to swagger, see? Brotherhood struts and dresses like kings in whatever fashion they like, and people are so scared of 'em they're half defeated before the Brotherhood even draws a knife. Now we have to do the same. It's war up here." She tapped her forehead, and Thog nodded with small, defined movements, her little chin jabbing the air. "As for Uslar, he reported the bow maker just laughed at her. Said they knew all that already. Somebody's been watching us since we took the pirate base at the mouth of the Sartoran Sea."

Inda groaned, reached for his knife and spoon (he still didn't like forks, though he'd seen them often enough over the years), and was about to dig into the fast-cooling braised chicken and cabbage before him when Thog flicked her gaze upward, eyes narrowing.

Inda tightened, shifting his weight, hands poised—but it was Fox.

His mouth, as always, was sardonic. He would meet death with sarcasm, that one; but right now his manner was tense. "There's something you had better see," he said—in Marlovan.

"Now?"

In Dock Talk, "Barend awaits you at the chart maker's off the quay." Back to Marlovan, "It is a matter of family honor."

Inda's spoon clattered to the table and he got to his feet, face grim. He walked out, queue swinging, boots clattering, scratching with exasperation at his ear, this time unaware of how every head in the place turned to watch him. Jeje repressed a flutter of laughter at Inda's obliviousness.

Thog rubbed her small hands together, her expression apprehensive. Seeing that she wouldn't speak, Jeje said, "What's wrong?"

Fox dropped down at Inda's place, his fine-woven black wool longcoat open, the gold-tipped edges of his shirt laces swinging. Then he leaned back, arms crossed, studying Thog with his usual lazy mockery. Jeje had rarely spoken to him, and this was the first time he'd actually sat down anywhere near her. He was tall—towering over them both—hard-muscled though lean in build, always dressed in black, which, it was said, he preferred because it didn't show blood in battle or dirt in everyday life. Jeje knew he washed his shirts every day in the good water, that his cabin was cleaner than most, his manners neat, unlike Inda who never noticed what he wore or ate.

The silence was too long. Fox was staring through those nasty winter-sea–colored eyes of his at Thog, and Jeje held her breath.

But when he spoke, it was to both of them. "Inda sent Barend and me to scout for news. Barend thinks that the best news is to be got in whatever dockside taverns are closest to the water, but I believe that the truth—what the mainland merchants call the sved—is easiest found at charthouses."

Thog whispered, "Yes."

Fox watched the reflection of the fire dancing in her eyes, reminded of pinpoints of fire in her black eyes after that long night on the water at The Fangs, when she had deliberately and single-handedly set up Boruin's pirates to burn to death aboard their own ship.

He looked away, and only then could he think. "We decided to go to the charthouse first. We found an old fellow in charge who speaks Iascan. He has the latest chart of the islands and the coast north of the Narrows, and when he unrolled it, I saw on his finger a silver ring set with a big square emerald. Carved on it was the Algara-Vayir symbol, an owl in flight."

Inda found Barend standing outside the charthouse, his posture a startling change from his usual slouch. He stood there with his feet apart as though he wore cavalry boots, his back straight as if fitted into the tight gray military coat that he had never actually worn. One thumb was hooked in his crimson sash, whose color Inda recognized for the very first time was that of the Montrei-Vayirs. Barend always wore something crimson, whether a silken shirt in summer or a crimson knit cap in winter or this old sash for liberty trips. Until now Inda had assumed the crimson to be part of the bravura costume of the pirate, but Inda now saw the ironic significance of that color.

"Here." Barend held out on his palm a heavy silver ring.

Inda stared down at the owl carving. Disbelief—sick certainty—made his body go hot, then cold. The last time he had seen that heavy signet it was hanging around his mother's neck—

Mother. He mouthed the word. His mother would never have relinquished that ring alive.

"No, no," Barend said quickly, jolted by the extreme pallor of Inda's face. "It's not what you think. Though it's bad enough," he added in a rough voice very unlike his own. "Take it."

Still numb—blood icy—Inda bent and scrutinized the ring. No, it wasn't his mother's—the carving around the big stone was more elaborate than the plain leaves bordering the emerald on the one his mother wore, seen every day for ten years. This was not his mother's ring, but older by a generation.

He closed his fist around it, meeting Barend's eyes as the waves of terror died away.

"Here is the proof that the Montrei-Vayirs, in the person of my father," Barend stated in the words of someone who has planned what to say, "betrayed the Algara-Vayirs." He now held out an old, worn, unfolded chart.

No, a *map*.

Inda took it. Chart notes marked the coast, but those were quick notations, smudged and fading, written in the silver-point of the chart keeper. Marks that could be erased. The map was drawn in age-browned, cheap traveling ink, by a distinctive hand, the words written in Iascan. It showed the way to Castle Tenthen, noted the roads around it, and listed probable defensive positions and numbers: it showed someone, in other words, exactly where and how to attack his father's castle.

Inda's tongue had gone dry, his throat tight. He worked his jaw, then forced himself to meet Barend's bleak, unsmiling gaze. "You recognize the hand?"

"It's my father's, all right. I've seen a thousand orders written by him. Copied the boring ones for writing practice, before they decided to send me to sea."

Inda let out his breath. His fist clenched so hard the metal of his father's ring cut into the thick calluses on his palm. "This ring—the map. This was taken by the pirates who attacked our castle thirty years ago," Inda said.

"Sent there by my father." Barend lifted his head, his sharp, triangular face looking more ratlike than ever in the scouring wind, with his short-lipped mouth drawn down at the corners. "Only one thing I can do. Either get my father to face yours, or face him myself."

They stood there on the edge of the road where it met the quay, moss growing between the bricks, the icy wind humming low in a weathervane atop a low storehouse building. Behind them the charthouse stood, shuttered against the rising weather; overhead thick bands of gray clouds were lowering. The air smelled of ice.

Inda sighed. Barend's stance reminded him of the way he himself had stood that terrible day so long ago, on the parade ground before Dogpiss' body on the bier. Barend knew he was in disgrace and nothing Inda could say would change that. The years, the distance, had all vanished, and both of them felt the weight of Iasca Leror over those mountains to the north, and the hand of Anderle-Harskialdna gripping their lives and flinging them once again to the winds.

He said, at last, "Speaking as an Algara-Vayir, I declare the matter must rest until we have finished dealing with the Brotherhood, who lie between us and home."

Barend struck his fist against his heart, and Inda did the same before he realized his arm had moved.

In silence they walked back to the main street.

The two women looked at Fox in total incomprehension.

Fox frowned down at the table, grunted, then surprised Jeje by answering. "You may as well know." His teeth showed in an unpleasant smile. "And I may as well spare him questions he obviously doesn't want to answer, since he hasn't told you before now."

Jeje's heart thumped. "Go on."

"You do know that Inda is the son of a prince—in Marlovan his father is Adaluin of Choraed Elgaer, right?" Fox asked, lounging back in his chair, arms crossed.

"Right. His real name is Indevan Alga—blah-dee-blah. So?" Jeje said, since Thog wouldn't speak.

"The Algara-Vayir device is an owl in flight. They wear it here on their formal clothes." He unfolded one arm long enough to touch his chest. "And on their shields. And the stone on the ring is carved with the owl so that when you press it into a seal, it leaves an owl impression. Rather like a sved, but the owl sign is bound by honor, not magic."

"I know what you mean," Jeje said. "Go ahead."

Fox sighed. "Well, you don't, really, if you have to ask. You see, years and years ago Inda's father's family, his first family, were all killed in a pirate raid on their castle. This man was there. He told me all about it. He was young then, and set to have adventure, though it turned out he didn't have a taste for slaughtering civs. So he took his skills as a chart maker and set up shop here decades ago." Fox looked out the window at the ghost-lit snow falling softly. "He was a cheery, gabby fellow. Told me about the attack, showed me their map, which he kept as a reminder of his pirate days, and then showed us the ring, which their leader had taken off a beautiful young woman after he killed her."

Jeje sensed there was something missing, that Fox was avoiding it. Though he was difficult to comprehend, and always prickly, that change she'd seen in Inda's face when Fox said those words in Marlovan emboldened her to speak. "And?"

Fox glanced her way. His eyes had gone narrow and nasty again. "It was Barend's father, the king's brother, who hired these pirates—a secret their leader was paid to keep." Fox made a derisive gesture. "But he died of drink not long ago. And before he died, he paid his debt to our chart maker by giving him the owl ring."

"Barend's *father* hired them?" Jeje repeated. "Weren't they all Marlovans together?"

"Marlovans, yes. But not together," Fox said, his smile really nasty now. "You could probably say that we're a little like Delfs: we band together best when attacked from the outside. Otherwise we make do with one another. So, the king's brother provided them with a map to find the Algara-Vayir castle. Said they could take anything, they just had to kill the family. The leader surprised the beautiful princess carousing in a tower room with the prince's brother and their favorites among the castle guards, whom we call Riders. All drunk as pirates, when they should have been guarding the castle. Said he would rather have taken the princess along with him—she offered to go, begging for her life—but business was business. They were paid to kill them all."

Jeje glowered. "All right, it was bad, but it was also thirty years ago. So what? That happened before Inda and Barend were born. So why did Inda look like someone had ripped his heart out?"

"It is a matter of honor." Fox opened a hand. "Which is, you will probably observe, about as definable as the weather, to which I will have to reply that it is also as powerful."

Thog whispered, "I understand."

Jeje glared at them, half rising from her seat. "Wait! Wait! Understand what? Are they going to do something stupid? I'm going to personally wring their necks if they try fighting a duel or some idiocy like that!"

Fox patted the air in a languid gesture. "Calm down, calm down. They won't lay a hand on each other. But unless I miss my guess, they won't speak to each other either, until the matter is resolved, unless it relates to the battle we face before they can get home to resolve it."

Thog nodded in slow agreement.

Jeje smacked her hands on the table. She saw people at the other tables glance her way; she fumed, leaning forward and forcing her voice down to a whisper when she wanted to yell and stomp at the unutterable madness of Marlovans, of the world. "The only *resolve* that makes *sense* is for them to go together and *kick* this father of Barend's off the *highest* tower of his *castle*."

Fox grinned. "If only it were that easy." *If it were that easy I would be on a throne right now.*

Jeje eyed that grin, recognized the self-mockery in it. "Marlovans," she stated. "You're all crazy."

Chapter Twenty-two

"THERE'S only one I'd trust to stick it with us and not stab us in the back if the fighting gets hot," Tau said the next day. "Or to refrain from looting all over the countryside if we do manage to win." He turned his thumb up, indicating the building behind him, but Inda still saw it as the Marlovan gesture of approval, and had to make that unsettling mental sidestep. "Little private room top of the stairs. Name is Swift. Says he will bring us a fleet of three: his son's raffee and a couple of fast, tight trysails."

They stood outside the Dancing Sun, a long, low inn that, from the looks of it, had managed to stay prosperous despite Pirate Island's violent changes of ownership. The porch was long with sturdy posts; during the summer it was probably quite pleasant to sit out here and watch the sea crashing on the rocks below and the ships sailing in and out of the harbor. Now a row of scrub-aged children stood at the mossy stone wall, their gender indistinguishable in their sturdy winter coats and boots and mittens. They tossed pebbles into the sea down below, their laughter sounding like the cry of gulls.

Inda's brow furrowed as he watched them.

"You don't like the idea?" Tau asked, always quick to catch changes in mood.

Inda snorted as he surveyed the harbor town below, its jumble of roofs wearing a light coating of snow. Ice definitely on the way. They would have to sail soon, before the wind shifted north for the winter and the Narrows closed up with ice for months. The weather and wind were holding steady now, but that could change any day.

His breath clouded as he said, "Children. Below. Reminded me. I meant to get the small ones to stay here, if it was safe—"

Tau's watchful gaze eased into irony. "I heard about that. You apparently made a fine speech about safety."

"Which no one listened to," Inda admitted.

He grimaced, remembering Nugget holding hands with another scrawny tube of a twelve-year-old girl, this one with vaguely Chwahir features, who—Nugget explained with passionate accusation—had been forced to be a cabin girl on Sharl's flagship. And though it *wasn't her fault,* no one wanted her here. So *of course* Inda would take her, *wouldn't* he, *wouldn't* he, her *very own age*—

And when he delivered his carefully thought out speech, Nugget wailed, "You *promised* Woof you'd *never* leave me *behind!*" Her wail so loud that people poked heads out of doors down the hall at the inn where they'd stayed.

And Mutt appeared, scowling in accusation. "How old were *you* in your first battle?"

Inda wanted to say much older, thought back, then realized in surprise he'd been about their age. "But that was different—it was a mutiny, not facing the entire Brotherhood of Blood."

"But the marines were right after. And you could have fought them—"

"Yes! You would have, if they hadn't gone west!" Nugget shrilled, bouncing on her toes, Pilvig bouncing with her, black eyes wide.

"And you can't make Uslar stay," Mutt added. "Thog would never allow that."

"The idea is to give you all a choice to stay—"

"But we want to be with yoooooooou!" Nugget wailed.

And so he'd given in. And still felt guilty.

So he shook his head. "What's this Swift want?"

Tau opened his hands wide. "Revenge."

"Don't they all," Inda retorted, rubbing his mittened

hands together. His wrist ached. He'd been practicing hard that morning with the new barbed wrist guard, before Nugget and her new friend had confronted him.

"Yes, but this is personal. There's bad history between him and Marshig. And he's got probably the best information of any on this island. We're not sailing clear—they will outnumber us by two to one, at least—but Swift seems to think we can bring it off. Come listen to him."

Tau led the way inside and up a narrow staircase to a private room built like a captain's cabin—same dimensions, smooth wooden floor, low ceiling, windows across the back shaped like stern windows. Four people awaited Inda, who studied each one. First was an older man, balding, with a thin fringe of white-streaked black hair. He was the only one seated, near the fire; behind him stood a tall, strong young man some years older than Inda, and to his right a young woman Inda's age. They both bore a distinct resemblance to the seated man with their brown skin, narrow cheeks below watchful dark eyes, and high-bridged noses. The fourth, leaning against the window, was a very young man, also dark of hair, but with pale eyes and a challenging smile.

At the same time they scrutinized him, this short young fellow about whom so many surprising stories were spreading: he won all his fights, and he used fire not only to attack—like the Brotherhood—but to punish. Like kings.

"I'm Swift of the *Swift*," said the older man. "And these are the captains of my consorts, *Silverdog* and *Moon*."

Inda said, "You say we're outnumbered. But you want to join us. Why?"

Captain Swift leaned forward. "We sift the news of you as carefully as you do of us." His accent brought Testhy to mind; he had to have originated on the Toaran continent, northwest of the Land Bridge. "Marshig and I began in service together. Mids in the Damondaen navy. But he was thrown out before half a year. You probably heard about his crimes, and his rise to captaincy and to command. In the Brotherhood that's done by treachery and being faster and more vicious than anyone else. But I can tell you this: he still does not understand that in the end treachery and viciousness will only carry you so far. In a battle when it be not predator chasing prey, fear seldom stands against discipline."

"Ah," Inda said, leaning forward. "Ah."

Three days of mad labor, day and night under a canopy of lamps, and Inda's fleet set sail. When they had sunk Pirate Island behind them, and the purple-black juts of the Narrows loomed on the horizon, Inda signaled for *All captains*.

By noon they were on board. Inda bent over the big map in his cabin, tracing the last dogleg before the open sea of the west, the Toaran continent curving out toward the setting sun, and Halia jutting northward, giving way to the great Iascan plains. "According to Captain Swift here, they have upward of thirty ships. Tell them?"

Swift looked around at his new allies. "We counted the red sails going north to join Marshig and his fleet of eleven. Thirty in all, not counting a few small craft. We do not know who maybe joined him from the north, coming down from over the strait. Not as many, as apparently that fleet took a terrible beating at the Nob."

The woman spoke up in broken Dock Talk, "They was taking it out on the coast here ever since."

"Trying," the younger of Swift's captains said, with a sardonic lift to his brows. "The horse boys been handing it right back. What you can say is the Brotherhood has destroyed all trade. Nobody goes into any western harbor except on attack. Pirates or Venn get 'em out at sea."

Tau drifted along the back of the cabin, watching the people. He knew he was useless in making military plans. He'd go where he was ordered and do whatever had to be done. Where he was of use to Inda was in observing the individuals who made up the captains of Inda's fleet.

And what a fleet! *If we manage to survive, what will history say of us?* Tau wondered, watching the night-black heads of the three Chwahir captains bend near Inda's sun-streaked brown head, a startling contrast to Fox's ruddy waving hair strictly schooled into its long queue; on the opposite side of the table was the silvery-black braid of old

Captain Swift, tied with a ribbon Colendi-style, though he had come from the continent of Toar. *Will the stories go out reducing us all to faceless and equally disreputable pirates?*

He laughed to himself, glancing past the Chwahir to Tcholan and two hand-picked mates from Freeport Harbor who were now captains of the three old, round-hulled brigs Inda had bought the day before.

"What I figure is this." Inda looked from face to face. "They know we're coming. Makes the most sense to be waiting right on the other side of the Narrows. They'll know we'll sail with the wind, on flood tide. So they'll have the position of strength, squatting in the bay waiting for us to emerge one by one. And Swift says that Marshig's usual strategy is to send his worst in. Then charge our flank—" Inda shook his head impatiently. "Tack in from both sides for the kill."

A pause as everyone glanced Captain Swift's way, then back to Inda. He frowned, organizing his words in his mind. He'd spent the previous day working out exactly what he'd say. These people were all much older than he— Swift had said casually a couple days ago, "You scarcely look twenty, Captain Elgar. Your experiences don't seem to have aged you outside of a few scars."

Inda did not want them knowing he was younger than that by a couple of years. Though he felt stupid at the idea of dressing flash, he had taken seriously Tau's words about part of success being in the mind, of being how one was perceived. That meant he had to sound older than he was. And more assured.

He glanced down at the map. "What we don't have in strength we have to make up in trickery. They will have been told about Boruin's defeat. Might expect us to use a fire ship. What I hope will not be expected is that all three brigs will be fire ships. And they'll come out behind me."

A muted intake of breath.

"But you filled them with supplies," Captain Swift said.

"Right," Inda said. "Necessary for the ruse to work. You know as well as I that at least one spy is ahead of us, sailing something fast and small through the Narrows right now to report on everything we did in the harbor."

The Chwahir fleet commander spoke, his accent so flat it was impossible to distinguish any emotion behind his words: "How do you see the order of battle, then?"

"The *Death* goes in the lead. So they see Boruin's famed trysail. See the crew at the ready. The three come right behind me, with real people moving about on their decks. When they start closing in on me, then the three can split their line and do the most damage. That means the three cannot look like old firewood, but must appear to be fighting ships ready for battle. Marshig's ships will probably be in at least two lines in order to keep us from fleeing. I want the fire ships to break the first up so thoroughly the second line can't move in concerted attack."

The Chwahir said, "You will take terrible damage."

Inda sat back. "Probably. I'll shift to the *Vixen* when we've broken the line. Then Fox commands the *Death*."

Glances Fox's way. He straightened up and leaned against a bulkhead, looking far more like a pirate than Inda.

"But there are too many of us, and we will be too spread for me to count on commanding from *Vixen*. Therefore I'm dividing you into three fleets, and if you cannot see my signals—we'll use flags and screamers both, for as long as we can—then command goes to the fleet captains. Your orders are to divide their lines, board, carry, set fire. Jeje, your fleet of scout craft has the same orders. I want the enemy scouts put to work for us, either as fire ships or to carry boarding teams, or to foul their hawses. So your scouts will have extra crew to board and take as many as you can."

Jeje signified agreement. Inda was speaking for the others to hear; they had already planned her part out between them, deciding whom she'd take. She was going to get most of the younger, more disciplined fighters, capable of independent thinking—new crew would be under Fox and Dasta.

Inda spread his hands. "Work out your signals, fleet captains. The only way we will win is by concerted action. Marshig has numbers. We'll have discipline."

Tau wondered if anyone saw the Marlovan in Inda now—the narrowed gaze, the aspect of command. *But they*

*want to see command, they rely on it. You can only follow
someone you believe will lead you through to life, to light, to
safety.*

Inda said, "There are two things that could destroy our
plans at the outset. The first is the Venn. No one has reported any sightings, but that means nothing. We all know
they can navigate in the deep waters, so they can appear
where they want. If a huge force of them come hull up in
the west, I will turn and run. Thirty pirates with no habit of
order we might be able to take on, but a fleet of Venn warships, drilled for years, will destroy us as mere drill."

Inda saw acceptance, and continued. "The second possible destruction of our plans could be the appearance of
Captain Ramis and the *Knife*."

Dasta spoke from the other side of the Chwahir captains. "He's by way of an ally, yes?"

Inda shook his head. "He's been fighting the Brotherhood commanders, that much we know. But we don't know
why. One of the few consistent stories about him is that he
then sends them straight to Norsunder. So I would not call
him an ally. Not when he might be recruiting. Pirate-style,"
he added, when he saw subtle signs of unease in his listeners. "No asking for agreement, that too I heard; he just
sends them beyond the world. If he's taking warriors for
Norsunder's future battles, then his purpose is so far from
ours that in his eyes we might be no different from Brotherhood. He could blast us out of the world because we
know how to fight."

Silence, except for creak of the hull and the moan of the
wind in the rigging.

"So if you see his black sails, you run. I will, if I can. Now.
Fire ships. No towing empty gigs. That'd give away the plan.
If we do attack at night—flood tide being late this time of
year, Swift says—then the crew can drop off once the
course is set and *Vixen* or the sloops will pick them up. But
our captains have to steer right into the enemy. Then light
the fires. Last, escape as they can."

Pause. Everyone thinking of winter's cold, and the horror of how fast icy water could take you down. Riding a fire
ship into battle, jumping into water trusting to be pulled

out, then sitting in a tiny scout craft, trying to dodge the
second wave of attacking ships . . . that required either fa-
natic dedication or cold-eyed courage.

"We'll call for volunteers for that," Inda stated.

"I'll lead one," Barend said from the far side of the circle, his hands behind his back, his manner the same
strange, remote distance he'd maintained ever since the
day they'd first docked at Pirate Island, the week before.

Now *that,* Tau did not understand. You listened to people, watched them, learned their language and their man-
nerisms; after time you thought you could predict them
under any given circumstance. Then, quite suddenly, they
did something unpredictable, totally out of your experience of them.

The night of their landing at Pirate Island Jeje had privately told Dasta and Tau what Fox had discovered. The
fact that Barend's royal father had sent pirates against
Inda's father was certainly terrible, but not exactly recent
news, Inda's old sailing mates had agreed in their low-
voiced conversation on the masthead. Since neither Inda
nor Barend were even remotely involved with what had
happened a generation before, it made no sense for them
to have come back from that charthouse as if someone had
died, and rarely speak to one another ever since.

Barend spoke to no one, in fact, existing as if an invisible
wall had closed him off.

Tau was startled to hear Barend's voice now: "I'll lead."

Inda turned his way. Their eyes met, cool remote gazes,
revealing nothing. Then Inda struck his fist to his chest.

Barend ducked through the cabin door, and his quick
steps diminished down the companionway of the *Death.*

Tau sighed, feeling that life had slipped into a dream,
and an ugly one at that. Here he was, heading straight
toward the entire Brotherhood fleet waiting clustered beyond the Narrows—and beyond that lay the coast, specifically Parayid Harbor, his old home.

"I may as well be next," he said. No, he heard himself say.
And knew it was another attempt (and it would be equally
unsuccessful) to make a kind of internal restitution for that

day on the deck above them when he'd cut down unarmed Boruin—and took pleasure in the act.

Tcholan spoke up from the back of the cabin. "I'll take the third."

Inda looked up, his brown eyes tired. The appraisal there was quick, and kind, and finally grateful. "Thanks, Taumad. Tcholan." And to the others, "Barend, Tcholan, and Taumad will steer the fire ships. The rest of the week we'll make our fire ships seaworthy. Believable from a glass. Weather permitting, we enter the Narrows eight days from now. Now, let's go over the signal plan . . ."

Twelve days later they sailed in a row between the huge, dark-rock palisades and sheer cliffs at the narrowest part of the passage, a grim, watchful trip that in places was almost like shooting down a river seldom touched by the sun for six months at a time. Another couple of weeks—maybe a matter of days—and the waters would be full of ice. It was dangerous enough now; they'd had two northerly squalls, with more promising to come. If the wind hauled around at last and stayed in the north, within a couple of days they'd smash to splinters on forming icebergs.

So they sailed as fast as they dared in a long, snaking line within a cable's length from one another. Everyone on watch tended sail with haste and solicitude, evidence of their dread of the grinding scrape of rock on the hull or the sudden thud that would give them a heartbeat's warning that the ship was about to founder, flinging everyone into near-freezing water, rescue impossible before they turned numb and drowned.

Fox now captained the *Death*. He was captain because Inda had put him there, an irony he contemplated as he walked the command deck, gazing up from time to time at the sheer cliffs walling them in on either side. Walls that forced him in only one direction, toward the battle that Inda wanted to fight.

Dasta was now the acting captain of *Cocodu*. His fight

team had formed around him as crew, steady independents and privateers all. They appreciated Dasta's even-tempered steadiness, and readily adopted his unswerving loyalty to Inda.

Faint sounds of singing came from that ship now, the rise and fall of voices in an Old Sartoran winter song, as they hauled their mainsail around tighter.

The *Death* was so narrow and sharp of keel the crew seldom had to touch brace or sail. Yet they were all there on deck, sailors waiting by the halyards already laid along, mittened hands tucked in armpits or in pockets, breath clouding, as Fox continued to walk the command deck, a ceaseless, restless pacing broken only by his occasional scans of the heights through the glass.

Inda also watched the heights for the expected signal fires as they sailed north. The sounds were the creak of wood, the hum of wind in the ropes, the racket of sail, and the continuous screeling wail of the armorers' treadles as they worked to hone sharp the steel weapons of each ship, the noise echoing like shrieks up the cliffs. When they anchored for the night, the sounds were the roiling surge and hiss of the sea, and far away the faint hooting cry of unseen birds.

Jeje, skimming the *Vixen* between two of the fire ships, hauled up on the lee of the first, and Thog and Uslar climbed down, both looking tired. The ruse crews had been working day and night—at night under weather awnings, lamps shrouded, so that spies on the heights peering down saw nothing but a row of ships under weather awnings. There was no evidence that under three of the long row of ships, straw-stuffed old fabric and worn canvas being fashioned into the semblance of hands hiding in rigging and along the deck.

Thog dropped to the deck, wringing her fingers, which were pricked all over with tiny blood spots. It was difficult to sew with numb fingers, but she couldn't work with gloves. Her palms were covered.

"Here." Jeje pressed a cup of mulled wine into her hands.

Thog thumped onto a hatch cover, enjoying the warmth

as the weak sunlight vanished with perceptible speed. A whirtler from Inda's flagship arced up. Time to anchor for the night.

Jeje waved at the Fisher brothers, who set about anchoring bow and stern. From below came the delicious smells of food. Uslar, who had been learning Sartoran recipes from Lorm, had joined Nugget in fixing supper. Uslar's breaking voice and Nugget's high one drifted topside, happily wrangling over the best method of cooking fish fillets.

"Will the ships be ready?" Jeje asked, when Thog had at last taken a sip, and her face looked less drawn.

That short nod, a jab of chin toward collarbones.

Jeje stared up at the clouds wreathing the snow-blue heights as the last of the light vanished. "So what'll you do with your share if we win?"

Thog glanced Jeje's way. "If we live. You will stay with Inda, yes?"

Jeje had posed an idle question, or at least she thought she had. Thog's quiet question shifted the mood, exposing the real question Jeje had not asked—had not let herself think.

But she was not a coward, and so she faced it now. "If we live. I'll crew with Inda long's he commands." She considered that, and liked the sound of it. And as Thog did not agree—or disagree—she said, "I like his purpose. It's a good purpose, fighting pirates. I thought after we sank the first one there off Freedom Islands, there are people who will see old age now, with this one gone."

Thog whispered, "I count them. Each time I kill a pirate, I count the lives I save."

The outsides of Jeje's arms prickled. "How—how do you determine the number?"

"By how many died in my village, killed by each pirate."

Thog's black eyes were huge, with no hint of humor.

Jeje let her breath trickle out and groped for ease again. "And when we got to Pirate Island, I liked the way people looked at us. Everyone fears pirates, but no one is doing anything. Except we are. And they know it. I can see it in the way they looked at my ruby." She flicked her ear. "And got out of my way."

Thog stared into her drink.

"And you?" Jeje asked. "I take it you will not stay." She hesitated again, but could not force the words to try to talk her into it, skilled as she was.

Thog set her empty cup down and spread her fingers flat. Then said in a low, fervent voice, as if making a vow, "If we live, then I shall go home and find some land, make a garden, and each night when I lie down I will know that I will never again fear the dawn bringing red sails on the horizon."

Jeje sighed, glowering into her own cup. The truth was, she liked Thog, respected her ability, but she would never again truly trust her. Not after that terrible, deliberate fire on Boruin's consort.

Thog knew and accepted it.

Two days of slow progress were broken once when a ship farther down the line, heeling too far in a sudden gust of the wind howled down the canyons, struck a jagged rock that tore a hole in the hull. It was soon plugged, with carpenters from five ships working as desperately as the ruse crews worked to finish their ghost crews aboard the fire ships.

Inda spent the rest of the day aboard the *Vixen,* going from vessel to vessel to inspect and to review plans. Each ship was ready, eyes on him, tension evident in hands, faces, lips. Heartbeats pulsing in necks, temples.

He returned at sundown to the *Death* and said to Fox, "We're ready."

The last act was to soak those brigs with oil, something that Thog oversaw. Again it was done under a canopy the last night before the attack; under all the other canopies, people not on watch sat on deck despite the cold, doing the things that people do when sleep is impossible: talking, playing cards, singing, even dancing.

When they anchored, a signal fire glowed, golden and sinister on the heights. Inda watched the light steadily through his glass until the light blinked once. Twice. His heartbeat quickened. They had nineteen ships all told, including the three false ones and four scout craft. If the blinking varied three times at the end of the count, they were blown. If four, perhaps their ruse was safe—

Eleven . . . twelve . . . fifteen . . . blink-blink, blink-blink. Four blinks in a different rhythm: four for the small craft. Some of the tension gripping his neck eased.

". . . and listen to 'em, yowling away like that."

The voice was distinct in the frigid air. Inda walked aft. Ah. The singing of the Sartoran and Sarendan independents on *Cocodu*—this time accompanied by Tau on a stringed instrument someone had brought. Tau played a counterpoint to the complicated rise and fall of those voices, glissades of three-note chords every first and third beat. The sound drifted faintly over the black water churning by.

He nodded to Gillor, who had the command deck watch, saw her nod back and then pull her scarf up closer to her knit hat as she paced back and forth, keeping on the move so she wouldn't go numb.

Inda dropped below, welcoming the warmer air. Most of the crew was gathered around the magical Fire Stick blaze in the center of the crew's quarters, some honing weapons by lamplight, or sewing links under their coats. No one was asleep; the hammocks were rolled and stowed along the rail, the deck clear except for those sitting about.

From the look of his flushed face and glistening green eyes, Fox had been drinking; he held out mulled wine to Inda, who took it, drank, felt the bite of distilled rye underneath the wine. Warmth spread through him. He drank again, and again. The weight of home, so close, and yet forbidden, ceased to oppress him.

". . . then you are a fool," came Fox's voice, soft, but with a cruel edge of amusement.

"*You* dance at weddings?" asked Knotfist, one of the older privateers hired at Freeport Harbor. "Dancing is for women!"

Fox turned his head. "Barend. Let's show them."

Barend was there, out of the firelight. He wouldn't dance, not when he was in private exile. But that didn't mean he couldn't drum.

A sudden tapping in an old pattern, unheard for years, forced Inda's mind back to the night Dogpiss died. Barend hadn't a drum, of course; he thudded knife hilts against the decking.

Ching! The shivery sound of steel being drawn from scabbards caused every head to turn, and there was Fox, holding his preferred fighting swords, two very fine sabers made in Sartor, with slightly curved tips after the fashion of the Marlovan riders.

The blades rose high, flame reflecting redly down the cool bluish watered steel; then Fox flung them down, one pointing north and south, the other crossing east and west, and before the echo of their ring died away he lifted his head and grinned, teeth showing. "Inda."

War dances were usually performed in pairs. Inda set aside his wine, wondering if he even remembered the steps. Barend's drumming increased in speed and volume, a galloping rhythm that brought everything back, including the sounds of boys' voices and the scents of the fields, and horses, and the sharp aroma of rye bread baking.

Inda's heels drummed the deck in counterpoint as he and Fox stamped and spun then swept their hands down to pick up the blades, whirling and clashing them together. And Inda was a boy again, a scrub among his friends in the sweet-grass summer of childhood.

The pirates found inspiration in their commanders' deadly grace, the leashed power that was all the more threatening for its easy control.

They finished and Inda's memory vanished at the roar of approval that went up. Several of the crew promptly pulled knives and started trying to reproduce the pattern.

"Again! Let's have it again!" one roared.

"I give in," Knotfist cried. "Teach me that! I'll dance that one at me wedding, and no mistake!"

"No," Fox said. "It's a war dance. Tomorrow we go to war. After, I do a victory dance. Those're fun, too."

Inda looked around, feeling ill at ease. He retreated to the cabin. *It means nothing to them,* he thought. *I shouldn't have done it.*

He looked down at the owl ring on his hand, plucked so many years ago from his father's wife's dead body, worn for the decades since then as an expensive trophy without meaning. Inda groped mentally for meaning now, but other than the vague memories of his father that rose—with or without the ring—there was no inward conviction, no seeing the ring as symbol of honor, of family. It was just a hunk of metal, and he looked up and away, feeling the impulse to yank it off and toss it into the sea.

His gaze traveled up the rough gray sea cliff toward the bleak winter sky pressing low overhead. He knew he wanted justice, but he also knew it wouldn't happen, not when the mystery behind his disgrace led directly back to the will of the Harskialdna, brother to the king. Justice was difficult enough to define, but honor, outside of the word *trust?* Maybe the concept of honor was mere pretense, as Fox insisted.

But Barend believed in honor, and what's more, he wanted to go home again. For his sake Inda had to go through the forms. Supposing they lived through this pirate battle, he would have to send Barend to his father and Tanrid.

Inda sighed. His fear was that the Adaluin might insist on the old life-for-a-life ritual and tell Tanrid to slay Barend. No, Inda decided. His father would ride directly to the king—if he still lived.

If his father still lived.

So if Tanrid was now Adaluin . . . Inda tried to envision his brother as a grown man. His image of Tanrid was of a towering, hard-eyed figure of seventeen—which did not seem so old any more. And his last memory of Tanrid was his calloused fingers tousling his hair, like he always tousled the castle dogs' ears. Tanrid had believed in justice, in his own way. And honor.

And vengeance. What was it Tanrid said that one day at Daggers? *Never show mercy to pirates.*

Inda looked down at his shaking hand. Odd. He was not aware of fear, just that endless stream of possibilities. Anticipation, and sorrow for the unrecoverable past.

One more drink, though he knew it would not numb the memories, and then he returned to pace the deck and watch out the rest of the night. They were as ready as they ever would be, and perhaps he could sleep through the day until the tide turned, carrying them out to battle.

Chapter Twenty-three

KNOTFIST was the first one to die.

Under the rapidly fading light, the *Death* rode the rolling green swells of the outflowing current, leading the line to the attack.

As they emerged into open ocean, arrows arced down from the last of the high cliffs—to clatter against the shields that the crews raised.

When the last of the rocky dragon-teeth was safely passed, there was the enemy. Two enormous half-circles of ships, all stripped to fighting sail, tacked very slowly against the wind and current, so tight nothing could slip between them and get away.

"We're gonna die," someone muttered as the icy wind whistled and moaned through those last jagged rock towers, serrying the hissing hail of arrows that were not even aimed, just shot. Some with fire, some not, but just as dangerous because they were difficult to see.

Arrows clattered on the shields overhead and at the sides. A few thunked into the hull. One skittered across the waiting barrel of newly made arrows, then clattered to the feet of Gillor, who, laughing, stood up and shot it back.

The rest puckered the surface of the gray sea and then vanished in the swirling white-water surges and eddies caused by the rocks they had now cleared.

Knotfist crawled out on the bowsprit with his glass to

count the enemy. An arrow thunked squarely into his back from the heights behind them, and he fell without a cry, vanishing into the churning gray water.

Inda's crew hunkered behind the rails—trembling, fingers gripping weapons with white-knuckled intensity, tongues licking numb, dry lips—but long drills held them in readiness.

"Orders, orders, orders," someone whispered over and over, and those who heard *order, order, order* gripped that thought hard despite the looming threat of chaos and death.

At the bow, under a shield-covered net, Inda stood with his glass trained on the enemy, closer, closer, until he could see faces in the last of the light—

"Wait . . . wait . . ." *Range.* "Now!" Inda yelled.

The rail bow teams popped their heads up, the masthead teams leaned out, and arrows hissed over the black water, each aimed at a living target. Silhouettes tumbled from mastheads, booms, and yards as the *Death* drew near, nearer. Inda gauged the boarding crews lining up eagerly along the rails of the lead ships. "Disperse!"

Signals screamed skyward. Sails flashed. The ships behind the *Death* fanned out.

Inda's head ached, but he kept the glass to his eye. Barend, Tau, and Tcholan sighted on that tight line of pirates, and checked that the sails had been tightly bowsed in place before they emerged from the rocks, the sail crews dropping aft to the boats on the lee side.

The three watched the *Death,* nearly hidden in the black-lined cloud of arrows concentrated on it, hearts thundering in their ears.

Sailing, too slow—
—sky—where's the wind—
—need to pee—
thirsty—
water?—
sweat—ice—dive will kill me—
Jeje, where are you?

Shaking hands slipped waiting ropes over the helms, binding them hard in place, and Tcholan and Barend almost at the same moment dropped a bucket of smoldering, rum-soaked knotted rags below the open hatch where whiskey fumes rose. And then, their bows nudging between pirate bows, they crawled—shielded from view by festoons of old netting—to the stern rail. Last each kicked over the waiting fire buckets onto the oil-slick decks, and then, under the deadly sheets of arrows whizzing overhead, they dove overboard.

Foosh! Barend's and Tcholan's ships torched skyward at exactly the same moment. From the pirate ships on either side rose a roar of shock and fear, followed by the blow and curse-punctuated commands; Tau's ship sailed on— had the oil not been enough? It winnowed between two big brigantines under a thick shower of fire arrows, pinpricks of gold arcing through the dark from both sides— then it too exploded into a sky-scorching tower of flame, the shock sending clots of burning sail, rope, and blocks dropping onto the brigantines' decks.

Inda jammed the glass tighter to his eye. Yes—a slim form dived from the stern just ahead of the firestorm, golden hair briefly fire-limned.

Instinct yanked at him—he flipped up his waiting shield. Arrows thudded against it. Beyond question, he swept his glass round, called out two more commands, sent up signals, and then pirates closed on the *Death,* a boarding party swung down, and Inda's detachment vanished into an eternity of shouts, steel, the stink of blood and shit, the grip of pain and fear.

"Hard over!" Fox shouted.

They slipped between a burning trysail and a huge brigantine with cut booms extended. Brigantine!

Inda twisted around, whipping the glass up. *Marshig's ship is a big rake-masted brigantine, named the* Bloodfire, *with black and gold fire on the red foresail,* Swift had said.

Red sails, but the device was two crossed swords.

Fox called out another command. Inda felt the deck lurch under him as the helmsman threw the ship hard over. The sail thudded, then tautened. Two big forecastle caravels bore down. Though Inda had the current, the pirates now had the wind. They edged closer, boarders ready.

"Assault crew!" Inda yelled. "Signal the *Vixen!*"

Inda's picked crew of fighters lined the rail, weapons gripped. *Vixen* cut close and they dropped in, the deck shuddering under each thud. Loos had the sails taut as the last four jumped down, and *Vixen* plunged into the dark waves, gaining speed with each surge.

Inda led the way up the tumblehome of the first caravel before the pirate boarders could swing over to the *Death*. Inda launched straight into the attackers.

Fox watched pirates fall away before that steel-hot savagery; those who ran were chased and cut down by the assault crew.

Leaving his band to finish the pirates, Inda leaped over the rail into the tender, sweeping the horizon with his glass.

Fox also did a sweep. But—so far—no Venn. He watched Inda again. *What does he see? Is it possible to make sense of smoke and noise?*

"Two trysail on the weather beam!" called the lookout.

Ah, Fox breathed. *I don't see the shape of battle, but I do see an immediate fight.* He ran to the weather rail and began shouting orders.

"There," Inda shouted, pointing at a cluster of smaller ships attacking Swift's *Swift*. Jeje and Loos yanked the tiller over, feeling the wood vibrate through their hands.

"Bows up," Inda croaked. "Each cold shot to a target. Each fire to a sail. Right down the middle, steady, steady . . . Ready to board!" His voice cracked on the last word, and Nugget appeared at his shoulder, holding a cup of water, grinning as though they were on a picnic. Inda gulped it down; despite the thin, freezing sleet he was hot, sweaty, trembling with fatigue, but his heart thumped fast. No Venn . . . no Venn . . . no Marshig, unless he was on the other side of the battle.

He picked up his bow. As they neared the first of the red-sail schooners, he put a foot up on the rail, slapped an arrow against his bow, and took aim at the man at the tiller—

"Loose!"

It was Nugget's arrow that arced out first, twanging overhead. Inda ignored the thrum of bows and peered up at the tiny masthead. "Get a shield!" he yelled at Nugget.

She waved her bow, laughing.

"Fire arrows ready," Inda shouted. All around him was the clack of firepots, the hiss of sleet on smoldering leddas oil, the rattle of arrows against bows. "Shoot!"

Five volleys, each hitting a target. The schooners heeled before they could prepare the sixth. But Inda had already forgotten them. He'd spotted their leader. "Boarders!"

After they took the schooner flagship, he climbed up the mast, sweeping the seas. No Venn. No Ramis, either.

Where was Marshig?

He slid down, signaled for his crew to assemble on the bloody deck. Jeje had sailed to Dasta's aid so they lowered the schooner's launch, one of the new hands at the tiller, Inda in the bow with his glass, sweeping, sweeping—then using it to point. "There! Two closing on *Silverdog*—" He could get there faster than *Moon*—

Dawn lit the undersides of vast clouds, a cold, wintry pale light; smoke drifts obscured tangles of burning ships. Tattered sail of red and white. Struggles surging back and forth on decks. Little boats with oars plashing—some fleeing, some reinforcing. Inda, wearily leaning on the taffrail of the high-sterned scout craft they'd just taken, fumbled again for his glass.

He blinked away the sting of sweat and ash and stumbled around in a circle to survey the entire field. Ah, there were the black sides and white trysails of the *Death*, which was shockingly damaged, its lines blurred from the number of arrows protruding from hull, masts, every surface. But then it was the flagship—it would be the main target. Fox was a tall silhouette on deck, difficult to make out in the haze of smoke as he supervised the crew dousing fires and repairing lower sails.

Inda searched next for Jeje, trying to remember when the *Vixen* had parted from them. There'd been that brig on the other side of the schooner, and he'd taken his boarders directly over, and oh, yes, there was a whirtler from the *Death,* and *Vixen* had sailed away as Inda was in the middle of hot fighting. By that time he and a squad of Chwahir boarders, appearing out of the smoke and fighting grimly and brutally with straight swords, had taken the brig. Both the *Death* and the *Vixen* had vanished into the murk.

So Inda had gone aboard the Chwahir flagship, and then—

He scrubbed his sleeve over tired eyes. He couldn't remember the next fight, or the ones after that. Didn't matter. He was here. And he was ready to swear he had done a full circle of the battle, without sight of Marshig.

He whipped around the glass for the thousandth time.

North. Mostly clear of ships.

East: clear, too, except for burning wrecks—the flames, so bloodred and sinister at night, now pale but just as sinister. Several red sails against the horizon, running for the coast in the freshening wind from the southwest.

West? Burning ship, beyond which little else could be made out; fog drifted over the water in the middle distance, worming softly to the northeast.

Back to the trysail.

A break in the fog revealed the fire-scorched captain's deck. Fox leaned on a sword, cloth twisted around both arms and one leg. He scanned in the opposite direction, then swung around and straightened up. He lifted a hand in salute, which Inda returned. Fox was not unhurt, but he was alive.

Then the fog drifted aft and the *Death* faded to a vague silhouette. Inda swept his glass again, counting sails, each now backlit in the rising sun: white, red—no, that wouldn't matter. He couldn't remember how many had he boarded on his own, leaving sketch crew on each to hold it. Impossible now to determine who had taken what. Or who lived.

Why were they all staring southwest, into the wind?

Inda turned to the southwest, stumbling as his head swam. He braced his feet on the wet, cold deck; he couldn't see anything past the high sides of a burning brigantine. Aft rode the schooner that he'd taken before dawn. Gillor leaned at the helm, her long, silky blue tunic slashed and tattered, her blood-soaked sash wound around one arm. He caught her eye. She gestured and three of his secondary boarding crew started hauling the mainsail around while Gillor pulled the wheel over.

Inda bent to the tiller of his scout, wincing as a cut he'd gotten sometime during the night protested the movement. His left arm was mostly numb, but he hauled the tiller over with his aching right, and then peered again, and his jaw locked when he saw the fleet of six big brigantines tacking up from the eastern side of the Narrows, huge red sails belling in the brisk west wind, the lead ship with fire in black and gold on the foresail and streaming in a long banner over the ship from the mizzenmast. Brigantines untouched. Fresh, ready to fight.

They'd been hiding. All night long.

"Inda!" Fox shouted across the water. "He's coming for me—I'm sending up screamers for a defensive line."

A quick sweep of the glass showed Inda what Fox was not saying: there probably were not enough ships left whole for anything but a token defense.

"Signal for the small craft. Keep the consorts busy," Inda hollered back, his shoulder sending lances of pain up his neck and arm at every word. "I'm going after Marshig."

He motioned to one of his crew to take the tiller. Behind him an arrow arced up, whirtling into the wind. A second from the trysail, fainter, a third from farther out; the *Death* ran the single-stripe flags for small craft, and those within sight began to haul around. Ragged, exhausted, his fleet was still following orders.

Marshig had waited in a hidden bay on the east side of the Land Bridge, watching through the night and counting on the wind to rise with the sun, his plan to attack whoever was left afloat. *He likes to be in at the kill.* Inda had underestimated what that meant.

You think you've won, Inda thought. *But if I can get to*

you I'm going to kill you on your own deck. He threw down the glass, not caring that it shattered, and groped around for his sword—for any sword.

Then a low cry from the schooner off their weather beam caused him to look up, stumbling against the tiller rope.

"Where did *that* come from?" It was Gillor's accented voice—he still couldn't figure out what her accent was, and she wouldn't tell anyone. She too sounded hoarse as a crow. "North, Elgar. North by northwest."

Inda fumbled his way forward and stood on the bobbing bow, oblivious to the cold white spray drenching him. He stared as three ships sailed out of drifting wisps of fog to the north: two schooners, led by a square-sailed warship with a high, curved prow. On the masts of all three, etched against the bleak gray sky, black sails.

Black. Not white or red. Few pirates flew black sails for long; the sun and weather tended to turn them a ridiculous streaky green, but these were the black of a starless night, and as Inda watched in skull-numb amazement, all three flashed their sails with thrilling precision, and the three slanted southward toward the six oncoming brigantines.

"That's Ramis and the *Knife*."

Someone else, farther aft, croaked in terror, "He's comin' after us."

"No," Gillor called. "No, he isn't. Look!"

Inda looked down. *Vixen*—fire-scarred, hull bristling with arrows, its summer mainsail now flying, its two winter sets having been destroyed—had pulled up on his lee. Jeje had a bow slung over her shoulder, her clothes were grimy from smoke, and around her lay arrows in a moat.

Inda looked for his glass, realized it was broken.

"Here."

Vixen glided closer, and, judging the waves nicely, Jeje tossed her own glass over the surging seas. Inda glanced down, distracted: there was one brother, where was the other? Why was one of the new hires at the headsails? Inda's left arm did not work; he caught the glass in his right, raised it, focused on Marshig, who was instantly identifiable.

Marshig stood with his feet braced apart on his captain's deck, his glass trained north on the *Knife*. A tough-looking older man, gray hair, short, squat, powerful arms, but now he looked afraid—Inda could see the diamond-studded hoops at his ears trembling and winking in the dawn light as he turned his head and shouted orders to the mate on watch.

They were about to see Ramis in action.

Before Inda could form an order, the *Bloodfire*'s sails began to haul around in jerks, and the ship leaned heavily as it plunged around to the east—and the mouth of the Narrows.

Abandoning the battle.

Gillor cried, "Blood and death! Watch him run!"

"What's happening?" Jeje cried in a high, sharp voice completely unlike her own as she leaped to *Vixen*'s low prow and balanced there, staring.

No one answered. All stared southward, battles ceasing, fires smoldering, as the air over the bay at the mouth of the Narrows began to shimmer.

The shimmer was vast, glimmering with eerie sparkles high up in the wintry sky, a sinister glistening that intensified as exhausted combatants wiped eyes and tried to force a sense of familiarity onto the strange rain that was not rain.

Desperate human cries echoed from the distant palisades as Ganan Marshig, Commander of the Brotherhood of Blood, screamed orders. Inda and his squads were too far to the north to hear, but *Cocodu* and the Chwahir at the southern extreme of the battle heard the harsh voice echoing off the rocky cliffs, the keening note of terror making everyone's nerves sting. The six brigantines' sails jerked then filled with wind, bows plunging with the rising swells. Though the helmsmen strained, the six ships sailed straight for that gleam, which now began to hum, a high sound that became a deep, steady thrum that caused bones and teeth to vibrate.

Lightning flared, ripping down from the scattering clouds to the water, sending spray high into the glimmer where for a moment the suspended drops glowed crystalline, and then the whole vanished, leaving a gaping fissure into an utter absence of light.

Only the water seemed undisturbed, though one could not see it past that vast and terrifying opening. One by one the six ships sailed from light and life into an unknowable, and final, tenebrae that would thunderstrike the dreams of those who witnessed for the remainder of their lives.

And when the last ship had been swallowed into that ineffable void—its crew screaming as they ran about, some flinging themselves overboard to be swept along by the foaming waters—the opening between the living world and Norsunder's timelessness vanished, leaving waves, clouds, and the wheeling seabirds high above.

Dripping blood onto the deck, Inda lowered the glass, too stunned for thought.

Jeje shuddered, sucked in a deep breath, then deliberately turned her back on the bay. "Inda," she called across the little distance between *Vixen* and Inda's craft.

He looked down into her face, usually a smooth brown, the straight black brows that always signaled her emotions without evasion or falsity. Inda took in the dark marks under her brown eyes, the stress lines emphasized by smoke grime, thinking, *So she will look when she is old.*

"You should know this," she said, her naturally low voice rough as a hunting cat's growl. "After I left you I got a whirtler from the *Garth,* which had gotten separated from *Cocodu.* Seems they were on the far south wing, where you put them, and some local in a little ketch came up. Rowed up. Said they had pirates hiding in galleys in two of the inlets over yonder, waiting to attack any boats that tried to land." She waved vaguely at the rocky coast, where Inda could now see smoke lazily rising to brush against the underside of the clouds. "So Tau led a few of ours to fight 'em."

Inda knew Jeje had to have a reason for speaking as she did, though he was too tired to find it. "And?"

Ramis' ships tacked, all at once, sails flashing yet again. Jeje kept her back to them, as if not seeing them would ward against an attack; a battle she could face, but against that terrible magic she had no defense. If Ramis intended to smite them through that black rent in the universe, she did not want to see it coming.

Inda would face it, and fight it if he could. So he squared his stance as the three ships tacked steadily in his direction, cutting off the *Death* from view.

"Tau?" he asked sharply.

"Hasn't returned that I know of. I have Barend below. Mutt patched him up. He's asleep."

"No he's not." Barend emerged, smoke-blackened, arm bandaged. "You better wrap that," he added, in a steadier voice, pointing up at Inda's left arm.

Inda looked down. Oh. "It can wait," he observed, as if of the weather. "The right hurts worse," he added, flexing his fingers, which sent a throbbing from wrist to shoulder.

Then Jeje gasped. "He's coming *here* . . . he's—I think he's after *you,* Inda." She scowled at the *Knife* as if a glare could drive it back. "How can that be? The pirates all went after the *Death* like you thought they would—everyone thinks you're on the *Death*." She considered what she'd seen during the time she'd sailed beside the trysail in case it needed aid or transport. "They think Fox is you. Wherever he was on the ship, that's where the arrows all flew, and the boarders tried to get to him—"

Gillor cut through Jeje's exhausted ramble. "He's definitely coming for us."

"Couldn't be," Inda breathed, numb with disbelief. "The *Death* is the flagship—they know it, they know the *Cocodu*—"

The *Knife* bore up, the enormous curve of its prow towering over them. Gillor had loosed the schooner's sails to keep it out of the great Venn prow's path.

Inda tipped his head back, saw ordinary humans scrambling along yards and shrouds—fast, efficient. Aft on the captain's deck, in front of the two-man whipstaff that steered the Venn ships, stood a lone figure, hands clasped behind him. Within a very short time—there was nowhere to go—Inda gazed up at Ramis the One-Eyed, whose face was livid purple all down one side, that eye covered with a patch. It was hard to look past that scar. Inda didn't even try, as the man faced him across the intervening waters, brought one gloved hand up, and made a slight sign.

The two men at the whipstaff leaned hard into their

crosspieces, and the *Knife* heeled over. From the fore-
topgallant masthead there was a sharp *twang* and an arrow
whizzed across the water to thunk into the mast a forearm's length from where Inda stood. Ramis called across in
accent-free Iascan, "Meet me at Halfmoon Harbor above
Ghost Island. You'll find a chart there."

Inda gritted his teeth. "I will not take my fleet into Norsunder willingly."

The one-eyed man retorted, "Had I wanted you, Indevan Algara-Vayir, you would be gone." He even pronounced the name correctly.

"Oh shit oh shit oh shit," someone behind Inda was muttering softly in a high, breathy voice. The mast creaked
above, and Inda thought of Nugget. He didn't see her on
the *Vixen*.

His focus splintered. He pressed the heel of his right
hand to his forehead, forcing his thoughts into order. Then
he staggered, not from the deck's movement but from a
sudden wave of dizziness as he reached for the arrow.

It had paper wrapped around it. "We have taken damage," he said, sounding far away to his own ears. "And it is
winter."

"Repair first," came the reply across the widening gulf.

Inda croaked, "Where? We heard the coast has been destroyed." *The coast of my homeland—where I was told I
cannot return.*

"You will find what you need north at Lindeth."

"The Venn?"

"They watched," came the answer. "Until midway
through the night. They stood off to the west."

And that explained where Ramis had been during most
of the battle. His timing, then, had been extraordinarily
close. Possible questions splintered into more questions,
the shards spinning away and vanishing into the fog of exhaustion before Inda could catch and hold but a single, inescapable truth: he had yet to deal with Ramis, and the
Venn.

But he did not have to do it now.

Ramis turned his head, and Inda glimpsed brown hair
tied simply back and an everyday woolen sea jacket before

the *Knife* heeled again, tacking away northward into the wind that was, at last, shifting into its winter path.

Inda stared witlessly, thinking over and over, *How could you have known who I am—and where I was?*

"Don't give your orders yet."

The voice came from the *Vixen*.

Inda turned. Staggered again.

"Before you start northward, I wish to be put ashore," Barend called, his voice flat.

Inda faced east and saw the long, uneven line that formed Parayid Harbor and beyond that Fera-Vayir—and north of that, Choraed Elgaer.

Inda looked down at Jeje's exhausted face beneath its smears of smoke grime. "Where's Loos?"

"Down below. Took a couple of arrows."

"Nugget?"

"Insisted on going with Tau. I would have had to tie her up to stop her."

Inda sighed, feeling sick right down to his bones. He forced himself to look up. One order at a time. First a person. Then a ship. He was a commander, he must command.

"Barend, Jeje will take you to Parayid. Jeje, search for survivors who might have gone ashore. When you're sure they are all accounted for, meet us at Lindeth. My guess is we'll need a week or so to get supplies and finish the repairs we cannot make on the way up the coast."

Jeje nodded agreement, lower lip caught between her teeth. She would never tell Inda how Barend had shivered and wept when they first pulled him out of the water after he'd led the last boarding party to take a huge brigantine, one whose decks had run with blood. He'd called for the last of their oil and set it afire, then dove overboard for the second time that night. When they'd pulled him up, he said with almost voiceless anguish, *No one should see what I saw below*, and then, as he trembled with fear while they bound his wounds, he whispered over and over, *I must go home, I must go home.*

Barend walked aft on Inda's scout, his eyes bleak, and Inda forced himself to move, to twist the ring from his hand, and pull from inside his clothing the map he'd worn next to his skin ever since Barend bought it from the chatty old chart maker on Pirate Island.

He handed both items to Barend. "Go to Tenthen," he said. "Go with my good will," he added, hoping that the words would mean something to his father and brother, unseen for six years.

Barend folded his fingers into a fist and brought it to rest against his heart, then leaped over to the *Vixen,* which plowed coastward on the strengthening wind.

Inda lifted his head, saw Ramis' ships already hull down in the northwest, heading straight out to sea. Of course he knew deep-water navigation. A powerful sorcerer from Norsunder—assuming that's what he was—would know that.

Inda forced himself around again to survey the remains of the battle in the strengthening morning light. All red-sail ships had lowered their red banners. He was in command of the remains of the Brotherhood as well as his people still afloat. *I've won,* Inda thought, but he felt nothing.

Mutt appeared at Inda's side. "Come on. Let me bind that wound before I have to scrub the entire deck. And how did that Ramis know how to find you anyway?"

No answer.

Chapter Twenty-four

THE news that the red-sailed pirate ships that had been striking along the coast were sighted heading south gave the Sierlaef his new excuse not to go home for Convocation.

"It's Elgar the Fox, coming up from the Land Bridge to meet them, that's what everyone says," Nallan had added to the end of his report on his ride east a couple of weeks before.

The Sierlaef knew that shifty look. "And?"

"They say Elgar the Fox is Indevan-Laef Algara-Vayir."

This was not the first time the Sierlaef had heard that rumor. The same claim had been in everyone's mouth in every harbor, ever since late autumn—with muttered insults and sidelong glances the Sierlaef's way for his failure to prevent their damned fish-smelling shacks from being burned.

That made him furious. It was easy to order battle on the plains, where you can see the enemy advancing. But it was impossible to prepare for attacks from the sea, which could come without warning at any point along the shore, a length equal to two months' hard ride. And it wasn't as if his forces hadn't killed plenty of pirates—even burned a few of their ships, the times they'd been at a harbor when the red sails struck. But no, that wasn't *enough,* it didn't *count* for the times they missed an attack—

No use arguing inside his head. Or even with Nallan.

Indevan Algara-Vayir! He could barely remember the boy himself. One of the many scrubs surrounding his idiot brother years ago, but for some reason his uncle had taken a dislike to him. Wanted him disgraced. So he'd done what he was told—and it was not his fault the other scrub slipped and died.

He hated remembering that summer. Hated any mention of Inda Algara-Vayir because the name reminded him of that Noth boy, lying dead in the stream bed.

No one had ever said Inda was dead, just vanished. And the "Elgar" was too close to Choraed Elgaer to be coincidence. The news—rumors or not—had made him uneasy. "You go. Find out," he'd said, then touched his own chest. "South. Coast. Inspect."

And so Nallan had ridden off, leaving the Sierlaef to his real task: finding Joret Dei.

The Sierlaef sighed as he rode along the snowy trail, his Honor Guard talking quietly among themselves behind him, passing back and forth a flask of distilled rye to warm themselves up. Now, with weeks to think about it, he didn't really care who Elgar the Fox was. His biggest concern was that the coastal war not end before he found Joret; the war gave him his excuse not to return home. Because he would not return home until he found her—and while he could force his uncle to cover for him, he knew his father would be angry indeed if he found out his true goal.

The last place Joret had been was at the Cassad citadel, for a wedding that he'd forgotten about. By the time he found out she'd been invited for a protracted stay, it was too late to ride east over snow-clogged roads, ostensibly to honor the newly married pair. But that time, word was she was preparing to leave.

That was two weeks before; six days earlier one of his subsidiary Runners sent east to watch the roads had reported a big cavalcade with Cassad pennons riding toward the middle plains. He'd turned right around and rode back as fast as the snowstorms would let him.

Middle plains!

The question that galled him now: Was it possible Joret would dare to ride to Darchelde?

Oh, but the *women* could cross the border into Montredavan-An lands and it broke no treaty.

The Sierlaef brooded as he rode along, not seeing the slushy ground, the snow piled along the sides of the road—forced labor from the locals, commanded by scouts a day ahead. He could feel his father's and uncle's anger at his not being at New Year's Convocation, for not marrying Hadand. Well, he was in command of the west, and they'd put him there. So they had to deal with the consequences—

A screamer from ahead broke into his thoughts. He held up his hand, and his Honor Guard pulled up, the horses' ears twitching. The horns came: Marlovan. He grimaced, disgusted at the racing of his own heart. Must have been all that thinking about pirates earlier.

Marlovans, from the east—not going north to Convocation.

It had to be the Cassad party. At last.

And Joret.

He raised his fist and his entourage began to trot until they topped a gentle rise and saw the white-draped river valley of the Marlovar below. There they were, numbering at a rough guess at least three ridings, with a jumble of lackeys at the back. A tall blond was at the front: Tanrid Cassad, heir, once one of his own Sier-Danas, though the companions so carefully put together for him by his uncle hadn't lasted much beyond the academy days.

The Sierlaef looked past him, and his heart drummed when he made out a female with glossy black hair framed by her hood and eyes the color of the summer sky. *Joret.* At last, at last. Frustrated desire gripped him so hard his hands trembled.

The parties closed far too slowly. Then he had to wait while they mouthed their way through the formal deferences. He didn't listen. Why had she stayed in Cassad for months? He watched Cassad with Joret, furious at the possibility that she could take *him* as a lover, a skinny, rat-faced Cassad. Anger burned up his throat until he finally turned his attention to the tall, heavy-faced, pale-blond young woman riding on Cassad's other side: Carleas Ndarga, Cassad's new wife and Joret's old friend. He knew that from the days when Joret was with his mother and he'd set Nallan to find out whom Joret spent her free time with, and where, when she wasn't attending the queen.

The Cassads worked hard to hide their dismay at this surprise encounter.

Joret frowned straight ahead between the hairy ears of her mare.

"Well, this is a surprise," Cassad said, struggling for ease of manner. "Though I suppose anyone out will have to meet on the king's roads, as you can't find any of the others." He indicated the smooth expanse of snow to either side of the road.

Only his wife laughed, her voice sounding to the Sierlaef like the caw of a crow.

"The surprise," Cassad continued, with the familiarity of the old companion days, "is in finding you here."

"War," the Sierlaef stated. "Sea." For an exhilarating moment he pondered riding off with her. No, he had to get her the right way. He couldn't even claim the honor of escort, not with only nine of the Royal Guard and a handful of his own Runners at his back. Impatience and frustration made him shift in his saddle, causing his mount to sidle and whisk his tail.

"Ah," Cassad said, after a covert glace of appeal at his wife and her friend—which both stonily ignored. "Well, we won't hinder the king's business—"

"Where?" the Sierlaef cut in, with a circle of his hand.

Cassad turned his face up at the cloudy sky.

Disgusted with her spouse's weak attempt to thwart the prince, Carleas said, "Joret has received an invitation to spend some time with Shendan Montredavan-An in Darchelde. We wished for news of the west, so we came along as her Honor Guard. At the Jarl's request we are accompanying her as far as the border."

Darchelde. As he'd figured. Where he couldn't go—the treaty that kept the Montredavan-Ans inside kept him outside.

"Well," Cassad tried again. "We all want to avoid being stranded by any coming snow—"

"Camp," the Sierlaef stated. It was a command.

They all heard it. So despite the fact that he had no claim whatsoever on Joret, he had issued a direct order.

He would be king, he had the right.

And they had to obey, or be in the wrong.

The thought of being mired in a tent with the Sierlaef made Joret angry: there was no semblance of choice left anymore. The king's son was using his rank to force them to comply with his wishes. Whatever it was he thought, the truth was that she'd just lost her freedom. Embarrassment and regret were swept away by rage.

Her color was high, her straight gaze intense with repressed emotion when at last the four of them sat around the fire in the royal tent. Carleas kept her expression strictly controlled. Poor Joret! One look at her glare helped quell that flutter of laughter behind her ribs.

It fell to Carleas to maintain conversation, a semblance of friendship and ease, but all the rest of her life she'd insist she knew what it must be like to push boulders up a mountain with your hands tied behind your back.

It began all right, with Cassad and the royal heir exchanging war news, but the name Elgar the Fox brought the talk to a halt. The Sierlaef, misreading a quick look between the women, was stunned by a horrible idea: that they knew about Indevan, that Joret was being saved for him.

He could scarcely contain his fury. As he poked at the food his Runners brought he thought he'd figured out the Algara-Vayirs' secret plans. They had to know that Indevan was masquerading as a pirate, and once he defeated the red sails, he could return in triumph and until then, Joret would be hidden with the Montredavan-Ans, where the Sierlaef couldn't get at her unless he broke the old treaty. And wouldn't they love that! They were all allied against him, *all* of them!

He set aside his plate and stood up. Carleas almost dropped her knife, she was so startled by the sudden slit-eyed anger in the heir's pale face. She stuttered to a stop— no one was listening to her anyway—and the Sierlaef took hold of Joret's arm. "Talk."

The others labored to think of something to say, but he jerked his thumb at the tent flaps. "Out."

The Cassad pair withdrew, grim and silent until they reached their own tent.

The Sierlaef had already forgotten them. He was alone, at last, *at last,* with the one thing he'd ever wanted in his life that hadn't been his for the asking. He reached for her other arm, which hardened under his fingers. Her whole body had tightened to rigidity. Lust seared through him; his grip turned to a trembling caress, moving up her shoulders toward her face.

She jerked away. "You dishonor me," she whispered.

Astonishment made his mind reel. As always words galloped through his thoughts, too fast for his tongue to catch and form, making him more angry and frustrated. "Q–q–queen," he managed, choking in his efforts to force his tongue not to stutter. "Marry."

"Then you dishonor Hadand, she I call sister."

"Marry a prince. C–c–colend. Bren. Fuh–fla–Fal." He clenched his jaw, waved eastward. "Make 'em allies."

"Iasca Leror wants her as queen," Joret said, her color high, her breasts rising and falling beneath the thick wool of her robe. The thought of her body under those clothes nearly killed him. "We need her, especially during war."

"You." He held his hands out to her. "Queen."

She struck his hands away. He felt the spark of her touch, brief as it was.

Would it have been any different if she had flung herself into his arms, as had Dannor Tya-Vayir last time he stayed in the Yvana-Vayir castle? But then he'd never found Dannor attractive, only convenient, and finally not even that when she started hinting around about becoming a royal favorite, and how she might "help" him by finding out who his enemies were.

Perhaps the question could not be answered. He certainly would have denied it. The one thing he was certain of was that as future king, he could not possibly dishonor Joret with his love. Not if he did everything right. "Marry," he said again. "Make things g–g–good with Hadand. Come back. You be ready," he added, mentally assembling a mighty force in the royal city and riding to the Montredavan-An border. To damnation with pirates and rumor-chasing. His strength lay at home.

He was the future king and no one could stop him.

She heard the determination in his voice and vowed, eyes stinging with anger and repressed tears, "I will fight you every day of my life."

And saw the corresponding tightening of desire all through his body. Her threat was a horrible mistake, his reaction made that clear. And it was too late to take it back. She saw her error now, how her steadfast denial had made her more desirable. His hunt had made her into a prize he would do anything to win. So either she dishonored the Algara-Vayirs by obligating them to fight over her, or she dishonored herself by surrender.

She could not fix her error, but at least she could save lives. She shifted her gaze: surrender.

He took hold of her shoulders, and she forced herself to stand unmoving under his touch, while the sweetness of desire, the anticipation of fulfillment rushed through him. "Agreed? Say it."

She clenched her fists at her sides. "Yes."

While Joret wept silent tears of fury in her bedroll and Carleas sat beside her stroking her head in wordless sympathy, far to the south, Jeje sa Jeje reduced sail on *Vixen* as they slid into Parayid Harbor. As Mutt and Viac brought the scout craft to, Jeje grimaced at the destruction that was plain even under starlight.

She docked where the capital ships used to, back when trade was permitted, then helped Mutt secure the cable fore as Viac and Barend secured aft. The harbor was nearly empty, a strange sight.

Torches bobbed at the far end of the dock. A crowd coming as fast as they could.

"Well that looks bad," Barend said, his breath clouding.

"If they're pirates, we can lie," Jeje said. "Tide's about to turn—we can get away. Nothing around that can chase us."

Tired as she was, she'd forgotten until now about the possibility that remnants of the Brotherhood might still hold various ports.

Someone in the approaching crowd shouted in a masthead bellow, "What news?"

Not a lynch mob, then, or pirates. So, what news to tell them?

Jeje and Barend stood wearily, lost in memory. The unhurt Fisher brother sat by *Vixen*'s tiller, tired and despondent.

They'd spent a long, tense day in the lee of *Cocodu*, repairing her after sending up their wounded and getting in some supplies. Dasta had called down that Loos breathed, though he had not woken, had not even stirred. Then the scout ship from *Silverdog* arrived with Tau and half of his band, the rest either lost, wounded, or dead.

Nugget was in that second group, having launched herself into a fight armed only with a knife.

Tau says he saw her last curled in a ball, the side of her clothes dark with blood, but still alive. Despite hot fighting around them he'd handed her down into a pinnace with the other injured and told them to go ashore, Dasta reported, his voice cracking on the last word.

Inda sent Tau to the shore to find out where that pinnace had landed. He was turned away. Treated with distrust and fear by an armed mob guarding the beach. To them, Elgar the Fox and his crew were Marlovan pirates, scarcely less sinister than Marshig the Murderer: what would they do in their triumph, and who could stop them?

And so Tau had thrown to the beach the gold Inda had sent and begged that it be used to take care of the wounded; then he'd rowed back to sea, watched from the shoreline by tight-faced villagers gripping weapons.

The rest of the day had been even more bleak as they tried to find out who lived, who died, who was badly hurt. Watching Inda try to comfort the sobbing Pilvig, and poor Mutt, hunched into a knotted ball of grief as he summoned together the remains of the fleet, lit a bonfire for their dead—a bonfire that glowed to life from ship to ship, all except the Chwahir.

Finally, as the tide shifted, the remaining Chwahir ships drew together, diminished crews already busy repairing the terrible damage, as they risked the Narrows to sail back to their homeland. Jeje's eyes stung when she remembered her last glimpse of Thog and Uslar at the stern of the flagship, standing there so still.

"Did you see the battle?"

The crowd had reached them without either realizing it. Jeje's neck twinged as she straightened up, eyes blurry and body aching with exhaustion.

"What happened? Who won, the red sails?"

Iascan! After all this time, to hear Iascan again spoken by someone besides themselves! Barend and Jeje turned to each other for clues, each overwhelmed with emotional reaction as the crowd closed the distance, their faces curious, intent, wary—but not threatening.

"We won." Jeje's voice cracked. "Red sails lost."

"Elgar the Fox, it was Elgar the Fox?" someone cried.

"Yes—"

"Did he duel Marshig?"

"What happened?"

"How many did ye sink?"

"Did the red sails get any of you?"

Pressed on all sides, she began to talk about the battle, warming to the subject when she saw the eagerness, the delight, even admiration in the surrounding torchlit eyes. Admiration! From Iascans! She permitted herself to be swept along, her tired body briefly refreshed by the tide of goodwill. Viac and Mutt stayed behind, each too exhausted, too grief-stricken even for bragging—or eating. All they craved was the oblivion of sleep.

The Parayid Harbor folk took Jeje to one of the few standing inns, plying her with food and drink as the growing crowd competed against each other demanding battle details and trying to impress upon her how terrible it had been there. Burnings, stealing, no trade, sudden attacks, and the Marlovan king's men always at least a week away—evil Marlovans—no, at least they did send warriors as promised, but just to the harbors, angering the fisher folk along the shores—"Is Elgar the Fox really a Marlovan?"

She vaguely noticed Barend stiffening at the sight of a tall man on the periphery, an ordinary man with short, pale hair and tradesman clothing.

Jeje shrugged them away. She was trying to explain that Elgar the Fox was *not* a real pirate—though, yes, a Marlovan—when Barend drifted back a step or two out of her sight, then wove through the crowd to confront his cousin's man. "Vedrid. Why are you here, and dressed civ? If the Sierlaef sent you—"

Vedrid looked both ways, then said in Marlovan, "I am Evred-Varlaef's man now. And I came south in a fishing smack when I heard of the impending battle. You were there?"

Astonishment silenced Barend. He opened his hand.

Vedrid paused, uncertain. Then: "Is Indevan-Laef with you?" He indicated the sea.

"Laef?"

"His brother is dead and he is now the heir."

"Oh." Barend did not know what to make of that, so he just went on. "Yes. That is, he's with the fleet, trying to—well, never mind that. Why?" Barend's voice hardened with threat.

"Because Evred-Varlaef sent me to locate him," Vedrid said. "It is his command that I find him. Take him to Evred-Varlaef, who will himself bring him back to the king."

"Inda is on his way north," Barend said in a low voice. "You can't possibly catch him—no one around here will dare set sail, not after what happened. What we saw. Inda is going north to Lindeth Harbor to refit, and then back out to sea."

Vedrid hesitated. When last he'd seen Barend Montrei-Vayir, he'd been a skinny little rat of a boy watching the summer academy games from the castle windows and covering expensive paper with drawings of horses. Now he was tall, thin, and hard as a beech, his bony triangular face scarred above one eye and along his jaw, his hair tied in a sailor's queue. He wore pirate gold at his ear—a bloodred ruby dangling from it—and his clothing under his open coat was covered by the loose, embroidered, and exotic long vest of the east, only he bore at least as many weapons as a warrior of the plains riding to battle. "Do you go northeast?" Vedrid asked.

"Yes. But not to the royal city. I ride on a matter of honor to Tenthen, castle of the Algara-Vayirs," Barend said formally, and Vedrid saw starlight flicker in an emerald on Barend's gloved left hand: a silver signet ring. A prince's ring.

Shock, instantly suppressed. Vedrid said, "I'll have to ride up the coast after Indevan-Laef, then, and try to catch him at Lindeth. Will you ride with me until our roads part? I can arrange mounts for us both. We had better exchange news, I believe, Barend-Dal."

Barend agreed, and so Vedrid led the way to one of the hastily built travel houses where he had left his gear.

He was not at all a stupid man, but he was so straightforward he was unaware of Nallan watching from an adjacent building, shielded from view.

Nallan had been shadowing Vedrid for two days, ever since he saw the Runner he'd always hated arrive in one of those rickety old boats that had scudded south in the wake of the pirate fleet. He recognized Vedrid instantly despite the short hair and civilian dress. Vedrid, supposedly dead on the road to the Marlo-Vayirs! He'd seen the bloody coat himself. And what was the truth behind *that?*

Something treasonous—with Vedrid at the center.

Nallan had spent the two days wavering between planning to kill Vedrid and hoping he could be caught in some capital crime, which would lead to his bleeding his cursed life out at the flogging post, Nallan rejoicing in every lash.

He cursed under his breath when a passing torch in the hands of a young girl briefly lit their faces: Vedrid was not consorting with pirates or Venn—he had found the long-missing Barend Montrei-Vayir.

Nallan could not hear their talk—the low voices of conspiracy—but in a sense it didn't matter. He could not raise a hand against Vedrid now, not with Barend-Dal at his side. So he was left perforce with his original orders. He would ascertain the true name of this Elgar the Fox, and then he would carry that plus the news of Vedrid's (and surely the

Marlo-Vayirs') betrayal back to the Sierlaef, who would decide what to do.

A week later, Whipstick Noth stood beside Jarend-Adaluin in Tenthen's hall, and watched the range of reactions from Inda's family and liege people. Barend stood beside Whipstick, also watching.

The old prince held up the Algara-Vayir war banner, tattered and ancient and sun-faded as it was, saying, "In one week's time we shall ride to the royal city, and there I shall demand the blood price of Anderle-Harskialdna Montrei-Vayir, to be given in justice or taken in justice."

Silence, except for the scraping of feet. Some, mostly the old folks, were angry; the tall, brawny cousin (what was his name? Branid?) looked sullen; everyone else looked somewhere between stunned and fearful.

Jarend-Adaluin held up the ring and the map. "Here is my proof of Anderle Montrei-Vayir's treachery against us."

Cousin Branid kept licking his lips and watching the faces around him, uncertain how to respond, wondering if he would be left in charge or if he should ride with the warriors. He wanted both, badly. Maybe he should challenge that Montrei-Vayir rat-face to a duel? He was such a skinny runt. If he slayed the rat-face, maybe people would follow him at last.

"We will make ready, and in a week we will gather here to ride to war." The Adaluin thrust the banner into a holder in front of his judgment seat, where it would stay until he picked it up for the ride. Then he walked out, one gnarled old hand gripping his evidence, the other leaning on his wife.

With three exceptions the people in the hall were busy striving to be heard and listening to no one else, and so did not see the prince and princess sidestep into a short chamber where the Adaluin sank wearily into a chair, staring beyond the walls as he murmured, "I will have justice for the dead."

Whipstick was the first exception. He stationed himself

outside the door to the little chamber, guaranteeing them privacy as he winced inwardly. *I'm afraid you will not last out the journey, my poor liege*. He hated to remember how Jarend had wept soundlessly when Barend Montrei-Vayir stuttered and stumbled through his news after his arrival. After which the Adaluin sat up straight, his lined, weather-worn face reddening with hope as he said, "Inda is coming home?"

It was right after Barend replied, "No. He sailed for the north," that the Adaluin seemed to age past his nearly eighty years as he whispered, "My sons are gone." And then, after they gave him something to drink, even lower, over and over, "My Joret, my Joret"—his long-dead beloved first wife, aunt to the Joret he'd brought up to marry his son.

It was Fareas-Iofre, Whipstick knew, who had gently roused him, reminding him that only at his hands could there be justice. The word appeared to have infused him with life again—but for how long?

Barend Montrei-Vayir was the second exception. He steered between the shouted questions from Algara-Vayirs he did not know, ducked into the hallway where he'd spotted Whipstick, and joined him. "Well, that's done." And, when Whipstick made a sign of assent, Barend added wryly, "Now I don't know what my part is: to go home and fight for my father, or against him. The king will have to decide."

Whipstick shook his head, grimacing in sympathy.

Cousin Branid was the third exception. He lurked behind a knot of arguing relatives (his grandmother was the loudest) as he noted all the knife hilts in the rat-face's clothing, the scars, the stance. The way he stood reminded him of Tanrid, like he was ready for a fight. Maybe it was strut—like the pirate clothes. Well, if this rat-face Barend Montrei-Vayir offered any insult, that's when he'd challenge him to a duel. That was the plan. If he dishonored the Algara-Vayirs in any way. Otherwise, ignore him. That's the way to treat a strutting pirate.

Barend never even noticed him.

He left Whipstick on guard and wandered the length of

the hall where Inda had lived as a boy. He was wondering
how he was going to tell Inda that his brother was dead,
and if he should describe how his mother, after hearing
about the battle, had said only, "Is Inda coming home?"
And when Barend had to tell her that he was sailing for
Lindeth and then the Ghost Isles, she had not responded,
just looked as if someone had struck her.

A little later Whipstick met with Tdor and Fareas-Iofre,
who said, "I don't know what will happen, but this I do
know: Hadand and Ndara have to be told the news. First
that Barend is indeed alive. Second that the Adaluin is
coming for blood. They can warn the king and the
Harskialdna if they feel it's right. Chelis, you shall ride
now, and go like the wind."

Tdor said, "As for me, I think I'd better ride for
Darchelde with the news that Savarend is alive. We can't
write it in a letter, we don't have any codes to say it right.
It's better spoken." She paused.

Fareas-Iofre murmured agreement, knowing that toil-
some as the journey would be for Tdor, news of a son's
being alive was too priceless a gift not to give to another
mother.

Tdor added, "I can also warn Joret. She might want to
come home."

*Everyone knows the Sierlaef is going to come here look-
ing for Joret—or trouble,* Whipstick thought. *We'll need allies.* But there was no time to send anyone to Fera-Vayir
Harbor to ask his father, who was in command of the defense there, for advice. He had to act on his own, and now.
So he ordered his personal Runner—his cousin Flatfoot
Noth—to ride north to Cherry-Stripe Marlo-Vayir, who
would know where Evred was and could be trusted to send
someone to report to him.

Fareas-Iofre stood at her window watching Tdor's departure, but her mind ranged far ahead as she pondered. In
the next room her husband lay on his bed, falling by consent under the mind-numbing peace of sleep-weed. A

whole night of reawakened grief and old rage had left him exhausted, barely able to walk.

She remembered how Barend Montrei-Vayir had stumbled and stuttered to answer her question "Is Inda coming home?" How like his mother Ndara he was, not just in looks—he had taken after the Cassad side, not the Montrei-Vayir—but his immediate and obvious wish to make things easier, even for an older woman he did not know.

But Barend's well-intentioned, fumbling words about honor and the mysterious Ramis' equally mysterious demands and the needs of ship repair had flowed past her. It wasn't that she didn't believe them, she did—insofar as Barend obviously believed them.

No, to her Inda's actions were a kind of communication, cast in a code perhaps only mothers could decipher. He had been sent away alone, except for a guard he probably never knew about—a kindness from the king—and had returned years later at the head of a fleet to fight the pirates who had been tormenting his homeland.

So Inda sails north to Lindeth, Fareas thought, struggling against sorrow. She must not grieve. She'd raised her son to one day bring knowledge and enlightenment to his father's principality, but events had overrun her benign plans. Yet some lingering sense of the great works she had given him to read must have remained, because she perceived honor shining behind his actions, like the moon's silhouette crowned by fire when it crossed the sun.

Of course he had honor. Not just the false sense that was so often in the mouths of those who meant merely precedence, or preference, or vanity, or demands. It was true honor, which was just another word for trust.

He will be back, she thought. *I will believe he will be back when he perceives a need greater than whatever order they gave to keep him away.*

Chapter Twenty-five

WHAT later became known as the Conspiracy of Hesea Spring was really a latticework of accidental encounters and impulsive decisions.

A great winter storm smashed down a glittering ice shroud over the plains, day after blinding day, as messengers crossed in all directions, unseen under the gray-white sky.

Flatfoot Noth reached the Marlo-Vayirs' castle first to discover that the Marlo-Vayirs were not yet back from Convocation. Unfortunately Cherry-Stripe, though future Randael and thus traditionally left at home, had gone with the Jarl of Marlo-Vayir and Buck.

Disappointed but not surprised that his dreary trip was to be prolonged, Flatfoot downed a meal, then set out again. He followed the king's road toward the oldest known Marlovan town, Hesea Spring, where three great roads met: the east-west, north-south, and the older Iascan road that cut from the royal city northwest to Ala Larkadhe through the plains. When the snows were bad, the old granite markers along these roads were about all the guidance you would get.

The great stone posting house at Hesea Spring was nearly as large as a castle, but single storied except over the stable, the older part of the house built in the days when Marlovans sat on mats and ate with knives off shallow wooden dishes. The most common meeting place for travelers in winter, it was built around a hot spring: this year, in fact, the Marlo-Vayir brothers had appointed it the place to meet Cama Tya-Vayir after his stay with the Yvana-Vayirs for Hawkeye's wedding. (Cama was also a future Randael, but he was home as seldom as possible—and no one who knew his brother Horsebutt, or his equally horrible future wife Starand, questioned why.)

A few days later—the day Tdor reached Darchelde ahead of a blinding four day blizzard—Flatfoot arrived at Hesea Spring from the west not long before the Marlo-Vayirs arrived from the east. Each obscured from the other by falling snow.

Flatfoot tiredly scanned the pennons planted outside, saw the great blue and yellow eagle banner belonging to the Jarl of Yvana-Vayir, along with Hawkeye's more unpretentious banner. The Yvana-Vayirs! Weren't they supposed to have spent New Year's at home for Hawkeye's wedding? Why would they be riding south now, in this weather? For no good reason, of course.

Mad Gallop Yvana-Vayir didn't see his marriage to the king's sister as a step down for her, but a step up for him, Flatfoot's uncle, Dragoon Captain Horsepiss Noth, had said. *He's been ambitious since our own academy days, and I wager he'll make trouble about his half-royal boys if he can.*

Frost. That's what they used to call it during his academy days, when someone strutted his rank. The sad thing was, Flatfoot thought as he stabled the loaner horse from the Marlo-Vayirs' Runner stock, Hawkeye wasn't the least full of strut, much less frost. Nor were the young twins, Hawkeye's brothers Badger and Beaver.

He thawed himself in the common room, trying to decide whether to wait or to push on, when horns announced a cavalcade arriving.

In his rooms not far from where Flatfoot sat, the Jarl of Yvana-Vayir heard the horns as well. He had taken all the good rooms along the southern wing for himself and his sons, the rooms that overlooked the road from the royal city; he'd also filled a quarter of the barracks over the stable with the enormous Honor Guard he'd seen fit to bring.

"There's the Marlo-Vayir blue and green," he said, rubbing his hands as he peered out the window of his chamber into the courtyard at the modest-sized company riding in with a clattering of horse hooves and shouted orders. "The falcon banner! Means Hasta himself is here. Heh heh! Good, good."

Hawkeye and the twins were silent. Their father had been acting strange ever since the wedding, his latest oddity being his sudden insistence on accompanying Cama Tya-Vayir when he rode south to meet the Marlo-Vayirs here at Hesea Spring. That, and his bringing two flights of warriors as an Honor Guard. One flight was usually enough for an entire family; a wing—three flights—was against the law. They were one flight away from treason.

"I must see if Hasta knows we are here," the Jarl said.

"In case the Jarl of Marlo-Vayir was too blind to see our pennons," Badger cracked as soon as his father was out the door.

Hawkeye had been thinking the same thing, but it did not show respect to say it aloud. He snapped his fingers and turned his thumb down. Badger sighed, and Beaver grimaced in sympathy.

After an uncomfortable silence—there'd been a lot of them on this ride—Cama said, "Guess I'll shift my gear down to Cherry-Stripe."

He hefted his saddle bag over one broad shoulder. Cama had grown into a very tall, powerful young man with a deep, husky voice. That, his eye patch, and his long, glossy night-black horsetail made heads turn. Badger and Beaver saw him go with some relief, for though they liked and admired him, so did everyone else, and over New Year's Week he'd gotten all the female attention that they had anticipated for themselves.

Hawkeye watched him walk out, feeling uneasy. He sensed he was riding on shifting ground, but he couldn't see the danger, only feel it.

Then he remembered that Buck would of course be with the Marlo-Vayir party, and he said, "I'm going as well."

The twins retreated to their room and began pooling

their coins. Now was the time to make an expedition into the town on the other side of the spring to seek the sort of fun they'd missed during New Year's Week.

Hastred Marlo-Vayir limped into the posting house, grim with pain. His leg hurt worse than ever, clear up to the hip, and he wondered if he'd ever ride again. His mood soured when he recognized Mad Gallop Yvana-Vayir's voice: "That you, Hasta? How was Convocation?"

Hasta didn't want to answer, he wanted to get to a bed and lie down, but he would be damned for all eternity before he'd let Mad Gallop, who'd been the barracks cockstrut all during their academy days, know that. As he tried to summon up friendly words he was distracted by the sight of an unknown Runner approaching his sons.

"Isn't that Horsepiss Noth's boy?" Mad Gallop asked, squinting at the familiar form: all the Noths were blue-eyed, square-faced, bodies lean as whipcord and strong as steel. "No, can't be; t'one is dead, t'other is—" His voice changed, "with the Algara-Vayirs. Ho! You, Runner!"

Flatfoot turned, surprised. His face then smoothed into blandness in a way that made the Jarl of Yvana-Vayir, watchful and wary, instantly suspicious.

Flatfoot thought rapidly. He was supposed to report to Cherry-Stripe before riding north to Evred, and here he was. Whipstick had never said anything against Hawkeye or his family but neither had he told Flatfoot to give them his news. An ordinary message he wouldn't mind repeating, but the nature of this particular message made him reluctant. He took a couple steps backward, as though to retreat.

Both fathers saw the reaction and they frowned, one in pain and irritation, the other scenting the trouble he'd come hunting.

Mad Gallop said, low, "Hasta. I know we might have had our differences when we were boys, but the fact is, it's time to unite, time to unite. I have bad news." And, louder, "You! Come here!"

Flatfoot saw the lordly finger, hesitated, then muttered something to Cherry-Stripe, who whistled soundlessly.

That whisper gave form to Hasta Marlo-Vayir's pain and

irritation. Talking secrets with his boys, was he? No, he wasn't! "Come here, Runner," he said.

With two Jarls commanding him and no orders to the contrary, Flatfoot had to obey.

"Now, who are you and what have you to say to my sons? I shall hear it, too."

A few words into Flatfoot's report, Mad Gallop stopped him. Here they were in the broad, wood-floored entry hall, more than one pair of curious eyes and ears turned their way. "We'll go to my rooms."

Cama, still with his gear on his shoulder, followed the Marlo-Vayirs and Yvana-Vayirs back to the latter's rooms. There everyone listened to the news that Anderle-Harskialdna had once hired sea brigands to attack a Marlovan castle and kill everyone in it. And he'd gotten away with it. Until now. Jarend-Adaluin was raising his war banner and riding on the royal city.

Old news never died when it concerned kings.

"They have proof?" Hasta Marlo-Vayir asked at last, and when Flatfoot told him, he frowned. In truth, over the past years he had come not only to distrust his old friend Anderle—now Harskialdna—but to dislike him. Had he always been so arrogant? Why had he never noticed? Until now it had seemed disloyal to even think such thoughts. "Treachery against the house of a prince. Bad for us all, for where will it stop?"

"Just my thought," Mad Gallop said, rubbing his hands again. "That's why I came south—that is, I have my own news, but it touches treachery as well as our old friend, if you follow me."

Treachery? By the king's own brother? The Jarl of Marlo-Vayir rubbed with a fist at his aching hip, not certain what to think.

"I know what I have to do," Hawkeye stated. "With your permission, Father, I will cut short my leave and ride straight to the north. Evred-Varlaef will need a report."

"No," his father commanded. "No, you will remain by my side." Again, his strange smile, evocative of anticipation and triumph. He never thought to have everything he desired delivered so neatly to hand. "We will need your skills at the royal city," he said. "I will send trusted men north to the Varlaef, I promise you that," he added, and turned to Flatfoot. "I suggest you get yourself back home to Tenthan Castle. Tell your cousin that the Jarl of Yvana-Vayir will see to the righting of matters."

Flatfoot realized he'd been dismissed, so he saluted and left, standing in the courtyard as he considered his dilemma. The Jarl was going to send someone north to Evred—that part of Whipstick's orders would be seen to. Meanwhile, Flatfoot smelled trouble.

Yes, time to go home indeed.

Inside the chamber, Mad Gallop dismissed the Noth Runner from his mind and addressed Hasta. "This tale of Anderle-Harskialdna's treachery was unknown, but it is also old news. Now, hear me. What is new to us are the words of Vedrid the royal Runner about the Sierlaef's covert assassination of Tanrid Algara-Vayir. Hawkeye questioned Vedrid himself."

"Assassination? Vedrid?" Hasta repeated.

Cherry-Stripe beckoned to Cama and they withdrew to a window while Hawkeye's father made him repeat the story to Hasta Marlo-Vayir.

Buck walked over to his brother, grimacing.

"We're in trouble." Cherry-Stripe groaned softly. "We never told our dad about Vedrid."

"Vedrid? Isn't he the Sierlaef's Runner?" Cama asked.

As briefly as possible, Buck related what had happened.

Cama whistled once, then shook his head.

Cherry-Stripe, thinking of the Sierlaef and capital crimes, said uneasily, "What do you think we should do?"

Cama sighed. "So that's why Hawkeye's dad's been gloating, and the boys've been mum. Listen, Cherry-Stripe, whatever your dad says, Mad Gallop is on some kind of secret mission, and it's all tied up with the Sierlaef and Vedrid somehow. I don't know the details, but I do know this: you won't be the only ones in trouble, if there's going to be trouble. And Hawkeye's dad is looking for trouble. He's got two flights of warriors, and he came here seeking allies, I see that now. You're the only Jarl family, so you're it."

"What kind of mission would have to do with Vedrid's story?" Cherry-Stripe asked uneasily. Life was pretty good at home. If you ignored the war in the north that had never quite ended and the pirate attacks along the coast. But the real truth was things *could* change, fast, and for the worse, and right where you think you're safest. He'd learned that when Dogpiss died.

They glanced across the chamber at Mad Gallop's wide, manic grin.

Cama said, "A mission that he's going to take straight to the royal city," he predicted, and no one denied it. "I don't know what he thinks he'll get out of the king and the Harskialdna, but I do think we had better let Sponge know."

Cherry-Stripe scraped his boot heels on the tiled floor. "Mad Gallop told Hawkeye he would send messengers north."

"When? Saying what?" Cama glanced in growing doubt at the Jarl's manic grin. And came to a decision. "Look, I think we need some of *us* in on whatever's going to happen." "Us," they understood, were their academy mates. "I can ride north, talk to Noddy, maybe Tuft. Flash, if I can find him. All on the way to Evred."

Cherry-Stripe glanced again at the men talking and conviction seized him; for once he knew the right thing to do. "Go find Noddy. He can spread the word. Tuft's too far out of your way. Then gallop for the north and tell everything to Evred."

Buck added, "You're alone, under no one's command at this moment. They can't stop you if they don't see you."

So Cama departed quietly through the back door. He saddled his horse and set out on the north road not long before Yvana-Vayir sent his four most trusted men north with orders spoken only into their ears.

Ostensibly they were to escort the disgusted twins back home. But their secret orders were to continue on to Evred-Varlaef at Ala Larkadhe—and there take their place in history by assassinating Evred-Varlaef Montrei-Vayir.

Badger and Beaver Yvana-Vayir, their Runners, and

their four escorts reached the northern road, kept clear by ancient law, half a day behind Vedrid on his long toil northward to report to Evred that he'd found Indevan-Dal at last, and that he was sailing north to Lindeth.

A fortnight of hard weather later, the Sierlaef made it home.

Hadand Algara-Vayir, raised in the royal castle as the Sierlaef's future wife, sat in her rooms reading.

The door banged open and her betrothed strode in, snow-soggy coat swinging, yellow hair hanging wet and tangled down his back.

She rose in a swift movement, her small, capable hands reaching for her knives, then falling away when she recognized who he was, her wide-set brown eyes questioning.

The Sierlaef liked Hadand. She'd always been kind to him, pretending he did not stutter, secretly doing his reading tasks for him in the schoolroom. The age of change had kept her short as he'd grown hands taller; her growth had been outward. She'd kept her trim waist, but was quite broad in hips and bosom. Most of his old academy mates admired her, and the Sierlaef had been pleased to see her admired; until he'd seen Joret, he'd been content enough to marry her.

He reflected on these things, and how sensible she'd always been, as he closed the distance between them. Then he stopped, hating the struggle to speak clearly. But he must. Now, of all times, he had to be understood.

She remained silent as he glared down at her with those angry green eyes she'd braced herself all her life to endure. To deflect. He had never struck her, but he'd beaten Evred and Barend frequently enough that his presence in the schoolroom had felt akin to impending thunder all the days of their childhood.

"I will marry Joret, and you'll get an honorable treaty," he said, having planned that much, and practiced it over and over to get it out in one piece, with no tremor.

She gasped. "What?"

"Marry. Joret. You and I. Go to Father together. You marry a p–p–prince. Trade. Alliance. All with honor." He got that out with utter conviction—there was no going back, not now. He'd promised Joret.

"Have you, uh, seen her?" Hadand groped wildly for the real world, which seemed to have slipped sideways, leaving her in a terrible dream.

"Yes. She waits." He scowled as he mentally rehearsed his words, then said, "Go bring her back. Three of us. Go to Father. Everything right." He was tired, having run day and night, using all his horses and forcing people along the road to give him theirs. But desire was stronger: now that he'd told Hadand, it remained only to gather a suitable force, ride to Darchelde, get Joret, and ride back and marry her!

He started out, leaving a puddle of melted snow on her floor, then stopped. "Don't talk. Till she's here." He left.

Hadand said nothing until she saw him ride back through the gates with half the Royal Guard—already severely diminished due to the necessity of guarding the coast, the eastern border, and the north. She sped straight to her aunt Ndara's rooms.

Anderle-Harskialdna arrived back from a morning at the royal horse stud, and when he heard that the Sierlaef had arrived, stormed up to Hadand Hlinlaef's chambers, and then left again—this time taking half the Royal Guard— the Harskialdna was livid with fury. Not only had the heir acted with no discernable semblance of sense, he hadn't even left a message explaining himself, and no one could tell the Harskialdna why.

The Harskialdna paused long enough to rework the watch schedules with his seriously diminished defense force, then ran upstairs, nearly colliding with Hadand. He was going to stop Hadand, looked at her red eyes and compressed lips, and let her pass. His wife would know. The women shared all their secrets.

He stalked in to confront her.

Ndara-Harandviar rose from her paper-piled desk, her

plain Cassad rat-face closed as always. How he hated her! She said, with obvious reluctance, "It was nothing. The Sierlaef insulted her. He can explain himself to you and the king as soon as he returns."

"If it was nothing, why does he need to ride out again the day he arrives home, taking half the Royal Guard with him?"

"Ask him that. I never saw him."

"You're lying!" His hands trembled with pent-up rage. "Nothing but conspiracies everywhere!"

She flushed. "Address the Sierlaef about that. You're the one who raised him. He doesn't trust any of us, or talk to any of us. That was what you wanted, was it not?"

The words were no less than the truth, despite her sarcasm.

He stood there fighting his rage, wanting to strike her down, smash in that despised rat-face. But he could not blame the damned women and their whispering conspiracies for his failure with the Sierlaef.

He stalked out, flexing his hands against the nearly overwhelming urge to hit something. Yes, he had raised the Sierlaef, and so if anyone was to blame for his strange behavior, the Harskialdna knew it was he. Only how had it happened? Discipline, training, long-sighted planning, those he had taught the boy. And how his uncle would always be at his side—a Royal Shield Arm—to protect and guide him in those shared long-sighted plans.

All carefully worked out. All ceaselessly and scrupulously seen to—just to lose him over that stupid girl. Because what else could it be? The Sierlaef fobbed off his father with reports that the Harskialdna knew were composed by Runners, but in truth the heir cared nothing for the embattled coast, for trade problems, for diminished resources or men spread too thin. All he thought about was Joret Dei.

Chapter Twenty-six

THE Sierlaef's forces had begun their second day on the main road heading south. During those two days the men wondered what the Sierlaef was after now as they watched him pacing restlessly at every stop, snapping his fingers and whirling his hand to get the horses changed faster, get everyone fed faster (and the men themselves to finish eating on the road if they didn't eat as rapidly as he did). No one spoke to him, of course; since Nallan was gone, they did ask one of his other Runners, only to get a shrug and "All I know is, we're off to Montredavan-An land" in return. That made everyone uneasy.

Late that second day the outriders signaled a lone Runner approaching.

The Sierlaef stopped his cavalcade, his heart beating hard when the anonymous blue tunic and black woolen cap resolved into Nallan. He held up his hand flat to keep the men in place and rode ahead for privacy.

Nallan rubbed his gloved fingers over his cold-numb lips, then said, "Vedrid's alive, dressed civ. He met with Barend-Dal, your cousin. He was in a sea battle, led by—"

The Sierlaef waved his hand impatiently. Right now he had no interest in sea battles. "Vedrid. Said?"

"I don't know. Could not get near without them seeing me. They talked a long time along the northern road. Then

Vedrid sent Barend-Dal to the east into Choraed Elgaer.
Vedrid rode north along the coast."

Vedrid alive! The Sierlaef shivered with the neck-
gripping chill of impending threat. It could only mean one
thing: treachery. No, *treason!* Treason from the Marlo-
Vayirs! And Barend, the sniveling little rat, no doubt racing straight to Tenthen Castle to blab to the Adaluin, and
from there he'd gallop home to tell the king whatever
Vedrid had yapped about Tanrid Algara-Vayir's death.

The Sierlaef raised his hand again, this time with two fingers up to summon the flight captains forward.

When they halted, side by side, he had his words ready.
"You. Go to Darchelde. Escort Joret Dei. Royal city." He
waited for the man's acknowledgment, hand to heart, then
turned to the second one. "We go back." Then he waved
them off. To Nallan, he said, "Take two. Kill Barend. Before. He reaches r–r–r–royal city. He's a pirate," he added,
and watched the horror in Nallan's eyes.

He hadn't meant to lie, it just came out. How easy!
Everyone was afraid of pirates. "Ride."

Two days later the Sierlaef and his tired force finally spotted the towers of the royal city stitching the gray-white sky
to the snow-covered plains on the horizon.

The men were tired, relieved—and annoyed. Four days
on the road, no explanation for the trip or the return.
While bedding down that first night, under the cover of
darkness, more than one of them had muttered variations
on, "Good taste of what life'll be like under a new king."

The others shushed the mutterers, not in defense of the
Sierlaef but for their own safety.

The Sierlaef noticed nothing. Now that he was in sight of
home, he slowed the pace. He hadn't figured out how he
was to explain Tanrid's death to his father. Even if he'd
managed to gain time by ridding himself of Barend, it was
only time, not freedom from trouble. If the sniveling little
toad had indeed gone to Tenthan Castle in Choraed El-

gaer, the Adaluin would soon be galloping north with a war banner to demand his blood.

Angrily he considered various explanations, always coming back to the fact that he shouldn't *have* to explain. He was the future king. It should be enough.

To anyone else he could say that, but not to his father.

His uneasiness was at first allayed when one of his outriders came plunging back down the road toward them, mud splashing up to either side.

"Big force," he said, striking fist to heart, his breath in clouds. "Marlo-Vayir and Yvana-Vayir banners, northwest. Looks like at least a wing altogether."

Marlo-Vayir? Aldren-Sierlaef thought immediately of Vedrid, not killed by Buck after all, and knew he was in trouble. Not soon. Now.

"At the g–gla–glala—run!" he shouted, sending his startled horse plunging. He kicked the stallion's sides and galloped for home.

After nearly three long, grueling weeks on the snow-covered roads, Vedrid rode his tired mount in through the gates of Ala Larkadhe, lying far to the north of the royal city and the royal heir charging for home just ahead of retribution. He had used old Runner trails and a few trusted contacts for changes of mount, which had put him more than half a day ahead of the Yvana-Vayir men with their secret orders.

For the last distance he'd used the road closest to the coast so he could stop in Lindeth Harbor, and sure enough, there was the low black pirate ship he'd glimpsed in Parayid what seemed so long ago, riding far out on the bay. He did not risk changing his horse or even eating. He did risk one brief conversation to gather information, then turned eastward to the old city built at the base of the mountains visible in the purple haze from the harbor, Ala Larkadhe.

It was not far, though it seemed far to one tired and cold and hungry, riding a plodding horse that was equally tired, cold, and hungry.

When he reached the castle, he left his drooping mount at the outer stable used by visitors and castle folk other than the military and Runners. Stable hands took one glance at those sweaty sides, the lowered head, and closed in around the animal.

Satisfied, Vedrid shuffled toward the gate. In civilian dress he did not draw the eye; he waited until a group of merchants went in to discuss a matter of trade with the kitchens. The sentries still scrupulously counted them, checked for hidden weapons, and a bored herald apprentice wrote names and belongings down on a long list, then turned them over to a Runner-in-training to be taken to the kitchens.

Security was even tighter than it had been at his last visit.

When it was his turn, Vedrid brought out a sealed letter he'd prepared as he said, "I'm here from the harbormaster in Lindeth Harbor to deliver a bill to Runner Toraca."

The sentry waved in the direction of the white tower as he said, "There's the door. Runner will take you to him. Wait there if you don't see a Runner. Don't wander around unless you want to be either bitten or questioned under white kinthus, whoever gets at you first."

Several Runners waited inside the round room, a Fire Stick making the small chamber bearable; from the smell they were drinking cinnamon cider with a generous dollop of bristic. All was quiet, orderly, and warm inside the glistening white tower, a contrast to the blue cold of the snowy city and the mountain heights above.

He was duly handed over to Nightingale Toraca, who greeted him with raised brows in his lugubrious, houndlike face as scout dogs sniffed all over his muddy coat, their ears flicking. "That real or an excuse?" he asked, taking the paper.

"Excuse. Evred-Varlaef said not to write, only to speak to—" A sudden yawn seized Vedrid and his eyes watered. "Speak to him."

Nightingale led the way four steps at a time up to Evred's tower office, where Evred looked up from a desk almost covered with neat stacks of paper.

"Indevan-Laef Algara-Vayir is here," Vedrid said, too tired for preamble, his thumb angled toward the west—and as it happened the doorway.

"He's *here?*" Evred got to his feet, peering past Vedrid into the empty doorway.

Nightingale poked his head out, looked both ways, then shut the door.

"Coast," Vedrid said, pawing vaguely behind him. His hands were numb, his gloves sodden. "Lindeth. Been here for a week, I discovered this morning." He yawned again, and stretched his hands to the fire.

"A *week?*" Evred repeated, a flush of annoyance reddening his cheekbones. "Why have I not received a report from my guard there?"

"Because they don't know." Vedrid gestured at his own civilian clothing. "They accepted me as a messenger from the Guild Fleet in Bren. Your men don't seem to know one ship from another, and Elgar the Fo—that is, Indevan-Laef, was not permitted ashore until their business was at an end. Which it is today, according to the harbormaster's chief scribe. They need to settle about the captured ships—"

"Captured ships," Evred repeated, perplexed.

"From defeated pirates. There was a pirate war in the southern waters, against the red sails, and he won."

Evred frowned. "Lindeth has known a week, and no word reached me of that either?"

"There were no Runners in Parayid Harbor when I was there. I came directly north—the roads are mostly snowed in. Any Runners sent by anyone else have to be at least a day or so behind me."

"But that doesn't explain the silence from Lindeth," Evred said, and for the first time Nightingale and Vedrid saw him really angry.

His resemblance to the king was striking, and Vedrid squeezed his eyes shut, trying to think, then shook his head. "I was there a short time. It was the scribe who told me, and that only because he thought I was from Bren. Whatever the reason, the harbor authorities kept the news to themselves. I'm not certain even the regular folk know.

Maybe they wanted to wait until Indevan-Laef's fleet left. The scribe referred to them twice as pirates."

Evred's brow cleared. "Ah. Perhaps they expect trouble from me for their harboring of pirates—either that or they anticipate some sort of wicked Marlovan collusion with the wicked pirates." His tone was wry, almost humorous, and the flush faded from his face, but no one smiled.

Vedrid said, "So maybe a messenger will come when their 'pirates' are safely gone. Oh. I should have told you before, I met Barend-Dal at Parayid Harbor—"

"Barend? My cousin? Alive?"

"He was with Indevan-Laef. But he rode inland while Indevan-Laef sailed up here. Anyway, I began to say that Indevan-Laef himself is coming in on the late tide, to settle the trade of captured ships for repair and stores. Then they expect him to be gone on the tide's ebb."

Evred stared at Vedrid, realizing he did not even know what a tide's ebb was. "Today. Inda in Lindeth. Leaving Lindeth. Then . . . I must go now."

He must go right this moment, but hard on that conviction was the equally strong one that he did not want a clutter of guards, questions, explanations.

Ah. His blue coat.

He sent Nightingale for the coat and to Vedrid he said, "Go to the stable. Two fresh horses. Stop for something warm to drink. I know you are tired, but you must take me to him and I do not want anyone here or in Lindeth to know. Afterward you will have time to rest, I promise."

Vedrid made another of those pawing motions toward his chest in salute, and turned to obey.

Presently two Runners rode out through the gates past four men in Yvana-Vayir yellow and blue entering the city, but neither party stopped. The Yvana-Vayirs, who had only glimpsed the king from a distance and had never seen his sons, were intent upon their purpose. They knew they were about to make history, and had no interest in a civilian or a Runner in unmarked blue.

Evred-Varlaef recognized the blue-and-yellow eagle stitched over the hearts on their coats, and decided whatever message Hawkeye was sending could wait.

The world could wait.
It was time to keep his promise.

Evred never clearly remembered that journey down
through the snowy hills to Lindeth Harbor. Only impressions remained: the color of the light on the snow, sometimes gold, sometimes blue; a trail of animal tracks winding
away toward the hills; the sound of his horse snorting, its
breath clouding and then falling. The smell of snow giving
gradually over to that of brine as they neared Lindeth.

His own heartbeat, drumming in his ears.

His mind, repeating what he would say. *That justice I
promised the king will provide.* Did that sound too full of
frost? He was certain his father would agree to the justice—yet he had never spoken to the king on the subject.
How about this, then? *Come home. You are now the heir,
and you are needed in Choraed Elgaer.*

And Inda would say . . . what would he say? Memory
kept sliding back to the eleven-year-old boy. "What do you
think, Sponge? How about we try this ruse next game,
Sponge? We always have to have a backup plan, Sponge!"
It seemed impossible that Inda could have become a pirate—but who was he now?

They reached the snow-covered outskirts of the new harbor, which consisted of streets neatly laid out with an eye to
defense. The plan was one of Evred's own, based on an old
Sartoran record. The Lindeth guild leaders and harbormaster had fancied having their new buildings patterned on
Sartoran design; the style being two centuries out of date
mattered not a whit to either Marlovan or Iascan.

They slowed, Evred timing his ride across the sentry
path until the outer perimeter guard would be too far away
to easily make out his face. He did not look right or left, relying on his blue coat to keep him unnoticed. And it
worked. The Lindeth people paid him no attention, other
than a few scowls at the coat that marked him out as a
Marlovan messenger—a spy, as they said among themselves.

Vedrid kept an anxious watch ahead, for the weather

was lowering and the water looked gray and choppy. "That black one is his ship," he said at last. "Tide's turned—it's coming in now."

Evred lifted his head and saw the long, low, raking black-sided vessel riding far out in the bay in the midst of several other ships. It drew the eye immediately, a sinister ship that could only belong to pirates. He fumbled for words. "Why don't they come all the way in to the docks?"

"Harbormaster wouldn't let them. Ah! That's got to be his boat." They peered through the soft haze of drifting snowflakes as a small boat dropped down to the water from a huge wood-and-rope structure at the side of the black ship. The snow prevented them from seeing who climbed down into the boat. All they could make out was one, possibly two shapes, and long sticks that were proba-bly oars.

Evred felt snow touch his face, cold and numbing. He ig-nored it as he sought a vantage from which to observe the rowboat now working its way slowly toward the shore. This end of the harbor city was mostly smoothed ground below the high street along the ridge, marked off by small stone plinths awaiting spring, when there would be more money to commence construction on the larger buildings. Until then, the high street served the cluster of little cottages thrown together in no order above and below, much as they'd found the Nob last spring.

So it was easy to see with an unimpeded view. Evred stopped his horse in a half-finished archway connecting two warehouses and stared at that distant boat, over-whelmed by a wish to speak to Inda alone, with no wit-nesses. Not even Vedrid. There must be no alarms, no mistakes. "Take the animals to warmth and food, and see that the sentries do not come this way."

Vedrid obeyed. Evred gripped the rough stone of the archway as he watched the oars dipping and rising, dipping and rising, the green breakers surging around the boat in a way that made him feel unbalanced and a little sick.

*   *   *

That same surging gray-green sea was a calm swell to Inda and Tau as they rowed in toward shore.

Tau said, now that they were away from the ship and all the listening ears, "You're really lifting anchor to sail north?"

Inda sighed. "Taumad. The man said 'Meet me at Half-moon Harbor above Ghost Island.' If I don't go there, he'll hunt me down. And where would I go?"

"Anywhere else in the world, for a start."

"Will that really get me away from someone who can rip a hole in the sky and sail right out? Probably with the wind ordered to blow right behind him?"

Tau uttered a vile curse; Inda, surprised, grinned as he leaned into the oars. His shoulder still pulled, but it was healing. By the time he reached the Ghost Isles he should be back at his old speed and strength. He shifted his thoughts from that to Tau's first question. "The Brother-hood is effectively gone. But we're going to have to face the Venn, who set them against our land. You know they were watching. They are watching still. I can feel them on the horizon."

"If," Tau said with rare acerbity, "you 'feel' anything, it's too many bashes on the head. We did what we set out to do. Let others clean up the remaining pirates and take on the Venn."

"Who?"

"Well, it seems to me that that would be a job for kings, who do have the money and ships for that sort of game."

Inda retorted, "So while the Venn are hunting me down, I do what? Or don't you believe they'll be hunting me down?" As Tau sighed, Inda almost added, *Go home if you like,* but that would be cruel. Though Tau had said nothing at all, Inda knew from Jeje's private report the day before, when the *Vixen* caught up with them, that Tau's mother's pleasure house in Parayid Harbor had been reduced to snow-covered ash, and his mother was gone—apparently abducted by pirates. Tau had no home to go to.

He did not speak, but Tau guessed the direction of his thoughts, and cursed again.

Chapter Twenty-seven

IN one of those unnerving coincidences of history, the same day—the same watch—that Vedrid and Evred-Varlaef rode down into Lindeth Harbor, back in the royal city the Harskialdna prowled outside his own rooms, brooding.

Still no sign of the Sierlaef. The night of the Sierlaef's thunderbolt appearance and disappearance the Harskialdna had confronted Hadand, but she said only, "Ask him when he returns. He ordered me not to speak, and is he not the future king?"

Another evasion from another conspiring woman, damn them all—

"Brother."

Anderle-Harskialdna whirled around. There stood Tlennen-Harvaldar, the king. His face was difficult to distinguish in the fading winter light. "It has been several days, and I have not seen you."

"No. I spent most of the day with the armory master."

"My son apparently arrived the day after I saw you last and took half the Royal Guard away again. Why have you not reported this to me?"

The Harskialdna forced a smile. "I've been waiting to find out the reason first. It seems he was here and gone while you were in that trade meeting with the Adranis and I was overseeing the royal stud. Since I had no more than that to report, I did not want to interrupt you when you were shut up with the guild leaders the other day, and yesterday with the tax men. So I have been attending to my own tasks while I await either him or a message from him."

The king laid his hand on the doorframe outside his personal chamber. "We need money for our defense and mages back for spell renewal," he said, his expression bleak. "The Adranis are claiming that war negates our old treaty."

The Harskialdna scowled. The army already complained about the rain-resistance on their coats fading; there were signs of other spells beginning to lose their potency. At first he'd dismissed the subject, but as time wore on and they could not get messengers in or out of the kingdom, it began to become clear how many little spells they had previously taken for granted.

The king said, "Until I can settle with the Adranis there is the problem of finding mages to come here, then of finding money to pay them. It requires compromise, and money that we do not have, not with so much of it going to the north for supply and rebuilding."

"As for the communication problem, there should be news from the coast soon. Maybe today," the Harskialdna said, shifting the subject. "The last messenger from our southernmost harbor reported a mass migration of pirates toward the Narrows, and everyone there was talking of a possible ship battle."

Tlennen said, "When they come, interrupt me in whatever I am doing. I need to know what happened."

Anderle-Harskialdna was relieved. But then the king added, "I also want to know if the rumors about the commander of the sea defense being the Algara-Vayir boy are true."

The words were like a punch to the Harskialdna's gut. He'd exerted himself to keep those rumors—not that he believed a word—from being voiced here. How *could* Tlennen know? Jealousy spurted its familiar and caustic acid into the roiling pit inside the Harskialdna: his brother's accursed mate Sindan had not been home for over a year, staying in Ala Larkadhe to protect Evred, and the Harskialdna himself opened every dispatch brought by Runner to the king. Including Sindan's.

"I believe those rumors are false," the Harskialdna stated, all the more firmly because of his doubts. "Mere rumor, spread by those whose ambitions have been thwarted, by the disaffected—" He stopped there, knowing his brother would want to discuss why Marlovan Jarls who had recently sworn their year's oaths would be disaffected.

"I was weak," Tlennen said, so low his brother almost didn't hear it. "Too weak to face what I did not want to see." He retreated into his room and closed the door.

What did *that* mean? The Harskialdna had reached his own rooms when one of the young Runners-in-training dashed in, panting from his run the length of the castle. "Heir's back. At the gallop."

Indeed, there it was, the sound of horns. War horns, faint and far away. Why would the Sierlaef be blowing war horns? Many horns—signaling an entire wing—

The Harskialdna paused long enough to thrust his fighting knife through his sash and then started down toward the stables, meeting the Sierlaef halfway. "Those horns—not you?"

The heir was muddy to the hip and white-faced with emotion. "They're coming for blood," he said, clearer than he'd ever spoken. "Coming for me. Yvana-Vayir, Marlo-Vayir. Wing. At least." His mouth twisted with threat. "You. M—m—make it r—r—right."

War horns again, louder, and a young Runner dashed in, stumbled to a stop, and thumped his fist to his chest. "It's Yvana-Vayir and Marlo-Vayir, with war banners," he announced breathlessly, more excited than afraid. "Three columns, looks like three flights—"

The heir pulled his knife. "Vedrid lives. Blabbed."

"Go to your rooms," the Harskialdna commanded, and he waited long enough to see the heir retreat. His heart thumped against his ribs, and ideas—words—plans tumbled through his mind. He knew Mad Gallop and Hasta, had known them since they were ten-year-old boys down there in the academy scrub barracks. If he could soothe whatever it was that got them hot, it would renew his hold on the heir. All this sped through his mind as he ran to the listening chamber above the great hall; he'd decide on his strategy after hearing what they were saying. They'd come through the great hall first, if they were waving war banners around. He could calm them down by prolonging the ridiculous formal palaver of their ancestors—

"Empty! The coward! Probably lurking over in his office at the guard barracks. You, take your riding upstairs, and find the traitor Aldren-Sierlaef. You to the guard barracks, and you upstairs, find the Harskialdna and kill him!" That was Mad Gallop. His next words stunned the Harskialdna. "Strike the traitor down. You, find the king—"

"Wait." That was Hasta, hoarse with pain. "Hold hard! You never said anything about assassination. Only justice, and not against the king! *He* hasn't—"

"Justice demands a new king," Mad Gallop replied. "And who better than my son, who is also son of a princess?"

"But the king hasn't—"

The Harskialdna didn't stay to hear the argument. A wing of warriors against the depleted Guard, and most of those not at their post, but heading toward the barracks to sleep? He knew in bone and nerve and viscera that his life was over. He who thought and planned ahead had been taken completely by surprise, and not by the pirates, or Idayagans, or even the Venn, but by conspiracy where he had not watched for it.

Here was the end. But he would not die alone.

He ran to the door of the one he hated most, whose secrets and plans had always eluded him. He kicked open the door to his wife's rooms and saw her seated, hair wet, her bathrobe draped around her. She was in the act of writing on a little square of paper. "Conspiracy!" he snarled, advancing. "And you're at the center of it!"

"Center of what?" she snapped as she backed to the wall.

When he saw her fling the little square of paper into the fire he released that lifelong hoard of anger in an inarticulate roar.

Her hands brushed over her wrists—to find them bare.

Her weapons lay in her room with her clothing. Rannet, her personal Runner, was weeks away.

She was alone and unarmed, her other Runners busy on duty.

"You never. Lay with me. In life." He reached for her, she dodged in an expert, flowing move, but her hair, usually neatly confined, swung out in long wet ribbons. He caught a lock and yanked viciously, and she fell to one knee.

He wound his hand in her hair, then, with his other hand pulled out his knife and stabbed her again and again.

Her arms rose, white hot shards of pain shooting through her as she warded the killing steel with bare flesh. "You," he snarled, stabbing furiously as he tried to reach her neck, her heart, her gut. "Will. Lie. With. Me. In death."

Shock—pain—the swift flow of hot blood made her head reel. She kept her arms up as she struggled to free herself. The last word—death—rang in her ears as the cruel knife lacerated her, scraping on bone, until a single thought jetted upward through the rising black tide: Barend.

I must protect Barend.

Purpose pushed back the billowing blackness. Old lessons guided her failing body. She ceased trying to regain her feet, but sagged suddenly, and his hand loosened its grip on her hair—

Ah, there! His boot knife. She fell forward, closed her bloody hand round the hilt. She was beyond question, beyond hearing: as the Harskialdna straightened up, his body tensing at the clatter of footsteps rapidly approaching, she gathered her remaining strength, though by now the roaring in her ears deafened her and flowering black spots as well as blood blinded her eyes.

But instinct fortified by years of hatred and honed by the ritual of drill drove her steel up between his ribs and straight into his heart.

The door slammed open then, and nine men ran in, each determined to be the one to earn his name in the ballads for dispatching the traitor. They hacked at Anderle-Harskialdna, whose hands scrabbled feebly at the knife in his ribs; it was only when they finished that they noticed the woman lying nearby—but she was already dead.

*   *   *

The noise of screams and clashing steel terrorized Kialen, Evred's betrothed, who had been passing softly along the hall to take embroidery silk to the queen's rooms.

Hadand appeared from somewhere and shook her. "Kialen! I heard shouting. Who was it? Where?"

Kialen could only point, her cold fingers trembling.

Hadand turned her head at the distant shouts of men. Trouble, that much was clear. She gazed desperately into Kialen's frail, heart-shaped face, took in the terror rounding her eyes, the tense high brow, and forced her voice to soft urgency. "You must go hide in the secret chamber. Now! I have to protect the queen. Kialen, do you hear?"

Kialen's thin hand groped, closing around Hadand's wrist. Her frail body trembled violently as she assented, always obedient, for did not obedience make the shadows go away?

"Go now, little sister." Hadand bent and pressed a maternal kiss on those slender fingers, and waited until the weird, distant focus in Kialen's enormous pupils altered to awareness. To comprehension. "I'll be with you as soon as the queen is safe."

Kialen seemed to hear, her brow smoothed, and she began to glide away, so strange and childish, though they were the same age. But Kialen—so unlike her Cassad cousins—had never seemed to age past her tenth birthday; she just got stranger.

When she vanished around the corner, her steps soundless, Hadand hurried away.

Kialen drifted silently to an alcove, but stopped again and backed against a wall at the iron-shod clatter of running men. She closed her eyes and shrank into the shadows as five Yvana-Vayir riders in yellow and blue tramped down the hall.

They ignored what they took to be a child cowering in the corner. They spread out, swords at the ready as they began kicking open doors. The first suite, across from Hadand's empty chambers, belonged to Aldren-Sierlaef.

He was there, alone. His hazel eyes narrowed when he saw the Yvana-Vayir colors instead of the Marlo-Vayirs' but he did not speak. Just drew his knife.

The men exchanged uncertain glances, each waiting for a sign from the others. To kill a prince! They knew the penalty if their lord lost, but if they won, it would mean promotion, maybe even land of their own—and perhaps their names mentioned in the songs that would be written about their Jarl for future drums.

Still they waited for one another to move. The Sierlaef, for all the bad gossip about him, never had anything said against his courage.

They studied him now. He was tall and strong and all five remembered those stories about his winning a battle against overwhelmingly superior numbers of Idayagans when he was barely out of the academy.

"Now," said one, with a sideways glance, and they charged.

Even charging they waited for one another to be the first to strike and so the Sierlaef ripped his knife across the lead man's throat and on the backswing opened the belly of a second one.

The remaining three shouted and lunged at him. Two, each now determined to be the first to strike, fouled one another's blades. Aldren-Sierlaef backed up, hoping to get to the doorway so they couldn't come at him from the side.

The last man wheeled and blocked the door as the other two found their footing and attacked more efficiently.

And so, though the heir fought hard, he took more wounds than he gave. He managed to strike one himself and shove another into his companion's downswung blade, but by then he was dizzy from blood loss. The first assailant dropped hard, kicking senselessly. The second folded to the floor in a faint. The Sierlaef slashed the man's throat to finish him, then stumbled back through the doorway to his bedchamber. The last man, who had stood in the outer door to block it, now charged after him and arrived before the Sierlaef, who was breathing harshly, faint with pain and rapid blood loss, could get the door closed. The man whipped his cavalry sword in a vicious uppercut and buried the point in the king's son's heart.

The noises the Sierlaef made, the way he fell to his knees onto the carpet and then half rose again, groping with his knife, thoroughly unnerved the man. He did not see the promise of reward so much as the flogging post if he were caught here, and so he flung down the sword and ran.

The Sierlaef lay on the crimson carpet his grandmother had given him, where when he was small he'd loved to work his toes after a long bath. It was soft under his cheek, and so he lay there, his gaze on that cavalry sword gleaming dully so far away. Aware of only pain and thirst, of anger, because he knew why they had come. The king had a right! But slowly the world began to diminish, all meaning narrowing to that sword. If he could just reach it—

Ah. His hand touched steel, and he gripped it until all pain, anger, and question washed away in the coolness of night.

Kialen watched the man with the blood-stained blue-and-yellow tunic run by, looking neither to the right nor the left. Terror kept her there in the welcoming shadows, where comforting voices whispered from far away.

If she waited, still and quiet, maybe they would sing.

Hadand had sent Tesar the shortest way to the arms mistress; they met outside the queen's rooms. "Fighting," Hadand said, breathing fast. "Why doesn't my aunt order the city bells to lockdown?"

The arms mistress said, "Not invaders. Yvana-Vayir, Marlo-Vayir. And one of our own scouts just arrived with the word that Choraed Elgaer is coming."

Was this screaming and fighting related to the news about Barend that her mother's Runner had brought from Choraed Elgaer? No time to find out—these warriors were *here*. In the castle itself. Hadand pressed her knuckles into her eyes. The women trained for generations for these moments. "My place is to guard the queen. Until we get orders from either Ndara-Harandviar or the king, you defend yourselves only if attacked. Otherwise, remind them that to draw weapons in the king's house is to be forsworn."

"If they fight?" the arms mistress asked, her emotions betrayed only by the sharpening of her voice.

"Since these are Marlovans, try to disarm and disable, not to kill, unless they try to kill you. Then strike swiftly. Take no commands from any one of them, no matter what rank."

The arms mistress agreed, gripping her knife handle.

"Go now to secure all the public halls. Don't let any Marlo-Vayir or Yvana-Vayir men cut any building off." And to her own women, "Guard the hall outside the queen's chamber—bows as well as knives. Let no one in. Let no one *near*." Back to the arms mistress, "And you'd better send a girl to ring the bells for city lockdown. My aunt can always countermand, but having the city quiet seems a good idea."

Everyone agreed—the city knew that lockdown meant *Get behind your doors and lock them.* Anyone out could, and would, be struck down without question.

The arms mistress loped off, issuing orders to the women who had assembled in stairs and archways, waiting in silence.

Hadand glanced back but saw no sign of Kialen, and hoped she was safe in the hidden chamber. *I should have brought her,* Hadand thought, but then she shook her head and opened the door, smoothing down her gown. Kialen's mind was slowly drifting to a place none of them knew, far from the real world. Any violence she witnessed might shred the last few threads of her hold on sanity. And what if these attackers came to kill the queen?

On Hadand's entrance, Queen Wisthia felt some of her terror ease, only to be replaced by a rush of anger. She too had heard the war horns, the shouts, the running feet. "What is it?" she demanded.

"I do not know. But with your permission I will find out. My women are on guard—"

Wisthia rose to her feet, a tall, elegant woman who even after nearly thirty years of marriage to a Marlovan still

moved, dressed, and especially thought like an Adrani.
"Don't leave!" she commanded. Her own women stared,
shocked and frightened. "Don't leave me alone with these
barbarians. I always knew they would turn on one another
like wolves in the wild. Worse, because wolves do not train
their young with steel."

The low, venomous voice went on and on, releasing
decades of pent-up emotion. The Adrani women who had
followed their mistress into her long exile forced themselves to sit silently, stitching with exquisite care the butter-
flies on sashes, the new fashion from home, each stitch
counted out in heartbeats, as if order could be restored by
will alone.

Hadand sat motionless, trying not to hear the trembling
voice whispering invective against her people, as she wondered where Ndara was—and the king.

Taumad and Inda lifted the oars, rode a wave, then back-
watered the boat to the newly-repaired dock. They shipped
their oars.

Captain Ramis had been right about Lindeth offering
anything they needed by way of repairs, either free or at
bargain prices, once they heard the news. Not that they'd
believed Inda's people. Several boats had sailed with them
for protection, southern traders known in Lindeth Harbor,
and it was to them that the Lindeth people had listened.

Inda had seen during the very first exchange that their
gratitude for the defeat of the pirates was tempered by
fear. The harbormaster himself had visited each of the fleet
of traders that had followed Inda north. Some had lowered
boats, just to boom them up again after the harbormaster's
gig rowed away.

When at last the harbormaster was brought to *Death*,
the harbor folk's upturned faces were pale but determined
as the harbormaster stated that Elgar send one person
ashore—not himself—to negotiate. He could only come
ashore to pay just before his departure and none of his
crew was permitted ashore at any time.

"We've had too much destruction here," the old harbor-master said, his gaze shifting uneasily from Fox to Inda. "Don't want more, so we're not telling anyone who you are, and we won't let those traders that came in on your stern come ashore until you're gone."

Inda wondered who he thought would attack and then realized with a sick sense the harbormaster was afraid of the Marlovans that Inda had glimpsed on patrol through his glass.

Inda did not want to tell them why he himself felt obliged to avoid the Marlovans, so he just agreed.

He'd sent Dasta to negotiate, as he'd been raised by bee-keepers a little farther down the coast. Dasta—wearing a sashed sailor's smock and deck trousers, his sun-browned features unremarkable, his manner slow and easy except on the deck of an enemy—seemed the least piratical of the crew.

When Dasta returned, leading a fleet of supply boats and carpenters, he had reported, "When we're done loading you'll deal with the guild mistress. They are all afraid of you."

"I gathered that."

"As for news, no one knows anything of interest to us. They don't communicate with the Marlovans except if they have to. The pirate attacks have kept them fairly isolated. They were full of questions about the Brotherhood's defeat."

Inda's mind returned to the present when the boat bumped up against the floating dock. He and Tau tied the boat up, then looked at one of the barnacle-stippled pilings to check the flow of the tide, mentally gauging how long they could stay ashore.

Tau climbed up the seaweed-wrapped stairs to the pier. Inda stamped on the new planks of wood to get the feel of land under his feet again; he tried to envision the old harbor and the Pims' hiring table, but too much had changed.

Home. He was on Iascan soil again, though briefly. And not under his name, so he was not strictly breaking Captain Sindan's orders, but oh, the familiar smells, even in winter, cast him right back again to that terrible summer day when they first arrived here . . .

Inda had been silent too long. A glance showed Tau that Inda's gaze had already gone distant. So Tau led the way up

the dock toward the jumble of small houses patched together with wood and stone, their rows of windows, some
dark and fire-marked, jagged teeth of glass still thrusting
up or down, others alive with a dim golden glow.

Inda, blinded by the stream of images and emotions of
the past, did not see the transformed harbor, much less individuals in the present, but Tau—on the watch for the
king's gray-coated warriors—measured each pair of eyes
he encountered, then moved on when he saw no threat.
There was no threat, for example, in the steady hazel gaze
watching them from the shadow of one of the archways.
Tau glanced at the red-haired young man long enough to
note and then dismiss the plain coat of Runner blue; then
they were past.

That hazel gaze belonged to Evred, who'd recognized
Inda instantly, though in that broad-shouldered young man
in the loose-sleeved heavy linen shirt and long brown
rough-woven winter vest there remained little of the
eleven-year-old boy he knew. Inda had not grown very tall,
but he was at least as broad through the chest as Evred, his
face scarred, his hands big, his walk a rolling stride that set
his long brown queue swinging, his golden hoops dancing
at his ears, rubies winking with bloodred light. But the expression of those wide-set brown eyes was the same guile-
less inward gaze of the eleven-year-old boy, and Evred
hesitated; in the space of a single breath the world fractured into starbursts that whirled and spun and then
locked together into a new pattern that left Inda limned in
invisible white fire.

He shook away the reaction, meeting the wary gaze of
the tall, golden-haired young man at Inda's side. Evred half-
raised a hand, then he too was overwhelmed by memory:
Tanrid's dying voice, *Find Inda,* and his own promise, *I will.*

In that moment Inda and Tau turned the makeshift corner at the newly built Sailor's Rope Inn, its freshly painted
sign swinging above the door, and followed the lane between the half-repaired houses that they'd been told would
lead to the guild mistress.

So when Evred dropped his hand and said, "Inda?"
there were only incurious Idayagans to hear; traffic moved

along on the high street beyond the stone archway but Inda and his companion had vanished.

Furious with himself for being a fool, Evred dashed up the street toward the harbormaster's, for of course they would go there.

The vagaries of wind, weather, roads, and horses had thus brought Yvana-Vayir's four assassins to Ala Larkadhe on the very day that their lord attacked the royal city, though neither party could have foreseen such timing.

And so, while the assassins were dismounting below the weird white tower, far south in the royal city Tlennen-Harvaldar emerged from his rooms to the sound of shouting and the clash of swords. He thought: *Pirates attacking the castle? No, for those are Marlovan horns . . .*

He ran to his son's rooms. Shock stopped his breath in his throat when he saw the bloodstains and shattered furnishings. On the floor lay four blood-covered bodies. Little lights sparkled across Tlennen's vision when he recognized the yellow-blue livery on the dead.

He stepped around them to the bedroom beyond and there his son lay sprawled on the crimson rug on the floor, fingers gripping a fallen cavalry sword.

Three swift steps and he knelt by his son, whose face was peaceful in death as it never had been in life. Tlennen touched the long lashes resting on Aldren's lean cheeks, the brow almost smoothed of the faint creases of frustration that had shadowed his son's efforts to communicate all his days, and anguish ripped through him. For an excruciating time he could not breathe. Tears of horror, of anger, most of all of the bitterest regret welled up through years and years of anxious waiting, and watching, and standing aside because custom demanded it, exigencies of kingship required it, and his brother's platitudes and talk of duty made it easier to postpone another struggling conversation in which he and Aldren shared so very little.

Shared so little beyond flesh and blood. *Heart of my heart, and now you lie dead, and it is forever too late to make amends*. Sobs shook Aldren's father, tears burned down his face, dripping, unheeded, onto his son's brow. He rocked back and forth, the world narrowed to anguish, until faint sounds roused him.

Yvana-Vayir. The old ambition.

Evred.

"Evred." He whispered the name, urgency breaking the paralysis of sorrow. He rose to his feet while scanning around him, but of course there would be no pen or paper in Aldren's rooms.

There was always paper in his own pockets.

He picked up the blood-smeared sword and slashed his own arm, using his own welling blood and the nail of his forefinger to scratch out the words "Protect Evred."

The sounds came nearer. Quick, quick.

He jumbled the paper together and thrust it into the locket he always wore, twin to the one Jened Sindan always wore. He completed the spell as the door slammed open.

In Ala Larkadhe Captain Sindan was finishing his personal drill with the arms master in the barracks. He felt the magic summons and brought the sword bout to a close. Still in work shirt and breeches, he stepped outside, ignoring the cold, where he retrieved the locket and pulled out the paper.

He stared down in shock at the sticky, reddish smears until he made out the two words scratched so awkwardly: "Protect Evred."

It was then that a young page appeared. "Captain Sindan! Messengers from the Jarl of Yvana-Vayir. They insist on seeing Evred-Varlaef."

The message transfer was immediate, but no one else in the kingdom save Ndara-Harandviar had access to magic transferred messages. Any message from Yvana-Vayir, therefore, had to have been dispatched weeks ago. Logic denied any connection between this blood-smeared exhortation and the unexpected arrivals, but instinct brought Sindan upstairs at a run, the king's message still in his hand.

He reached the archive as a young Runner-in-training stopped outside the great carved doors, saying cheerfully to four men in Yvana-Vayir colors, "Well, since he's not at mess or drill or his rooms he's got to be in there reading. You can knock, and if he doesn't come out, you can give your message to Nightingale, his Runner, who's down at drill—"

Sindan lifted his hand and the youth backed away. Sindan moved to the archive doors and set his back to them. "I am Sindan," he said, knowing the Yvana-Vayir armsmen would recognize his name, if not his face. "You can give your message to me."

The four looked at one another, and their spokesman said, "It's a personal message. From our lord."

"About treachery," added another, licking his lips.

Eyes, hands, manner, suggested anticipation of violence.

"He cannot be disturbed," Jened Sindan stated, crushing the bloody paper in his fist.

"Let us knock, and he can tell us himself, king's Runner," said the spokesman, who was thinking, *The king must be dead by now.*

"No," Sindan said, and tucked the paper into a pocket.

Four swords were drawn; Sindan already held his.

"Get out of the way," warned one, who felt uneasy at four men in their prime facing a single old fellow of near seventy—though one with a hero's reputation.

"No," Sindan said again. He gripped his sword in one hand; in a swift move he grabbed a boot knife with the other and settled into a defensive stance.

The four exchanged a look and charged.

The young Runner felt at his sash. No knife, not for boys on inside castle duty. He ran for help.

In the royal city, there was a quick tap at the queen's door.

Hadand motioned to her women on guard, and one called for identification. Hearing a woman's voice outside, Hadand said, "Let her enter."

One of the queen's night maids slipped in, her face

twisted in terror. She ran past Hadand and flung herself
down at the arm of the queen's chair, her skirts billowing
around her, and whispered.

"Dead?" The queen started up. "My son is *dead?*"

She pushed past her women, all crowding around her
now, their voices shrill as they asked questions no one answered. The queen stalked to her bedroom and shut herself
in.

Her women stood outside, stricken, fearful, incapacitated by the sound of sobs, a sound the older ones had not
heard since their first days in this place.

The Sierlaef, dead?

It's a conspiracy, Hadand thought, and because there
were no orders from Ndara-Harandviar, who would herself have come first to the queen, Hadand had to push
aside questions—disbelief—and take action.

She motioned for the inside guards to remain at the
ready, then slipped out, signed for the hall guards to follow,
and ran for the throne room. If indeed a conspiracy had
turned into action, surely someone would end up there.

Chapter Twenty-eight

EVRED dashed through the jumble of cottages to the harbormaster's newly finished building at the high end of the street. Those who recognized him stopped in their tasks.

"Prince Evred?" the harbormaster's chief scribe asked, afraid at the intensity in the prince's face—hectic flush, tight mouth, wide stare—when he'd always seemed so calm and remote.

"The captain of that black ship out there. Where is he?"

The scribe hesitated, unwilling to be the one to speak, and turned to his colleagues. Most shrugged, many of them in honest ignorance.

The scribe wondered if the prince's sudden appearance had anything to do with his conversation with that Guild Fleet fellow this morning—so easy to talk to, that fellow had been, so interested; the scribe had spent the day since anxious that he'd said too much, especially after the fellow vanished without talking to the harbormaster at all. "I do not know anything except that the harbormaster went to a private interview." *I won't say too much now,* he thought.

But the chart mistress, an older woman, glanced up from her desk, brushing back a strand of gray hair. "At the guild mistress', wasn't it?" she asked, looking vaguely around the room. "Were they not handling those affairs there?"

Evred flung a "Thank you," over his shoulder and ran

out. He dashed back up the hill, dodging people, horses, wagons, dogs, chickens, and mittened children.

He was fairly certain the guild mistress lived in the jumble of half-built houses beyond the new inn with the nautical sign; if not, Evred at least knew where Inda's boat was tied up. He'd go to the dock and wait there—all day, if need be.

He'd reached the archway where he'd first glimpsed Inda, and was looking about for the inn with the sailor painted on it when a hand gripped his shoulder. He started violently and whipped around, a knife in his hand. A passing woman gasped and dropped her roll of cloth; a tradesman backed away hastily, almost falling under the wheels of a cart.

But Evred did not see them. He glared at Vedrid, whose gaze flicked from the knife to the fury in the prince's face. He backed up a step and saluted. "Evred-Varlaef. You must come at once."

Evred looked around, his mind floundering to find sense in the sudden whirlwind of sensation. "What?"

Vedrid opened his hand toward Nightingale, who stood with three sweaty horses, looking pale and wide-eyed. "I was at the perimeter on watch, as you ordered, and saw him riding at the gallop," Vedrid said in Marlovan, aware of the staring harbor folk.

Nightingale spoke in a quick, low voice. "After you left, Captain Sindan was attacked."

"By—"

A quick look. "Yellow and blue livery. He's—" Nightingale shut his mouth and shook his head, unwilling to say the word *dying,* but they saw it in his manner.

Evred closed his eyes. War, need. Duty. First the sound, then the sense. He had missed his chance—his single chance. The self-hatred caused by this inescapable realization was so intense it was physical. *I let him go.*

There would be no justice yet again, and this time because he was the fool who had lost Inda.

But he was a fool with duty before him: he would simply have to find another time, another way. He opened his eyes and became aware of curious eyes surrounding him. Including a pair of his own guards veering from sentry patrol, surprised and dismayed to find him there in Runner blue.

"Surprise inspection," he said. "Carry on." And to Nightingale and Vedrid, "Let us depart at once."

The king knelt by the side of his dead son, unaware of the time that had passed, until a riding of men wearing Yvana-Vayir yellow and blue slammed the door open and dashed in, spreading out, swords and knives in hand. They clattered to a stop, staring at the king, at the dead heir, and one another, their purposeful movements now uncertain. The man before them was unarmed, and unhated; he was the same king they had seen at a distance a month ago, taking the yearly sworn oath of their own Jarl.

Though they'd cut down the king's personal Runners in his chambers, this was the *king*. No one wanted to be the first to strike.

Tlennen-Harvaldar got slowly to his feet, his hands empty, and met each pair of eyes.

"Our Jarl ordered us here, Tlennen-Harvaldar," said the Yvana-Vayir riding captain, who had the most ambition.

The king said, softly, "Are you forsworn?"

Looks, uneasy stances, and then another said, his gaze midway between the king and his captain, "Not to our Jarl."

From the doorway came Mad Gallop's voice, "Kill him!"

Yvana-Vayir's men stepped forward, but no one raised a weapon. Mad Gallop bawled, "Anderle, my son!"

Hawkeye joined him, grimacing at the name he hated. Tlennen-Harvaldar looked old, his gray hair disheveled, a golden locket hanging against his robes. Old, and he was the king.

The Jarl's gaze moved back and forth. "You ignored your brother's treachery, Tlennen," he said, every word loud, as if loudness made it more true. "You always protected him. Even when he was wrong. That's the weakness of family sentiment. The times demand strength. Strength of will. Starting here."

Tlennen shook his head slightly. "If you take the crown, Yvana-Vayir, I hope you are wise enough to see before I did that its weight warps will. And strength. And vision. So that what seems right can be the wrong decision, and you are left forever making amends—or compounding your errors."

"Hear that?" Mad Gallop demanded, glaring at his hesitant men. "Hear him admit he's wrong? In a king, is that not treason against our forefathers?" And when the king said nothing, the Jarl turned to his heir. "Execute justice, Anderle," his father ordered. "Kill him!"

Hawkeye gripped his sword, looking past his father to the king, whose face was still wet with tears of grief, and he shook his head. "He did not betray us."

"I will have you, king!" Mad Gallop shouted, drops of spittle dotting Hawkeye's grimy coat.

"No," Hawkeye said again. "He's the *king*. It was the Sierlaef who—" He stopped at a familiar sound from outside.

War horns reverberated, echo after echo.

A shout came from somewhere below: "Algara-Vayir green!"

Mad Gallop bellowed in rage; Hawkeye stared at the king, at his father, at the men, recognizing his own reluctance in them. They were waiting for him to act.

So either he disobeyed his father, or he committed a far greater wrong and obeyed him by killing the king.

Nothing he could do here was right—except getting help.

So he turned his back on them all and ran.

He didn't get far. On the first landing he nearly ran down Buck Marlo-Vayir and hound-faced Noddy Toraca, who had been brought by Cama. They had been racing up the stairs as fast as he'd been descending. Hawkeye stumbled to a stop.

Before anyone could speak, Cama and Cherry-Stripe clattered down the hallway, having come up the main staircase. Cherry-Stripe had his sword in hand.

Noddy said, "Hawkeye's in it?"

Cherry-Stripe pointed his sword. "You attacked the king?"

Hawkeye, sick almost to the point of dizziness, shook his head. "No. It's my father's plot. Look, he's got the king in the Sierlaef's rooms right now. The Sierlaef's already dead. I think the Harskialdna might be, too, or he'd be here. My father sent an entire riding after him. I swear—on my honor—I did not know what he meant to do." His voice broke at the end. "I can't stop him—he *ordered* me to . . . I don't know what to do."

They stood there, questions in all their faces as Hawkeye struggled to command his emotions.

Buck jabbed his sword toward Cama and Noddy, who had arrived from the north moments after the big cavalcade, having ridden in their muddy trail most of the way. "You didn't go north?"

Cama said briefly, "Noddy sent Runners. Faster—they know their trails. We thought we might be needed here."

Buck turned to Hawkeye, then looked away from the tears in his old academy mate's eyes. He hefted his sword. "To the king."

He and his brother ran upstairs, followed by their own Runners. Cama remained, his one good eye narrowed in cold anger, Noddy next to him. Both with swords drawn and ready.

Hawkeye cast down the weapon he realized was still gripped in his hand. "It's my father's plot. Not mine." He squeezed his eyes shut, wrenched by guilt and remorse. *I never should have told him.*

Noddy sighed, leaning on his sword. It seemed it was his job to guard Hawkeye, though no one was giving orders. "Truth is, I don't know what to believe. Rousted out of bed by Cama here the very morning I get home from Convocation, my own Runners sent at the gallop—not even a change of clothes—northward to Sponge, us riding day and night. Blood all down the hall that way." He jerked a thumb up and backward, his long, jowly face wry. "Has the world gone mad?"

"Not the world," Cama commented, lifting his head at the sound of shouts, adding sourly, "Just us."

The voices neared. Cherry-Stripe clattered back down the stairs, grimacing. "It's all over," he said. "King's

dead." He expelled his breath in a whoosh. King dead—
no one in charge. Cherry-Stripe tried to marshal his
thoughts. The Jarl of Yvana-Vayir was a king killer, but
here was his son. What to say? The ballads sure didn't
give any hints about this situation. "Hawkeye, your dad
and his men ran off down one of the other hallways. Any
idea where to?"

Cama whistled. "This damn castle is enormous. We could
run around a week and never find them. What now?"

Hawkeye wiped his eyes on his sleeve. He drew a short
breath. "Any of you know if the king had time to give orders to Ndara-Harandviar before my father and I got upstairs? Where's Hadand?"

No one even thought of Queen Wisthia.

Cama jerked his chin over his shoulder toward the stairway leading down. "Women have the lower passageways
guarded below. Saw 'em taking over behind me. Are there
any women up there?"

"No," Noddy said. "We didn't see anybody."

"King's Runners are all dead in his chambers. Not all of
them armed." Cherry-Stripe grimaced.

Hawkeye said, "This floor and above are all the royal
residence. Hadand will have all the public hallways and
landings guarded."

Cherry-Stripe remembered Hadand at their very first
academy game, doing knife tricks against her brother Tanrid. And his last two years at the academy, how she'd commanded the siege games and won. He remembered some
of the things Sponge had said about her. "Buck went off
looking for Hadand—"

Buck Marlo-Vayir appeared right then, leaping down
the stairs four at a time, and almost ran Hawkeye down before he fetched up against the rail. "No one up there, except women guarding the queen. Wouldn't listen, wouldn't
answer questions. They drew their bows on me when I demanded to talk to Hadand," he said, breathing hard. "So I
ran. Stopped to take a squint through the big windows
overlooking the garrison side. From the colors on the men
I'd say the Algara-Vayirs are here, and they're surrounding
the garrison buildings. Women on the heights, all of them

with bows drawn, aiming down inside. Would your father go to the garrison?"

Hawkeye shook his head slowly. "I think—I think he'd go to the throne room. We came there first, then straight up to the king's rooms, after he argued your dad down, Buck. He'll take the throne according to the old forms. In my mother's name."

Cherry-Stripe said, with conviction, "Then that's where Hadand's going to be, if she isn't up here. She's gonna turf him out."

"Father'll kill Hadand-Edli if she gets in his way," Hawkeye whispered. "I've got to try to stop him."

Above, reverberating off the stone walls, the castle bell began the deliberate, slow toll of lockdown, soon echoed by the city bells, faint and farther away.

The four looked up, then at one another. Hawkeye stooped, grabbed up his sword again, then began to run, using the servants' stairs, the others now right behind him.

Hawkeye stayed in the lead, hesitating only once or twice. He always seemed to know where the women would be, and how to avoid them. None of the others knew—and he did not tell them—that his father had had their castle rebuilt on the same model as the royal residence wing for their mother when they first married. Hawkeye had grown up being told it was romantic gesture, but he knew now his father had built himself a king's residence, and so he knew how it would be guarded.

Buck Marlo-Vayir muttered to his brother as they ducked down a narrow stair, "Did you see it the way I did? The king didn't even have a weapon. The way he fell, it's like he opened his arms to the blade."

"It's the blade for us all if Mad Gallop wins," Cherry-Stripe retorted, skidding on a rug and stopping himself with both hands against a wall, then launching himself after his brother.

They rounded a corner and pounded down the flagstone hall in the guest wing where the Jarl families stayed during Convocation.

"If so, we'll take as many of 'em with us as we can," Buck promised.

They reached the service entrance to the great hall, which was opposite the throne room, the two separated by a huge arched passage. These two vast chambers each had enormous iron-studded doors that would have been barred and held against the onslaught of enemy invasion in the old days.

Now the doors stood undefended because the Harskialdna had only considered this area first priority on the Guard roster during Convocation; pending specific orders the sentries' standing orders were to stay at the walls if the city bells tolled the lockdown.

So no one stopped them as they raced down the middle of the great hall, which was cold and empty, the massive tables still set out for the Jarls and their liege men, the dishes long since carried away. A trace of cabbage and rye aromas lingered in the frigid, motionless air.

Cama took the lead, but paused at the mighty doors at the other end. He and Buck shouldered them open and they ran across the passage between the great hall and the throne room. Those doors stood open.

They dashed in. There stood Hadand—flanked by two women—on the dais before the vacant throne, under the Montrei-Vayir banner. A cluster of men had gathered before the broad, shallow steps. Men with weapons drawn, some of the swords blood-smeared. Men, women, and swords were highlighted in the slanting shafts of sunlight from the clerestory windows along the walls to either side—they looked, at a glance, like one of the old tapestries.

"Stand *down*," Hadand ordered in the voice of one who has already said it several times.

"I have no quarrel with you, girl. You must let me pass," the Jarl of Yvana-Vayir stated, his voice, like hers, trembling from excitement, fear, determination.

Already ideas raced through his mind—set aside his son's recent marriage to that detestable young snake Dannor Tya-Vayir—Hawkeye marries Hadand, mortars the Yvana-Vayir kingship with the former heir's betrothed, daughter of a prince—

Hadand was struggling to comprehend what had happened and to think ahead, but this man was not giving her time to think. So her reasoning had narrowed to a single fact: he must not be permitted to sit on the throne.

Neither wanted to see the other dead. And so they held to the old forms, she standing on the dais before the throne, he below the steps on the stone floor, facing her, his feet in the place where the Jarls had stood to make their vows before the throne ever since Marlovans first captured this castle. "The king is dead, as is his brother," he said, raising his voice. *Be strong! Kings are strong!* He set his boot upon the first step. "Who committed treachery against the kingdom, against your own family." Another step. "The Sierlaef, at his uncle's orders, had your brother murdered!" He took the final step then, and stood on the dais looking down at Hadand, who did not move away from the throne; her women glided forward to flank her, their arms, like Hadand's, in the sleeves of their robes.

The Jarl of Yvana-Vayir ignored them. He raised his sword. "I now claim the throne in the name of my son, who is half Montrei-Vayir. And I warn you for the last time, stand aside!"

Hadand braced against the sickening sense in the pit of her stomach at the proximity of violence when there was no violence in her mind. She bit her numb lips, her face blotchy from the cold, from emotion, but her brown eyes were steady. "There is an heir. Evred-Varlaef."

The Jarl was not listening; he'd shifted his gaze to his sword, and the blood there. In his dreams, the Jarl had raised his sword just so, but Tlennen had surrendered to him as he stood there triumphant, surrounded by loyal men who cheered, who drummed. What happened was the king's unwavering gaze as he faced that killing sword—the flinch of pain as the steel juddered into living flesh—

The Jarl gripped the sword to steady himself. The king was dead. *I will be king, then my son. All I need to do is get this girl out of my way. If she will not obey me, she is no use. She's better off dead.*

". . . Evred Varlaef." He realized she'd spoken.

And the Jarl of Yvana-Vayir laughed, a triumphant little laugh that caused Hawkeye to gasp. Hadand's chin jerked up; she saw Hawkeye's face, the sudden and shocking realization there, and her mouth thinned.

"Father, don't!" Hawkeye yelled.

Furious with his son, the Jarl brought the sword down at the girl.

"Evred," Hadand whispered, and forced her watery knees to stiffen.

As the Jarl's bloody sword came down toward her in a killing strike, her body obeyed with all the strength and speed of years of determined drill.

Steel scraped on steel, warding the Jarl's sword mid-arc; the smooth deflection took him by surprise. He staggered, his balance off, and a jab of anger tightened his grip. He snapped the sword back, lunging straight at her, but Hadand-Edli had become a whirl of robes impossible to hit.

She deflected the Jarl's blade again, twirled within his defensive space, and in the same circular motion sliced one knife lightly across his throat, too lightly to kill. Then she buried the second knife up to the hilt in the shoulder joint on his right side, all between one heartbeat and the next. His sword clattered on stone. He brought his hand up to the spurting wound and fell to his knees.

His men started forward. The two women stepped silently between them and Hadand, their blades out, angled along their forearms, sharp and gleaming and steady.

Hadand cried, "Stand down in the name of Evred Montrei-Vayir!" just as Hawkeye shouted to the Yvana-Vayir men, sword out, "Hold!"

Then he stepped forward to where his father knelt, groaning and wheezing over and over, "Kill them. Kill them, boy. You. Be. *King* . . ."

Noise at the back of the room brought them all around. A riding of men in green coats ran through the double doors and fanned out, weapons raised: Algara-Vayirs.

Behind them appeared four Marlo-Vayir liege men and the Jarl. "Barracks is under guard," Hasta said to his son, wheezing slightly after having run, his bad hip aching.

Buck motioned the four liege men to surround Hawkeye and his father.

"Coward," Mad Gallop glared up at his son. "Coward."

Hasta grimaced at him, took in Hadand at the throne, and looked away; Hawkeye faced Cama and the Marlo-Vayir brothers, offering his sword, hilt out, his expression bleak. "Listen. Whatever happens to me, one of you had better ride north, make sure your Runners got there, Noddy. If Evred is alive, he's the only one who can hold the kingdom now."

"I'll see if my horse is still saddled," Noddy replied, relieved to have a clear duty—and even more relieved to get away from the tears in Hawkeye's eyes, the pain and embarrassment in his friends' faces, the angry ravings of the fallen Jarl. "Looks like it's back on the road for me."

Chapter Twenty-nine

JAREND-Adaluin, come to seek justice, found himself standing next to his daughter in command of the royal castle.

Elsewhere in the castle his men and the Marlo-Vayir and Yvana-Vayir armsmen, kept apart by the expertise of armed women, all stood about eyeing one another uncertainly. This lasted until Hadand asked Cama Tya-Vayir to go through the castle ordering any guards not on duty to report to the barracks, in the name of the king. She did not say which king. By then Jarend-Adaluin—listening to the disjointed exclamations from those around him as he stood at his daughter's side—had figured out most of what had happened, and he ordered his own men to escort the Yvana-Vayirs under drawn steel to the garrison prison.

Tradition and common sense guided Hadand and her father in their dazed attempt to restore order. First one by one and then in an ever increasing flood they issued orders. Tesar stood by Hadand's other side, blades out, and the Adaluin's gray-haired old Runner took up position behind him, sword in hand.

*   *   *

And so, riding back at the gallop from Lindeth Harbor to Ala Larkadhe, Evred Montrei-Vayir went, unknowing, from being Evred-Varlaef to Evred-Sierlaef.

About the time he arrived at the white tower, his father stood unresisting before the steel of Yvana-Vayir's ambition, and his son became Evred-Harvaldar.

In Ala Larkadhe, the Guard was out, weapons at the ready. Visitors had been summarily ejected. Evred dismounted at a run and dashed inside, forgetting that he wore a coat of unmarked blue.

His people looked at him in amazement. Much later he discovered that people thought he'd escaped the assassins by cleverness. At the time, he listened to the jumbled words shouted at him from all sides: Yvana-Vayir men always passed through before—said they had a verbal message, Jarl to prince—fight—Sindan defending the archive door—assassins all dead—

Sindan lying in his bunk dying, repeating Evred's name over and over.

Evred dashed through the barracks to Sindan's private chamber off the officers' duty room, which he rated as King's Runner Captain. Evred had seen death often enough during the past two years to recognize it in the blue lips, the unfocused eyes, even if he hadn't seen the great crimson stain across Sindan's shirt as he lay there on the narrow bed.

"Ev . . . red . . ."

Evred flung himself down at the side of the bed. "Uncle Sindan. Try not to speak."

But the one good hand groped for his, and paper pressed into his fingers. The sharp-sweet scent of blood clogged Evred's constricted throat. "Necklet," Sindan whispered, in Sartoran.

Necklet? Had he gotten the word wrong?

Sindan's fingers moved to his chest, feeling restlessly, then slipped to his side; the effort had defeated lifelong and patient strength of will at last. Evred, staring down in misery and question, saw the glint of gold at Sindan's neck. He reached down, feeling with gentle fingers. There was a long chain. Up came a locket smeared with red.

Aware from just beyond the reach of the physical world that he had discharged his last duty, Jened Sindan gave a sigh and died.

Evred straightened up, the bloodstained gold loose in his fingers. "I have to send a message to my father," he stated in a flat voice, and walked upstairs, motioning for Nightingale to flank him.

No one followed or spoke. Most of the Guard were too busy searching out other assassins, and finding nothing but cold shadows and curious and speculative looks from the locals here with their demands and complaints.

Evred ran to his rooms, but before he sought pen and paper, he remembered the paper in his hand and opened it up. It, too, was blood-smeared and gritty from being crushed. He could barely make out his own name. After close examination directly next to a lamp he realized two things: that the other word was "protect" and that it was not just smeared with blood, but written in it.

He dropped it onto the table. "Where did this come from?" No answer, of course. He looked up at Nightingale Toraca, who stood in the doorway facing outward, knife in hand. "Summon Tlen. He's going to have to take command here. I have to go home," he said. "Now."

While he was packing his belongings—the locket tied with care in a square of silk, just as it was, to be given to his father—and issuing orders for Flash Arveas as aide to Jasid Tlen, a short ride coastward in Lindeth, Inda sat in the guildmistress' house.

He and Tau had been kept waiting. Then they'd had to endure a long and tedious but exact list of goods and services rendered, first donations and then those for which he was expected to pay. Each item was ticked off by clerks for the guilds and the harbormaster.

At last it was over, just as the tide was about to turn. Inda studied the faces around him. "That's settled, then?"

The harbormaster, the guild mistress, and the others who had insisted on attending this meeting all murmured assent.

Inda pulled a purse from his winter vest and counted out the heavy silver six-sided Sartoran coinage. Two or three people leaned forward. Most everyone recognized Sartoran coins, but they were rare this far west.

"I believe that's the equivalent," he said. "According to the value table your own people sent me."

"Fair enough," said the harbormaster, a gaunt, austere man who had been born when Lindeth was free and who remembered the conquering Marlovan king fifty years before. He knew that Lindeth Harbor was by far getting the best of the bargain, and his innate honesty jibed at him until he said, "From all the reports, what you have thus given us in sail-craft, we are probably in your debt."

The guildmistress, even older than the harbormaster, pursed her lips. Then said defensively, "We must pay for those services that were not part of the donation agreement, and it must be done now, as you are sailing. We do not know how the ships you left us will value out."

Inda flicked open his hand, palm up—a Marlovan gesture, from the long-ago days when it was important to show no concealed knife. But Iascans no longer knew what it signified.

Tau observed the subtle signs of distrust and wariness after Inda's gesture, as Inda said, "I am not arguing, but I do need to go, if you want to see the last of us."

The others stirred, some of them avoiding others' gazes. Inda had recognized that the long wait was partly the back of the hand at Marlovan pirates and partly what they'd consider prudence—to release him just in time for the tide to turn so he'd not stop anywhere on his way out. "Listen," Inda said. "Many of the Brotherhood ran. They might try something new, so get those ships repaired and don't relax your watch."

The harbormaster looked grim. "We will continue to keep night as well as day watch, you may be assured."

Inda flicked up a hand. Most of his cash reserves were now gone, but his own ships were in a fair way to being repaired. The last things could be done by his own carpenters under sail. More important, each ship was laden with goods against the long journey ahead.

He looked around, saw questions in some faces.

"May we ask your plans?" asked the old guildmistress.

Inda knew distrust when he saw it. And so, to whom would they pass any answer? "Whatever I do will be far away from here."

Exchanges of looks. Inda turned to leave.

A tall, black-haired young man, who had lounged against the side wall during the whole interview, watching from under lazy eyelids, straightened up and stepped in Inda's path. He said in flat-accented Marlovan, "We know who you are." The words were Marlovan, but the verb endings Iascan.

Inda gave him no more than a glance, stepped around him, and walked out. Tau got up and followed—or began to.

The lounger's hand shot out and gripped his arm. "Is he really Elgar the Fox? The son of the Prince of Choraed Elgaer?"

Tau looked down at the fingers gripping his arm, waiting until they loosened and then dropped. The man backed up a step, hands held up in mocking apology.

"Ask him," Tau replied, and closed the door behind him.

The harbormaster looked up wryly. "Well, Mardric?"

Mardric shrugged. Obviously whoever that scar-faced pirate and his pretty companion were or were not, Elgar the Fox hadn't the remotest knowledge of or interest in the Resistance against the Marlovan conquerors. Except that that short young fellow—he'd swear he was even younger than the princeling up at Ala Larkadhe—was not the tall, red-haired commander clad in black that the traders he'd visited in secret at midnight had all insisted was in command of the flagship that defeated the red sails.

During the time the pirates had been kept waiting Mardric had slipped out once to hear from the spies he'd sent to observe the two at the pier and then on the main road, where the gray-coated Marlovan sentries patrolled. Elgar and his golden-haired mate had made no attempt to speak to any of them. They had also walked by the Marlovans without the latter betraying any sign of recognition. He was certain it would be the same on the way back.

"I'd call that a waste of breath," the harbormaster added.

Mardric laughed. Indeed. So much for his plan to try to hire or lure these pirates—especially if led by an exiled Marlovan—to do some fighting against the Marlovans for Olara! But he never admitted defeat—out loud.

He said, "I'd call it a good try."

The harbormaster turned his head. "Well, Mistress Pim? You're the only one who has seen their Lord Indevan Algara-Vayir. Was one of those men he?"

From a side room came a straight-browed young woman. "Yes," she said. "The short, ugly one. He hasn't changed much since I found him in that pirate harbor in the east, except to get uglier." She touched her jawline.

"Ugly? Not at all," Mardric drawled. "Perhaps not as finished as his golden-haired mate, but pretty enough, despite the scars." He was thoroughly enjoying the unspoken disgust in Ryala Pim's face, the revulsion in the guildmistress': their firm stance on the moral high ground obviously did not include the possibility of pirates being attractive.

Sure enough, the guild mistress said in her precise, disdainful voice, "But we still don't know if he's Elgar the Fox."

The harbormaster nodded. "Anyone might wear black, but neither of them is red-haired."

Ryala Pim said with disgust, "That Lord Indevun called himself Elgar when he hired on our ships. He is a Marlovan *and* a pirate. You can't tell me he paid for that black raffee out there, nor did he earn what he sent to repay me."

"Ah, so you spurn the pirate but not his money, eh?" Mardric retorted.

Ryala Pim flushed. "My mother says money is money. It has no wish or will. And we were owed." Several nodded silently from the background.

Mardric dropped his voice, affecting seriousness. "Whoever he is, if we can't make use of him, he's better out in the ocean drawing the Venn out there than drawing them here."

"True," said the guild mistress. "We have enough of both, pirates and Venn. And Marlovans."

"We do owe him a debt," the harbormaster stated. "I mean the coastal harbors."

"We won't forget that," the guildmistress said. "But that doesn't mean we owe any of *them* allegiance." She pointed through the tightly closed window, past which a pair of Marlovan guards rode by on their ceaseless patrol. "I say, don't tell them anything about the pirates, whoever they are."

And everyone agreed.

Outside Inda and Tau dropped into their boat and caught the last of the tidal flow. They were carried out to their waiting ships, which soon set sail for the unknown waters of the northwest and the legendary Ghost Isles.

Chapter Thirty

*S*TONE, cold stone, all around. Does it see? Does it hear? Does it remember? Kialen pressed back against the gritty wall, terrified by screams, shouts, clangs of steel, until the sounds drowned in the rising and falling melody of "Alandais Lament." It was old, older than the stone. So old and so secret Mistress Resvaes, who had come all the way from Sartor a couple of years before, would have been shocked to hear it echoing down the darkened hallways— not that it could be heard by any in this world.

Kialen shivered beside the wall until the only sounds beside the distant voices were the bells. No longer the terrible slow tolls of emergency lockdown, but the *dang-dang, dang-dang, dang-dang* of Daylast.

Night had fallen. She could move again, unseen. Safe from killing steel.

Her hands and feet had gone numb. Slowly she glided away, a wraith in the deepening shadows. Her own thin voice joined in the song.

"*. . . and the gates did open, and there was a new world, radiant with beauty and peace.*

"*And after the humans came, bringing sickness and greed, hunger and pain, the elder kind did sing: O human women, is sorrow borne in your seed?*

"*No, elder kind, the women answered. We love, we laugh, we spin, we make, but we need plenty for peace. And they*

*gave the women plenty. We need magic for peace. And they
gave the women magic."*

Her sweet, breathy voice keening like a reed in the winter wind, Kialen left the silent stone and drifted from room
to room, where glowglobes had lit in response to the fading of day. There lay the Sierlaef, darkening blood
splotches against the bright crimson rug, surrounded by
those he had slain. Near him the king, so still, face toward
his son. She laid upon each desecrated breast a single white
lily, unseen by any in this world, and then passed out of the
room, singing.

*". . . and elder kind said: We have given you magic, we
have given you plenty. Yet human kind spreads terror and
pain, and we ask again, O human women, is sorrow borne
in your seed?"*

Through Aunt Ndara's room.

*". . . and so the women turned their hand against men who
burned with desire for children."*

There was Aunt Ndara, lying next to the Evil One.

*"They turned their hand against men who mated with the
weak by force."*

Kialen straightened Ndara's arms, so terribly slashed
and slashed again. She pressed a kiss upon her cold brow,
then resumed the lament.

*"And last they vowed to turn their hand against those who
make war . . ."*

Kialen unfastened the locket round Ndara's neck, obedient to a promise made long ago. She laid a last lily down
in her aunt's quiet hands and bore away the locket, still
singing, as she stepped into Hadand's silent rooms.

*". . . when Norsunder came, with promises of life and
power and an end to the silent war of time."*

There she laid the locket down, and then she retreated
to her own bower, full of lilies, bright as spring, gleaming in
a sun from very long ago.

*". . . and we strove, and they strove, until all the singing
disirad stilled, and the sky wept and the sun shone no more
on human make."*

She took from a secret casket a vial of the dream-flower.

"And the elder came yet again, and sang to those who

were left, O human women, we shared with you our world, and you have nearly unmade it, tell us the truth at last: Is sorrow borne in your seed?"

Still singing, she paused only long enough to gulp down the sweet liquor in the vial, and then lay upon her bed. She sang softly now, lilies gathered in her hands, until the ancient melody was joined by other voices, sweet voices, high and clear and good, voices bearing her away on a sighing tide, as her breast rose and fell one last time.

"Is sorrow borne in your seed?"

Chapter Thirty-one

EVRED was met two days outside of Ala Larkadhe by Noddy's Runners, who had been dispatched the day that Cama reached Noddy. They were the first to alert Evred that there might be trouble in the royal city.

He commanded his host to hasten.

They were met more than halfway home by an impressive cavalcade of armsmen belonging to three houses, led by Noddy Toraca himself, Tuft Sindan-An, and Cherry-Stripe Marlo-Vayir, who had insisted at the last moment on accompanying Noddy. Tuft had joined with a flight of his father's men when Noddy and Cherry-Stripe passed through his family land.

They took turns telling Evred everything they knew, though it took a couple of days to make sense of the splintered accounts. But before they saw the winter-bound city on the horizon he had assembled a fairly accurate picture of what he'd find.

In the meantime he had to contend with his own emotions.

His father was dead. Grief chilled his spirit when he thought of never seeing him in the archive poring over a text, the talks they would never have. At least he would not have to tell his father about Jened Sindan. Once or twice he considered tossing that stained locket away into the snow, but instinct stayed his hand. He had assumed that it was a love-gift of his father's, but there had been far too much urgency in the way Sindan had hung onto his life just to say that one word.

The last day of their journey, his entourage, knowing they would soon reach the royal city, broke out their House tunics and weapons, everything polished and shining. Evred put on his old gray academy coat.

Noddy appeared at his tent flap, resplendent in a rich brown tunic with a crimson marmot: Khani-Vayir colors. "Gray?" His straight brows lifted. "I'm not much for strut in the ordinary way of things, but this does seem to be the time."

"When you left," Evred said, "I had a crown waiting. You of all people ought to know how quickly things can change."

Noddy pursed his lips. "There is that. But they'd have to get past Hadand-Edli first."

Nobody else said anything. The earlier freedom had vanished, and everyone, from friends down to armsmen, now maintained a scrupulous distance that Evred felt almost as an invisible wall forming by universal will. He was separate now, he was a king. Their behavior invested him with the power of kingship; he had done nothing yet to grasp it.

He was mulling the nature of power when they sighted the royal city. Armsmen were posted all along the walls: Montrei-Vayir crimson mixed with the sky blue and dark green of the Marlo-Vayirs, and the brown and crimson of Khani-Vayir. All wore black sashes. To Evred, that indicated a universal desire for order.

The city streets were crowded, cold as it was. When he passed, cheers and fists against hearts were proof again that that mysterious act of will on the parts of people he had never met had transformed him into a king.

They rode through the great gates of the castle to the central courtyard and stopped at the passage between the great hall and the throne room. The big iron-reinforced double doors to the throne room stood open, black-sashed guards at either side to hold back the crowds of city folk gathered there despite the freezing air. More cheers, more fists thumping chests as he and his entourage passed inside, joining all those already gathered there. Someone blew the bugle-call for the king's arrival, and all fell silent. Evred could hear breathing, felt the weight of gazes, as he walked up the broad stone steps of the dais.

Hadand waited at the side of the throne, dressed in Algara-Vayir green except for a black sash. At her left, in Shield Arm position, stood Cama Tya-Vayir; Evred knew it was he who had taken control of the Guard. To her right stood Buck Marlo-Vayir. Both wore formal House colors.

Hadand greeted him with her fist against her heart.

He held out his hands to her, met those wide-set, honest brown eyes, and felt a faint shock when she drew in a small breath and her eyelids gleamed with sudden tears. But they did not fall as she briefly touched his hands. "I have kept everything as it was," she said so only he could hear.

Evred opened a hand, already distracted, for every pair of eyes watched him, each face a mirror of questions, demands, exclamations held in check.

He lifted his voice. "Let the word be spread through the kingdom: as is traditional, the coronation will be held Midsummer's Day."

A tumult of voices rose, echoing off the stone to a skull-shattering roar. Evred walked off the dais through the narrow door at the side, followed by those who had awaited him there. Hadand's Runner shut the door after the last, diminishing the noise to a distant roar.

"Where is Jarend-Adaluin?" Evred asked, turning from one to another.

"Went home. Declared justice given. Took his banner. And Joret," Cama said, his voice rougher than usual. "We've been holding the Yvana-Vayirs in the garrison, and *their* Runners." He glanced upward with his one eye on the word "their," and Evred knew he meant the Runners of his brother and uncle. "The few left alive."

More mess: so the old Jarl hadn't died of the wounds Hadand had given him. Damn. And what would he do with his brother's Runners? His uncle's?

"Take me upstairs," Evred said to Hadand. "Everything else can wait."

The two of them left the anteroom, followed by their

personal Runners, who shut the outer door and guarded it, as signals went from female to male guards. In concert they began conducting people out of the throne room and to the gates.

Neither Hadand nor Evred spoke on that long journey to the upper level of the residence.

They walked through the doors locked for more than a month and shut their Runners out to guard. A muffled thump had to be Nightingale setting his back to the door; they heard Tesar's low murmur as she introduced herself and took up a stance beside him.

They were now alone. In Aldren-Sierlaef's rooms the smell of old blood hit them, and Hadand moved to open windows to the freshening flow of snow-laden air. The bodies had been Disappeared, but the blood and disarray lay untouched, unwanded, so that Evred could witness it.

"I have reconstructed what must have happened," Hadand said after a long pause. "Different bands of Yvana-Vayir armsmen went after your brother and uncle, probably at the same time. Aldren took down four of them before a fifth got him. Your father came in right after—but I think you know the rest."

Evred grimaced. "Noddy and Cherry-Stripe did not know what happened to my uncle, but assumed he was dead."

"Yes." She pressed her fingers briefly against her face, her fingertips against her closed eyelids. Then she dropped her hands and opened her eyes. "I found your uncle lying in Aunt Ndara's inner chamber. He had died of so many cuts I can only guess that an entire riding came after him, too many for him to fight. He had one of his own knives in his ribs. He fell very close to her. She too was considerably cut up, but mostly about the arms, except for a long one on her neck and several on her upper back. In short I don't know if Ndara died by assassins' blades, or by his hand. The Yvana-Vayir men we questioned insisted she was dead when they saw her." Hadand hesitated, unsure whether or not to share her speculations about Ndara's death.

"I think I'd rather not find out the truth, since it changes nothing," Evred said, and when she opened her hands in agreement, "Was there much fighting otherwise?"

"Very little. I sent my women to hold the castle as soon as I discovered there was trouble." Hadand added wryly, "As for the Guard barracks, I suspect the Marlo-Vayirs and Yvana-Vayirs did not want to fight one another any more than they wanted to fight us. Not when they'd been riding together for over a week."

"And the Guard?"

"My father rode up and took over. Ordered them all to stand down. Half of them were exhausted, having been riding through the snow for days with the Sierlaef. They'd just gone off duty. The others were tired from doubled watches. Nobody argued."

Evred could imagine their confusion, the consternation that there was no invading enemy, only Marlovans, and which colors would be the enemy? "So the Marlo-Vayirs did not know about Yvana-Vayir's plans?"

"Not a hint. Mad Gallop only talked of justice. The Jarl of Marlo-Vayir ordered his men to stop the Yvana-Vayirs after their Jarl gave his orders to kill. I think certain of the Yvana-Vayir captains knew the plot. Had promises of future glory. The captains give confused testimony, some saying they had an idea, some swearing they didn't, but once the killing began, they all knew they had crossed that inward boundary between treason and what one called making history. He talked a lot about that, I gather. 'Making history.' It seems to be defined by killing. You will not have a pleasant task, judging them."

"No. So this assault took you, too, by surprise?"

"Completely." Her color changed again. "All I knew was that the Sierlaef had apparently—well, it no longer matters. I'd heard two days before from Chelis about Barend and the owl ring, and that my father was coming with a war banner. If he did appear and throw down a war pennant before the throne, that would be king's business, but I'd had my women on alert. So everyone had been going about armed with their bows and we let the Guard think it was drill. Thus we were able to deploy fast."

"So I must first examine the Yvana-Vayirs," Evred said, feeling a band of tension tighten around his skull. It was a familiar sensation, the one he'd felt whenever he had to sit in judgment between Marlovans and Idayagans. "Before I do, I'd like to hear your conclusions."

Hadand drew a shaky breath. "I believe the plot began and ended with Mad Gallop Yvana-Vayir. Hawkeye was as surprised as the Marlo-Vayirs when Mad Gallop announced his real plan—and hinted that someone was sent against you."

"It's true. Sindan died instead."

Hadand recoiled, shock and sorrow widening her eyes. "I thought . . . I thought he was . . ." Her voice trailed off.

"Left in charge of Ala Larkadhe? I don't think I could have prevented him from coming home, had he known about—" Evred waved a hand toward the bloodstained rugs, then rubbed his forehead. *Kill the king.* Anger burned into fury behind his ribs, but he had to get control. Think, not feel. He'd seen the evidence of letting emotions control actions. Seen it and lived it in his own mistakes. "You're certain Hawkeye knew nothing?"

"As certain as I can be. He refused at least twice, in front of witnesses, to obey his father's will. Surely Cama told you that?"

"Yes. But I wanted to hear it from you." Evred opened his hand, then turned slowly, looking from object to object in the room. She watched him covertly.

He was so tall, his austere profile so like his father's, and yet so unlike. His dark red hair waved up into its clasp and hung down to the small of his back, his hands were the long, fine hands of his family, roughened by daily drill. He was her own dear Evred in his academy gray, yet he wasn't; there were faint lines around his eyes from his long rides in the northern summer sun, from whatever tensions he'd endured during that time. Though only twenty he was a man grown, and despite the ravaged chamber, despite her awareness of the many waiting outside to demand the new king's attention, her heart fluttered in her ribs like a caged swift. She fought the urge to step closer to him, to hear his breathing, to smell his scent, to look up into his eyes. To touch him.

But he didn't want her. He would never want her.

She forced her mind away from awareness of him, disgusted with herself. *Here he stands, not a handbreadth from where his father bled out his life, and all I can think of is . . .* She shied away from even that much acknowledgment of her emotions. "Maybe if people weren't already tired of the demands of war there might have been more trouble," she said, because this was what mattered to him most, and he would need her help. "Under all the talk of loyalty and oaths I hear a fear of chaos. People want you to fix what's wrong. And there's a lot wrong."

She paused, and he gestured agreement. She resumed, her even tone and the flow of words now sounding rehearsed to him, who was sensitive to every subtlety in her voice.

"After that first week we had ridings appear from Ola-Vayir, from Stalgrid Tya-Vayir—the one you call Horse-butt—from friends and foes of your uncle, some demanding fulfillment of secret promises your uncle Anderle had made, others demanding justice in the form of more lands and grants. But my father's warriors and Cama and the Marlo-Vayirs forced them all to sheer off. Cama stood at my shoulder looking tough, and he had the Guard drilling in the open, armed, at all times." She smiled briefly. "Cama was my Shield Arm. Joret arrived," she added after a pause. "Your brother'd sent men to Darchelde to fetch her—doesn't matter why—"

"We know why. Was there trouble with Darchelde?"

"Not a bit. Joret said she had promised the Sierlaef she would come, in order to prevent bloodshed."

Evred knew Hadand too well to think that the mention of Cama and then Joret were unrelated. "What happened with Joret?" he asked quickly. "No trouble with Cama, surely?"

Hadand sighed. "I had some fears for a time that she would follow poor Kialen, for she felt that she had chosen dishonor rather than risk causing civil war. Your brother wanted to marry her, you see, which made her sense of dishonor more unbearable—the fact that in marrying him she would turf me out as queen."

Evred made a warding gesture. "Why didn't she just take a knife to him?"

"Because she knew that, by his own strange reasoning, he was doing the right thing, the 'honorable' thing, by offering to make her a queen. So she was grieved and confused and ashamed. But then she met Cama." Another little smile. "The only bearable thing in a terrible month. When they're together the heat could banish winter."

Evred pinched his thumb and forefinger to his nose. "No. Not Cama and Joret." He dropped his hand, smiling wearily. "I should say, under ordinary circumstances, what you call heat couldn't happen to two finer people. But his family—*her* family—"

"Exactly," she said, looking grim. "If Horsebutt found out, he'd try to force Starand out and gain alliance with Choraed Elgaer by insisting on a marriage. And Starand, of course, would go home to Ola-Vayir, wailing and insisting she'd been dishonored—she would love nothing better than a clan war in her name. She would in fact do anything for that much attention. So Cama and Joret had just a few days together, and when my father went home, she went with him, and Cama stayed by my side."

He sighed. "Honor again. What a cost."

Hadand's smile faded. "Honor indeed. I just hope they don't pay the price the rest of their lives."

Evred shook his head, then moved to the next painful item on his list. "What about Kialen? Where is she? You said 'follow'."

"Dead. But not by violence. We found her lying on her bed. Tesar insisted she smelled distilled white kinthus in the room, and there was an empty crystal vial on the nightstand next to the unlit candle. Though I don't know how she could have gotten it, as Tesar acted as Runner for her, too. She couldn't bear to take a stranger as Runner. Anyway I'd told her to hide. I had to get to the queen. My first duty was to guard the queen," she added, her voice going high.

"I know. You could not be everywhere at once. Poor Kialen! I don't think she spoke a single word to me in the year before I was sent north. Yet I tried to be as gentle with her as I could."

"Oh, Evred, I tried so hard to make her happy, but she

got stranger and stranger, like she half lived in a world we
didn't see." Hadand's voice trembled. She made a fierce effort and stilled it. She looked up, blinked, then turned to
the fire. "Aunt Ndara confessed to me not long ago that the
Cassad family had decided she was going the way of a mysterious Cassadas great-grandmother seldom mentioned,
who saw and even spoke with ghosts. I did my very best to
try to keep her with us, but when she wasn't in her own
dreamworld she was always afraid. I should have kept her
by me at the end, but I didn't know if they'd come after the
queen, and I did not know what she would do." Her face
was averted.

Evred moved to where he could see her. He could feel
the effort she made to marshal her emotions.

"At least Barend is recovering," she said, glancing his
way and attempting a smile.

"Barend! Vedrid told me he had returned, but subsequent events so overtook me I completely forgot. And the
others never mentioned him."

She said reasonably, "Well, your academy friends don't
know him, do they? He showed up the day after, when
everything was upside down. He was more dead than
alive."

"What happened to him?"

"From the beginning? He was taken by pirates. He was
with Inda when they found out about your uncle's betrayal
of the Algara-Vayirs. Barend can tell you all that. Your
brother apparently sicced Nallan onto him, along with two
others."

"To murder him, I take it?"

"Yes. But the Sierlaef made a mistake, it seems, in sending only Nallan and two of his own spy hirelings against
someone who has been fighting against pirates for ages."

"Nallan," Evred repeated with distaste. "As well he's
dead. I would hate to sit in judgment over him—to labor to
be fair when I have always despised him."

Hadand said, "Well, Barend killed all three of them. But
in his hurry to get here he traded his steady old mare that
Tdor and Whipstick had wisely given him, tried galloping

over ice, and he and the mare fell. Barend's leg was shattered, arm broken. The horse did much better, merely bruised knees. Somehow he managed to get home. Poor Barend," she added. "He wanted so badly to ride for the north to rejoin Inda at some harbor. The stairs defeated him—he tried to leave, and we found him in a faint outside the stable. The only other good thing I can claim to my credit is my thinking of Aunt Ndara's Runner Ranet to nurse him. She returned a couple of days after the deaths, and when she discovered what had happened—she had not been here to defend Aunt Ndara—I was afraid she would take her own life as a kind of expiation, even though she probably could not have saved her. Even though she was sent on some mission by Ndara herself."

Evred gave a faint grimace. "But they have been like sisters since Ranet was assigned to be her Runner when they were small."

"Yes, and Barend loved Ranet like an aunt. So I assigned her to nurse him. We were already desperately overreached anyway. And she has recovered enough to find purpose in life, I think. But Barend, well, he could use some cheering."

"Yes," Evred promised, his heartbeat quickening. Barend was alive. Here. And he had been with Inda.

Hadand brushed shaky fingers over her brow, pressing as if to hold in a headache, but then her hand dropped. "At least dear Aunt Ndara had the joy of knowing Barend was alive, even though she never did get to see him."

"Good."

"Let me show you the king's rooms, which are untouched. I left your father's and uncle's papers for you. Evred, Iasca Leror is in trouble. Mage spells weakening, no mages from the Adranis, tax money flowing north or to the coast and leaving things undone here. It's not going to be easy to hold the kingdom, especially if we face more war. You know that the pirates were defeated, but the Venn sailed away. They were apparently not in the battle, just the pirates. The Venn are untouched. Surely they plan something else."

"Yes, but that can wait. We've enough to consider here. One more task before we face the others."

She fell silent and Evred walked with her to the royal chambers. There she waited in the doorway while he wandered about, avoiding all the bloodstains on the floor, where the king's own Runners had died defending an empty room as the king had been in his son's chambers. He examined little things: a hairbrush laid aside, a robe tossed over the back of a chair for later. His father's house slippers by his bed. Everything in readiness for another day, one that would never come.

Finally they walked into the king's bedroom, where a magic fire burned quietly in the grate, untended for a month. The room was warm, unlike all the others, plain, the few furnishings old and well-kept. There Evred turned to face Hadand, and pulled from his pocket the silken square. She remained silent as he unwrapped it. "Sindan wouldn't die until he gave me this."

She drew in a slow, audible breath. "So you know, then."

"Know what?"

He watched her color change.

"About the magic lockets."

"No. Tell me," he added, thinking, *Yet another secret.*

She searched his eyes, which had gone remote, and sensed the change in his mood. "I did not know that the king and Captain Sindan had a pair," she said. "The only pair I knew about was that belonging to Aunt Ndara and Ranet. It was Aunt Ndara's secret," Hadand added, emphasizing the words. "I was sworn never to tell anyone. The lockets transfer messages. Your mother brought them as gifts for her and your uncle when she first came to this kingdom as a bride—she did not know our marriage customs. Your uncle, of course, despised the idea of 'lovers' lockets.' But I found this on your father and set it aside for you. Somehow he got a pair as well." She crossed to a carved cedar-wood casket on the mantel. "It holds the twin to Sindan's locket."

Evred made no move toward the casket. "Do you know how they work?"

"I know how Ndara's works. They are probably the same."

He joined her at the fireplace, where he laid Sindan's locket in the cedar-scented wooden box with its mate.

Hadand said, "Any other questions?"

Evred led the way out. "My mother?"

"She has not stirred from her rooms. She would like to see you," she added, following him back into the study. "And she wants to be reassured she can go home."

"Home," he repeated, shaking his head. "I will see her after we are done here."

Evred walked into her field of vision; she turned away, busying her hands with piles of papers that lay on the king's desk, senseless stacking and patting. He was in arm's reach, but he couldn't see her face, only the top of her head, the neat part in her brown hair. She was quite short; not so long ago she had been the taller, the wiser, the stronger. She still was wise. And her strength was the kind he needed most.

"Hadand," he said.

She glanced up, those eyes so very like Inda's. The resemblance jolted him, and for a moment he lost his own trail of thought. He forced the memory away and saw Hadand's distant, sad gaze go to the window so that her profile was outlined against the bright golden sunrays slanting in.

"Hadand, why won't you face me? Is there something that I've done?" He added, "That I should've done, and have not?"

She shook her head, then turned away.

"Hadand, please look at me," Evred said. "You have held the kingdom for me. Not so easy a task."

She did not deny it. Neither did she look at him.

"Hadand, I thought about this matter during the long ride south. It might not be what either of us expected, or even what you would want, but will you marry me? If you like I shall enumerate all the reasons. But I really believe it is the best thing for the kingdom. It's your skill, your mind, your wisdom that Iasca Leror needs. That I need."

She had turned her back. At first he thought she was angry, but he saw the shaking of her shoulders, and he stopped, bewildered.

But then she stood up straight, her shoulders squared. "Excuse me." Her voice was firm, if a little rough. "Just— being in these rooms. Of course I will. I do agree, it is the right thing for the kingdom." Her voice was too brisk, too unnatural.

"It is the only thing I am sure about." He held out his hands. "We've known one another all our lives," he said, hands turning outward in a gesture of distress. "You know I would never interfere with you in personal matters. All I ask for myself is truth between us. And when the right time comes, an heir we will train so there never again is a problem like the one we face here."

"Yes," she said, and swiped her wrist across her eyes as she turned around. "Yes. And so shall it be."

"We will marry Midsummer's Day, at the coronation, for you will be Gunvaer to a Harvaldar, since it's clear that despite any wishes of mine the war is not ending."

She said, "I fear you are right."

"I want to know the state of things well before then. When they all come to make their oaths, they will be demanding this and that of the Sierlaef's awkward young brother who knows nothing of kingship, and I don't want to give more than I get." He looked wry. "First I must deal with the Yvana-Vayirs, though I hope if I stall long enough the old man will die. Maybe I should offer him a knife."

"Do," she said, her brown eyes serious. "I wish I had not stayed my hand. It would have been be so much better. But he was an old man, a Marlovan, and my instinct was to wound, not to kill. Then I couldn't reach down and finish him off when he was on his knees before me, his weapon fallen. Not in front of the eyes of his son."

He agreed, relieved to see the tension fade from her forehead, from her small, expressive hands.

"All right. Then let us order the royal bonfire. And I've got my own promises to keep. Then we'll take a look at the trade papers while we await the last reports from the coast . . ."

*   *   *

And as the days turned into weeks, and he never again
saw that strange torment in her expression, he grew easier
in mind, deciding it had been her grief over the many
deaths.

Chapter Thirty-two

Chapter Thirty-two

THEY lived in their childhood rooms while the royal suites were refurbished, the papers from the king's study having been moved to the old schoolroom. One by one the expected formal rituals were performed, all of them painful for different reasons.

The first was the funeral bonfire for a war king and his Harskialdna and son, carried out—as Evred's coronation would be—at midnight, the throne room lit with torches. They did nothing to warm the high-vaulted stone chamber, men's voices rising and falling in the ancient Hymn to the Fallen, the voices of the women in the gallery echoing in an eerie descant. Evred did not sing; his throat was too tight. All he could think was, *My father. My father is dead.*

Evred's mother stood behind him, and she too was silent; at the end, she pressed his hand, her fingers trembling.

Wisthia and the others left, but Evred and Hadand walked together over to the barracks, where Runners from all across the kingdom had gathered. Once again Evred endured the heart-wrenching chant so movingly whispered, sung in wavering tones with abrupt silences and bowed heads, in memorial to Jened Sindan, Captain of the King's Runners, who had died as he had lived, defending the king and his family.

Evred could not sing at all, his throat was still too tight;

the sting in his eyes intensified, and when he heard Hadand's muffled sob on the women's side, his tears began to flow.

He was still standing there, eyes closed, when the Runners all withdrew. Only Hadand remained.

When at last he drew a long, audible breath, she said, "Do you want to be alone?"

"No. Thank you."

They did not speak as they walked upstairs to their childhood rooms.

The next day he had to deal with his father's personal possessions, and once again Hadand was at his side. It did not take long. The king, austere his entire life, had not owned much. His aesthetic pleasures had been bound up in the archives, and in ancestral furnishings and banners that would remain untouched.

His clothes, and the even more modest belongings of Captain Sindan, Evred and Hadand packed with their own hands. That night they and Barend held their own private bonfire; none of them wanted to pack away their personal belongings to some attic, as most families did, or to have them reused. Evred said he wanted to burn them all cleanly, and no one disagreed.

Barend brought his parents' effects, and Hadand the Sierlaef's. They and their personal Runners stood in silence watching them burn until their smoke rose and mingled, leaving only ash.

The queen did not attend this private ceremony.

That was the last private ritual; it was then time for the public displays of justice, beginning with the personal Runners of all four dead. It turned out to be easier than expected. Retren Waldan, the Harskialdna's chief castle spy, had died by many knife wounds half a day's journey away, which indicated two things: one, he'd abandoned his master, and two, someone had hunted him down. Probably several someones.

The Harskialdna's surviving Runners revealed under kinthus that they had not been in on their master's secrets. They rambled on about rumors that worried them, but their duties had been unexceptionable, carried out scrupu-

lously, for the Harskialdna had worked others as hard as he
had worked himself.

Farnid, the Harskialdna's personal Runner, was still
stunned and distraught. He barely seemed to comprehend
the offer of a life pension, which was given to all the others
with the exception of Ndara-Harandviar's Ranet, whom
Hadand had taken onto her own staff.

And so Evred and Hadand worked through all the rest,
ending with the Runners and armsmen belonging to the
so-called Conspirators of Hesea Spring. Most of them were
shot. Last of all was the execution of the Jarl of Yvana-
Vayir, who neither conveniently died nor accepted the opportunity of a quick, quiet suicide.

And so they had to execute him. Evred forbade the ancient tortures. The flogging was grim enough, a disgusting
spectacle at which he and the Jarls, or their representatives,
had to be present: he left Hawkeye in prison to spare him.
Why had the old man not accepted the offered escape
from this horror? Had he perhaps thought that his fellow
Jarls would rise against the young king and put him, or his
son, on the throne? If he did, he was disappointed. No Jarl
came except for Hasta Marlo-Vayir. They all sent a representative, silent testimony to their rejection of the actions
of Yvana-Vayir. If they had respected him, they would
have come to watch him die, then given him the accolade
of the Hymn, and songs over drums. There were no
songs.

After that Evred was closeted a long time with Hawkeye
Yvana-Vayir, who emerged not only with his title and hold-
ings intact, but as the interim Royal Shield Arm, until
Barend could be trained to take over.

Once that happened, he would go home at last as the Jarl
of Yvana-Vayir. His father's cousin (who had strenuously
resisted and resented Yvana-Vayir's pretensions; thus the
Jarl had never included him in any of his private plans)
would serve on as Randael until the twins could finish their
training and take his place, leaving him to honorable retirement. The Jarls would thus see that the new king gave
justice to his liege men rather than vengeance.

Cama and Cherry-Stripe and Noddy returned to their

homes—Cama to marry Starand Ola-Vayir as duty required.

Spring was coming, and what would that mean in the north and along the coast? No one believed the pirates were gone. Barend had reported to Evred what the mysterious Ramis had said about the Venn watching the battle. They decided that Barend would go to the coast after he recovered and organize what defense he could.

Those were Evred's greatest worries. His greatest joy came on the quiet nights after the first day of spring, when the first warm rain pushed in from the sea. By then Barend was beginning to hobble around; meanwhile he'd become an unexpectedly deft aid with the unending paperwork. The three sat together, Barend, Evred, and Hadand, in the old schoolroom, comfortable with one another as they always had been when the Sierlaef was not present. They often worked late into the night, and then, when the mulled wine was served, usually it was Hadand who asked questions about Barend's life at sea, and especially about Inda.

Barend did not try to hide his sorrow at being landbound. He never tired of talking about his sea adventures, responding to the unfeigned interest the other two expressed. The only reticence he privately decided on was talking much about Fox, because of the ancient enmity between the Montredavan-Ans and the Montrei-Vayirs. Not that he thought Evred would make trouble ... but Barend had learned early in life that the least said on some subjects, soonest mended.

Besides, it was clear to Barend that Evred didn't want to hear about Fox—or Walic, Coco, or Barend's time aboard the pirate ship before Inda was taken. Evred wanted to hear about his old academy friend from boyhood.

So Barend talked a lot about Inda.

Evred seldom spoke, but he listened. Hadand, sensitive to his every mood, saw in his relaxed face how much he enjoyed these stories. She prompted Barend to remember the

smallest details about Inda's words and actions on the
ships, with the people, in the battles. They listened to all the
details of the surprise mutiny against Walic. The horrifying
fight against Boruin. The Sartoran Sea battle on New
Year's Firstday.

And finally they talked about the Brotherhood battle,
and the mysterious rip between sky and sea. They went
over every aspect until Evred, watching Barend shove bits
of paper about on their old, scuffed nursery table, began to
comprehend a little about the ships and their movement.
He began to recognize Inda's style in battle planning; it reminded him in subtle ways of Inda's boyhood plans, though
he could hardly define the resemblance. But they discussed
that last battle endlessly as the fire crackled softly on the
grate, speculating about what lay beyond that rip from sky
to sea.

It wasn't much, Hadand thought wistfully. These quiet
evenings of talk seemed the only pleasure she could give
Evred, who worked so hard and so willingly, cognizant always of others' needs but asking nothing in return.

Nor did she ask anything for herself. When she entered
a room and Evred looked up and smiled his quick, unguarded smile, and Barend made an easy joke as they settled into companionable work—warm and safe and
content despite the icy winds outside—she hoarded the
moment in her heart. And resolutely, consciously grateful,
thought: *I am happy. I am. I am.*

PART TWO

Chapter One

EVERY hand aboard Elgar the Fox's fleet scrutinized the jagged circlet of rocks that surrounded the Ghost Isles, but few of them were watching for ghosts.

Vixen, sailing ahead of the rest, ran up a signal flag.

From the foremasthead of *Death*, the lookout hailed the deck. "No sign of attack!"

Mutt—suddenly grown tall and gangly—flung Inda's cabin door open to report, "No attack in sight."

Their first sighting of the Ghost Isles caused universal relief. All they had to navigate by in deep waters were the stars and the sun. And when the sun was behind clouds, which happened often this time of year, their lives depended on the magic-made sun-tracker guarded in the binnacle from watch to watch. It showed with a tiny dot of light the sun's position on a mirror-black piece of concave magic-bespelled glass.

But relief did not last. Not with their destination being a notorious pirate base.

The *Death* heeled hard, sending water foaming over the railing; the approach was treacherous with hidden rocks.

Inda braced himself absently against the table as he bent over his chart. To Mutt Inda looked almost *old*, his face sun-browned and scarred, sinister golden hoops at his ears, glinting with the blood-bright rubies. When his face wore that expression—brown eyes narrowed, mouth a thin line, jaw taut—he seemed not old but curiously ageless to the rest of his crew, none of whom knew that his eighteenth birthday had passed last fall.

Inda studied the chart he'd been given in the Delfin Islands. The Delfs, though ferociously independent, had been open in expressing their gratitude for Inda's defeat of the Brotherhood by offering refitting, supplies, and these charts.

Inda said, "Mutt, tell 'em to prepare for attack."

Mutt whooped, spun about, and scrambled up the ladder to the long, narrow flush deck, yelling "Prepare for attack!" with the same joy he would have yelled "Prepare for liberty!"

He flung open the signal box and snatched up the flag that would soon have the rest of the fleet falling into attack formation, fighting sail set, the tops full of archers, weapons out, all watches ready to handle the ship, repel boarders, or board, on Inda's command.

The journey northward between winter storms had been spent in drill, because Inda had not known what to expect at its end. These islands had been pirate-held for more than a generation. Supposedly the Ghost Isles, like Pirate Island down south of the Narrows, had been liberated by Captain Ramis of the *Knife*. But that news was at least four months old.

"We'll make a night landing," Inda said when he reached the deck.

Gillor, the mate on watch, laughed in anticipation, her curly black hair blowing in the wind.

Some of the crew covertly watched Fox, who turned away, his expression caustic. But he said nothing.

They reduced sail, tacking steadily westward as the current tried to carry them north. When the sun touched the horizon, lighting up a pathway of broken golden light over the western sea, they hauled their wind once more, sailing with care between the two sets of tall, green-spotted volcanic rock-fangs that cut the waters directly south of Ghost Island. Moon Island, their actual destination, lay directly to the north, but was unreachable by any other route, surrounded as it was by a deadly barrier reef just below the ocean's surface.

Quietly they drifted northward, the deck watch constantly trimming sail against the variable island winds. Hands posted on either side of the bow alternately swung out their leads and called the depths. Everyone else stood or sat or crouched motionless at their stations on deck, silent, wary of a trap.

The sun vanished below the western horizon. They glided slowly through more rock clusters. Ghost Island itself was a tall mountain ringed by dense greenery, its heights lost in cloud. As they slid by, many watched the island from their battle stations, though nothing spectral could be seen. But they had grown up hearing stories of the ghosts who supposedly gathered there.

Inda saw no ghosts, a matter of indifference to him. There was enough danger from the living.

Ghost Island passed gradually behind them, revealing the main island, now fast darkening to a silhouette against the starlit sky. Lights glowed into existence all along the harbor—the warm yellow of lamps, the glistening white of glowglobes—a silver and gold necklace that looked peaceful enough. But then so would a trap.

There were no estuaries. Halfmoon Harbor was a natural bay, a socket for the finger of Ghost Island. The bay and the island it belonged to, like Freedom Isles far away in the eastern seas, wore a different name with every new power that claimed it. Moon Island was the name inscribed on the Delf chart Inda had bought from the Delfin Islanders, Skull Cove on an old chart he'd found aboard his trysail, and a hundred years ago it had been named after some king or other who'd sent a troublesome son there to get rid of him.

Inda and his small fleet eased in on the tide under bright stars, the wind soft but steady. The faint smell of smoke rose from the oil-soaked twists of old canvas in the clay pots on the yards for the bow crews. Shields lay tight along the rails, ready to be grabbed on signal. Halyards had been laid along for an instant flash of sail, the defense crews standing silently by, weapons to hand.

As they rolled in on the easy waters, torches dotted the far end of the bay, jogging together into a row of points.

"Spill wind," Inda said, and the deckhands on duty silently loosened sail. The way came off *Death;* the scout *Vixen* slanted round, glasses trained on the bay. They saw small fishing craft, masts bare, but no sign of the tall, three-masted, square-rigged Venn warships with their distinctive curved prows.

Or Ramis' Venn ship with its night-black sails.

The row of points resolved into a longboat, oars rising and falling with ritual precision.

On the deck of *Cocodu* a cable's-length away, Dasta stood on the rail, watching Inda for a sign, one calloused thumb rubbing absently up and down the outer leg seam of his old drawstring trousers, the other gripping a shroud.

The longboat drew up on the lee of the *Death*; the rowers lifted their oars in one motion. Torches held upright down the middle of the longboat cast red light on upturned faces. An old woman stood in the stern sheets. "Elgar the Fox?"

"Yes."

She spoke a curiously singsong version of Dock Talk. "Captain Ramis, who cleaned out the last of the pirate vermin, bade us invite you in. Your crews are free of us for a full moon-cycle, during which time he says he comes back."

Ramis is not here. Silent faces turned Inda's way, most of them remembering their last glimpse of Captain Ramis casually ripping a sky-high rift out of the world, then sending the six of Marshig's fleet sailing into the black and timeless damnation called Norsunder.

Inda said, "How do we know your words are his message?"

"Captain Ramis said you'd be asking that. He said to surrender to you this . . . thing."

Inda motioned and two of his crew boomed out a basket suspended on a rope, into which the object was put. Up it came, everyone watching as it was brought to Inda. He took out—a book. A heavy one, with thick linen pages. He moved to the binnacle light, opened the book, and glanced down at the thick brown writing. It was in many languages, some of them incomprehensible. Then this must be the infamous oath-book of the Brotherhood, each crew member's name signed in his or her own blood.

The Brotherhood would never let that out of their hands by choice.

"Prepare to anchor," Inda said to Fox; then he hand-signaled to Dasta on the *Cocodu*, a cable's-length away.

The woman sat down in the stern sheets and the launch returned to the bay.

Inda looked down at the world-famous book everyone had heard about. Left here by Ramis—more like discarded by Ramis, who smote Marshig out of the world. And then said to Inda, "Meet me at Halfmoon Harbor above the Ghost Isles."

"We'll stay here the night," Inda said, and returned to his cabin below, not hearing the sighs of relief, the questions, the muffled laughs, and ribald comments of his crew who, now that danger had been averted, anticipated pleasure. Not seeing the tension in Fox's lounging posture, his considering gaze—and Tau watching them both.

Chapter Two

WHEN the rising sun began to spread glorious color over the eastern sky, Inda emerged from his cabin. "I'll go ashore first, with a picked band. If all is as they say, we'll have general liberty, rotating back to the ships watch by watch at three-day intervals."

He paused, and the sailors, young and old, looked out at the peaceful jumble of houses, all whitewashed, with wide arched windows and flower boxes and pretty little balconies.

Inda and his picked crew dropped down into the *Vixen*. They landed without incident and were led to a main street lined by those whitewashed houses made of formed brick with open shutters painted in bright colors. Flowers grew everywhere. The houses were mostly small, two stories only, and many of the windows had no glass in them at all. The tile roofs projected outward into awnings to ward the ferocious sunlight here on the belt of the world.

Inda glimpsed balconies and broad windows, most of them open; enticing food smells drifted out, fragrant with complicated scents of fruits, spices, and above all, the heady scent of fresh-roasted coffee drifting on the breezes from the hilltop plantations.

Inda walked up a narrow redbrick street, off which opened tiny courts containing fountains and bordered by equally tiny gardens. The zigzagging street of tiled houses and colorful gardens made a pleasing patchwork leading the eye upward to a long, low building on the highest hill that overlooked the inner bay. Not one of the curious people of all ages who came out to look at them was armed.

"Up there be Pirate House," a young man said to Inda in a distinctive, singsong Dock Talk, indicating the imposing building atop the hill. "You stay there."

His faint emphasis on *you* and his tone made it plain that no one else wanted that house.

Inda sent Mutt to signal general liberty, hooked the book under his arm, and walked the rest of the way up the hill, many of the unseen watchers muttering variations on "He's so young!"

Including a girl whose admiring tone caused her grandmother to retort, "Young? Yes. So was Marshig of the Brotherhood of Blood thirty years ago when he had half the city torched as a result of a bad bet."

The third morning after their arrival Fox found Inda lounging on the highest balcony at Pirate House, watching the low-flying birds skim the placid waters of the bay as the noise of people going about their business rose on the soft air, punctuated by laughter. The breeze drifting lazily through the open windows was perfumed by the thick growth of sugar stalks all over the island—the main trade item.

The little town was extraordinarily beautiful, as you'd expect in a place warmed by direct sun all year round. On land, the equator was marked by high, nearly uncrossable mountains full of magic that distorted both distance and time; at sea, the weather was warm, the winds changeable, bringing different scents from all directions.

"You don't look like someone who's had two days of liberty without having to pay a flim," Fox observed, dropping into a woven basket-chair.

Flowers were everywhere: growing, patterned into the furnishings. The houses had little shaded balconies off nearly every room, overlooking the bay, the hills behind the house with their lush greenery and unseen waterfalls, or the rooftops of the town interlocking in a complicated pattern down the hillside.

"That's because liberty, so far, hasn't included much sleep," Inda said.

Fox's mocking mouth deepened at the corners in amusement, but his gaze was steady and acute. "Is it possible you've finally recovered your wits? Realized it was stone stupid to come here?"

Inda retorted unheatedly, "You can't really think Ramis appointed this as a meeting place for a duel or a trap. If he'd wanted me he could have taken me easily enough when I was bleeding out my life on that scout in the middle of our wrecked fleet."

"Setting aside what he might or might not want, from what I understand the fight he had with the Brotherhood holding this island was bloody enough." Fox glanced over his shoulder. "Did you ask around about that? I did. Islanders helped Ramis by turning on their former masters. Wasn't so much of a fight as a slaughter."

Inda had heard much the same. "Yes, and?"

Fox propped a booted foot on the edge of a low table and tilted the chair back. "The locals might decide to serve us the same turn, and why not? Who's to stop them? I sleep with a knife, don't you?"

"Of course," Inda said impatiently. "Been doing that since I was twelve. Except when I was aboard *Coco* and you had my knives." His fingers stroked absently over the white scar leading down to his jaw. "I am more disturbed by Ramis' actions during the winter then by what happened here." Inda spread his hands. "From anyone else it would be a gesture of alliance. From him—someone from Norsunder—his motivations, as Tau says, become murky. His actions don't make sense. I need to know why he did it."

Fox expelled his breath, the chair thumping forward again. "Why are you giving him moral ascendance? Because without his timely appearance we might have lost?"

"We still don't know that," Inda said. As he put himself back inside his mind at the time, the room seemed colder, even darker. "If I had managed to get to Marshig and kill him—"

"And if his crew hadn't promptly scragged you on the spot," Fox interrupted, at his most caustic.

Inda threw his hands out wide. "But don't you see? It wouldn't have mattered what happened to me, as long as I did defeat him. From everything I heard, Marshig didn't hold them out of loyalty. And it doesn't sound like he had a trusted first mate they'd follow if he died. Should there've been a smooth transfer of power—no evidence of that ever happening in the pirate book or in the stories about them—yes, the rest of you would have been massacred. But if they hated him—if they all scrambled to be the next leader—well, you could have taken piecemeal any who didn't just run."

"But you would have been dead. Or near it, unless they all lined up behind you, and why should they? You had nothing to offer them," Fox said, shifting to the real subject. "But you're going to do it again—this time against the Venn, who are far tougher. And you want that one-eyed shit's advice. Why? Even if they know, back in Iasca Leror, do you think anyone cares?"

Tdor would care, Inda thought. *My brother. He was the one who told me to fight pirates.* But he said nothing.

Fox pinched the skin between his eyes. "Could Barend have talked you out of coming here? You won't listen to me!"

Barend's name caused a cascade of bitter memories that Inda usually tried to avoid, leaving him, as always, feeling intense but unspoken regret. "That's because you're never serious about anything I think is serious."

Fox snorted.

Inda gave Fox a rueful grimace, too pained to be a smile. "There you go! Nevertheless. Whatever I plan to do or not do, Ramis appointed this time and this meeting place. I didn't. We all know he can hunt me down wherever I try to hide if he wants a little easy recreation."

Fox flipped up the back of his hand—but he didn't deny it.

Inda gave his scar a last rub. "Anyway I'd much rather

face danger on neutral ground if I cannot pick a battlefield
I know. Someone that powerful, I have to find out at least
if he's an enemy. Or not. Last thing is, yes, I've been wild to
talk to him ever since the first mention of his name." And
when Fox glanced skyward in mute disgust, "I wonder
where Barend is."

"You mean you wonder if he's alive."

From the street laughter rose, a clatter and unmusical
twang and trill of musicians finding the same note. They
launched into a celebratory melody, accompanied by the
cling of brass finger cymbals, unheard by both.

Fox regarded Inda, who stared beyond the wall into the
east. Contempt did not override Inda's convictions, just
made him go silent and stubborn. Fox made an effort to
control the anger that burned the more cruelly at any evidence of idealism, and waved a languid hand. "You blame
yourself? You didn't force him to go ashore with that
damned ring." He added savagely, "I wish I'd kept my
mouth shut."

"But you wouldn't have." Inda's eyes narrowed as he
considered Fox.

"No?"

"No. Next time you got drunk, it would have come out."

Fury blazed then died, leaving the familiar self-mockery.
Fox heard his father's voice—drunk, late at the end of another long night of exile—discoursing on the meaningless-
ness of honor in his big, beautiful prison in Darchelde, far
from the Marlovan center of power. He gave a soft laugh.
"Yes. You're probably right."

"Come here," Inda said, rising to his feet. "Let me show
you this thing close up. Tell me what you think." He led he
way over tiled floors, each broad, six-sided tile painted with
intricate designs, mostly highly stylized birds and animals.
He said, "How are the *Death*'s hands comporting themselves? Dasta had to brig half a dozen from *Cocodu* the
first night, but it was mostly drunken fights."

"No problems after I thrashed a couple of Walic's former crew for interpreting the generous bounds of our invitation here to include stealing from that armorer halfway
up the other hill. You should see his work, by the way. I'm

surprised you haven't already. It's sweet stuff, knives as balanced as our own from home, the steel almost as good."

Inda gestured, a wave of the hand that could mean anything—or nothing. "I will."

This house had once belonged to the local governors, before pirates had taken the place and executed the governing families in the main square off the dock. It was the highest, and the finest, on the island. Too fine to burn, an old servitor had told Inda when he first entered. But the islanders who had been forced to labor as servants for the Brotherhood had silently carried off everything valuable that the pirates had brought in, leaving only a few worn pieces of furniture sitting on the beautifully tiled floors.

They'd also left this room containing the pirates' charts and maps on an old, battered table with ivy vines carved down the legs. The rolls lay next to the big bound book that Inda had been given on their arrival. All untouched until Inda handled them—the old man had warned Inda that the pirate chief had told them there were poison spells on everything there—only Ramis, a mighty mage as all knew, dared touch anything. Since the pirates had never been known to use magic, Inda suspected the "poison spells" existed only in imagination, and as soon as he was alone, he'd experimented. Nothing happened.

"This is what I've been doing by day. Reading that book. And studying these charts of every continent. Including the coastline of the Land of the Venn."

Fox turned away with a violent motion. "Venn!"

Inda spread his hands. "They were watching that battle. I didn't think about it before, what it meant. You can't attack someone's allies, however mistrusted, and not draw their attention. The Venn have to be coming after me."

Fox cursed; Inda grinned, taking that as corroboration.

"So—why don't I go after them first, and while I'm at it, clear the strait?"

"I knew it." Fox slammed a hand down on the table, making the maps and the heavy book jump. "I knew you were going to do something even more stupid than taking on the Brotherhood. Which would have killed you, you know it yourself—"

"But it didn't."

"—and if you think I believe those your only two choices—stay to get killed by Ramis or go after the Venn and be killed by them—you really are a fool," Fox stated.

Inda snorted. "No one is going to have freedom on the seas until the Venn are reined in." And at Fox's obscene gesture, he said, "No one. I'm not just thinking of us."

"Us?" Fox repeated, hands at his chest. "Iasca Leror is not in your thoughts? Who comprises this 'us'?"

"The southern half of the world, for a start," Inda retorted without any of Fox's heat. "If no one will follow me, I wonder if Ramis would take me on his crew, if he's going to fight them. That is going to be one of the questions I put to him."

"If no one will follow me." Of course they'll follow you, no matter how stupid your intent. Fox gazed at him, angry, so angry he couldn't speak—until he recognized he was mostly angry with himself, not at Inda, who had never asked for command. Who had, when he was sixteen years old, seen the moment to mutiny and led it.

And everyone had followed, because he'd figured out where everyone fit. They'd followed him against Boruin and a dozen other lesser known pirate predators and, finally, against the Brotherhood.

If he didn't think those who were left would follow him now, maybe it was time to for Fox take the lead—and without the Brotherhood's habitual violence.

Fox picked up the great oath book. "Do you know what this thing is?"

"Yes." Inda had spent an entire day reading it. The book not only contained names famed and feared written in the pirates' own hearts' blood, but records—stories of accession, plans, sometimes notes on this or that kingdom's strengths, all in the hands of former chiefs. And a map.

"This book *is* the Brotherhood. No, it's promise." Fox hefted the book, his eyes wide, the pupils so dark they reflected the brilliant light from the windows in pinpoints of gold. "It's possibility. You could rebuild the Brotherhood, make it far greater than it's ever been. You can take this thing and do anything you want." He set the book down beside Inda.

Inda left. He crossed the wide, tiled room to the balcony, sat on the low rail, and gazed out over the bay. Little pleasure boats had launched out, glass aboard refracting ruddy fire. The silken air carried voices rising and falling in song, horn and string instruments weaving melodies in counterpoint.

Fox leaned against the shuttered door, holding the Brotherhood's oath book. "Anything else is the act of a fool."

Inda's profile was pensive. His head lifted slightly, his breathing arrested. Fox had been ignoring the music, but a single melody persisted in being heard; then he had it. That song was the Marlovan Hymn to the Dead.

Except the tempo was wrong, the emphases and the words that drifted up were not the old, old ritual words sung over fallen warriors, but a silly romance about some fool longing for a woman gone to sea.

"You said I'm never serious. I am now." Fox laughed, a scornful sound, more irony than humor. "Meaning is what we make it," he stated. "There are no absolutes except for death. If there really was such a thing as honor, instead of a convenience for exalting one's own purpose, you and I would be home."

Inda looked up. "You mean your family would hold the throne."

"Yes." Fox opened one hand. "The point being that Iasca Leror's present royal family is founded on a dishonorable act, the craven murder of my great-father in the night while he slept. But as always, 'honor' is defined by those in power. In Iasca Leror, it's defined by the ambition of the Montrei-Vayirs. And everyone, including your own family, followed right along." He smacked his hand on the book. "Use it! Those damned bloody pages are not just promise, but power. Whatever the hands think of the old Brotherhood is irrelevant. If you call your whole fleet together and sign your name in that book, they'll line up right behind you, because you stand on the wreck of Marshig's empire. Your fleet of five would expand fast, upon old reputation as well as current success. Faster, because you have the knack of drawing people to you. Use it," he said again.

Inda looked up into Fox's wide, intense gaze. "Why should I?"

"Because meaning is what we make it," Fox repeated. The song below had ended. "The Brotherhood of Blood can be anything you want it to be. Make war on other pirates if you wish. Avoid the hapless and helpless, if that is your nature. There are plenty of grasping kings and guilds whose trees can use some shaking. Shake 'em, take what you knock down. Build your own empire."

Inda looked out at the deep sapphire blue of the bay. *Meaning.* He had five ships under his command and all the wealth of the Brotherhood of Blood, if the notes and map he'd found in the book did not lie. Several generations of accumulated booty was supposedly secreted across the bay on Ghost Island. The map had been carefully drawn; he had already memorized it.

He *was* the Brotherhood now. He sat here in this house, served by strangers who looked at him with sidelong admiration, and some apprehension. Both nights he'd had his pick of the handsome young women who strolled by just to look at him. All of them laughing, all of them willing. The first one brought a basket of fresh fruits of amazing variety: he had counted eight different types of grape alone. *Just don't ask their names,* Jeje had said, walking by on the arm of a young man nearly as handsome as Tau, only dark. The last he'd seen of her was that valedictory grin.

And he hadn't asked any names. He got up in the morning from that vast bedroom downstairs, and when he walked to the bath the pretty young woman with whom he had shared fruit, wine, and his body smiled and left. No demands, no expectations. A night of pleasure, of passion, given not because she liked Inda as a person, or liked his looks, but because he had commanded a successful battle against their hated foe—he knew it as well as she did.

"Meaning. Power," he murmured, now in Marlovan. Odd, both words carried slightly different connotations from the same words in Iascan.

"Life, death, and power," Fox said, breathing fast. Smiling in challenge. "That's all there is. Why not enjoy them?"

Inda turned away, leaving the book—and the question of the future—behind him. "Let's get something to drink."

"Liquor?" Fox asked derisively. "Even I don't drink just after dawn."

"No. Coffee. It's the best I've ever had. I think it's better than Sartoran, even. I want some now, and I'm going to fill the galley with bags of it when we go."

Three weeks passed, marked by intermittent storms. One morning the sky cleared after a thunderstorm, and there in the bay beyond the pier rode a single ship with a high, curved prow like the head of a swan, its masts tall, the slackened, drying sails square. And black.

Ramis of the *Knife* was here.

Chapter Three

ON the morning after his conversation with Fox, Inda had walked down to the shore behind the dock, weapons in hand, to start the daily drills.

Many of his crew were reluctant to rise early from their pleasures just to struggle and sweat, but drill had become a part of their lives. The fight against the Brotherhood had imbued most of them with the conviction that pleasure would not last beyond their share of the pay Elgar had handed out once they left Lindeth. Either they'd go cruising again or someone would come after them. Inevitable as rain. So their lives depended on readiness.

And then there were those who came out because Fox entered their comfortable pleasure houses, strong-arming them out of bed without ceremony or pity.

So for three weeks Inda's crew reported for daily drill on the broad beach before the pier to which their ships were moored.

The morning they spotted the *Knife* anchored out in the bay the sailors stood about in uneasy groups, fingering their weapons and staring, until Inda's sharp whistle—and Fox's freely dealt buffets—brought them into line to begin.

A boat from the *Knife* glided in. A scar-faced man leaped out, and while his boat crew rowed back he remained on the beach to observe the sword and staff drills.

A riff of self-consciousness tightened muscles, sharpened focus, and those of Inda's crew who had been slow or reluctant now put forth all their effort.

Ramis One-Eye watched, while everyone watched him. There wasn't much to look at beyond the spectacular purple scarring down one side of his face, a black patch covering that eye. His brown hair was neatly clubbed, his height was above medium, his clothing a plain linen shirt under a long vest belted at the hip and loose trousers stuffed into boots. His manner, the easy control of his movements, all indicated to their practiced eyes one with lifelong weapons training, though he only wore a knife in a sheath at his black-weave belt.

Inda saw that his crew was more distracted than focused and gave up. "Tomorrow a double," he said, wondering if he'd be alive to lead it.

The scar-faced man lifted a hand toward Pirate House, and Inda fell into step beside him.

The brick road leading up was scarcely wider than a path; there were no horses on the island, only goats, cows, bulls, dogs, and cats. Plump felines trotted along fences and balconies, each wearing a collar of sweetly tinkling bells, for apparently the mice were pets as well. Everyone walked, or was pulled in little flower-decorated carts by fat, well-groomed goats with flowers decorating their halters.

As the two passed by in silence, the windows and doors of the shops and houses crowded with curious folk; only the local dogs and cats ignored them, indifferent to the matters of humans.

Everywhere flowers bloomed, and music—Inda had discovered that the islanders made music day and night, with any excuse—wound complicated melodies through the cool breezes.

Ramis did not speak during that long walk. Inda spotted Tau lounging in the doorway of a tiny house, watching with unsmiling intensity. How had he gotten there so fast?

Then Dasta appeared at the top of the hill, still breathing hard as he casually whittled some pale wood. He had armed himself for battle—all his old mates had, apparently running up one of the back streets. They eyed Ramis with open speculation.

Inda and Ramis reached the house. Ramis said in Iascan, "We will go up onto the balcony so that your followers will see that you are safe."

Inda flushed, though he didn't know why.

Ramis glanced over as they walked inside. His good eye was hazel in color, its expression wry and acute. "You do not seem to appreciate," he said, "just how rare is freely given loyalty. I suspect you've had it all your life."

"Loyalty," Inda repeated, leading the way upstairs. Fox's voice came back: *There is nothing but life, death, and power.*

Ramis sounded amused. "What else would you call it?"

Inda feinted with Fox's credo: "There is nothing but life, death, and power."

Ramis laughed as they entered the chart room.

Inda flushed again.

"I forget how young you are," Ramis said. "Well, when I was young I understood the world, too. Until the world ended." His voice had not changed; the scarred face, his reputation, were far more convincing than a dramatic alteration in tone ever could be.

Inda's neck tightened with a heightened sense of danger. "Are you in truth a Norsundrian mage?"

"What will you really know about me if I say yes?"

"That if you come from Norsunder you cannot have fought the Brotherhood out of any moral conviction. Therefore you could do to me and my crew the same thing you did to Marshig and his Brotherhood captains, if it suited your convenience. And so I should be suspect of your motives for this meeting."

Ramis' good eye narrowed in amusement. "But would you not have come to those same conclusions had I said no?"

"Dhalshev of Freedom Island was right," Inda exclaimed, exasperated. "You do answer questions with questions. Here's one that you can answer plainly. How did you cause those ships to vanish like that?"

Ramis opened one well-shaped, rough-palmed hand, then clasped it with its mate behind his back. "I am watched by idle eyes from the Garden of the Twelve." He shifted briefly to the archaic Sartoran when he named Nor-sunder's power center. His accent was startling, almost singsong. "The former chief of the Brotherhood attracted those eyes by a degree of treachery achieved by very few. I was merely the agent of time and place."

"What do you mean?"

"I mean that the Brotherhood of Blood was in the midst of a noisy and vicious struggle for precedence, noisy enough and vicious enough to catch and entertain those idle eyes I spoke of. The necessity of meeting your coming fleet was the only thing unifying them. Ganan Marshig planned it all carefully, sending enough of his worst enemies within his fleet against you for you to destroy one another so that he could emerge and finish everyone off on both sides."

"Then I was right," Inda exclaimed. "If I could have taken him—"

Ramis raised a hand, and Inda fell silent. "The Venn also knew it," Ramis said. "For they had a spy on board Marshig's ship. This is why they rode there in the north, watching. Their plan was to prevent any of your fleet from escaping Marshig, until I drove them off."

So if Marshig hadn't gotten him, the Venn would have. Inda felt sick. "Why did you not let them finish us? Was that not entertaining enough for Norsunder?"

"No, it wasn't," Ramis said. "Too easy."

There was no understanding his motivations, Inda thought. Or those of the mysterious inhabitants of the Garden of the Twelve.

Ramis said, "As for what I did, it was time for what you might think of as a demonstration of consequences—not just to the pirates, but to the Venn. I'm sure you will agree it was most effective."

Inda's breath huffed out on his "Yes." He breathed out again, trying to ease the tightness in his neck. "And so . . . Marshig, and the Venn spy as well, and everyone else on board those ships have been taken into the heart of Nor-sunder?"

"Oh, not the heart," Ramis said, smiling a little. "Marshig and the remainder of his fleet are in one of the borderlands . . . we can call them holding areas, far from the heart—though even 'heart' is a misnomer for a place beyond time and physical space. Those who command merely have use for him, no interest."

Idle eyes. Archaic Sartoran. The casual power of some unknown hand ripping a curtain between this world and Norsunder vast enough to swallow six capital ships. Inda felt very much like a scrub again.

Ramis glanced at the table, his one brow lifting. "Ah, you saved that, I see."

The oath book. "I was reading it." Inda looked at the amusement still deepening the corners of Ramis' mouth, and decided not to add anything about power or interest. He didn't think the one-eyed man would be impressed.

"Did you know that Gasthjanju, the one who wrote the long records, got faint at the sight of his own blood? Used to line up his followers to donate theirs when the poetic urge seized him." Ramis picked up the book, hefted it, and then with a flick of his strong wrist, he spun it into the glowing remains of the fire.

Inda gasped. Ramis' single eye met Inda's, his smile gone. "Don't tell me you had limited your vision to perpetuating this absurdity?" He pointed at the curling pages, now burning in blue and gold flames. "The legends grown around the Brotherhood will no doubt produce fleets of greedy or disaffected people in the future, and they'll fall to death and defeat after fighting their way to a pinnacle of stupidity. Is that really how you wish to squander your life?" Before Inda could say anything, he indicated the glass doors. "Come. Show yourself on the balcony. They are all watching."

Inda stepped through the doors, looking down. There was Tau, now with a half-hidden bow team behind him. And Jeje too, also armed with a bow, black-haired Gillor next to her, hefting a cutlass. Fox was there as well, at the intersection with the side street, his fighting scarf hiding his red hair, his knives not in their sheaths but in his hands, visible as cold steel gleamed up the inside of his forearms as he leaned casually in an arched doorway watching both entrances. No doubt with bow teams hidden out of sight but ready to attack either entrance on a signal.

Inda backed into the room, observing, "Fox wants a fight."

The man didn't respond. Instead, he closed the door-length shutters, then flicked something silver through the air. Inda caught it. It turned out to be a piece of metal, thicker than most coins, with carving on both sides. "Say '*Knife*.'"

Inda said it, and a black wind ripped sight from his eyes, burned away skin and bone, then restored them, all in the space of a heartbeat. He staggered, his vision clearing, to discover he was not in Pirate House but standing on the deck of a gently rocking ship. His entire body tingled unpleasantly, though the sensation faded fast.

Forward curved the high prow of a Venn ship instead of the angled bowsprit of southern vessels.

He was aboard the *Knife*.

Sailors moved about, ignoring him. Inda stared around in amazement, then faced Ramis. "So that's how Ryala Pim vanished so quickly!" And frowned at the memory of the shipowner's daughter accusing him of piracy and theft after the loss of the last of the Pim trade ships.

Ramis gestured toward the silver disc Inda gripped in his fingers. "Transfer token." Ramis gave Inda a slight smile. "For sale everywhere but at the west end of your continent."

Inda rubbed his forehead, trying to press away the last of the transfer reaction. "Expensive?"

"Very."

"And leave you feeling like a mountain fell on you."

Ramis gave a silent laugh. Behind him, Ghost Island rose from the deep blue of the water, its mountain crowned by cloud.

Inda sighed. "Are there really ghosts there?"

"I thought you knew what was real and what was not?" Ramis retorted. But not cruelly. He moved aft to the binnacle; Inda was distracted by the sight of a real Venn whipstaff—what they called a koldar—instead of the wheel common to all ships of the south. This straight spar was as tall as the two mariners standing at it, both attentive despite the ship being at anchor.

Ramis retrieved a glass and moved to the rail, which was pale gold oak carved with a pattern of leaves. Inda looked around again. The *Knife* was beautifully made and scrupulously clean. "Look," Ramis said, holding out the glass.

"I did when I first arrived," Inda said.

"You did not expect to see anything. Look again. Do not tell your mind what it is to see."

Inda did not question him. Somewhat apprehensively he leaned against the rail, raised the glass, and swept that coastline once again. He viewed white sand gently molded by wind and rain, and ferny plants, and glistening rock with striations of many colors.

"Look again," Ramis said from just behind him.

Inda blinked. The coruscation was not the rock but lay over it; when he gazed into that sun-bright shimmer, the sparkles resolved into many figures, faint outlines as if formed of smoke and sun refraction.

Ghosts?

He could almost make out individuals: men and women, children at times, some dressed in outlandish fashion, walking, drifting slowly as a dream, forming in shafts of dazzling light, then vanishing in blue shadow.

Wonder bloomed, withering into chill. This was no life, only a distortion of life. "I don't understand."

"There are places all over the world where the temporal bindings, shall we say, are very thin. This is one."

"I can't count them. Why are they there? What do they do?"

"I suspect they find themselves there, the ones who are not bound to a place by their own passions or will, however fragmented. I was reliably told that the single trait they share is violent death. I was also told that those who do not find a reason—however that can be defined to a ghost—to cleave to a specific place any longer will eventually wander here, gathering, drawn to others of their kind. Human beings are by nature social when they are not busy murdering one another. Their numbers increase until those who first lived in this world before we came notice them. And send them out beyond the temporal bindings."

Inda drew in a deep breath, now searching those glimmering forms for fallen shipmates. Was that Yan, there, on the shore, watching? Sunlight dappling the water dazzled his vision and the form, familiar or merely seeming so, was gone. Inda lowered the glass, and blinked away the blue afterimages leaping across his vision.

For a moment he felt a presence at his side, as if Dun the Carpenter—killed by Fox when Walic's pirates attacked their ship—stood at his shoulder, sword in hand, as he had just before his death.

Inda turned his head and saw only the rope-and-metal shrouds webbing down to the rail, supporting the towering mainmast, and beyond the rail, the calm blue sea.

A flush of foolishness burned his ears as he faced Ramis. "Why did you bring me here?"

"What do you want?" the man returned.

Inda fingered his jaw, looking out to sea again. Easier than meeting that steady gray-green-brown gaze. "The satisfaction of a good fight. Why not? It's what I'm good at. Most of my crew believes there is no real meaning past that . . ." The words, almost convincing to Inda when contemplated during the nights since his conversation with Fox, seemed absurd now, when he considered that strange shoreline nearby.

"What do you want?" Ramis repeated.

Inda's mind began sifting words, images, and he faced Ramis once again, this time with a narrowed, considering gaze. "What do *you* want?"

"Freedom," the man said, smiling a little.

Inda thought over their conversation and put together the clues. He said, "You mean Norsunder . . . runs you in some way?"

Ramis said, "I made a very bad bargain once. They will let me live as long as my actions provide entertainment, after which they will exert themselves to destroy me."

Destroy? Soul-eating. Not just the unthinking invective of anger, the real thing—that which comprised damnation, another word used so freely, with no thought to what it meant. But Inda had read enough to comprehend a little: to be violated not physically, but in mind and memory. Each secret routed out and devoured, each memory. First your will and then your identity stripped deliberately away by those who savored terror and resistance, consumed by those Ramis had referred to as "idle eyes" until you diminished to . . . what? Nothing? Or did some essence remain, terribly, in the heart of the enemy, for all time?

Ramis said, "This will be our only meeting. Ramis of the *Knife* will vanish within the year. My value as entertainment has waned, and my harvest has garnered them enough for their present wants. So I ask again, what do you want?"

Inda's awareness shifted to that rapid flow of images, possibilities, connections, the running stream that pushed into the future and became a path: a plan. That, once acted on, became real. Ramis, whoever he was, whatever his past, had in reaping souls for Norsunder's mysterious rulers managed to do the world some good.

Inda said, "You could have beaten Marshig. Taken over, run the Brotherhood yourself. Attacked Iasca Leror yourself. Even taken over as king."

"Yes."

"And Norsunder, wouldn't they like that?"

"If whatever I did was sufficiently entertaining, of course."

No moral truth lay there, yet Inda sensed its presence underlying the man's words, like a lake beneath parched land.

Ramis said, "I ask for the last time: what do you want?"

"I want to go home," Inda whispered.

Ramis did not reply to that, just returned his gaze steadily as the rising salt breeze fingered their hair and clothing.

Inda looked past him to the ghost-ridden island, where no living soul willingly walked. He thought past his answer, his true answer.

Even if I can't make meaning, I can make nets. As always, when he thought of the net-making of civilization, there was Tdor's child face, steady and true. The Venn intended harm to his homeland as much as the pirates had, so wasn't it net-making to get rid of them if he could?

"The Venn," he said. "They are looking for me, aren't they?"

"Yes. I believe there is a considerable force on its way here right now."

They have a spy here? Inda almost asked, but the answer was obvious. As well as the answer to *How do you know?* A Norsundrian would have access to information as well as magic.

So Inda said, "What can you tell me about the Venn? Why us? Why now, and not thirty years ago, a hundred years ago?"

"There are fierce political divisions in the land of the Venn," Ramis said. "Due partly to the need for better land to feed a breaking empire and partly to ambition. But these problems lead to the fact that the Venn system of kingship is at stake."

Inda's mind streamed with images, questions, possibilities. "The Venn created the piracy problems here in the south," he said. "I mean, besides their using the Brotherhood as their front-line chargers to weaken coastlines, Iasca Leror especially," he said, and when Ramis inclined his head, his manner implying conditional agreement, Inda said, "Their stranglehold on trade—forcing the southern kings to comply with their tolls and rules—brought on piracy. No one can raise a fleet big enough to get order on the seaways. The Venn smash them first."

Ramis said, "All true."

Inda stared sightlessly at the island, then faced Ramis, who had waited patiently, his one-eyed gaze uncomfortably acute. Inda said, "Who is my chief enemy? Their Prince Rajnir?"

Ramis said, "Among the Venn you have three. Prince Rajnir needs a war triumph to win back their king's regard; he has problems not just in the Land of the Venn, but much closer to home. Your second is Hyarl Fulla Durasnir."

"Hyarl," Inda said. "Sounds like our 'Jarl.' "

"The titles, similar in meaning, share the same root. He commands the southern fleet of the Oneli, the sea lords. The Oneli is the oldest and most prestigious of their forces. He would actually like to see an end to further invasions, but he does not make those decisions; he is oath-sworn to carry them out once made."

Inda was briefly distracted by a word that sounded so unfamiliar. His mother's lessons about the history of language made him wonder if the word "Oneli" had vanished from the Marlovan version of Venn when the latter turned inland after their exile and adapted to the plains.

"The Hilda—the army—has been traditionally seen as support, which causes its own tensions. Durasnir is the most able commander they have had in generations, which is why the king sent him south to accompany Rajnir."

"That's who I—we—a fleet, I mean—would face in battle. Assuming I can raise a fleet," Inda said, and on Ramis' gesture of agreement he laughed at himself inwardly. He had to be dreaming, talking so easily about raising fleets and personal enemies in the world's most dreaded empire. Digging his thumbnail into his palm, he said, "That's two. You mentioned three."

Ramis lifted a hand northward, a gesture Inda could not interpret because he was distracted by memory of Ramis making a similar gesture to rip a hole between sky and sea.

"Your third," he said, "is a mage. The Venn call them dags. Erkric seeks to become the Dag, the supreme magic-wielder at the side of the future king. It was he who negotiated with Ganan Marshig to loose the Brotherhood against the south. He is aware of you now, and would do anything to destroy you."

Inda realized he'd drawn blood and wiped his hand down his old, scruffy deck trousers. The other palm was equally damp, he discovered: sweat.

"There is no one else trying to gather against them?" Inda asked.

"The answer is complicated," Ramis said.

Inda retorted impatiently, "What forces are trying to fight the Venn? I don't see any complication in that."

Maybe not, but Ramis seemed to consider the question further before saying, "Forces. Those in the north are disorganized, and not well led," said Ramis. "Here in the south all that stands against Venn sea power is the Guild Fleet struggling to form out of Bren, but now that the Brotherhood has been materially defeated, their purpose, to fight the red sails, is—according to the Venn—nullified.

The Venn have made it clear there is no more reason for the Guild Fleet to exist. The guilds themselves are split over this question. The only thing they agree on is this: if the Venn ever deem them a threat, they will smash them."

Inda said, "How can they not know that the Venn are the biggest threat to trade, bigger even than pirates?"

"They do know. But doing something about it is another question entirely." Ramis turned his palm up. "The guilds involved are not stupid people. Their ships are not well led as a force. And they know it. The Guild Fleet expeditions have been mostly confined to watching Venn Battlegroup maneuvers on the pretext of pirate-watches and noting down various outrages in hopes some king will back them."

But the Guild Fleet still existed. Inda needed a big fleet to even consider going against the Venn. The Guild Fleet needed leadership.

Ramis turned his gaze westward, and Inda sensed that this extraordinary conversation would soon be ended. "Tell me how the Venn navigate in deep waters."

"It is a system run by magic, connecting each ship to certain established sites in a webwork over the world. Their ship-mages—the sea dags—tend to the navigation, showing each captain where he is on the water in relation to land and to other ships."

"They can spot us by magic, then?"

"No, they need sight just as you do. But because of that network their sea dags can reveal their position to the others, as well as the positions of ships they sight to others of their fleet."

"So what we need to do to master that navigation is capture not their captain or mates, but these mages—dags?"

"Yes. But be aware of this: the dags transfer away if it looks like the ship they are assigned to might be taken. It's an imperial order they always obey. And if a dag is incapacitated, it is the captain's job to kill him or her. And the dags agree to a spell that kills them if they are given white kinthus—all measures to protect the secret of their navigation. A last fact: Venn captains, like your Marlovan warriors, are always men, but the dags can be either sex."

Inda rubbed his jaw again as he tried to figure out which question to ask next—or if he dared ask a personal one.

"The tide is on the make," Ramis said. "I must be on my way."

Inda looked around. The sailors were busy preparing to set sail, as if they'd received some sort of invisible signal. "I suppose the Guild Fleet will not kill us as pirates out of hand if I contact them."

"The Venn would probably wish them to do that, but those whose voices currently prevail will welcome with open arms, and open pockets, the one who defeated the Brotherhood."

Open pockets. Inda recalled what Ramis had said about the writers of the Brotherhood of Blood book—he'd read it. That meant he, too, knew about that vast treasure supposedly buried on Ghost Island.

"The treasure is real, then?"

Ramis looked across the glittering water. "It is real. The few who knew the extent of it no longer live. The world expects the Brotherhood to have treasure, but the whereabouts and the amount have remained a matter of hot debate. There are kings who suspect the size of it and thus would willingly kill anyone to discover its whereabouts."

Inda drew in a slow breath. He'd at first disbelieved in the existence of treasure; from his limited experience pirates spent loot as fast as they took it. But the Brotherhood was old, older than he'd thought, however violently it had changed its captaincy, and there had been those in its twisted, extremely violent past with an eye to empire building.

So if the kings find out I have it, then they can join the Venn in hunting me, he thought, grimacing.

He dismissed that for later consideration, and turned his mind to his immediate situation.

"And then what, if I do join with the Guild Fleet? Am I being set up for your 'bad bargain'?"

"It's a necessary question," Ramis replied. "But no. You would have to do a lot more than you've done to come to the notice of those who tarry in the Garden."

"Are we being watched now?"

Ramis's mouth was grim. "Their gaze is elsewhere, or we would not talk with this much liberty."

A man who could predict his own death with such calm certainty had to be listened to.

"As for my own motivations," Ramis said, "consider how many of our kings and heroes appear to define honor by the worthiness of their enemies. Things will change only when honor is defined by our works."

He plucked the metal from Inda's fingers, touched his shoulder, and the black fire took Inda again, leaving him standing alone in the chart room of the Pirate House, feeling as if his bones had been stripped from his body and his muscles unstrung.

He leaned against a wall until he could stand without falling. The reaction passed fairly quickly, then he opened the shutters. His friends waited outside, patiently guarding what had been an empty room. He would go out and speak to them, and deal with protests, arguments, and exclamations, but not yet.

First he got his glass and watched the black-sailed *Knife* glide out of the bay—and out of his life.

And so, as the *Knife* vanished behind Ghost Island, Inda thought about treasure—that is, about vast amounts of someone else's wealth—and what he'd seen happen to those who craved it. *Kings would kill . . .*

Inda rubbed his jaw. *Kings.*

He realized what Ramis had said, and what he had implied.

Kings. The first problem was going to be Fox.

Chapter Four

THE next morning the five aboard the *Vixen* studied Ghost Island's approaching shoreline. Only one of them searched for a glimpse of the walking dead.

The sun was not yet up but already the early morning fog had broken into gentle wreaths of mist, faintly throwing back the blue and warm yellow-pink glow from the eastern horizon. The water rilled outward behind the *Vixen* in a long, slanting wake, the ripples reflecting subtle shades of blue.

Five pairs of eyes spared the beautiful curve of the mainsail a glance or two as it shivered in the strengthening breeze, then returned to contemplation of Ghost Island.

Jeje couldn't accept the notion of ghosts. She gripped the tiller, testing tide and wind against the wood's resistance, then again lifted her glass to give the island, which rose in a dark mass against the skyline, one last sweep. Ghosts. Huh. Made no sense. If something had no body, of course you couldn't see it! But the locals on the main island had been quite matter-of-fact about them. *Oh, yes. The ghosts walk on yon island. No one goes to that island.* Too often, they said, the living who did go never returned.

To Jeje that strongly suggested dirty doings from those who walked, talked, and breathed. Now *that* made all too much sense.

Well, now it seemed the *Vixen* was going to test the truth

either way. Something during his interview alone with that sinister Captain Ramis had caused Inda to appear at each of their dosses last night, ordering them to be on the *Vixen* before dawn.

Moreover, something was *wrong*. She sensed it, and because she didn't believe it could be these convenient ghosts, she studied the other four covertly, trying to identify what had caused the uneasiness in her gut.

They were all watching that shoreline as early morning banished the shadows and picked out details of thick greenery, rocky inclines, waterfalls, white sandy beaches. Nothing human walked there, though brightly colored birds sailed in the sky and skimmed the water. No living human beings in sight—or dead ones, either.

Jeje decided she might as well speak first. Test matters. If the others just laughed, well, there were worse things. "I don't see any ghosts."

Dasta, tall, wiry, and sun-browned, shrugged. "I don't think there *are* any ghosts."

Inda was sitting on a barrel, watching the coastline through a glass. "There are."

"What?" Dasta and Jeje spoke at once.

"But we won't see them, because we don't want to see them."

Fox's eyes narrowed to slits of green. He drawled, "I take it you have seen ghosts?"

"Just once," Inda replied, still scanning the beach. "Yesterday. When Captain Ramis took me to the other side of the island, on board the *Knife*."

Silence again, then Tau said in a cautious tone, "Inda, you realize we never saw you leave the Pirate House. When exactly were you on board the *Knife?*"

Inda looked up at a row of faces that expressed a range of emotions from concern to disbelief. He snorted. "No, I'm not mad. He took me by magic transport. And sent me back by same," Inda said.

"And while you were there he talked about ghosts," Fox said, lounging against the rail on the weather side of the bowsprit, arms crossed, fine drifts of red hair escaping from his long four-strand sailor's queue and ruffling in the wind.

"Yes," Inda said, and raised the glass again.

Fox's gaze was safely on Inda, so Jeje scrutinized his long, lean body. He always wore black and always went armed; there was the faint bluish gleam of polished blackwood hilts at the tops of his boots and in his loose sleeves when he lifted his hands.

Jeje wasn't sure what to think about Fox even after a year of traveling with him. Fighting the same battles. Sometimes taking his orders, despite the fact that she and Dasta and Tau had been with Inda six years. Despite Fox having been with the pirates who initially captured them.

Tau had said it was because Fox was a Marlovan, like Inda. He'd also said there was a connection between the name they used for him—Fox—and the strange, raptorish golden fox face on their fleet banner that had caused Inda to be known across the seas as Elgar the Fox. Fox and Inda had never talked about that anymore than they had about their past.

The sail-hum changed in pitch as the teasing breeze shifted. Jeje leaned into the tiller to compensate. Those forward adjusted with the heel of the ship, all with the ease of long habit. They glided over the still water, the island appreciably nearer.

Inda still sat on a barrel, glass to eye. Unlike Fox he wore a battered old shirt, not even a vest as the weather would be hot as usual, and worn deck trousers. His feet were bare, his sleeves rolled—

Sleeves. Jeje looked at those powerful forearms, much more pale than the rest of his visible flesh, and recognized what was out of place.

It was the first time she'd seen Inda's arms bare, at least since they were newly-hired deck rats of twelve and fourteen years old, years ago.

Inda's profile was mild as he watched that island. Some of the islanders had not believed he was the fleet commander and mastermind of the Brotherhood's defeat, insisting that Fox, with his sardonic gaze, his sinister aspect, was really in command. Inda's face was broad at the forehead, his brown eyes wide-set, his face boyish despite the scars. His unruly brown hair escaped his sailor's queue in curling tufts. He looked like a ship rat perched there on the barrel.

Were the others armed? Dasta, wearing deck mocs, old trousers with a weather-worn sash, and a vest without any shirt under it, had two knives thrust through the sash, and one strapped to his leg above his right moc. Jeje had her own trusty knife in her sash. She felt naked without it. And because Inda had been so mysterious the night before, she'd added another under her tunic, strapped to her thigh over her loose trousers, out of sight.

Jeje wondered if Tau was also armed—and just as she thought of him, his golden head appeared at the hatch, and he came up bearing four of her wooden, broad-bottomed mugs, two in each hand, their contents smelling of brewed herb with one of the island spices. He carried one to each person: Inda lowered the glass and murmured his thanks, Dasta grinned. Fox ignored Tau, who set his mug in the center of a coiled rope. Typical behavior from both. Despite their mutual antipathy Jeje thought they not only moved a lot alike, sometimes they seemed to think alike.

Tau brought Jeje her cup, his golden gaze narrowed with laughter. Jeje lifted a shoulder, carefully careless.

"There." Inda pointed with the glass. "Beyond the three trees twisted about one another. There should be a lagoon."

The sun had risen abruptly, as it did here on the belt of the world, and was fast burning away the remaining fingers of fog. Jeje drained her cup, her other hand gripping the tiller as she eyed the short promontory thrusting out into the water. It was scarcely higher than her mast, mostly a tumble of barnacle and dung-bespattered rock. Grass grew along the ridge of the promontory, culminating in a curious sight—three trees of a species none of them had seen before, twisted around one another, the gnarled branches ending in broad, feathery deep green fronds. Small wavelets lapped up against the rocky cliffs; ripples in the surface beyond the cliff's edge indicated an abrupt rise in the seafloor.

"Leads," Inda said.

Unnecessarily. Dasta had the stowed leads in hand. He gave a set to Fox. They stood at either side of the bowsprit, casting the leads and measuring, not calling out—they wouldn't unless the shallows threatened the keel.

The water was so clear Jeje could see the bottom, and schools of fish, silvery blue and silvery green, darting about. She wondered if merfolk avoided this island as assiduously as did surface humans.

Inda and Tau hauled the mainsail sheet aft. They glided around the promontory and, as demure as a duck, the *Vixen* drifted into the broad lagoon on the height of flood tide.

They spilled wind. Fox and Dasta joined Jeje to brail up and furl the sails, Tau and Inda at the windlass, letting the anchor fall the right moment so the *Vixen*, losing way, headed around broadside to the shoreline. No other craft was in sight.

"Come on, let's get the skiff down," Inda said.

Each of them saw wariness and question in the other faces as they boomed down the skiff. All except Inda, whose expression was remote.

Leaving the *Vixen* behind, they rowed for shore.

Jeje sat at bow oar, determined not to speak again. Inda was never moody or sour, but sometimes he just wasn't *there*.

The ripples of surf carried them the last distance. They shipped their oars and jumped out, the water briefly cool on their legs as they pulled the skiff up onto the beach. It was scarcely past sunup, but the air was so hot they were breathless.

"Where to?" Dasta asked. "What are we looking for?"

The distinctive ice-shivering *zing!* of steel caused them to whirl around.

The corners of Fox's mouth were wry as he laid the blue-steel Marlovan blades on a flat stone, and sat down to pull his boots off. Jeje remembered what Dun, their marine carpenter, had told them not long before he was killed by pirates: *Marlovan steel is made with many flat sheets of metal, folded and refolded in a method kept secret by the Iascans. The Marlovans conquered Iasca Leror just to get that steel.*

And Tau had added, in a whisper, *Meaning our gallant Iascan ancestors were superior armorers but not warriors.*

Fox dumped water out of each boot, wrung out his socks, put them back on again, and resheathed his knives.

Inda had been surveying the thick greenery crowding down to the beach. "Ah. There. Has to be the path."

He started off at a run, kicking up white sand behind him. They followed, Jeje—being shortest—last.

Tau dropped back to match his pace to hers. He said softly, "Did Inda tell you why we are here?"

She swiped a hand over her damp hairline. Jeje was not beautiful. Never had been, never would be. She cut her fly-away dark hair off with a knife as soon as it grew long enough to tickle her neck; her golden earring, with its single ruby gleaming, swung free against her narrow jaw. Jeje was short, boyish in shape, muscles flowing like a hunting cat beneath her smooth brown skin. She was grimly practical, looking at the world with trenchant humor from under those straight black brows.

Not in the least matching the world's standard for beauty. So what was this new vagary in the comedy of human nature that made her so damned attractive?

Sex Tau could get anywhere, any time. And whether it was because he was a bawdy-house brat or it was just his own innate flaw, he could enjoy sex—very much—but never was any emotion attached. He had watched from a sympathetic distance as Jeje struggled to overcome her adolescent craze for him, settling into this tranquil friendship he had come to value more dearly than diamonds.

He restrained the instinct to touch her. He would do anything to avoid losing her friendship, which he would if she were to fall back into the brooding obsession that had made them so unhappy. And so he looked away before she could catch his glance.

"No," she said, her voice deep and rough. It had always been the deepest voice among them, boy or girl, but since her teens she'd not only been muscled like a hunting cat on the prowl, her voice sounded like one—quite ravishing. "But I'm not blind."

Tau laughed under his breath. They two then were the only ones who'd seen what Inda had stashed below *Vixen*'s deck: bolts of the cloth they used for light-air sail.

He saw Jeje marking the way and dropped obligingly back.

Jeje, like Fox and Dasta, was memorizing the landmarks as they pushed up a narrow trail through thick green ferny growth. Here a distinct pile of rocks, mossy though they were, there a lightning-struck shell of one of those broad-fronded trees. Up along hard switchbacks into the rock hillside, affording the occasional glimpse below of the peaceful sand, undisturbed by any feet but their own. They smelled brine, wet sand, the heavy scents of flowers, and the fresh tang of savory herbs.

No sign of ghosts.

For a time they walked single file along a cliff, everyone looking down with some care. The skiff seemed a child's toy in the lagoon below, and beyond the *Vixen* lay, looking small and fragile through the heat's haze.

"Here," Inda said at last, pointing to a waterfall.

Fox looked at it, then down at the rocks it thundered and foamed over, and wiped his brow. "Here?" It was the first time he had spoken.

"Behind the water," Inda said. "At least, so the map said, before Ramis cast it into the fire." He grinned.

They eased along the slippery path, which was scarcely wider than their feet, not caring that some of the waterfall spray dashed over them. It felt good.

Farther, farther, another step, a sudden sharp turn to the right and there was a cave, smelling of wet stone and mold.

They sloshed inside.

One of Dasta's feet slipped on slime, and he scrambled to recover. "Should we go back for light?"

"Nearly there," Inda said. "We'll let our eyes adjust—Ah!"

They stopped. Their night vision gradually picked out the rocky cavern, with its old limestone drip-spikes hanging down from the root-pierced ceiling. Weak blue light from the water-curtained mouth of the cave revealed a black hole against what felt like the northern end opening out into the sea.

"We'll have to feel our way, this first time," Inda said. "But there are supposed to be steps hewn into the rock."

And there were—broad, uneven, slippery, but unmistakable steps hewn by human hands centuries ago.

Down they trod until they reached a rocky cavern hollowed out by water millennia before, smelling of brine and mossy stone. Overhead the rock had been scoured by water, layer by layer, so that it curved in uneven bands all the way down to where the surf surged in under a rocky lip. Light glanced in as the tide slowly began to ebb, but they could hear the treacherous roar and crash of water splashing over jagged rocks outside this great cave before it foamed in under the lip, tidal height sending rills of water across the cave floor in a surge that clinked and chinged softly as it was sucked back out under the stone lip.

The light was wavering, greenish, but strong enough to pick out in cold gleams and glitters the man-sized piles of gold, gems, kingly objects made of rare metals, that heaped and spilled in horse-sized mounds over the rocky floor, scattered by the unending flow of water. Here and there lay the whitish-green bones of the dead, all of them lying in attitudes that suggested an end not by supernatural means but by the usual human violence. Tau stared, feeling oppressed by the hot, pungent air, the greenish light, by the miasma of greed and betrayal and murder that seemed to permeate the cave.

Jeje stared down at the pebbly ground between surges, where the splintered wrecks of small boats tangled with yet more skeletal remains. In a world where bodies were usually Disappeared after death, these silent remains of old pirate feuds appeared especially sinister. Maybe these were the supposed ghosts, Jeje thought, seeing the old bones pitch back and forth with the current underneath the surface waters. The theory made sense, it was eminently practical. But she had to admit to herself that she wasn't convinced enough to speak.

"Brotherhood," she whispered, and echoes hissed back at her. "Probably attacked one another over this stuff."

Dasta straightened up, his hawk nose lifted as he sniffed around. "Either that or the captains who had the treasure brought in killed those who did the carrying. Secret stays with one person."

Jeje nodded. "And that would explain why they left the bodies here. Because you cannot Disappear the person you murder."

"Or they were left as warnings." It was the second time Fox had spoken.

Dasta stared at the treasure, then swung his head toward Inda, his brow furrowed, brown eyes concerned. Inda never did anything without reason.

Fox said, "Well?"

Inda lifted his hands. "Here it is. No one else seems to know about it. Marshig and his favorite captains are gone, and so is the Brotherhood's single map. Ramis burned it yesterday. So, it appears, the entire wealth of the Brotherhood of Blood is now ours."

Fox propped a boot on a rock, leaned his elbow on his knee, and stared down at Inda.

Inda jumped off the last stair and splashed to the first mound. He kicked at a small pile of gold, sending six- and twelve-sided coins tinkling unmusically down the pile before they *plink-plunked* into the shallow water.

Then he looked up at each of them: Tau, Dasta, Jeje. Fox. "And so we either use some of it for my plans and leave the rest to the future, whatever that may bring, or you turf me and take it. You all know how to get here, and all four of you are armed. I'm not. If you don't want to follow me, go ahead and kill me now—I don't want to be watching my back forever. Not against any of you."

Tau saw it first. Everything—the journey, the gold, Inda's peculiar orders that it be only the five of them, in secret, and that they were to go armed—had all been made just for Fox. Dasta was astonished, Jeje affronted.

Inda wasn't paying any attention to her. He watched Fox—as did the others, one by one.

Fox lounged above, halfway down the stair—in command of the only really defensible position in that cave full of treasure. The single ray of slanting light caught ruddy highlights in his red hair, and illuminated one sharp cheekbone. Otherwise he was nearly invisible against the dark rock.

Inda said, "Ramis said that Venn warships are on the way."

No one argued.

"I want to launch tomorrow if I can, the next day if necessary. East into the strait while the weather holds. I want to get to Bren by midsummer. The Guild Fleet has its headquarters there. My plan is to take command of them, if they are willing, and build a fleet to clear the strait—and the southern seas—of the Venn."

Fox moved his hands, but not to grasp his knives. He straightened up and clapped slowly, derisively. "A very pretty speech. And now, it seems, your loyal mates are waiting for me to betray you. Is that it, loyal mates?"

Jeje flushed, crossing her arms. Dasta looked down. Only Tau returned his gaze, a mirror of his own mockery.

"I want to know if you are with me or not." Inda turned from Fox to the others, opening both hands toward the piles of treasure. "Here's the wherewithal for your plans. All you have to do is turf me out first. I'm not even armed." He put his hands on his hips. "If it's going to happen, I'd rather it be now."

Fox gazed down at Inda, or rather beyond Inda. Plans? What plans? He'd made some wild statements, fueled by drink, about a pirate empire, but surely Inda did not—

Empire—

Fox drew a slow breath. His head ached; he wished he could breathe. He did not believe anything without material form was any threat. And yet he seemed to hear a whispering, a soughing of voices just audible above the hiss and surge of the sea, and Inda's form blurred curiously, as if he were doubled—either that, or some non-physical presence stood behind his left shoulder.

Mere trick of vision. From hunger, thirst, the thick, hot air. He knew that. Yet he swallowed—twice—as he faced the fact that, once again, Inda had been ahead of him.

Empire. Not a pirate empire at all. A treasure that the son of displaced kings could use to hire and field an army to retake a kingdom taken by treachery, now grown into an empire.

His skull rang as if he had put his head inside a great bell.

"Pirate empires," he drawled—relieved his voice sounded normal—"are for you to make. I'm far too lazy."

Trying to hide his relief, Dasta squatted down to poke at a golden pitcher that was carved all around with firebirds.

Tau thought: *Inda, you really are an innocent. You have changed nothing.* But he did not speak.

Inda looked up, then away, then up again.

"We'll spend the rest of the day loading the *Vixen*. That should give us enough to buy us a kingdom-sized fleet, in addition to whatever the Guild decides to give us."

Then Dasta said, "But loading all this gold'd take days. I take it you aren't planning to tote the whole stash."

"No."

"So," Dasta said, "did you want to just leave it here?"

Inda waved a hand. "It's been safe enough until now." And with a wry look that did not single out anyone in particular, "According to all the histories, gold—this much gold—tends to take care of itself."

He started back up the stone stairs.

The rest of the day was long, hot labor broken by stops for drinks from the waterfall or another of the pure, sweet streams trickling down toward the sea, and brief, breathless exchanges.

The others all seemed to want private converse with Inda.

Tau included. But he knew how to bide his time.

He stitched together a new set of bags for the sackloads of treasure they'd brought down the trail, his fingers nimble from years of sewing. He could even sew without having to watch what he was doing, the better to covertly observe Inda and Fox talking low-voiced under the shade of the last tree before the blinding white sand of the beach. The tendons on Fox's hands stood up as he gestured violently, his stance tense. Inda shook his head from side to side and repeated something over and over.

Fox said something sharp in Marlovan.

Jeje came up behind Tau. "Harskialdna. What's that mean?"

On her other side, Dasta flipped his palms skyward before returning to stacking loaded bags.

Tau said, "It means Royal Shield Arm."

Jeje frowned. "I hate it when they talk in Marlovan. I don't know why—I never mind other lingos I don't know."

Fox flung himself away, hesitated, then dashed up the trail for another load. Tau stitched, Jeje packed little bags with gold, Dasta tied off and stacked the bags. No one spoke as Inda joined them.

Dasta caught up with Inda on his fourth trip back. "You have a plan?" He looked around, then added, "I'm with you, no mistake about that. But the Venn. You *know* they're far bigger than the Brotherhood ever was. They're, well, an *empire*. Up there in the north." He swept his hand outward to take in the entire northern hemisphere.

Inda grinned. "Bigger. Drilled. Equipped. We can't go to war against them with pirates, we'll need a military force this time, or as near as we can get."

Dasta heard the hesitation in his voice. "But?"

Inda ran his sleeve over his forehead. "But first we need something better than those sun-trackers, which don't allow for wind or current. To meet the Venn and expect to win we must find out how they navigate in deep waters. We will have to capture one of their sea dags. That's their name for mages that navigate their ships in deep water."

Dasta whistled. "So we won't need gold, nice as it is; we'll need magic?"

Inda said, "Short of a dag coming forward to volunteer, which I don't see happening, we'll have to find one any way we can."

Jeje's conversation with Inda was even shorter.

It was late in the day, which Jeje had spent rowing back and forth with a skiff full of bags of gold and jewels. She'd loaded them into the hold of the *Vixen* herself, stowing them to keep the vessel in just the right trim. The sky was now full of tiny marching lambkin clouds, presaging one of the sudden storms that boiled up out of nowhere in this part of the world. She followed Inda down into the skiff, where they set their last load at their feet.

As she took up oars, she eyed him with her straight black brows meeting over her nose, and said abruptly, "We heard Fox. That is, we heard Marlovan, and I thought 'Harskialdna' was cursing, but Tau says it means Royal Shield Arm. I'd feel better if I know what a Marlovan's idea of a Shield Arm is, royal or not."

Inda leaned into the oars. "It isn't a 'royal' Shield Arm, it's a war king's Shield Arm."

"A war king?" Jeje snorted. "That does sound *just* like Marlovans."

"Go ahead and regard it as a curse, if you like," Inda said, giving her a brief, sardonic grin—a rare expression for him. "He was using it scornfully, if that helps."

"No," she said stolidly, but Inda only smiled and put his back into rowing.

Jeje repressed a sigh. Inda wasn't going to say anything more. He never talked about his past. Despite whatever had forced him away from his home all those years ago, he still thought like a Marlovan.

She bit down hard on her lip. While she didn't regret that sting at the Marlovans, she regretted saying it to Inda.

They rowed six, ten strokes, sending the boat skimming over the pure blue water of the lagoon, and then Inda gave her an apologetic smile. "Take it this way. Fox is haunted by worse ghosts than any on this island. They are all his ancestors."

Jeje opened her mouth to say that that wasn't any answer at all, that it left her with more questions than she'd had before. Then she thought the better of it.

Tau's conversation was last, and shortest of all. They had just set sail as the sun dove toward a fast-moving line of clouds on the western sea, the sky over the island behind them deepening to indigo, lit by stars more brilliant in color than any of the gemstones they had left behind. Fox was below, Jeje at the tiller, Dasta tending the sail.

Tau joined Inda, who stood alone at the bow of the dangerously laden scout craft, looking across the deep blue water toward the distant twinkling lights of the main island's harbor.

Tau said, "You can't think your offer back in the cave resolved the question of ambition and greed once and for all?"

Inda's eyes narrowed. "You mean Fox."

Tau opened his hands.

Inda flicked a grin. "Course not. But I think saying it
straight out like that—well, if Fox does change his mind,
he'll tell me." He tipped his head. "Probably argue."

And so I underestimated you. Or Fox. "Is Ramis going to
come after us?" His forefinger slashed between sky· and
sea.

Inda leaned his bare forearms on the rail. "Ramis told
me that he expected to be gone within the year. The way he
said it cost me a lot of thought last night. We don't, after all,
really know what life and death even mean in Norsunder.
But I'm sure of this, he spoke the truth to me, and he and I
will never see one another again."

Tau said, "Right. Then in that case, let us get this hoard
of yours aboard the *Death* before the weather swamps us
and saves the Venn any effort."

Chapter Five

LONG, low, rake-masted, and black-hulled, the *Death* rode in the midst of Inda's small fleet out in Halfmoon Harbor, the raffee *Cocodu* on one side, the two schooners on the other, the sketch crews battening down against the coming storm.

Gillor checked forward and aft to see that everything was bowsed down and furled except for the storm sail on the foremast, ready for the blow swiftly devouring the northwestern sky.

"Sail hai!" called someone from the foremast.

Gillor peered toward the harbor. The clouds seemed to touch the top of the hills; at least the wind would not drive them into land, she reflected, but safely seaward. "Bearing where?"

"Direct astern. *Vixen*."

Gillor leaped to the shrouds, impatiently raking back the black curls that had escaped from her queue. Her scalp and her neck were sticky from the breathless heat. She'd wanted to signal for more crew, but Inda had been definite last night when he put her in charge of the ship. *Pick a crew you can trust, the fewer the better, and hold the* Death *until the* Vixen *returns,* he had said.

Vixen—usually as swift and graceful as a reed skimmer— wallowed up on the lee, so low the choppy seas kicking up ahead of the storm winds were washing down the deck.

The *Vixen* hove to, its sails brailed swiftly by the captains who'd taken it away.

Inda vaulted over the side a moment later, his face gold-lit, then shadowed by the light of the swinging binnacle lantern. "Dismiss the rest of your watch below. Ride out the storm," he ordered. "Let's get relieving tackle to the helm before the wind rises. We have some fast unloading to do."

The small crew, on watch since the night before, did not question—they seemed glad to vanish below, leaving the storm for the new watch to deal with.

Curiosity spiked yet again at the promising chink of metal in the little bags that Jeje, Tau, Fox, Dasta, and Inda brought aboard as swiftly as they could, staggering with the heavy weight while waves dashed against the railing, kicking high surges of water that the wind then poured, hissing white, down the deck. The wind shrieked on a higher and higher note through the rigging.

But the heavy little bags came on, until Gillor, her jaw locked with tension, feared that the *Vixen* would smash against the *Death*. But she said nothing, only stood at the helm, hands gripped tight, her body set against the groaning, shuddering wood.

Inda judged his mysterious unloading to a nicety.

Just as Gillor was ready to despair, Jeje's regular crew were brought out of *Death*'s wardroom and dispatched to help Jeje sail *Vixen* around to the lee of *Cocodu* to drop Dasta there, Tau going with them. Fox brought up two more of the crew to take station at the foremast.

The lightened *Vixen* raced over the waves, vanishing in the silver-gleaming spears of rain that momentarily flattened the sea, lit by blue-white lightning.

Gillor was soaked to the skin within about three breaths. Inda joined her at the helm, tested the tension of the relieving tackle with one palm, and took up station on the weather side, Gillor shifting gladly to the lee. Together they fought to keep the ship pointed up into the wind, bracing themselves, tired as they were, for an all-night fight; summer squalls frequently lasted that long in the southern waters. Here on the belt of the world they were usually short, coming in waves; though one wouldn't last long, you wouldn't know if another squall, and even a third, was following rapidly after.

The storm passed swiftly after dropping showers so thick and warm they'd had to turn their faces leeward so they could breathe, and they could not see Fox and his hands at the foremast.

At least this storm was alone. Rumbles and flashes moved southeast, leaving a pure, rain-washed sky filled with the jeweled gleam of multicolored stars and a thin sliver of moon rising, and they'd only made a little headway.

"West wind," Inda said, his voice husky with tiredness. "Spring is really here, and we have the wind right where we want it. If it stays steady we could reach the middle of the strait by midsummer. Two months at the outside."

Gillor said, "We're leaving?"

Inda said, "Soon as we can. Listen, Gillor. I ask that you keep to yourself what you saw and heard."

She realized then that she'd been the only one he'd trusted to see that unloading. She swallowed. Even after all this time, she wasn't used to trust, did not know how to respond to it.

But Inda went right on, as if he didn't expect her to speak—or swear an oath. "We're going to find the Guild Fleet. I'll give everyone a choice, whether or not they want to fight the Venn." And when she hesitated, he smiled. "You don't have to decide now. We've got until summer before we reach Bren. Meanwhile, I'll send Tau to pay our shots and see to last supplies."

Gillor laughed. "That one, he could talk Norsunder into peace and plenty."

The swinging lamp made it difficult to see Inda's expression before he turned away, stopped, then turned back. "When did you sleep last?"

"Night before. We came aboard just after the midnight watch. I stayed on deck. Thought that was your order."

"Go below. I'll take the helm until the change." And, seeing her hesitate, Inda added, "I need the time to think."

She raised a hand as she trotted down the still-streaming gangway. He watched her hip-swinging stride, a privateer's stride. Such a conversation after an order would never have happened in the Marlovan military and he suspected it was the same for any navy. Could he successfully use the shifting nature of authority common to the pirate life to defeat the tradition of hard-drilled obedience of the Venn military?

Fox's voice rose above the hissing of the diminishing waves, ordering the green flag hoisted to the top of the mainmast. The watch-change bell tinged; the lookout lanterns were hung once again, and the remainder of Gillor's scant crew emerged, most refreshed from sleep. They began setting sail so they could beat back into the inner harbor and opened the hatches to air the hot, stuffy cabins below.

Inda watched idly as Fox oversaw the work. He knew he could not take independents and privateers against the Venn—arguing, fighting, side-switching independents, owing allegiance to no one, their goal usually confined to immediate wealth and the prospect of squandering it. Sometimes the division between independents and pirates was a very narrow one indeed.

So he needed discipline, but that required consent first. So how did one get the consent of pirates?

Inda felt the wind dying and knew he could tie the helm down and slacken sail, but it felt good, tired as he was, to lean against the polished wood, feel the ship creaking sleepily underfoot, sniff the clean air with its tang of the sea. The treasure stowed below in the captain's private, locked hold had stiffened the *Death* slightly, setting it by the stern so that the masts raked even more sharply back. Big as it was, it would handle like a scout in most winds, and he would need speed and agility.

He would need speed.

"I'm going ashore." Fox leaned against the rail, Gillor's tired crew standing by to boom down the launch. "I can name those who'll stay with us and those who'll run. Let 'em run with my goodwill. Most of them are worthless. But some of those who'll ship out with us might see fit to kick up some trouble before the morning tide. I want to be able to return to this island without getting my throat cut, so I might have to break a few heads to remind them of their manners."

Fox would only take a couple of crew to handle the launch; he was capable of doing his reminding on his own. Everyone in the fleet—probably on the island, by now—knew that nobody outfought him and his Marlovan steel.

"There were also a few possible hires," Fox added.

Inda heard the question in his statement. "Tell them the new plan. If they still want on, find out their experience."

Fox lifted a hand, and presently the launch splashed down, raised a sail, and eased away toward the shore, faster in the variable breezes than the *Death* making its way at a stately pace back toward the harbor.

Inda remembered he was going to send Tau, and ran up a signal so that *Cocodu* would come up on the lee.

Then he leaned his arms between the spokes of the helm. Either his fleet followed him or not. Either Fox challenged him or not. No use worrying. Just go on.

So what was first in "on"? Supplies to be seen to. Weapons. Then drills. A mage to be found, new tactics to be designed and practiced.

He thought of these things as little threads stretching across the empty loom of the future, a loom built like the ones he'd seen every day in Tenthen Castle at home, before he was sent to the academy to train in military command, with Sponge and Noddy and Cama and Cherry-Stripe.

And Dogpiss—

No. Forget the past. You cannot change it.

Look to the future. Which ships to send where. Crew, training. What he'd say to the Guild Fleet organizers when he reached Bren. Where to seek what he needed to know about the Venn. Whom to trust to what task. Warp. Weft.

He picked up the glass and swept the harbor, more for something to do than anything else. To his surprise he saw one of the little hired boats set out into the choppy seas. He straightened up as it sped toward them, slanting with the wind.

The lookout yelled, "Boat ahoy!"

"Hire!" came a woman's voice.

Inda looked down at the battered hired coracle bumping up against the trysail's smooth hull.

"Come aboard," he called.

A short, bandy-legged, weathered woman scrambled aboard and swung her patched, worn sailor bag to thump on the captain's deck. Even in the darkness there was no mistaking a Delf. Impossible or not, he seemed to be getting a Delf as a volunteer.

She faced Inda. "Fibi Rumm by mother relation of Fussef, cousin-second to Niz Findl."

Inda grimaced. "If you are looking for Niz, I am sorry to have to tell you that he died by pirates' hands. I told his family when we stopped at the Delfin Islands a couple months ago."

Fibi poked her beaky nose forward, a gesture that brought Niz strongly to mind. "So the word is," she replied without any hint of sentiment. "The Fussefs decided to send another o' us. Me you'll be needin', especially if you take on one o' them square-sail Venn shits."

Inda stared into pale eyes in a face whose age was impossible to guess. "How did you know that?" he asked.

She shrugged one shoulder. "Figured us Delfs, Venn's next. Makes reason, ye'd finish what ye start."

Inda smiled. "Welcome aboard. We sail on the ebb tide tomorrow."

"What's a Harskialdna? Besides a war king's Shield Arm, whatever that means?"

In the *Vixen*'s tiny cabin Jeje, Tau, and Dasta crowded around the little table, now that the worst of the storm was over, and they were no longer needed on deck.

The two scuttles were closed, the cabin door shut tight.

Tau sat back tiredly, his long hands open and loose, golden eyes reflecting the fiery lamplight overhead as it swung to and fro. "I haven't told anyone this—didn't seem to be a point. But the night before we took on the Brotherhood, I found Barend on deck. It was after that sword dance exhibition. He was alone—remember how isolated he kept himself? Just sitting there drinking and staring up at the fox banner on the *Death*. I asked its origin, and Barend was drunk enough to actually answer, instead of bowsing up like they usually do."

Dasta sighed and Jeje snickered. "Go on."

"He told me it used to be the personal banner of the Montredavan-An heirs to kingship but now they use it at some academy where they train their commanders up from boys. The one Inda was apparently in before he came to us."

Jeje shrugged. Her people, fishers for generations, had no interest in the plains-riding Marlovan warriors, their kings, or their academies. To the coastal folk the Marlovans' single virtue was that they avoided the sea.

Dasta ran his thumbnail back and forth along the wood grain as though it helped him plumb his memory. He said, frowning, "Aren't their kings called something else by way of family name?"

"Barend's name is Montrei-Vayir."

Dasta grunted. "Fox. Banner. *Our* Fox, you mean."

Tau laughed softly. "That's right. Anyway, Fox, our Fox, is the descendant of the displaced kings."

"So that's what Inda meant," Jeje said. "I think. He said Fox is haunted by his ancestors. Something like that."

"I won't pretend to know Fox's mind, because he's as close as Inda. Closer, in many ways. But what we have topside are a son of disgraced kings and a disgraced son of a prince."

Dasta dug harder into the wood grain.

Jeje groaned. "So what? So *what?* Who cares about a bunch of dead kings, or even living ones?"

"Patience," Tau said, raising a mock-admonitory finger. "When we overheard Fox accusing Inda of attempting to become Iasca Leror's Shield Arm, you can perceive some of the scope of the insult, perhaps."

Jeje hated this kind of talk; she didn't know why. On second thought, yes, she did. It was because she loathed the idea of kings. In her view, they were no better than anyone else. Underneath all the jewels and velvets and so forth was skin and bone, they ate, they farted, they snored like anyone else. But their passions didn't affect just one or two people, they affected whole kingdoms of people—people who might never see a king in their lifetime—a concept so fire-scorchingly unfair it made her itch all over.

"Inda's not doing any such thing," she said crossly. "Inda's going up against the Venn because they've all but destroyed ship trade. We all know that."

Dasta glanced from one to the other, his nails working away at the grooves in the grain.

Tau grinned across the table at her.

"Don't we?" she asked, less belligerently now.

"How much has Inda ever told us of his motives?" Tau sat back. "My mother always used to tell me that people put different values on sex at different times: sex with our people at the pleasure house, sex with others outside of it. Though she was talking about the way they came at the price of exchange, I've come to the conclusion that she spoke a general truth. That is, people put different values not just on others' lives, but their own, and the exchange isn't always money."

Dasta pointed a calloused finger. "You think our Marlovans don't value our lives? Or their own?"

The swinging lamplight gleamed in Tau's eyes, twin golden flames. "I don't think Inda has any value for his own life. Not at sea. That might be one of the reasons he's so formidable a fighter in battle, though we can all see that Fox has the edge on skill. Just barely, now that Inda seems to have gotten his full growth at last—he might not be tall but he makes up for it through here." He drew a line across his own chest.

Dasta said, "He wants to go home. I always thought that," he added in a low voice. "Wondered why he didn't after we sank the Brotherhood. But he never even went ashore, except before we left, to pay our shot."

Tau shrugged. "Let's say Inda can't go. Not because of some threat. Or even a price on his head. That wouldn't stop him if he had sufficient reason."

Jeje nodded. Anyone who had seen Inda in battle could believe that.

"It's a question of honor, which means—here I'm guessing—he really does have to have sufficient reason, something that supersedes whatever it was that disgraced him."

Jeje sighed, restless again.

Dasta rubbed his bony chin. He said, "All right. Makes sense. But why would he want to go home if they are all such shits?"

"Because they aren't. Only the king's brother and his first son are. Barend spoke well of Inda's sister, Hadand by name. She will apparently one day have to marry the royal heir. Barend loves Hadand. Says Inda does, too. And she loves him, misses him terribly. So does Barend's paternal cousin Evred, the king's younger son. Barend called Evred 'Sponge,' I cannot imagine why. Anyway, Barend spoke even more highly of this cousin Evred, or Sponge."

Jeje drew in a sharp breath, remembering Inda's first day or two on board. How he'd been staring at the bucket of red sponges just pulled up from the sea, his face drawn with pain.

"This Evred-the-Sponge being the one who is supposed to become the Marlovan Royal Shield Arm, if his brother doesn't kill him first."

Jeje snorted as directly overhead seabird feet skittered on the deck. "Figures. The ones Inda misses are the ones who have no power and are probably even dead by now. When it comes to kings, bullies *always* win—because kings *are* bullies."

Dasta laughed. "So says Jeje, who knows what's what."

Tau grinned, and Jeje flushed. "Find me one single exception if you don't believe me."

Dasta yawned. "Who cares? We're never going to meet any kings. Or queens. Rain's over." He opened a scuttle and peered out. "Looks like that might be your signal, Tau, aboard *Death*. And I want to get some shut-eye while I can. You know right well that tomorrow, if Inda or Fox don't set us to rousting our crews out of the bawdy houses, we'll be grunting supplies aboard in that heat, stowing, and making sail, all before tomorrow's ebb." Dasta grinned, an unexpectedly nasty grin that was the more startling because his expression was usually so mild. "Anyone who comes aboard drunk on my ship is gonna wish they was under a Marlovan king."

Chapter Six

MIDSUMMER'S Day was a month and a half away for the southern half of the world.

In Iasca Leror's royal city this year it meant a coronation. Not that Marlovans wore crowns. The only metal involved was the steel of swords. But the closest word for kings becoming kings in Iascan was "coronation." Before taking Iasca Leror, the Marlovans had been commanded by chieftains, usually selected after extremely violent competitions among the three ruling families and anyone else ambitious—or mad—enough to challenge them. But coronations happened in castles, and when the Marlovans took the Iascans' castles, they adopted many of their customs.

So there would not just be a coronation, but a wedding as well.

Sentries patrolled ceaselessly along the towers and walks, men looking outward, women guarding inward. Memory of the winter's bloodshed was fresh enough that the sentries were extra-vigilant in case certain Jarls thought they might try their hands at king-making with more success than Mad Gallop Yvana-Vayir had had.

While the vigilant sentries walked under the brilliant sky, pausing only to wipe their damp faces, Queen Wisthia sent a messenger from the residence wing to locate Evred and Hadand.

The queen so rarely disturbed anyone, preferring during

the long years of her marriage to remain in the stronghold
of her private rooms, that Evred and Hadand, who had far
too much to do and far too little time in which to do it, immediately left their respective tasks. They met in the hall
on the way to the queen's rooms.

"Do you know what the problem is?" Hadand asked.

His brow furrowed as he observed Hadand's worried
face. "I do not," he said. "I thought you might."

She opened her hands, flicking him a glance. Though he
had grown up with her and once would have said he knew
her better than anyone, save only his cousin Barend, he
could not account for this new habit of hers. If one could
call it a habit, that quick, anxious look into his face, followed a heartbeat later by a studied calm, her attention on
a distant corner of the room. Or a window, he discovered,
as she peered out at the alley leading to the old tack rooms
back of the stable's outbuildings.

"She's not spoken to me of it," Hadand said in a low
tone. "Not even about changing rooms. Nor would I ask,"
she added in haste. "My own rooms are fine until she goes
back to Anaeran-Adrani. If she goes?" She looked up in
question.

He said, "She's mentioned no change in plans."

During her very first interview with Evred after the
slaughter of the royal family during winter, Wisthia had
said, "May I go home?"

They were now in earshot of the female guards posted
outside the queen's suite across the hall from the king's
suite, where Evred would take up residence in a month's
time. The door to the queen's sitting room was not opposite the king's. Wisthia had chosen an entryway at the other
end of her suite, and so Evred and Hadand kept walking
down the hall. The guard women saluted, palms striking
over their hearts.

Entering the queen's chambers was like walking into another world. Hangings on the walls; low, stuffed chairs; the
scent of carefully nurtured foreign blossoms; the distant
sound of soft woodwinds and metal-stringed instruments,
all were designed to recreate her Adrani home.

Evred had always found his mother's rooms alien and

cloying; Hadand was used to them, and had even come to appreciate the artistry in their design.

Queen Wisthia, tall and thin, her hair grayer than it had been in winter, gestured from her inner chamber. A maid-servant curtseyed to them, a gesture Evred found odd, though he'd seen his mother's servants do it all his life.

"My dears," said the queen, as Evred kissed her hands in the way she had taught him when he was small.

Evred said, hoping to please her, "The highest mountain passes have been clear for at least a month. You can go home whenever you like."

Wisthia looked at her only living son, and again re-pressed the surge of sorrow for what might have been, what never could be. The truth was, they had nothing to say to one another. After his birth he'd been locked into the Marlovan way of upbringing as had her first son, who had willfully pulled away from her to embrace his uncle's war teachings. The prospect of enduring that rejection yet again had caused her to avoid Evred once his Marlovan educa-tion had begun; consequently he had grown up regarding her as a benevolent but distant figure, removed from any of his concerns.

Both wanted it to be different, but it wasn't.

So she said, "I will stay to see you take your place as king. For my own pleasure, and because I think it right. I will depart directly after. But I have a last pair of requests before I prepare for that departure."

"Please speak," he said, courteous and remote to her as always.

Hadand, acutely sensitive to every shade and timbre of his voice, heard the regret that he would rather have hidden.

"I would like to take Hadand with me, for a visit."

"Me?" Hadand exclaimed.

"To preside in her place here, I would have you invite Fareas-Iofre of Choraed Elgaer."

"My mother?" Hadand whispered; then she closed her mouth, thinking, *Mother never leaves Tenthen Castle.* The next thought was: *Would she if she could?*

Evred opened his mouth to deny the request as impossi-ble, but the queen forestalled him. "Think on it for a time, my

son." She added with a wry smile, "I know that your negotiations with my brother for the treaty renewal have stalled."

Evred and Hadand could not prevent reactions of surprise, subtle as they were: no more than his putting his
hands behind his back, and her eyes turning upward to his,
but Wisthia saw these things. "I have stayed most straightly
out of Marlovan affairs, for your late uncle negotiated
specifically for my noninterference when I first came here,
but I cannot help knowing a little of what concerns my
homeland."

Evred said, "It is true, the negotiations have stalled, and
I do not know why."

"Well, I can find out. I will carry your interests in my
heart as much as I can. And I believe that Hadand, visiting
as a queen as well as my brother's niece, might rekindle
mutual interests."

"But is it safe?" Evred asked. "What if—"

He gestured, not wanting to accuse his mother's relations.

She took his meaning at once, and said dryly, "Only a
Marlovan would think of hostages. But believe me, my son,
whatever vagaries my brother indulges in now that he is
king, he is not mad. No one beyond the Iascan border
would dream of threatening you: they are fearful enough
of your people charging down upon them as it is."

"I don't want more wars," Evred said, faintly accusing.

"So said your father, once upon a time," she retorted, but
without anger. "As for Fareas-Iofre, if Hadand's well-
respected mother is here overseeing the queen's duties, it
might go a long way toward establishing a sense of continuity with the older people."

Hadand drew in a slow breath. She had always known
that the queen was intelligent, well-read in Sartoran history and poetry, but she'd always thought her to be as distant from Marlovan politics as the clouds from the
windblown grasses below.

Evred said slowly, "I can see possible benefits, though
our rulers have seldom left the borders. Hadand's visit
would have to be short, as early fall can bring snow to the
high passes." He turned to Hadand, adding, "And if she
does not wish to go, then there the matter must end."

Hadand met his inquiring hazel eyes, so concerned, so scrupulous—and so free of the heat of desire. She tried to match his concerned, equable tone as she said, "I will go. I might be able to learn something of benefit that I can bring back." Her reward was Evred's smile.

He said, "Very well." And to his mother, "You spoke of two requests?"

Wisthia's acute gaze moved from one face to the other, then she said, "I wish to have Hadand accompanied by Joret Dei." Another surprise. "I realize that Joret is officially designated as the wife-to-be should the Algara-Vayir heir come home. What was his name?" she asked, watching her son under lowered lids.

"Inda. Indevan-Laef." Evred said, his voice flat and a little husky.

The queen continued, "But young Indevan, I am told, is nowhere in Iasca Leror, and while I hope he may one day return, I think Joret deserves time away. This past year or so has been a hardship for her, through no fault of her own."

"Hardship." A diplomatic understatement, considering how close the Sierlaef had come to tearing the already tense kingdom apart, just because of unrequited lust.

"We owe Joret. Let us offer her the choice, shall we?"

Hadand thought rapidly ahead. What would her mother say? Of course she'd think of duty first—but surely Tdor was capable of leading castle defense. More than capable, as Whipstick Noth was capable of territory defense, especially with his formidable father, Dragoon Captain Noth, stationed not far away. It was a possibility, startling though it sounded. "Permit me to write the letter."

The queen nodded. "As it concerns your mother and your foster sister, I think it appropriate. But you must convey my personal greetings and best wishes. Make it clear this is not any kind of summons, only a request. From me."

Hadand struck her fist over her heart.

Evred said, with his customary courtesy, "We will send it with crown Runners, the better to speed them." Everyone considered the distance to Choraed Elgaer, far to the south, and how hard the Runners would have to ride

in order to bring them back in time for Midsummer's
Day.

He kissed his mother's hands, saluted Hadand, and left.

Hadand waited as the queen outlined more details to be
included in the letter. She scarcely heard. Her gaze was out
the window, down toward the stables where she saw, right
on time, three figures sneaking by.

"There they go," an old Runner grumped as he hefted his
basket of reeking oil-wrapped torches and started up the
next flight of steps toward the north tower.

His companion, another gray-haired man who'd been a
Guard before a skirmish with brigands ruined his riding,
grunted as he shifted his basket to his other shoulder to
ease his bad leg. "Do they really think nobody sees 'em?"

They paused on the landing, peering down through the
arrow slits of the main residence wing toward the warren
of walled courts below, leading to the huge stable complex.
No hint of a breeze, even up here.

Below, Cama Tya-Vayir, Noddy Toraca, and Cherry-
Stripe Marlo-Vayir strode fast along a narrow accessway,
the ringing of their high-heeled black-weave cavalry boots
echoing up the stone walls.

"*He* doesn't see," the first man said. "All that matters."

The second one, fighting a sharp twinge in his knee, massaged the spot with one gnarled hand as he reflected. "No.
He wouldn't expect anything."

Everyone knew who *he* was, but until he gave his oath as
king, no one knew what to call Evred. Strictly speaking he
was the Sierlaef, the heir, but his brother been Sierlaef too
long for people to shed the prejudicial associations.

The second man hefted his load of torches, glowered at
the remaining stairway, and cursed under his breath. "What
I'd like," he said in an undertone, "is my grip on the shithead
who decided war kings have to do coronations at midnight."

Below, the three walked faster, Cherry-Stripe glancing
behind him, his long yellow horsetail swinging over his
shoulder and back.

Above, on the inner castle walls, stood two women and a girl, the women part of the Queen's Guard, the girl newly arrived from far south, here for the queen's training.

The sun beat down on their heads, and even though the women's summer robes were now mostly made of the new light fabric, a mixture of their old linen and the plentiful cotton brought from Idayago, those robes were worn over high-necked linen shirts sashed at the waist, and sturdy loose trousers. All three were already damp with sweat. Not that they paid any attention.

"Mmm-mmm," said the tallest and oldest of the Queen's Guards, looking down at the three young men with deep appreciation.

"Why are they alone like that? No Runners or anything?" the new girl asked.

The two older women grinned. "A secret meeting. Look, there goes my choice out of all of 'em, right into the old tack rooms." She pointed a bow-calloused finger down at Cama, whose splendid body was enhanced by the gray coat of his ancestors, tight to the sashed waist, the wide back-slit coat skirts swinging against his boots.

All three gazed appreciatively at his long horsetail of curling black hair, the sharp-cut bones of his cheeks and chin, the fine mouth below the dashing and slightly sinister black eye patch.

"Who *is* that?" the girl asked.

"Oh, that's Camarend-Dal of Tya-Vayir," said one of the women. "They call him Cama. He acted as Harskialdna after the Conspiracy, before handing it off to Barend-Dal."

"There's young Cherry-Stripe," the second woman said.

"And they call that third one Noddy, I've heard, though no one knows why. Like Cherry-Stripe, they all get these names in the academy."

"I know," the girl said with an air of vast experience. "My brother came home called Dogbreath his first year, and now he won't let anyone use his real name."

"Noddy looks like one of the track-hounds," the first commented. "Some might say he's not as easy on the eyes as Cherry-Stripe and Cama Black-Eye, but I'd take a gallop if he was offering just fine."

The words were no sooner out of her mouth than she caught the affronted glance of her duty mate, and they turned guilty glances to the girl, who was in the long, sturdy smock and loose trousers that looked much like what her brother was no doubt wearing over at the academy. She was probably fifteen, the usual age at which the girls who would be future Jarlans or Randviars came for their two years of training with the queen's guard, and while everyone knew girls reached the age of interest before the boys, at fifteen some were still a long way off. Proper was proper: you didn't talk about sex before someone in smocks.

The serene smile of this girl made it clear that she was envisioning nothing more intimate than a horseback ride on the plains next to an agreeably handsome fellow; the first guard said, somewhat hastily, "So anyway that's part of 'em in on the secret meetings. The organizers, you might say."

"Secret meeting?" the girl asked, a little worried—remembering the bloody stories the second year girls had told her the first night after her arrival—but mostly excited. Secrets were always interesting, but they were twice as delicious when they concerned people of rank.

The other two laughed. "Secret in a way, young 'un, only in a way. They're here instead of at home because they are *his* Sier-Danas, see? Only one that doesn't know is *him*. He was a second son, see, and he always does everything proper, so he just ordered twelve drums for the coronation. His Sier-Danas, well, they're going to make sure it's done the way everyone else sees as proper."

"Oh," she said. "Does Hadand-Edli know too?"

"Of course!" said the first.

"It's she who worked out the details, as 't should be."

The girl clasped her hands. "And she'll be Gunvaer, too, and not have to wait until she's old, because everyone says the old queen is going back over the mountains." She used two different words for queen: for Wisthia the Iascan *Sarias*, taken from Sartoran. But Hadand was a Marlovan queen, a fighting queen, so they used the Marlovan *Gunvaer*.

"All as it should be," the girl said happily, for she loved romance. She added in a rush, "The second-year girls told us that Hadand and the new king were ever so close, all their lives, though they were each intended to marry some-one else. It's like one of the old love ballads!"

The guards' eyes met over her head, and the first one said, roughly, "Hadand-Edli is a good woman. She deserves to be happy," though no one had been arguing.

The two guards hefted their strung bows and resumed their patrol, no longer speaking—leaving the girl, on her very first watch, wondering how she'd managed to offend them.

Chapter Seven

"INDEVAN-Dal is dead!" Spittle flecked the old woman's wrinkled lips. Her mottled face, hard-furrowed with decades of anger, contrasted nightmarishly with that of Joret Dei, who stood against the window wall of Fareas-Iofre's formal interview chamber, her remarkable blue eyes blank.

Marend-Edli, once Randviar, jerked a gnarled thumb in Joret's direction and said, "He's long dead. Give it up, Fareas. Joret should marry Branid. Now. Branid should have been Branid-Laef ever since your boy Tanrid was killed, but you can fix that now. Give my grandson the title, marry him to Joret, and he can take up his proper place as heir to Algara-Vayir. That Noth boy can be Branid's Randael, and Tdor here can marry him and be Randviar as before."

Fareas-Iofre spoke, cool and austere. "My son is Indevan-Laef, not Indevan-Dal. His becoming heir was my husband's decree. You were there. You heard it. And I will not believe Inda is dead until I am shown proof."

The old woman gave an ugly laugh, more of a harsh, humorless caw. "There's never any proof at sea. Unless you've found a fish that carries letters?"

Standing at Fareas' right shoulder, Tdor bit her underlip, her hands hidden in the sleeves of her robes gripping hard over her wrist sheaths. *Inda is not dead*, Tdor thought furiously. *You just want him to be, you old carrion-eater.*

Joret's eyes met hers, and Tdor saw anger in the flicker of her long lashes, the tautness of her high forehead. But Joret did not move or speak, and she was the subject of this confrontation between the princess of Choraed Elgaer and the Randviar of two generations ago. So Tdor remained silent.

Fareas-Iofre said, "How many years did all Iasca Leror believe the Harskialdna's son Barend-Dal dead at sea? But he returned alive. My son Indevan was seen a bare five months ago, no longer than a fighting season on land, and I have every reason to believe he lives yet."

"Lives? Maybe. But not here, taking up his responsibilities. Word is he prefers a pirate's life," the old woman said, her scorn undiminished. "*My* grandson will do his duty. Uphold the family's honor. But you must cede him his rightful place." And seeing Fareas' compressed lips, old Marend shook her head. Her voice stayed gruff with emotion, but no anger, for once. "I know what it is to have to give up. To give place. Your Jarend turfed my husband and me fifty years ago, after his own father died. Jarend put his brother Indevan and his wife in our places. As was right. He inherits, he trained Old Indevan. A brother should be Randael to a brother. That's the Marlovan way."

She paused, and Fareas-Iofre opened her hand.

"And I said nothing when Jarend-Adaluin's first family were all killed by attack thirty-some years ago. I said nothing when he should have taken my son as his heir and my nephew as Randael, instead keeping his old Rider Captain as Randael and marrying you. It was need. The Rider Captain had more experience than my son, who was just out of boyhood, and my nephew a mere babe. But now your sons are gone and Branid is full-grown in the eyes of law. If he marries Joret and takes his place as Laef, everyone has time to learn his ways, and he will learn your husband's ways before Jarend dies, as is right and proper. Branid is Algara-Vayir," she added. "Who has more right?"

"No one," Fareas said. "Outside of Inda. I must consult with my husband—"

Marend-Edli snorted, a disgusting liquid sound. Her ever-ready anger was back. "Who does what you tell him—

when he can be made to hear anyone outside of his ghosts." The old woman's eyes narrowed. "Take another six months. A year, if that eases your conscience. But after that year, whatever happens will be on your head: you can transfer the title peaceably or not. As you choose." She twitched her robes closer about her meager body and stalked to the door, her silent Runner, nearly as ancient but strong as a century-old ash, walking silently after her.

Tdor watched her go, angry disgust her foremost reaction until she thought, *Will that be me in fifty years? Old, ugly, doing my duty until I'm displaced, then disappointed again and again?* She winced, remorse cooling the anger like snow on fire.

Through the open door Tdor and Joret caught sight of Branid lurking in the hall—tall, broad, blond, his customary sulky expression twisted into anxiousness as his grandmother stalked past him. "What did they say? What did Joret say?"

They could hear his voice diminishing before Chelis, Fareas-Iofre's Runner, shut the door.

Fareas lifted her head. "Whipstick? You heard it all?"

The inner door leading to the Iofre's private room had been open a crack. It opened and tough, wiry Whipstick Noth stepped through. He seldom revealed any emotion, but his bony face now twisted with derision. "Enough," he said. "She threatened you."

Fareas-Iofre turned her palm up. "She gave herself away."

Tdor said, "Everyone has been talking about her promises and bribes. Now we know toward what end."

Whipstick said, "No one would follow Branid otherwise."

Tdor said, "No one will follow him at all. But some might think they can run him if he inherits Jarend-Adaluin's place."

None disagreed; Fareas just looked tired. "She and my husband have hated one another for more than half a century, so she won't dare to disturb him," Fareas said. "And without his agreement, nothing will change, and she knows it."

Unspoken was the alternative: that the Adaluin, whose health was more frail with every winter he survived, might die before Inda's return. He spent his winter days prowling the upper rooms, seeking the ghost of his beloved first wife, which had departed after the death of the Harskialdna.

He was out on his duty ride now, the weather being clement. They had all been glad to see him take horse; he strengthened during long summer days in the open air.

Whipstick said, "Fareas-Edli, a royal Runner appeared just after Marend-Edli came upstairs."

No one spoke, but the subtle signs—no more than tight shoulders, a fast glance or two—revealed their apprehension. There'd been far too much bad news conveyed by royal Runners over the past year.

Whipstick said, "I bade her wait in the watch room, Fareas-Edli."

"Bring her in, if you will."

A swing of coat skirts, the twitch of a long brown horsetail, and Whipstick was gone. Fareas studied Joret, who had not moved from her place next to the window, the summer sun glinting in the blue highlights of her silken black hair. She stared out the window, her brow troubled.

It was not Joret's fault that once again a man was making trouble on her behalf. She was cool, sober, hard-working, and in spite of her astonishing beauty she was quiet and self-effacing, the opposite of the aunt she so closely resembled. The older Joret, the Adaluin's first wife, had been the opposite: lazy, capricious, loving luxury and ease. Her single passion had been to live as the center of attention and desire, and to that end she had exerted herself.

Joret had never been seen to exert the smallest sign of attraction to anyone. She did not even visit the pleasure houses. Yet ever since she'd reached the age of consent she had been, like her aunt, the center of trouble—first the king's son and now Branid at home. *Beauty is a weapon*, Fareas thought. *Even if she doesn't use it, it cuts on its own.*

Whipstick opened the door, letting in a royal Runner in a blue tunic, the gold crown stitched over her heart indicating that she bore an official communication.

The Runner held out a message, and Fareas, Tdor, and

Joret recognized on her forefinger the plain ring, inset with a small emerald, that indicated a message from Hadand.

Fareas-Iofre opened the scroll, then exclaimed softly. She handed the letter to Joret; dusky rose bloomed in her smooth, honey-colored cheeks, then faded.

Joret handed the letter to Tdor, who glanced at Fareas in question, saw a slight nod, and moved so that Whipstick could read over her shoulder. In surprise they discovered two breaks with tradition: an invitation to Fareas-Iofre to see her daughter crowned and then stay—and an invitation to Joret to accompany Hadand and the former queen, among whose women she'd spent a year, to Anaeran-Adrani.

Fareas-Iofre studied her hands, noting with part of her attention how old they looked. No Iofre had ever left Tenthen Castle as far as she knew, but times had become so strange. Why this invitation from a queen she had never met? No clue in the letter, but Hadand would tell her if she went.

So should she go?

Peace had come to Choraed Elgaer at last, except for these troubles in the family. Whipstick and Tdor could be trusted to protect not only Choraed Elgaer but also Jarend-Adaluin. In an extreme emergency, Captain Noth at Fera-Vayir Harbor could ride to their aid.

Added to that was her strong wish, always, to see her daughter again. She felt almost as strong a desire to meet Evred, this young man who had sent her copies of precious historical manuscripts, she suspected written out in his own hand. Yes, it seemed good to go.

She lifted her head and studied each young face. Whipstick's bony countenance did not express much; Tdor looked worried, then thoughtful. Joret stayed mute, her color heightened.

"Shall I wait outside?" the Runner asked.

"No. You are Hadand's own Runner, are you not?" Fareas-Iofre said kindly. "You may hear our words, which will not take long; then I promise you food, drink, and rest, before you return."

The runner struck her fist over her heart and retreated

to stand next to Chelis, who knew her. The two exchanged brief smiles, knowing they would be able to talk later.

At last Tdor said, "Joret, Carleas Ndarga wrote to say that Honeytongue insisted on a bridal trip to attend the royal wedding because Hadand had invited Cama." "Honeytongue" had been the nickname for Starand Ola-Vayir when they were girls in the queen's training: Starand had had a penchant for sweet-talking any new girl long enough to winnow out any secrets, later to be held against her, or spread all over just for fun.

Fareas said, "The Jarlan of Tya-Vayir probably agreed just to be rid of her for a time."

Tdor looked unhappy, and Joret knew what she was thinking and did not want to say: *Will it be too painful for Joret to see Cama again, especially if Starand is present to cause strife?*

Joret said, "Honeytongue can do no worse to me than the trouble Branid gives me here."

Tdor hesitated. Branid's habit of spying on Joret every chance he could get, to the extent of attempting to bribe her women to let him by when Joret was in the baths or inventing excuses to visit her in her rooms, was personal. Starand's craving to be the center of attention had grown since they were all girls.

Whipstick said, "Branid wants Joret more than he wants Choraed Elgaer, I believe."

"Which means it might ease our problems here a little if you go," the Iofre said. "But Joret, this is not only an invitation to the royal city. You would be taken over the mountains to a kingdom no Marlovan has ever seen."

Tdor considered the idea for the first time. Joret to *leave* Iasca Leror? And Hadand as well? Marlovan queens never left the kingdom! Tdor felt strange, anxious at the idea, but she stayed silent. Hadand would want Joret's company on such a journey. They had been close all their lives. What surprised her was that the queen, at least according to the letter, had issued the invitation herself.

Joret struggled with conflict. She tried not to remember the fire-bright attraction to Cama Tya-Vayir that, within a day's talk and laughter shared, had flared into love.

Her eyes half closed and a soft, tender smile, utterly un-like what the family was used to seeing in steady, sober, ca-pable Joret, made Whipstick catch his breath. His shoulders shook with inward laughter as he thought, *If she did that on purpose she could kill at a hundred paces. I won-der if that old queen sees her as a weapon? Ah, the Iofre does.* But this was women's business. No one had asked his opinion, so he kept silent.

The lovely color faded along with the smile as Joret squared herself to face the truth that she and Cama had faced at the end of their glorious week together. They lived at opposite ends of Iasca Leror and Choraed Elgaer had enough problems without Horsebutt trying to use his brother's relationship with a future princess to further his ambitions. Like trying to set aside Cama's marriage to the hated Starand Ola-Vayir, who was quite capable of racing home and demanding a clan war—if she could be at the very center as the Wronged Bride. The Jarl of Ola-Vayir, far to the north, had his own ambitions: he and his family felt that Olara and the west end of Idayago would round out their territory nicely.

Joret had had enough of that kind of trouble, being stalked in her home then chased around the kingdom by the Sierlaef. She and Cama had sensibly chosen duty and honor—but their week of joy had nearly been destroyed by the intense pain of parting.

Joret's voice had never been sharp, but it was now. "I will go."

The others stared at her.

Joret took a deep breath and said, "I would like time away. Not from you. Branid will never leave me alone. And as long as I am here, he will make trouble. Let me go away for a time. See if that eases his . . . desire." Her brows quirked, her faint smile was sad. "Who knows? Maybe I will like this far country. In which case, if Inda does come home Tdor must marry him, as was always intended. And Whipstick, you would be able to choose a wife, as you would have, had the king not sent you here instead of to the dragoons."

Fareas was amazed to see Tdor's eyes tear, and she wondered how many secrets she had managed to miss, she who prided herself on her vision.

She looked anew at these two girls, born of mothers she had never met, girls she had raised from their second year, while her own dear Hadand had been raised in the royal city, with all its dangers, except for those precious Name Day visits until she was fifteen. That was the Marlovan way, and the only recourse women had after the age of fifteen was the steady stream of letters carried back and forth across the kingdom by their Runners.

Girls.

She was wrong. They were no longer girls, and she could not choose for them. They were young women, already directing their own lives, making choices from circumstances she no longer oversaw. "Midsummer's Day is less than a month away," she said, rising. "And the fastest Runner with fresh horses along the way takes two weeks. We had better plan for four weeks' journey. Which means we must leave by this week's end."

She turned to Whipstick and Tdor, standing side by side. "I shall leave you with the Adaluin to guard Choraed Elgaer." She smiled. "And we will invite Branid to lead the Honor Guard that accompanies us. If he wishes to strut about the royal city and call himself heir, he is welcome to. It will keep him from making trouble here. Now, everyone to work: we have a lot to do."

Chapter Eight

THE puddles had begun to steam after a sudden, violent summer storm when the rain-washed west wind carried the sound of trumpets.

High in a tower above the royal castle's garrison the conspirators paused in their last rehearsal, listening. Horns from the outer perimeter riders, faint but distinct—fast triplets in two separate chords. The fanfare for runners was a single set, for Jarls two sets of the same chord. Three chords for the royal family.

Two chords for princes.

The Algara-Vayirs are here. Cherry-Stripe Marlo-Vayir noticed that several covert, sympathetic looks were sent Cama's way.

"I'd better go." Cama strode out.

As his footsteps rapidly diminished the others exchanged looks, everyone reluctant to speak first.

As usual it was phlegmatic Noddy who broke the silence. "Better ride shield," he said.

They caught up with Cama, who gave them one unreadable glance, but said nothing.

Cherry-Stripe followed Cama's swinging black horsetail down and around the tower's worn stone steps. He wondered again how Horsebutt Tya-Vayir, Cama's brother, could be so damned different from Cama. Usually easygoing, he felt a pang of angry resentment when he remembered the ride to the royal city. It should have been fun, but was ruined by Starand's constant complaining and bickering: she had the smallest tent. Cama ought to sleep with her, since they were newly wed. The food was boring. The pennon-bearers didn't give her proper precedence as new Randviar of Tya-Vayir. Even little Mran, Cherry-Stripe's betrothed, could not distract her though everyone had given Mran credit for trying.

Cherry-Stripe snorted a sigh of impatience. You grew up knowing that Jarl families did not pick their wives or husbands. Most got along fine, some turned into love matches, like Cassad and his Carleas or Buck and Fnor. Then there were ones like Dannor and Starand—one Cama's sister, the other his wife.

As they launched through the door and started across the huge garrison complex in the direction of the main gate, Cherry-Stripe dropped back, elbowing Noddy Toraca. "Didn't Horsebutt once dally with Starand?" he asked.

Noddy glanced over, his long face, as usual, as expressive as a scout dog's. "She's not bad looking. Besides, there she was—and his wife sure never wanted him." He grinned; his wife, the popular Imand, had been tight with her Runner since they were all here at training.

Cherry-Stripe snorted a laugh. "Idea of Starand in my bed is like, I dunno, picking at a saddle-gall."

Noddy made his turtle-shrug, familiar from childhood. "She uses sex for intrigue."

Cherry-Stripe grimaced. "Who cares?"

Noddy laughed. "Horsebutt. Probably that father of hers as well. But Imand will at least keep Horsebutt in rein. He never crosses her, despite all his strut before the Jarls, now that his father is dead and his mother went home to Sindan-An. It's Imand who's gonna run that land one day. You watch."

The young men passed through a lichen-dotted archway, then Noddy lunged ahead and caught Cama's arm. They stopped, and when Noddy jerked his chin toward the wall, they peered down through the crenellations into the passage to the stable.

Starand had planted herself at one end. Hadand, wear-

ing a fine linen undergown, stood at the other, arms
crossed. Flanking her were tall, strong Carleas Ndarga,
married last autumn into the Cassads, and little Mran Cassad, who barely reached Hadand's shoulder.

Hadand glanced up at the fellows, then ignored them.

Starand seemed to be unaware. She shook her golden
braids back and said with dramatic disdain, "Stand aside,
Hadand." Then, as Starand's Runner took up a defensive
position at her left shoulder, "Or I'll have to go through
you."

"Try," Hadand invited.

She stood there in that white linen undergown, no
queen's over-robe yet. It was difficult to see if she wore her
sheaths under the broad sleeves . . . but her stance had altered to Autumn Wind.

Starand glowered. From Autumn Wind a woman could
launch at least four of the Winter attacks—all of them offensive—and two Ice defenses.

Starand slid a glance at the others. Well, they made as
good an audience as any for the other line she'd thought up
and practiced, and she hoped they would get it right for the
future songs. "I know Joret Dei is your foster sister, but to
ignore her treason is to commit treason yourself." And
when they didn't react, she added nastily, "It was with your
own husband, ahhh, that is, had he lived—" Starand cursed
at the fumble, and pushed on louder and faster when Carleas snickered, "had Joret not betrayed him by luring him
into dalliance, the kingdom would be whole. And now she
seeks to lure mine, at the cost of—"

"Horseshit," Hadand stated.

Mran turned away, shaking with silent laughter.

Carleas, tall, very strong, said in her mild voice, "Honeytongue—that is, Stara," she corrected herself, obviously.

But Starand saw as well as everyone else the quick grins
indicating that everyone used the hated nickname instead
of the Stara that she'd demanded.

Carleas crossed her arms. "Here's the truth. We all pity
you if you can't catch the eye of your own husband."

"And whose fault is that?" Starand began angrily.

Three women said at the same time, "Yours."

Starand turned crimson with rage.

Hadand said, "Cama is as free to pick a favorite as you were when you crooked your finger at Cama's own brother."

Again Mran muffled snickers.

Starand gaped. Who'd been gossiping? Oh, yes—*Dannor*. Cama and Stalgrid's Norsunder-cursed sister Dannor, now married to Hawkeye, was fifty times nastier than Joret Dei, but she would never dally with Cama. Starand flushed. "What I do at home affects no one. Joret Dei was committing treason when she tried to oust you! And she's going to do the same to me!"

"You know as well as anyone here that Aldren-Sierlaef chased Joret clear around the kingdom, or if you don't, then know it now," Hadand cut in.

"Get out of my way!" Starand demanded. "She brought dishonor to your Choraed Elgaer, and now she's going to dishonor my family. I shall demand justice before the throne—"

Carleas covered her face with her hands. "You idiot."

Hadand shifted, and two black-hilted knives dropped into her palms.

No bluff, then.

Starand's face contorted. "You wear your knives in your own castle, Hadand? With all these guards?" She waved her own blade at the silent women behind Carleas and Mran. "What are you afraid of?"

Mran's lips whitened and Carleas frowned.

"I wear them all the time. Everywhere," Hadand said, her tone slightly amused, her wide-set brown eyes mild. "Which is why I'm never afraid."

It forced them all to remember the last time she'd used her blades—right there in the throne room, the entrance to which was not fifty paces away.

"Then what is *she* here for, if not to make trouble with Camarend?" Starand demanded, waving a hand in the direction of the castle gates.

"Joret Dei is here," Hadand stated, "on personal invitation from Queen Wisthia."

"That's a lie! And I'll proclaim it before the throne—"

Whispers from behind; people were coming.

And so Hadand said, "My first act as Gunvaer was meant to be far more benign. But necessity demands decision. You are *not* going to use your own jealousy as an excuse to stir up entire clans into feuds over imagined affronts. Because they *are* imagined. And every woman here knows the truth."

She paused as Carleas and Mran turned their thumbs up.

"Therefore, Starand Ola-Vayir, you are herewith confined to Tya-Vayir for the extent of your life. You may guard its castle and its inhabitants as Randviar, and if your husband is selected by mine to serve somewhere else, you will go to guard that castle, but you will not stray from its bounds, and never again enter the royal city upon pain of death."

Silence met these words. Starand, opening her mouth, saw no woman protest.

Nor did Cama, whom she saw standing above them on the wall, a row of men beside him.

Hadand added, "Tesar, appoint a suitable escort, and remand her to the custody of Imand Tlennen, Jarlan of Tya-Vayir."

Starand trembled, aghast. No one had defended her. *No one.* "Imand hates me!" she wailed.

"Everyone hates you," Hadand said. "Because the only thing you have ever been consistent about since we were girls was making yourself hateful. Go."

On the wall the young men backed away and approached the stairway more slowly. No one looked at Cama, though he could feel the sympathy of his friends.

The clatter of horse hooves echoed from the castle stable yard beyond the stone arch; Cama and the others dashed through the arch, where they found the women waiting.

Hadand led the way into the stable yard to greet the newcomers, pausing as the enormous cavalcade came to a halt on the rain-swept stones, hooves sending steaming puddles splashing.

At once the stable hands ran to the horses' heads.

Evred himself appeared a moment later, having heard

the horns and run down from the study. Like his friends he was dressed in his old gray academy coat. Busy as he was, he would greet the Algara-Vayirs in person.

Cama and the others closed behind him in shield position, and Hadand deferred, the other women waiting behind her. It was Evred's place to speak the formal words of welcome to her mother, who rode at the front with her Runner on one side and the Algara-Vayir pennon in the hands of a young Rider on the other.

As he spoke, she looked past her mother. Behind her rode Joret—next to Branid? Hadand stared in surprise at the big, arrogant yellow-haired young man dressed in a formal green-and-silver House tunic, despite the rain and the long ride.

The formal welcome now over, Joret leaped down from her saddle and grabbed Hadand in a damp, convulsive hug.

"Branid?" Hadand whispered as Branid loudly claimed precedence over someone from a minor House who had arrived at the same time as the Algara-Vayirs.

Joret swiped back her dripping hair. "Your mother asked his escort. Better than leaving him home to cause trouble."

Hadand's lips parted as they glanced at Fareas-Iofre, who had dismounted and was overseeing the disposition of their party.

Hadand comprehended it all at once. The other family having already deferred, Branid harassed the stable hands and their own Riders with unnecessary orders. "I just got done deflecting Starand, who seems to want a war in her name. I don't want *him* sparking off clan wars with people who don't know he's only a horse fart, but I cannot ask Evred to exile him to Choraed Elgar for being stupid."

Joret's rare smile dimpled her cheeks. "Get somebody you trust to shuttle him between the pleasure houses and the wineries, and he'll be little trouble."

Hadand began to laugh, but it died when Joret's blue gaze shuttered and every muscle in her body tightened. Hadand knew she'd found Cama in that waiting crowd.

Evred said, "Welcome, Joret. My mother is above. She awaits your pleasure."

Hadand stepped away, leaving Joret facing Evred, and so

she had a perfect view of the young men ranged alongside one-eyed Cama, who looked impossibly dashing in that black eye patch with his long curling black hair. Cherry-Stripe and Noddy gazed at Joret in silent appreciation of her beautiful body in its clinging wet clothing, her stunning complexion glowing with rain-washed color. All of them transfixed, that is, except for Evred, whose hazel eyes were kind as he chatted easily with Joret about the journey.

And does that not sum up the irony of my life, Hadand thought, her emotions swooping like summer starlings: her own Evred, nearly as handsome as Cama and the only love of her life since childhood, framed by his friends who were trying politely to veil their lusty appreciation for Joret's beauty. But in Evred's face there was only tranquil courtesy.

She shut her eyes.

Fareas, watching her daughter with the hunger of a mother long separated from her child's life, saw with dismay a closed countenance where once there had been transparent openness.

As if she felt her mother's stare, Hadand opened her eyes. She saw Fareas' loving face—older, thinner, her un-hidden worry—and they flung their arms around one another.

From over her shoulder she caught Evred's gaze. He flicked his eyes in the direction of Branid, his brows faintly raised in question. Hadand made the briefest grimace, and responsibility transferred from one to the other in that instant, comprehended by both.

"Come, Branid-Dal. Join us in a glass of wine while you wait for the Runners to get dry clothes laid out," Evred said, knowing who he was although they had never met. Hadand had brought home bitter stories about Branid after her Name Day visits ever since she was small.

No sign of that now as he smiled, opening his hand toward his friends, then led the way back inside.

Branid strutted after them, glancing backward to see who was aware of his being thus singled out by the future king. Finding he was not the center of attention, he started in with loud commentary in a mixture of flattery and bragging that would very soon wear on them all.

Hadand led her mother and Joret up to the queen's chamber.

Queen Wisthia awaited the women in her empty parlor with exquisite silks covering the walls, now showing faded spots. The furniture that had stood there for decades was now on a wagon train plodding eastward. As soon as this last interview was done, the waiting servants would strip the walls, too, and begin shifting the new queen's furnishings in, so Hadand would begin her first night as queen in the queen's rooms.

Wisthia surveyed her rain-drenched guests. Joret smiled back, her color heightened. Fareas was thin, aging, careworn, her brown gaze the direct and assessing expression that had become so familiar in Hadand.

"Thank you for bringing Joret," Wisthia said, taking Fareas' hands briefly.

Fareas looked at the queen's eyes, saw a curious sadness, the intensity of need, and sensed there was some extra meaning intended. It would take time before she comprehended that Wisthia, having accepted her own failure as a mother, harbored hope that Evred might find a mother in the woman who had birthed Hadand and Inda.

Hadand escorted Fareas-Iofre and Joret to the guest chambers to change to dry clothes, then returned to her rooms for her splendid overdress of scarlet and gold. Montrei-Vayir colors—the kingdom's colors. From now on, she belonged to others. That meant the needs of the kingdom must come before her own.

During the great dinner in the vast hall across from the throne room, Wisthia presided one last time, Hadand at her right hand, Fareas at her left, Evred at the far end. Down either side sat all the Jarls and Jarlans, save those who were prevented by trouble in the north or old age from the long ride. Everyone seemed determined to promote an atmosphere of good will, perhaps mindful of the violence of winter; at either end Evred and Hadand observed who was speaking to whom.

*   *   *

Midnight.

Torches burned along every wall.

Beyond the castle the plains, contours faintly reflecting back the golden glow, were empty. No enemy lurked within a month's ride, but the vigilant sentries gripped weapons as the rumble of drums thumped in the summer air all around them.

Then, as the castle bell tolled midnight, the clangor was drowned in showers of shimmering brass glissades as trumpet after trumpet echoed from every tower in the city, playing the thrilling triple-chord fanfare of "The King's Charge."

Within the throne room the heat was exponentially more intense. All eyes turned to the massive double doors, hearts beating fast as the fanfare's echoes died away. The drums high on the balcony above, six to a side, shifted to the galloping beat of "King's Triumph," first one side and then the other. In through the doors strode Evred Montrei-Vayir, horsetail swinging, light glinting richly off the long crimson-and-gold battle tunic of his ancestors, chain mail jingling, the ring of his boot heels slow and sustained, exactly on the beat. Four, five, six steps he took, and then without warning the great two-sided war drums—as tall as the pairs of strong young men playing them—thundered a counterpoint, and those closest saw Evred flush at the accolade.

As he walked the length of the long throne room, past all the gathered leaders, more drums joined from those hidden above, riding by riding, nine by nine, until there were eighty-one drums pounding the beat back and forth until the rolling rumble pulsed in blood and bone. Step, step, straight to the dais where Hadand waited, a sword in each hand, four armed men standing in a diamond shape behind her.

She raised the swords, points toward the sky.

A shout went up from all around: "Hadand-Gunvaer! Hadand-Gunvaer Deheldegarthe!"

She flushed then paled, for she too was given an unexpected accolade.

Evred smiled in pride and triumph; she was not just hailed as Gunvaer, war queen, but as Deheldegarthe, the protector of the kingdom.

Tears stung her eyes, but she braced herself, lifted her chin, then tossed both swords high into the air.

Wisthia closed her eyes.

Fareas watched those slowly turning blades, every nerve in her body singing.

Tesar held her breath, remembering the cuts Hadand had gotten the first two or three days she practiced the Sword Throw without gloves.

Down they came, spinning slowly. Hadand's hands reached up—and she caught them by the crossguards, whirled them expertly down to her sides, arms clamping the flat blades against her waist, the hilts offered to her mate, her war king.

Another shout reverberated off the stones.

In peacetime she would have handed him the swords, and he would have held them point down as he listened to the Jarls, but a war king was expected to make war: his coronation must follow in the manner of long tradition.

He slammed the swords together over his head.

Clash-innng!

A blue spark arced away. Hadand stepped aside as Evred whirled around, striking at the man behind him. The Jarl of Ola-Vayir was still strong enough to meet that powerful swing. He whipped up his sword in an overhead block. *Crash!* Exactly on the beat two sparks glinted, and the Jarl stepped away and lowered his blade.

Evred whirled and swung. *Clang!* rang the blade of the Jarl of Jaya-Vayir from the south, for the third time striking a spark, and old men as well as young nodded and smiled.

Then he whirled and Hasta Marlo-Vayir, determined to hold up the reputation of the west, met Evred's blade with such an enthusiastic strike the sparks shot upward, causing a cry of delight from the watching Jarls as, last, Evred stepped directly before the throne where his Shield Arm

stood—his cousin Barend—and again a spark twinkled as
Barend forced his healing arm up to meet that blow with
his sword. But meet it he did.

And then the double blades crashed to the ground, one
lying north-south, one east-west. Hands high, Evred began
the war dance. The intricate steps spun him in and out of
the squares, steel winking and glittering in the reflected
torchlight.

On the second round the other four joined, throwing
their blades down—north-south, east-west—at either side
of the square made by the new king, and all five of them
whirled and stepped in perfect time with the drums, the
older men's horsetails and long coat skirts swinging as
briskly as the young men's, for they, too, had practiced for
months.

They stopped on the very same beat as the drums, the silence so sudden the echoes rang up the ancient stone.

Then a great shout reverberated, so loud and solid a
body of sound that the watchers' skulls buzzed.

For that moment they were one kingdom, united into
one heart, one will. But fast as the echoes died individual
minds returned from the sound-sustained center-point to
their accustomed boundaries. *Heat—thirst—hunger—
tiredness—how long until I can get free of this crowd—oh,
yes, the Jarls have to come forward—where's my place—*

They shuffled forward in strict order of precedence, oldest titles in front—except for the Montredavan-Ans, exiled
onto their own land.

But the first vows belonged to Hadand and Evred, he as
guardian of the land and she as guardian of everything
within the walls of the royal city and overseer of the
women who guarded every castle in the land. Her shoulder
bumped against Evred's muscular bicep. He had grown so
tall. Hearing his breathing, smelling his distinctive scent
fired her belly with longing as they stared out at the torchlit faces and spoke their vows together, their cadences
matching perfectly.

She forced her awareness away from him, an act of will
since she could not control her body's simple but insistent
homing, direct as the return of a bird after winter.

An act of will to ignore the sound of his breathing, so that her breathing did not match its rhythm. An act of will so protracted that everything blurred, leaving only the vague memory of her face aching as each Jarl, new and old, stepped up to speak his vows with right hand laid flat over heart. She and Evred had worked out with care the concessions they would grant each speaker. He spoke well, though his voice grew rough and husky from thirst; hers was little better. Tired, distracted, she by his proximity and he by the reactions he saw in the faces before him, despite their private resolves to stay aware of everything, neither saw the glower, so like his daughter's, in the eyes of the Ola-Vayir Jarl. They did not see Horsebutt Tya-Vayir's calculation, or the glee in Branid Algara-Vayir's face as he spoke for Jarend-Adaluin. They did not see some of the Jarls fade back to the periphery to exchange quick murmurs of conversation.

Three people grieved in secret.

Cama and Joret on opposite sides of the throne room avoided so much as a glance at the other though they could feel each other's presence as a fire more intense than summer heat. But they had promised, and each knew that to come together again would make the parting just that much worse.

The third was Barend, bracing himself against the heat, the rhythmic shouting. He forced a grin, trying to kindle joy in his heart for Evred and Hadand, who had been dear to him since their shared childhood in the schoolroom upstairs. But the joy would not come, though they looked so happy. Nor could he admit it, not when he stood at Evred's left as Harskialdna, Royal Shield Arm, the position most coveted in the land besides kingship. He knew Evred meant it as an honor, and he knew that Cama and Hawk-eye and all the others would strive to help him to learn what he needed to learn, but the truth was that he would never learn it. Nor did he want to.

While Evred and Cama and his friends were boys at the academy learning the land warfare he was now supposed to command, he had already been long at sea, and that was where his heart lay. Not in this hot, stuffy castle, smelling of

sweat and stone and the pungent, sun-dried grass of the
plains. He longed to pace the deck of a fast ship, out in the
free winds and the ever-changing ocean, a longing so unbearable he could not fight it as the sound of the drums
that accompanied the Jarls out of the throne room thundered in his teeth and bones. Inside his ringing skull his
mind rode the wind, seeking the rake-masted trysail *Death*
that had to be sailing, sailing, somewhere in the world, and
on its deck Inda and Fox, Jeje guiding the *Vixen,* Dasta's
Cocodu within hail . . . oh, how he wished he were there!

Chapter Nine

"**D**AMNATION!" Inda smacked the taffrail.

A summer storm had tumbled up the river valley bisecting Bren, throwing about spectacular lightning and thunder. Just as the fleet entered Bren's harbor the rain sheeted down with the density of a poured pitcher, warm as the humid air. This coincided with the sliding of *Death* past Bren Harbor's inner island, making it even more difficult for the lookouts to see if the Venn, or pirates, or anybody, lay in wait to attack.

But that is not why Inda cursed. Fox was in charge of the defense, if defense was needed.

Inda dropped from the companionway into the waist and glared at the three youngsters before him. All three gangling, unprepossessing, beginning to grow out of the roundness of childhood.

Mutt surreptitiously flipped up the back of his hand at the other two, the girl hired at Pirate Island, the boy at Ghost Island. "What's the problem here?" Inda asked. "No. Let's be specific. Which one of you little walking turds greased that rope?"

The looks back and forth, furtive, feet shuffling on the wet deck, reminded Inda so forcibly of his scrub days the urge to laugh was almost overpowering.

But he couldn't laugh. So he did his best to look stern. "Never mind. No one wants to squeak. I can understand that. But you have to understand this. The Venn might be lying in wait somewhere nearby, out of sight."

Mutt sent a look at the others. "So? Then we smash 'em."

"With ropes greased?"

"Storm'd loosen it," Pilvig said—then clapped a hand over her mouth.

"I see. So you planned it carefully, then," Inda said to the red-faced girl. She was quick and clever, round-faced, dark-haired—she was half Chwahir. Had been Nugget's hire, and her best friend. "A storm is coming—you grease the rope with leddas oil, Mutt comes off watch, falls to the deck, everyone laughs—and the water cleans the rope."

Pilvig's eyes rounded, making it clear she thought Inda was a mind reader.

Again the impulse to laugh.

Jug, the new boy (whose ears made the nickname obvious and inevitable) jerked a thumb at Mutt. "He struts. Just 'cause he was on Walic's ship."

"I do not!" Mutt retorted. "*You* strut, with your stupid uncle bein' a mage, as if we believed any of those stories—"

Pilvig's higher voice cut through the boys'. "You think you're so sharp a blade, with your uncle and your ghosts on Ghost Island. Nobody sees ghosts. And you can't take the place of *anyone*." She blinked rapidly, flushing.

Still grieving for Nugget, that much was clear. He remembered how long he'd grieved for Dogpiss, but he had to either bridle them or lose them. "Peppered spud-gruff. Itch weed in the hammocks. Missing trousers. What else has made the trip from Ghost Island memorable?"

Three pairs of eyes found the deck full of hidden meaning.

Inda sighed. "Orders. Every sting is going to net you a full day as lookouts. All three of you. Starting now. One on each mast. You can come down when the sun sets."

"But—" Mutt began.

Inda waited, doing his best to emulate Master Gand's expression from his scrub days. Mutt decided that pointing out dawn was half a watch away was not a good idea after all.

"Get."

They scrambled out and by the time Inda reached the deck, none of the three were visible. As Inda finished a circuit of the deck the rain lifted momentarily.

"Barge away from the dock," came the lookout's voice from above.

Mutt leaned out, his sailor's queue sending drops down into Inda's face, and added, "Someone thinks he's a king."

"Your lookout duty," Inda informed the three mastheads in a carrying voice, "includes silence. Except for sightings."

Cackles and hoots sounded around the ship as the rain started again, hissing against the sails as they rode the last way into the estuary on the height of the tidal flood.

When the lookout reported the barge clear of the ships anchored in the harbor, Inda picked up the glass from the binnacle and snapped it out. The Guild Fleet barge leaped into existence, silhouetted against the rain-dimmed glow of harbor lights, lamps swinging from its grand canopy. Oars rose and fell, all manned by burly fellows who were probably warriors in guild colors.

Inda lowered the glass. The rain was heavy but warm, but his crew waited in expectation; he knew—could almost feel—the spyglasses trained on them from just about every capital ship in the harbor, and probably most of the traders as well.

"Flash," Inda said.

Fibi the Delf, the new hire who had already been promoted to captain of the tops, took over in her unlovely crow squawk. "Halyards! Downhaul! Sheets!"

Inda glanced up at the wizened, bandy-legged Delf. Fibi stood on a boom watching the hands at the sails.

Since the day Fibi had come aboard talking of his plan, which had apparently been debated in family councils on the Delfin Islands—a plan hardly a day old, and spoken of only to his captains—Inda had been thinking about the nature of news. He'd come to the unsurprising conclusion that news spreads the faster when it affects you. He hadn't heard anything at all about home for a couple of years because whatever happened in Iasca Leror held no interest for anyone else. It was as if the Venn blockade had made the entire kingdom vanish from current time, if not from the physical world.

Thuddud! With a whooshing whump the sails flashed, all at once.

A royal yacht couldn't have done better, and his crew knew it, for they'd drilled often enough, first under Walic's cruel first mate, then under Barend, and now under Fibi. Flashing sails during action meant tight maneuvering, and you could manage it if you had enough crew to fight and sail. Inda's proprieties had been shaped by the scrupulous first mate of a trader, so he rarely gave in to his crew's taste for flamboyant approaches outside of battle. Today was an exception: flashing sails was also a demonstration of power, of control, even a threat.

Approving looks came Inda's way for this indulgence. None of them but Tau guessed that he was apprehensive at his first encounter with mainland officialdom, an apprehension the more severe since he'd sent *Vixen* in ahead with a message to warn the Guild Fleet of their arrival. He did not know if that had been a bad decision.

Fox stood on the bowsprit, oblivious to the rain, one elbow casually crooked around a taut stay, his glass sweeping the low hills constantly for any sign of danger whenever there was a brief lull in the rain. Bren was built at the mouth of the Ban, a broad flat river that flowed northward onto the many little islands reaching into the strait. Fox knew the hills could be hiding full wings of warriors waiting to attack—but not before the trysail could escape, once the tide began to ebb. Nothing he'd seen in the water was faster than his ships.

He swept his glass around again, knowing he wanted treachery to be awaiting them: threats, even an attack. Anything that would drive them back into freedom so they were not trapped in this meaningless obligation. But there was no sign of treachery. Not when you needed it. *Can* treachery ever be convenient? Or was that expedient? He laughed softly to himself, and blinked rain from his lashes before looking into the glass again.

At the same moment, far to the west, Hadand walked beside Evred up to the newly furbished royal suites, directly across from one another now. The new door to the queen's rooms had been hinged and set during the previous watch. It smelled of the fresh coat of linseed oil and rosin varnish the carpenters had put over it to protect the old carved wood.

They stopped in the hallway.

Evred said, "I think it went well enough, don't you?" He reached for her hands, kissing each on the palm.

"Neither of us dropped a sword," she said, trying to match his light tone. "And no one tripped, fainted, or challenged anyone to a duel. I would call that a success."

He gave a soft, appreciative laugh, then said, "Get good rest. You've earned it." He opened his door, the light within reflecting in his eyes, on his smile, then the door closed behind him and the light was gone.

She unlatched her door and stood on the threshold looking in. There were her familiar furnishings, trying bravely to fill too large a space. She could hear female voices: Tesar supervising something in the far room.

From behind, in the king's rooms, came the rumble of male talk, punctuated by laughter. Oh, nothing intimate. If she listened hard she could pick out individual voices: Cherry-Stripe, Noddy, Tuft Sindan-An, Rattooth Cassad, and Barend. His cousin Hawkeye, here as the new Jarl of Yvana-Vayir. All the voices of Evred's inner circle, joining him for a private celebration. No doubt planned long ago.

She turned away at last, and discovered her mother waiting patiently and alone in the archway leading to the bed chamber. Impossible to hide her tears from her mother.

Fareas-Iofre held out her arms, and Hadand walked into them. A hard squeeze, and then Fareas-Iofre softly shut the door on the laboring servants, and held Hadand by the shoulders. "How long have you been yearning after him, my darling child?"

"Oh, I don't know. I think since he turned sixteen." Hadand sniffed.

"Does he have a favorite?"

"No. It's all friends in there. But one day he'll find one, and maybe he'll even fall in love, and it's too much to hope he'll be a Jened Sindan."

"He," Fareas said, and sighed.

"Right." Hadand sniffed, wiping her eyes on her crimson velvet sleeve. "No hope for me. Meanwhile I have to worry that if he does find someone, and it's for life like the rest of his family, it will be a—a Branid."

Fareas chuckled. "Do you think Evred so blind, then?"

"No. But love is blind. And cruel."

"So speaks the wisdom of old age," her mother teased, and hugged her again.

"Oh, Mama."

"Love is also sensible, if you let it be. A love that is not returned does not flourish."

Hadand wiped her eyes. "So what do I do until then?"

Fareas smiled. "You find another kind of love."

"You told me on my last visit home to never form a bond with the pleasure house men, and so I've been scrupulous about never seeing one longer than a month or so."

Fareas opened her hands. "It's good advice if one also has a relationship with one's husband. But if there will not be one—as I didn't have one—if you find yourself cleaving to someone, as long as he has no ambition to interfere with your duty, keep him."

"You have one, then?"

They hadn't seen one another since Hadand was fifteen, and their last conversation had encompassed the dangers of lovers, sex, and duty. But because Hadand had not reached the age of interest, her mother had said little about her own private life; Hadand only knew that once or twice a week her mother had gone with some of the women to the pleasure house in the nearest town.

Fareas said, "I had one. I always visited him, he never came to the castle. It was a good relationship for nearly fifteen years. He retired to marry the spring before last." She stroked her daughter's hot forehead, and brushed a tear off her lashes. "So find a favorite, if you can, with whom you share laughter and affection. You and Evred will have children eventually, and that will bring another love, one both vast and deep."

Hadand wiped her eyes against her mother's breast and gave a watery chuckle. "Sensible advice. I wish it wasn't so hard to be sensible!"

"It will be easier come morning," the princess promised. "When you begin your travels to a new kingdom and the discoveries that await you there." And mentally she saluted Wisthia for long vision indeed.

Oars rose and fell, bringing the Guild closer with every stroke. On board the *Death* Jeje stood in the waist, looking up at Inda on the captain's deck. She knew it made sense for him to keep Kodl's original crewmates safely aboard, in case the warrants the Pims had issued all over the continent against him had additions of their names as well, but she'd hated to see *Vixen* shoot ahead the day before.

She knew the Fisher brothers were competent to command it. But somehow it had, even if only in her own mind, become *her* scout.

Tau drifted up next to her, the swinging lamplight hiding, revealing, hiding his amusement. "Why the frown? You think the Fisher boys have sneaked off with the *Vixen*?"

She looked at his face, and knew he was aware of the real reason for her gloom. And because he would share her exile, she continued the joke. "Well, either that or they've been arrested, and I'll have to go rescue them," she grumped. "*And* get my—the *Vixen* back."

Tau laughed softly at the fumble. She felt heat in her cheeks, thought of the long separation ahead, and sighed.

Tau said only, "Here come the Guild Fleet people."

They had been standing out of the rain, which slanted across the deck so hard the droplets splashed back up again, brief golden flickers in the reflected lamplight.

"Barge ho!" the lookout yelled.

Fox and Inda met on the gangway above Tau and Jeje, both rain-sodden. "Be prepared to slip the cable and sail on the ebb," Inda said in a low voice.

"Everything's laid along," Fox responded, unsmiling. "I take it the three mids are mastheaded for the duration?"

"Till sunset," Inda said.

"You don't want me to thrash them?"

Inda grimaced in disgust. "Save that for the enemy. If it

doesn't work to masthead 'em—" He waggled a hand. "Extra work will steady 'em down."

"A thrashing would be faster," Fox retorted, but Inda had already turned away, the matter forgotten.

The ship gave a slight lurch at the thump of the barge on the lee side. Inda and Fox fell silent as the arrivals hooked on. No one else spoke as the visitors climbed up.

Inda raised his glass. No *Vixen* following the barge.

The first one up was Perran, the Cooperage Guild Mistress for Bren. Tall, attractively stout, with a pair of intelligent, handsome gray eyes, she was at thirty newly come to her position as head of all those who made the barrels, boxes, and trunks with which ships were fitted. The Coopers were one of the five guilds banded together to form this fleet.

She had insisted on going first, though once she was on the deck of what everyone claimed was a pirate ship, her attitude was wary, even defensive as she studied the pirates for their leader Elgar the Fox.

Her gaze passed the shorter one with the old clothes and the unruly brown hair and stopped on the tall, black-clad one leaning negligently against the rail. That one had to be the captain. She felt her throat constrict as she stared at that hard, sardonic expression, its blade-sharp bones dramatized by the sharp yellow light of a swinging lantern. She clasped her hands tightly together.

Guild Fleet Master Chim stumped forward, squinted up into Fox's face, and said in heavily accented Dock Talk, "Ye could've saved me bad leg an' come ashore."

Perran gasped. Such direct speech never happened in meetings between the Guild and the city, where delicacy and the appearance of compromise were vital. But Chim was an actual sailor, a retired captain.

She endured another pang of shock when the formidable captain stepped back, making an ironic gesture toward the short, scruffy one standing next to him that she'd dismissed before. Now she studied him. He was her height, scarred face, broad chest and shoulders, sodden deck trousers, bare feet, a rough old shirt with no laces that looked like this rain was the only washing it was likely to get.

This young man in his turn assessed her from unexpectedly mild-looking wide-set brown eyes. Then he turned his gaze onto Chim as he said in old-fashioned court Sartoran, "And be arrested and dragged off to the local dungeon?"

Chim cackled, shooting a triumphant look at Perran, who had believed that someone with a reputation half as formidable as Elgar the Fox's would never deign to acknowledge inconsequential impediments such as laws.

Chim then rubbed his jaw. This short, scruffy one, despite the reports, appeared to be Elgar the Fox—either that or the pirates were running a little ruse of their own. He knew how to test it.

He said, "I thought as much. No, no. Well, maybe the king woulda pretended to arrest ye, but the prince wouldn't have none o' it. Not the hero sank the Brotherhood. Now, that brings us, so to speak, to ye. We know ye as Elgar the Fox, but d'ye be this young lord out o' the west, what was it, Indovin Ala-Grubber?"

Inda said in a hard voice that his crew usually only heard when they were in action, "That was my name at birth. Elgar will do for now."

Chim had guessed right and all the rumors about a mysterious red-haired leader were wrong. Interesting. "And I, me boy, am Guild Fleet Master Chim. Fleet Master though we never actually did put out a fleet, thanks be t' ye." He chuckled, noticed no one else laughing, which made him chuckle the more. "Well, well. I brought this here paper." And from his tunic Chim pulled a flattened scroll, which he held out. "She paid for a sved and all." When Inda took it, he touched the seal that glittered faintly with magic.

Inda ducked under the binnacle housing to ward the rain and examined the paper, which was written in both badly copied Iascan and the Brennish script, with a Sartoran abstract below. Ryala Pim had rescinded her charges of piracy, the date the year before.

The year *before*. So why hadn't they told him that when he was getting his supplies last winter in Lindeth Harbor?

Because it didn't matter to them. He was a Marlovan pirate, to be gotten rid of as fast as possible.

Fleet Master Chim added, "City nosers in the guilds

voted to keep yer boys off the scout hostage, but they'll be freed in a trice soon's we step safe back ashore."

Inda handed back the paper. "Whatever we decide, you're safe enough with me, as I promised in the message they brought you yesterday."

Guild Mistress Perran felt words forming about the validity of pirate promises, but (though they had been spoken at length and in heat all the previous night) she now kept her lips closed.

"Come into my cabin, where it's at least dry," Inda said, and they followed him, the Fleet Master looking around with open appreciation, the Guild Mistress not hiding her fearful expectation of seeing bloody weapons or other hideous sights. Her gaze caught, and lingered, on that tall, striking redhead who lounged with casual menace just off the companionway.

He smiled slightly. She flicked her gaze away then back again, and counted at least four knife hilts in plain view. She wondered if he really was the pirate captain pretending for some reason not to be, then forced herself to turn her back.

She heard soft laughter behind her.

The cabin was low, clean, almost barren of furniture.

They sat at the table, clothes squelching. On it rested a splendid chart of the strait. Elgar did not seem to mind everyone dripping onto his clean deck, but no one leaned over the elegantly detailed chart—they had too much respect for such beautiful work.

Chim thumped his hands onto his thighs with a liquid smack. "Will ye be usin' your name again?"

Inda flipped his hand over, palm down. "I'm Inda Elgar."

Chim grunted with approval, then said in Sartoran, which was easier understood than his Dock Talk, "As well. None of us said aught to anyone in the city about that." Pointing to the paper. "Fleet business. Handled strictly by Mistress Perran here. Nobody but the two of us and one clerk, she being even more close-mouthed, know. We don't want that damned Prince Rajnir siccing Durasnir onto us."

"Hyarl Durasnir, Commander of the Oneli," Inda repeated, remembering Ramis' words about the three Venn most dangerous to him. Now to test Ramis' words a little. "Didn't Durasnir lose a big battle at the east end of the strait almost ten years ago?"

"In oh three, yes. But Durasnir wasn't in command, him being away north. Came in at the end, too late to clean 'em all up. Word is, he kept young Rajnir—who was a boy at the time—from total annihilation, though that might be rumor. But we do know this much—Rajnir lost the battle himself."

"Ah."

Chim made a spitting motion toward the north. "Then he contacted the pirates." He switched to Dock Talk, addressing them all. "They'll come after ye if they sniff out ye bein' Iascan. Embargo's tight. More tight, after what ye did to their red sail bully boys out west. They demanded we disband the fleet. We's arguin' that, on account of the fact that not all the pirates been there. Whichever way they decide, the facts is, the western sea's full of Venn now, we hear. We know the strait is—we saw Durasnir's big fleet runnin' west right before the summer winds came."

Inda thought, *Just as Ramis said: coming for me.*

Perran turned her attention to Elgar the Fox and saw a smile brief and frightening. For the first time, she believed he was who he said he was.

He said, "The Venn are in the strait because they're looking for me."

"Yes." Chim nodded vigorously. "Reports from the west are he's comin' back down the strait. Maybe a month behind ye. Maybe faster." He bobbed. "Always expect 'em to be faster than ye'd think. Another reason I hope yez setting sail soon's we finish talking."

Inda turned his palm up, a peculiar gesture Chim could not read. "That's my plan."

"Good. Officially, see, the king's throwing ye out of the harbor on account of yez bein' a pirate. But not clapping ye in irons on account of ye defeatin' the Brotherhood, long's ye don't set toe on land. But official, d'ye see, ye cannot land in Bren. All them Venn spies out there with their glasses trained on us now just got to report seein' ye go, soon's our barge unhooks."

Chim paused, saw Inda open his hand again, his expression unsurprised. Relieved at how reasonable this young pirate was, he leaned forward, elbows on the edge of the table, chin up to keep his dripping hair away from the chart. "So, to yez plans. Goin' pirate again, or against the Venn?"

Inda's smile sharpened at the corners—resembling that of the black-clad young man lounging just within view. "I want to clear the strait for free trade."

Chim cackled, slapping his knee. "Don't I know solid gold when I sniffs it!"

Jeje and Tau exchanged looks, Jeje wondering how you could sniff gold, but she didn't speak. She liked this Chim more by the moment, and felt a corresponding easing of the pain bound tightly around her heart at the prospect of what was coming next.

Chim said, "As to our fleet. We've ships promised us. Many good ships. Spoken out loud as promised for a fight against pirates, but in secret, d'ye see, for rising against the Venn. What we don't have is a leader. Some want t' be boss. But none of 'em know fighting, not well enough. I don't, and I beat off pirates four times during me years takin' goods down to Sartor and around." He squinted at Inda as the lamps swung back and forth. "Yez kinda young, yes?"

"I started early."

Fleet Master Chim gave a bark of amusement. Mistress Perran jumped.

Tau lifted his brows. She obviously believed the rumors—and would pass them on unless Inda convinced her they were not bloodthirsty pirates.

"Yes, ye did, if half the stories be true," Chim said. "Now, here's what. We lost seventeen ships last year. Seventeen! In me young days, we didn't lost seven in as many years. Seventeen, ten to the Brotherhood, but yez took care o' that. The rest vanished, and we think it's been the Venn. And here's why we's getting volunteer ships. One at a time, but getting 'em! That damn Prince Rajnir keeps upping the tolls, and worse, far worse, there's rumors east and west that he's formin' up for a second try."

Inda leaned forward, his gaze steady. "A second try at taking land? If so, where?"

Fleet Master Chim raised his hands. "Ye know rumors. About as shaped as water. Some say he's goin' after Chwahirsland, bein' so close to the eastern thumb o' the strait. And some say no, he wants land in the west."

"Like in Iasca Leror?" Inda's eyes narrowed.

Chim flapped a hand. "Some say that, some say here, others say north. What we do know is he's been taking ships into his fleet, mostly up around Ymar and Everon, above where the Chwahir thumped him hard in oh three."

"Hearing, you keep saying. Do you have any who have been along the coast themselves?"

"No." Chim shrugged. "No one wants to land. They have ways of knowin' ye, everyone keeps sayin'. Maybe on account of them cursed sea dags, though our contact in the Mage Guild says no. Anyway." He bent forward. "D'ye think we can clear the strait of 'em, and if so, how many ships ye need?"

"At the moment I don't need ships as much as I need information. I must be the one to get it. I've got to watch them, find out how many, learn how they move, how they attack. And if he's training warriors, where and how many."

The Fleet Master shook his head. "So said Berda Lham last year, fast privateer out o' the eastern islands—and she been the first to vanish."

Inda waved a hand. "Which is why I don't ask any of your people to do that. I'm seeing to it myself. What I need from you are the best charts of the other side of the strait that you can get. Look here." He pointed down at his chart. "We have every inlet on the south side, every river, most shoals and reefs, with all the notes on what birds fly where, what color the water is, and so forth. But the notes on the north side are sparse."

The contrast matched their own charts: the north side largely unknown along the crucial harbors, where the Venn forbade any but their own ships to anchor.

"We'll be doing some of our own charting as we cruise, but anything you have that can help would be most welcome."

Chim thought of privateers, smugglers, and independents. He still had some contacts among the older ones. "How long ye need?"

"I don't know. Let's say we meet here in a year, and meanwhile you raise the biggest fleet you can."

Chim smacked the table again. "That I can do, like I told ye. We'll get a rumor goin' o' the guilds building a trade fleet, one that can withstand pirates. So when word gets out, what the Venn hear is 'trade.' If ye hear different, I need to know."

Inda waved in agreement. "I'll leave a couple of people here to run drills. You'll call it defensive practice. Fleet maneuvers can't be taught inside a harbor anyway, so that training will wait until, if, and when we sail as a fleet."

"Good. Defense, yes, everyone will believe that."

"Second, I require my people to be decently housed and treated."

The Fleet Master held up his hand. "I can make 'em me official assistants, so they can stay at Guild House, and draw pay, same as harbormaster's clerks. We already worked all that out. If they act as clerks, the Venn won't notice 'em."

"My last demand, that the drills be done to my requirements, or they're worthless."

Fleet Master Chim fingered the braids in his beard, then cackled. "I like it." He said to Mistress Perran, "Ye won't get a fairer offer, not if ye live five hundred years."

"I know," she said, but she braced for the pirates to demand gold, grants of land, ships, and stores. Then she cleared her throat, glancing doubtfully up at the red-haired one whose expression was a masterpiece of provocative insolence. She asked in Sartoran, "Ah, who is going back to shore with us?"

Inda and Fox regarded one another, their faces equally guarded. No one knew what the conflict between them was, though they'd heard sharp voices in muffled Marlovan behind the shut cabin doors. Tau suspected the conflict related to that day in the treasure cave, even if it hadn't begun then.

Inda lifted his hand toward Tau, who sighed inwardly,

and with a rueful smile stepped away from his favorite observation post by the stern windows.

"Taumad will act as your liaison with captains and civil authorities. He can also teach our weapons drills," Inda said.

Perran's first thought had been intense gratitude that that redhead with the hateful smile was not one of those staying. But her thoughts flashed into flame and then ash when a golden-haired vision stepped forward, haloed by the lamplight. She scarcely noticed the short young woman who took up a stance with stolid resignation beside him.

"Jeje sa Jeje will teach weapons drills, and if we get that far, she can conduct the fire-team and defense drills. She can also work with you on the strategy we've been developing with smaller vessels."

The Guild Mistress tried not to gawk at the golden-haired Taumad. Were his eyes really gold, too, or was that a trick of those swinging lamps? "Have you a family name?"

"The last one my mother favored was Darian. We've tried several."

Tau waited expectantly.

Change the pronunciation to "Daraen" and it meant— " 'Friend' in archaic Sartoran," she exclaimed. And laughed, realizing that she was struggling against her own expectations, and not against real people. She said in a firm voice, "Welcome to Bren, Jeje sa Jeje and Taumad Darian. If our business is concluded, shall we use the remainder of the inward tidal flow and return to shore?"

Chim chuckled in glee as he followed Perran onto the deck. Fox sauntered after them, leaving Inda alone with Tau and Jeje in the captain's cabin.

Inda studied their faces. "This Guild Mistress Perran obviously doesn't trust us as far as a fart smells in the wind. You two really are the best we could have here. Here." He reached into his battered chest, then withdrew a small bag that rattled slightly: gems.

Tau took it in silence as Inda said, "You know your orders, and they don't change. But I have a request. Private. Just for me. Find out anything you can about Ramis of the

Knife: where he was born, where he came from, where he trained. Where he is. Anything."

Jeje swallowed hard. A whole year on land. Well, not completely on land, but it may as well be. Once she would have rejoiced to be with Tau, but now she only felt the prospect of separation and oh, how it hurt.

The faint wince around Inda's eyes was familiar from when he was twelve. Regret? Sympathy? In an effort to lighten the mood, she said, "At least you can use your name again, when the Venn are not around."

"No," he said, so soft it was almost a whisper. "That paper means someday, if the Venn are defeated, I might be able to land anywhere else on the continent. Nothing is changed at home. I'll see you in a year." His right hand came up, flicking to his heart, then he paused, frowning down at his fingers as if they'd sprouted fangs. "Better get your dunnage over the side before they sail."

He left.

"That went well," Tau said.

Jeje couldn't even laugh. Instead she leaned against a bulkhead. "I feel sick."

"You didn't make anything worse than it already was." Tau dropped the irony. "We've known him all these years, and we have to accept that whatever happened to exile him is staying inside his head. He won't let it out by talking." Because her expression did not ease, he thumped her lightly on the shoulder, a companionable thump that she appreciated because he so rarely touched anyone. "Let's go. They won't want to row against the flood tide."

They shifted the gear already piled down to the barge, careful that their own people handled the booms. Nobody on the barge was to notice in the midst of their various bundles an old, stained barrel that was packed tight with treasure for the purchase of their own ships. Jeje saw to that.

They felt the turn of the tide. The Fleet Master gave the sign for the barge to strike for shore.

Tau and Jeje moved sternward out of the way, but while Jeje wistfully watched Inda's fleet set sail, Tau turned his back.

In his mind, they were already gone. As he eyed the approaching harbor in the weak blue light of another day, his thoughts fingered their way into the future: they would land, get this damned barrel to their rooms and appropriately hidden in a jumble of old clothes and sail-making gear. Jeje would make friends with the Guild Fleet staff. Tau would go straight to the pleasure houses, where one could always begin finding out the very latest news.

And as summer slipped into winter, Jeje would train whomever they found to train, and maybe buy ships, and he would buy . . . information. Wherever and however he could find it. Then he'd sort it for word not just of the Venn, and of Ramis of the *Knife* as Inda wished, but also of a woman taken in the west by some pirate, a gold-haired, beautiful woman who might or might not go by the name of Saris Elend, or Elend Darian, or something similar, playing off the words *grace, butterfly,* or *queen*—but never, it seemed, the name she was born with.

Chapter Ten

MOUNTAIN terrain seldom traveled by humans made for particularly slow journeys, but Hadand never found it tedious. Her world had been confined to either end of the plains of Hesea until now, mountains being seen as a jagged line on the horizon. At times they looked down from cliffs so sheer and high that raptors riding currents between their narrow road and the distant ground below were mere dots. Sometimes they gazed over a soft cotton carpet of clouds hiding the world, while mountain peaks, smelling of pine, gleamed all around them in the bright sun, islands in a sea of slow-foaming white.

There was little talk of a private nature on that journey; it was not until they began descending toward the vast river-plains of Anaeran-Adrani that Queen Wisthia began to instruct them during their first night at an inn, where the plates and silver were like those she'd preferred in her own rooms.

"I said nothing to Evred because I cannot be certain, but the true story behind my brother's not marrying Tlennen's sister Tdiran may have affected more than the Yvana-Vayirs' lives," she said abruptly, after dismissing her women. "It might lie behind the unsuccessful treaty negotiations."

Hadand and Joret stared in surprise at the queen. Wisthia had been so withdrawn in Iasca Leror that one seldom thought about her when not in her presence; when you were away from her strangely decorated rooms, it was difficult to remember what she looked like. But the tall, thin woman who had been so plain, so unmemorable all those quiet years in Iasca Leror seemed to alter before their eyes each day they drew closer to the land of her birth.

Her thin brows arched, expressive of irony. "First you must get a sense of my brother's character. He was always given his way, always, in everything, large or small, from the day of his birth. He was not sent as a page to Sartor, as is our custom, because he refused to go."

"We were told he never saw Evred's Aunt Tdiran, that he'd already formed another alliance," Hadand said.

"He didn't. That much is true. What your family did not know was that on one of the trade missions, my brother sent two of his personal friends disguised as servants, who reported back that Tdiran was plain and thin. My brother wanted a beautiful bride, one with an attractive shape, and refused the marriage. My father, who was dangerous and subtle in every other regard but in matters pertaining to my brother, gave in. The resultant trade treaty—requiring the Adranis, for Tlennen's lifetime, to pay for sending mages over the mountains to Iasca Leror for spell renewal—was an expensive compromise, but no one wanted to risk war with Iasca Leror. Which was why my father broke his own rule and escorted me to the border to meet Tlennen and Anderle, when Tlennen and I wed."

Hadand drew in a slow breath. "I see. So that might be why your brother has resisted renewing the trade treaty?"

Wisthia nodded. "Exactly. What we must contrive is to prevent my brother from finding out how desperate is the Iascan need. I sent two of my ladies-in-waiting ahead last winter, as soon as Evred promised I could return. They await us at a private house belonging to an old friend, who is expecting us. There we will find all the latest fashions. We will practice the newest customs of court. We will not arrive as a queen without a land, a barbarian queen, and a girl who should have been a princess, all dressed in the fashions of thirty years ago. We will arrive at court in glory, all to enhance Iasca Leror's prestige."

"Our prestige is her prestige," Hadand said later to Joret, when they met in the tiny sitting room between their two equally small bedchambers.

Joret considered, then said, "Are you being critical?"

"No, because I believe in her goodwill. She wants Evred to succeed as king. Perhaps I should say it this way: my prestige is her prestige."

Joret made a sign of agreement. "And since I have no rank, my part of the prestige is to be the decorative hand-maiden?"

Hadand smiled. Then, "Is that unbearable?"

Joret laced her fingers around her knees and closed her eyes, for the first time not warding memory, but welcoming it.

Welcoming the cherished memory of almost stumbling over Cama's long legs outstretched in front of the old reading chair in the archive the day after the Conspiracy, because she was looking up at the shelves of scrolls and books.

The laughing apologies, the tingling warmth that traced over skin and trickled through her veins for the very first time when she met his gaze.

How strange life is! That the same appreciation and warmth she had seen in others' eyes most of her life, and had been offended, indifferent, and occasionally repelled by, could set her on fire when seen in a single dark eye.

She cherished the flurry of impressions that followed: his strong hands righting her, the puff of his breath on her ear; the laughing, breathless apologies. His husky voice as he admitted he was there not to read history so much as to look up the proper bugle call for a returning second son who was not heir but king, just so everything would go smoothly when—if—*when* Evred arrived. They would believe he lived until told differently: his voice deepened when he said that.

Cama's masculine scent as she reached past him to set her book down; the angle of his head as he listened appre-

ciatively when she explained she always read the oldest
histories when she was upset over things in the now: how it
steadied her to remember other people long ago had much
the same problems and somehow survived.

He hadn't shifted the talk to her eyes, or her hair, or her
figure, though she felt as if each of her features was bathed
in golden light, a light experienced only in his proximity . . .

She cherished the memory of taking him to her guest
room. First encountering Hadand, who had taken a single
look—her brown eyes shifting back and forth twice—then
expertly fended off anyone else, just so they could be alone
a little while.

Cama and Joret had so much to do, as Joret had to go between the Adaluin and the Guard and Hadand, and he had
the prisoners to oversee and the Guard to reorganize, yet
they found time for a first kiss. A first embrace. The cherished memory, impossibly dear, of him lying in her bed, a
long strand of his hair caught in his eyelashes. Even the
small heel-shaped scar around his ruined his eye had become impossibly dear . . .

And then—

And then—

And then the decision to part, as honor and duty required.

She opened her eyes, to find Hadand's sympathetic
brown eyes as steady as the candle flame.

Joret said, "No. It is not."

Far to the northeast, the thunderstorm Inda had been waiting for boiled out of the west at last.

They'd spent nearly two weeks skulking in a inlet east of
the Danai harbor. It was a difficult inlet known to smugglers on *Cocodu*, carved out of the desolate land of cliffs
and treacherous coastal reefs and rock-strewn headlands
between Chwahirsland and lands to the west. The Fangs
lay eastward at the narrowest point of the strait and were
guarded by Venn warships. It took no awareness of grand

strategy to guess that the Venn would have set a trap for Inda's fleet once they came down the strait; Inda's lookouts, posted on the cliff tops, twice spotted Venn patrol fleets under sail.

But even the most watchful ship cannot see much farther than the waters directly ahead of it in the middle of a vast summer storm sweeping directly down the strait and out into the great seas beyond.

In the meantime his crew had not spent the hot, breathless days in idleness. The two schooners were transformed into aged fishing smacks by laboring sailors during the day. During the evenings they drilled.

The light changed just after dawn, brightness hardening to the peculiar blinding glare that makes one's eyes ache, turns the sea's color a restless green marked by choppy waves. All ships struck down the upper masts and set out storm sails.

And for a long day and half a night they fought as hard as they had last winter against the Brotherhood, only this time not against inimical pirates but against the dispassionate cruelty of high, chasing waves, punishing winds, bands of rain that hit from the side, roaring as loudly as the thunder directly overhead.

They saw no other ships—including one another. They were grateful only to be afloat, having passed not only the Venn (who had mostly withdrawn to the shelter of harbor on the eastern side of the strait) but the tall, misshapen rocky spires called The Fangs, against which many a storm-driven ship had smashed before.

When the bleak sun rose behind a streaky eastern sky that second morning, shining on a rough gray sea, Fibi of the Delfin Islands stretched her aching body and then stretched her arms between the spokes of the wheel. She looked around at the ragged clouds stretching from horizon to horizon. No other ships in sight.

She leaned on the wheel, rejoicing in the faint warmth of the sun and the fresh breeze that brought a hint of cold northern wind, a promise of winter, but none of the suffocating air presaging thunder. She was too tired to think about anything but the ship beneath her feet. She pressed into the wheel, feeling the ship's vibration resonate through her bones and teeth, trying to descry any judders or creaks that would warn of damage to keel, hull, or mast.

No sickening shiver of a wrung mast. Movement on the deck caught her eye; Inda trudging to his cabin at last, after standing on the foredeck since the onset of the storm. Gillor stopped him, said something. Inda snorted a kind of laugh, the short, breathless bark of the very young man he really was; like all young males, no matter how tired, his interest awoke on the instant.

The two vanished into the cabin together, watched by Fibi with approval. She liked young Inda, she liked Gillor. And best of all, she knew there was no romance between them, only the fun of the moment, no expectations. No trouble, therefore, for the crew. If anything, Fibi suspected Gillor's guarded heart yearned for that red-haired blade Fox, but those green eyes of his never rested on any crew member, man or woman, with desire. Only with unyielding expectation, whether the drill was ship-handling or fighting. An expectation set at a high standard which he himself met, so they all exceeded themselves in trying to match it.

Expectation. Yes.

She leaned her cheek against one of the spokes as she studied Fox, who prowled along the gangway as if he had not been on his feet since the day before, his sharply boned face highlighted by the rising light as he squinted up at the sails. She closed her eyes, thinking *bide your time . . . bide your time . . .* then jolted when a hand touched her shoulder.

Sleep had almost taken her. She lifted herself away from the helm, which she had been handling entirely by instinct. Every bone and muscle ached.

One of the young sailors waited, someone who looked slightly more rested than the rest, and so she relinquished the wheel and retreated down to her hammock, later not remembering climbing in.

She woke when firelight flickered on her eyelids. She was up, feet on the deck, hand fumbling for a weapon, when she recognized Mutt. "Inda wants ya," he whispered.

Fibi worked her dry mouth, suspecting (rightly) she'd been snoring. "We cleared the Fangs, yiss?"

"We're safe of the Chwahir coast."

"Fleet?"

"*Vixen* hove up not long after you went below," Mutt said, following her to the deck. "Spotted *Cocodu,* hull down, foremast gone. Schooners stayed together, *Vixen* found 'em about noon. Now Loos is out scouting our perimeter, Inda's orders, in case the Venn are searching."

Fibi stepped up on deck to a vastly different sea than that she'd gone to sleep on. Blue, placid waters reflected the smiling sky; a cable or two away, sailors were lowering a new foremast onto *Cocodu.* Voices drifted over the water, sounding almost like gulls. She paused at a rain barrel, took a deep drink of water kept magically clean, and then strode up into the cabin, where she found Inda and Gillor looking tousled but rested, Dasta tousled, and Fox neither. Not that he ever relaxed enough to appear tired. His face was just harder than usual as he leaned against the bulkhead, arms crossed.

Behind Fox, big, dark Tcholan stood at the stern windows, looking out at the work aboard *Cocodu.*

Inda had the chart spread out under the swinging lamp.

"Fibi," he greeted her as she dropped onto the bench opposite, Mutt flopping down to sit cross-legged on the deck next to her.

Inda leaned forward, giving his captains a fast assessment. All looked alert, if not rested. Fox, he knew, would sleep after this meeting, but not until then.

He said, "We slipped past the Venn."

Fox shifted. "They'll come looking."

"Right." Inda thumped his fist on the chart on the table. "So the plan is to use all the talk to our advantage and to keep them looking. I want news going out about us all over the seas." He opened his hand, sweeping it to take them all in. "We are going to split. I'll appoint a meeting place next spring. If you're there, I'll have another plan. If not . . ." He opened a palm.

Dasta thought of the bag of jewels and gold sitting in the cabin aboard *Cocodu,* then realized what Inda meant. It jolted him inside, made him feel queasy, the way the ship feels when it wallows on a windless sea. There was one big bag of treasure for each ship—enough to buy outright a couple of warships and outfit them right down to the smallest rat, promising a year's pay. Dasta thought back to the confrontation in the treasure cavern on Ghost Island, and for the first time he really considered what Inda meant: either they did what he wanted, or . . . they took the treasure for themselves. And then what?

Inda looked up, pointing a finger at him. "Dasta. You are now confirmed captain of *Cocodu,* instead of acting."

Dasta glanced in surprise at Fox, just to meet his usual ironic smile.

"You were the next hired, Tcholan, and since you two and Gillor are same in skills, we're going in order. Tcholan, you're acting captain of *Death,* and Gillor, first mate. Take sail for the Fire Islands, and roust every pirate you can find. I want raids, and stories of raids, going all over. If you can also attract a fleet of likely prospects, all the better." He turned back to Dasta. "But you're going to be Elgar the Fox, see?"

"Me?" Dasta smacked his hands against the smooth skin of his chest, his former speculation windblown in the face of this new surprise.

"You *and* Tcholan." Inda waved over at Tcholan by the stern windows. Tcholan looked up, flashing a rare, brief grin. "You two didn't see the Guild people come aboard us in Bren, but they went right up to Fox. Rumors had to have picked Fox out from the fight against the Brotherhood."

"But you were in command," Dasta said, rubbing his jaw.

Inda shook his head. "There isn't all that much command in that kind of battle, I told you that before. You set things up, and about all you can do after the first smash with the enemy is scout around dealing with the pieces. As far was what people saw, I don't think many saw me. I was mostly on the scout craft, going from ship to ship, and Fox was seen on the deck of Boruin's famed black-sided trysail and boarding some of the bigger pirates, and he does stand out."

Everyone observed Fox's mocking tilt to the head.

Dasta grimaced. "But neither of us has red hair." He didn't need to point out that they were about as unlike Fox as any in the crew: he himself was rangy and tall, hawk-nosed, eyes, skin, and hair a similar shade of sun-bleached wood; Tcholan was the same height but powerful in build, his skin chocolate brown, his hair long, black, luxuriant.

"So you make sure you're only seen from a distance. And you wear a black fighting scarf and black togs."

"I hate black," Dasta mourned. "Hotter 'n fire in summer."

Inda snorted. "People see what they expect to see. We'll use that by making rumors. You two have to trade off being Elgar the Fox, wearing black and sailing under the Fox banner. Gillor, you as well, if you can be seen from a distance."

Gillor made a flourishing gesture with her hands in a kind of ironic half bow.

"You attack no one but pirates. Gain a fleet if you like, but tell them nothing. Communicate through others, hold aloof. You have to be Elgar the Fox, because that's the only protection we will have." He turned his thumb toward Fibi, Fox, and himself.

Dasta scratched his salt-laden scalp. "You mean you're going out in disguise?"

"Yes." Inda turned his attention to Mutt, who still squatted on the deck. "You, Pilvig, and two of the other new mates are going to crew *Vixen* and make a run to Freedom Islands. Your job will be to spread rumors of the fleet's success, talk about us rousting pirates at Fire Islands, and talk to Commander Dhalshev."

Mutt's eyes rounded. "Do I lie to him?"

"No, but you won't tell him everything."

Mutt fingered his scruffy braid, then said, "Will he even talk to me?"

"He'll recognize the *Vixen*. Will want real news. I'll go over what you say and don't say before you set sail, but it's important to remember, talk to no one else about our plans. Where we are. You'll be getting plenty of offers to join our fleet, if I guess right. Only take the ones Woof or Commander Dhalshev vouch for."

Mutt felt dizzy. He knew he was tired, but it wasn't that. He loved the idea of being in command of *Vixen,* and he loved ruses and secrets and action. But he only loved it when Inda was right there nearby. "Where will we meet you?"

"Meet us at Danai on Flower Day." Inda turned his head. "Dasta, you've got to be drilling them all winter."

Springtide. Mutt nodded, thinking, *At least there's time for fun before we meet the Venn. If we meet the Venn.*

Chapter Eleven

THE elaborate terraces of the Adrani royal city, cut into the side of forested mountains, looked strange to Hadand, especially from the inside of a carriage—a hot, jolting, stuffy wood-and-canvas box. She leaned over to Joret. "Impossible to defend once an enemy gets inside the city gates."

Wisthia, sitting across from them, said, "Remember. No Marlovan in anyone's hearing."

Joret opened a hand. Hadand saw the tension drawing tight the fine skin of the queen's brow, and said, "We're agreed. Sartoran only, until we master Adrani."

Wisthia smiled a little, then turned to survey the city of her childhood, seen again after all these years. Very little had changed other than the layout of the formal gardens. It all looked exotic yet congenial, after the ubiquitous stone of Iasca Leror.

Her expression softened into reverie. Joret gazed out the other window, her profile impossible to read. Did she like this completely indefensible city? Hadand had to admit that the gardens all looked lovely, as did the artfully shaped waterfalls and canals—apparently emulating the famed canals of Colend's royal city with their pretty brick banks, but how would one defend such a place?

Joret, framed against the window, was even more strik-ing with this artistic greenery as background, like some-

thing from an old painting. Maybe it was that gown selected by Wisthia's friend, a baroness—which was a new
title to Hadand and Joret—named Lady Ialari. This gown
the baroness had insisted was the very latest fashion with
its low square neck, the draped ribbons and lace, the
smooth line of its bodice flaring out into arm's-lengths of
rich silk. In the two weeks they had stayed at that lady's
private home, Hadand had learned a great deal about that
mystery called "fashion."

There was no fashion in Iasca Leror. People wore what
they had worn for generations, aside from occasional alter-
ations of stitching along hems and seams; the only change
that Hadand could name was the men's preference for
fighting in the plain gray long-coats over the old, bright
House tunics that were now reserved for formal occasions.
As for the women, you could inherit a beautiful robe from
your grandmother, wear it at a formal House celebration,
and be admired. Not here, where, they were earnestly assured, to be seen in the same court gown twice would earn
scorn. The waste of that had at first scandalized Joret and
Hadand, until Wisthia explained that all but the most
wealthy had their overgowns taken apart and remade with
differing trim after each wearing, wasting not fabric but the
efforts of teams of seamstresses.

"Lest you think it frivolous and meaningless," Wisthia had
said on the first day, "look here. These are the fashions of fifteen years ago." And they stared at the sketches of clothing
shaped around bodies of massive size, the lines broad and
impressive. It looked very fine, especially if one wished to
appear larger than anyone else around one, Hadand
thought—but how could one move with any celerity?

Wisthia had said, "Look at it in pieces. That stiff lace ruff
about the neck is to hide extra chins. The huge quilted
sleeves increase the proportion of the arms to match that
of one's body, if one has a very large girth. These fashions
were preferred by my brother and his wife, so everyone
had to wear them."

Joret was shocked into speech. "Even in summer? One
would die of the heat!"

"They were uncomfortable, I am told, yes."

Hadand said, "Are their bodies in truth so large beneath the clothes? I remember being told that the queen was beautiful; does this mean that for the Adranis beauty is measured by size?"

"She was a slim beauty when she first came. All the letters I got claimed her to be, even from those who very shortly had little reason to like her. But years of rich food affect even princesses, if they do little else besides eat through the day and night. Anyway, look at the current fashions."

The new fashions looked light and airy, perhaps too airy to Marlovan eyes. But once you got used to the idea of men's clothing being tied on by clusters of ribbons and the women's dresses fitted in the bodice so you could see their shape, you could perceive a grace in line and design.

"That," Wisthia said, "is the effect of my nephew."

"So Martan-King and Nalais-Queen no longer lead the fashions?" Joret asked.

"Titles first, my dears. And only when you refer to them. To their faces, you must use the honorifics: even I must address my brother as Your Majesty. We will practice that. As for your question: no, they no longer lead fashions." Wisthia smiled again, an enigmatic smile that reminded Hadand once again how very little they actually knew of the private thoughts of Evred's mother. "It is my nephew, Prince Valdon, who leads the fashion now," she said.

Joret shook her head; Hadand said, "What does that mean?"

"We shall find out," Wisthia promised, smiling.

Inda and his fleet separated that day, as soon as the *Cocodu*'s shrouds had been tightened down and the sails raised.

The last he heard of Dasta, as he climbed down into his gig with a bundle of Fox's clothing under his arm, was, "I hate black. It's hot!"

Fox was lounging against the rail of the schooner *Skimit,* which was to be Inda's home for this next cruise. "It doesn't show dirt, and better, it doesn't show blood," he called down with no sympathy.

Inda thumped the rail next to Fox, and flashed his rare grin. "Remember, you are invincible!"

Dasta's reply was lost as the coxswain gave the command to start rowing, but they knew it was both pungent and idiomatic.

Inda found Mutt lurking at his elbow. Mutt's mute expression of worry, of trust, made Inda feel old—he had to remind himself he had survived a mutiny and was expected to lead in all but name a band of marine defenders when he was a year or two younger than Mutt. "Just remember, don't blab," he said, and then he stepped closer. "Woof will be there, soon's you land in Freeport."

Mutt's brow puckered. "What do I say about Nugget?" He added, tentatively, "Pilvig offered to tell Woof. They were hammock-mates all last winter."

It hurt to remember Woof's sister, barely thirteen that winter, her happy laughter, those tousled yellow curls. She'd been so gallant, so thirsty for adventure—even in the midst of battle she apparently couldn't believe anything could happen to her. The other young ones had obeyed the orders she'd been too reckless to heed about shields and defense.

"Good for Pilvig," Inda said, not adding how glad he was that the youngsters had resolved their feud. He knew how much he would have hated such a comment at scrub age, seeing it as condescending. "If Woof asks for details, she must give him the truth, ending with the fact that we don't know if she recovered. But Nugget's tough. And Parayid Harbor would be a good place for her, if the villagers took her there. We liked it when we had liberty there. Tau knew the people. There'd be plenty of work with the rebuilding, so they'll need hands."

Mutt's throat worked in his skinny neck. He turned away. "I'll tell Pilvig. And get my gear."

The transfer of belongings did not take long. Mutt, too, was given a heavy bag of pirate treasure whose clinks had been smothered inside a small barrel. Inda and Fibi were exact about what sort of hires to look out for, once Dhal-

shev had vouched for them. They also described what to
say to them, to which Mutt listened with narrow-eyed concentration. Young he was, his only weakness was a penchant for practical jokes—and inexperience at making the
decisions instead of carrying out the results.

And so Mutt sailed away on his first command, the oldest of the four youngsters, all recent hires except for Mutt.
Only Jug was staying aboard Inda's schooner; he was fifteen, and Inda needed to ask him some questions—though
not yet.

Inda watched Mutt standing there so proudly at the tiller
as he called something to Pilvig. She crouched on the masthead, her black hair twisted into cub-ears that bobbled
when she turned her attention downward to listen. *Vixen*'s
beautiful curved mainsail tautened, the slim scout craft
taking wing.

Inda turned away. All the orders had been given. Now it
was a matter of waiting to see if they would be carried out,
or if circumstances—and ambition—would destroy his
plans.

That, or the Venn, Inda thought, turning his attention to
the squalid *Rippler*, wallowing slack-sailed on the water as
it awaited the last transfer.

A hard thump on his shoulder. "Let's do it if we're going
to," Fox said, looking unfamiliar in Dasta's old vest, his
drawstring trousers, the skin of his arms and chest pale. But
even now, he would not go in bare feet, which were impossible for fighting, he insisted. Below the wide, ragged hems
of the trousers were his black-weave cavalry boots.

No matter. If they stayed with his plan, Fox would never
leave the deck.

"Let's go," Inda echoed.

After the promise not to speak Marlovan, the Iascans fell
silent, and Wisthia watched with nervous tension as they
rolled past low gates, pretty gardens, discreet buildings
with climbing, flowering vines hiding the bare stone.

They had progressed up the slow switchbacks to the

palace that lay along the top tier. And now to find out what message her brother was sending her.

Wisthia had not told Hadand and Joret about the gates; she was not certain why. Pride, probably, she acknowledged with an inward flinch.

But here at last they were, rolling past the outer palace annexes with their familiar spreading terraces and wide windows, and inside the first court.

No more than she expected. To have stopped her outside of that would be the deadliest insult, and though her brother had inevitably changed over the years, at least he hadn't gone mad.

Through two vine-covered archways, under glass-windowed buildings, and into the second court, the nobles' court where the nobility who came with royal invitation were greeted.

Up on one of the walls someone signaled; Wisthia could not see it, but she felt it in the check of the driver on the horses. The pause was very slight, and the girls did not notice, or at least did not question, before the coach resumed rolling. She relaxed as once again they moved sedately under an archway and along the narrow road at the pinnacle to the private royal court. Well then. No insults, at least. She returned with her old status, that much was clear; the rest would be easier.

Her slow breath of relief revealed to Hadand that they hadn't been told all, and there was significance in where their carriage was ordered to stop.

The last court was within the building complex itself. Wisthia smiled. Hadand understood that the inner court was a mark of prestige, invisible unless you knew. How subtle, how dangerous!

The carriage halted. Someone opened the door, letting in the fresh air that the Marlovans, used to traveling by horseback, had craved. They disembarked, waiting to the right and left as previously arranged, so that Wisthia could step into the center.

Holding the door was a tall man wearing a livery that looked both impressive and impossible to fight in, Hadand thought. The main color was a deep violet, almost black, with highly stylized white swans embroidered down the sides of the sleeves, their necks entwined. These sleeves had broad white cuffs, as did the straight trousers; the herald himself wore a stiff hat that was not a helm, but resembled one. A single white swan embroidered on the front of this hat seemed to identify him; Hadand saw Wisthia's eyes lift to it before she faced the man.

He was older, his bow low and practiced. He spoke rapidly in Adrani, too rapidly for Hadand to get more than a word or two; Wisthia said in clear Sartoran, "My royal brother and sister invite us straight to court, expressing a kind wish not to postpone so long delayed a reunion, but if you wish to rest and refresh yourselves first, they will await our pleasure."

Hadand could tell from the queen's tone, the tiny smile at the corners of her thin lips, that this was the greeting she had hoped for.

Hadand knew that it was important that the barbarians be heard speaking Sartoran. "I hold myself ready, if that is your wish, Your Majesty."

"And I, too," Joret said.

Hadand and Wisthia watched the sober herald stare at Joret and then shift his gaze, the effort visible. Joret was thinking: *We were told to wear our very best traveling gowns, after which we sat motionless in the coach for a short drive. Rest and refresh from what?*

But she straightened her spine, even though she felt exposed in this gown with its tight bodice and open neck. This had to be what pleasure house girls felt like, except they were within the confines of their house of business, and they knew what to expect. Joret did not know what to expect, other than what came next would not be war, except perhaps of words. It was clear from the swift exchange between the queen and this herald that she and Hadand would have to practice far more: the Adrani words were spoken too swiftly to follow.

But then they were moving, and she was relieved at this chance to stretch her legs. She tried to walk with the quick, scudding steps the queen's friend had shown them, but gave up after two long corridors, all with wood panels etched with gold leafing in swirling patterns, and some kind of beautiful milky-white stone forming swans diving, gliding, posing with their pretty necks arched. She and Hadand gradually lengthened their paces until they were walking with their customary long strides, their skirts billowing despite their straight-armed attempts to hold them still.

Cushioned little chairs lined the last hall, all of them with the low rounded backs that reminded Joret of harps. Chairs built for wide skirts, for people who did not expect attack from behind. No raptor chairs here.

Down broad marble stairs. Marble was even more beautiful than described, a translucent stone veined with faint colorations.

And then great carved double doors were thrown back by twin young men dressed exactly alike, small swan-hats on their heads. Wisthia walked in, tall and proud, the two Iascans behind her in what both thought of as Honor Guard position. Then they didn't think at all.

Joret blinked at all the color within, a brilliant display that resolved into ranks of men and women, all in clothing far more elaborate than hers—something she would have thought impossible a moment before.

Hadand gave them all a single sweeping glance, her attention drawn to the two people on the thrones, difficult to make out among all the gilt and carvings and rich folds of fabric.

The herald spoke in Adrani, pronouncing their names in the middle of the stream of words, Joret's name third. Then with a whisper and a rustle the entire room full of people made their bows.

At first Hadand and Joret had laughed at the notion of bowing—of sticking your butt out at the hapless person standing behind you—but these courtiers made it look good. It was in the bending of the knees, the way they held their backs straight as they inclined their heads.

Now Joret fell in behind Wisthia and Hadand, who, being queens, walked side by side up the carpet, which was again a deep violet, only now the swans were faint outlines worked in pure silver, toward a dais on which were two couches.

"Bow," Wisthia barely breathed, and Joret realized the other two had begun the movement they had practiced so long. She performed her bow, then straightened up.

Hadand regarded the woman of impressive size with the painted cheeks and lips, who reclined on her couch-throne in a gown glittering with ropes of pearls and clusters of diamonds. The gown was decorated by a profusion of silken roses and loops of ribbon as well as glittering gems, the skirts so voluminous they draped over the back of the couch and down onto the floor, rich, gleaming lengths of exquisite fabric.

The king was larger than his queen. He wore a spectacular embroidered cloak obscuring half his body, like the queen's skirts, so long it trailed two men's lengths before him on the floor. His nose was purple from drink; that, at least was a familiar enough sight. Mad Gallop Yvana-Vayir had had the same purple nose, though he'd been less than a quarter the size of this man.

The royal pair spoke ritual words of welcome, using Sartoran, the language of civilization, but their accent was unfamiliar, and Hadand and Joret struggled to comprehend.

Wisthia was stationed at the queen's right, Hadand at the king's left, and Joret was bade stand at Hadand's side—as all eyes turned to watch her.

For the remainder of the formal court, which was a long series of ritual speeches, goings and comings, flattery, music, capped by a meal at a long table in an adjacent chamber equally as large, Hadand observed those clever, smiling faces. Jewels winked, betraying subtle movements made by courtiers who were covertly observing the newcomers. Especially Joret.

Hadand saw the expected admiration, interest, curiosity, except for the pretty, artful blonde at Wisthia's right, who watched Joret from beneath her eyelashes, her mouth tight with . . . anger? Hatred?

Wisthia ignored her. She kept her attention on her brother and his queen. Her quiet smile, the tone of her soft voice as she spoke to them in Sartoran, convinced Hadand that Evred's mother, powerless in Iasca Leror, had indeed laid deep plans for her eventual return to her homeland. Plans she had imparted to no one.

When at last they withdrew to ready themselves for the evening's entertainment (which, Wisthia warned them, would not be materially different from the morning's, just with more music—maybe dancing, certainly gambling) Hadand wanted to discuss her observations with Joret. But Joret was absorbed as she admired the scrollwork rippling artistically in drapes and crimps along the vaulted joining walls and ceiling. A quick glance showed most of the Adranis admiring Joret's profile.

Hadand decided for now to keep her thoughts to herself.

At nightfall, when they were alone on the sea, Dasta signaled and Tcholan rowed the short distance to *Cocodu*.

They were exhausted from the storm and its aftermath. There was plenty to do on both ships, but at least they were seaworthy and could survive any but the worst storm.

Tcholan glanced back at *Death* riding quietly on the mild swell, lamps strung along the deck as the night watch continued repairing the rigging.

He hooked on and clambered up the sides of the *Cocodu*. Dasta was waiting, the lamplight painting his skin gold as he led the way into the cabin. He wore Fox's black trousers, but no shirt, and he'd scrounged a vest from somewhere with added pockets, which carried his spyglass and a few other oddments.

Inda's big Eastern Seas chart lay open on the table, a lamp holding down each corner.

They sat down together at the table and for a moment looked at each other. "You ever expect to be a captain?" Tcholan said presently.

"No," Dasta admitted, then laughed. "I've been sitting here wondering if I ought to get drunk, or play around with maps and pretend to be Inda."

Tcholan laughed. "Yes. Yes."

Dasta sighed. "Jeje told me, when she made her run to Freedom, she kept asking herself what Inda would do. So I tried to think the same." He smacked the chart. "See, if we use the sun-trackers we can go straight east to Inglenook.

The more I think about it, the more I suspect we'll find *Sea-King* there, and maybe even some of Walic's old gang."

Tcholan grimaced. "Why would you want them? I thought you told Inda none of them were worth going after."

"We couldn't take the ship with all those spies o' Walic's aboard. Not after that fight, and the storm." Dasta ran his fingers lightly over the islands. "But what if, once they found out Walic was gone, they got the spies overboard?"

Tcholan leaned forward. "Keep talking."

Dasta did—with much back and forth, doubts, shrugs, curses, and then, "Let's ask Gillor when she's off watch."

"Let's. Three guesses at what Inda would do are better than two." Tcholan squinted at the chart. "I hate this kind of thing. I want a clear order. Get your fight band up the side of that ship and take it. That I can do. D'you think Inda ever felt this way? Like being captain is puttin' someone else's clothes on?"

"Like these?" Dasta stuck his legs out, grinning, then grimaced. "Tight across the hips. Wish Fox had the sense to wear drawstrings." Dasta frowned at Tcholan, who was bigger all through his body. "These won't fit you at all."

Tcholan laughed. "I know, already tried. Sails gave me some black cloth from the flags chest. Good linen cloth. Always carries extra, he said, on account of Fox, if his shirts get ripped up. He's particular, he said—won't wear summer-sailcloth, like the rest of us. Got to be linen."

They both contemplated Fox.

Tcholan went on, since Dasta hadn't laughed. "Wearing Fox's clothes—even if they aren't strictly his—makes being a captain a put on, for me, outside as well as in here." He hit the heel of his hand against his forehead. "Maybe easier to think of it as puttin' a ruse on."

"I've an idea for that, too," Dasta said, tracing round and round the Inglenook Islands on the chart. "Inda said before we sailed, the outfit is part of war in the mind. Like the earrings. You know what would make us look real, real good? I mean make us look like that Ramis, except for that business about the holes in the sky?"

Tcholan made a warding sign. "*Big* business."

Dasta chuckled. "So here's what. We time our attacks at Fire Island—first you, then me. We attack one then the other on opposite sides of the island. Get us a cutter like *Vixen*, to go between us. Then the pirates think Fox is everywhere. War up here, see?" He tapped his head.

Tcholan considered. "Good. Gillor has some tricksy ideas, too," he offered. "She was on privateers before Walic got her. They're good at ruses." He rose. "Got to get back. Too much to do." He paused at the door, then faced Dasta again. "I was born on land. Parents painters—pa did wall murals, ma did porcelain. I spent my days grinding colors. Sitting outside trying to sketch trees. Always looked like bread dough on a stick. Pa smacked me. Said try harder. I hated trees. Told Ma one night if I never saw another tree again, I'd be happy. She took me to the city. Ended up at sea." He hesitated. "And here I am."

Dasta laughed. "My family was beekeepers. Figured on the sea, there were no bees."

Tcholan left, chuckling, shaking his head. "No bees. No bees," he repeated in a low voice as he rowed back to his new command.

Chapter Twelve

THE sun lightened the east as Fleet Commander Hyarl Fulla Durasnir finished his weapons warm-ups. He glanced skyward, something all Venn did as a matter of necessity, even those fixed here in the south year after year. The horizon all around was clear. Unimaginable at this season in the Land of the Venn, when autumn brought surprise storms howling like a pack of wolves nearly every day. But then this was not even autumn at home, it was spring—another cruel, stormy season, warming reluctantly.

Harsh as Venn was, it was home, and Durasnir missed his home. He hated it here in the south, hated its smiling seasons, its small, smiling people who looked up at him with imperfectly hidden hatred, fear, scorn. *Those huge Venn, stinking of spice, how stupid they are!* They used to say so openly, not knowing he knew their language as well as they did, while they did not know his. Every time he returned to the Port of Jaro after a cruise his hatred seemed to intensify a little more. And it was always at its worst the day after he regained the shore.

He reached the baths before the lazy locals were even out of their beds, and finished before anyone else came through the door, wringing his long yellow hair, now shot with gray, in the summer air. Another thing you did not do at home, unless you wanted your hair to freeze and break off, all in the time it took to draw three breaths.

But there was no use in thinking of home. He was here, in Ymar, living on the rocky walls overlooking the Port of Jaro, the rising sun revealing row after row of whitewashed stone houses as the shadows sank down toward the waterline and then vanished altogether for another day. After a long, fruitless spring journey he'd rejoined his wife and young son yesterday, which was good. They would be awake and awaiting him now.

He rolled his hair quickly and clipped it up on the back of his head, then ran up the steps into his meeting chamber, sensing something amiss before he reached the door. Ah. No sounds of breakfast, the quiet chatter of family— instead the silence due to the presence of strangers. Or superiors.

There was only one superior to the Commander of the Oneli—the sea lords—and that was Prince Rajnir himself. But there was one equal to him.

And indeed it was a tall, slim silver-haired man who placed hands together, head tipped politely, as Durasnir entered the room.

"Dag Erkric," Durasnir said, hands open. "You honor my house."

"Your house honors me," Dag Abyarn Erkric said, indicating the family sitting motionless on the eating platform, their food rapidly cooling. Durasnir's glance took in his rigid wife and knew that she'd offered to share and had been refused. No one could eat, or even move, until the Dag took his business out of the eating chamber.

"You will pardon my intrusion when I explain that I am here at the prince's command," the Dag said. "There were enough survivors of that storm appearing along this coast to convince him that Elgar the Fox slipped entirely past our blockade. Therefore the prince desires an immediate sweep-search of all possible inlets as well as the coast, every male from fifteen to thirty, every masted craft, checked for the identification medal."

Durasnir was silent as he considered the scale of this order. A local search would ordinarily fall within the duties of the Erama Krona, the Arm of the Crown, the prince's personal guard, who had their own training, their own command structure, and were thus answerable only to the prince. Or it would fall to the Yaga Krona, the Eyes of the Crown, the mages with a similar duty; they reported to Dag Erkric, who was answerable only to the prince.

But because of the prince's anomalous status, the Erama Krona and Yaga Krona were few in number—enough to guard the royal residence and very little else.

Therefore such a search would fall on the shoulders of the navy, in particular the marines, already in use as supplemental guards, much to Durasnir's regret. But the king, as yet, had not sent occupation forces. And so everyone had to make do with what they had.

There was no avoiding a direct order, but one could ask a question. Durasnir said, "Was there any evidence Elgar the Fox would turn northward—all land held by us—and not to the south, which is not held by us?" *In other words, is there any evidence that Elgar would do anything so profoundly stupid as to land on our side of the strait?*

Erkric's lips pulled down in amusement. "The prince is convinced that this Elgar, having defeated the pirates, is marking out the prince himself as his next target. Therefore, it is I who come, and not a messenger, as evidence of his wish for dispatch. It is by the prince's command." He used the royal modality.

It is what Rajnir would do. "There is nothing more to be said," Durasnir replied. "But it will involve every ship and man, so large a search. The fishing fleets alone will not be able to sail for days and days while we sort them."

"Ah, but the prince thought of that. Count Wafri will take charge of all land searches north of Jaro. It is the area the prince gave him to oversee, after all. The prince wishes Count Wafri to be given more responsibility in government. He feels it is a gesture of good will to the Ymarans. Your orders are to sail west in case they went to ground at the start of the storm and have beat up into the winds toward Bren."

Durasnir made a gesture of agreement without speaking. Dags interfering in military business—again. And he sent haring off for yet more months, to come back to what changes next?

But he would not reveal his intention to check these orders. He had reason to visit Rajnir to report; that would suffice. "Very well."

"Then I will depart at once, and leave you to your morning meal." Erkric made the Dag's bow again, this time to the degree of respected equal, rather than as Prince's Voice. Then he made a sign and vanished, the displaced air swishing through the room.

Durasnir knelt across from his wife. Brun gave him a tight look that promised questions, and plenty of them, but not before Halvir. Instead, in her smooth, quiet voice, she oversaw Halvir's eating until the boy made that abrupt change from interest in food to restlessness that characterizes the two-year-old. And Brun summoned his nurse.

As soon as the door was shut behind them she sat down next to him. "Well, Fulla? Shall we begin addressing him as '*the* Dag'?"

He let a laugh escape him. "He wants it now."

"I know. But the king will have to direct me to give him that coveted article." The lines in Brun's face deepened with her hatred of Erkric, a hatred become implacable since the discovery of the treaty with the bloody-handed Marshig. No one believed that to be Rajnir's idea—he would never have thought of such a thing. So it had to have been the Dag, and of course the prince would welcome any idea that would bring back his heirship to the throne of the Venn.

"If Rajnir becomes king," he reminded her, "it will happen."

Brun's face tightened. But she said nothing more about Erkric's ambitions to be decreed The Dag of the Venn, the highest of all mages, above Houses. "What lies behind this search?" she asked.

"Oh, I believe the search is what it appears to be, though the Dag, and not the prince, is probably the instigator. Dag Erkric was badly disturbed by the rumors that this Elgar the Fox has dealings with Norsunder through Ramis."

Brun set her spiced leaf aside. "I never thought I would be glad of such tidings—"

Durasnir laid his finger to her lips. "Ydrasal in deed," he

said in a whisper, "means Ydrasal in word and in thought." He made the sign of the tree.

"Though our actions lead away from the path of Ydrasal," she stated, and countered with the gesture of warding Rainorec—*Venn-doom*. "I'm silent. Never fear. But I live to see the summons come for us to go home." Her eyes, seldom soft, were bright with a sheen of tears that she would never let fall. She was far too angry for that.

"I fear it is a quick repast I must make," he said, sitting back on his mat.

Brun bowed her head, accepting the implied rebuke in the change of subject. Though their chambers were promised by the sea dag Jazsha Signi Sofar to be free of spy spells, Signi was just a sea dag, and not to be compared with the likes of Dag Erkric in power.

So Brun studied her husband, unsure how much of the truth she could burden him with and not dishonor herself. She could not say aloud how she was coming to hate Rajnir, who had grown up in Durasnir House playing with their first son, daughter, and the kin-children. Rajnir who had shown such promise, and who had been whispered about ever since he turned fifteen and was proclaimed heir to the throne, though others had previously been spoken of. No one knew the truth behind the heirship choice, but they did know that nine years ago, when he turned sixteen, he led the more impatient sons, including their own Vatta, into a disastrous ship battle that had gotten most of them killed—Vatta among them—at the callous and cruel hands of the Chwahir. Which led the king to rescind the heirship, causing a storm of conflict among the Houses at home.

Durasnir ate one muffin, drank one spice-milk, and then rose. "I must go report on my findings at the Ghost Isles," he said. "And prepare for this new cruise, which I trust will at least be short."

The harbor at Beila Lana on the east coast of Ymar was long and narrow and also shallow enough to limit the very large ships; thus it was a favorite of the fleets of small fishing craft that in larger harbors got shoved out into the worst anchorage and services.

"That's why I want it," Inda had said when they were discussing the best place to land.

They sailed slowly up the channel. Fox had been silent since they sighted the harbor. "The Port of Jaro has got to be too well guarded, even if the news would be firsthand there," Inda said.

"Firsthand," Fox repeated. "Rajnir is probably crouched on a rock right now, glass to his eye, watching for you. He's got to figure we survived the blow."

Inda flicked his hand up. "That's what I'd figure, too. But surely he'd think we'll stay safely on the Sartoran side."

"Surely?" Fox mocked.

Inda ignored him. "So we try this coast. I'll take Beila Lana, you go up the coast a way."

Fox crossed his arms. "What 'news' is it you have to find on your own?"

The crew shifted uneasily, all except for Fibi, who watched Fox without any change of expression. As always Inda took Fox's sarcasm as an honest question.

"If I knew I could send someone. I want to see them. See their ships. See them handling the ships. Hear them talking. Hear their gossip, especially if they talk about home, or land, or their marines. Ramis said they are far from united. That usually means talk, doesn't it? If so, I want to be around to hear it."

"Speaking Venn so well," Fox said, gaze skyward.

Inda sighed. "It's supposed to be a lot like Marlovan. If I can't puzzle it out after I hear enough of it, I'll give up." He jerked his thumb back. "But first we sell this load of fish!"

Fox peered under his hand at the sea.

Fibi chuckled as she squinted through the spokes of the wheel at the two commanders, standing side by side at the rail. Inda was convincing as a fisher mate, with his wide-set, mild gaze, his curly hair escaping his sloppy four-strand queue. His powerful chest and upper arms were common to forecastlemen all over the world; his old shirt, stitched by his own hand, had no laces, his deck trousers were baggy at seat and knee, his brown feet bare and tough. "But change you them rubies, first," she said, and chuckled again.

Fox and Inda both looked up, clapping hands to ears. Only pirates wore these big hoops; Brotherhood wore them large enough to support diamond drops. And by now everyone knew that Elgar the Fox's pirates who'd killed pirate ships wore rubies.

"Glad you reminded me," Inda said, letting out a breath. "Sailor rings."

Sailors who wore earrings kept them modest to avoid being accused of strut—or piracy. Gold at your ear was a good way to guarantee at least some money if one was shipwrecked and made it alive to a foreign shore. Or if one left a ship without pay for whatever reason or drank up one's earnings and slept through the ship's departure. You could always sell gold. But those rings were always finger-sized, to differentiate from the swinging hoops of pirates.

And so, as the schooner sailed the rest of the way down toward the long dock extended out into the channel, Inda sat in the cramped cabin below. He pulled out his earrings, removed the stones, and cut one golden hoop in half, then hammered each into a finger-sized circle.

Jug dropped down through the hatch. "Fibi said you wanted me?"

"Yes." Inda worked the golden wire, twisting one end into a loop. "Tell me about your uncle. What kind of mage is he?"

"Illusion," Jug said.

"Illusion?" Inda repeated, looking up.

Jug wriggled. "Don't you know anything about mages?"

Inda sat back. "I know something about the spell renewal mages," he said. His mother had taught him a great deal about them.

Jug deflated a little. "Oh. Well. Illusion mages work at the playhouses."

Inda thought about that, remembering Tau telling him a long time ago about actual places where people paid to see plays. When small Inda had read Old Sartoran historical plays without knowing that they had ever been performed.

He frowned at Jug. "What do you yourself know? Can you do magic?"

Jug shook his head vehemently. "No! The basics are boring, and it takes forever. Illusions are easier to learn, my uncle said, but the magic doesn't last. It fools the eyes and ears, and then is gone. So they make illusions for plays." And, seeing Inda's puzzled brow, he said, "You know, in the play it rains, so he makes rain. There's no wet, but the audience sees rain. There's a banquet, so he makes it look like there is food on a table, and as long as the players don't forget and put their hand through, it looks real enough."

"Illusion." Inda's brow cleared. "Is this akin to natural illusion, like the shimmer above flagstones on a summer's day?"

"Yes. Because they don't change anything, it's easier to be an illusion mage. But it's not good for much else. In fact, you're not allowed to use it for much else. If you use it for crime, for example—" Jug drew a finger across his neck. "The rules are strict. Why, you can't even play jokes! Not really. No fun in that!"

Inda said, "Two kinds of mages. So . . . what type would a navigation mage be?"

"Oh, the real one," Jug said, extracting the maximum out of his pose as expert, though in truth he wasn't sure.

And Inda, experienced with the young if not with magic, suspected as much. "Thank you, Jug."

The boy swarmed up the ladder to the deck, and Inda heard the quick smack of his feet running forward as, from aft, came Fox's familiar step.

Shadow obscured the sunlit hatch, and Fox dropped down a moment later. Inda was fixing the earrings into his ears.

Fox whacked the fold-down table up with a careless swipe, latched it into place, and dropped onto the bench facing Inda, hands on his knees.

"Inda," he said. His expression was always sardonic to a lesser or greater degree, but when he was angry he seemed to take up all the available space. "Inda. You are not even twenty. Why in damnation are you determined to take on the world's most powerful empire?"

"Because no one else will," Inda said, meeting Fox's angry gaze.

Fox cursed as he made a sudden gesture, as though backhanding Inda's words. Then he said, "So why don't you take that misplaced impulse and raise me an army to retake Iasca Leror?"

"Why?" Inda retorted.

"Why," Fox repeated scornfully. "You don't think any one of us would be better than those damned Montrei-Vayirs?"

"Only one I hate is the Harskialdna. And the Sierlaef. But that was personal. What matters is that the Harskialdna couldn't be too incompetent if he's managed to take and hold Idayago. And Olara. Despite everyone around Halia being against him. Can he?"

Fox flipped up the back of his hand. "Go chase your Venn. I hope they kill you."

Inda snorted in amusement, pushed past Fox, and climbed to the deck, leaving Fox to reflect on how seldom anyone had seen Inda laugh. Quite different, in fact, from the ten-year-old Inda who'd stopped at his home for a couple days on his way to the academy for the first time, trading cracks with his sister Shendan, and laughing at all their funny stories.

Rajnir had taken the building at the highest point on the ridge overlooking Jaro. It had once belonged to the Ymaran harbormaster, and was—most Venn thought—an inconvenient building in all ways. But it did boast one feature absolutely unknown in their homeland, a tower with windows all the way around. Including in the west. No building had doors or windows in the west in Venn, or not for long: the endless killing ice storms that scoured the western part of the Venn homeland had created cities blind on one side.

In nearly ten years Rajnir had never tired of watching sunsets from this tower. In fact he liked the small room so well during the balmy summer months that he conducted most business there, causing inconvenient jams on the narrow switchback stairways leading up and down, tirelessly guarded by the Erama Krona, the Arm of the Crown.

Stairs he did not have to use. Dag Erkric had fashioned him a transfer square. If one could bear the transfer magic—which was not too gut-wrenching just from the top of the building to the government center at the foot of the ridge—it was considered a mark of distinction to be granted the Access Spell.

Durasnir had never asked for the Transfer Spell, partly because he felt the exertion of the long climb was good for his body, but mostly because the long climb and descent gave him time to think uninterrupted.

He reached the top, found the expected pair of armed Erama Krona on guard, dressed in white and wearing the Tree as their device. They saluted him, a salute he returned with grave respect.

He passed inside. The tower room was unchanged since he'd left. This was not always the case. Nine years ago, after having negotiated the trade and protection treaty with the elderly queen of Ymar, he'd sailed for the homeland on the order of the king, leaving Rajnir behind to settle the details that should have brought north all the goods they so desperately needed. The king had been so pleased with his new heir!

But on Durasnir's return everything had changed: the queen had recently been found dead in her summer palace above Beila Lana, and out at sea Rajnir was losing a battle against a combined force of Everoneth and Chwahir—usually each other's deadly enemies—that Durasnir just barely kept from being a far more spectacular defeat.

Then the very day he returned from that disaster, ahead of the limping fleet, he found winding down to flower-bedecked barges the strangest funeral procession he had ever witnessed: the queen's entourage moving slowly in a fluttering shower of white flower petals tossed by locals, led by white-haired morvende who sang and chanted complicated threnodies that haunted his dreams. They had all entered the barges and sailed away—without returning.

He still did not know the import of that day, but he sensed he would one day find out.

After that it had taken a year to rid Ymar of the Everoneth who had overrun the kingdom of Ymar on the pretext of defending it and to settle the old nobles on their estates and keep them out of trouble. Except for one.

Who was standing with Rajnir at the window. Next to the prince's bright head and long body was a short, slim figure, also fair-haired, well-dressed. They were talking low-voiced; then came the quick, almost breathless laugh of Lord Annold Limros, the Count of Wafri—the only Ymaran noble to ally with the Venn.

"Greetings, my prince," Durasnir said, and bowed to Rajnir, hands together, then opening.

Rajnir turned, smiling, his lips shaping the words "Uncle Fulla," but a quick look and he retreated, as he always did in the presence of others, into protocol. "Hyarl my Commander," he said, palms touching together briefly.

"Greetings, Count Wafri," Durasnir said, with a short bow.

Wafri bowed to exactly the same degree. "Commander Durasnir," he said, his smile wide.

A small anomaly. Wafri had claimed to be Rajnir's age exactly—he even looked younger than Rajnir—but he was five years older. Durasnir had discovered the fact during an examination into the count's background, done as a matter of course with any foreigner the prince invited beyond the formal interview chambers. He'd attributed the anomaly to vanity, and so had never troubled to tell Rajnir, who wanted an age mate after he lost so many at the disastrous Chwahir battle. Wafri certainly was a handsome fellow, who spent a great deal to secure the latest Colendi fashions, all velvet and lace. He looked barely twenty, being short and slender, his hair clipped in the Colendi fashion so that it curled on his brow and over his ears, which made his head look rounder.

"I am sorry you did not capture Elgar the Fox." Rajnir returned restlessly to the window. "But tell us what you did discover."

"Little," Durasnir said. "We reached the Ghost Isles a

week after his departure. I stayed just long enough to gather information. He was there a month, and he did indeed meet and talk with Ramis. They were seen together walking through the harbor town."

Rajnir frowned. "So which one commands? More to the point, is Elgar the red-haired one our contact in Lindeth reports, or is he the Marlovan prince's son who led the mutiny in eastern waters? Or are they one and the same, as Erkric surmises?"

"That I could not discover." Durasnir hesitated, then decided not to share his theories, at least not yet.

Durasnir still did not know how Wafri and Rajnir had met; one of the questions concerning the events of nine years ago was the fact that the old queen had died under problematic circumstances—some said smothered—in her summer palace, which was the gift of the Limros family. Wafri's own family. And when Durasnir found Rajnir out at sea, he had this young count with him, as they'd become not just allies but friends. It seemed impossible that so vain and pleasure-loving a little man could be any way connected with any of these events, but Durasnir was by nature cautious.

So he kept his report general, omitting his surmises. "Elgar the Fox spoke with no one other than Ramis during his stay. His people said nothing of import. Mostly wild talk about their battle against Marshig's forces. But they all said the same thing: the battle ended when Ramis rent a hole out of the world and send Marshig and his five consorts to Norsunder."

Rajnir frowned. He was angry that the fleet had pulled away from the pirate battle, but it had been on Erkric's insistence. "Ramis is a Norsundrian mage," he'd said, standing on Durasnir's deck. "None of us can withstand his magic." And Durasnir had had to obey as the prince had given Erkric precedence in any matter pertaining to magic. Rajnir therefore had himself to blame, as they'd both obeyed his orders.

"So we returned, our raiders sweeping both coasts, but discovered nothing before the storm was upon us."

Rajnir whirled around, pacing the length of the small room. "We need that Transfer Spell. Surely Norsunder's mages, though formidable, are not the only ones who can command it. Entire ships! We need it. I told Erkric if he finds that spell, he will be the Dag. Not only Dag of the Venn, but of the world." He whirled again, stared anxiously out the window as Wafri's dark eyes flicked from one to the other, his smile never diminishing.

Rajnir pointed down below. "See the game those children play? We've been watching them. I cannot comprehend what the rules are. Wafri says they change little from generation to generation. Is that not astonishing?"

Rajnir beckoned, and Durasnir joined them at the window, which was warm from the morning sun. He gazed down onto one of the broader terraces, where a scattering of Ymaran children played a game involving ropes being swung in circling arcs. Children ran and jumped back and forth through the arcs, tossing wooden balls to one another through the ropes in complicated patterns. Their mouths opened and closed in unison, suggesting a chant, as around them Venn children watched from one side and a few Ymarans from the other.

"Their children do not mix with ours," Rajnir observed.

"They will," Wafri promised.

Rajnir rounded again, his gilt-edged tunic skirts swinging. "I won't declare myself king of Ymar."

It was an old argument. To Rajnir kingship was meaningful only in one place: the Land of the Venn.

Wafri bowed, hands spread, palms up in the Venn style. He gave his quick, characteristically cheery smile. "I should take my leave," he said. "Will not my search be more efficient if I am seen supervising?"

He almost always phrased his opinions as questions. Durasnir had noted this the few times he'd been in Wafri's presence.

"Ah! Yes, yes, yes," Rajnir replied, shooing with his hands. "Go. Find him. If you find him, I'll make you a, what, a duke?"

Wafri's lips parted. He gave a happy chuckle, then said, "We counts always held that we were as good as dukes. Our titles are oldest, not borrowed. Most meaning." He chuckled again.

"But meaning changes," Rajnir said, smiling.

"Well spoken, O Prince!" Wafri bowed. "We no longer count everything, though *counting is knowing what you have*, as it says in Old Sartoran over our arms. The wise old sayings are ever true."

"Go count every stranger who landed on our coast," Rajnir said, making his quick motions again. "See if the medallions were worth the expense."

Wafri bowed elaborately, and, still chuckling, moved onto the gold and white tiles of the transfer square. A flick, a puff of air, and he was gone.

Rajnir smiled at Durasnir. "I know you think Wafri only plays about, but he's educated. And smart. He is never boring, and oh, I do get so bored, sometimes, waiting to go home." Rajnir paced to the wall and back to the window. "Waiting for Hyarl my Commander Talkar of the Hilda to say the army is ready. Waiting for the Dag Erkric to say his magical mysteries are ready. You are the only one who does not tell me to wait for what amounts to personal reasons."

"You know what I think, my prince. It is for the king to decide when and where we move next."

Rajnir raised a hand. "I know. And I know that you are in some ways right. But since my goal is the same as the king's, is it not right that I choose the time, the place, the means? Is that not the action of a king?"

Durasnir hesitated. The answer was obvious, but the consequences so fraught. So he sidestepped. "If Count Wafri does find someone he suspects is Elgar the Fox, I wish to be there when he is questioned."

Rajnir hesitated, then turned to the window again, a restless, jerky movement. "Erkric thinks each is most effective when wholly bent on his task."

Durasnir hid his flare of anger. "I appreciate your Dag's insight," he said. "His observation matches mine. But perhaps he has not considered my orders from the king."

Rajnir gripped the windowsill, his back tense. "I hate it when you two disagree. Hate it!" When he turned around, he was anxious again. "And I always come back to this: I am disinherited. The Dag keeps telling me it's a test. You think it is a test?"

"I never thought it a test," Durasnir reminded him. "That does not mean you cannot win back the regard he once gave you, the regard of a father toward a chosen son."

Rajnir's eyes, pale blue as a dawn sky, flickered at the word *son*. Then widened, and for a moment his face spasmed in bewilderment, even fear. And cleared. "Yes, yes." He breathed. "Yes, the Dag also says that. And so you do agree. Do you?"

They'd had this same exact conversation a year ago. Durasnir said, "The king has not written to me directly. You must remember, you went to war against his orders."

"Ten years," the prince whispered on an exhaled sigh. "A mistake ten years ago, or very near! Vatta—your own son—and the others all agreed it would be fun to surprise you with a win against the Chwahir. Even Wafri wanted to go because he'd never seen a battle, wanted to see Venn might in action. But we were sixteen!" Rajnir shook his head. "No, no, we've been in this place too many times. It is my disgrace to remove, my decision. So it shall be."

And Durasnir had to respond, "So it shall be."

He had one thought now. "My prince. You will contact me if it transpires Elgar is found here?"

Rajnir's expression altered and Durasnir saw the old habit of trust, almost of relief. "You'll know what to do," he said. "Yes. Yes."

Durasnir let his breath out only when he reached the stairs and began the long trip down.

Inda's schooner joined the others at the long, floating dock whose smell indicated it was for fish selling and unloading. While the locals and Fibi were busy, Inda quietly and unobtrusively slipped away in the small boat, soon to be lost in the boat traffic around the main wharf.

While the locals counted out their earnings, Fibi stretched, then paused when she discovered Fox standing at her side. "It's all reasonable, his plan," she said.

"Reasonable," Fox repeated with slow derision. "That's why I hate it." Unsmiling, he vaulted over the rail into his boat and rowed to the *Rippler*, which was soon unloaded, and sailed away.

Chapter Thirteen

BY the time Inda reached the end of the dock he'd intercepted some strange looks.

When he reached the broad brick-tiled quay the looks followed a pattern: a glance at his chest, and then his face. Their expressions puzzled, wary, or even suspicious.

He scrutinized the front of his shirt. Nothing amiss.

On the other side of the quay stretched a long row of market stalls, some tents, others fold-up stands. He headed to a hitching post with a half-barrel trough between a couple of tented fruit stands. Four horses were tethered at the post.

The smell of horse made him homesick, but for once he did not get lost in memory. His sense of danger was far too heightened. When one of the horses lifted his head and snorted, Inda gentled him, letting him sniff all over him as he peered over the animal's broad back—

Necklaces. They wore round silver medals on chains. Everyone, down to children of maybe ten or twelve. It could be a fashion, but he didn't think so. There was no art to those plain chains, the hammered discs, only utility.

There were the Venn guards, dressed the same way the Venn marines had been when they boarded the *Ryala Pim* on Inda's second cruise: heavy V-fronted, slit-sided tunics, as long as the Marlovans' coats but not open in the front, belted instead of sashed, with long, straight swords in sheaths at their sides attached to baldrics. They wore helms and high boots, but not with the high heels made for standing in stirrups; Inda risked another glance, wondering if the Venn were mostly foot warriors, not mounted.

They were big, most of them fair-haired, vigilant as they walked down the street, eyes busy everywhere.

Inda turned his back as they drew abreast of him, and bent down, easing the horse's foreleg so he'd shift his weight and lift his foot. Inda inspected his shoe and used his finger to clean around the frog of the animal's foot as the footsteps passed up the street.

He took his time, then moved to the other foot, in order to give the warriors time to—

"What are you doing?"

It was a woman's voice, brisk, wary.

And she spoke in Fer Sartoran—"New" Sartoran. Inda had heard Ymar's language called that, and relief flooded through him. It was recognizable Sartoran, only . . . flatter.

He indicated the horse's forefoot. "Standing funny, he was." He strove to match her accent, but he knew he sounded foreign. He wished he could do accents like Tau. "I work with horses."

She shrugged, hefting her basket. "He is newly shod. But if there is something wrong, I do thank you. I will have it seen to."

Inda bobbed his head the way he'd seen a couple of the sellers on the dock do. Then he backed away, hunching slightly to close the gap in his shirt.

The woman mounted and he forced himself not to look after her. He had to get one of those necklaces.

Why hadn't anyone known about them? He remembered Chim's words about no one landing this side of the strait. But surely not every fishing smack, every boat—

Worthless questions. He had to hide his front until he could get one.

The market stalls sold a wide variety of things. Farther down were at least four rug makers, and he remembered being told Venn sat on platforms before low tables. Good. Something everyday—and big. He'd buy a rug.

He yanked at his vest to pull the front of his shirt together, tightened his rope-sash, then ambled to the first rug stall. The proprietor looked surly; the next one was tended by a girl. He'd separated from the treasure some northern coinage; now he brought it out of his pocket, frowned as if choosing between two rugs, and then pointed to one. "That'll do."

The girl named a figure. Inda held out his coins, and she lifted her brows in surprise, then said, looking at him with more interest, "You have lots of money, I see."

Then he remembered being in a similar market in Sartor when he was twelve, and how you were expected to negotiate prices. That was not the case in Freeport, or anywhere he had been dealing.

So he grinned. "Not mine. I was ordered to buy it. By the steward," he added, when she seemed to be waiting. The word came to mind from his long-ago days at Tenthen Castle. He could pretend to be Fiam, or have a similar job, but did he remember all the household terms in Sartoran?

"Your master must be rich," she said, grinning. "Here. Take this one. It has a far better nap. Real worth closer to the price, and near the same color. Better, it has the Water Spell on it."

"Water Spell?"

"For your ship?" she said, her voice now slow and kind: she'd figured him out; he was stupid.

Well, he'd been stupid before. Of course she'd peg him as a sailor—his queue and earrings. So much for the castle steward!

"Thank you," Inda said, setting the coins on the counter as he felt the rug. He had no idea the worth of the coins there.

The girl took what she needed. Inda pocketed the remainder, then rolled the rug and hefted it over his shoulder so it draped in front of him, and with a smile that the girl returned, he walked down the quay, staying behind a clump of sailors as he neared the modest building with the ubiquitous white flag that marked it out as the harbormaster's.

He slowed at the sight of a long line leading down from one side. The people in the line, mostly men, of all ages, looked uniformly scruffy.

He walked parallel to the line until he reached the end, where there was a boy about Mutt's age.

"Which line is this?" he asked in Dock Talk.

The boy looked up glumly. "Identification." His hand gestured toward his neck. "And we have to pay for it! Talk about thieves! But they put you into prison if you don't have one." He frowned at Inda's rug, then said, "What, did you get swamped by the storm too?"

So they were refugees from the big storm, blown north—exactly as Inda had expected! He got in line behind the boy, figuring he had plenty of time to fabricate a good story. Yes, this was going to work out after all, he thought.

"Here, who wants a roller?"

The boy called, "What's that?"

Someone farther up the line called back in Khanerenth-accented Dock Talk, "Round-breads, spiced cheese with tomato bits. Grilled fish extra."

Hands went up, people offering a mixture of coins. Inda paid—saw the boy looking wistful, and without asking ordered two, then got back in the slowly shuffling line.

They'd passed inside the gates when, without warning, the twenty or so people who'd gotten into line behind Inda were shoved violently forward, a protest turning into shouting and shoving.

The ring of steel blades being pulled from sheaths ended the shouts. The mail-coated men who entered, shields up, swords out, were not Venn. They were mostly shorter than the Venn, mostly dark-haired, wearing yellow surcoats. On their chests was emblazoned a stylized clover leaf in intersecting circles.

"Against the wall!" the first one shouted, and when everyone in line looked bewildered, he started using the flat of his blade to whack people on arms and heads.

The line merged—some trying to hold their places—into a mass against the inside fence as the newcomers spread out, watching everywhere. Inda let his rug slide to the ground as the boy in front of him kept saying over and over, "Who are they? What's happening?"

Inda stood poised to run—leap the wall—but from beyond it came the sound of a fracas.

"Women out," the leader said, the sword point indicating girls and women in line.

Most departed, some cursing, others looking wooden, the last ones casting worried looks back.

One older woman stopped before the leader. "Can't I wait with m'brother?"

"Get out."

"What is this, an arrest? We're not thieves!" a big, brawny redhead demanded.

"March!" the leader said.

"But we didn't—"

The leader flipped up his blade and used the hilt to club the man down. Stepped over him. Said in flat-voweled Fer Sartoran, "You are all under arrest by my lord, the Count of Wafri, under direct order of Rajnir, Prince of the Venn. You have anything to say, say it to them." He stepped aside and kicked the unconscious man. "If anyone here thinks his life worth sparing, bring him along. Anyone not in line, and quiet, gets killed. Now move." He started away, then said, "Repeat it in your sailor lingo, but as you move. And if I see a single weapon, you die right then. No question, no comment."

Whispers started up. Some explained but most cursed and commented as they were marched back through the gate and up onto the quay. There Inda saw Venn and the men in yellow deployed along the quay. There were patrols on horse, all armed with bows, and others walking as a third group stopped every man and checked his necklace.

Inda looked around for any chance of escape.

None. Whoever had ordered the search knew how to do it right. No one could even hide in the tents. A patrol emerged from one and marched directly into the next: the walls poofed out—batted by hands—and the proprietors scurried around trying to right upset tables and displays.

So it was time to be quiet, stupid, dull. A sailor on leave. And watch for his moment.

Someone said, "I don' know any more than you do! Obviously they's looking for a man."

Sick with certainty, Inda thought. *They're looking for me.*

*   *   *

Durasnir walked out onto what the Ymarans had called the Royal Dock. It was now reserved strictly for the barges of the other eight Oneli—Venn sea lords—capital ships out in the bay now, and for Durasnir's own *Cormorant,* the royal flagship.

He found eight lieutenants waiting for him, as he'd expected: ever since the green flag had been hoisted atop the tower up on the ridge, his fleet had been readying for sail, though they'd only returned the day before. Behind them, apparently impervious to sun or wind, stood old Valda, Chief Sea Dag—also as he'd expected. Chief Sea Dag Valda gazed out to sea so all he saw was her aged profile and her iron-gray hair.

What he did not expect to see was the small, spare, sandy-haired woman at Valda's side.

He made no sign he was aware of either of them as he issued orders to each lieutenant. The plan, as he explained, was to spread the fleet to keep the search as quick and efficient as possible.

Midway through the line, he felt the tap of his communication case: it was Rajnir's signal.

He held up two fingers, and everyone backed out of sight range. Those with orders departed in their barges to their ships to relay the orders; the four remaining lieutenants and the two sea dags waited in silence.

He pulled the golden scroll-case from his belt pouch and removed the little scroll.

Rajnir's sprawling hand, instantly recognizable, covered the little square of paper:

> *We already have hundreds! The storm must have driven every fish boat in the strait northward. Erkric says it will take days to sort through just the redheads. Why so many?*
> *Ah, he said just now redheads are common in Sartor and over on the continent of Toar. He says for me to add being fast stops warning going out. Didn't you say*

that yourself? So move fast! The Dag says if we do find Elgar, he will preside in your place at any questioning—it is rightly a matter for the Yaga Krona, as it concerns my personal safety. He says to add that you can interview him after the dags are finished. Compromise!

Durasnir stared down at the paper until he knew he had a grip on his temper. Then he crumpled it, threw it into the sea, and watched the rice paper disintegrate.

When it had vanished he resumed giving the orders, and at last turned his attention to Chief Sea Dag Valda.

Ydrasal: no word without honor. "You are aware of the prince's orders with respect to the dags?" he said.

Valda inclined her head. "I received orders from Dag Erkric. We are to assist in the questioning when called upon, under the direction of Yaga Krona Dag Ulaffa."

Durasnir's gaze flicked to the sandy-haired Dag Signi, whose still body conveyed tension and denial in every line.

"I asked Prince Rajnir to contact me if he did find this Elgar the Fox," he said. "Dag Erkric now deems that unnecessary, according to the prince." He touched the belt pouch where his scroll-case lay. "The Dag will preside. We—that is the military—will have this person, assuming they do find him, after Erkric and the Yaga finish."

"Ah," Chief Sea Dag Valda said, and addressed a few remarks in the dags' version of Sartoran to her companion. Then she faced him. "I am assigning Dag Signi to the land search here in Jaro," she said, an open hand to the sandy-haired mage. "To assist Dag Ulaffa."

Signi was long known to Durasnir, from the days when she was Jazsha Signi Sofar, the dancer-in-training. Known and once loved, and Valda knew it as well.

Signi had not moved, but now her posture was different: one shoulder down, her attitude cooperative. Strange, how she did that—Durasnir had never gotten used to the way she communicated without word, almost without moving. Though the heat had died many years ago, he carried tenderness for her in his heart.

"Very well," he said, understanding what could not be

said. And they both understood him: Signi would be watching out for his interests as much as possible.

He descended into the waiting gig then, and the dags departed without a look back. But his mood had eased.

Inda watched for an opportunity to break away during the long trudge up a smooth brick road that led up behind the harbor to a garrison.

There was no chance. They were conducted in tightly controlled groups by mounted guards, all armed with bows, swords, knives. They were taken to the stone garrison, and down a few steps—

And Inda was unprepared for the blow that caught him by surprise: the smell of the prison.

The other men all looked fearfully around at the narrow stonework corridors and cells. Inda breathed that cold, moist air that smelled of stone and mold, and he was cast right back to his feverish, grief-stricken days in the garrison prison after Dogpiss' death. Before the king unaccountably sent Captain Sindan to whisk him away to the coast and aboard a ship.

The memory was so vivid Inda—who had meant to watch for a chance to escape until there was no possibility left—walked without noticing down the few steps, through a massive iron reinforced door, and into a cell along with twenty or thirty others.

When the door clanged shut he jumped, irritated that he'd managed not to notice the route in. How could he escape if he didn't remember what was on the other side of that wooden door, how many guards there were, where the entrance was?

Several men jostled him, all wanting to look through the barred door to the corridor. A few shouted questions at the guards busy herding other prisoners to the cells farther down. *Clang. Clang. Clang.* Three more clangs, and those cells were filled.

Inda sat on the mossy stone floor with his back to a wall, listening past the useless speculation of the men around him. A pair of passing guards were talking in that distinctive flat Sartoran as they clattered past the cells: "How many more?"

"At least two hundred, but some said we'll be sorting for redheads first . . ." And then their voices merged in the general hubbub.

Redheads. So that rumor persisted on this side of the strait as well. Inda lifted his head, hopeful. All right. He had time to get a good story figured out.

When the lookouts on the two schooners first spotted each other, Fibi and Fox ran to the bows and raised their glasses.

As they drew near, Fox stood on the bow with his glass, leaning out with one hand gripping a stay. Fibi knew he was searching for Inda beside her on the *Skimit*. She'd been doing the same in hopes Inda had ended up on the *Rippler*.

She shook her head. Saw Fox's hand drop, the violence in his abrupt turn, his leap to his deck matching her own mood.

The two ships met where Inda had told them to meet—on the eastward side of the northernmost islet above the little cluster north of Beila Lana. Fox was too impatient to wait until they'd drawn alongside; as soon as the *Rippler*'s bow passed the *Skimit*'s he used a line and swung himself over, dropping onto the deck.

"Where is he?"

"Not here," Fibi retorted, crossing her arms.

Fox's eyes narrowed, he tensed, then stilled and wiped a hand up over his face, his expression changing from anger to bleakness. "You did check."

"Every day, three days," Fibi answered. "Like he ordered. Then us voted, and did another three days, though by then they knew who us was. Could see 'em marking us, along o' the other fisher craft waitin' on someone ashore. Then night of the third us was takin' another vote when one of them Ymaran fishers hailed us." She paused, looked around.

The crew had all gathered aft on both schooners, which

bobbed up and down, sails slack. No one made a pretence of not listening.

Fibi sighed. "She—captain-owner o' the *Lark*—sez word is, they rounded up pipple. No. Men. With no identification medals. Got magic sveds on 'em." She made a motion, like tugging something around her neck. "She sez, starting 's morning, any craft left out in the water was bein' pulled in by the warships. Captains questioned. So us voted. Came here." She frowned. "Thing is, us don' know what story Inda be tellin' 'em on shore. Or even what name he'd give."

"Right," Fox said. "You did right." He gazed westward, as if he could see through the empty islet and beyond the sea haze to the Beila Lana harbor.

Fibi snorted. "So. Inda's orders is: you command. What's yer command?"

Fox did not mistake her tone for either friendly or obedient. For a long time they stood there on deck, neither giving way. The crew watched. The only sound was the *plash-plash* of water against the sides fo the ship and the creak of wood.

"Let's go below," Fox said abruptly.

"Yes," Fibi said. "Let's."

Those on deck tiptoed so there wouldn't be a thunder of bare feet right above the captain's tiny cabin. But they hadn't gone more than a few steps before the scuttles slammed shut on both sides of the hull below the rail. *Clack! Clack!* Followed smartly by the thunk of the stern windows.

So much for nosing in; the snoops gave up and returned to their duties.

Below, Fibi plopped back in one of the two wooden chairs on either side of the small plank table that had been let down and eyed the younger man.

Fox said derisively, "You can spare me the speech. I already know you don't trust me, and don't know why Inda does, and you're going to argue with every order that doesn't match exactly what you think Inda would want. But before I have to hear it all, let me ask you if you've considered why Inda's plans have always been conditional?"

"Already know that," Fibi said, tipping back in her chair

in a way that would be dangerous for anyone but a Delf. Their balance was too good for that. "He's trying to convince you while he's convincin' hisself. Easy enough to see."

Fox's brows lifted in surprise. "It's not at all easy to see," he replied. "I didn't see it myself until more recently than I'd like to admit."

Fibi pursed her lips. Because he'd been honest, she refrained from the far more pungent reply she'd been readying next. She said, "You been too busy thinkin' on yer own plans. So let me ask you. Why's his cabin on *Death*'s well as here got nothing personal in it?" She indicated the bare cabin, to which she'd not added anything visible.

Fox shifted to the bench below the stern windows. The bed had been neatly folded back so the table could be let down at need.

He stretched an arm along the planed sill below the windows, tapping his fingers in one of those distinctive rhythms Fibi had heard from time to time—from both Fox and Inda.

All the arrogance had gone out of his manner, though she couldn't have defined how. He was long and well-shaped, the loose cotton trousers and the vest accentuating his lean, hard-muscled contours. His skin, once pale, was now uniformly honey-colored.

She turned her attention outward, listening to the water splashing. Judging from the roll of the schooner, the west wind was gradually picking up. Feet thumped back and forth overhead, everyone doing what they were supposed to do.

"Same reason as mine, I expect," he said at last, facing her again. "Some day—assuming I'm alive—I will weaken and go home. Maybe he will, too, despite all that foolery about honor."

Fibi looked disgusted. "If *he* goes home, it won't be because he's gone weak," she stated, and Fox wished he hadn't said as much as he had.

She saw at once that she'd made a mistake; the derision was back in his face, the arrogance in his shoulders and the way he held his head. "The others is going to want to run a rescue. Ye'll have trouble with any orders that run counter."

Fox got to his feet, bending slightly under the low deck above. "But I want Inda back as much as you do. More," he said sardonically. "He's an important part of my plans."

She knew better than to ask what those were; she'd brought on that irritating manner, and so she just sat there stolidly.

Seeing no reaction, Fox flicked the islets chart closed and reached for the bigger one showing what they had of the southeast corner of the continent Drael, with Ymar mostly blank. "We'll take your fishers at their word and assume that the Venn will be investigating any suspicious craft. So we're going to go on being fishing boats. But what we'll do is set up a series of rendezvous on different dates, *Skimit* on the south coast, *Rippler* under Spark's command on the north." He tapped the chart. "As you search, may's well complete the chart as you can."

"So where's you gonna be?" she asked.

"Rescuing Inda," he said, "is my affair. I am going in alone."

Chapter Fourteen

THE first couple of weeks were the worst, Jeje thought at the end of her first month.

Not that the boring days since had been much improvement. At least she no longer woke thinking the ship was still because the wind had died.

The harbor bells rang the watch change. Inside the Guild Fleet office everyone begin chattering, stretching, yawning, preparatory to leaving. Jeje finished counting up the hash marks on the tablet, wrote the number under the column marked off for beckets, blew on the ink until it didn't shine, then laid down the pen. She was going to close the book, then remembered she had another load of supplies to count up and enter for that ship before she could move on to the next, so she left it open for tomorrow's first chore.

A sudden silence caused Jeje to look up, and sure enough, it was Tau coming down the stairs from where he'd been put to work writing letters and updating accounts, his handwriting being clear and fine.

Tau wove through the other workers, all of whom watched him, some openly, some surreptitiously. As usual he seemed oblivious.

In silence she fell in step beside him. Her shoulder blades twitched. She knew the others were watching her now. And she knew what they said among themselves, which wasn't very flattering.

As soon as they were out on the street, he asked, "How are the supply lists?"

"Boring," she stated. She'd found it mildly interesting, how the Guild Fleet kept record of everything the convoys they arranged started out with and came back in with. Her interest hadn't lasted long.

Tau said, "Can you bear it here?"

Jeje didn't look up at him, but at the crowded street, everyone coming out of shops, some of which closed, others that traded watches. Noise everywhere.

"We have to, don't we?" she mumbled.

Tau sighed. "Let's go somewhere we can talk."

Jeje shrugged. What was there to say? She hated living in the harbor. She hated the smell of mud and horses and rotting vegetation in the summer heat, especially after a huge storm like the one last week.

She missed her friends, *Vixen,* the freedom of the sea. Chim was funny and full of interesting stories, but she saw him rarely now.

No. Think of the good things. Well, the bearable things. She was learning the language fast. Actually, she discovered that except for Sartoran, most words in Dock Talk were Brennish—which made sense, seeing as how this was the biggest harbor on the strait. Harbor folk switched between the two languages a lot, depending on what they were talking about; inland people stayed with Brennish, but she could pretty well follow most of what they said now.

She did have Tau's company, at least in the mornings for drill and for some meals. But nothing else, since he'd taken to going out at nights and staying out later—she supposed at the pleasure houses. Though every morning before dawn there he was outside her room, waiting for their morning drill.

Yes, that time was good, when they ran through Inda's and Fox's drills up on the roof directly over her room.

She snorted. Everyone at the Fleet House thought she and Tau were lovers, and here they'd never even kissed. All they did was practice fighting.

"Problem?" Tau asked.

She was so used to being ignored all day that she had forgotten how to carry on a conversation. It was too easy to get lost inside her head for an entire watch.

She wasn't about to tell him what she'd been thinking. "I hate being stuck on shore," she said—so obvious there was no answer.

And Tau did not answer. He knew when he was being deflected.

He also had a good guess why, so instead he indicated they turn left, where a lane led off the main street and curved up onto one of the low hills. Jeje followed reluctantly. The nicer places were on the hills, leading gradually to the long ridge overlooking the harbor where the king and his nobles all had their fine houses. Jeje hadn't ventured that far inland, though sometimes she looked up at them in the morning light, when the line of the ridge stood out sharply.

The lower hills were where prosperous merchants and ship captains or owners could be seen eating at little tables set in carefully nurtured little gardens. Flowering trees dotted the hills and clustered thickly between the buildings on the ridge: everyone who could have them seemed to like garden plots.

Tau navigated without hesitation, which didn't surprise Jeje. "Here," he said presently, indicating a pretty intersection of two curving lanes. Delicious smells filled the air; the four corners all had different kinds of eating establishments, one Sartoran—or so the sign said—one Colendi, one Ymaran, and the last local, its sign a name, not a place. All low buildings with lots of windows half obscured by flowering shrubs.

"What's Ymaran food like?" Jeje asked, glancing at the blue-walled building as he led her into the cream-yellow Colendi one.

"Not much different than anything you get along the coast," he said. "Their claim to fame is a kind of baked apple dish that the old queen supposedly liked, with hot cream whipped with honey poured over it."

"Yum," she said, but did not dispute his choice.

The proprietor, a young man their age, gave Tau the

smile of intimates and waved toward the terrace. Tau gestured his thanks, and soon they had a secluded little table, flowering shrubs on two sides, one side open onto the lane, the other a narrow view of the rest of the terrace.

"I don't really like Colendi food," she admitted.

"How often have you had it?" Tau responded, leaning his elbows on the table, chin on his hands. He did not stare directly at her—which she hated—but turned his head slightly, ostensibly to watch the other tables.

"Just in Freeport. Inda and I went once together, when we came back with our first big pay. Called Taste of Alsayas—"

"That place," Tau stated, "ought to be burned down. Colendi food! It's leftovers smothered with over-flavored sauces so you won't notice that the chicken has been twice-boiled."

"Oh."

He grinned. "Some of our brethren at Freeport like spicy food—for them good taste means spices so hot you can't actually taste the food, only the burn."

Jeje snickered. "All right. But what should I try?"

"Kerrem will bring the best. Don't worry about the food. Let's get back to our situation."

"Which is a big nothing," she said. "How am I supposed to be finding people to train when I can't even get anyone at Fleet to talk to me, much less strangers?"

"I'm about to take care of part of the problem, if you agree with my idea," he said. "It's certainly easy for me to be upstairs writing out records and second-copying convoy letters for Chim, but it's a waste because I only learn what he learns. I believe we can rely on him to tell us any news we need to know."

Jeje nodded.

"And so, if you agree, I'm going to head farther up the hill," Tau said, with a flick of his chin over his shoulder. "The kind of information I think Inda really needs—to say nothing of my own need—is to be found in court circles."

Jeje blew her breath out. "Do the nobles even have bawdy houses? I thought they summoned their own favorites."

Tau chuckled. "Some do, some don't. There are very discreet, very exclusive places, but that world is bounded by strict laws of confidentiality. I don't actually plan to confine myself to those."

"So how else can you get anywhere near court people? You might be able to get the fancy clothes, but what about the rest?"

"You mean I haven't birth, wealth, or position?" Tau asked with a pretence of affront, and when she chortled, he said, "Not a problem—if I am quick, clever, decorative, and connected with the world of the theater."

Jeje pursed her lips in a soundless whistle. "That's something I've never even seen."

"You will, if you like," Tau promised. "As soon as I get myself ensconced where I think I need to be."

"Never mind. I heard a couple of people talking once. You can't even get past the doors if you don't wear fancy duds. Can you see me in a big dress with a lot of lace and feathers?" She dusted her fingers over her neck and head.

"You would be charming," Tau said, grinning again. "In any case, feathers are not in fashion. Nor for that matter is lace. It's unpatriotic right now to wear lace, which mostly comes from western Colend, as there have been disputes in high places—most notably, the new King Lael of Colend unaccountably does not favor the crown princess' suit." He said it with a mocking air. "Braid and embroidery are now what everyone who wishes to be thought in style wears."

Jeje sighed, falling quiet as the young man brought plates and set them down. He gave Jeje a perfunctory smile, then addressed Tau: "Spring vintage?"

"Just a glass apiece," Tau said, knowing Jeje never drank more.

The food was fresh fish, perfectly grilled. The sauce was light, with complicated flavors of sweet and tart; she could identify no single ingredient.

"Hoo," she said.

"Told you!" Tau's smile was completely unchallenging.

Jeje put her fork down. "I feel stupid," she admitted. "I don't know the half of what seems necessary."

Tau also set his fork down, and then he did something he never had before: stretched out his hand and lightly touched hers. "Not stupid. Never that. Inexperienced in these matters, yes. But your strengths lie in other directions."

"Counting up blocks and beckets?" Jeje fought the impulse to let her hand lie in case he'd do it again. She pressed her fingers to her forehead and rubbed. "I would have believed that about inexperience when we were small, but I've been in enough bawdy houses by now to know that most of those people don't know half what you know. But your mother's place was only a harbor house like any along Rosebud Row."

"Yes. I am only myself beginning to realize just how much knowledge my mother had that I can't easily explain," he said. Then he leaned forward. "I mean to find her, Jeje. I realize Inda's search must come first. And yet I suspect—it's only instinct, though strong—his search for information and my own might not be as unrelated as one might reasonably assume."

He hesitated, and two wine glasses appeared before them.

Kerrem said, "Are you going to Asfar House tonight?"

Tau gave his head a quick shake. "I promised Eris I'd come to her musical. I need to practice."

"If *you* do, none of us have a hope," Kerrem said, and then was gone.

"There you go again." Jeje pointed an accusing finger. "Expert in yet another thing."

"Not really." Tau sat back, the wineglass cradled in his hands. "I've had a minimum of training in a wide variety of skills, but I did inherit my mother's quick ear and eye. Most of these people, like me, play for fun, and many don't hear how very much better someone is who's had a lifetime of training. That means practice." He smiled. "And listening."

Jeje heard about half of what he said. As she ate, she thought about how very rarely Tau talked about anything personal. But she'd seen on her single visit how close he and his mother were despite their very different attitudes and very strong wills. She said tentatively, "I hope you can find news of your mother, but . . . well, Parayid is all the way in the west, and wasn't she taken by a pirate?"

Tau nodded, not speaking as a couple stood nearby, waiting for a table to be cleared.

When they were seated, Jeje spoke again. "You didn't have a dad, did you?"

"Magic birth. And no. No relatives left on her side, either. Or, if still alive, none she ever owned up to."

"The more I think about it, the odder it seems," she said. "I mean, where in Parayid did she get her training? There not being much, oh, courtly custom in Iasca Leror." She grinned.

That unexpected, wicked grin, framed by long dimples, was so ravishing. Tau had to grin back. "One of my very earliest memories is her saying our name was now Darian. *Daraen—friend in Sartor—what could be more appropriate for us?* That's exactly what she said. I think my interest in languages stems from that time."

Jeje set her fork down. "I never had fresh peas this good. How do they fix them so they don't moosh? Never mind, it's not like I'll ever cook anyway." She sat back, tasting the wine. Her brow cleared. "Good!"

Tau sipped his. It was delicious, complex in flavor in a way that complemented the food, didn't overwhelm it. But he only drank half; tonight he would begin his campaign, and that meant his head must be completely clear.

"The question of my departure from Fleet lies before you," he said.

Jeje snorted. "Oh, Tau. I'm really going to say no, you have to stay right in the Fleet House."

Tau smiled in apology. "I will be back to practice with you, that I promise."

"Good. I can do it on my own," she said quickly. "Though Fox said it's better with a partner."

"Certainly. When we are called upon to begin training people—though I don't see how any more than you do—we've got to be in fighting trim."

She grunted an agreement.

He opened his hands. "Done?"

"You mean you need to get going," she said, looking around.

Dusk had fallen, soft and unnoticed. The eatery people

had hung paper lanterns all around the terrace, and the windows on the lane glowed golden.

"I'll see you at dawn," he promised.

Her throat was tight. She managed a nod and a careless shrug, and forced herself to be the first to depart.

Leaving him looking somewhat wistfully after her. But he knew she would be fine—in fact, if he was gone from Fleet House they might treat her better. Not that he'd say anything about that—it was just the sort of comment he loathed himself.

So instead he used the money he'd changed earlier while doing an errand for Chim and went to pick up the new suit of clothes he'd ordered a few days before.

It was time to go on stage.

Jeje did not look back. She tramped back down the lane to the harbor and its familiar strong smell of fish, brine, old wood mold, and stale beer.

Since she'd never spoken to anyone at Fleet House, she knew nothing about the harbor other than what she'd already observed while roaming about. The air was warm and still, and her fast march made her hot and sticky, which added to her vile mood.

When she reached the bottom of the road that led to the older part of the harbor, she looked around, her hair swinging into her mouth. She spat it out, but it stuck to her cheek, tickling horribly. Impatiently she yanked out one of her knives, gathered her hair in back, and then sawed it off.

The coolness on her neck was a relief until she turned her head—and her earring smacked her cheek.

She'd forgotten the earring. That was why she had been letting her hair grow—to hide it.

"Argh." Furious with herself, she flung the bits of fine dark brown hair into the mud and stomped them. They vanished in the sludge at once. Then she walked on, peering through the darkness past jumbles of old and rotting ship gear and rickety storehouses in search of a tavern where she could get a good dark beer. Maybe she'd at least be able to sleep, even if it didn't improve her mood.

Faint slants of light drew her in one direction. Few people moved about in the deepening shadows. It was getting so dark that she heard more than saw them.

She reached a broad street parallel to the quay, dimly lit by the lights from the windows of low, ramshackle buildings. Outlined in the weak light were five men, some shambling instead of walking, oblivious to puddles and debris. One roared after stepping in a pile of dog shit that no one had wanded. He sounded drunk.

A thin figure slipped through them—a cutpurse. At Freeport cutpurses were rare, as there was nowhere to run. Gambling was the usual way to get others' money—

"Hey, all alone?" A raucous voice broke her isolation.

She sidestepped in a quick, smooth move, hands near her weapons. The speaker was a big, burly man who stank of old sweat and stale wine. Bad wine.

He stumped forward, peering at her. "Izzat a ruby on yer ear, girl?" He turned his head and bawled, "Larian! Col! Here's the fortune you were wantin'—"

She sidestepped—straight into a puddle. At the sound of the splash he turned on her far faster than a drunk had any right to. She felt his fingers brush her cheek before she backed away.

"Gimme that ruby, girl, an' you can go. Whaja do, steal it? Fair's fair—"

"Don't," she said. "Don't try me. I'm in a really bad mood." And as he made a swipe at her again, rage burned through her. "No, I change my mind. Go ahead. *Do* try me," as he grabbed for her again. Duck, *thump!* A fist straight into his gut. "You can only make me—" He lunged. She sidestepped, tripped him, smacked his ear openhanded as he fell. "—Make me feel better."

He yowled a curse, and his two friends came on at a stumbling run. Jeje laughed, and yes, her bad mood had vanished. Danger—action—it was like being on *Vixen* with pirates trying to board, only the ground was hard under her feet, and she had no tiller to tend.

She smacked the first assailant, kicked the side of the

knee of the second, who whirled and fell, howling and punching the air.

The other two scrambled to their feet and tried to rush her together. A palm-heel to the midsection of the first and a forearm smack against the nose of the second sent them after their friend.

She jumped over them, started walking, and saw a small crowd gathered. Her hands moved to her knife hilts but dropped when a woman crowed, "Fine work!"

"Hey, Col, what's it like to receive 'stead o' give?"

Laughter from the shadowy figures, as someone small darted down, feeling over the groaning drunks in search of their coins.

"Come, stranger, I'll buy you a drink!" a man invited.

"If it's good dark beer," Jeje said, wary.

"I know where to get some," the woman promised breezily. "What's that accent? Western, are ye?"

"Out o' Freeport Harbor," Jeje stated firmly.

The man whistled, and the woman said, "No wonder yer walking around alone here like ye was a queen in a garden."

"Here? What's wrong with here?" Jeje asked in Bren.

The woman shifted out of Dock Talk to Bren. "Well, the King's Guard don't patrol here any more. Not since the shore guilds and the tax collectors have been at daggers over the taxes," the woman explained. "So the guilds got their own hires, but they don't come down here to the quay. None patrol here, as it's mostly old storage. Empty as trade's so bad. We call it the ghost yards."

The man said, "And trade bein' bad, there's a lot of old hands can't, or won't, get another hire, so they jump people and drink off what they steal. Like Japsar, there, and Col and their new mate. Lots of 'em hide out here inna ghost yards."

The woman said, "Col used to be a good sheet-anchor man, but not with the drink and Japsar's gang."

They'd reached a rough-stoned alley lined with small, shoddy-fronted shops and a low-roofed, rambling tavern bright in all its windows, which were of different sizes. The buildings were all lit outside with a variety of lamps, lanterns, and here and there an expensive glowglobe—a ready-made sort of street lighting.

Jeje was aware of whispers spreading the story behind her; it was quite a crowd that walked into the tavern, called Lower Deck, decorated with nets draped from the ceiling, fog lanterns, and barrels used to support tables. Jeje liked the look of the place at once.

"You're mighty young, aren't you?" the woman asked, and Jeje looked up into a weatherworn face probably ten years older than she was.

She shrugged, hands out. "You have to start some time."

They laughed at that, and a round of mugs came forth; they asked her name and in a jovial hubbub told her theirs, what they did when on hire, and what ship they'd been with last, everyone talking at once.

Jeje kept trying to follow, but every time she identified the last speaker someone new spoke. She barely had time to learn that the woman's name was Thess and the skinny teenage boy behind her with the same color of rusty brown hair was her son Palnas when the doors slammed open, smashing into the walls.

The tavern went silent as Japsar walked in, muddy down one side. At his shoulder lurked Col, holding his nose, and behind him Larian, a balding, furtive man holding a dagger. And behind them five or six others, all armed.

"Here, you," the tavern owner shouted, striding forward so fast his apron flapped. His voice was the roar of a deckhand as he snarled curses ending with, ". . . and I meant what I said, Japsar, you pay up your score before you set foot in here."

"Just you bide," Japsar said thickly, looking about, then sneering when he saw Jeje. "Just you bide, and there won't be any trouble. Me and this girl here got some score of our own to settle."

Thess made to stand in front of Jeje—she was a head taller, and brawny—but Jeje pushed past. "We got no score," she said. "You tried to take my earring. It's mine. I earned it, so I defended it. We got no score."

"You stole it," Japsar said. "So that means yer a liar as well as a shit-eater."

"And you," Jeje stated, "are a stinking drunk."

Again Japsar moved fast, grabbing a plate off a table and slinging it toward her face.

Jeje batted it aside with a fast forearm block, not watching as it crashed to the floor. Japsar brought a cutlass from under his long vest. He charged Jeje, as all around people exclaimed, chairs skidded, mugs thumped down—

The man at Jeje's table started up, but Thess put a hand on his arm. "Wait."

Jeje shut them all out, her forearms crossing as she whipped out her blades. She took a single step back, met Japsar's charge with a round-block and a hard kick to his knees. He bellowed, whirling his blade. She ducked. The blade passed overhead with a hum. She jumped up, ramming her knife-handle under his chin. His head snapped back, and she kicked him straight into two of his gang; they sidestepped, jostling into the ones behind them, and Jeje waded in, blades nicking Japsar's gang in a blur of movement that backed them into the doorway. Those in front retreated; the ones behind shoved forward until they all burst inward, staggering.

Everyone began to fight.

She leaped to block Col, and a gray-haired woman slung a small keg at another of Japsar's gang; Jeje stayed in the center, kicking, punching, shoving, but as yet she had not killed anyone. *Crash! Thud! Smack!* Figures rocked back and forth, knocking into furniture. The tavern keeper briskly moved about, smashing mugs on bobbing heads. The fight was soon over, most of the gang lying unconscious, a couple moving and groaning—the rest having fled back out into the night. Jeje's partisans hadn't dealt any deathblows, and she was glad her instinct had been right to wound and not to kill.

The tavern keeper stood nearby, wringing his hand.

"Sorry," Jeje said. "Do I, um, owe you—"

The man laughed. "Why d'you think I use these?" He smacked a barrel and kicked a fallen net. "Easy to come by. They'll help me get shipshape." He flicked a hand toward Thess and the others who'd brought her in.

"I'll help," Jeje said. "I'm a fast hand with a net."

Talking and laughing about the fight, the regulars all pitched in, their manner so efficient Jeje suspected that fights were more frequent than not. She helped with a good will as fresh beer was poured out for everyone by the tavern keeper's daughter, who was about Jeje's age and height.

It did not take long. Some of the men dragged the unconscious ones out and dumped them in the street; pity for their state only went so far. Others helped scrub down the wooden floor, the barrel-tables were righted, and a fresh supply of old, rusty fog lamps brought out from the back to replace the broken ones.

By the midnight watch-bells the room looked as it had when Jeje entered. Thess sat down across from Jeje. "Ruby—fighting—that would put you with Elgar the Fox, I'm thinking."

Jeje's neck tightened with prickles of danger.

She and Tau had talked for a long time about what to say and what not to say—but that had been weeks ago, and Jeje had half forgotten what they'd decided. She busied herself with her beer as she recalled what they'd agreed on, then said with her best attempt at indifference, "I'm not with anyone now."

"Why not?" asked the gray-haired woman whose use of a beer keg as a weapon had accounted for at least two of the gang.

Jeje said, "Well, for one thing, Fleet Master Chim did mention something about defense training. For future convoys."

The tavern owner narrowed his eyes. "Convoys," he repeated.

Thess said in a slow, meaningful voice, "Convoy defense."

The gray-haired woman added, a hand beside her mouth—as if everyone around wasn't able to hear quite clearly—"So that would mean somebody would be hiring people for such a thing?"

These people were not exactly subtle—but neither was Jeje. She grinned. "Well, I'm working for Chim now, at the Guild Fleet House. Word is, there might be hiring for such a thing. Hiring after training. As it happens."

Thess patted the table. "So ... where does that put ye? I mean, was it ye bein' blind, or was it ye bein' convenient, like, this fight o' yez?"

Jeje snorted. "I didn't know about ghost yards, if that's what you mean. Truth is, I was walking off a sulk. I miss being out at sea. Anyway what you call the ghost yards looks like the south end of Freeport Harbor to me." She got to her feet. "Speaking of Chim, and jobs, I should be turning in."

"Hope you'll be back," the tavern keeper said. "Thanks for helping out."

"We'll know where to find ye," Thess said, saluting with a flick of fingers to her forehead—the salute to a captain on her deck.

Chapter Fifteen

FLEET Commander Durasnir spent several exasperating days coordinating the reports of various unidentified southern craft, many of whom lingered along the harbors in an effort to reclaim missing crew. It was taking far longer than he'd expected to board and inspect each and then issue identification medallions.

By the end of the second week, he hated to walk into his wardroom where the big maps were and his subordinates, used to his customary calm, hated to see him loom—he was tall, even for a Venn—in the doorway, his blond brow furrowed and light eyes narrowed.

He loathed the sight of people who should have been tending meaningful duties scurrying back and forth from the maps to the table, laboriously listing the names of countless little craft that dags reported after each search, then sticking corresponding pins into the maps.

Durasnir knew that the general questioning had begun on land, a headache of logistics: having to feed, guard, and issue identity medallions to countless angry strangers. Their task was no easier than his.

Durasnir stood alone in his inner cabin, staring out through the stern windows at the choppy seas of the strait. The Fangs jutted in the distance.

Instead of discouraging Prince Rajnir and Dag Erkric, the enormous number of prisoners the sweep had gathered was deemed significant. Rajnir had written via magic message the night before: *If we don't have him, surely we must have some of his fleet. They can tell us much.*

Even the Count Wafri, Rajnir reported, was enthusiastic.

The Venn guards separated out all the redheads or anyone who could be described as having reddish hair. No explanation.

The next few days in the cell, the men around Inda were angry and afraid. No one had done anything wrong, they kept protesting every time the guards came down into the corridor. When the guards did not listen, they told one another over and over again.

The noise from the other cells seemed to encourage those who wanted to shout in protest, an escalation of yells that ended abruptly the third night when apparently someone in one of the last cells organized some kind of breakout attempt. Inda and his cell mates heard a sudden, violent fracas, the sharp, high voices of men, followed by thuds and the crash of an iron door being slammed.

More guards came running.

Five men were carried, some struggling, out of the garrison. A little later they were returned hanging limp in the hands of the guards, all of them bloody and moaning, their faces bruised. They were thrown back into the cell, all without a single word spoken.

Things were quieter after that.

The prisoners settled down; they arranged space with the practiced efficiency sailors learn on shipboard, sleeping head to foot as if they had hammocks. By day they mostly squatted, some gambling with wooden buttons pulled off their shirts. Most talked, a few slept, or sat staring at the iron-barred door. One man scrupulously kept count of the meals, offering guesses at the passage of days to anyone who would listen.

Inda waited, watched, and listened.

Gradually everyone in the cell learned everyone else's

name. Inda had thought out the most uninteresting story he could, choosing the name of a former shipmate, Fassun, because it was an Idayagan name. He hoped his accent would pass for Idayagan. A Khanerenth or Sartoran name and his western accent might raise suspicion. He had to convince them he was just another fisher, like most of the men around him. He listened to the way they spoke, what subjects they talked about, how they used words, sometimes repeating their phrasings. He practiced on the others the rare times they spoke to him. No one seemed suspicious—or even interested.

Eventually the redheads were questioned. The ones they kept were housed separately. The others were let go, though Inda and the rest in the garrison prison did not know that, so tension stayed high.

The interrogation of the non-redheads began. When the men from the first cell came back—no one from the non-redhead group was permitted to leave yet—people yelled in Dock Talk from the cell doors, "What's going on?"

"They're lookin' for someone," a man yelled back.

"Quiet," the guard snarled. "In."

They only got through the other side of the corridor that day. One of the last men pushed back down the corridor to his cell said to the faces pressed against the iron-barred doors, "Word is, they's lookin' fer a pirate!"

General laughter rose at this, and because the night guard didn't understand Dock Talk, the sailor got thumped before he was shoved into his cell.

The next day they came to Inda's side of the corridor. Inda's heartbeat sped up, but he kept his steps slow, his hands loose. He'd taken care to position himself in the middle of the group; some fought to go first to get it over with, others seemed to want to be last—the ones who talked least, probably thieves or the like, Inda guessed—as if that was any kind of protection.

They were guarded closely as they marched up the corridor. Their destination was not through the front door, but deeper inside the garrison. Inda did his best to keep track of the turns, stairs, and halls.

They were directed into an office and lined across the back. Guards in yellow—swinging cudgels—walked along their rows. Anyone who moved got a hard rap.

They were summoned to the front two by two; there were two desks, two questioners, each attended by a herald busy with his quill. Between both groups stood a man dressed in a long blue robe whose purpose Inda couldn't guess. This man observed, then did something on the desk that Inda couldn't yet see.

When the two rows of men in front of him had been processed, he realized that the robed one was a dag. After each prisoner had been questioned he muttered over coin-sized metal circles. The faint luminescence of magic glowed around the medal before it was clipped to a chain and hung round the prisoner's neck.

Then it was Inda's turn. The guard was another of the ones in yellow, a young man roughly his own age, who looked weary and bored.

"Name?" he asked, in Dock Talk.

"Fassun."

"Family name?"

"Son of Fassun the rope-maker."

"Where are you from?"

"Idayago."

"Town?"

"Hot Springs. Village east o' the pass," Inda said, having made that up. He couldn't remember any of the Idayagan names he'd seen so long ago when he'd studied his father's maps.

He watched the herald duly write it down, and hoped that there were too many prisoners for such details to be checked. Surely the Venn did not have detailed maps of Idayago?

"How long you been out of Idayago?"

"Six years. Horse boys took it, so I stayed east. Hired onto the *Skimit*-fisher, as an all-purpose hand, promoted to bosun-mate in charge o' cordage."

The young man opened his mouth, but the dag touched his arm, bent down and whispered something, then straightened up, his pale blue eyes never wavering from

Inda's face. Inda tried not to stare back at the dag, who was a tall man, maybe thirty, with short fair hair.

"Where'd you get all the scars?" the questioner asked.

"Pirate attacks. Two. One five years ago, one a year ago. They played around with us, last time. Rescued by a warship out of Sarendan."

The questioner, the dag, and Inda watched as the scribe wrote all that down. Then the questioner glanced up at the dag, who made a very slight shake of the head.

The scribe pushed forward a medallion, the dag looked down, whispered, touched it, and magic glittered around it.

The scribe clipped a cheap chain on, handed it to Inda, who put it on. He saw a number on it that corresponded to a number on the paper.

As he turned away, from the corner of his eye he saw the dag lean down, dip a pen into one of the inkwells, and draw a green line below the word *scars*.

Chim and Jeje sat on the porch of his favorite eatery, a grilled fish place frequented by ship captains and officers on the street built along the foothills below what she thought of as merchant territory. They gazed out at the forest of masts out in the harbor, then he pointed at the one cleared space. "I know they talk rough about Prince Kavna's yacht buildin', but most of 'em don't see that he did it to give 'em jobs."

Jeje nodded. "Thess said as much." She peered out at the fabulous yacht recently launched alongside its own dock. It was twilight, so only the lines could be made out. The yacht was already graceful as a swan. Jeje had heard about the carving and scrollwork all over it, inside and out; it would be a dream ship. Something that also probably would never ride the sea, at least not until the problems of the strait were resolved, if ever. But many, many former sailors had been employed building it, and worked alongside skilled crafters carving, painting, making every aspect as artful as possible.

Chim grunted. "So how yer classes goin'?"

"They're enthusiastic now," Jeje said cautiously. "Funny, I was so careful to say only what we planned. That I could train defense if there was a convoy hiring as protection. Nothing definite. But they come every day, each day a couple more. They think there's going to be hiring."

"Well, not so far off," Chim admitted. "Word is, the prince is arguing with his father and sister about that. Thinks Bren ought to take the lead. Get the old trade line going again."

"The Venn can't possibly forbid it," Jeje said.

"Not forbid. That'd catch the eye o' kings for certain. But stop 'em, charge a stiff toll, so stiff the goods cost too much to sell again."

Jeje sighed. "I forgot that aspect."

Chim chuckled. "That cuz ye been a pirate too long, girl. Pirates don't pay no toll." He chuckled at his own joke.

Jeje smiled perfunctorily. She was tired. Up early every day with Tau. She worked all day, then drilled her convoy defense hopefuls until it was too dark to see, in a square well guarded from nosers, over behind the tavern.

She was relieved today was Restday. For some of her people it meant family time, others a night for carousing. For her, a precious night of early sleep.

Chim said, "Speaking of high places, how's Angel doin' with the Comet?"

"She's interested," Jeje said. "That's about all he's said."

Chim chuckled again. "That boy o' yez is as good as a play all by hisself."

"Not my boy," Jeje retorted, but without heat.

"Mebbe so, mebbe so. Leastways he's out o' our hair at Fleet. Less exciting w' him gone. But I notice the others don't treat ye like a horse turd on the street anymore."

"No, they actually talk to me once in a while," Jeje said briskly. "Nothing like people pitying you for being thrown over by a beautiful fellow to get them to see you as human."

"Aw, they're not so bad," Chim said, chuckling wheezily. "Just, he never gave any o' 'em a second look, and there he was, walkin' out with ye every day."

"I know," Jeje said. "Well, speaking of walking, it's time for me to walk to bed. Tomorrow will be another long one."

Just about the time she sank gratefully onto her pillow, Tau examined himself in his mirror, and then trod lightly downstairs to begin the next phase of his campaign.

He'd gone to the theater every night for a week to watch and listen to the performer known as the Comet. A nickname that some said was for the beauty of her voice—like a bright star arcing across the sky—others insisted it was for the brightness of her pale blond hair. A few thought the name was for her quick, birdlike movements, and in private a number of people had wryly told Tau it was really for her temper.

Tau had found out at Wisteria House that she was courted by everyone of high status and low, that she was spoiled, moody, choosy, and difficult to please. She'd had diamonds given her by dukes. Poems written to and about her. Music written for and about her. Paintings of her and for her, by artists whose prices would buy an entire house on the lower hills. She'd radically changed the fashions twice, once by refusing to wear a style she'd gotten tired of and then by appearing at a court function in something she'd designed on a whim. Even the crown princess wore her fashions, though it was said she cordially hated the Comet. But if she really did say that, it was nowhere in public.

Everyone knew the Comet's tastes: she hated the Colendi (no one knew why), she hated current Sartoran plays and traditional music; there was a long list of foods (Sartoran) and colors (dark) and scents (floral) and songs (historical ballads) and places (Colend, Sartor, the west, the north, and any island) she disliked.

So here was Tau, dressed in an elegantly tailored Colendi long-coat of the most severe black. At the high neck and the turned-back cuffs gleamed the snow-white complexity of the finest Colendi moth-gauze lace. His trousers were black, fitted at the hip and dropping in a long, gradually widening line called sea-mode after the sailors' deck trousers—also Colendi. They, land-bound, seemed to have a penchant for things named for the sea, which suited Tau's purpose. He wore fine-weave Colendi court dancing shoes, also in black. No ornaments whatever, except the discreet diamond in one ear replacing his piratical gold and ruby hoop, since there was no disguising the hole, and his hair, which had only grown to his shoulder blades, and was tied back with a narrow black ribbon in the Colendi manner.

He picked up the forty-eight stringed tiranthe he'd been practicing with for days and took it downstairs.

The moment Mistress Rosebud, the proprietor of the house, saw him, she gasped and made shooing motions at him. "Colendi! That's Colendi courtier dress! Taumad, you don't dare! Not in my front window, when *she's* coming tonight—"

"Please," he said. "Let me try."

She fanned her plump face. "You'll ruin me, if she gets angry." Mistress Rosebud was as shrewd as she was good-humored. "I can see what you're doing—a campaign of opposites. It might intrigue most. It will intrigue most," she corrected, her gaze running down his length. "That line suits you beautifully, Angel, dear. But that's others. Who knows with *her*? The one thing we can predict is her temper! No one has crossed her successfully. She'll declare my house outside, and no one will dare to cross the threshold, and I'll have to go back to baking pies . . ."

Tau smiled. "I think—I really believe I know how to manage."

So far the campaign had worked: he had avoided her for a week. He'd been invited not only to theater parties, but a court affair, just so people could watch them meet, and he'd taken care to leave as she arrived.

Two days ago the tide had reversed. She was now coming to places where he had agreed to perform, or had accepted invitations. And again he took care—employing friends as lookouts—to leave at her arrival. Not overtly. As friendly and smoothly as possible, but so far he and the Comet had not come face-to-face.

His friends from the musicians' gathering, who had willingly served as his lookouts, were all gathered in Madame Rosebud's main room, where they'd volunteered to play background music to his tiranthe.

Madame Rosebud sighed, her hands up in surrender. She shook her head slowly as she bustled away.

Tau took up his chair in the front window, where some-one was always on duty playing or singing or reading po-etry. That was Wisteria House's distinctive signature: musicians.

He sat down, letting the fine coat fall open as it would. Put the tiranthe on his lap, and began strumming the diffi-cult triple-beat chords of a Sartoran ballad, shifting from major to minor key.

He heard a soft moan—"*Not* Colendi?"—followed by muffled laughter from his friends, who began playing a lovely air that ran counterpoint to his ballad so the two musical lines were distinct, but did not clash.

The night watch-bells rang. If he was right about the Comet's being by now thoroughly intrigued, she ought to for once be on time.

He closed his eyes and concentrated. He would never be a great musician, but with care and practice he could make such showy pieces look effortless. Beyond the shimmering chord changes came the rustles and whispers of arrivals. A bustle that stilled into the almost hush of many people squeezed into a small space.

He smelled the distinctive pepper-poppy scent she wore.

"Colendi," she exclaimed. "You were not aware of how tired I am of their haughty posturings, Boy-Named-Angel?"

While listening to her sing, Tau had amused himself try-ing to find words to describe her voice. He didn't like any-one else's effusions. To him her voice sounded like a wide ribbon of molten silver, though he knew others would con-sider that just as effusive.

But he was not a poet. What he could do was quote poets . . . "I observe everything but the obvious," he said, with his eyes closed. His hands strummed glissades in the minor alaf key.

A little intake of breath, and the Comet said, "People did warn me you were arrogant."

Tau changed chords then said, "I ask myself why people waste time saying behind one's back what is true?"

She laughed. "So you admit to being arrogant?"

"No. We're never arrogant ourselves, nor are we out of

fashion. Those qualities are purely reserved for others."
There, he thought, is *your bait*—

"You appear to be," she retorted, "less mystery than mode."

And Tau came back with the next line, "Whichever has the least influence." Then he stopped, and smiled, and opened one eye.

She stared, her dark blue eyes huge, her lips parted, then she finished the exchange in a somewhat breathless voice, "Oh, I so agree. Influence is terrible enough, but good influence is the worst of all."

As everyone around her made little noises of appreciation—one woman sighed, "How very clever she is!"—the Comet added, "Will you join me? We shall find a cozy place to talk. Just the two of us."

Tau waited until her admirers finished their sycophantic compliments: "Oh, but you must let us all hear!" and "How else shall we learn the art of conversation?"

Tau drew his fingers down the tiranthe, then laid it aside, stood up, flicked his fingers down the faultless coat, and held out his hand.

With dainty grace she placed hers on his, and they walked out, admirers trailing the Comet; from behind came the sound of Mistress Rosebud thumping into a chair and calling for her fan.

The next morning he told the entire story to Jeje, who laughed appreciatively, then said, "So I suppose the rest of the time you gave her the old 'night to remember,' and no, I don't want to hear any details."

"Not at all," Tau said, ducking her knife, and whirling up to tap her on the collarbone—to find her beside him, her knife tip pressed lightly against his side. "Ooof!"

"She gave you a night to remember?"

"She tried. But I kept her at arm's-length. Until dawn. Kiss on the fingertips. And a rosebud. She hates roses, remember."

Jeje chortled, then sidestepped and kicked at Tau's kneecap.

This time he was ready. He feinted, swooped, got behind Jeje and put his knife under her chin. "Oh, Inda. The things we do for you."

Jeje tromped Tau's dance shoes with her bare feet and elbowed him efficiently in the ribs. He grunted and let go, and she said, "I hope he's having more fun than we are."

"This isn't fun?" Tau asked, lunging.

Jeje skipped back, made a swipe at his belly, which he blocked. "It would be fun on the deck of *Vixen*." She feinted low, struck high, and he tapped his neck below his ear, acknowledging the blow. "Here, everything's work."

"Heh." Tau grinned.

And when Tau trudged to his current lair to sleep until the night's campaign, and Jeje marched off to another day of tallies and lists, a lone, tired figure with short pale hair walked into town behind a row of market-bound wagons full of produce.

Vedrid, Runner to the new king of Iasca Leror, Evred-Harvaldar, lifted his head, saw the harbor city at last, and let out a sigh. It had been a very long journey.

Chapter Sixteen

ON Inglenook Island, the lookout slammed the newly hammered door open. He stood on the threshold of the southern room, trying to get control of his breathing. He'd run all the way to the old ruin, now half transformed into a house.

Eflis yelled, "Careful with the damn door, I just hung it myself!"

The boy waved a hand violently. "Two capital ships hull down, comin' in!"

"Where?"

"South-southwest."

"On the wind." Eflis dropped the chart she'd been copying, grabbed her glass, and strode through to the wide bank of windows—the main reason she'd chosen this room for her own, despite it being only half roofed. She stopped at the westernmost window. Snapped open the glass. Looked—and jumped. "Shit!"

The hammering above ceased, and an upside down head appeared in the narrowing gap.

"That's *Coco* back, and I'll give my oath it's Boruin Death-Hand's trysail with it!"

Two hammers clattered to the wood planking overhead, and footsteps retreated rapidly.

Eflis ran back into the other room, grabbed up her

weapons belt, and pounded out, yelling for everyone to get aboard the *Sable*.

Halliff met her halfway down the trail. His face was drawn and old with fear.

"Boruin's *Spear*," she said. "And *Coco*."

"But Walic's dead," Halliff said hoarsely. "We know that."

"So's Boruin," Eflis reminded him. "Torched by Elgar the Fox. If he's comin' to torch us, it's not going to be without a fight."

The bells were ringing on the *Sable* and the *Sea-King*. Pirates ran down on either side of the two captains, who stood on a little outcropping, Eflis with her glass. "He can't attack us with two ships."

Halliff exclaimed, "Eflis. This madman took a *single ship* against Boruin's fleet. And he *burned them all to death*."

Eflis sighed as the small boats launched out into the bay. Between the two of them they had twenty small craft, ten sloops, seven schooners including Eflis' large schooner *Sable,* and Halliff's raffee, the *Sea-King*. Surely that would be enough even for a fire-slinging madman with only two ships, capital ships though they were.

If, that is, he only had two capital ships. What might he have beyond the horizon, or sneaking around to the north side of Inglenook?

She beckoned to one of the carpenter's mates and issued some quick orders. Halliff stood there, a tall, stooped figure with lank gray hair, his narrow face tight with fear.

Supposedly he and she were equals. But she'd realized soon after reaching Inglenook, limping precariously after that grandmother of a storm two years before, that Halliff had lasted so long under Walic because he was unimaginative and unambitious. He was the perfect sailing master—he took excellent care of his ship. He did not come close to her idea of a real captain.

"Let's get out into the bay," she said. "Get some fighting room."

Neither of them thought of trying to defend the island—they never fought on land.

When she reached the rudimentary dock—which was

nothing more than some old boats lashed together with planking hammered over them—she found her first mate, Sparrow, waiting.

Sparrow held up her hand. "He's got a parley flag out," she said, hooking her thumb over her shoulder.

Eflis whipped up her glass as one of the schooners drifted across her field of vision. She exclaimed in disgust, then jumped down into the gig. Sparrow snapped her fingers and the gig crew bent to the oars, soon skimming them over the water to the *Sable*, where the two women clambered up and ran to the foredeck.

This time the two ships were clear, running parallel, stripped to fighting sail, but both flew the single white flag that offered parley.

Eflis cast an exasperated look toward the *Sea-King*, but it didn't really matter how slow Halliff was. She knew she ought to wait for him and discuss their next move, but she also knew he was not going to do anything but worry and the final decision would be hers.

She lowered her glass. Sparrow waited, so still the chimes braided into her black hair did not ring. "We'll answer, but I want the blue *above* the white."

Sparrow whistled, and now the chimes rang sweetly. "You think Elgar the Fox is going to come aboard us? If that's really Elgar the Fox."

Eflis shrugged. "He came here. I want to know why, but not enough to hand him my head aboard his ship. It was bad enough before." She grinned. "The days are over when the Brotherhood, or those who wanted to join 'em, forced you to come aboard them, eh?"

Sparrow smiled, then said, "Yes, but you'll remember it was this fellow who tromped 'em."

Eflis wavered, then stiffened her resolve. "I don't care. So far, I don't see anything else with him. Blue over white." She smiled, remembering that it was supposed to be Elgar the Fox who'd rid the world of Walic—and Coco the Monster in Human Form. "Make the cabin nice, will you, Sparrow? If he really does come aboard us, I want him to sit and chat, and maybe tell me how they killed Coco."

Sparrow snorted. "Long and lingering, I hope. It was her favorite kind o' game, after all."

Aboard *Death,* Dasta and Tcholan watched through their glasses. The fight crews waited, armed and ready. The sail crews kept the sails loose, their progress slow. Presently the answering signal went up not on Halliff's raffee, as they'd expected, but on the biggest of the schooners, the one with the spiky five-fingered black leaf on the foresail.

Dasta turned his head. "Gillor?"

She came forward, took a glance. "That's Eflis of the *Sable,*" she said. "Word is, her family was on the wrong side in the Khanerenth War and she ended up turnin' pirate. Walic used to try to recruit her, but she said she would join the Brotherhood on her own."

"Brotherhood-style pirate, then?"

Gillor shook her head. "Not the way I heard. Oh, in the beginning she talked wild. Took risks, and Emis Chaul o' the *Widowmaker* took some interest in her. She talked the talk w' him, but most said she was doing it to keep him thinkin' she was an ally. She really only was interested in Khanerenth navy and trade. Revenge, like." She grinned, then added with satisfaction, "Coco hated her because she's young and pretty."

Gillor laughed to herself at the sharpened interest Tcholan and Dasta revealed. She waved the glass. "Blue over white—they want you to go aboard them."

Tcholan whistled. "So they're interested. You were right."

Dasta rubbed his beak of a nose, wondering if the pretty Eflis was planning a trap. But this was his idea. "Unless you want to, I'll go. You stay here and be Elgar."

Tcholan said, "You go. You talk better with strangers."

"Remember the fighting scarf." Dasta motioned for his coxswain, who waited a few paces away. "One rumor we don't want going out is that Elgar now has black hair and skin the color of chocolate."

"Face away and fighting scarf, hai," Tcholan promised,

and Dasta signaled for the ship to be anchored as the coxswain got his crew together to lower the gig.

"Here he comes," Sparrow said, peering through the scuttle. She rose on tiptoe, then frowned. " 'He' as in a man, but if that's Elgar the Fox, then all the rumors are wrong."

Splashing, voices, and then the gentle thump of a gig nudging the hull, and the women sat down on the pillows before the low table.

Shortly thereafter the cabin door opened and one of the hands motioned in a tall fellow who was brown of skin, hair, eyes. Hawk-nosed, long-bodied, he moved with an easy slouch. He wore just a vest and wide-legged blue and white striped deck trousers. A knife at his belt. Bare feet.

"You can't be Elgar the Fox," Eflis exclaimed in disappointment—though she rather liked his looks.

He was a little taller than she, and despite the slouch he had the muscle expected of anyone who was fighting under a captain as famous as Elgar the Fox, but there was no arrogance in his face. Instead, the curve of his mouth, the shape of his brown eyes, hinted at a sense of humor. She remembered that beautiful golden-haired fellow Coco had kept as a pet, and wondered if they knew one another.

Dasta gave a comical shrug. "What can I say? I follow orders—he stays on board in case there are problems."

Eflis snorted. "Well, it does make sense, seeing there are forty of us all told, and two of you," she said, more sharply then she really felt. But it was good to try to take the lead here, since the infamous Elgar wasn't actually on board her ship. "Or do you have a trap awaiting us over the other side of the island? My scout will report on that soon," she added, as Sparrow, standing behind Eflis, silently indicated one of the pillows.

Dasta dropped down cross-legged with the ease of one used to sitting on the floor. "Your scout won't have anything to report. There are just two of us. But the Fox remembered Halliff from before, wondered if he was looking to rejoin another fleet, and wanted to see a little action."

Eflis and Sparrow expressed surprise.

Dasta felt the atmosphere change. He'd seen at once that they were not only disappointed but annoyed to see him instead of the expected mysterious black-clad Elgar the Fox.

The tall blonde regarded him thoughtfully. The short curvy one with the dark, braided hair silently poured out spiced wine into three cups, let him pick one, and then took one and sipped—all long-established pirate custom.

Dasta hoped that he hadn't managed to pick a poisoned one, and sipped at the same time she did to indicate goodwill.

The gesture had been futile at least as often as it had really been an indication of good faith. Everyone knew that. But the women accepted it anyway, and when Eflis took her glass they raised theirs in salute. They all drank.

"I'm Eflis," the blonde said. And with a tip of her head, "Sparrow, my mate." Sparrow gestured, which made the chimes in her braids ring.

"Dasta," he said. "First mate on the *Death*."

Sparrow plopped down next to Eflis. "Is that what he calls Boruin's trysail? Kinda swag, no?"

Dasta grinned. "We couldn't decide whether to rename it *Boruin's Death*, *Majarian's Death*, or *Pirates' Death*—then Fox ended it by telling us it's *Death* and to stop yapping and get it cleaned up." His voice hitched at "Fox" but then he was clear. Whew. Whatever it was about that banner that got Fox and Inda crossing names was just as well, but he'd have to watch himself.

The women misconstrued the slight hesitation in his voice. "He must be worse than Walic," Eflis observed.

Dasta knew a hint when he heard it. "Not at all like Walic. For one thing, he never leaves anyone behind unless they are too wounded to sail. Or I'd be aboard the *Sea-King*," he said, his smile vanishing. His voice took on that timbre, hard to describe, that convinces one the speaker believes what he says.

"But he did for Marshig," Eflis said.

"Good command," Dasta returned. "Better than Marshig's trickery. Though it did help that Ramis of the

Knife appeared and took them into Nightland. But if he hadn't, I fully believe Elgar the Fox would have killed Marshig on his own deck. He might not have survived it—don't know what his crew would have done—but at least Marshig had no chance either way."

Sparrow said, "So that rumor about the rip in the sky is true?"

"I was there," Dasta said. "I saw it." He shut his eyes. The women waited, the sounds of the crew above muffled, the water against the hull. "Hard to describe. Don't have the right words," he finally said. He had their complete attention. "It was black beyond it, a black of night with no stars. Sometimes, during the day-watch, I think I dreamed it. I was tired. We'd been fighting all night. But no, that's the easy thing. Not the truth. It would be comfortable to believe it wasn't real. But it was. It happened. Those six ships sailed right into a night beyond night—into damnation."

Sparrow twitched her shoulders. "Strange. You use that word as a curse, but when it actually happens, the meaning changes, doesn't it?"

"They all went?" Eflis asked.

"Yes," Dasta said. "We saw it. A lot of Marshig's crew tried to dive overboard, but they got swept on through that hole anyway. I hope never to see anything like that again."

Another pause, during which Sparrow poured more wine. She found this Dasta utterly unexpected.

Eflis leaned forward. "Before that. Your Fox, as you call him, burned Boruin and her crew to death. Even Marshig never did that—though if you ask me, some of the deaths he and his captains dealt out weren't much better. But those were one at a time, usually personal, like. Not entire crews."

Dasta ran his nails absently along the grain of the table. "I think . . . I think I'd have to let him explain that to you," he said slowly. "I'll say this. What he intended was to send the crew in their boats to the Chwahir coast, or wherever the current took 'em. Not Boruin. Majarian. They died fighting. Idea was, leave the crew to Chwahir justice, as they'd preyed mostly on Chwahirsland. But things happened otherwise. Wasn't his intention."

Sparrow thumped her elbows on the table. The chimes in her hair rang, reminding him of Gutless, who'd come to Halliff's ship a time or two: the braids and chimes, he'd been told, were a fashion from one of the countries over on Toar across the land bridge. He wondered if they'd known one another, a thought that made him uneasy.

"So what you're saying is he doesn't have control of his crew?" Sparrow asked.

Dasta rubbed his nail back and forth on the table a couple more times, then lifted his hand. "Oh, not at all. But there were, huh, things going on, you might say. Had to do with the Chwahir on board, for one thing."

Eflis sat back, knees up, her hands clasped loosely around her knees. Her gaze was lowered thoughtfully so he let his eyes linger appreciatively on her. Pretty! Gillor was usually reliable, but to call this tall, strong-looking woman "pretty" was to call a big feline a kitten.

"Chwahir," Eflis finally said. "Huh. I usually take as I find, but some o' them are strange, like. So you're here because?"

"Because though we did for Marshig, the cost was high. Fox wants to play with the Fire Islands pirates now. They get in the way of Freeport independents too often, and you know we're affiliated with the Freedom Isles. So we're looking for anyone who wants to have some fun with us there. Equal shares on any loot."

Sparrow said warily, "He doesn't take captain's share, then?"

Dasta suspected what was coming next was a question about the Brotherhood treasure trove. So he gave Inda's deflection, "He says there are plenty of rich pirates out there. Everyone fights. And everyone gets rich together or everyone loses."

Sure enough, Sparrow said, "So I take it there wasn't any mysterious hoard?"

"Ghost Islanders never saw a wink of it," Dasta replied with the ease of truth. "And Pirate House—where Marshig lived—had been completely stripped right down to the floor tile by the time we got there in spring."

Eflis snorted. "I never believed in any treasure anyway.

What pirate hoards treasure? You get it, you spend it. Forget the treasure. So what you're offering us on his behalf is equal shares if we join his fleet? What's the command line?"

"Plans his, though ideas are listened to. But sometimes he goes off on investigations on his own. He also rides one ship, then the other. Fleet commander, with captains on each, so he's free to move around. We carry out his orders as if he's aboard us." He glanced at Sparrow's chime-braided hair, then away. "No torture parties or any of that, if that's what you're thinking. Thing is, if you like that sort of thing on your own ship, probably better sheer off now."

Eflis grimaced. "Truth? I hate it. I want a good fight. I hated Coco—everyone hated her. I hope she got what she used to dish out." She added casually, "And I hope that pretty fellow with the long golden hair gave it to her."

"Tau cut off his hair," Dasta said. "Because her fingers had been in it so much." Eflis and Sparrow gave little nods of complete comprehension, which Dasta found interesting, as he'd never understood the meaning of Tau's gesture. "As for Coco, Elgar set her adrift. With a couple of Walic's worst. We don't know what happened to them, if they didn't make it back here." He waved toward the island. "We weren't all that far out when we let down the rowboat."

Eflis showed her teeth in disgust. "They never fetched up here. That is, we don't know what happened between your taking of Walic's flagship and our own arrival. When we got here, Halliff had survived a mutiny on his own ship. Half of his crew was dead, all Walic's known spies. A few of Walic's old fleet—the small craft—came back rather than drift on the ocean and die, because they didn't have supplies. Not a one squawked at the change when Halliff and I made an alliance. And there was certainly no sign of Coco."

"So who's your prey?" Dasta asked.

"We were going to take on traders to Geranda—no Brotherhood holding that road. Compete with the Fire Islanders for any traders not Venn. Wouldn't mind getting rid of the Fire Islands soul-suckers."

"But you wouldn't take on the Venn themselves?" Dasta

asked, watching appreciatively as Eflis stretched and yawned.

"Even Marshig didn't take on the Venn warships," she said, wiping her eyes. "And they always accompany their traders."

"They that tough?" Dasta asked, thinking of Inda's quest for information.

Sparrow laughed, pouring out more wine, then kneeling beside Eflis. "Warships are warships. Venn are rough water, yes. But the reason we won't touch 'em is, they got those sea dags. That's what they call their mages."

"What can a mage do, even if called a dag? I never heard that mages fight." Dasta asked, watching as Sparrow laid a casual hand on Eflis' shoulder. Then brushed her fingers against Eflis' neck in a caress. And when Dasta flicked a look up, he saw awareness in her eyes.

Mate, not first mate. Ah.

Eflis made a wide gesture, apparently oblivious to this little interaction. "You don't know why no one ever goes north? Why the Venn never gave up those prows, even though they can't rig 'em well with jib sails?"

Dasta said, "So I'm a southerner. Tell me."

Sparrow grinned. "A bowsprit makes a nice handle for the big monster squids of the deeps. Prow doesn't. Also, prow is a signal to them it's Venn, so the squids don't attack."

"Why not?"

Eflis said, "Because the sea dags talk to them."

Chapter Seventeen

TWO days later, one of the big Venn guards came down into Inda's prison corridor with a host of the ones in yellow.

The Venn said in Dock Talk, "Those with the following numbers come to the front of your cell." His accent jolted Inda. It was unexpectedly like Marlovan. "Anyone else stay to the back. Make a wrong move, you kiss the ground." He hefted his cudgel then slammed it against the iron door.

Silence.

He motioned to one of the others, who commenced reading out the numbers. It took a long time, especially when some exclaimed, followed by hisses and curses from those trying to hear. With fearful and angry looks men shuffled forward and back, no one knowing if it was good news or bad news to have your number called. Or, as a fellow near Inda muttered without moving his lips, "Bad news or worse?"

When the range of numbers neared that of the group in Inda's cell, his fellow inmates stilled. Each held his medal, many gazing down with furious concentration as if the numbers might change. Then, as numbers were called or skipped, the men separated slowly, many reluctantly. Inda's number was passed over. He stayed in the back. *Scars*. He knew what that meant: suspicion. But he said nothing.

When the Venn finished, the questions started, spoken first. When the guards ignored them, some began to shout. The guards moved down to the next cell; when a couple men pressed their faces into the bars, demanding answers, one of the Venn snapped out his cudgel and smashed their knuckles.

The bellowing ceased. Numbers were read out for the last of the cells down their side.

After that, the Venn moved back to the first cell. This time they unlocked the door and let the men out one out at a time, each checked against the list.

Sudden noise as a man tried an escape—voices, scrabbling; the horrible thunk of a weapon on a skull, followed by a thud. Then the door was relocked.

No one else tried anything. Presently the last of them were gone. The Venn departed and the cells, emptier now, were left alone until the evening bread and cheese were brought and pushed between the bars; someone else brought the pitcher of water to replenish the bucket soldered to the wall by the door, the communal cup hanging on a string.

The fear and questions of the first week were back again.

Inda sat where he was, back to the wall, working on his story as he ate.

"We've got a problem," Nathad said, dropping down opposite Thess in the Lower Deck, the tavern in the ghost yards of Bren Harbor that had become Jeje's favorite retreat.

"Not Japsar again! I thought Col had a talk w' him."

Nathad shook his head, beckoning, and the regulars came closer, most of them just off work and waiting for Jeje the Pirate to come down from Fleet House.

Haelec, the proprietor, set down two fistfuls of mugs, and stepped up, wiping his hands on his apron.

Nathad sidled a shifty look around then said in a low voice, "It was Japsar who heard 'em, and this time I think I believe his stories. Col says he's tryin' to stay sober. So's he can join us."

"Don't trust him," Marn—the gray-haired grandmother—said. "Least, not till he's been sober at least a month."

Nathad waved a hand. "We can talk over Japsar later. This is the thing. There's some fellow nosing around the taverns along Anchor Way, askin' about Elgar the Fox."

A brief silence, during which half of the gathering sent wary looks at the door.

"Who is he?"

"That I don't know. But Col says his accent is a lot like the Venn."

Thess made a fist and pounded it on the table. "That don't sound good at all. You think it's a Venn spy, then?"

" 'Cep' what's he want?"

"We need to find out," Nathad said. "And not tell Jeje—she might vanish on us. See, I figure this. If she's goin' to all the trouble to train us, and Chim, well, he's backin' her, there's some kind o' plan afoot. And we're gonna be in it. Jeje's talked around about jobs, ships. Careful like, but you know what it is?"

Thess waved a hand. "Already figured that out. Elgar the Fox is gonna be hirin' for his next fight, and he don't want pirates. Who would, for choice?"

Everyone signified agreement.

"They'll want us if we're good," Thess said. She grinned. "I plan to be real good, because I want in." She frowned. "So . . . this spy. I think we need someone to spy on him. Someone real friendly like, if he's close as a clam. Take their time. Palnas!"

Her son was at the far side of the room, setting up a game of Cards'n'Shards. "Yeah, ma?"

"I got me a job for you, boy, so get over here."

"Good thinking—" Nathad began, but was interrupted by Marn.

"Here comes Jeje. Mum, everyone! We take care of this matter ourselves."

*   *   *

Despite there being fewer prisoners in the cells of Beila Lana jail, this time the interviews were more extensive, so it took a couple of days to work down the rows.

Everyone waiting noticed that there was another change: this time some men came back, others did not.

"What's with the ones don't come back?" someone asked early on.

"Lettin' em go," a young man responded. "I saw it, man before me in line. They chased him right out." He laughed. "They don't like me because I used to trade out west."

"Get inside," the guard ordered him.

"I'm goin', I'm goin'."

Clang!

Inda's turn came the next morning. This time he was alone in the long office, with the same dag listening, though a different, older, officer did the questioning.

Inda gave them the same information, and when asked to describe the pirate attack, he told the story of Walic's attack on his convoy, ending with his being struck unconscious. He saw recognition in their faces when he named Gaffer Walic, and described his raffee. As rescuer he described the *Nofa*, the Sarendan war ship that he'd encountered on the way to attack Boruin.

When they were done, the officer addressed the dag in quick, idiomatic Venn. Inda listened, frustrated: he caught a couple of words, but not the sense of the talk. The dag responded more slowly, and this time Inda recognized two words: *pirate* and *captured*.

Four armed guards had brought him out, and four took him back to the cell, and locked him in.

He sank down at the wall; the others did not address him as the next was taken out.

He did not come back, nor the next, nor the ones after that.

Inda was left alone in the cell.

When the guards passed on to the next cell, Inda put his hands over his face, resolving: *Next time, I fight.*

* * *

The Comet faced Tau.

They were alone in her house, because he refused to take her to his room. She had a spectacular mansion—a gift from a duke—on the hill, the lower rooms of which had been decorated sumptuously and were used frequently for her entertainments. But the third floor was her own private space, and there they were now, not even a servant in sight.

She sighed, throwing her gloves down onto a table inlaid with pearlescent stars and comets. She dropped onto the satin couch, leaned her head back, and watched him as he walked slowly around, not touching anything, but examining the furnishings as if evaluating them. "You really are an angel face," she said, draping her skirts so that the folds outlined her form. "You are the only man I cannot construe."

"Construe." He bowed, Colendi style, his hand flourishing up in a satirical salute. "Am I an old language or a verb?"

"Everyone is a verb," she said. "When we dwindle to a mere noun, we die. Do stop hiding from me. Take off the mask. You already see through mine. I am grateful for your goodwill," she went on, raising a hand before he could speak. "Yes, it's a pretense about my hating Colend, and yes, it's because I steal freely from the best of their old plays for my wit. Why not? It's wit, free for the taking. So what if I claim it? If I were able to be witty on my own I would write all my own songs and plays. Anyway, all the minds who thought those lines are long dead, so they can hardly complain of my theft. I want to know how you knew. Are you in truth an actor, then?"

Tau shook his head, smiling. "No. I really was raised in a pleasure house, just as I said. Except my mother read to me from the greatest plays and made me recite them back as a way of training my diction. She said once that current Sartoran plays had all the taste of yeastless bread, because the queen feels that no play ought to be performed that has not a useful lesson to teach. And current Colendi plays were too full of private innuendo—trying to out-clever the clever—so she used the older ones, which are as airy as pastry and as full of the complexity of good taste. But unlike pastry they are ageless."

Comet laughed and clapped her hands. "I should love to meet your mother."

Tau's smile vanished. "Perhaps," was all he said. "But let us discuss ourselves."

"Oh, don't tell me there's some horrid reason you won't sleep with me," she said, tucking her feet under her bottom and patting the place beside her invitingly. "Don't let it be something dreary that I will hate."

Tau smiled again. "Nothing dreary. Shall we negotiate a deal, you and I?"

She sat upright, eyes narrowed. "Oh, Angel, you're going to be like all the rest? I am not rich—everything is gifts, and if you don't know the nobility, you had better learn this: they can take back the things they give so easily, and all on a whim. There's no recourse. No argument. If for some reason you cease to entertain them, they snap their fingers, and hordes of muscular minions appear, and your appearance of wealth disappears. So don't name some hideous price. I won't listen." She laid her dainty fingers lightly over her ears, taking care not to disarray her charmingly arranged hair.

Tau waved a hand to and fro. "I don't want your money. I have enough of my own. More than you do, as it happens." He strolled toward her, bent, and kissed her fingers.

She took hold of his wrists and tried to pull him down beside her. She had longed to kiss that mocking mouth for days and days, a longing that had intensified to hunger. "You're rich?"

"Very. But not in this kingdom." He gave her that lazy smile, then turned his wrists slightly, breaking her grip.

She sighed again, saying with undisguised desire, "No one else shall wear white and black. I am determined on that much."

He shrugged expressively, and she loved it even when she was exasperated at his deflections. He was every bit as beautiful as she was herself, but he never looked in mirrors, never responded to compliments, never gave in to desire. "Tell me your deal," she said.

"It's simple, and I don't think you will suffer by it. I want you to introduce me into court circles," he said. "Especially Prince Kavna's."

Disappointed, she groaned. "Oh, you *are* like everyone else after all. Court!"

"Yes." He bowed.

"And Prince Kavna! He's fat, did you not know?" She threw her arms wide. "Fat, and obsessed with the sea, of all things. That and government and justice. He's as enticing as your Sartoran yeastless bread."

"Nevertheless."

She sighed again. He regarded her with that ironic smile. Giving in to impulse, she got to what really mattered: "In return I get you?"

He threw his hands wide, mocking her gesture.

When they came next for Inda, he was ready.

He listened to the lock click, positioned himself. As soon as he was outside the door, he'd strike. He knew where they stood. If he could just get hold of one of their weapons—

But this time they entered the cell two by two. He backed up a step, off balance, out of practice. How many days had it been since he'd drilled?

Go.

He launched himself forward, twisting between the first pair.

The Venn were good. He'd hardly exchanged three blows when he felt threat from behind, whirled, faced the second two—

And the first one clubbed him efficiently behind the ear. He dropped to his knees, his vision splintering into flickering stars. A foot on his back slammed him facedown onto the stone. Someone wrenched his hands behind him.

He thrashed violently, but they were too many and too experienced. His wrists were tightly bound, and a hobble put around his ankles, which would prevent him from taking a step larger than his forearm.

They pulled him to his feet and pushed him out. Shuffling awkwardly, he was herded in a new direction. The room this time had no window. That same fair-haired dag in the blue robe was there with a Venn officer as well as one of the yellow-clad ones. This latter sat at a side table, with pen and paper.

"Fought, did you?" The dag said in Fer Sartoran, his mouth derisive; Inda realized then that this man was not a Venn dag, he was an Ymaran mage.

Inda did not know which was more dangerous.

He hesitated, and the mage said with heavy irony, "It will seem even more suspicious at this point in the proceedings if you pretend not to understand Sartoran."

"I did nothing wrong," Inda said, striving to match that accent. "Don't know why I'm here."

"We are here to determine that," the mage responded. "Since, as you say, no crime is involved, you could be on your way more speedily if you answer my questions fully and completely." He gestured to the chair before the desk. "Sit down."

Inda shrugged his shoulders and wiggled his fingers behind him. "Rather stand."

Two of the guards behind him gripped his arms, wrenched his elbows out, and thrust Inda into the chair so his hands were behind the back. The chair back cut excruciatingly into Inda's arms; he could not move.

"Now then," the mage said. "First item. Tell me where you learned court Sartoran of the last generation?"

Inda grimaced. "Dunno what it was called. That's what I learned when I was small."

"In an Idayagan village? Son of a rope-maker?"

Inda said doggedly, "We all learned it."

The mage addressed the Venn officer. This time Inda caught more words: "Satisfied? . . . Drink."

And the Venn waved a hand.

The mage sat behind the desk. No one spoke. Inda twitched uneasily, trying without success to ease the strain on his arms. A short time later the door opened and someone entered. The air he stirred brought a familiar smell: kinthus.

He tried not to swallow, but one man jerked his head back by his sailor's queue, another pinched his nose. When his mouth opened on a gasp they poured in the liquid. And though he choked and gagged on at least as much as he swallowed, they kept pouring until the mage said, "I think that's enough."

Inda felt the effects almost at once, as he hadn't been given a morning meal. The familiar cloud of unfocused detachment settled around his thoughts as he fought his own mind, saying over and over, *I am Fassun, I am Fassun.*

But when the mage asked next, "What is your name?" Inda heard himself murmur, "I have to say I am Fassun, I have to say I am Fassun. Have to say Fassun, and a little village, because I don't remember any of the town names on the map—"

"Tell me your name when you were born," the mage ordered in Sartoran.

"Indevan-Dal Algara-Vayir of Choraed Elgaer," Inda said, and smiled at the Venn's intake of breath, the sudden alertness in the guard at the table, and the way he jerked around to face the mage.

Who said, "This is a province in Iasca Leror?"

"Principality," Inda corrected gently.

"So you are a Marlovan."

"Yes."

The mage made a slight gesture at the guard in yellow—a twitch of two fingers—then said, "Tell me how you ended up at sea?"

Out it all came. Under the mage's patient questioning, Inda told them about the academy, Dogpiss, his exile, the *Pim Ryala,* the mutiny, the marines, his days on Gaffer Walic's ship. That mutiny. The attack on Boruin. The preparations for the attack on the Brotherhood.

He talked until his throat was hoarse, but the mage listened closely, and the guard in yellow wrote swiftly at the desk.

The attack on the Brotherhood took the longest, because the mage wanted every detail about Ramis that he could dredge from Inda's memory. When he'd answered exactly the same way three times, the mage breathed deeply, wiped his forehead, then said, "And you never saw him before?"

"No."

"So you did not take his commands?"

"No."

"Nor he yours?"

"No."

"Yet he desired you to meet him at Ghost Island? Tell me what you did with him there."

"We walked to the house. He told me to come to the balcony, and when I did, he said I am used to loyalty—"

"Did you and he talk about the Venn?"

"Yes. He told me there are splits in the Venn government. He said the system of kingship is at stake. He told me the three most dangerous Venn to me are Hyarl Durasnir, Commander of the Oneli; Prince Rajnir; and Dag Erkric."

This time the intake of breath was from the Venn observer; the mage and the guard met each other's eyes briefly, their expressions indicative of intent.

"Go on," the mage said, after a questioning glace at the Venn.

"He told me that the Guild Fleet has no leader. He took me aboard his ship by magic transfer, which felt like—"

"Just tell me what he said on board his ship. Did he give you orders, or a future meeting place?"

"No. He said he would be dead within a year. We would not meet again. He showed me ghosts. He asked me what I want."

"And you said?"

"To go home."

The mage sighed. "You did not see Ramis again?"

"No."

"So you left Ghost Island and sailed down the strait?"

"Yes."

"Looking for information about the Venn? About Prince Rajnir, say?"

"Anything I could find, though mostly I wanted charts—"

"Did you get any information, or charts, when you stopped in Bren?"

"No. They had nothing. Their charts of the northern side of the strait are as blank as ours." Inda's voice was a mumble by now. "So I wanted to come here and chart the north coast myself. Count Venn ships. See them maneuver, and—"

The mage said, "So the storm drove you through The Fangs and you came here to spy?"

"Yes."

"Why are you spying on the Venn?"

"To gather information. Chart the co—"

"For what purpose?"

"So I can free the strait for southern trade."

Another intake of breath.

Inda's mind had drifted into the kinthus dream state that left emotion behind. So he watched with detachment as the mage glanced at the Venn, then—longer—at the guard in yellow. And said, "I believe we are done."

The officer dressed in yellow got to his feet, drew his knife, and in a swift move gripped the surprised Venn officer with a forearm under the chin; the man was off balance for the heartbeat it took for the other to rip a knife across his throat from ear to ear. The man jerked—slumped as blood flowed—the mage motioned to the ground in front of Inda.

The two yellow-clad guards at the door sprang forward and helped the officer bring the Venn around the desk. They dropped him at Inda's feet, where he flopped, blood pooling on the stone floor.

"Get the other," the mage ordered.

The door guards left. The mage stooped, drawing his blue robe carefully aside, and checked the dead Venn. Then he moved to the officer's table. He tidied the papers scattered there, and began to read.

Time measured itself by the quiet hiss of papers being turned over as the mage read through them all.

Presently he said, "Get your pen. Rewrite this last page. I want the same handwriting, the same sense of his words, but under the that list of his three most dangerous enemies you will say that at Ghost Island Ramis commanded him to assassinate Rajnir."

The scratching of the guard's pen was the only sound, and then he looked up. "Do you think that's true, about Ramis dying?"

The mage shrugged briefly, more of a twitch. "The only safe observation is that nothing Ramis ever says or does is what it seems. Even death. That much we can surmise from the very little we've learned about him. But for our purposes, this will do."

He took the sheet of paper with Inda's real words, folded it neatly, and slid it into his robes.

Inda's body had gradually sagged forward, his muscles unstrung as in deep sleep, but his mind observed in helpless horror when the guards reappeared, dragging a young man roughly Inda's size and age. Inda never saw his face, just his unprotected neck and dangling brown queue as they lugged his dead weight around Inda's chair and, at a gesture from the mage, dropped him near the Venn. He'd been stabbed several times; the blood was slick and dark.

The officer in yellow pressed the bloody knife into the young sailor's lifeless fingers. He pulled off Inda's medal, hung it around the neck of the young sailor, whose medal was removed and pocketed. The mage pulled his blue robe aside again, knelt carefully, and arranged the limbs of the murdered victims. When he was satisfied he rose and stepped back.

Then at last he flicked his fingers toward Inda.

"Take him."

One of them hauled Inda to his feet, another swathed him in one of their own cloaks.

Inda was carried out. Muffled voices spoke in Sartoran, then two in Venn. "Attacked . . . had to kill him . . . one of our men severely wounded, clear the way!"

Inda was bundled into some kind of conveyance. Heavy men in jingling chain mail sat on either side of him, forcing him upright. From outside came a sharp command, the clop of horse hooves. The conveyance jiggled and jerked.

He'd drifted into a troubled, pain-limned sleep when he was abruptly woken by hands gripping him roughly by the arms.

Once again they hauled him out, and as his feet fumbled for purchase on the ground, someone said, "Up in the stone room."

Inda was dragged up stone steps. The stair edges hit the

top of his feet, scraping them. He felt it; the kinthus was wearing off, though his legs wouldn't move properly. Zings of red lightning shot up his arms.

But then he was flung facedown onto a bed, and a warm tenor voice exclaimed with breathy excitement, "Oh, well done! *Well* done! I never believed he'd actually be here. How very expedient, how fitting! Promotion for you all, I promise. But take the ropes off him. He needs to sleep. I will have him fresh and ready to work."

As Inda's numb hands were loosed, the voice laughed softly. Then all the footsteps clattered out.

Inda was left alone, lying facedown on a bed.

The door closed, the locked clicked.

Chapter Eighteen

HADAND was thinking about beauty, art, Joret, and the Adranis after a long succession of days, each one much like the one before.

And again she said nothing about the matter when Joret joined her in her chamber. It was noon; they generally had the mornings to themselves, for apparently most of the court slept until then.

Joret was reading a record written by one of Wisthia's ancestors. She sat there on a hassock, one leg tucked under her, dressed in a blue silk gown which Wisthia had herself picked out, trimmed simply in white lace with tiny golden ivy leaves embroidered at the edges of the lace; Joret did not like what she considered fuss. Her gleaming black hair was pulled high with a small wreath of silk flowers braided in. She hated the great concoctions of wire and lace and ribbon that were the fashion. To her own eyes she was simply but adequately dressed. To Hadand, who admired the clean, graceful line of her neck, the shape of her head artfully enhanced by that single arc of white silk blossoms, Joret looked like someone from another time, another place. "Taste" was a new concept to the Marlovans: the ability to discern what is aesthetically pleasing. It was a fascinating concept to Hadand. Even more fascinating was the realization that Joret's discriminating taste seemed to be innate, though she described it merely as perceiving balance in colors, shapes, and lines.

A sharp pinch in her ribs recalled Hadand's attention, and she gave Tesar a glance of reproach. "Why did you pull those bodice strings so tight?"

Tesar pointed at Hadand's back. "Because the ends do not meet. We'll have to remake the dress."

Hadand sighed. "Am I putting on extra flesh, then?"

Joret looked up. "I know I am. At least my arms feel like those squashy arms I see around us." She ran her hand over her fitted sleeve. Hadand frowned at her own arms. Had the familiar curve of muscle diminished to the soft line she disliked seeing in others? She gripped her silk-covered arm, was reassured by the muscle she found there. That was another strange thing about beauty, or at least, its perception in different people: she and Joret did not like the shapeless arms on the women here, but the women just as clearly thought their own muscular arms unpleasing distortions.

As one particular lady spared no effort to let them know.

Joret went on. "I picked up my knife again this morning, and I was out of breath in a trice." She pursed her lips. "We can't possibly be getting old, can we?" She made a comical face.

"If we are old in our mid-twenties, I hate to think what we will call ourselves at forty—or eighty."

"We won't talk about age at all, but about the past." Joret's cheeks dimpled as they only did when she was being ironic.

"In any case, it's the result of a month without drill," Hadand said. "That and all those butter-potatoes with every dish, and cream in every pastry. This food tastes wonderful, but it sits heavily in the stomach in a way that our rice and cabbage doesn't. Twice, now, I've had to drink steeped ginger-leaf before I could sleep."

"So have I," Joret said, with her sudden chuckle.

"Well I now resolve: no more cream cakes, delightful as they are. At least, only one. And tomorrow, no matter how late I get to bed, you must not let me sleep late, Tesar. It is time to resume dawn drill."

Joret turned her thumb up. "I'll meet you. Gdand told me days ago she found a place to work in an empty chamber off the lower baths. No room to practice the bow, though." She wrinkled her nose, and glanced out the window at the garden. "How fun it would be to organize a defense here."

Hadand laughed. "With whom? I suspect some of these women who are even younger than we are would fall down if you asked them to run five steps. Not that the men are much better. Their arms have little more shape than the women's, under all that silk. And the way they mince about, as if more than ten or twelve steps requires a carriage to bear them!" She stood up and looked at herself in the mirror. And frowned. Were those shadows at the corners of her chin, or was she putting flesh on there, too?

She felt a pang of sympathy for the queen. Had it been swift or gradual, the taste for cream cakes that led to one extra, then two extra, until now at least six was an expected part of a meal? Did rank do that to you, or was it this strange life, with nothing to do all day but sit about in fancy dress and watch one another for signs of presumption, and maybe dance in a slow, gliding step to the constant music? Imposing the queen certainly was, beautiful, too, but it took the strong arms of two footmen to help her from her throne, and she walked with the same slow effort that Hadand herself would use if she were carrying a pair of laden saddle bags over each shoulder.

Joret's face appeared above Hadand's in the mirror. "Why the frown?"

"If I carried as much extra flesh as the queen, I could never have defended the throne last year. But then such a notion of defense seems to have never occurred to anyone here."

Joret laughed. "They think their smooth necks and shoulders charming. As perhaps they are. At least, that Lady Fansara has dropped several comments about the utter lack of charm of laborers' arms, and the stalk of dockside sailors."

Fansara—the blonde who had stood out from the very beginning for the utter lack of warmth in her welcome.

Though a very pretty woman, and one their own age, she obviously did not like foreigners. Or at least did not like Joret, Hadand reflected. Fansara paid Hadand the courtesy due a queen in a smooth, sweet voice that reminded Hadand very much of Starand Ola-Vayir at her worst.

"My portion of Fansara's style of compliments have all made some sort of reference to barbarians," Hadand said wryly. "Though nothing direct enough for me to be able to think of an adequate response. Do they really consider Iascans to be barbaric? Sartor doesn't have these fashions either—everyone keeps mentioning the austerity of their court—so is it just me looking for insult?"

"If you mean Fansara, she's cruel every time she opens her mouth," Joret said. "She's far worse than Dannor Tya-Vayir, even."

"It was Honeytongue that I was thinking of, that spun-sugar voice. Before Fansara began about laborers' arms and barbarians."

Joret put her head to one side. "Why is it, do you think? I remember distinctly the first day Dannor arrived at the queen's barracks and discovered that a future Jarlan hadn't automatic precedence. How angry she was! But Fansara hasn't that problem. She's First Lady. And her brother is the most powerful duke!"

Hadand had studied the map. Bantas was one of the biggest duchies over on the Anaeran side of the great river. She said, "Precedence is never enough for some." She yawned. "In one of Wisthia's records I discovered that the origin of their primacy was in the granting of a thumping great tax on the porcelain profits that come from that region. So they're not the oldest family, nor do they hold their titles longest."

"Why should that make a difference?" Joret asked.

"I cannot begin to understand. It's plain to see that Fansara craves power the way the queen craves pastries."

"She was considered the first beauty of the Adrani court. Until we came." Tesar gave Joret a wintry smile in the mirror.

Joret's gaze lowered. She loathed that kind of talk.

"Well, that explains at least a part of it," Hadand said,

trying to be practical. "If you regard your face as a counter in a competition, then a better face is going to debase your counter in your own eyes, will it not?"

"Why think that way at all?" Joret whispered, and moved to the window to stare out.

Tesar rolled her eyes at Hadand, who opened her hands. They knew Joret—she wasn't going to change.

Tesar shifted the hairbrush in her grip. "What's said downstairs is that Lady Fansara and her bother's wife, the Duchess of Bantas, fight from cockcrow to sundown. Lady Fansara won't marry any of her suitors; she has her eye on Prince Valdon. And the king and queen want her as crown princess—has to do with that same porcelain tax."

Hadand pursed her lips. "Everyone talks about Prince Valdon. What he does, what he likes, what he says. Whom he's courting. But isn't that some princess up around Colend, or thereabouts? That's what I heard someone saying yesterday, when complaining about how boring it is waiting for him to come back."

"My nephew arrives back in a week."

The voice came from behind. Hadand and Joret turned. Gdand, on guard outside the door, had opened it, and Wisthia entered, elegant in a draped mauve gown. "I suspect we shall see some changes."

"I hope so. That's another thing that worries me," Hadand admitted. "It's the waiting, for no one has said anything to me at all about the treaty. They give me precedence, at least in all the court ritual, but where is the real work done?"

"True," Joret said, expression pensive. "We see the king and queen reigning all day, but when do they rule?"

Hadand sighed. "I've listened to the whispers of those courtiers who line the way from the dining chamber to the anterooms, waiting to ask for favors, but those appear to be personal business. Otherwise never a word spoken about anything beyond food, music, dancing, and pleasure. Is it possible the king and queen don't really rule, that everything revolves around this Prince Valdon, like the planets in the sky around the sun?"

Hadand thought of the locket on its golden chain between her breasts, and her nightly ritual, when alone, writing to Evred on tiny squares of paper. It all had a peculiar intimacy, despite them being so far apart—despite her having to write, in essence, *No news yet*.

Wisthia considered Hadand's distant gaze and Joret's interested one. "Some of the real work of government seems to have gone to my nephew. My brother presides over final decisions, but most of the work leading to those is done by Valdon. So our protracted wait is not aimed at you—everyone murmurs in private to me about it."

How strange, Hadand thought. A king who merely wants to look like a king, but not do the work of one. Why be a king at all? She could not imagine Evred in a similar position.

Wisthia smiled. "You should see some changes within a day or two after Valdon returns."

As Tesar brushed out Hadand's long brown hair, Hadand and Joret exchanged unself-conscious comments about how heavy it seemed, to wear one's hair on one's head, but it did look rather pretty, didn't it? Wisthia laughed inside, a buoyant laugh, as she admired the blue-black sheen of Joret's hair.

At noon, Valdon Shagal, Crown Prince of Anaeran-Adrani, reached the eastern border mountains and rolled into a royal posting inn to change his horses. There he found his cousin Randon waiting inside the very best private parlor that his outriders had arranged for him earlier that morning. They sat down in comfortable chairs before a bow window that looked onto a broad square made of patterned brick, into which the main road emptied.

"How goes the chase?" asked Lord Randon, pouring a glass of the waiting ale. "Rotten, I take it from your lack of cheer. Good!"

Valdon looked askance at that grin. "What now?"

"One word." Randon lifted his ale in toast. "Joret."

"Joret! I've had five golders already, all mentioning this 'Joret.' " Valdon tapped the discreet waistcoat pocket that housed the fabulously expensive golden case wherein chosen friends—with expensive cases of their own—could send letters by instant magic transfer. "Let me tell you, I've had it with beauties. The royal palace in Alsayas was full of 'em. Lael did what he promised to do, soon's he got his throne: he surrounded himself with every beautiful woman in Colend. And don't they just know it!" Valdon whistled.

Randon laughed. "I've heard about Lael's garden of roses."

"You know the real reason they're called roses? Thorns, every one. Each thinks she will be empress. And though he's as much as said he will never marry, they each think they'll change his mind." Valdon shook his head. "Anyway, if you want the truth, I was through there as an excuse—Mama being what she is, only a journey to Colend would silence her about this marriage business."

Lord Randon kissed his fingers and flicked them out in an airy gesture. The queen had insisted that if her son didn't marry Lady Fansara, then only a woman of impeccable lineage would do, preferably a Colendi or Sartoran.

How about a family that had married among both? He shook with laughter and anticipation as Valdon said morosely, "I rode all the way to Mearsia to try to talk Dascin into marrying me—figured, since she's a princess, she *might* be almost as acceptable as a Colendi duke's sister in Mama's eyes—but she won't have me. Or rather, she won't have Mama, Papa, our court, and all the rest."

"Wise woman. I like her already."

Valdon grinned. "Then go court her! I told her I'd send some likely candidates for consort. You can furnish the example of worst choice."

They laughed. Randon heard his own turning to gloat, and turned his head aside to scrutinize that brick square out the window.

An open carriage rolled by, filled with young ladies in their hastily donned, very best clothes. The owner tugged on the ponytail of the driver, who slowed the horses even more, and all four ladies glanced through the window at him and then eyed his companion with speculative smiles. The royal livery on the outriders, the royal arms painted on

Valdon's open racing carriage, had obviously caused a local stir.

"Damn," Valdon said, brooding. He gave the young ladies an absent salute, but his mind was back in memory and he never noticed the smiles or the pretty, beribboned dresses. "Two things I learned, being a page under Queen Servitude during those miserable years in Sartor: how to scrub floors and how to laugh. Dascin and I laughed a lot during our page days—and we had some good dalliances, those long afternoons on bare stone when we were supposed to be contemplating the real meaning of service."

Randon whistled. "Another reason to be glad I wasn't born a prince. My single visit to Sartor was bad enough. I think being a page for five years would have driven me to drink."

"Except there isn't any drink." Valdon sighed. "I may yet have to give in and marry Fansara."

Randon made a gag face. "Don't do it. You haven't seen her as much as I have these past few years. And when you do, she's courting you with all her might."

"But the porcelain pact—"

Randon waved a careless hand. "Take my word for it. Bantas will seal it for another century if you get Fansara off his hands for good."

"Well, that would mean I have to marry her, yes?"

Randon tossed off the last of his ale. "If you do, I'm off to Sartor. Sitting on benches and eating cold food would be preferable to her tender rule."

"And you're trying to talk up another willful beauty?"

Randon shook his head. "Joret isn't like that."

"So she has enough manner to hide her nature. Fansara did too, I remember, when she first came to court. Before my mother made a pet of her." He set down his glass, frowning at the golden liquid catching the light reflected in the diamond panes of the window. "Truth is, we're all like that aren't we, to greater or lesser effect? Raised to sell either our rank or our faces for advantage, and then spend the rest of our lives taking that advantage as far as we can."

"Val." Randon's pleasant, mobile face drew downward

in a pretense of sourness. "You're brooding. It upsets me. If *you* think yourself constrained to do anything you don't want to, where is the hope for me?"

Valdon laughed as his page appeared at the door and bowed, signaling that his carriage was ready. "All right. I have nothing to brood about. Promise you will talk no more of beauties, for I've had enough of them."

Randon placed both hands at his heart, and followed the prince out. They stepped up into the superbly upholstered royal carriage, leaving behind the pages to pay the shot and drive Randon's less racy equipage—in addition to Valdon's closed carriage, used in case the weather turned bad—at a more sedate pace.

Valdon whistled to his pair, who pricked their ears. A flick of the reins and the horses dashed out of the inn yard at a splendid trot.

For a time neither spoke as they bowled up the well-paved road toward the mountain pass that would lead toward home, and all the decisions that awaited Valdon there. While the prince inspected the state of the roads—which were justifiably famous for their excellence—his cousin brooded on the character of courts.

Presently Randon said, "Speaking of Sartor, did you hear whom Queen Servitude finally picked as heir?"

"Lael told me! After all the gabble about her wisdom and insight, she's gone and crowned that hypocrite Lissais. 'Service to the Kingdom.' Oh, they'll learn what 'service' is as soon as the old woman finally croaks. Probably that day."

"But it's said Princess Lissais sleeps on a stone floor just as the queen does."

"Don't you believe it. Dascin and Naryan of Mearsia swear any oath you can name that she locks her door and forces her servant to sleep on that bare floor. She gets the warm bed. Heirs! I don't know about this custom Sartor has of picking heirs. It only seems to make people lie and scheme the more. Maybe those Iascans have it right, that the older brother rules, the younger one runs the warriors."

"Except they fight just as much. And it's not talk, it's steel and blood. Look at your Iascan cousins last winter!

King, uncle, older brother, all murdered at once, and the younger one comes home to a waiting crown."

"So he couldn't have done it himself."

"His sweethearts did it," Randon said, nodding wisely. "You know they're all tail-chasers, everyone says it. The men go out for six months into the fields and romp with each other. Leave the women all alone. So it has to be true. I can't imagine anyone leaving J—women behind by choice."

"Then if the men are all tail-chasers, the women have to be skirt-chasers. Which means your J—woman won't give me a second look no matter how handsome she is."

"Not she! You can't be that stunning and chase girls."

"If you think that, then you've forgotten Great-Aunt Tirthia," Valdon stated. "The toast of the city, what, sixty years ago, said men belong in the stable and not in the salon? If you didn't get that lesson every time you misbehaved as a boy, I sure did. Anyway, as for your Joret, she's probably the Iascan royal cook's daughter. Not that it matters to me anymore, but it would to Mama and Papa. I'm going to marry Fansara and drink myself purple along with my father."

Randon grinned, and uncorked the gloat he'd enjoyed until the right moment. "Oh, no. Your horse-faced cousins over the mountain apparently don't pay any heed, but Joret's one of the Deis. The *western* Deis. Descended from Adamas Dei of the Black Sword himself—a line going straight back to Connar Landis of Sartor. She could walk into any court in the world and claim precedence of just about everyone."

Valdon looked askance. "They don't pay any heed, over the mountain? Of course. It's because the Deis are all mad—they talk to spirits, and what, bay at the moon? Your Joret probably keeps hedgehogs as pets, and flings peas at the servants when she's at home."

Randon laughed. "They aren't Marlovans, is all. Live way down south, in the area most recently annexed to Iasca Leror—and there was some old connection with the disgraced Montredavan-Ans, so the current government pretty much ignores them."

Valdon whistled, then he groaned. "Doesn't matter. She can be perfect, her family can be perfect, but the way my life has gone so far, it only means we'll hate each other on sight. You'll see."

His gloom made his cousin laugh the harder.

Chapter Nineteen

HYARL Durasnir, Commander of the Oneli, was sitting down to the Restday meal with his officers when the summons-tap of his scroll-case alerted him.

He excused himself, indicated his chief lieutenant should carry on as host in his place, and withdrew to his private cabin off the grand wardroom called the hel, after their formal gathering halls in the Land of the Venn.

The scroll was written in large, angry slants: *Send the ships home. Come now. Elgar dead.*

He touched the paper to a candle flame and watched it burn. When he was certain that his relief would not show, he returned to the wardroom.

The officers fell silent, scraped back their chairs, and stood.

"We are ordered back to Jaro," he said. "And I must transfer. Battlegroup Captain Gairad will assume command."

They saluted. He withdrew to his cabin. Took out the transfer token he was required to always carry on short cruises or long. Braced himself—and sound, sense, and spirit were wrenched away then restored with equal violence.

He swayed on the transfer square tiles, eyes closed, until the shivering stopped.

When he opened his eyes he found himself in the Port of

Jaro tower room, two fully armed Erama Krona at the closed door, dressed in white with the Tree of Ydrasal on their chests, their faces impassive. Rajnir stalked between them as if they were walls, scarlet with fury.

Erkric frowned behind him; at any time he was slim to the point of thinness, his silver hair gradually receding from an already high brow, but he seemed gaunt as well as tense. Attenuated, Durasnir thought, as he recovered from the last of the transfer malaise.

Behind them waited Commander Talkar of the Hilda, boots wide-planted to steady him. His jowly face was taut, his forehead hazed with the faint sheen of sweat caused by the reaction to long magic-transfer.

Rajnir thrust a scroll at Durasnir. "Look at that, Hyarl my Commander! I was right! I was *right,* he was *here.* And he's *dead.*" He rounded on the Commander of the Hilda. "It was your Armor Chief Skir who managed to lose a fight with an unarmed man. What are you training your Hilda in, dying?"

Durasnir winced inwardly. There had never been much amity between the Oneli and the Hilda. The sea lords, as the most ancient of Venn military forms, despised the land warriors as land hungry and short-sighted. Incapable of Ydrasal, the Tree on the Golden Path—the highest Venn aspiration. The army regarded the sea lords as arrogant without just cause. Despite that inherited bias, some individuals among the Hilda had earned Durasnir's regard, and one of them was Talkar.

Talkar stated in a voice devoid of emotion, "Skir was a capable warrior." His eyelids flickered, as if to repress a meaningful glance toward the Erama Krona, and Durasnir knew what he was thinking: Skir was trained for war, not for the duties of a guard and gatekeeper, spy and interrogator, as were the Erama Krona.

But no one ever said anything to or about the Erama Krona, unless on the prince's order.

Erkric said in a low voice, "I wonder why it is that only our witness died, and how many of Wafri's guards were also there, in addition to the Ymaran mage?"

Unperturbed, Rajnir waved a dismissive hand. It was his

Dag's duty to be suspicious of anything and everything. "Everyone knows mages don't fight. It took all the yellows to bring Elgar down, and Wafri says they lost one. So Skir might not have been so clumsy. Except in permitting the pirate to get his belt knife. But damnation! Elgar was *here*—and coming after *me*. Perhaps it's just as well he's dead."

Erkric bowed his head in a grave nod.

Rajnir said, "You never would have trusted him. I know. You said it nine times nine. Yet I did so wish to send this man against those accursed Marlovans. *I'm* certain he would have embraced the opportunity to turn on those who betrayed him. Read that."

He thrust papers at Durasnir, who skimmed them with the rapidity of years of report reading.

When he looked up, he said, "*Ramis* ordered him to assassinate you?"

"You see? You see? I was right!" Rajnir exclaimed, turning to each of them, arms outflung, blue eyes wide and angry. "Even so, had we had him first, I cannot help but think he would listen to reason. He might not like us, but look how his own people turned against him. The enemy of my enemy is my friend, eh?"

Erkric lifted his silver brows in question. Talkar remained still and expressionless; Durasnir read in that wooden expression thoughts roughly concurrent with his own: Ramis had been mysterious, even sinister, in his successful evasions of various Venn traps military and magical, but never once had he done anything stupid. Sending Elgar the Fox to assassinate Rajnir was stupid.

But you did not tell a prince that.

What Durasnir could question out loud was this: "He was under the influence of kinthus and he attacked a man?"

Rajnir paused, then frowned. "You're right." He pivoted, tunic swinging. "Dag?"

Erkric opened his hands. "I confess that aspect had not occurred to me either, but then I only had the briefest moment to glance through the papers because we were busy examining the bodies and dealing with the release of pris-

oners and so forth. We do not know how long the questioning continued, or how much kinthus they gave him."

Rajnir sighed. "Since it happened in Wafri's garrison,
we must be content with what we were told. I see it as a
matter of good faith. I have said I would begin to trust
him with some governing responsibilities, and it seems
well to begin now, with an event under the shadow of his
own castle."

No one spoke. Durasnir was watching the Dag, whose
upper lip twitched in the briefest sneer. It was enough to
make his reaction clear, if not his thoughts.

Rajnir had retreated to the window. "Even if his men
are not as efficient as ours." He glared at each in turn. "I
have tried to turn a badly handled situation into triumph;
I ordered a day of celebration for tomorrow. The bells will
be ringing the celebration carillons come morning. We will
pretend we are pleased—Wafri certainly was pleased to
have ended the threat to my life. You could see how happy
he was, and maybe relieved too. I suspect he was frightened that he might be next. Though he has wonderful
ideas, he's never pretended that he has the least skill in
war craft."

"Indeed." Durasnir's tone was dry.

Fox's vigilance was rewarded on the second day he cruised
just beyond Beila Lana harbor in his gig. A fleet of fishing
craft and a couple of small traders sailed out on the tide—
the first in over a week to leave the harbor.

Fox tried to speak to the smallest of them; two wouldn't
answer his hail, kept going full sail, one's captain yelling
from the stern through cupped hands that Norsunder
could have Ymar and everyone on the whole damned continent of Drael.

The next obligingly slackened its courses, and several
men his own age and younger crowded to the side, many of
them raising the wide-bottomed cups common to ships
around the world.

"If yer crazy enough to be goin' in, ye'd better have one

of them necklaces," a boy with red hair called, jerking his thumb toward his own bobbing throat-knuckle.

"Necklace?" Fox shouted back, remembering what Fibi's captain had said.

"Them damned Venn have got every single Ymaran listed—and any that trade in Ymar—on their damned lists. If you don't have a necklace, yer as good as signing over yer liberty to a cruise in the box." He mimed being stuck behind bars.

"How do you get a necklace?" Fox asked.

"Ye stand all day in line, and then have to pay for the pleasure!" The redhead spat over the side. "If ye want it, ye can have mine. Save yerself some trouble. Not to mention a pocketful of good money wasted on those soul-eating Venn." Back of the hand toward the shore. "We're never comin' north again. Ever."

"Thanks," Fox called. "I have to land and find one of our mates, got lost after the big storm. What can I expect?"

"I almost lost half me crew," the oldest one shouted— the captain of the fisher boat. He snorted. "Last time I let these worthless rats ashore for liberty. Some fresh fruit! A little sex! And we're stuck out on the drink for days with half the crew behind bars."

"Well it was worse for us," one of the young men bellowed, buffeting the fellows at either side of him.

"No, it was worst for me!" the redhead roared. "Grabbed the boys like me first—just because we got red hair!"

"But they let ye go first," retorted the other, and the others hooted and crowed in enthusiastic agreement. He was short, blond—looked like he was probably the captain's son. " 'A little sex?' Penned up with fifty other men, no bath for a week. Nightland liberty, I call it! And for no reason, other than some shit about pirates. Like we're a terrible pirate ship!" He pointed to his nets, and one of the others sang, unmusically, the chorus to an old pirate ballad, joined raggedly by his mates.

"But at least they did let 'em go," the captain yelled over the buffoonery. "And we are, too. I won't breathe free until I sink this accursed land behind us."

"Here!" The redhead tossed something metallic down

onto Fox's deck. He laughed. "Yer name is Red Mendin out o' Lands End if they ask. I'll never be back there again. Hope ye find yer mate."

They saluted one another, then the fisher—its crew singing—put before the wind and sailed off.

Fox hung the medallion round his neck and raised his own sail, cursing steadily as the craft picked up speed.

Redheads. Pirates. Inda had walked straight into a trap.

Prince Rajnir's Dag, Abyarn Erkric, transferred to the Dag Hel just off the garrison terrace in the Port of Jaro. While the whoosh of displaced air ruffled round the room the dags rose and bowed, hands open.

The etiquette was dags waited until the transferred one recovered and spoke first. Especially a superior in rank.

Erkric thus had time to take in the wide chamber with its row of western windows. Every Venn seemed unconsciously to gather on the west of any building that had windows, where the long light of afternoon slowly turned gold before it faded; it was a luxury absolutely unknown at home. Even those who professed to be, and were, homesick displayed this weakness, he had discovered.

The light through those open windows painted bright rectangles down the long length of the worktable, illuminating the stacked lists of prisoners, the status of each neatly written in various colors of ink.

"You are finished," he said. "Elgar the Fox is dead. You may return to your regular duties."

Ulaffa, the Yaga Krona Dag, had been given charge of the sorting of reports and information. He folded his gnarled hands. "How did that come to pass? Our people were painstaking in following orders."

"*Our* people were," Erkric repeated, emphasizing "our." "Count Wafri's mage and men chanced upon the Marlovan, who apparently rose up and slew our observer. The Prince and I inspected the scene ourselves. It appears that all happened as Mage Penros reported, and the prince pronounced himself satisfied." His opinion of Penros was conveyed with nicety through the title *Mage* instead of *Dag*—a nicety that only the Venn understood. "The Prince has ordered a day of celebration tomorrow."

He paused. No one spoke, so he transferred away again.

"So much for my hunches," Anchan said, laughing as she chucked her list into the empty fireplace. "I really thought that insolent redhead who said he was from Fal had to be their Elgar."

"Oh, he was from Fal," Byarin said, ripping his list before he threw it down after hers. "I've been in the south once."

"The significance of that being?" Anchan prompted.

Byarin was never averse to lecturing his fellow dags. "Fal is a tiny country in the middle wastes down south. They habitually challenge you, or me, or each other, or the birds—not to mention the air itself—to a duel if they feel the whim. The babies go armed, the grandmothers fight so much the city squares are reserved for duels."

Everyone laughed.

"Insolence," Byarin said, waving as he headed toward the door, "is the proof you are a Faleth. Politeness will get you killed as a traitor." And he was gone.

"So that's why we've never heard of the place," Egal boomed, towering over the others. "They must be dead before they get a day's travel from their own border." With a billowing of sun-touched blue, he whisked himself out.

Jazsha Signi Sofar took more time to gather her lists. As most of the others dropped their papers into the fireplace, she cast an eye down her neat columns. Across from her, old Ulaffa sat with his hands loosely laced together, his bushy eyebrows knit.

"Did you ever see Mage Penros' reasons for keeping lists?" Signi addressed him in her quiet voice.

"No," Ulaffa said. "I was told that I should not expect him to report through me, that the prince gave the count freedom to run his investigation as he saw fit, as long as we saw any results. As, apparently, we did."

Apparently. Hint given, hint received.

Signi bowed, stooped to lay her papers on the others, and left. Ulaffa watched her go, and then took the Fire

Stick down from the mantel, dropped it onto the pile of paper, and spelled it to flame.

Fox had never told anyone he spoke Venn.

It was a family secret. Though he despised secrets and despised his father, most of all he despised the treaty that had put his family in the inescapable prison of their own home.

The Montredavan-Ans all learned Venn because they believed that the easiest defense is to know your enemy. They had all read copies of the letters their great-father Savarend had written to the King of the Venn, and the replies: the last from old Savarend in effect giving the back of the hand to Venn's offer to make the Marlovan plains a favored province if they aided the Venn in conquering the Iascans. Fox, by age ten, had memorized the last letter from the Venn King, promising that the Venn would come one day, in force, and there would be no favored family or province. Instead the Montredavan-Ans would be the first to die.

The morning Fox set foot on the quay at Beila Lana, bells were ringing carillons from all the towers.

The market was closed down. Groups of people in bright, festive dress moved briskly about setting up tables, benches, and a temporary stage—all the organized chaos of a celebration.

Fox searched around for someone young and inoffensive looking. A line of sturdy boys was busy unloading barrels of drink from a wagon, passing them from hand to hand, and stacking them beside a long table being set with cauldrons and huge plates of skewered fish. Fox sauntered up, and when the last barrel was passed down the line, he tapped the last boy, and asked him in Venn what was going on. The boy's glance lit first on Fox's chest, where the medallion hung, then lifted to his face.

The boy was relieved; Fox observed that relief, and his tension racked tighter.

The boy said in stilted Venn, "I do not well this language

speak." He shifted to Fer Sartoran, adding with a return of his initial wariness, "You're a foreigner, I take it?"

"Not from too far," Fox answered in the same tongue, with a fair try at matching accent. "Just returned from fishing up the coast. Got blown farther by a big storm."

The boy's brow cleared. "That storm," he said, "brought Elgar the Fox. Prince Rajnir has declared a holiday to celebrate his death."

Fox's hands gripped together behind his back. "His death? I take it there was some kind of public execution?"

The boy patted the draft horse, then wiped his forehead on his sleeve. "No, not at all. My cousin in the guard says they were supposed to keep him alive. Something went wrong. Cousin said the others were talking about how he jumped the Venn noser." He looked around furtively. "Killed him, wounded another guard. Unarmed, too! They said he was worlds fierce."

"So . . . no one saw this attack?" Fox asked, unwilling to believe the obvious unless forced to.

The boy shrugged. "Just our count's guard. The Venn Dag came and inspected, Prince Rajnir inspected, everyone inspected before the bodies were Disappeared yesterday."

"How did they know their prisoner was Elgar the Fox? Had they ever seen him?"

The boy laughed. "No one had, and you should've been here the day they dropped on us and searched. *Hundreds* of fellows. More. Most of 'em sailors blown in on that storm. Word is it was even worse down at Jaro. The Venn and our own guard come in all of a sudden, chased off all the female sailors, and in one swoop marched the men off to the cells." He waved behind him at the stone garrison above the harbor. "And did they gripe! First the Venn wanted redheads, then it was every boy and man over ten and under fifty. Everyone't didn't have a medal."

"Seems miraculous they found their man, if no one knew what he looked like." Too sarcastic? At the boy's questioning glance, he added with a fair assumption of regret, "Too bad I missed seeing the fun."

"Word is, they had the entire fleet out and all, but they

was down below Jaro, so we didn't see 'em all take wing. It's a fine sight! But they're comin' back. Business as usual after today."

"So . . . did your cousin say that Elgar the Fox told everyone who he was?"

The boy rubbed his nose. "Some said kinthus was used, and they'd have his medal, I guess—they gave 'em all medals before they even questioned 'em, I hear. Only *they* didn't have to pay!" He slapped his chest. "In any case, the important thing is, today's no work, all fun—and yesterday Restday! Two days off work is no bad thing. And the word is, the Prince is only givin' out drink in Jaro, but here the Count is payin' for eats and musicians. All day as well as tonight! We're goin' to have dancing and contests—you arrived at the right time!"

Fox responded in kind, and after a little more conversation, he moved on down the quay, passing directly under the garrison tower ringing its merry carillon.

Fury burned cold through his veins. He walked for a time without seeing, as he struggled to come to grip with the impossible. Kinthus! No one lied under the influence of white kinthus. So Inda was dead, and his great plans blown like smoke. But . . . who inspected? People who didn't know him . . . Fox recognized the fact that he did not want to believe what appeared to be the truth.

One thing Fox did know. He would find out who those guards were, Venn or Ymaran, and after getting the details of Inda's murder he would choke the life out of them one by one.

Chapter Twenty

INDA lay on the narrow, wood-framed bed, gazing up at the window far above him. It was a square window, probably big enough to get through—if one happened to be as tall as a tree. He examined it in the clear light of the glowglobes set high on the stone walls at either side of the cell.

The sound of the lock clicking broke his thoughts.

"Listening to the bells?"

He recognized that voice.

He flipped up his legs and sat with his back to the wall. Acknowledged and then as swiftly forgot the distant ringing of the carillon. His attention shifted to the richly dressed young man who walked in. He appeared to be near Inda's age. His skin was smooth, his cheeks and chin round. His fair hair was cut short, which made his head seem rounder than it was; his eyes were dark brown, wide with curiosity. His broad smile curved on the verge of laughter.

He had small, neat hands framed in turned-back velvet sleeves embroidered with golden clover leaves. Despite the long dark blue velvet fitted Colendi long-coat, Inda's first impression was that he was short, but as the fellow came forward with a quick step, Inda realized they were about the same height. Despite the situation he couldn't help a flutter of laughter—he never thought of himself as short.

"Those bells are celebrating your death," the fellow said in a jolly voice, as though Inda would share the joke. "Hear

them? Did you know those carillons are Sartoran-cast, and
we play the same rings as they do in Eidervaen?" He spoke
Fer Sartoran, but his accent was much less flat than what
Inda had heard from the people and guards, and more like
the Sartoran his mother had taught him. Court Sartoran is
what the mage had said.

Betrayed by my knowledge, Inda thought, laughter
gone.

Wafri paused and studied his prisoner. Excitement—
anticipation—warmed him. "My dear friend Rajnir is probably stamping around in his tower having one of his
tantrums, but I cannot help that, can I? I wouldn't want to
see you wasted leading his army against your countrymen."

The Marlovan had been hunching in a wary knot, staring
at his drawn-up knees. At the word "countrymen" he
flicked a glance up. Wafri smiled, pleased with the reaction.

"So . . . what? Are you going to let me go, then?" Inda
spoke for the first time.

"Oh, yes," Wafri chuckled softly. "Of course! As soon as
you sweep Ymar clean of these soul-rotted Venn, and restore our land to us."

Inda recoiled, an inadvertent gesture that klonked his
head against the stone wall. He rubbed his scalp and said,
"What? Who *are* you?"

"I am Lord Annold Limros, Count of Wafri." He laughed
silently again, thoroughly enjoying the opening moves in
this little duel of wills. "I give you my name as well as my
title because we are of similar rank. My grandmother was
younger sister to the old queen, who everyone thought was
going to live forever." He gave Inda a happy, open-
mouthed smile, and swept his fingers to his forehead and
outward in a curious gesture.

Inda rubbed his jaw. Despite the laughter, the friendly
voice and manner, Inda sensed danger. "Did you kill her?"
he asked.

Wafri did not react with anger, affront, or even surprise.
He shook with laughter, his eyes closed. "Such a question!
Why are you the only one who ever asked right out? I assure you she died in her bed, pillowed in sleep." More of
that silent shaking.

Inda felt warning tingles in his hands, at the back of his neck.

Wafri opened his eyes wide. "She gave away the kingdom. Did you know that? *Gave* it to these Venn. Oh, some fought after she died, when the Everoneth came to our aid. But it was too late by then; it took only a year for them to run the Everoneth back over their border and tame the rest of us. If we'd combined and fought earlier, before they were already here—" He shrugged, hands gesturing with grace. "But that was nigh on ten years ago. Now it is time to take Ymar back again. I can't do it alone. I wasn't born to war, and my guard, though loyal, is small. The Venn permit me barely enough to keep the peace here in Beila Lana." Again the smile as he added, "Rajnir honors me by using County Wafri for his army training."

He paused, as if waiting.

The distant clangor of the bells filled the silence, and closer—just beyond the door—the rustle of cloth, a whisper or two, a footstep. Guards, waiting on call.

Wafri said, "But *you* were trained. So you will lead Ymar to freedom. I will take the throne, and I promise I will be very good to all my people. Everyone will be happy! Except perhaps for the Venn. But they can go off and chase your countrymen. Don't they like fighting, too? They can fight until the last shit—doesn't matter if it's Venn or Marlovan, they fell out of the same wolf's arse—is left to be wanded away."

Inda tensed, ready to spring—

"Don't move," Wafri said, his smile vanishing.

He stared at his prisoner, who'd tightened in an eyeblink from the hunch to poised stillness. Danger flashed through Wafri, a kind of near-pain that—within limits—he enjoyed. But only when he was in control. "Don't move, Prince Indevan."

The rustling from behind the door had abruptly ceased. Inda did not have to see the waiting guards to know that they were alert, ready to rush inside at a word.

An uneven flush of some indefinable emotion stained Wafri's round cheeks. "Is that not correct, you are called Prince Indevan?" Wafri asked, rocking back on his heels, his brow puckered, as if he were afraid of committing an error of etiquette.

"No," Inda said, sitting slowly back. Judging from the sounds, Wafri had an entire riding waiting right behind that door. *If I jump this blathermouth, they'll kill me.* "My father's the prince, my brother the heir. I'm only a second son."

Wasn't the brother dead? Wafri paced the length of the cell as he tried to remember what Rajnir had told him.

His new coat gleamed richly in the slanting shaft of light from the window above. He wore several fine rings; they glittered and flashed as he passed in and out of the light. They distracted him, so he put his hands behind his back and concentrated for another turn or two.

Wafri did not remember, but even if he could and the brother was truly dead, he decided not to give the Marlovan the delightful news that he was a step closer to his father's throne unless he got some information in return. "You must listen to me. I treat you with civility, you will observe. I want us to be friends!"

"Like you are with your shit Rajnir?" Inda retorted.

"Oh, oh, quite right. It does sound false in me, does it not? I confess I like Rajnir. We share many similar tastes; I do not wish to harm him as a man. If only he were not a Venn prince! It would be different if we were truly equals, if he did not use my title as if it were a pet name, and reward me with bits of my own kingdom and expect me to be grateful. He cannot help not being as smart as I am—and he is so grateful for my ideas." He shook with silent laughter.

Inda was not aware of his expression changing, but Wafri's quick eyes caught something, and he raised a hand. "I assure you, he does listen. It takes very little to suggest new ideas, like his sea battle nine years ago. But he did not die with the rest! His faithful hound Durasnir prevented that. Then the brilliant notion of preserving his men by luring pirates in to do his work for him."

"*You* did that?" Inda exclaimed.

Wafri laughed softly. "Yes. I thought it would make him hated everywhere and bring me allies. But it did not. His dag loved the idea, though. Rushed right out to make the contacts and the treaty—for reasons even I cannot discover. Surely not mine." He sighed, lifting a hand in an airy gesture; his dark velvet cuff fell back, revealing the snow-white fine-weave linen of his shirt sleeve. "Yes, Rajnir has been generous and kind. And he can be led. Is that not rich? A prince as follower? But not easily, not easily at all. His moods are like the weather, and then there are his two fierce watchdogs."

Wafri looked toward the high stone ceiling, his manner ruminative, though his fingers trembled.

Then he stopped by Inda's bed, smiling down at him. "My metaphor is not precise. Durasnir is more of a mossy boulder. Dangerous only if you stand in its slow, inexorable path. If you watch out, it's easy enough to stay out of his notice. But Dag Erkric? Ah, he's more like lightning. I do not understand him at all, except that he's dangerous."

Wafri began pacing again. "After all, they are all Venn! We cannot escape that even Rajnir is a Venn. They are large, they take up too much space. They stink of the dreadful spices they use in their food, some say because their land is so cold you cannot taste anything otherwise. Imagine cooking anything with vinegar! When wine goes sour here, we throw it away." He made a soft noise of disgust. "How can anyone take seriously a supposed aristocrat whose cook offers anything that includes vinegar as an ingredient? I feed my lowest servants better food than that."

He stopped prowling about and regarded Inda. "Don't tell me. Marlovans use vinegar?"

"Over grilled fish. Don't cook with it."

"Well. You see? You are different. More to the point, you are the enemy of the Venn, and Rajnir is afraid of you. He fears no one else except his king, and I really think that Erkric is also afraid of you." A sudden smile again, his round head tipped in question. "Do you know why?"

Inda did not, but he had decided he'd better stay mum.

"Come. Talk with me! I will answer any of your questions." Wafri held his hands out, rings glinting. "Anything! Go ahead. Ask me."

Inda said, "I want to go home."

"You can, you can!" Wafri studied the stubborn face before him, so young a face, so free of guile. Those two long scars, one down the side of his cheek, another along his jaw. He wondered what action had caused them; he wanted to know what it had felt like. He wanted to touch them.

He put his hands behind him, wiping them on his coat. "I promised you. You can go as soon as you rid me of the Venn. Did you not come for that purpose anyway?"

"No, I came to learn about them."

Wafri whisked around and paced back. "I will tell you anything you like." He spoke in a different tone now, his words precise. Inda sensed that his nice diction was a measure of the emotions Wafri was trying to control.

Wafri laughed again. His laughter, so gentle, was no longer humorous, it was the laughter of expectation. Of desire. "I am the only Ymaran noble not confined to my land. And I have managed to keep this palace—the very palace my forebears gave the crown as a gift."

Inda crossed his arms, the sense of impending danger stronger now.

Wafri tipped his head again. "You do not speak?"

Inda jerked up one shoulder. "What's to say?"

Wafri's hand rose, palm flat, fingers toward the sky. "There is so very much to say. 'Yes, Lord Wafri, I will help you recover your kingdom. I will be your friend.' And I did say you shall leave, did I not? Once we are rid of our mutual enemy." His color heightened. "You will not disappoint me by uttering fatuous moral platitudes—not when I have your written confession of your willingness to hire yourself as a mercenary."

"That was defense."

"And so is this plan of mine! So is this plan, don't you see it? We are a conquered kingdom! My being here, now, is a sign of my goodwill, you *must* see it."

"I might have if your men had set me free and didn't murder some poor sailor and leave him there with one of those medals. Then write lies about what I said under questioning by your mage. Goodwill would mean you and I talk on neutral ground, each free to walk away."

Wafri waved a finger back and forth. "No, no, that might

work in the ballads, but in real life?" He extended his hands toward the south wall. "In real life we woke up one day and the Venn were there on the horizon, eighty-one capital war ships full of warriors, and all their attendant craft full of mages and spies." He flushed again. "I want you as my friend. You will remember that. I want an ally—your resolve joined with my resolve. I shall settle if I must for the abject submission that results from the motivation of pain." He clapped his hands together, twisted, flexed them, then forced them apart. "My invention that way is whimsical. Do not put me to that exertion." His voice roughened.

Then he started. Slapped his pocket and pulled out a long golden tube, which he clicked open.

Inda sat up straighter, curiosity briefly subsuming his profound unease.

Wafri took out a small scroll of paper, read it, and then laughed again. "How rich! Rajnir expects me in his tower right now, to celebrate your death! Is that not rich with irony? How I love intrigue."

"That thing sends messages?" Inda asked.

Wafri's eyes widened in surprise. "Do you not have scroll-cases? They are most useful for messages, but one must answer at once if the enemy calls. You and I will discuss our plans further when I am free again. Sleep well. Is there any food you especially like? Do you need more blankets? I want you comfortable—I so wish to show you my palace, my *royal* palace. Rajnir does not know it, but I will rule from here as king. The Venn desecrated our royal city. I will never set foot in it again. All my treasures are here—and my weapons." He indicated the cell with another of those open-mouthed smiles. "Contemplate, in your leisure, what I said about friendship and will. I have a princely room waiting for you. All I need is your word you will serve as my commander and free Ymar."

When Inda did not answer, Wafri sighed and walked to the door, which was ajar. "I am summoned to Prince Rajnir," he said to those waiting outside as he took from his pocket a transfer token—Inda recognized that from his experience with Ramis.

He vanished. The door slammed shut. The bolt shot home.

Inda buried his face in his hands.

Then pulled them away.

Sulking wasn't going to free him. Being ready was—and he'd been sitting for days.

He got up and once more examined the door. It was solid. There appeared to be no peepholes.

Well, if there were, so be it.

He moved to the middle of the cell and began to work through his Odni drills for the first time in far too many days; his muscles protested, but that was good.

What was better was that the familiar movements brought Hadand's voice to mind, and his mother's, and Tdor's—for a short time, he could close his eyes and pretend he was back home in Tenthan Castle, surrounded by those he loved.

"Is anything wrong?" Whipstick Noth asked Tdor as soon as they were alone at the end of a long day of harvest duties outside Tenthen Castle.

Tdor had been standing at the foot of the stairs leading up to the family's rooms. She looked down at the candle in her hands, then glanced his way. "I received a letter from Fareas-Iofre in the royal city."

Whipstick knew that—he'd seen Chelis, the Iofre's personal Runner, arrive.

Tdor busied herself with transferring the candle to one hand and reaching the other into her robe to extract the letter from her pocket. She and Whipstick were good friends, but she never could bear to tell anyone how she counted Inda's birthdays off.

Nineteen, she thought. *Somewhere in the world, he's turning nineteen. I hope he's not alone.*

The thought made her eyes sting. Furious with herself, she drew in a sharp breath, then said, "She doesn't have much to say. She's very busy with the Queen's Guard and the training. Everything as Ndara-Harandviar had it, or as

close as she could come, she says. She sees Evred seldom,
but when she does—mostly very late at night, when they
are free of duty—he always asks her to help him translate
more of the Old Sartoran taerans. They study together."
She waved the letter. "Do you want to take it to read?"

Whipstick listened to the sound of her voice, as well as
the sense of the words. Tdor had her back turned, and he
knew her well enough by now to recognize from those
tight, stiff shoulders that she did not want to talk.

"Your summation is good enough." He added, "The
prince wants us to stage one more harvest-time defense
drill before the Riders leave. We can plan it in the morning."

"Very well," was all the answer he got, then she ran upstairs, leaving him staring up at her braid swaying against
her narrow back.

It was a day and a night later when Wafri returned.

Again the door was left slightly ajar. This time he was
wearing scarlet, with extravagant sleeves thrown back over
his shoulders and connected by a handsome gold chain.
The false sleeves revealed a tunic embroidered with gold
and scarlet, sashed with black. Beneath he wore long
straight trousers of black embroidered down the sides with
scarlet in the same pattern as that on the shirt.

Inda sat up, alert and tense. Wafri's eyes were wide, the
pupils enormous, gleaming with reflected light from the
glowglobes overhead. "It is time to decide," he said. "Either you choose freely to join me or I must persuade you."

Inda said nothing.

Wafri drew in a hissing breath. "Every king adds his
work to history, or he becomes nothing in the roll of time.
I will add our freedom. My vision is attainable, and you will
attain it. But the time is now." He smiled, head tipped
slightly, his hands out, rings of gold and ruby glittering.

"I won't be forced to anyone's will," Inda said, and once
he'd said it, his heartbeat drummed his blood through
tense limbs.

With a chiding beckon Wafri summoned men through the doorway.

There were four big ones. No pretence, then, at a fair fight. Yet Inda tried. He leaped off the bed, twisting in the air. He took out one's knee, sent another crowing for breath by a blow to the middle, and was rounding on the third when the fourth clubbed him with wood from behind.

He was not struck unconscious. Later he'd recognize the skilled precision of that blow and those that followed. Then the guards forced him to his feet, one on each arm. The other two struck their swagger-sticks to each elbow joint, and when the pain of those blows arched his back, a fist directly to his ribs folded him abruptly. The same ribs broken nine years ago, and now rebroken; he did not notice the subsequent blows to his face and gut.

Wafri called a cease. The point was lost if the victim was not aware of the proceedings.

"It's your ribs?" he asked, but Inda could not answer, just hung there in the guards' grip as blood dripped from his nose.

Wafri gestured for the men to free him, and Inda dropped so abruptly the side of his face caught on the wooden frame of the low bed, laying his cheek open as he tumbled flat on the floor.

"Put him on the bed," Wafri ordered, and in accusation, "I don't want anything broken—you know that."

"Ribs weak, my lord," was the stolid answer. "Didn't hit him hard enough."

"Go away. I am quite disturbed. I need him awake, and able to talk to me. Go away. All of you, and next time use the pain spots instead of pounding with your fists. Send Penros to me."

And so Inda woke looking up at the intent face of the mage who had questioned him as Wafri said, ". . . only his ribs. Leave his face. He will keep one scar that is mine."

Once again Inda was offered drink laced with kinthus, but this time he drank it down without hesitation, and presently the red glowing pain round his middle receded.

And, while he lay there, the mage slowly and softly intoned magic, over and over, until Inda drifted into light sleep, as, band by band, the hot wires of pain cooled and then faded. The cracked ribs were magic-bound, and then his middle bandaged. Beyond him Wafri kept vigil.

Inda woke briefly when the mage finished. Penros rose and staggered, his face drawn with exhaustion.

Wafri pressed his fingertips together. "When can I have him again? I require his full attention."

"Give him at least a day. Two would be better," the mage said hoarsely.

Inda slept.

Noren woke when a heel nudged hers in sleep. She snorted, sat up, discovered Whipstick beside her in her bed.

She grinned. Poked him.

He propped himself up on his elbows, hair in his face, eyes bleary. She picked up a lock of his hair from where it lay beside his elbow, then pulled her own braid around, idly comparing the similar shades of brown as he rubbed his eyes. But then he pulled his hair out of her hand, fumbled on the floor for his hair clasp, and fingered a horsetail up onto the back of his head.

"I must have been hot, eh?" Noren joked.

Whipstick grinned, and turned a shoulder toward her, where she saw fresh pink scratches. She chortled; they liked a tussle as part of sex. But usually Whipstick was awake and long gone before dawn.

He leaned back, crossing his arms behind his head. "I was awake a long time thinking about Tdor," he admitted. "Why is she so unhappy? We were as strong as we've ever been on the harvest drill yesterday. Stronger, with Branid still in the royal city, so he wasn't interfering with the Riders on the attack."

Noren sat up and shook out the coverlet, pausing to admire the owls in flight she'd embroidered along the edges. She'd discovered that stitch-work was relaxing at the end of a long day, and it looked so pretty when finished. While her finger traced the silken smoothness of her stitches over the owls' outstretched wings, she considered, then said, "If I tell you what I think it is, you can't say anything to her."

Whipstick curled his lip. "Name one time I've been a blathermouth."

She grinned briefly, then said, "It's Inda."

Whipstick's eyes widened in surprise. "Inda? If she received a message—"

"No. It's his Name Day. Every year she gets like that when it's the time of his Name Day. It only lasts a week or so, then it's gone. Till the next year."

Whipstick drew in a slow breath, his brow furrowed as he thought back. "You're right. I never noticed that."

"She'll be fine next week."

Whipstick played absently with the end of Noren's braid. "Maybe we should, I don't know, see that she gets some time at the pleasure house, or something to take her mind off Inda? Though why she should worry about him like that—" He stopped.

Noren said gently, "The way you go all cold and hard and distant every summer, around the time your brother died?"

The faint shadows of bitterness that had tightened in his thin face at the word "brother" smoothed, and then he smiled reluctantly. "I didn't think anyone saw that."

"Oh, Whipstick, why do you think Tdor always suggested a field run or extra liberty for you? Things to keep you busy, to gallop those days past the faster?" She snorted. "Would you like it if she said in a scolding voice, 'Whipstick, I think you should take your mood to the pleasure house'?"

"Tdor doesn't scold. But I can see what you're saying. Pity words and good advice would be worse. No, I'm mum."

"Besides, she really isn't one for the bawdy houses. Some aren't, you have to know that. She goes once in a while, but she said no matter whom she tries, it takes forever to warm up, and then afterward she just feels sad."

Whipstick shook his head, then got up and retrieved his clothes from where they'd tossed them the night before. "I never thought the Marth-Davans had one-person crazes like the Montrei-Vayirs."

Noren waved. "Tdor is Tdor. It might not be Inda so much as the fact that Tdor isn't one who can have sex without love. Right now she doesn't love anybody but her memory of Inda. Until that changes, and in the way of things it probably will—she knows that, has even said it— what can we do but leave her be? She'll be laughing again next week. You'll see. And you'll forget until next year."

Whipstick paused in the act of shaking out his shirt. "Not if the prince and princess decide we should marry. We've not that many years until we reach twenty-five."

Noren's heart constricted. *If that happens, Tdor will give up hope of Inda coming back.* Then she shook away the bleakness. "Let's get down to the baths and not borrow trouble. If you haven't any work today, I certainly do—and Tdor will be wondering why we're lolling about."

Chapter Twenty-one

PRINCE Kavnarac of Bren arrived late at the Comet's house and was ushered at once to the chair reserved for him. As always, his place was in the center of the gathering, which meant he had to rein his impatience.

He found music boring at the best of times. He could appreciate in a small way the Comet's remarkable voice—it reminded him of water in the sunlight—but he did wish that the songs wouldn't go on so long.

This time it was at least just the Comet singing, accompanied sometimes by the young fellow they called Angel—and Comet referred to as her Angelface—other times by a group of musicians in the background while Angel quietly tended to food and drink in place of a servant. Kavna noted how gracefully he managed the silver and crystal, never making a noise, never moving swiftly. He served unobtrusively, without marking any special deference to anyone whatever their rank.

A longer silence than usual after the soft knocking of knuckles on the chair arms clued him that the concert at last was over. The Comet rose from her seat, shook out her gown of rose and golden spangles, and was shortly surrounded by her admirers.

Good. Kavna rose, knowing that his bulk, if nothing else, would eventually draw Angel's eye.

When Kavna saw the scan of Angel's honey-gold eyes, he jerked his chin toward the alcove.

Angel continued at an unhurried pace around the room, taking away empty goblets, setting out plates of fresh fruit. He reached the alcove and stepped in without having drawn any attention; everyone else was gathered around Comet, voices rising and falling.

"She'll keep them busy," Angel said, sounding amused.

Kavna waited, but Angel said nothing more. This unusual fellow with the golden eyes and hair, dressed in severe black and white, did not court, defer, insinuate, or flatter.

Maybe the beautiful didn't have to, Kavna thought with grim humor. Beauty was its own aristocracy, after all.

Kavna said, "Listen. Chim has been hinting around that you're connected with Elgar the Fox."

A tiny indrawn breath was the only reaction Angel made. Then he said, "And?"

"And, well, you're probably aware of the conflict about taxes and patrol and harbor hiring and the rest of it." He barely waited for a nod. "So some of my guards have family in the sea guilds. They patrol when off duty. Volunteer. Just today one of them brought me word that there's some spy nosing about for information on Elgar the Fox. The harbor folk in turn apparently set a spy on him—they think he's a Venn."

"And?"

"And there was mention that one of our beached captains was going to kill him. They think they're doing the right thing. But if the man really is a Venn spy—and I know we have at least the one, if not more—if he disappears, how much trouble will the Venn will bring on us?"

Angel looked out at the quiet city lights below them. "And you're telling me because . . ."

"Because apparently no one wants to tell your compatriot in Fleet House about that young woman with the black brows who's training half the beached hands. They think she'll vanish if there's trouble, so they want to make the trouble go away."

"Tell me where," Angel said, and Kavna did.

They left the alcove and Angel resumed arranging dishes as if the conversation had not happened.

Comet had been watching. She trilled, "Your Highness! Come settle this wager, do!"

Kavna resumed his court manner, dealt with the laughing courtiers who wanted his attention while trying to think up something to say to get that Angel moving.

But when he managed to break away, his remonstrance ready, it was to discover that Angel was gone.

Tau was, by then, halfway down the hill.

He had learned the general layout of the city, including the fact that there were areas it was not safe to walk unless one knew where one was going.

He made only one stop, to the cousin of his friend Kerrem, who was one of the new recruits under Jeje. Kerrem had begun bringing this young cousin to the practices, where her eagerness, her longing for adventure and action, reminded Tau painfully of Nugget. She often ran messages.

The family was at supper; he asked for her, and she was at the front door in moments.

"Your justice house," Tau said. "I need to be taken there. Do you know where it is?"

Her face changed from eager to fearful.

"Prince Kavna himself sent me," Tau murmured, with a glance over her head to where her family, so far unaware, were busy passing plates, talking, laughing.

She pulled the door shut behind her.

"Thess and Palnas don't like what the captain's going to do," she whispered as they began to walk fast.

In the light of the street corner glowglobes, she was clearly terrified, glancing back many times, a quick movement that sent her brown braids smacking her skinny shoulders.

They sped down alleys and twice through yards—one stable, one wheelwright—to where the smell of brine permeated the air, the wood, the stone. No more glowglobes, not here in the ghost yards. Down a dark alley to a low house whose windows were mostly blocked so that only a chink of light escaped.

"It's here they do their justice," the girl whispered. "It's

the old sailors' rest, you know, when we're too old to ship
out—"

"I know what a sailors' rest is," Tau said.

The house, made of rotting timber, was no better at
blocking sounds than the windows coverings were the
light; the angry voices, the sounds of violence caused the
young girl to stop, her shoulders hunched. Poor little creature, Tau thought. Not like Nugget after all. Was that a
good thing?

He waited until the pang of regret eased, then said, "It's
all right. You run home. It's better if I go on alone."

She straightened her back, and said with somewhat desperate bravery, "I'll help."

Tau smiled. "No, I promise you I'll be all right. Go home.
Don't tell anyone you were here."

She hesitated, and when Tau reached for the door, she
fled, her tough bare feet smacking on the mossy stones.

Tau waited until she was out of sight, made certain his
knives were loose under his lace cuffs, and then kicked the
door open.

Everyone inside froze. A bleeding figure lay on the floor
in a circle of men, their faces startled, some angry, a couple
fearful. The biggest and oldest flushed with fury.

"Who are you?"

"I am sent by Prince Kavna, Captain Wenald," Tau said,
pitching his voice to be heard.

The name was better than a weapon.

The burly man paused in the act of drawing back a foot.
"The prince?" he repeated.

"I am to take this man into custody, by the order of the
prince."

The others exchanged uneasy glances, and when Captain
Wenald scowled, another man, after a scared look Tau's
way, whispered something that included the word "Angel."

They did not answer. Captain Wenald had spent eight terrible years chained to a pirate galley with the tacit permission
of their Venn allies. He burned for justice—but not at the
cost of the prince's ire. Everyone knew that Prince Kavna,
unlike the king and the princess, was the sailors' friend.

And so he motioned his men out, and he started to follow, then stopped on the threshold the light from the single lamp cutting across his heavy face. He glowered at Tau. "If we ever see him nosing around again, we won't stop."

"I understand," Tau said. "Thank you."

Wenald slammed the slat door in answer; from beyond it the sounds of departure dwindled.

The man was fair-haired, dressed like the locals. He lay, breathing with difficulty, his hands over his face, which was swelling into distortion.

Tau winced. Every sign of a broken jaw.

He bent and whispered, "Lie quiet. They will not be back. I will, with help."

And so poor Vedrid lay, wondering if he'd dreamed that soft, kindly voice.

His life had gone from bad to worse after spending days slinking around these filthy streets, avoided by most and distrusted by the few who did take notice of him. His story about a cousin named Elgar had not convinced anyone, but he hadn't known how to lie any better. A year ago, the Fleet House had readily given out information, but now, for no reason he could discover, the words "Elgar" or "Fox" caused everyone to clam up tight.

He'd been about to give up. Only the thought of Evred-Harvaldar's disappointment had kept him trying another day, and another, until he'd been set upon without warning this very evening, and dragged here, while these madmen screamed at him for being a Venn spy. They hadn't listened to him—just knocked him down and started kicking him while shouting "Spy! Spy! Venn shit of a spy!"

Now he was aware only of an endless sea of red pain, drowning him in waves. He was moved, which caused lightning flashes of new pain in his broken feet, in his jaw; for a brief time he sank into the cool darkness. When he woke, he gazed up blearily at a fair face lit by a candle.

"Drink," the voice said in a soothing tone.

He did not question. When a strong hand lifted his head, he tried to get his broken jaw to move, and almost passed out again. Patiently, a drop at a time, the man—had they really called him an angel?—got warm liquid into him, and the pain gradually began to recede.

He slept, half aware of the whisper of magic. Tau had brought the prince's own healer, who used magic to bind the broken bones and to give what ease he could.

Vedrid woke again in time to hear, "He must rest. Magic only holds together the broken bones. Time and nature reknits them."

"I will see to it."

Vedrid might have slept again; when he woke, the fresh scent of steeped listerblossom leaves was in the air, with a tinge of the bitterness of green kinthus.

Angel held a cup to Vedrid's lips. This time he could swallow without killing pain. An agreeable lassitude stole over him, and Angel set aside the cup and smiled. He asked questions in a couple of languages, but Vedrid shook his head minutely. Then he said in Bren, "Who are you?"

"Vedrid."

Angel's brows rose. This time he spoke in perfect Iascan, "Vedrid is not a Venn name."

"No . . . Iasca Leror." It hurt to speak, but he wanted to cooperate with this lifesaving Angel.

"Ah. What are you doing here?"

"I'm . . . Runner. King. Order. Find. Elgar. Fox. Or news." Pain through his skull made him break out in sweat.

Angel looked up, then back. "He is very far from here. It might be best if you were to return to your king, and tell him that Elgar the Fox is out on the sea far away, and will never return."

"Yes," Vedrid sighed, and there was no mistaking his relief.

The kind voice went on. "You are here with some people who will care for you, but you must promise not to leave until you feel strong enough to go straight from here to the border, and then back again across the mountains. And do not return. They believe you to be a Venn spy."

Vedrid was too weak to nod. He sighed again.

Warm fingers touched his. "Remember. You will find money waiting for your journey. But do not pause, or speak to anyone. Just go. Tell your king that Elgar the Fox will never return to the west."

Chapter Twenty-two

FOX lay on the Beila Lana garrison roof staring up at the Venn flag, a black shape against the starry sky. He'd climbed up before dawn, darkness being the only time he could reach this vantage unseen.

It was the perfect hiding place once he was in position. All he had to do was wait for his target to get off duty at the midmorning watch change. The man would come through the narrow passage directly below to enter his room, where Fox could land on him without being seen by the sentries on the walls behind and above. Or—he hoped—heard by the man's roommate asleep in the small chamber beyond the door at the end of the passage.

After careful listening and a few questions to under-servants and messengers, he'd discovered that this was the man who'd killed Elgar the Fox.

So he'd be the first to die.

But that meant a long, wearying morning lying flat on old stone, peering down at the passage between a slanting roof and a rain gutter at the occasional sounds of footsteps. He was sheltered from the tower sentry walk above by another slanting roof. The garrison was picturesque, with its jutting towers and many levels and uneven rooftops, but as an unbreachable military establishment it was a disaster. Fox figured the Ymarans knew nothing about clear fields of view, at least judging by this part of the garrison, where the low-rankers were housed. There were some Venn guards—far more effective judging by their stations—they seemed to be restricted to the garrison prison and the officers' headquarters.

Promptly at the dawn bell, the day-watch emerged from their rooms, leaving the passage and the tiny court empty. Fox lay back again and watched the light come up, first outlining the flagpole with thin color. Slowly the strengthening light warmed the banner from gray tones to green and white and blue and gold: the figure on it appeared to be a flame, but was actually a great tree, highly stylized.

The banner waved and snapped in the rising wind. Fox wondered who had decided on that pattern of interlaced roots that resembled a crown, and how long ago. The Venn had supposedly been sea folk who'd sailed a fleet of longships through a world gate millennia ago—so why did they choose a tree? It seemed to have something to do with the concept of Ydrasal, which his mother had never been able to explain satisfactorily. It wasn't honor, nor was it the imperative to sail out and conquer for the greatness of the Venn, but appeared to fall somewhere between, with an emphasis—that his mother had been quite sarcastic about—on clear sight, honesty, and above all choosing the greater good over risk to oneself.

As with all fundamentals, the Venn knew what it meant so well no one had ever defined it, at least in any of the written materials possessed by the Montredavan-Ans. One had to divine it by inference and examples given.

Ah well. Fox turned his head to study the little court and the old buildings, which had been haphazardly amended over the centuries. He figured that this area had once been a castle brewery.

The midmorning watch bell rang at last. Fox knew his officer had switched to the midnight watch. He should be along soon—

Steps.

He rolled, face pressed between the roof tile and rain gutter.

To his surprise an old, frosty-haired mage in a white robe

had entered the tiny court, but instead of moving on, he stood right there. A mage! *Move along, old man.*

But the old man stood in the precise spot under Fox.

Fox cursed under his breath. It had taken days to track down the officer, learn his schedule, and map the garrison, all while remaining undiscovered.

Days! And now—

Approaching footsteps. The old man stilled. The officer appeared an arm's length below—and when he saw the old mage he stopped so quickly he rocked back on his heels. His face blanched.

"Mage—Dag Ulaffa?"

"I have only a question," the old man said in rather stiff Sartoran. "I do not intend a long interruption."

"I gave my report to Mage Penros," the officer said defensively.

Dag Ulaffa raised a hand. "Peace! I know. Our commanders are satisfied. But we did lose a man, whose family is grieved. I merely came by to ask, in all charity, if the young man wounded in your own guard is recovered." And as the officer's mouth rounded, Ulaffa added, "The young guard taken away somewhere, badly wounded? We had hopes he is recovered."

The officer's face had gone so pale Fox's anger vanished, leaving curiosity.

The officer flicked a fearful look to either side, moistened his lips, then said, "Please put all questions to our mage. Or the count himself. I know nothing."

"So your wounded guard was taken all the way to Wafri's palace? He does not seem to be here. That is well— I know that the count's Mage Penros is an accomplished healer," Ulaffa said soothingly. "I shall report, then, that all is well with his recovery?"

"Yes. All is well. And if there are any other questions, you must address them to the count."

Dag Ulaffa placed his hands together. The officer walked into the passage directly below Fox, who got a close view of beaded sweat at his hairline before he passed by, opened the door to his quarters, and closed it.

Ulaffa walked away; Fox never saw his face, only the untidy white hair.

Wounded officer?

"Do your Marlovans have those accursed skalts?" Wafri asked. "The first thing I will do when I take my country back is kill all those shit-brained Venn yammerers with their thousand-verse tales of who smote whom."

Inda shut his eyes. He couldn't move, much less prevent Wafri from sitting at his bedside. As long as the damned soul-sucker didn't touch his face or his hair again. That was the worst of it. The beatings were bad enough, but far worse was the stroking and petting afterward—that, and the hand feeding.

Inda had learned if he talked, then Wafri talked. If he didn't, he got petted like a sick child.

"Skalt?" he said, his jaw flaring with agony where the guards had rapped their sticks. Who knew there were places in your jaw that, when touched, went sun-bright with pain? The effort to speak made him sweat.

Wafri's dark brown gaze searched his face. "Shall I call Penros?" His brow furrowed in sadness. "Indevan. Why do you insist on prolonging what is so unpleasant? Never mind, I did promise not to ask anymore. I don't want to make you any more stubborn. I want you to think about the good things waiting for you. A bath filled with fresh herbs, and an experienced woman to tend you. Or do you prefer men? You shall have whichever you wish—both, if you like. Whatever you prefer to eat. Silken sheets—the room is ready for you now. It is dusted fresh every day."

Inda saw him lift his hand, and tensed all over. "Skalt?"

Wafri had seen how Inda hated to have his brow stroked. He struggled between the desire to touch his cherished commander and to comply with his promises. You show that you are in complete control, but then compromise a little, to give a taste of what can be won by obedience. "The Venn have these people much like heralds whose entire purpose in life seems to be to recite verses of the dullest historical poems. All the same rhythm, de-DAH-da, de-DAH-da, de-DAH-da." He tapped out a galloping rhythm on his silk-covered knee. "I assure you they are thousands of verses long, or seem to be when one has heard, for the hundredth time, of Falki Ax-Hand smiting yet another host of faceless enemies. And the strangest thing is, half of these fools know *all* those verses. I've seen Hyarl Durasnir, the Fleet Commander, who is far from being a stupid or dull man, whispering along with the sea tales."

He paused and smiled. Inda forced himself to say, "Sea tales?"

"Ah, those are far worse than the land battle ones. It takes a few hundred verses merely to name all their ships—and the history of each—before they even get to whom they smote. Did you know all their ships are named after seabirds? Birds and trees! What could possibly be more incongruous than these overgrown, vinegar-eating Venn and their birds and trees? Yet the Venn cannot hold the least celebration without skalts droning on and on. Much more pleasing are the hel dancers, I assure you—though they shroud themselves up so much you can scarcely tell if it's a man or woman inside those robes."

Inda gathered his strength. Wafri had the water carafe beside him, but Inda knew how much pleasure he got out of pouring it for him, even helping him to drink it. So Inda always waited until he was gone.

"Do you need a drink?" Wafri asked.

"No. Hel dancers?"

"Oh, that's the one bearable part of their endless ritual. They do everything in nines, did you know that? Yes, for someone told me you also group your warriors in nines. I cannot imagine why. You shall demonstrate for me, one day. Anyway, these dancers, men and women, are chosen very young, and they train for eighteen years. But only nine of a hundred are taken at the end of their eighteen years, can you imagine? What happens to those who train seventeen years and then are passed by? I should think they slit their own throats." Wafri chuckled. "But those who do become dancers, they are amazing to watch. The Venn hold their formal celebrations in what they call a Venn Hel—a vast hall, always with their tree banner—and there the skalts and the hel dancers perform. Nowhere else. At least, sometimes, I'm told, the skalts sing at private celebrations, but I broke Rajnir of that habit, and Durasnir and Erkric have never invited me."

He paused, smiling down at Inda, who forced his eyes open, forced his lips apart. "Dancers?"

"There's very little music. Sometimes nothing but a tapping drum. Yet when you watch them, you'd think there is a full set of strings and winds, and a herald-poet as well. They dance the tales the skalts drone so tediously. But when the dancers do them, well, you can see what the Venn consider their past glory. Perhaps, after we defeat the others, we can keep some of their dancers so I can show you. I already promised Erkric's papers to Penros. Why not keep some of their artists, even if we do not want their art?" He leaned close. "Bring the day for me, Indevan. Bring me that day."

Inda closed his eyes, trying not to stiffen, to alter his breathing. But hatred was so strong, his bones and blood rang like heated metal under the hammer. The shift of Wafri's rich fabrics, his breathing—which could become so passionate when the pain was the worst—the scent he wore, which was a subtle combination of pepper-tree leaves and orange blossom, these things had begun to invade Inda's dreams, turning mental escape to horror.

Fingers caressed his brow, the lightest touch. Inda flinched. Revulsion, hatred, irritation with himself for letting time pass. For revealing his reaction.

Wafri chuckled softly as Inda's cool, faintly damp flesh twitched under his hand. "Shall I tell you the truth?" he said, his tone intimate and tender. Inda's lashes lay on his cheek, only the tiniest quiver betraying his effort to control himself. A sweet flutter of elation caused Wafri to laugh again. "In truth I love this battle of wills. I am entranced enough to almost wish to prolong it, except I am not entirely free. There is the matter of my own masters, specifically one of those accursed dags questioning one of my men." His voice was now plaintive. "It could have been a gesture of consolation, but then, only this morning, one of Rajnir's Yaga Krona—in fact, not just any dag, but Ulaffa, second only to Erkric himself—asked one of my men how the wounded guard was recovering. Why this interest in a nameless guard?"

Inda said nothing. At first he had answered questions, though he knew he was trying to temporize, to postpone the beatings. That had made perfect sense. You did what you could to survive.

Until the night Wafri was rising from the cushioned chair his servants always placed beside Inda's bed, then took away again. As he got to his feet, Wafri said, "My single sea battle was so distant. Next time, tell me more about what it's like to be in land battle." And the next time he came, as soon as Wafri laced his fingers around his knees, rocking back and forth on his chair, Inda had begun with a long description he'd thought out earlier, which had pleased Wafri enormously. There had been only the briefest beating that night, after Wafri asked his usual question: "Will you be my war leader now?"

The following day Inda discovered himself thinking ahead to prolong Wafri's interest; how, in fact, he'd thought all day about how to please him.

So he'd shut up. Questions, he permitted himself. But no part of his own life: no memories, or plans, or feelings. Questions only, to get information, not to give it. Wafri held the reins controlling his body, but he would get no halter on his mind.

Wafri sighed, recalling Inda's attention to the present. "What I do know is that I cannot bear to lose you to Rajnir's grabby hands."

Inda said, pain flaring through his jaw, "So kill me."

Wafri grinned, then fingered a lock of Inda's hair. He'd had Penros dunk Inda's hair into an ensorcelled bucket earlier that day, as the smell of old blood, sweat, and the mold from the garrison prison had begun to offend him.

He did not know that Inda had felt far more degraded having his hair combed out than he had lying there in his own stink.

Inda's eyes snapped shut again, and Wafri laughed,

thrilled at the flinches that his prisoner fought so hard to hide.

"Never," he said, tasting the word. "No, I amend that. You are far too valuable alive, but if I think they will find you, I'd be forced to do it because I cannot bear for you to fall into their hands." He sighed. "Your hair is so coarse, probably from so many years of sun and sea. Would you like it cut? I assure you, short hair is the very latest fashion in Colend."

Inda said nothing. From the evenness of his breathing, Wafri suspected he did not care what happened to his hair. Few men did, he'd discovered. Not true with most women.

"I want you to remember that my admiration for you has never faltered, though you have often made me angry. But that is at the waste of precious time. We could have accomplished so much by now."

Inda did not answer.

Wafri gave Inda's hair a gentle tug, then let it go. "If anything," he whispered in that ardent, intimate voice, leaning forward, his entire concentration on Inda's face, his breath smelling of sweet wine, "your resistance enhances the prospective gratification of your consent." He leaned back, and spoke to be heard, with laughter roughening the edges of his words. "But you must talk again. I think next time we will use the kinthus. I discover in me a desire to know everything about your life, every detail. Everything you think. Your mind will close no door to me; perhaps your will may follow the sooner."

Then came the sound Inda had longed for: Wafri got to his feet. But Inda had learned not to relax or betray any reaction beyond what he couldn't help.

And his reward was the quick wisp of Wafri's slippers as he crossed to the door. "Penros! Good. I want you to do a general healing. I don't like how little response I'm getting."

Penros spoke in that detached voice of academic inquiry. "It's hard to do much about nerve centers when your men hit them so hard."

Wafri uttered his soft laugh. "Is that an oblique remonstrance for coming here too often? But you must know how time is against us."

Penros said, "I, too, am losing strength."

Wafri sighed. "I know the cost, my loyal mage, I know. Do your best now, and then I command you to drink a sleep-herb. Sleep through the night, and tomorrow as well. Tonight I must go to Rajnir; tomorrow I will have my time with Prince Indevan, but it will only be kinthus, and that I can manage with the help of the men. I wish for him to share his past with me, his most cherished moments, his dreams. Such conversations we will have! Do your best, and then to your well-earned slumber."

He left. Inda heard the quick steps recede despite the closer clutter of noises: the chair being taken away, the approach of the mage. He did not relax until that familiar *wisp-wisp* had receded out of hearing.

The mage's murmured spells sounded like Old Sartoran but the cadences and speed muffled distinct words. Inda had given up trying to pick out magic words; like those old taerans Tdor and Joret used to read, there was a context that was impossible to guess at by a few words here and there. That and the gestures. Often Inda's sight was too blurred to make them out. Now he listened to the gentle flow of words, the occasional rustle of cloth as the mage made his ritual gestures, and treasured his very small triumph.

He and Wafri had become a distortion of new lovers: each unfamiliar with the other's ways but watching hungrily to learn. Wafri because he wished to, and Inda because he had to.

Wafri had gotten very good at intuiting most of the motivations and reactions Inda strove to hide. But he had made one mistake, probably the most important one: he thought Inda's strength in resisting was a result of the healing sessions, and so he withheld them as long as he could.

He was wrong. Pain made Inda more angry, and anger gave him strength. It wasn't physical strength, but it was a strength that might, in the end, make it possible for him to choose the moment of his own death.

*   *   *

Tau sensed he was being followed.

He never ignored instinct, so even though he'd taken painstaking precautions, he took more. He loitered along passages that had reflecting surfaces, seeing nothing. He risked angering or missing his royal patron by being late, and doubled back via roof and drainpipe. Once he entered a house by using an open window, tiptoeing down a hallway past the oblivious family inside, and exited the front door as if he lived there.

He saw nothing, so he continued on, using the short route to Prince Kavna's appointed rendezvous at the back house beyond the Drapers Guild building. He sensed a shadow, so he opened the tall gate and passed silently through the quiet garden, watching and listening.

The only sounds were the rustling patter of raindrops on the flowers and leaves and the musical plink of drops in the wide, shallow fountain that magically stopped when rainwater fell into its pool.

The air was cool; for the first time in months the sense of impending winter could be smelled in the air, felt in the chill on wet skin.

Tau stopped in the shadow of a drooping fern and descried nothing untoward, so he ducked under the branch and rapped twice on the low door to the garden house.

The door opened a crack, then wider.

Tau slipped inside the room, which smelled of the mold and damp of neglect. Someone had made a brave attempt to make the room more habitable: nuts roasted on the hearth, wine freshly mulled with tart spices, and a twig of herb lay on the Fire Stick to spread a fresher scent through the warming air.

Kavna was alone, a stout young man dressed in well-made but unobtrusive clothing in a style favored by merchants. He had been reading while seated in one of two overstuffed chairs that seemed to represent fashions at either end of a century; between the chairs sat a sturdy table. The stone flooring had been covered with a worn carpet of dark blue with stars.

"The final word," Kavna said wryly as he set aside his letters, "seems to be that Ramis of the *Knife* does not exist.

My sister is tired of the subject, and has made that as close to a Royal Decree as she can without risking ridicule."

Tau had discovered that the prince was far more subtle than he seemed. "Unacceptable," he said as he approached the fire and stretched his hands out to its welcome warmth. "I saw him. More important, I saw what he did."

"My sister will have everyone know that if she has not seen such things as holes ripped in the universe, they are dreams and delusions for the simple. Unfortunately, I cannot, try as I have, and pay what I probably wasted far too much on, prove different: his land of origin seems to be at least twenty places, and everything else about him is mere rumor—"

The door slammed open. Tau had his knives out—Kavna stared, tensing as in walked the Comet, bedraggled and angry as a wet cat.

"Is *this* what you're doing?" she demanded, dismissing the prince with one imperious flick of her hand.

"This?" Tau retorted, mimicking her gesture. "How many reprehensible scenarios do you imagine that word includes?"

"None of which are true," the prince said, inviting her with a gesture to the other armchair. "Sit down, please, Mistress Arrad."

The Comet plunked down. She frowned, her outrage—which had been mostly theatrical—giving way to curiosity, though the real hurt remained.

The prince tipped his head, giving Tau a wry glance that invited him to speak.

"It's politics, not sex," Tau said.

As usual, he had uncovered what she wanted hidden. And that meant he knew of her jealousy, which she had worked hard to hide.

So she rose, tripped to the other side of the fire, and as Tau withdrew to stand behind the armchair she'd vacated, she held out her dainty shoes to the flames.

When no one spoke she sent a practiced glance back over her shoulder through dripping curls. "You could have said something. You know I am discreet."

"The matter we meet here to discuss is not mine to share," Tau returned.

"Nor is it mine," the prince added, unexpectedly. "It transcends us both."

The prince's civility almost ushered her into guilt, but she caught the edges of the metaphorical door and turned to stand at bay. "How many are in on this secret that isn't yours?"

Tau and the prince were both practiced at masking emotions, yet no one can completely rein instinct, and when they sent an interrogative glance toward one another, brief as it was, she crossed her arms. "Shall I step outside again so you can get your story straight?"

Tau flushed. "That's not ours to tell either," he said. "In fact, neither of us know."

"Either you trust me, or you don't. Tell me who is at the top of this supposed ladder of scheme and intrigue."

The prince tented his fingers, sending Tau a look that signaled, *It is yours to answer if you wish.*

Tau said, "Elgar the Fox."

Her eyes widened with disbelief, then narrowed. "Did that come to you as the most unlikely name, or the most impossible?"

Tau lifted his palms. "Believe what you will. And now that you know, to spare you the necessity of dictating terms for your silence, I will withdraw from your life, your service, your house. And the kingdom."

"Oh, no, you don't," she retorted. "Don't you dare. They come to hear me sing and to look at you. If you were another woman I'd hate you for that, but you aren't, and anyway they still come to me."

"Which is the most important thing," the prince observed, his fingers still tented.

"What does that mean?" she demanded, pushing the delicate fabric of her sleeve up past her wrists so she could extend her hands to the fire. Her gown was dark, and far more simple than anything she usually wore, which was a signal to the others that she had planned her campaign well.

They had not been clever, they had been clumsy.

The prince said a little more heatedly than he had intended, "That the welfare of the kingdom is of far less importance to you than its gifts."

The Comet shook out her pale blond hair, the droplets glowing before they hissed in the fire. "How tediously sententious that sounds!" She lifted her rounded shoulders, then added with faint humor, "But then I never do tell anyone what I really want, do I?"

Tau caught the change in her mood, and came forward, bending to take her hand. He kissed it smackingly.

"Eugh." She gave an extravagant shiver. "Your lips are cold. Spare me your frog kisses."

"How did you follow me?" he asked.

She considered them. They were really listening now; further, they were seeing *her,* and not what they expected to see. She'd made her point, and without either of them being drearily obvious.

"In pieces," she said. "You lost me a couple of times, but each time I marked where, and next time you left dressed like that—" She pointed to Tau's ordinary sailor clothes, the cap that covered most of his hair. "—I'd race ahead to where I left you last, in hopes you'd pass me by and lead on. Your twistiest evasions were always at the beginning."

The prince raised his brows, and Tau flushed, laughing.

"It took only three attempts to follow you," she finished. And, less triumphantly, "I was trained. But I left my home and that life. And no, I'll never talk about it. My voice gave me a new life, one I built with care."

Tau grinned.

She grinned back. "If it had been something honest, like your mother's pleasure house, yes I would have told you. But it wasn't." She sighed. "I know plenty about politics. I don't really understand the motivations behind risk for an ideal—I'm used to risk for gain. But though I cannot be loyal to a place, or an idea, I am to people. And I do communicate with prominent performers all over the continent, who have their own ways of hearing things."

Tau turned to the prince, hand open, a gesture the prince successfully interpreted as Tau's tacit acceptance of the Comet's implied offer. But the decision was his. Elgar the Fox's needs could be pursued anywhere; the kingdom's welfare was the prince's affair.

He hesitated only a moment. It had taken a long time to

discover her real name—Denja Arrad—back when he was first taken with her. Now he suspected that the name was as false as her initial interest in him had been. But despite it all, he liked her, admired her.

Could he trust her?

Taumad seemed to think so. And he had learned to trust some far more surprising characters.

"All right, then," he said. And with an attempt at humor, "At least we won't have to sit here breathing mold anymore."

Chapter Twenty-three

EVER since his return from the unsuccessful search, Fleet Commander Hyarl Durasnir had been rising before dawn—but not for his meditation watch, during which he had long been accustomed to working through the old weapons patterns as he let his mind range free. He was too busy for that luxury now.

The result was a sense of day-long physical as well as mental cramming. There was no help for it. The stream of reports and decisions that had been abandoned for the harbor search had dammed up, clogging the course of business, trade, cruises—everything. While Rajnir brooded at his window, encouraged by Dag Erkric to design a series of entertainments to lift morale, the labor of governmental log-jam clearance fell to Durasnir.

Despite the complexity of demands, delegated tasks, interviews, and reports, Durasnir found his thoughts returning to the private interview that old Dag Ulaffa had requested the day of his return.

The sea dags seldom interfered with land matters; the Yaga Krona were even more removed, involving themselves in daily affairs only when a matter concerned the welfare of the prince. Sometimes such "matters" led to jurisdictional bickering. The army and navy were customarily united in only two things: their oaths to the king, and their resentment of the powers granted the Erama Krona and Yaga Krona, whose chain of command ran parallel to everyone else's.

There were a few who never raised petty conflicts. Dag Valda, Chief of the Sea Dags, was one. The other was old Ulaffa, senior Yaga Krona under Erkric. Ulaffa spoke as Yaga rarely, but when he did, Durasnir always listened.

Ulaffa had come to him because Erkric was elsewhere; even Valda, he knew, had been summoned home to Venn. Ulaffa was therefore the ranking dag in the south, and Durasnir the ranking warrior.

So Durasnir had heard Ulaffa out. The problem was Durasnir did not take young Wafri seriously. There had to be a reason no one among the Venn knew the wounded guard who had been whisked away to Limros Palace. Patrol schedules were changed often, whether on land or at sea. It was not just humane but good policy to avoid anyone being stuck on night duty for months on end. The Ymaran guards had a different schedule rotation than the Venn and no one had paid much attention hitherto. The Venn guards looked down on the Ymarans. Said they had at best rudimentary military training, they were weak, soft, frequently drunk on duty, worthless for much beyond standing around wearing their lord's livery. But Prince Rajnir wished the Venn and the Ymarans of Beila Lana to work side by side, so they did—without much mixing.

It wasn't until late one night, as he lay awake beside his sleeping wife and took the time to think the matter through, that he finally identified what had bothered him.

The problem of the wounded warrior was not isolated.

First, there was the question of how Elgar the Fox could have attacked someone when under the influence of white kinthus. It was an accepted function of the herb for people to behave as if their limbs had been unstrung; most, in fact, couldn't walk at all until it wore off.

Second was his own private doubt. How could someone as preternaturally competent—if not to say longsighted—as Ramis of the *Knife* waste a commander on a mission that should have been given to those trained in covert and solitary action? There was absolutely nothing in Elgar the Fox's confession that indicated he had been

trained as a spy or assassin. It would have been far more
believable that Ramis would perform such an assassination himself.

That didn't even touch the question of motivation. How
would Ramis benefit if Prince Rajnir were assassinated?
Assassination would succeed only in turning the king's
eyes away from the northern problems to the south. And
that would result in him sending a force to descend in puni-
tive fury. Rajnir's plans were his own—that was understood in the Land of the Venn, while the Great Houses
were still stalemated over the choice of another heir—but
the goal of settlement and regulation of trade under the
aegis of the Venn was the king's will.

What he was fairly certain of was that the anomalies in
this situation, for once, did not have Erkric's guiding hand
behind them. Dag Erkric had been as surprised as, and perhaps more angry than Rajnir, which suggested he had in
fact wanted the Marlovan alive for his own purposes.

Now, lying awake on the first cold harvest night of the
year and gazing through the window at the icy sliver of
moon, he mentally reviewed Ulaffa's report on his interview with the Ymaran officer who had written out Indevan
Algara-Vayir's confession.

He was either angry or fearful, Ulaffa had said. *He did
not want to talk with me. So I approached him again, this
time with Dag Signi to witness, and she said he was mortally
afraid.*

Ulaffa, appointed by the king. And Signi, who had been
a hel dancer-in-training long enough to see revealed in
muscle movement what others tried to hide by artificial
stances, tones of voice. When Signi or Ulaffa spoke, Durasnir listened.

So, it was time to lay aside his work yet again, though he
loathed the prospect of more time lost, and the consequent
complications, delays, and tempers. He had better investigate this matter tomorrow.

He turned over and went to sleep.

* * *

One of the many evidences of Wafri's respect for Inda's putative abilities was the fact that he was never permitted to sleep in darkness. There were glowglobes installed high on the vaulted ceiling which never winked out.

So Inda did not know how long he had been imprisoned; he would waken and that narrow window high up would show blue or black, or the gray of cloud, rarely in succession. Sometimes golden light slanted in, stronger than the cool white of glowglobes, when the sun was right. There was no counting days when you fell asleep in dark and wakened in dark, or fell asleep in daylight and woke again in the same.

For a time he'd watched the window until he found that it made him too angry that it was beyond reach. Early on, when movement was still easy, he'd even wrestled the wooden bed frame up against the wall. He clambered up, despite how dangerously it wobbled, to discover that the edge of the window was still beyond an arm's length in reach.

So then he refused to look at it. He did not want to know if he could fit through it. He had no interest in night or day. What he watched was the door. He waited for a single slip on Wafri's part, such as a visit without a host of guards beyond the door.

That never happened.

What did happen was a sudden wakening under weak blue moonlight. Only this time Inda did not gasp, finding himself trembling on the bed in a sweat, his mind gripped in a nightmarish reliving of one of Wafri's visits.

Instead he sensed someone with him. It was that same strange sensation that he'd only felt in battle before. It was extraordinarily clear and sharp, like a poke inside his skull; despite the glass shards of pain in every joint when he moved, he sat up, looking carefully around the bright cell.

Empty.

He lay back gratefully, as always facing the door . . . and again that insistent mental poke.

But there was no raised sword behind him, no arrow whiffling through the air. There was nothing behind him except the wall.

So he looked directly up—and painful prickles ran from his neck down his arms when he saw, dangling from the window, a long rope.

He blinked. Rubbed his eyes. Opened them. The rope remained. One glance at the cell door. Shut. Locked.

Inda rolled over cautiously. At least he *could* move, after the last session with the healer. He climbed slowly up on the bed, trembly as an old man. Stretched up a hand—and his fingers closed around scratchy, twisted hemp.

Suspicion. Was this rope one of Wafri's tortures in a new form?

He didn't care. He'd go up that rope no matter what was at the other end.

The rope jerked twice in his hand. He lifted his other hand, gripped the rope, then lifted his feet.

It held firm.

So he began to climb, at first rapidly, but very soon he slowed, his hands slick with sweat, muscles trembling. He slipped, the hemp burning until he clutched with a death-grip that halted his descent. He swung slightly, then thumped against the stone wall.

The weakness made him angry enough for a short burst of strength, and though he weakened again very swiftly, at least he made it to the window, where two strong hands reached through to grasp his wrists.

He stuck a leg through and turned sideways. Then came the worst part, a pull through the narrow window. But Inda was so thin he squeezed through, though the stone scraped his ears and his chest.

And he was free. He collapsed onto flat stone, struggling for breath. He was too exhausted to speak, and too dizzy to open his eyes.

"How bad is it?"

Fox?

Holding out a flagon.

Inda forced himself to his elbows, caught his hair under them and collapsed again. Fox helped him lift his head and held the flagon to his lips; Inda sipped the bitter concoction, choked, then recognized listerblossom and willow among the flavors. Pain ease. He drank it down without stopping, then dropped flat again, eyes open. The blue-white crescent of moon revolved gently opposite Fox's bony face. "What?" Inda whispered. "No 'I told you so'?"

Even in the moonlight Inda looked terrible. "If you haven't done enough of that on your own, then you won't listen to any words of mine." Fox sat back on his heels. "Can you move?"

Inda gritted his teeth. "If it kills me." He sat up and clumsily began to braid his hair, but he winced and his hands dropped.

Fox took over, his touch impersonal. Inda dropped his head gratefully as Fox whipped his hair into a tight sailor's queue, wondering what kind of torturer made someone look as bad as Inda did, then had his hair washed? The idea made him queasy.

"I don't know how long this respite will last. What I'd like to do in departure," Fox said, "is indicate our royal displeasure. What do you say?"

Inda breathed in slowly. The dizziness was gone, leaving an almost hysterical euphoria. Fox! Here! How? Inda tried to frame a question, felt his emotions tumble, and shook his head.

Fox said lightly, "Inda, we are probably the most wanted two fighting men in this half of the world. I feel we owe it to the Sartoran continent to live up—no, really, to surpass—our reputations. After all, we do not want to risk becoming stale."

"I don't understand," Inda said.

Fox hung the flagon on his sash. The moonlight painted the bruises around Inda's jaw black. His visible joints—knuckles, wrists, ankles—were equally black and puffy. Suspecting it must be worse under Inda's clothing, Fox kept up the light words. A semblance of normality. "While you were loafing about down there, I was busy enough for the both of us. Wafri had a second perimeter on guard just for you when he was down in your cell. So last time he had all his boys at this end of the palace, I was busy laying down some gifts in thanks for his hospitality. And, a while ago, when the extra guard was dismissed to their hard-earned slumbers, I put in my finishing touches and climbed up to invite you out in hopes you'd like to join me in expressing our appreciation of the Ymaran style of entertainment."

Inda had become sensitive to voices in a way he never had been before. He heard the rage Fox tried to hide under the teasing, how it sharpened the consonants of the words he meant to speak so lightly. Inda forced himself to look up. Saw—lit in the cold moonlight—unguarded worry in Fox's bony face.

"I don't understand," Inda said again, almost inaudibly.

Time to move. Past time to move.

Fox abandoned the manner. "We need to cause a diversion so they won't chase us." He peered in all directions as Inda loosely turned his thumb up. "I figured we'd wreck this place. I've laid straw and oil in nooks and rafters and old stairways all over. Want to help?"

"Yes."

Intensely relieved, Fox said, "Think you can keep pace, or would you rather anchor somewhere while I take care of things here?"

Inda said, "I'll do. I feel better already."

Fox hunkered down so he could look into Inda's face. The distant ruddy glow of torches made his own expression clearer to Inda. For once Fox did not deflect with irony, or derision, or disbelief. He was serious and intent. "I don't think you are."

"I want to rip him apart," Inda said, and when he heard the tremble in his own voice, flushed with heat. He gritted his teeth and concentrated on his breathing until he trusted his internal hold, then said, "Will that turn me into him?"

"No." Fox's voice was husky. Inda's question spurted snowmelt through his veins. "Moral questions aside, he's not here. That's why I am. He's in Jaro, attending on Prince Rajnir, and most of his staff is asleep. There are half a dozen night guards, all right below here, outside your cell. There are a couple others down at the other end, but they're either asleep, or drinking and gambling. Typical civilian idea of security. So let's give them enough trouble to make them earn their pay."

Inda painstakingly got to his feet as Fox looped the rope and slung it over one shoulder baldric-style. They were on the edge of a roof. Below lay a sloping hillside, and far below that the lights of Beila Lana twinkled in a sharp horseshoe curve, the intersecting squares of golden lights in the middle shaping the garrison.

To Inda's left the jumble of slanting roofs indicated a long palace built around various courts and gardens. There were no guards on the rooftop. On his right was a newly-built wall, the stone pale gray. They were at the extreme end of the palace, then—in Wafri's playground.

Inda said, "Shouldn't we stay quiet?"

Fox led the way across the roof to a lower level. He put out a hand, and Inda stopped. "If you vanish," Fox said, reaching under a wide rain gutter, "Wafri will not only marshal every pair of eyes he can command to search for you, he will also lie to the Venn about the nature of the search. Because they do not know he has you. Had you. Ah, I see you are not surprised."

Inda flexed his hands. "No. He was proud of it."

Fox's teeth showed in his nastiest grin. "I really think the Venn ought to know what their boy is up to, don't you?"

Inda huffed, almost but not quite a laugh.

Fox pulled out something long and bulky, handed Inda a composite bow, a quiver of arrows, and a couple of knives in sheaths. He helped Inda get the sheaths on his wrists. Then picked up his own weapons.

"Ready?"

Inda found movement difficult—the pain in his joints kept flaring, prickling, then going coldly numb—but he told himself it was not impossible. The only impossible thing was another day, another watch, spent as Wafri's prisoner.

He was free. And he was going to stay that way, or die. Easy, when you thought about it that way. Move or die. Walk or die. Shoot or die. "Ready."

In the locked and guarded private suite of the royal residence, the pleasure dancers frolicked around the two young men who comprised their audience, poses enticing and artful, delectable perfumes drifting on the air, hips making slow and provocative circles as the chimes on their low-slung belts rang pleasant chords. For these two they wore nothing above their silken trousers and tasseled chain belts but bangles about their wrists, and diaphanous draperies attached to their headdresses that fluttered about them, revealing and veiling their charms.

Rajnir, Wafri, and the women were long familiar with one another—the dancers were superlative performers, and their two patrons were young, good-looking, responsive. And very, very rich. They were also capricious, as young, rich, good-looking lords tended to be. The leader of the troupe had been observing her patrons as the dance finished, and recognized restlessness in both. Restless patrons soon became bored patrons, who inevitably turned their attentions—and their largesse—elsewhere.

Wafri had been waiting impatiently for the first moment he could make a graceful exit. He loved the veil dances, but they had been familiar since he was sixteen; it was he who had introduced them to Rajnir, who had only been used to those sexless Venn hel dancers.

Dance in the land of the Venn could evoke the senses, but was always part of a larger context; the hel dancers dedicated their entire lives to inspiring their viewers to the golden path of Ydrasal. These dancers' art was confined to the pleasure of the senses. Rajnir's first sight of those veils, or rather the entrancing bare curves beneath the veils, had been as electrifying as a lightning strike: in the north, neither men nor women bared their chests in public.

Since then, after several years of summoning them whenever he could get time away from duty, Rajnir's feelings had dwindled to the ease of familiarity and pleasant anticipation. He had brooded for a couple of days over Erkric's mysterious request—really almost a command—that he give a series of entertainments as compensation for the hard work everyone had done in the land and sea search for Elgar the Fox.

He still found himself resentful of the mage's insistence. He'd thought a day of celebration had been enough, but Erkric spoke with conviction: personal attention was due everyone down the chain of command, on a succession of nights. Rajnir had decided he may as well begin with himself, with Wafri there to share in his favorite entertainment. Tomorrow was good enough to begin with the formal rituals in the Venn Hel for all the officers in Jaro, the day after that for those over the hill reorganizing Beila Lana.

He shifted impatiently on his cushion as the thumping drums brought the dance to a close. Why was he still sour? The dancers were good as always, but was Wafri paying attention to them? He kept tapping his fingers in that irritating way—

Having finished in a stimulating pose, draperies shrouding her body to a silhouette, the leader made a subtle signal. The troupe divided, running forward in tiny ringing steps to surround each man, their draperies blowing back.

Ah, Rajnir thought, attention thoroughly caught now. Hel dancers *never* do anything like *that*—and whyever not?

Soft hands massaged Wafri's neck and shoulders; someone else stripped off his shoes and stockings to rub his feet, and two others worked on each hand. He lay back and closed his eyes. Indevan could wait a little while, he thought with pleasant anticipation as the tutored hands began working inward toward his body. Indevan would not know when he would arrive . . . really, it was so exciting to contemplate. The man who had defeated Marshig the Murderer, helpless in Wafri's control. How he flinched when Wafri raised a hand! The thought made him rock hard, and he abandoned himself happily to his dancers, who were determined to sustain the bliss all the night through.

And so, when his scroll-case tapped, there was no one to feel it because the case was in his clothes. Which had been left behind on the performance floor.

There was no hope of making it through the palace undiscovered, not after Inda spied the Limros ancestral portrait gallery. He stumbled to a stop before the larger-than-life paintings, all framed in gold-threaded carved wood, in which Wafri's face was depicted in variety and multiplicity.

He stiffened. Hands out, fingers tense.

"Inda? We need to keep moving."

Inda did not hear. Fox touched his arm, to be flung off violently. Then, seizing the rest of the flagons of oil Fox had brought as extras, Inda flung the oil on every single ancestral portrait, tapestry, and wooden carving. He grabbed the hallway oil lamp that Fox had taken up as soon as they'd climbed in through a window. He slung it in a wide circle, breathing in great, shuddering gasps, as the blue flame sprayed outward, igniting tongues of fire.

Ruddy light glowed on his tense profile, head thrown back. Flames twinned and leaped, scattered and blended and roared, radiating withering, killing heat as the entire gallery—all gilt and carved wood, trophy swords mounted between the portraits, two ancient shields, and a banner with the clover leaf worked in gold between two tall windows—fed into the inferno.

Tiny sparks began to fly, drifting crazily around them.

"Inda." Fox touched his arm.

Inda recoiled, a knife arcing out—to stop against Fox's blade. Inda stilled, blinking at the crossed blades. Fox watched consciousness incrementally ease Inda's face, then sheathed his knife, and with his other hand jerked his thumb at the door.

They ran, smoke billowing after them.

There was no hope of slipping through unnoticed now. The smoke rolled down halls, causing panic among the sparse night staff in its wake.

But Fox had planned for that, too. They ignited each of his fire caches as they ran down the length of the old palace.

What he hadn't planned for were Inda's inspired additions.

Into the servants' wing they unloosed crates of chickens cooped for the night. In the main hall, where the minimal night guard converged out of instinct, Inda emptied a sack of dried peas, which sent the booted men slipping and slid-

ing. Dye overturned. A soup tureen poured down a flight
of stairs, followed by barrel hoops. Corn baskets waiting
for grinding thrown into the ovens, causing a spectacular
explosion of corn puffs sending the four bakers beginning
to make the day's bread shrieking for the beleaguered
guards, who were already trying to deal with screaming,
panicking servants. The chaos accelerated Fox's succession
of untended fires on landings, staircases, and halls into a
scale of unsurpassed domestic disaster.

They paused outside the guard hall, where the day shift
was asleep, though not for long, as the panic was slowly
building in the long palace complex behind them.

Fox indicated the row of neat pairs of boots at the foot
of each bed, moved on down the hall as he mourned in a
whisper, "Wish we could stop in the stable. These aristocrats! Can't bear the stink of horse. Stable is as far from
their living quarters as possible."

"Don't need horse shit," Inda said, the weakening darkness blurring his features. "Know something better.
Kitchen is right there." He ran back downstairs, Fox on his
heels. They dodged the screaming, fire-batting servants and
ducked into the larder.

Inda grabbed up two baskets of eggs. Surprised, Fox
took the last basket, and they drifted, soundless, down the
long barracks, inserting an egg into every boot.

Out the other end. They tossed the baskets away, and
were crossing the last distance to the tall gate to the road
and freedom, when Inda began to shake and shiver. They
dashed across a lit passage; Inda was laughing.

Laughing. First silently, then in gasping crows and
whoops. The abandoned laughter of a child of ten.

Behind them, the tide of panic reached the sleeping
guards at last. Fox had counted on the lack of any real drill
or training other than orderly marching; no one, including
the guards, seemed to know what to do other than yell
"Fire!" and run about looking for water—thieves—one another, as someone sped to the mage's chamber and tried
without the least success to shake him awake.

But someone knew enough to ring the alarm bells.

And so the guards responded by converging—some of

them squishing miserably—on the main court behind the gate, whose massive bar would take ten men to lift.

Inda and Fox hooked fingers and toes into the cross-pieces holding together the tall, rough wooden spars that made up the gate, not stopping until they hoisted themselves to the top of the wall. Inda still fizzed with wheezy laughter.

Arrows thunked close by. One hissed a finger's-breadth from Inda's ear, as whoever had rung the bell shouted orders in an attempt to marshal the swarming, yelling guards into a defensive line.

Fox glanced outside the wall. The road leading up to the palace was empty, dark, silent.

They unslung their bows, shook out their arrows onto the granite wall top, and began target practice on the half-dressed men down below, neither shooting to kill. Half were mere civs, and as for the guards, it was far more insulting just to drop them with an arrow in shoulder, knee, butt.

"Eggs?" Fox asked as a squad of men lumbered with a peculiar gait into position behind a wagon, driven by a screaming officer. The peculiar gait of men with egg sliming the insides of their boots.

Inda's wheezing ceased. His grin widened, and then with shocking suddenness his chest heaved on a gulping sob. Once, twice: crashing, lung-deep sobs. Inda whooped his breath in and held it, teeth gritted, as he fought for control.

Fox stared, helpless and appalled. Then swung around and glared down at the empty road as though he could will the last part of his plan into materialization.

"They're readying for a run," Inda mumbled, snuffling.

Fox whipped his bow up, smacked an arrow into place.

They loosed arrows in drilled succession, each shooting as the other drew, and each finding his mark.

The advance line staggered, straggled, and as the last arrow whacked into the commander's left shoulder a palm's-breadth from his heart, they broke and ran back for cover, despite the cursing and shouting of the staggering officer.

For a moment the court was empty.

"Not my idea, eggs," Inda said, his words quick, his voice husky. "But I think Dogpiss'd like it. D'you think he's a ghost? I hope he's not a ghost. I don't want him alone, bound to an island where no one goes, I want to think of his spirit in the sun, or beyond the sun, where spirits go out of the world, or the world that holds worlds, but then I wonder if he sees me. N–not—uh." Inda stuttered to a halt.

Dogpiss? Academy nickname. Has to be. Related to his exile?

Below in the courtyard the officer ventured out, one hand gripping the arrow in his shoulder, and with the other he violently motioned forward a new squad.

Inda shot. Fox shot.

Inda blinked rapidly as Fox cast a despairing glance back at the empty road.

"You know what the worst of it all was?" Inda began again in a running stream of words. "Wafri got tight against the seam when watching 'em scrag me. I could see it, what kind of madness is that, but Tau once said sex is like a persimmon pie, and I've always wondered what a per–per–persimmon was." Stop. Blink-blink.

Fox thought, *I uncorked this bottle, better let it pour.* "Persimmon pie being great if you like it—"

"—but poison if you don't. That's what Tau said."

And I thought it a family saying—no. "Carry on."

But Inda had control again, mouth a rictus, teeth shut. As if his break hadn't happened, though tears glistened on his cheeks, he kept shooting until the guards retreated behind cover, occasionally popping out for return shots. They were down to a last handful of arrows.

Inda frowned down at one, and was off again. "What *is* the tie between sex and scragging—even Kepa wasn't that bad—though we were only boys—no sex—anyway Kepa never petted anyone—that shit asked what my favorite color was! And I had to eat from his hand—which is why I got so scrawny." He clapped his elbow briefly against his ribs. "Brought all this fancy food, but I gagged on it. He hated that! He wanted me to beg for it. Tonight I was supposed to drink kinthus again and talk about when I was a boy. Why?"

Fox checked the road. Empty. "You say it—hear it said—but what do you think a soul-eater *is?*"

Inda's body jerked as if he'd been struck.

You also hear "My blood turned cold" said and think it a failure of imagination until it happens. Fox took aim with care. Shot the hat off a steward who had been sidling around a heap of hay. Then glanced back at the blue-shadowed road. Empty. "I hope no one thinks to waken the mage," he said when he knew his voice would remain steady. "I don't know what they're capable of." *Twang!* "Possessing someone's body is simple, relatively brief, and requires at least minimal cooperation; the desire to possess someone's mind and spirit—to take and use it, especially against someone's will—is what Norsunder is about. Ho! Another charge."

"I hope they take *him,*" Inda said, and shot a big, burly guard in the chest. It was the first deliberate kill he made.

I'll wager my life that was one of Wafri's torturers. He glanced back again, and this time breathed easy. "Ah! Not too early."

Up the road behind them trotted two horses—evidence that there were indeed honest Ymarans in the world. Though the cost had been two rubies from Fox's seriously diminished pocketful of gemstones, the boy Fox had bribed had indeed sent the saddled and loaded mounts, and then vanished as agreed.

While Inda loosed the remainder of his arrows—two of them deliberate kills, as a pair of the torturers charged the gate—Fox unwound his cord from his waist and then swiftly secured it. On his word Inda let fly his last arrow, and then the two of them rapidly descended the rope, Inda wincing and grunting all the way down.

When they reached the ground, Fox regretfully left the cord dangling—sailors' habit, spare your cord. You always need it. But there was no retrieving it now.

They mounted up, both feeling the pull of muscles they had not used for riding since childhood.

Inda slewed around, eyes wide and manic. "I won't ask how you managed that. But they have horses in there too, even if they have to run to the other end to get 'em."

"Where they will find every one of them hobbled by chain."

Finishing touches.

Inda snickered. They rode away, Fox reflecting with satisfaction that the fire ought to light their way for a considerable distance, and Inda wheezing as his head drooped lower and lower over the horse's neck.

AS usual, directly before dawn Jeje and Tau met on the roof above her room and they worked their way through their drills.

By now they were so used to one another as practice partners they thought nothing of the faint blue glitter of honed steel flashing a hair's-breadth from neck or heart. They threw one another and exchanged reports; they dropped, kicked, spun, rolled, and discussed the day's plans.

There had been one very bad near breach when Tau told her about Vedrid, the Iascan spy. He'd expected to be congratulated on his effective handling of the situation.

Jeje was furious. *I can understand the sailors not telling me,* she'd said. *Though all their reasoning was wrong. But you? And the worst of it is, I probably could have found out more from this Vedrid than you did.*

Tau reacted with surprise, disbelief, then embarrassment. Only the last one lingered—the rest vanished in his habitual readiness to laugh at himself. *But I'm the best there is at getting information,* he'd tried to explain.

Yes, from someone sitting across from you at a table, or in bed, or anywhere but lying there half dead. You probably scared him witless.

Inarguable. Probably true. Jeje was indeed hearing things in the ordinary way of conversation among ordinary people, who chanced to be somewhere in the vicinity of surprising things. Seafarers spoke freely in front of Jeje without her having to employ subtle arts of coaxing.

So he told her everything about the Comet, including what he'd surmised about her background. And as the sun touched the tumbled line of clouds in the east, revealing a murky, pink-streaked sky, she gave her brief nod of approval.

"We've got people, we've got information," she said. "Now what we need to work on is getting ships."

When the full light of morning revealed how bad Inda looked, Fox urged his horse out of the stream they'd been riding in to obliterate their trail, and led it up onto a grassy bank under a sheltering oak. "I think we'll halt here."

Inda did not speak. He slid off his horse, stumbled a few steps, and then dropped down onto the grass under the rusty-leafed oak. Fox unloaded the saddle packs of supplies, freed the horses of their tack and, regretfully, let them go. He stashed the horse gear deep into a thick, thorny shrub.

"Can still see the smoke," he said, pointing eastward. "I'm going to investigate. You stay here. Sleep. Eat. Plenty of stores in the bags. We'll talk about our next step when I return." He cast a cloak over Inda, looked down at those swollen knuckles, and added, "Don't lose this."

On a flattish rock he carefully set a plain gold band.

Inda was beyond speech. He flicked his fingers interrogatively, and Fox said, "It's one of a pair of summons rings. Amazing, the things we do not have in Iasca Leror. Not that we'd ever need magic rings for a couple of armies to find one another. I can find you again by that ring, so if for some reason you must move, take it with you."

He slid the other ring onto his finger and then faded into the forest shadows, leaving Inda to lie back, staring up at the blue sky through the autumn-bronzed leaves. Presently the tears came again, burning from his eyes and running into his ears, until he drifted into sleep.

* * *

Commander Durasnir walked around the smoking ruin of Limros Palace as Rajnir's own Erama Krona efficiently directed the regular marine guards in sorting people, animals, and in fire dousing.

The palace had been built at levels cut into a hill. Durasnir mounted to the highest wall to survey the countryside through his spyglass. He saw no sign of the mysterious hordes of attackers, who—after exhaustive questions—apparently numbered exactly two. At least only two were seen.

One by one the task captains reported to him: Ymaran guards secured and questioned; the wounded in the process of being treated. Fires mostly out. Horses safely picketed alongside the river on the other side of the palace. Servants gathered in a court well away from the burning central residence. Everyone awaiting his orders.

Ulaffa, as senior Yaga Krona, made his way through the laboring crews below, peering around. Durasnir climbed back down and met him in the central court.

"Penros has confessed," Ulaffa said, his grizzled white hair lifting in the wind. "He's under the influence of the kinthus if you wish to talk to him."

"What's the gist?"

"They did indeed have Elgar—Indevan of Iasca Leror—as a prisoner here. Wafri was personally conducting torture in order to force him to raise and lead Ymar against us."

"Penros was a part of this plot?" Durasnir asked.

"He was to be given Dag Erkric's chambers and books."

Erkric, whose whereabouts were unknown.

Durasnir would consider that later. Right now Rajnir was busy with Wafri, who had apparently crept away from one of their orgies at dawn in order to transfer home. Too late.

Durasnir and Rajnir had transferred in not long after to discover Wafri standing in the main court of his burning palace, the majority of his guards lying wounded around him, his people in a panic, everyone screaming of Elgar the Fox.

Durasnir remembered that stricken face, the naked terror as Wafri gibbered about a surprise attack. *I'll wager you were surprised.*

"Did Penros lie about the recorded interview as he did about the wounded warrior?" Durasnir asked.

"Yes," Ulaffa said. "He had the last page changed. There was no assassination plot. Elgar said he was here to gather information on us preparatory to a fleet attack to take back the strait. The substituted page of false information, Armor Chief Skir murdered—all were on the count's specific orders." Ulaffa paused, then added in a low voice, "The guard they claimed killed Elgar in Skir's defense was the murderer, which explains the terror that Dag Signi saw in him."

Durasnir grunted. "He has to know what we do to anyone who kills one of us." Plots—torture—the prospect of a grim execution of a man following orders—the orders and plots from a young, smiling liar pretending friendship. It all made him feel unclean.

He turned his gaze back to the gate.

Two. With a hundred of those distinctive spiral-fletched arrows: fifty each. The Ymarans—sixty injured in all, three dead—did not seem to appreciate the exquisite humiliation of those deliberately aimed arrows. Judging from the terrible aim evidenced by the bristling of spent arrows on the gate below where the two had sat, they probably thought those wounds accidental.

Durasnir was willing to wager his rank the three who'd been shot dead were Wafri's torturers.

He gazed up along the length of the palace, now mostly blackened ruins. Two men—and one of them in bad condition after how many days of Wafri's perverse attentions?

A sea battle against such an adversary! A truly worthy opponent.

He mentally reviewed the landscape as seen from the wall—no sign of retreat, the sea in proximity. Whoever had rescued Elgar would have a ship lying in one of the hundreds of inlets along the coast. A single spasm of regret tightened his heart, that he would not speak to Elgar. Torture! Disgusting. Reprehensible. Had Elgar been his own prisoner, he would have been given due honor. Durasnir indulged himself with brief, fanciful images: sharing the predawn meditation watch together, discussing strategy and tactics in theory then comparing battles they had seen, and battles they had studied; and when the king gave the inevitable command, Elgar would have gotten a clean death with all Venn lined up in formal battle dress, weapons polished, in respect to a worthy enemy.

Instead we will meet in battle. A clear and worthy goal.

So. He turned his attention back to the waiting mage. "We will not waste time and effort in a search—a second search, which would not do us credit."

Ulaffa pressed his palms together in silent but heartfelt agreement.

"I shall inform the prince that we're too close to the coast, and therefore too late. Elgar is surely out on the sea by now, in one of the hundreds of fishing craft still lurking about after the last search. I expect we shall see him leading a fleet before long." Durasnir waved a hand. "Get all the information you can from Penros, write up a report for Dag Erkric as well as the prince. I leave Penros to you dags to deal with as you will. Rajnir will deal with Wafri. I am returning to Jaro to order the fleet to readiness."

"There's no search," Fox said.

Inda had woken this latest time to low clouds, the cool, moist air that presaged rain.

Fox had been gone two nights and a day; Inda could count that far back, though he did not remember the ride to this quiet little grove of autumnal-colored oaks.

"No search?" Inda repeated. "Why not?"

Fox flicked out his hand. "No idea. The palace is empty, a ruin. The Venn appear to have marched everyone away. So they have no use for the Fire Sticks or some of the other things I scavenged. Like Wafri's jewelry box." He hefted his bag. "I'll strip the gemstones off, and bury the gold— the pieces might be well known. Gems are just gems."

A brief, vivid image of those rings on Wafri's hands

made Inda flinch. "As long as I don't have to touch any of it."

Fox eyed him for a moment, then said, "But first I will boil water and steep you some listerblossoms and willow bark."

Inda sat up cautiously. Though his joints still ached, a day and a half of sleep had helped. He was even hungry.

"I take it you told him about the treasure, then?" Fox asked. "If you want to wash off your prison stink in the stream, I found you some local duds." He held up a laborer's smock and some bag-kneed, patched trousers. He himself wore a similar outfit. "No one will look twice at us."

"Wafri never asked about treasure. Nor did the mage," he added, "when I drank the kinthus and blabbed everything else."

Fox snorted. "What rotten interrogators! And how much kinthus did they give you?"

"I don't know. That first day. He was going to do it again, right before you came."

Fox shook his head. "Too much at the amounts they use for interrogation used too often and your mind never comes back."

"I didn't know it could kill you."

Fox lifted a shoulder. "You probably haven't read any of the records of Norsunder's attack on the morvende, several centuries ago. My mother only has one antique record on brown, crackling paper, come down through my family's marriage with the Deis. They used to use kinthus in some kind of magic ritual. Supposedly could hear one another mind to mind." He tapped his forehead. "The way the Old Sartorans did. Again supposedly. I think that was the hyperbole of history—like they were all bigger and smarter and handsomer and more powerful than we are now ... yet they lost Old Sartor." He snorted. "Anyway apparently using kinthus and magic killed more mages than it helped with the hypothetical mental powers. What else did you keep from your interrogators?"

"Didn't keep anything." Inda looked away. "But they didn't ask about the treasure—or about you, if you're coming around to that."

Fox laughed silently again, and then produced a small flat pan. "Look what I found! Along with some of the spices in the abandoned kitchen. And some of our chickens who flew away flew back to their coop and were sitting in there as if nothing had happened, busy laying eggs. A few of the outlying buildings were only scorched. So we've got enough supplies here to rest for as long as you like before we need to scavenge again."

Inda had already decided what he wanted to do, but he wasn't going to talk about that yet.

"Eggs for breakfast, with some cheese. Wheel got melted on the outside, but I cut it away," Fox said, rummaging through the bag he'd brought, and bringing forth various packages wrapped in scraps of fabric he'd found in the ruins. "I even discovered a bottle of wine! And some pepper—"

"Don't want pepper," Inda said, too quickly, his stomach closing. "I'll burn every pepper tree in Tenthan if I ever get home. Orange—" His voice trembled, and he shut his teeth with a click.

Fox set the pan down over the fire he'd set between two stones; then he hunkered directly before Inda. "No, you won't," he said. He was serious, the way he had been the other night and never before. "You'll plant pepper trees in every court. Orange trees, too, though I doubt they'll grow. Plant 'em behind glass, and every day you wake up you sniff 'em and gloat because you are alive. Free. You survived."

Inda's tension slowly leached away, leaving him weary. "Right. Then when *you* go home you will not drink yourself to death like your father."

Fox jerked up. "Hah!" And laughed again, his old mocking laugh. "Is that your deal, then? If we ever go home, we'll hoard mementos of our experiences and triumph over 'em endlessly to the boredom of our progeny? My family already has a tradition of that. Began with the Venn King's letters in old Savarend's day."

Fox busied himself with the food. Inda eased himself down on the soft grass. Following the shifts in Fox's mood was like trying to track a butterfly during a lightning storm.

"Venn King?" he asked idly, gaze skyward between the

stirring leaves high overhead. "Does that have anything to do with the reason the Montrei-Vayirs turned on your family? Were your ancestors treating with the Venn?"

Fox used his knife to beat the eggs into a froth. "No," he said, grinning. "Boot's on the other foot. The Montrei-Vayirs were dancing around ~~trying~~ to placate 'em when the Venn King offered favored province rank if we did the work in taking Iasca Leror for 'em—with their help, of course. They were desperate in those days, too, for southern land. Old Savarend insisted if they were making offers they were too weak to take what they wanted. Gave 'em the back of his hand. They sheered off with a threat. And it was after they were safely gone that Anderle Montrei-Vayir turned on us."

Inda snorted.

Fox checked the crushed olive smeared on the flat pan. It was steaming gently, so he poured out his eggs and turned them slowly with his knife as he observed, "I know what it is you do, now. No magic, no mystery. It's a matter of mind. Most people, when suddenly overtaken by events that throw habit and training out the window, are helpless. Including me. Some—me—can manage if drilled enough. But your mind runs ahead, faster than events, and begins to shape them. Savarend was one of those. But it seems not to have passed down to me." He sprinkled his cheese onto the eggs.

Inda waggled fingers in the air. "It's like drawing. Some see the lines on the paper in their head, others don't. I see things to do, that's all."

"And you like to win."

Inda grinned. "I like to win."

They were silent as Fox regarded his cookery, decided it was done. He set the pan on the rock next to the homing ring. "Here, we'll share." He passed over a spoon. "So if you were to take Iasca Leror, how would you?"

Inda tapped the spoon absently on a rock in one of the Marlovan drum patterns they'd known from childhood. "Assuming they have to land, I don't know, depends on how big their fleet is, but let's say it's Wafri's nine times nine . . ."

They, Fox thought. *Not we. He's thinking of Rajnir and the Venn. He'll never lead anyone against the homeland. No matter who did what to whom.*

". . . fake attacks along the coast. Bring all the defenses there, like the pirates did. Then a strike team over the Pass to secure that. That would mean they could land huge forces in Idayago at their leisure. Then they don't have to extend supply lines over the strait, not with all Idayago's resources right there. So they come down through the Pass, and strike at . . . what was that city right below the Pass?"

"Ala Larkadhe."

"Yes. And Lindeth Harbor. Meanwhile our people hear about the Pass and race north to take it back, and those ships they used for the coast attack diversion? This time they land south, maybe Parayid, and march northward. Force us to defend on two fronts."

And so Inda would try to defend, but despite whatever had cast him out into the world, he would never attack. "Us," Fox repeated. "Inda, why don't you go home?"

Inda's face closed, and Fox thought with self-mockery, *Why don't you keep your mouth shut?*

But then Inda spoke, unexpectedly. And not easily. "I can't. I promised. It doesn't matter why," he added, as if to forestall an objection that Fox now knew better than to make. "I can't unless there is reason. I mean, a reason that supersedes the promise." He bent his head, scowling down at his hands as he mumbled, "Whatever others say, we have to live with ourselves. That's what my mother used to say."

That's what my mother used to say, too—and your mother and mine were friends in the queen's training, Fox thought. He could see in Inda's hunched, tense posture that he'd had enough, so he said as lightly as he could, "So what act of madness do you intend next?"

Inda straightened up, obviously unaware of doing so— he wasn't Inda anymore, who was still a troubled boy in so many ways. He was Elgar the Fox, commander of a fleet. "First, what did you tell Fibi and the others?"

"I set meeting places along the coast for both schooners. The last one along the coast opposite Bren on the full moon of Fourth-month. Assuming either of us is still alive."

Inda drew in a deep breath of satisfaction. "And you say you don't look ahead?"

"Maybe I'm learning?" Fox retorted. "Or maybe I've gone mad as well. Well, what is it you're hatching?"

Inda decided it was time to speak.

"It's just that I know where Rajnir's army is. I found it on the map you put in that saddlebag. Not even all that far—inland a way north. And you say they aren't searching for us? Why not go to Wafri's county and take a squint at what this army looks like?"

"Why not?" Fox mocked, hands open. "It's as crazy as any other plan of yours."

Inda ignored this frivolity, feeling better by the moment. "And then we travel south, scout the coast while we're at it. If they aren't searching, they aren't expecting us. So neither of us knows much about woodcraft, but we'll learn, eh, by the time we reach the central plains? And meanwhile, if Dasta and the others have stayed with the plan, there should soon be rumors about Elgar the Fox attacking pirates on the Fire Islands. Maybe sooner than later. Durasnir and his fleet can go chasing off there—about the time Dasta and Tcholan and whoever else they might raise go south to Freeport." Inda finished off his share of the food in a few impatient bites, then let his spoon clátter to the pan. "Listen, Fox, have you ever heard of scroll-cases? What an aid that would be! We could talk ship to ship . . ."

Chapter Twenty-five

MOST of the rest of Joret's story is widely known, for Valdon Shagal's *Take Heed, My Heirs* has long been one of the most popular royal memoirs.

But more than fifty years of conjugal besottedness understandably graces those first moments with poetic and dramatic joy that wasn't actually there. Valdon's record of their first meeting is too well-known to repeat here, and it is correct in all the visual detail: throne room, court in attendance, his mother presenting him to the Aunt Wisthia he had never met, and Wisthia in her turn presenting him to Hadand and then Joret.

He did not actually fall in love with Joret at first sight. It was the usual flash of attraction for her lovely face and figure—nothing that hadn't happened to her far too often.

Only this time she felt it at the very same moment he did, and they stilled, blinded by that sense that her most famous ancestor described as the sun meeting the waterfall and turning it to liquid light.

It took another month for him to fall in love with her honesty, her sudden bursts of humor, her clear but compassionate view of the world unmarred by courtly cynicism.

As for Joret, though she was attracted so strongly when she first saw the tall fellow who looked so unexpectedly like a dark-haired Evred, she did not believe love was possible anymore—her precious memories of Cama Tya-Vayir were too recent for that.

What she thought—when he turned away and she could think—was: *There is work for me here, and this is a man I could do it with. If he were free.*

Love came to them both: gradual, deep, and enduring.

Two things Valdon never recorded. One he passed over with diplomatic reticence. The second he never saw.

What he passed over was his midnight talk with Hadand in his mother's flower garden, a month after he arrived home.

Hadand had retired from that night's impromptu ball. (The difference between impromptu and planned balls was that one could go to the ball in one's evening gown, instead of retiring to change for the third or fourth time that day.) She had seen yellowing leaves in the gardens, and had been sniffing the wind anxiously every time she saw clouds. It was time to go home, except she had no treaty, despite Valdon's return home, and the way he vanished during most of the day to deal with overdue matters of state, only appearing at court at night. So far, his pressing concerns did not include her treaty. This mission was her first diplomatic challenge as queen, and it was a failure.

Once she'd unlaced herself from her heavy gown, and Tesar had taken it away to refurbish, she sat down in the pretty cotton-lace wrapper Wisthia had given her. The Adranis had glass doors—something Hadand had never before heard of. Hers stood open onto the fragrant garden, otherwise she was alone. She cut a tiny square of paper and sharpened her pen. Usually writing to Evred was a joy, but now she had to face the truth: it was time to admit defeat.

While she considered how to word it, the locket-magic zapped her.

She opened Evred's note and read:

> *Storms seen moving north. I hope you are back through the passes before winter. Found B. alone in room drinking. Admitted he wants to go to sea. Sent him to see to ship and harbor repairs, inspect harbors with eye to defense. Games began today, yr. mother pre-*

*siding. The girls love her. To save money I'm thinking
no more Tvei training. When can you come home?*

Storms moving north: it meant he too was watching the
weather. *He needs me there—but we need that treaty.*

She kissed the note—his hands had so recently touched
it—and then read it again, and shared his worry over
Barend.

She picked up her knife and began to trim the nib when
footsteps crunched the gravel outside the open glass door.
Well-drilled muscles brought her up and ready before she
could even think so she and Valdon gazed at one another
in surprise over the threshold of the glass door: he in full
court regalia, all silk and lace and ribbons, she in a wrapper
with a knife held at a lethal angle.

She set aside the knife, trying to hide the blush that
heated up her entire body, and said, with her back turned,
"I trust there is nothing amiss?" Her fingers nipped up
Evred's note and crushed it against her palm.

Valdon repeated, blankly, "Amiss?"

Hadand had not failed to notice how much Wisthia's
nephew looked like Evred. Valdon was darker, and his eyes
were blue, but the shape of his mouth, his cheeks and jawline, the long body, were all familiar.

He saw the blush she couldn't hide, and rueful laughter
crinkled his eyes. "Oh. I didn't think what my arrival might
look like." Now it was his turn to blush, and suddenly it was
possible to laugh, and to sit down, and to calm one's thundering heart.

She had learned by now that first assignations were usually arranged during the day—and if successful, people
arranged to meet for longer at night.

From there the rules became more subtle, and some of
them more fraught, depending on rank, expectations, and
families. As Hadand faced him, she thought of what her
mother had said once to Joret about the rules governing
relationships: *Nothing can tame the human heart.*

"And so?" Hadand asked, her voice unsteady; now she
wanted to laugh. "You came here thinking of me as . . .
what, a cousin? Perhaps as a horse?"

Valdon circled round the table, his head to one side as he laughed. "I thought of you as too removed for expectations of that kind and so my motivation was only to talk." He grinned. "You are so very formidable, you know, with your Marlovan walk and keen gaze. Everyone is quite intimidated. Including your obedient servant." He bowed with grace.

"So . . . what, you are hinting that you have changed your mind about dalliance?" she began, making the mistake of looking up. His eyes quirked just like Evred's, intensifying the resemblance, but totally unlike Evred was the unhidden desire there.

Her thoughts vanished into smoke. She looked away, expelling her breath in a whoosh. "No."

"Is it me, or politics?"

"Politics," she said, and there was no mistaking the honesty in tone and gaze. Then her brow puckered. "Besides, I thought you were interested in Joret?"

"Let's go outside," he said abruptly, and they slipped through the glass door into the private garden. Each of the suites in the royal wing had one, Hadand had discovered, bounded by high walls, and those obscured by levels of greenery. There was a splashing fountain in the middle, which would make it difficult to be overheard. Moonlight graced the well-trimmed plants and circular walk around the fountain. Insects chirruped in the soft summer air. "Interested." A direct look. "What a limp-prick word! Fascinated! Ensorcelled! But with Joret, I am beginning to believe it has to be life or nothing. Until then, why, a tumble with a handsome woman would be sweet, even if she is a queen."

"And you a future king," Hadand said, feeling that she must have fallen asleep and into a dream, without having lain down and shut her eyes first. After weeks of courtly ritual and platitudes, this conversation was enlightening and strange. And fraught with possible peril. "No, it feels too much like riding a runaway horse," she said finally. "The ride might be fine, but what about when it stops?"

"And we get thrown into the thorn bushes? Or to the wolves?" Valdon rubbed his temples. "In truth I don't know what I'm doing, except I discovered today—when I saw her at supper, and heard her capping quotations from that cursed archaic Sartoran poetry—I want her mind, I want her body, I want her to want my mind and body. Forever." He lifted away his hands and frowned. "And that was the trap, wasn't it? You and Wisthia, bringing her here? You had to know what a dilemma I'm in. They laugh about me from Fal to Danara, my old friend Lael Lirendi helpfully informed me recently. So here I am, a little drunk, very caught. By the both of you, in every way known to man or woman. The question is, what is it you want in return?"

The conversation had been strange before; now Hadand felt as if the shadowy ground had opened up, dropping her into another world entirely. She had not once considered what things must look like from Valdon's perspective—she who prided herself on careful scrutiny of all sides. She could not mention the treaty now. He would feel conspired against, even though she hadn't conspired.

"Joret and I knew nothing whatsoever about your situation," she said, the golden light from the distant windows shining directly in her eyes.

"Aunt Wisthia did," he said, his mouth grim, but that narrowing of anger had eased from his eyes. The humor was back. "And what, she thought I might be like my father, and fall for a beautiful face?"

"She never told us that if she did," Hadand said.

"So you think so, too."

"But Joret doesn't," Hadand said quickly. "She doesn't think that way. She never liked being singled out just for her face."

"What's Joret's story? I thought you people married off the girls at some absurdly young age."

"Betrothal. We go live with our future husband's family at age two. Joret had a betrothal," Hadand said. "My brother. He died." Her voice softened, as memory whirled her back to that spring breakfast before Tanrid rode northward as Evred's commander. How pleased he'd been! It was what he'd trained for all his life. Now he was gone. But so were those who had killed him. *Let it pass, let it pass.*

"Because of . . . circumstances she is free to choose for herself." Not *quite* true, but she knew there would be no trouble from anyone important at home if Joret made an honorable marriage over the mountains.

Valdon heard the affection in her voice. "Your brother? I didn't know you people had a strong sense of family— sending the boys off for years of training, and the girls being sent away even younger. Not that we serve as any great object lesson in that. Though it was different when my grandfather was alive. And I can claim *one* amusing cousin, who's been like a brother to me."

"Lord Randon," Hadand said, smiling briefly. Randon had made it abundantly plain that, much as he admired Joret, it was Hadand with whom he would most happily dally, something it had taken Hadand time to get used to. At home, her rank required her to make the first move if she wanted dalliance, but once she'd adjusted, he'd given her the first genuinely good time she'd had since her arrival.

Valdon did not misinterpret that smile. "I trust we're not about to hear of a war being declared?"

Hadand chuckled, a deep sound utterly unlike the carefully trained court titter—he found it very attractive. "No," she said. "I fault no one for different custom. And he makes me laugh. What, by the way, is a 'Marlovan walk'?"

"It's, oh, I don't know. Like this, a little." He parodied a martial saunter, his weight balanced on the outside of his foot. Then he grinned. "No man hears his own accent; do we have a walk?"

Hadand thought of her first impressions of the gliding, tiny steps of the women, the men's languid mince, and opted for diplomacy. "Very courtly."

Valdon turned around on the pathway to face her. She looked up, moonlight making plain her question. He sensed no deviousness, no triumph. If anything, an almost imperceptible sense of sadness. "So if there is no conspiracy, why won't Joret talk alone with me—or why doesn't she invite me to talk to her, if that's your custom?"

Hadand sighed. "Because we are guests here."

"Guests," he repeated. "Ah, back to politics."

"To put it bluntly, we are told on all sides that you will make a specific alliance, and Joret has too steadfast a sense of honor to trespass."

"Ah. Ah!" Valdon felt another of those unsettling shifts in perspective. The Iascans did understand honor, despite what had happened to their leaders the winter before.

And he had to be the one to speak.

He looked up at the peaceful stars, then down, and knew that his next words would commit him forever. "But there is no other alliance, not unless I choose."

"Is there not talk of some important tax grant?"

Valdon waved a hand. "That part is the easiest to solve. What would be the hardest is what I have to offer Joret: a pair of fretful, greedy sovereigns, a court renowned for its viciousness, where deviousness is regarded as an art. Where consuming everything and anyone good is their only intent. What I noticed first about Joret—well, second— was how free she is of guile. What I've discovered of her in company is that she is smart, honest, quick. Kind."

"All true."

Valdon held out his hands. "Imagine that! I've fallen in love with someone I've never had the chance to court. But what happens if we do court? More to the point, if she does want me enough to stay, must she either become worse than they, or else be ground to death by the court's teeth?"

Hadand watched the graceful winging of a night bird as she thought. The moment was poised to change all their lives. They both sensed it. She must not speak wrong. "She is a lot stronger than you think. Try her."

It was enough.

When Hadand returned to her room, there she found Joret, her wide eyes so steady the candle flames reflected in them in eerie pinpoints of light. She made no pretence. "He was here," she breathed. "What did he say?"

"He's actually free to choose and he wants you. Was afraid of conspiracy, but mostly he's afraid that the cruelty of this court will destroy you, or remake you into its image."

The corners of Joret's mouth deepened. "There's a third way."

Anyone familiar with history in that part of the world knows the results of the next morning's talk between Valdon and Joret, recorded for posterity: there is little point in repeating it, as they were both too guarded, too anxious, for it to have much charm. Their brief words accomplished one thing. They understood one another enough to begin to speak freely.

What he never saw was what happened after, when he hastened, his gait and grin unmistakable, up through the palace to confront his father before the official Rising.

He made no attempt to hide his elation—or the direction he had come from, and so gossip ringed out behind him.

Fansara of Bantas had expected a crown ever since her parents gave her a pony when she was five and said that queens must know how to ride with grace. Everything she had ever done was the action of a future queen.

Everything. There was no room in her mind, or heart, for anything except the prospect of power, and the exquisite anticipation of using it. Years of flattering that disgusting bore of a queen, listening to the wine-sodden beast who was now king, putting up with the neglect of their fool of a son while waiting for her crown: those were the price she'd had to pay to gain power.

But now, when she was about to succeed at last—everyone had said so, and deferred accordingly—there comes, along with that dried-up old raisin of a widowed queen, a blue-eyed daughter of the Deis bent on destroying everything.

Imagine her fury when Fansara saw clusters of courtiers hurrying and scurrying across the public garden toward the queen's wing for the Rising. She knew immediately something had happened, and paused only for a moment to check her reflection in a pond: yes, her peach silk looked queenly, her hair perfectly coifed, face smooth.

Inside the royal chambers the bright-feathered peacocks of court were circling around that Marlovan mare with her muscular arms and her stride like a quarryman. Glances Fansara's way, mirthful glances, without any semblance of goodwill, annoyed Fansara; when the others did not defer as she glided up to take the principal cushion, her irritation heated to fury.

The queen wasn't through with her bath yet—she slept later and later—so the women strolled idly about, or sat and nibbled the fresh bread and fruit laid out for them while they waited—for what? They should be seated around Fansara, as always. What had happened?

A sidelong glance from that fat little butterball from the Ashan plains. "Lady Joret, did the prince have any plans for today's picnic?" Her voice was shrill with triumph.

"If he does, I believe he will say so," was the reply, in that ugly accent from over the mountains. Joret sat down on a cushion—just any cushion, as usual, paying no attention to her position in the room—and reached for bread.

Fansara watched in horror as they others promptly sorted themselves out in rank order and took places around Joret. As if she was already forming a court!

Fansara rose again, on pretext of finding something to drink, and took her time cutting through the still-circling women, forcing them to defer. She stopped directly before the barbarian. "Tell me, *Lady* Joret. Is it true that Marlovan barbarians all eat with knives, like our meanest shepherds grubbing in the hills?"

Listen to that silence! Oh, I have struck hard!

Fansara smiled indulgently at the tittering on the edges of the crowd, rustlings of gowns, whispers. They all looked like frightened mice as they turned from her to the barbarian.

Who moved a hand to her sleeve. When she snapped her hand out again, she was suddenly holding a long dagger.

Women gasped. Some scrambled up, hands at their throats, some squealed and scurried away, leaving Joret alone there on her cushion.

Joret's wide, lambent gaze, the same color as the morning sky behind them, did not waver. "I will demonstrate how we eat," she said, her lips parting to show the edges of her even, white teeth.

And with slow, deliberate, delicate care, she sliced that

dagger through the bread so it fell into wafers. Then she brought the steel to her lips and licked it all down its length. A long, slow lick, so long and so slow it was unnervingly sensual, as was the way she used the dagger to flick butter over the bread. Then she cut it into tiny pieces, which she speared on the point and ate with that same slow, deliberate, measured care—the blade glinting this way, that way, and then again that shivery licking, now on both sides, all the way up to the tip.

The room was profoundly silent, the women watching with unwavering gazes of horror and fascination—several with a covert, though growing, admiration—until she finished.

They were shocked to discover that the queen was there, had been there for some time. She too had watched in appalled and fascinated silence. She was even a little afraid, as Joret calmly pulled back her lacy cuff to reveal the sheath, and slid the knife home with an audible *click*.

And so, a week later, while the Iascan queen was closeted with the Grand Council over the wording of her treaty, Fansara found Valdon at her shoulder in the evening, inviting her to dance.

She had dreamed about that long silver dagger for a week, and about Joret's blue, unwavering gaze. There had been no more comments about sailor's walks, or bricklayers, or really much of anything, and the dagger had made no reappearance, but all the women of court now knew it was there in her sleeve. In fact she carried two.

And so, when Valdon asked Fansara while they danced the length of the room to consider an appointment to Sartor as ambassador—as Lord Jasil was getting old and wanted to retire from the severity of life under the current Sartoran queen—she bowed to the inevitable and said yes.

Chapter Twenty-six

HARVEST moon hung great and yellow above the horizon on the first of the month. A late-autumn burst of summer weather had scoured the sky. Evred-Harvaldar's windows stood open to the soughing of the hot wind around the towers and down the stone canyons of the city. Hot, dry wind: good. His thought ranged eastward beyond the border mountains as he fingered the scrap of paper just arrived via the locket-magic.

Then he untwisted the paper.

Hadand's square, neat writing, a faint trace of her favorite scent—distilled from aromatic herbs—all brought her oddly near, yet reinforced her distance. He missed Hadand. Longed to talk face-to-face. And yet he had not brought himself to tell her that his father had actually had a set of three lockets. The third had been loaned on occasion to Runners trusted by the king and Jened Sindan; Pavlan, Sindan's cousin, had returned from the Land Bridge with it some weeks after Hadand left for the east. Evred pensioned the man off, sent him home, and hid the locket in the casket.

The reason he had said nothing stemmed from his ambivalence about the discovery of Ndara's lockets: a thirty-year-old-secret brought by his own mother, not to his father, but to Ndara-Harandviar, a woman Queen Wisthia had not even met. Implicit was a worldwide conspiracy among women—denied by them all—because it never occurred to Evred that the lockets could have had another purpose besides military.

Together, last spring, he and Hadand had tested his father's pair and Ndara's. They found that they were not interchangeable. The spells for the two sets varied slightly, and the magic only worked with the lockets and not outside of them. They could send objects tiny enough to fit, but they could feel the corresponding cost in magic. They'd agreed if they ever had to part on kingdom affairs, they would use the lockets—and so it had come to pass.

He frowned, considering his ambivalence; he trusted individual women, and yet he felt they had enough secrets.

He held the paper closer to the lamp and read the message.

Treaty: Valdon will get king to agree to send our mages back! But no warriors to our aid. Local dukes have only small forces to ride borders. Crown has none. V. says it wd. take years to muster an army, after separate agreements w. each duke. But V. promises they will not let Venn through their land for strike from east. I hope to leave sn., once everyone agrees on the exact terms: we await word from M.C.

M.C.: Mage Council. Evred twisted the note into a wick and touched it to the flame in the lamp, watched it burn, and realized he'd gotten used to lamplight, the glowglobes now saved for emergency use such as a Venn attack, their clear light being more reliable than fire. When the paper twist had burned nearly to his fingers he stooped to lay the smoldering fragment in the cold fireplace, then walked back to the window to gaze toward the northwest.

He should be triumphant, or at least glad, about the prospective treaty, yet his emotions were distinct: relief and melancholy.

Why was human nature so absurd? There was no other term, except maybe foolishness, for the way his mind stubbornly reverted to that single glimpse of Inda he'd had that day—the day of murder and assassination—in Lindeth Harbor. One glimpse, no words spoken, even. He had told no one, not even Vedrid, whom he'd sent off within a day to Bren to try again to contact Inda.

Disgusted and impatient with himself, he acknowledged this much comfort: at least no one knew what a fool he'd been.

The bell tolled the changing of the watch, and rhythmic clanks and clatters of sentries trading places syncopated the susurrus of the wind. Evred stared out at the sky, wondering if Inda saw the same stars that he did.

Disgusted by such asinine sentiment, he turned away from the window, but the self-loathing moved right along with him.

He strode to the door, yanked it open. Felt relief that Nightingale was the Runner on duty. "Heat Street, House of Roses," he said, without any preamble. "Dyalen. Request an interview."

Nightingale saluted, palm against chest rather than fist, indicating he was well aware that this was a personal and not a kingly matter. He left and Evred prowled around his rooms until Nightingale returned, this time with a thin woman in riding dress, her hair short and curly. The few years since they'd seen one another last had aged her subtly in the way some women aged—she looked less like a boy and more like a girl, not in build, but in the softened contours of her face. She must be ten years older than he, at least.

She saluted. "Evred-Harvaldar."

Dismissing Nightingale with a look, he said, "Never mind that. Sit down."

She did, and waited with her customary patience. During their time together, though it had been sex for pay, she had treated him like a person, not an object of business. And she had taught him to use the same courtesy toward professionals, something he'd come to appreciate only later, with experience. So, though he had no interest in her personal life, he said, "How have you been?"

A brief smile, a gesture of her strong hands that was curiously masculine—and he felt the faintest spurt of attraction. It had been far too long. Half a year—not since the murder-assassination—and all his experiences had been up north.

She said, "I'm retiring this year. The sex business is for the young. Going east to Nelkereth to raise horses. You?"

As always, brief, empathetic—and direct.

And so he said, "I want sex but I do not want favorites. I don't even want to know their names."

She put her hands on her knees. Down to business. "Male or female?"

"Male."

She asked some blunt questions which he answered as bluntly, then she stood up, saluted, and said, "Want someone today?"

"Yes."

"I'll set it all up."

He thanked her, she left and returned by unobtrusive byways to the House of Roses, where she went straight to the proprietor, her great-uncle. Because it was so late at night, the place was busy; she entered by a back way, listening with experienced ears to the sounds of merrymakers in the public rooms as she made her way upstairs to the office. "King," she said, when they were alone. "Discreet, no one with ambition," and she went on to describe what he liked in sex—not just from his words, but her own experience during her time with him, and she was far more accurate than Evred. "Someone now," she finished.

Her uncle tapped his fingers on the table, then said, "Who do you suggest we send as a trial?"

Dyalen said, "I considered that on the way over. There's something missing, something he didn't tell me, but I strongly suspect his heart is given. But no sign of to whom."

"Too bad. He might want a look-alike."

"No. Mistake. He's too much like the old king in other ways. If there is a someone else, the king may well be heart-fixed. No matter. Whoever the someone else is, he's not here. I think the king would hate a look-alike, so it's as well we don't know who."

Her uncle opened a hand. "You know him best."

"So try Fedran first, isn't he on duty tonight? He's not talky. Evred is quiet, though he has a sense of humor and Fedran's quick-witted. Evred relaxes if you catch him with a joke."

Her uncle summoned his Runner, sent the message. When he looked up, it was to see Dyalen at the window staring out at the moonlit sky, her expression not pleased so much as pensive.

He said, "Why the long face? We have the young queen's custom, and if we are careful, we might now gain the king's as well. The house will be made for this generation—and you will be getting your share, having set us up with the king."

Dyalen shook her head. "I've always liked Hadand-Gunvaer. And I liked Evred-Harvaldar when he was only the second son nobody paid the least attention to. Now he's king, and you know the first thing out of his mouth? It was to ask about me."

"Good custom," her uncle said. Smiling. "I wonder if there's any chance we can find out who the secret desire is."

Dyalen faced him, frowning. "You're not going to get into politics."

Uncle Kenrid laughed. "Politics! Anything having to do with human beings is politics. No, my ambitions have nothing to do with governments, wars, or lands. But if this mystery man shows up, everything will change. It would be as well to know who he is and plan for it."

She sighed. "It's not us I'm thinking of, but those two young hearts. Human nature being what it is, Evred-Harvaldar's mystery man is probably an utter snake. I hate him already."

Uncle Kenrid laughed. "Life will be interesting if the snake ever slithers in."

Thunder rumbled overhead and the rain turned to sleet as smoke rolled over the water from the burning galleys in the Fire Islands' main harbor. Dasta was, as usual, oblivious to the cold as he stood on the foreyard and watched intently. Far more galleys than he'd expected . . . boarding attempts repelled so far—too many, too many . . . Eflis, where are you?

In the west the sky was clear, the warm pale blue sky contrasting dramatically with the dark grayish-green thunder cell overhead. The distant sparkle of light on the sea made Dasta's eye tear; he blinked, and, yes! From the northwest a slanted line bisected the horizon. He blinked, and the line resolved into a tall, rake-masted schooner, impossibly fast, throwing up a magnificent feather.

The galleys noticed moments later—individual captains on the galleys recoiled, yelled, plied sticks or whips with fear-driven vigor. But no matter how hard they flogged the hapless prisoners chained to the benches in the galleys, none of them were as fast as Eflis with a wind at her back. *Sable*'s crew was lined along the upper rail of the sharply slanted deck, making the schooner even stiffer. It was Eflis' best maneuver; she judged the strength of those tall spars and the taut sails to a nicety.

Joy coursed through Dasta. He wanted to dance right there on the yardarm as the schooner slipped behind the galleys, cutting them off from the shore.

The *Sable*'s fire teams joined the steady and deadly stream of arrows: draw/shoot, shoot/draw. No falter, no flaw in aim. Pirates, never the galley crews.

And it was too much for the pirates.

A discordant horn blatted a signal, and the galleys began to retreat—or at least the captains ordered them to retreat, but by now the galley crews all knew what was about to happen, and despite the angry and desperate floggings, the screamed threats, most refused to lift an oar. Or they clashed the wood together, their rhythm so impossible the galleys did not move, only rocked in circles.

Everyone knew that Elgar the Fox freed the prisoners off all the galleys they took. So the horn signaling *Flee!* served instead as the signal for a general mutiny. More galleys crashed, bobbed, and drifted as the pirates abandoned the fight, and either leaped to other galleys that were moving, or dove overboard.

"Captains!" Dasta yelled—a command scarcely heard and not needed. Gillor was raising the signal flag herself.

And the fire crews shifted their aim to the individual pirate captains.

Joy thrilled along Dasta's nerves. It worked! *His* plan, not Inda's, had worked.

For weeks they'd used all Inda's suggestions, and they almost always succeeded. Again and again they'd hammered the galley pirates, though many of the fights were close, especially at the beginning when they had to guess at numbers and hidden pirate reserves.

But since they'd begun to win, locals forced to work for the pirates—or hiding out from them on the thick forested islands—had come forward with information when "Elgar" used a scout to make reconnaissance.

This bay was the lair of the second largest pirate gang, allies of Bendal Bonebreaker, the most prominent pirate chief on the island. The pirates knew *Death* and *Cocodu* by now. To flush them out they'd needed a ruse, and this ruse—to dress the merchant caravel they'd recaptured up north as a fat Sarendan trade ship and one of Eflis' schooners as its consort, both wounded badly after a big storm, limping to shore—had drawn out the pirates like bees to blossoms. *Death* and *Cocodu* had lain just over the horizon, as a mix of Eflis' and Dasta's and Tcholan's best fighters boiled up from the trader and schooner to take on the swarms of fast galleys.

That had been the tightest of the timing, and at first it had looked bad. They hadn't expected so many of them. But *Cocodu* and *Death* arrived in time to flank the galleys, and here Eflis came to cut them off from shore. *His* plan!

Inda had been right. The galleys counted on numbers, speed, and then savagery when they boarded. Fire team drills and maneuvering beat them every time.

Well, here was another win, but there was no time to gloat. Now for the long task of freeing the galley men and dealing with pirates and craft.

Below, Gillor signaled for the boat crews. And Dasta remembered where he was. *Who* he was. Nearly caught napping! Eflis was almost in range to identify individuals with a glass.

Dasta slid down a backstay—face away from Eflis' ship—and felt his command of the battle evaporating with his disappearance. He ducked belowdecks, and when he reemerged from a different hatch, he was Dasta again, and Gillor transferred command of the *Cocodu* back to him as she dropped into the gig and set up the sail. When she sailed from the lee of the ship she had on the all-purpose black shirt and trousers and headband they kept packed in the gig. Her back was to *Sable* and *Sea-King* as she sped away.

By now everyone knew that was Elgar the Fox going off to investigate, and the agreement with Eflis had been amended to include leaving him alone. "He'll come aboard when he's ready," was what she'd been told by all the deck-hands on *Cocodu* and *Death*.

She'd stopped asking, but Dasta knew her interest hadn't died away. So he was suspicious when she signaled for a parley.

Cocodu and *Death* anchored alongside one another to oversee the unshackling of the oarsmen in the galleys. Most were locals, with hapless former traders and defeated pirates mixed in. By now Tcholan—who was by far the best fight team leader, his team the toughest—had become the expert at sorting them. When Dasta waved, pointing at the *Sable*'s flag, Tcholan promptly signaled he'd stay. He'd rather oversee the sorting than dodge more questions from that flint-eyed Sparrow.

So Dasta rowed himself through gray sea, the hard, cold rain damping down the waves. Lamps glowed like low-lying fireflies all over the bay as Eflis' backup craft arrived and helped with the sorting. The galleys were stripped of usable timber as well as loot and anything else deemed worth saving, then they were sunk. The prisoners were sorted, some taken on as crew, most let go.

While all this work went on, Eflis and Sparrow had been busy. When Dasta arrived aboard the *Sable,* dripping wet, he was conducted down into the warm cabin, which was agreeably scented with hot wine mulled with orange, cinnamon, and cloves. The table had been folded up, and the floor spread with pillows and soft spreads of woven yeath fur.

Eflis beckoned with a smile and put a cup into his hands. "We thought we could celebrate another success while we chat," she said.

She was dressed in a loose blouse with a low neck, and her usual deck trousers. Sparrow, present as always whenever he or Tcholan met with Eflis, gave him a broad smile. Dasta looked from one to the other and at the cabin, and thought, *Hoo, if this isn't a plot of their own, then I'm a Venn*.

Tcholan had been up all night. Neither Dasta nor Gillor had returned, so he was forced to think ahead, relaying orders from Elgar the Fox.

He was hungry, thirsty, gritty, and more tired than all three put together when the dawn's bitter wind brought Dasta rowing back. One look at the smirk on his face and Tcholan knew what had been happening all night. It didn't help his temper any.

Dasta followed him into the *Death*'s cabin, where they shut the scuttles and windows. Dasta hadn't missed the sour expression on Tcholan's face, or the tired eyes, so he began with an apology.

"I didn't know they had a plot going. And it was a plot."

Tcholan sighed. "Both women?"

"Yes."

"All night?"

"Yes." Dasta grinned again. "Not that I was the center. Eflis was. But hoola-loola, it was fun enough! I've heard of three people, but could never see how you could manage it. They managed!"

Tcholan sighed again; his temper was fading, but if Dasta started swaggering the details . . .

"Anyway, they got to the questions this morning. Ever so easy and casual, but it was clear they'd planned it. They're more curious about Elgar than ever. If they don't meet him before long, it's gonna be all over. Listen. We got two problems, is the way I see it. It's that curiosity about Elgar, and the change of the wind. Winter's coming—I can smell it, can't you?"

Tcholan made the difficult mental shift from imagining *Sable*'s cabin to the prospect of winter. It banished the rest of his temper. Fair was fair, after all—he could have gone over the day before, but he hadn't wanted to. And it wasn't like Eflis and Sparrow had been lying in wait for Dasta in particular. It could as easily have been him, or Gillor. In fact, Sparrow probably would have preferred Gillor.

Tcholan grunted. "Winter."

"And word has to have gone out by now, since that trader we retook was on its way to Everon. Venn should know about it by now. And our orders were to winter at Freeport. If we sail for the Freedom Isles, Elgar can have ordered us there while he goes off scouting the strait. We buy the entire winter without him, and no more of this sneaking around. So here's my idea. See what you think."

Tcholan nodded. "Go on."

"We both be Elgar for this last one, to take down Bendal. We'll time it, see, and strike from opposite sides of the island. And then we go, whether we win or lose. Ah, assuming we survive. But I really think the entire island wants an excuse to rise against him. And if we get rid of 'em all, though there's no telling how things will settle out here, it'll sound good about Elgar, won't it?"

Tcholan's enthusiasm rekindled, faint but there. "Sure 'nuff, after all I heard all night on the galleys."

"Then let's see what Gillor says when she gets back from scouting. See, if we plan it exactly, I think we can bring this one off, and Eflis' people won't suspect . . ."

Chapter Twenty-seven

CHIEF Sea Dag Valda waited in Jaro's Dag Hel. The few dags who came and went paid their respects. Valda was revered at least as much as Erkric was feared. Most were surprised to see her, for they'd known she had gone north to the homeland.

Now she was back, and as usual no one said why. But sea dags were trained to work and think independently, for they lived isolated for long periods on extended cruises.

The first snow had fallen the night before; it had not stuck, and the rooftops along the bowl of Jaro were wet, not white, but the air was cold. The Chief Dag sat near the fire, working patiently at recopying an old magic taeran she'd brought from the north.

At last the dag she had waited for arrived, so unobtrusive one wouldn't notice her unless on the watch.

Valda beckoned, and Dag Signi saluted, her hands evoking not just grace but warmth in touch and then opening of palms, a gesture that was so stiff, so perfunctory in others. There were two other dags at work in the room, each absorbed in tasks. Valda said, "Come. I have news from your family."

Dag Signi made the peace sign again and followed her chief into the next room.

Signi knew that was a lie. Her mother had not spoken to Signi since the day she was called before the Chief Skalt and told that she would not be in the last year's nine in the hel-dance training. Seventeen years, their training group down to eleven. She and a young man were deemed not equal to the nearly impossible standard—and there was no gainsaying the decision.

They had treated her with the respect due to seventeen years of hard work. They had given her a choice of other paths to follow, and when she chose magery, they had cleared the way. But her mother, a hel dancer all her life, had turned her back on her daughter for her failure; her father had returned to Goerael when the war began ten years before that. She had not heard from him since, did not even know if he lived.

So her heartbeat raced.

Valda shut the door. "Did you perceive a change in atmosphere?"

The Chief Dag never asked frivolous questions. Signi said, "I did indeed, as soon as I stepped off the ship. There are far more of the Guard about. The Ymarans are subdued, even fearful, much as it was many years ago, when I was first sent here. What has happened?"

Valda pressed her thin fingers together. "I do not know the truth. The first rumor said that the pirate Elgar the Fox was alive after all and led a horde against Beila Lana, then burned the entire east coast. Since I arrived, the rumors have dwindled—the damage was apparently confined to part of Limros Palace, and Ulaffa told me in a private interview this morning that the horde was two men."

"Why would two men burn Limros Palace?"

"I do not know, and it matters little. What does matter is that people believe that the prince was under attack from this pirate on the direct order of the king of Iasca Leror."

Signi gasped, then covered her mouth with her hand.

Valda's old face mirrored the pain she felt. "Yes. Outwardly there has been a change: decadent, venal Ymaran custom is now deplored, and we are to return to the clean-living discipline of Venn life. But in command circles it is known that the invasion of Halia has been ordered at last."

The inner room had no windows, yet Signi felt the instinctive urge to look out to the sea, as if to find the entire war fleet lined in battle array.

Valda was too sorrowful to smile. "It will happen the spring after next. That is a secret bound by heart and blood."

Signi signified assent, the gesture deliberate with sincerity.

"Erkric was absent during the events that transpired. He says he was north, and I can attest to his presence before the king at the end of the time in question, for he was there when I was. And he secured the king's order for the invasion, though I do not know what he said to convince the king to reverse his decision."

Signi knew the king had been adamant about avoiding two major wars on different continents.

"This coming spring the army will march west and drill on the coast for invasion. The fleet is ordered to be readied for transport and defense, which means altering many ships."

Signi steadied her heartbeat, then said, "Fulla Durasnir?"

Valda murmured, "He approves. It is clear to see."

Signi thought, *We lost him; now the invasion will occur.* For a long time he had supported their wish for an end to invasions, the terrible cost in lives.

Valda added with indirect delicacy, "I suspect it seems an honorable solution to the growing problems here. He follows the king's orders, as he swore to do." She spoke in a whisper. "But, Signi, if we cannot win peace, then the time has come for the inner circle to act."

Signi's flesh roughened with chill. "You tell me because it is I who has been selected?"

"Yes. I had thought to be the one to go, but there is that variance in Erkric's words about where he was during the trouble with this Elgar."

Signi listened in worried silence. One of the dags' first oaths was to always tell the truth to one another. They dealt with so much power that every decision must be examined, every action explained. It was far too easy for human beings to be seduced into craving and then using power for personal means, first in the small things and then in the great. That much they knew from history.

Valda said, "I sense . . ." She hesitated, then made a gesture that Signi interpreted: it was a blurred version of the hel dancer's Rainorec posture, the ancient sign for the great doom that the Venn would face if pride and desire drew them off the golden path. And she said, "There has been too much talk about Ramis, and specifically about Norsunder. You know my fears that he will seek what he wants from them."

Signi nodded. Then said, "I do not argue, query only, but should not Halvic or Finni be as good to send, if not better? I know Halvic learned some of the southern tongues when he was young, and Finni is a teacher, so she could make clear what must be taught."

Even saying that much was dangerous.

Valda acknowledged. The mission she was sending loyal Signi on would probably mean death, and would definitely mean lifelong exile even if successful. The golden path to the Tree of Ydrasal required no less. "Halvic was sent to the northeast waters."

"Ah." He was the best Speaker to the Deeps.

"Finni has been attached by Erkric to speed along training of the new sea dags against this invasion. I dare not gainsay. We must make not a ripple in any water. Therefore you are to carry on as always, but you must sound every ship, and pick the one you think might be won to the cause. Even half to the cause," Valda said unwillingly, and Signi's heart squeezed at the thought of adding mutiny to her future oath-breakings. All to the greater good, alas.

There was nothing more to be said. She had known when she joined the conspiracy that it could mean her life. But the road to Ydrasal was golden in spirit, if hard and perilous in the world. Once you saw it, you must set your foot on it, and not flinch at risks.

They made the Ydrasal obeisance to one another, and departed without speaking again.

*   *   *

In the royal city of Iasca Leror, white and cold under the first big storm of winter, the Master of the Mint levered himself up onto his cane, frowning at the other guild counselors. His position as oldest—he'd now served under three kings—as well as his prestige as Master of the Mint quieted the others, as he intended it should.

They looked up. Jab of the invisible knife: there were now more gray heads than yellow or brown. They'd gotten old without him noticing. "It's clear that Evred-Harvaldar isn't coming to us today. Why argue about what it means?" he said.

"He didn't even send a Runner," protested the ironmongers' guild master.

The irascible wheelwright guild chief huffed, "An insult, surely? His father always—"

The Master of the Mint turned his back on the florid wheelwright and stomped out. Voices rose behind him; he sighed. Apparently gabbling your own unanswerable guesses without listening to the others was preferable to getting back to business.

Well, considering how grim things were for business, maybe they had a point. He would not feel better returning to agonizing about when the magic spells protecting the royal treasury—and the coin-strikes—would vanish. Or speculating on why the mages had not come, despite word of the prospective new Adrani treaty.

On he shuffled; his old sword wound ached during winter these days almost as much as it had when he first got it fifty-five years ago.

His granddaughter waited inside the door to the visitors' stable yard. The door opened and slammed five times as the master shuffled slowly down the hall; five times cold air blasted in, bringing the smell of wool and dog and horse, the sounds of shouts and clashes of steel from the Guard busy at work somewhere over the wall beyond the stable.

He reached her at last. "I visited Cousin Shel," she whispered. "Posted right up there." She pointed above their heads. "She says that Barend-Harskialdna arrived as the king was leaving breakfast."

"Ah." The master frowned at his granddaughter. "And?"

"And then a Rider appeared, and they all dropped everything. It was the king's First Runner, Vedrid, who used to be Runner for the Sierlaef so long ago. That happened right before I came to you." She gestured toward the stable yard and a swarm of young stable hands busy with the horses. Well, that explained where the king was, but not why.

"Then we'll go home." The Master of the Mint sighed. "Maybe it'll be good news for once."

While they made their way into the slushy stable yard, high in a tower room on the other side of the castle, Evred-Harvaldar shut a heavy iron-studded door with his own hands and turned to face Vedrid. "I thought you were dead," he said. "You have been gone a year."

Vedrid forced himself to stay upright by locking his knees. "I . . ." His brain clouded strangely, and he could not find the words, or form them.

Next thing he knew he was sitting in an armchair, something hot in his hands. The near faint passed, and he tried to drink, but the rim of the metal cup clattered unpleasantly against his teeth.

A shifting of cloth, breathing, and the king's hand, rough from years of daily sword work, guided the mulled wine to his mouth, where the welcome warmth flooded. Pungent spices and a sweet taste fired along his nerves.

"I should get used to you arriving half frozen," Evred said with a rare smile. "But never again will you be asked to leave the kingdom. You are restored to your rightful place in Marlovan life as my first Runner; you will choose the ones for those months-long missions."

Vedrid flushed with emotion, though he was too numb to express it.

But what Evred saw in his face was enough, though he looked grave. "How many horses since you slept last?"

"Six." Another sip. Protocol was gone in this new dreamworld. Vedrid leaned his head back against the king's chair, and his eyes closed of their own accord. "Six horses. I was desperate to get through the passes before the snows closed everything off until summer." He was drifting into exhausted sleep, and forced himself to speak. "And then . . . with home a day or so's ride away, if I pushed myself . . ."

"Talk. Just the gist, then you may rest."

Vedrid made an effort and opened his eyes, to find the king on one knee beside him, his face now grim. Alarm dissipated the shroud of exhaustion.

"He will never again come to the west," Vedrid said. "When I reached Bren last summer everything had changed, in ways I could not define. When I first went to Bren at your order, the Guild was open enough. But this time—" The man shook his head. "Nowhere would anyone talk about Elgar the Fox, unless it was to ask me questions about why I was asking. I know there are secrets, but I fear I am not trained enough to winnow them out. You need spies, Evred-Harvaldar, not Runners. The old man they call the Fleet Master followed me out and questioned me himself. I lied, said I was seeking a cousin. He told me to leave, he said he knew I'd been asking questions in the harbor. I stayed another week, trying to be more discreet . . ." He turned the warm cup around in his cold hands as he tried to ward that memory. "And it was a ship captain, one of the Guild Fleet captains, who set his sailors to ambush me. They dragged me into a cellar and they might have kicked me to death, but someone else intervened. I don't remember much. I had a broken elbow, broken jaw, smashed bones in both feet. Some of the memory might be mere dream. The one who stopped them was very much like a dream image of the golden angels of the old Sartoran New Year's songs. I think someone even called him Angel." At a sudden movement, a quick frown from the king, he raised a tired hand. "I know how it must sound. All I can tell you is what I experienced, wrong as it might be. In the dream this Angel gave me some drink to ease the pain, and spoke Iascan to me, and I answered—and then he told me, in Iascan, to leave and never come back."

The king's face hardened. "What did you tell this person?"

"I can't remember the exact words. And I have tried! Hearing Iascan, and that pain—"

"Was it white kinthus he gave you?"

"No. I know what that feels like," Vedrid stated, endeavoring to smile. "Lister-leaf, willow, maybe some green

kinthus. In any case he said clearly—this I remember—
'Tell your king that Elgar the Fox will never return to the
west.' When I healed enough to travel I left Bren."

Evred did not hear the last words. He remembered,
quite clearly, the golden-haired, golden-eyed fellow at
Inda's side that day in Lindeth Harbor. The same one?
Surely not.

Never again return to the west.

Someone who knew Inda, apparently. To gain a little
time he poured more wine and offered it to Vedrid, who
sipped once, then held it in both hands for the warmth.

By then Evred had mastered his emotions. "Go on."

"The northern mountain passes to Idayago are full of
hired bravos, some say forced on the Djedani by the Venn.
I don't know if it is true, but I do know it was impossible to
pass safely. I had to make my way south into Anaeran-
Adrani. That was very late in the harvest season. At once I
started hearing murmurs against us, even against their own
king, all about magic."

Evred opened his hand. "Go on."

Vedrid sighed. "It's easier to talk now. Thank you." He
set aside the cup. "Though I might sleep a week when I do
lie down."

"You will have that week. What did you discover?"

"The gossip about our coming over to make war with
magic aid I discounted as garbled repeats of some real
news. Thought I'd better find out what it was. For that I had
to make my way east, toward the capital, where I chanced
to fall in with vendors carrying Fire Sticks to sell for winter. They were angry at having to charge double prices, in-
curring the anger of the locals."

Evred-Harvaldar threw the cooled wine into the fire and
poured more from the pitcher on the hob. "Drink."

Another sip and warmth flooded the exhausted man.
"Winnowing out truth from rumor was not hard. The Mage
Council in Sartor decreed the Adranis won't get their own
spells of renewal except under supervision because of this
treaty of alliance they made with the evil empire to the
west."

"Evil . . ."

"Empire. That being us here."

"Whom do they see as the evil emperor of this evil empire? Ah, that would be me," Evred said dryly.

Vedrid grimaced. "I cannot tell you how angry that made me. But I revealed nothing."

Evred laughed softly as he moved to the window. "So I am the evil emperor now. A place I never thought to fill in the annals of our time." He turned around, making an effort to lighten the atmosphere. "Such news inspires me to regard the evil emperors of history with more sympathy." The tension he sensed was entirely his; Vedrid was trying valiantly to repress a yawn. So he said, "No matter. Continue with your journey."

"So then I started back. It took this long to get through the passes."

"I wondered why Valdon-Prince had not kept his word." Evred walked away, now thinking of the emptying treasury; Barend's bleak report; of the unrest among people worried about taxes, dwindling food supplies, fading bridge and fire spells, and who were exhorted to prepare for a war that always seemed to be coming but never arrived.

The embargo was an effective weapon, if you had the power and the will to maintain it. Another five years, and the kingdom would be too weak to resist a massive landing.

He swung around again. "Valdon is my cousin, and he will have had private conversations with my mother. Yet he, too, believes me to be an evil emperor?"

"No," Vedrid said. "There was nothing directly said, but he apparently campaigned strongly on your behalf, aided by Joret-Edli, until the king, pressured by these same mages, ordered him on an inspection tour of their coastal harbors to get him away from court. And Hadand-Gunvaer is being escorted to the border."

"By warriors?"

"Yes, that's what I was told. An Honor Guard, they called it."

"But they want to see that she gets to the border and doesn't go back? So that's why she's not here—if they let her ride alone, she'd be faster," Evred said. "I hope she doesn't get caught by the mountain snows."

"I suspect they will send a mage along. They seem to have spells for road clearing."

"Ah." Evred thought of Hadand on her way home, and some of the weight on his thoughts eased. Just for a moment. "Then there will be no help from my cousin, despite Valdon's goodwill." Evred's thoughts returned to the previous interview and Barend standing where Vedrid was now, equally cold and numb, his eyes weary and pained as he said, "Spongie, the Venn themselves have struck twice, scouting forays, against Olara and the north coast of Idayago. I think I'd better go all the way north and see what I can do."

Barend had been gone a week when, for the very first time, the trumpets on the city walls played the "Queen's Charge," which was the same as the "King's Charge," only the triplets were a cascade down instead of up the scales.

Hadand, tired and weary and cold, felt her heart lift at the sound and at the sight of home. Because for her, Tenthen had ceased to be home when she was a child: the royal city was home.

And to greet her there was not only her beloved, but her mother.

Evred was plainly glad to see her, though he deferred to Fareas-Iofre, who gripped her daughter in a long hug. Tired as she was, Hadand was aware of the women in their places, everyone looking alert and strong and focused, such a contrast to the decorative women of the Adrani court. She said two or three times, unaware of doing so, "It's good to be back. It's *good* to be back. Ah, it *is* good to be back."

She handed the treaty to her husband, who looked down at it wryly, then said, "We will consider it a gesture of amity on Valdon's part."

"Yes," Hadand said. "Do. He promised me in private that he would keep striving with the Mage Council. And as soon as he can, he will take a more active interest."

"What does that mean? When his father is dead?" Evred

asked. And with a mordant humor she had once thought unlike him, "I don't know whether to approve or—"

"There will not be any palace massacres," she said, trying to match his tone. And then, more seriously, "The king is giving over most of his powers of governing, one by one. He thinks them tedious beyond bearing. Val might see that they become more tedious and protracted, but I assure you that is the extent of his plotting." Hadand gave a tired laugh, thinking of Val's last surprise as he conducted her to the huge closed carriage she was expected to ride in to the border, surrounded by guards in their very finest armor and weaponry.

Hadand had been protesting that, no, really, despite the weather she would just as soon ride, when she climbed in and found Lord Randon waiting, finger to his lips, a picnic basket at his feet.

She chuckled at the memory, her gaze distant, her mouth tender. Evred hoped that she'd found some romance to liven her long, exasperating diplomatic mission.

Later on, Hadand and Fareas-Iofre dined together. The Iofre would leave for Choraed Elgaer on the morrow, so Evred excused himself, leaving mother and daughter alone. He sat instead in his study, writing letters about the treaty, a row of waiting Runners having readied their travel gear.

"It has been a good summer," Fareas said. "I have gotten to know your young man as much as he permits anyone to know him."

"He does hide himself, doesn't he?" Hadand said. "I was afraid it might just be from me."

"No, he has closed his emotions off from the world. He seems to regard that as part of his duty." Fareas slid her hands into her sleeves. "We sat together most nights—when he did not feel that duty required him to work from dawn to midnight without a single halt. When we were together, it was always in the archive, by his desire. I must say, he is the best student I have ever taught. He shares with

Inda such a thirst for historical knowledge, only his is the far-sighted interest of the man, and not the boy's wish for battles, excitement, and curiosities."

"Which would be Inda's too, no doubt," Hadand said. "Now that he too is grown."

"Of course. The thing is, though we touched on the lives and manners of countless monarchs, poets, and other famous names through history, he never once strayed into the personal. Courteous, scrupulous, ferocious in concentration, yes. It's hard to remember he is as young as he is; I felt myself talking to him as if he were his father, with decades of experience behind him."

"He's had plenty of experience." Hadand was upset, uneasy. "Maybe too much."

"Perhaps. But as far as I can see there is no true love in his life. Favorites, yes, occasionally; Chelis oversees the women on guard, which includes the list of those who may pass unchallenged down the halls. Including from your own pleasure house. Almost never the same man. And none of them are in his heart—it's seldom the same one twice in a row, and he never lets them spend the night."

Hadand sighed.

Fareas touched her daughter's hand. "You are in love—remember the Old Sartoran *thorned rose,* the passion that is not returned—but you must also love. Because he does love you, in all the ways except passion, and that is a love that must be encouraged, for his own well-being as well as yours. Remember."

And Hadand said, "I promise."

Chapter Twenty-eight

WHEN the spring melt began, Sea Dag Signi came at last before the Chief Sea Dag Valda and said, "We are ordered to sea, and I have found a berth on the *Bluewing Seeker*, scout for the *Bluewing* raider, attached to warship *Petrel*. This patrol group is assigned the mid-strait. As all warships sail west, this is the closest I could come to Sartor."

Chief Sea Dag Valda gazed through the western window. Soon the army would march toward that warm sun that set so slowly; lives and more lives would be sped from the light.

She pressed her fingertips to her temples, as though that would ease the hammer of tension inside her skull. She faced one of the most difficult decisions in centuries. It would be enough of a bramble for one lifetime, but a second terrible discovery had sent up its thorny shoots to block the golden path—both connected to the same secret, ramifying root of iniquity.

She made a gesture of command to Signi. "What I feared has come true. Witness."

Valda brought from inside of her robe a hand-sized polished steel mirror, a thing Signi recognized with dismay. The magic required to capture living moments and bind them in these mirrors was a complexity that taxed one to the extreme. Such tools were never used idly.

Signi forced her gaze to the mirror, which did not reflect

her face. She gazed instead into a light-distorted archway, skeined with shadows. Perhaps it was once a beautiful place—a terrace opening into a garden—the tile floor tessellated in patterns of blue and gold overlaid with highly stylized herons on the wing. Through the vine-covered arch a garden was crowned by three cypresses, the middle oval higher than the outer two. A dark point appeared before the arch, flickering outward like a thousand night-black moths; they vanished and Erkric emerged into the sourceless light.

He struggled for breath, recovering from a transfer even more wrenching than crossing continents; Signi knew then that this archway led to a place beyond physical space and even time.

"Gateway to Norsunder," Valda whispered, and Signi's body flinched, but her gaze did not waver.

Through the archway stepped a young woman. She was tall, her long, dark hair bound up in a complicated knot-work of silver from which hung tiny shivering pendants. Below the cold glitter of the headdress was a narrow, dark-eyed face smiling with malice. Her gown of raw silk, made high to the neck, gleamed with vermilion highlights and was fastened with clasps in a tulip motif.

"Yeres," Erkric whispered.

She said, "Ah, you are persistent, Venn."

"Determined." Erkric's voice was thin and breathy. Signi watched him fight for strength he did not have.

Yeres' lip curled. "Then you had better not bore me with speeches this time. As well my brother is elsewhere; he has not nearly my patience. What do you want?"

Erkric's voice cracked. "The wherewithal to make rift between sky and ground."

"And then?"

"And then you shall have anyone I send through."

Yeres laughed, a tiny high screel, like the death of a bird. "The rifts are closed."

Erkric said, "I need that magic."

"So do we," she said. "But those are games only played every century or so. You will have to cooperate with your Sartoran counterparts to lift that ward they struggled so hard to place. Or wait a few hundred years, until they forget again and cease their vigilance." ——

"If Ramis can have that magic, why cannot I?"

"Ramis!" Again the high, thin dart of laughter. "Think what you are about, Venn." She stepped aside and lifted her hand so that Erkric could see the garden and the shadowy figures seated within. The pale light haloed one figure, a tall one with white hair: a morvende. The strange light seemed to gather about him, but with no life or warmth. His hair, his flesh, his robe were all the white of the northern ice which, at the briefest touch, burns down to the bone. Signi was not ordinarily a fanciful being, but she had the sense that this morvende's lifted eyes would strike her dead.

At his feet knelt a man in a light gray robe, its lines fine and simple. His unremarkable brown hair was touched with strands of gray; his shadowed face was lowered, his hands resting flat on his thighs.

"Ramis," Valda whispered.

Signi wished to ask how she knew, but these captured moments did not wait, and so she suppressed the question. Just watched.

Erkric's breath hissed in.

"You really want magic that uses will as weapon," Yeres said, "but you have not yet offered us sufficient trade. I deplore your lack of vision."

And the mirror went dark.

Valda laid it carefully down. "Almost a month of my life I squandered, waiting in that place. I was protected by a circle of mages, and yet I sensed another shield—one I can scarcely define—when I was there."

"You identified that man in the gray robe as Ramis."

"Yes, for we met." Valda's eyes were wide with remembered shock. "My single visit to Roth Drael. The mages there do not trust us Venn, and I discovered why. Ramis transferred while I was walking from one building to another—no transfer tiles, no reaction. I recognized that robe from a wall painting deep below one of the buildings of white material, impossibly old, the writings the vertical Sartoran of ancient days." She gestured high to low, two fingers making a scissoring motion. "He is far older than any of us thought. He said, 'Abyarn Erkric has chosen the path of Rainorec.' "

Signi's startled gaze met Valda's. No Venn ever spoke of Rainorec before strangers.

"He then said, 'If you do not see, you follow.' "

Signi exclaimed, "How strange, for this man to come to you in such a way! Did you not suspect evil intent?"

Valda sighed. "I might have had I not already harbored my own doubts about Erkric. But even then, I must speak with care. It is far too easy to say, 'He is evil.' Does a man who was so kind to us all when we were young, who has always worked so tirelessly, wake up one morning and decide henceforth he will turn to evil?"

Signi said, "I believe I know your thrust. Did not someone among the Sartorans write that there is no human more dangerous than he or she who is most devoted to an ideal?"

"I have so read," Valda said, drawing a deep breath. "Yet are we not devoted to Ydrasal? I would amend it to say, 'those who will justify any means to serve their ideal.' Ideals are seldom evil—outside of Norsunder—and who can say what their justification is? But Erkric's ideal is no longer Ydrasal, which demands balance with all things; it has become the ascendance of the Venn, at any cost." She lowered her voice to a whisper. "Rainorec."

Rainorec—the doom of the Venn—did not always mean the same thing to everyone. Many felt that Rainorec lay in a shady future, perhaps the result of prideful but weak leaders being overcome by evil enemies; most ordinary folk regarded it as a term of disapprobation for adults, much as "naughty" is used for chiding children. Valda's mage circle believed that no doom was worse than that suffered by one too high, who held too much power, because the powerful, in falling, took everyone under their command with them.

Signi bowed her head, palms together in assent.

Valda touched the stone. "Durasnir, for example, hates Erkric, yet would defend his actions before the king saying—and believing—none more loyal to Ydrasal."

"I agree." Signi considered. "Tell me more about Ramis."

Valda set aside the mirror. "I asked how I was to see more than I saw already. Ramis said if I truly followed Ydrasal then I must witness in that place I showed you. It has taken me months to master first the magic, then to learn how to stay undetected in the realm of the spirit. I was protected by our circle in the homeland. One of us cannot manage alone. Even so, it takes us all at least a day to recover after such a session."

"Realm of the spirit," Signi repeated in a whisper almost without sound. "How do we contend with people who talk so easily about such things, who speak of waiting for centuries?"

"We do not. We must contrive with what we know." Valda brushed her hands over her face again, as if to wipe away the memory of what she had endured. "Erkric was thrust back here, in Jaro; he was unconscious, the servants spoke of blood." She touched her ears and nose. "I came away through the means I had learned."

Signi said, "Will he get such magic?"

"It is clear he was there before. You saw what I saw on this visit: do you not think he will go again, when he can, no matter the cost, until he gains what he desires?"

"Yes. But does such magic exist outside of Norsunder? There is no reference to it in our own archive, and I have seen nothing that indicates the Sartoran Mage Council has access to such spells."

"In the historical record there are references. It belongs to the ancient days, because it was systematically destroyed after what the Sartorans call the Fall."

"Can we act against the Dag? The intent of such spells is against all we do!"

"And yet Prince Rajnir has agreed to magical experiments. He is convinced such magic will achieve the king's will. Erkric uses the prince's anger. He will experiment on Count Wafri first, the prospect of which delights Rajnir. The Dag has," she said softly, "promised Rajnir Sartor, by subjugating Iasca Leror by magic after the invasion. The Marlovan warriors can be sent east to take new land for the Venn, and no one will be able to stop them."

Signi felt chill down to her bones.

"And Rajnir rejoices. He craves a brilliant success that will reinstate him in the grace of the king."

Signi gripped her forearms close against her body. "Then ... you cannot believe the Dag means to control Rajnir?"

"Why do you think the Sartoran Mage Council destroyed all evidence of such magic, long ago—before we even learned it in the Land of the Venn? Aside from the questions of what the Old Sartorans could or could not do by nature, what human being now can master that much power and not be warped by it? The gaining of power becomes, in a succession of small decisions, an end in itself—always for the right reasons."

Signi made a swift gesture evocative of desire. "At last, it is sufficient just to want. And so you must gain proof that the Dag ... walks the path of Rainorec?" She knew it was weakness, but she could not bring herself to give voice to the words: that if Erkric sought to assure victory over the Marlovans with the aid of Norsundrian magic, the next step along that path would be to subjugate Rajnir to his will so that, if the prince was brought to the throne of the Venn to replace the king, in effect Erkric would be king, with so much power no one could resist him.

Valda bowed her head. "That is my task. We have direful work before us because the need is dire. I cannot stand before the throne and accuse the Dag without proof. In the meantime, you must find allies on that ship, without mentioning the cause, because when I give you the sign, you must act." She looked old and afraid.

Signi said, "The sign will be orders that separate us from the patrol?"

"Yes. It might be a month, more likely longer. But when your *Bluewing Seeker* is alone on the water, wherever it is sent, you must act at once."

Valda made the sign of peace, returned by Signi. They knew this was probably the last time they would see one another.

*   *   *

Each day as the sun rose a little earlier Jeje had wondered which dawn would bring Inda back.

She had come to expect that, if he arrived at all, it would be at the head of a mighty fleet or with some sort of parade suitable more to a king than to a not-quite-pirate's exile.

But it was a quiet arrival, exactly a year and two days after they'd parted. A messenger appeared in Fleet House, waving significantly at Jeje before scampering upstairs to where Chim was busy with some captains.

That look was enough. Jeje's heart thumped, and her hands shook as she straightened her work area.

So she was ready when Chim came downstairs, summoning her with a beetle-browed glance. The messenger ran out, and before long the familiar tall, stout, gray-eyed Guild Mistress Perran emerged from the cooperage and joined them.

The three of them met Inda on the way to a cotton weaver's shop, where Chim was certain they could be assured of privacy. Inda paid the child handsomely. She grinned again at Jeje—she was one of the trainees, as were her mother and uncle—then vanished into the crowd.

Jeje studied Inda. Strange how you don't see someone for a year, and though you recognize him instantly, he looks different. Older. The planes of Inda's face were sharp, the boy long gone. Yet his sudden smile when he saw Jeje recalled the fellow rat of their days on the Pim ships. It was a sweet smile, an odd thing in so wary a face.

She did not yet know how glad he was to see her. More than glad. Gone forever was the blithe assumption of loyalty. Wafri had destroyed that. But each encounter with one of his friends who appeared when and where they had promised to be was as strong as any healing spell to his heart: first Mutt, and then Dasta and Tcholan, with the new fleet they'd been building up, all waiting for him at the Smuggler's Cove off Danai Harbor.

She scrutinized him again. He moved with the sailor's rolling gait, almost a swagger, his long, four-strand sailor's queue swinging. He wore his sun-bleached, much-mended unlaced fighting shirt under a long vest, despite the heat. Jeje knew he was fully armed.

She fell in step beside him, then laughed inside. It had never occurred to her how short Inda was compared to most mainlanders, though she still had to look up at him, being a full hand shorter.

They followed Chim up narrow stairs. The hot summer air was thick with the smell of spiced cabbage mixed with the aroma of too many people in rain-soaked clothing. Thunder rumbled in the distance; until this morning there had been no rain for days. Dust seemed to hang suspended in the air.

The waiting Guild Fleet members and six captains all murmured greetings, studying the famed Elgar the Fox with a mixture of reactions. They sat along the walls on crates and barrels, leaving the single plank bench for Inda and those who accompanied him.

"Are ye ready?" Fleet Master Chim asked Inda as soon as they sat down.

"No," Inda said.

Guild Mistress Perran gasped, then glanced Jeje's way.

"I've spent a year watching. Sometimes running," Inda said, the last part wry.

He looked older and tougher partly because he had a new scar, this one on the other side of his face. A long one, too, vanishing into his hair. Jeje shuddered. Hard as they'd drilled, those were only drills. Inda's presence made violence imminent again.

Guild Mistress Perran, who had come to like and trust the gruff Jeje, felt her mouth go dry; Chim thought of the Venn threats and subsequent royal decrees, the spies, interguild wrangling, dwindling funds, and, worst of all, interrupted trade, but said only, "Why?"

"They communicate by magic," Inda said. "I want some of those scroll-cases they use."

Chim and Perran saw their question mirrored. She said, "I know what you mean, but I've never actually seen them. Only aristocrats can afford them. The harbormaster has one, but it goes with the job, not with the person. Maybe in Sartor they are common, but that is a long journey, as you know."

"And costly. Damn costly," Chim scolded, his worries about vanishing funds goading him.

For an answer Inda stuck his hand inside his vest, brought out a heavy cloth bag, and tossed it into Chim's lap with a flick as though getting rid of something repugnant.

The gnarled old fingers stiffly undid the tie, and the contents spilled out onto the worn wooden floor. The Bren officials gasped when they saw the rich glitter of gemstones. Not ordinary gemstones, they saw at once. These were rare, rich, first quality in color, purity, and cut. A king's ransom. A kingdom's.

Perran looked up accusingly. "You *are* a pirate."

"They came from . . . a pirate," Inda said.

Jeje wondered what he had been about to say; Chim and Perran were too busy gauging the gems to notice the pause.

"Ah." Perran glanced up, with a knowing air. "Then you did clear the Fire Islands of pirates? All the eastern traders have complained about how bold they'd gotten since the disappearance of the Brotherhood. Rumor put you there, but no one knew for certain."

Inda turned up a hand. "Needed clearing. Now. The Venn always know where their fleets are, so in effect they are twice as fast as us. We have to send a messenger and then wait for response. Their messages go instantly."

"You are sure."

"Saw one used." Inda touched the new scar with absent fingers, then leaned back. "Any news here?" He glanced Jeje's way, and she knew he was thinking about Tau's absence.

"The Venn sniffed something out, somewhere," Chim said. "We're not blamin' ye—and if they blame yez for clearin' the Fire Islands, they are stupider than we thought. But still. Threats to us—we can only travel down the strait within close sight o' land, and only in singles, doubles if small craft. Threats t' the guilds. Spies. Which is why we're here, and not at Fleet House. Thank ye for sending a messenger," he added.

"It's not news that they're after me," Inda said.

Perran said, "We hoped you would be ready. Clear orders for action would resolve a lot of the problems that have beset us since winter and the resumption of the drills with no launch prospect in sight."

Inda said, "If we go now, we'll be slaughtered. We're going to need a hundred capital ships. Their core fleet is eighty-one warships, and each of those has attendant scouts and raiders. And that's just Rajnir's fleet. The king has far more up north and could send them at any time."

Chim whistled.

Perran glanced his way, kneaded her fingers, then said as briskly as she could, "I understand. Perhaps the magic communications, if they are something that we can locate and learn to use, would aid us now. The magic would summon our trade ships when needed."

Chim fingered his beard. "Hm. So. Yes."

Jeje, who knew him pretty well, recognized when he was serious and when he was trying to provoke by the language he spoke in. When he mixed his serious Sartoran with his broken Dock Talk, he was in a muddle. Like now. "We could in fact send out the ships we've collected, with our trained 'defenders' hired to actually defend. Make some money. Keep our owners happy. Get experience on Jeje's trainees. Guild-owned ships bein', ye might say, one thing, and owner-run ships another. Hum. Hum! Yes." He nodded.

"Then I'll get back to sea while the winds are good," Inda said. "And, short of a message, you'll hear from me again in a year."

Another *year*. Jeje clenched her jaw against complaint. She followed the others out of the hot little room and down the worn stairs.

While Chim's and Perran's voices faded into the distance, she became aware of a step at her side.

Inda said, "Where's Tau?"

"At the theater."

Inda frowned. "The what?"

"It's a building where they act out plays."

Inda wiped his brow, then shook his head. "Oh, yes. I heard about those last summer."

"I saw my first one here. I guess it's common enough in Sartor's royal city and Alsayas in Colend. Maybe other places. The players don't travel about. Instead, people come to them. Anyone who has the door price can come, once the court has seen each new thing."

Inda waggled a hand. "Tau?"

"I'm getting there. See, they don't only perform old ones, they write new ones, and furthermore, they put sneaky things in. Jokes about foreign rulers, or current unpopular people in court, and the like. You go to the playhouse to hear all the real news," she finished. "Tau, being Tau, is the favorite of the first-ranking woman player. She holds a kind of court after the new plays—there's one a month during the winter season—and everybody of any importance, land or sea, tries to get invited. They go, they drink, and they talk. Especially to the prince, who's on our side. So we get all the news, while Tau hands 'round the wine and makes them all laugh."

Inda whistled.

"So first thing: Tau hasn't heard anything but rumor about Ramis of the *Knife*. Anyone who's heard of him has nothing but rumor to pass on. Each wilder than the last." She added dryly, "Apparently the crown princess had decided he doesn't exist, and that Prince Kavna cannot spend any more money sending messengers to discover anything about him."

Inda grunted. "Go on."

"We train every morning, he and I. We do Fox's hand drills, which we haven't taught the others. But he went to sleep a few moments before your messenger came, and we're used to trading news, so I didn't want to wake him. I'll tell him anything you want me to say."

"Tell him that Dasta and Mutt were more successful than I'd thought. They met me at Smugglers' Cove with a good size fleet, but it's not nearly enough. Dhalshev is also recruiting for us, Dasta said—but again it's not enough, not to face the entire Venn fleet. It's going to take at least a year—more—everyone working together to build the kind of fleet that can take on the Venn."

Inda stopped right there in the street, forcing annoyed pedestrians to thread around them, and looked into her face. "You're unhappy."

"Not just me. Tau is as well, despite all the things I told you. We were hoping to soon be at sea," she finished in a rush.

Inda sighed, looked down, then up. "I'm sorry. But we can't be careless. I was. And got myself caught once, up north of The Fangs on the Ymar side. I'd be dead if it wasn't for Fox." A brief grin. "Escaped and made a mess of things."

Jeje made a face, uncomfortable, though she could not define why. "I hope that means you made the mess on them."

"Yes. But they did for me first." Inda went on before she could ask any questions. "There's a big war going on much farther north. Kingdoms allied against the Venn. My immediate goal now is to finish charting the north coast of the strait. Which has little travel on it. Now I know why, if the Venn are handing out orders against sailing down the middle like we used to. My other immediate goal is to capture one of those mages, which means taking a Venn ship," he finished. "Not a capital ship. Don't think I could. They rarely sail alone, and they're bigger than our biggest ships. With their magic connections, they can sail far ahead or behind, out of sight of any others—but one magic message and they sail fast to one another's aid. They have mages, and the mages have those communications as well as their navigation spells." His expression was bleak.

Jeje said gruffly, "It's that bad, eh?"

"But I've got one thing in my favor: I've got good charts of the northeastern coast of the strait. I need to chart the west, if I can—and find me a sea dag." Then he did a surprising thing—he bent and kissed her softly on the brow. "You could have been gone, and I would not have blamed either of you. But you were here." His voice went husky; to Jeje's surprise—and discomfort—Inda's eyes gleamed with a liquid sheen. He scrubbed his knuckles over his eyelids. "I don't know why I do that. It happened when I saw Mutt and the others, too." He stuck his hand in his vest and pulled out another, thinner bag. "That's for you two—it's the last of my take from Ghost Island. I won't need it now. I figured you had to be low, if you've been hiring ships and people. Use it however you see fit."

"We were indeed getting low. We have a huge pay list now." Then she had to ask. "That new scar. Ship action?"

A shake of the head. "I mentioned I was caught. By a local lord, supposedly an ally of Prince Rajnir. The little shit liked playing with his prisoners." When she flipped up the back of her hand in the general direction of Ymar he chuckled. "Fox came for me. On our way out, we decided we might as well make a suitable gesture—that mess I mentioned." He cocked his head, listening.

The noises around them were nothing more than the usual people on business or pleasure, many eyes turned skyward in hope of rain. But he sensed something, perhaps a change in the air, or even the tidal pull, some sea sense, perhaps, that a year on land had dulled her to. And then he was off, walking away rapidly, leaving her to wonder what that "gesture" had entailed.

Chapter Twenty-nine

"**I**CE floes," Mutt whispered into the speaking tube.

It was six, almost seven months later. Seven very long months, most of them spent running, sometimes chasing.

Now they were chasing, and had been for three days, a Venn scout ship.

About their size, it had separated off from the raider pack it had been sailing with, whether inadvertently or not. Inda had learned through rough experience to watch them for at least two days, his fleet strung out within mast-sight of one another, as they searched for consorts. They'd discovered that raiders systematically sent out the scouts in all directions, regrouping after a time.

This one had broken the pattern by continuing on to the west after its raider and the other scouts had swung back to the east on their regular route.

And so far, because they were drifting along the island-dotted, treacherous northern coast of the strait—fog-bound and moving under a single course due to ice—the scout seemed as yet unaware of their presence.

But they'd lost it in the fog.

Inda motioned to the waiting forecastle hands. "Booms."

In silence the crew got their long wooden booms and stood along the rail, watching for ice to shove away from the hull. On the jib two sounders tossed their weighted rocks, over and over again, counting the knots in the rope as they pulled them up, and flashing depth measure in finger signs.

They had learned long ago that rocks and fog made strange and unpredictable play with even the quietest voices, so no one spoke above a whisper. The business of guiding the ship through perilous waters was done by sign as much as possible.

Inda stood on the captain's deck of the *Death,* chin tucked into his silk scarf, nose numb, gloved hands shoved into jacket pockets for desperately needed warmth. Gillor was the mate on deck, her masses of curling black hair escaping from a knit sock-cap twin to his own—knitted for them by Lorenda in Freeport Harbor.

The heatless sun glinted coldly off metal and glass, riding above the northern rim of mountains way in the distance as they cruised off the coast of Llyenthur, across the strait from Bren.

"Lee-yin-thur ... Lya-shee-in-thur ... Lyah-*hin*-thur ..." Mutt whispered softly an arm's length above Inda, in an effort to get his tongue around the pronunciation. Should he shush him? No: Mutt's voiceless whisper made less noise than the rustle of water down the sides of the hull. To restrain his own impatience—the merciless grip of tension—Inda forced himself to consider the word and its roots. Sartoran had a lot of those "yah" sounds, but not with "l" and a hint of "sh" mixed in; that was the local accent.

They drifted under a cliff that looked startlingly like a melted castle tower, with its rough sediment layers and corrugated sea holes. On a high ridge behind the palisade a real castle stood, a shaft of sunlight emerging from the fog and glinting off highlights in the dull gray stone.

Inda tipped his head back. A private game he played inside his head, left over from his academy days: assessment of that castle's weak points and assembling a defense. Butterfly flickers on the extreme edge of his vision brought his head around, and for a moment he stared up into the intent faces of a trio of young ladies, aristocrats all, with their tight-fitting, embroidered coats, fine-woven cotton-wool skirts, their pretty hats, and ribbons streaming from one wrist. They walked along the edge of the high palisade not two ship lengths above him, outlined by the castle on the ridge behind them.

To the young ladies, the black-hulled, low-riding, rake-masted pirate ship below was something out of a dream. They stared in delight from one handsome male face to another, hungry gazes lingering on the molding of strong arms against jackets, long legs in high boots, the wild variety in dress that paid no heed to fashion but signified a life of utter freedom.

Then a fog drift obscured them, and when the swirling cloud passed the ship had vanished around a thin finger of rocky cliff thrusting into the sea. The ship was gone, carried seaward by the tide; they watched the towering masts swinging their way westward through the dangerous rocky spires, until fog shrouded them forever.

"Voices."

Inda had already forgotten the ladies. He, too, heard the bounced reverberations of angry argument; Mutt had abruptly ceased his soft whisper. There was no sound except the creak of wood, and the plash of water along the hull.

"Venn," Fox whispered, appearing next to him. "Knew it."

The helmsman pulled hard to the lee, and they rounded a sheer knife of stone reaching high into the air, water booming and splashing on one side. As they safely passed the rocky spire, the fog thinned and they glimpsed *Cocodu* farther out to sea. Inda grabbed the glass and swept the deck. There was Mutt, pointing up at the green flag, which dipped twice: nothing in *Cocodu*'s view, either around them as seen from the sea, or on the sea itself.

That meant no raider pack out in the strait—so far. But there was no cause to gloat. Right now the missing raider had lost its scout no less thoroughly than Inda had.

Voices again!

Inda and Fox exchanged questioning glances. The voices could have been fisher folk or settlers. Disappointment wrung a soundless oath out of Fox, who flung himself aft, striking the taffrail noiselessly with his fist.

Inda, resigned to yet another false trail, winced, aware now of hunger, cold, dull throbbing on his temple where

the most recent sword wound—earned on their last failed
attempt to take a Venn ship—had not yet healed, all things
he'd managed not to notice while they were on the chase.
He drew in a breath to give the order to haul wind, well
away from the dangers of unseen reefs, ice, and rocks—

And a loud scraping—the shearing of wood on stone—
stilled them. Shock, fear, helplessness made their hearts
thunder. They dreaded seeing stone punch up through the
deck and freezing green water swirl after it, to suck them
down to death.

The crash of a splintering impact that followed was even
more shocking—until they realized that the *Death* had
only scraped an unseen rock, but was floating free. The
smash was someone else.

"Venn?" Fox mouthed the word, green eyes wide with
incredulity.

"Has to be," Inda mouthed back, jerking his thumb over
the rail seaward, where they caught a brief glimpse of
Cocodu's topmast, on watch out in the strait; the *Vixen* was
scouting forward, *Rippler* south of *Cocodu*, *Sable* and consorts strung out behind.

A violent gesture from Mutt brought Fox up the mast almost at a run. He slid down a backstay moments later and
grabbed Inda by the neck, slinging him around.

"Venn. Reefed," he said directly into his ear, his free
hand pointing just off the lee bow.

Inda couldn't see anything, but that didn't matter. He
waved his hands, then pointed fore and aft, the gesture
gathering two boarding crews and dispatching them over
the side.

That was the hard part. No use in attacking with arrows
and cut booms—they had to board and take the scout before the mage vanished. So far all they had gotten for all
their care were wounds and chases from raider packs that
could sail out of sight of one another and communicate by
magic—and no mages. In a good wind that left little time
for any attacker—such as themselves. This formation had
nearly been their downfall three times until they'd learned
how the raider packs functioned.

Inda shook away memory. Gillor was put in charge of

Death with a firm gesture—her shoulders sagged with dis-, appointment—and Inda paused only long enough to arm himself before he dropped silently into Mutt's boat. Fox was already away; he hadn't even gone below to get his fighting scarf. The wintry light bleached his red hair of color as his boat launched soundlessly into the ice-green water.

Fox's crew dipped their oars quietly, pulling with crimson-faced effort. They slid along the lee of the reefed ship, against which waves smashed, and above, voices shouted unintelligibly. And was that the clash of weapons? Fox's fight team reached the beautiful arched prow as Mutt hooked on at the stern, and Inda led the way up.

Then over the rail, arms at the ready—

The jumble of images assembled into surprise: no struggle here to free the ship, but a mutiny!

Fox leaped to the deck at the prow, then someone shouted in Venn, and the mutineers turned and ran, weapons raised, to the attack.

Another voice repeated something three or four times, in a hoarse howl.

Fox yelled, "They're going to kill the dag!"

A blue-robed figure lay on the deck near the mainmast.

Blue robe.

Sea dag.

Inda bounded over fallen bodies and the clutter of ruined lines as two yellow-haired warriors jumped down from the upper deck.

Inda leaped over the fallen dag, deflecting the first Venn's downward stroke before it could cleave the woman's head off.

The Venn attacked savagely to beat Inda back, and the other stood at his shoulder as shield. They fought like drilled warriors, feet planted, using only arms; Inda fought like a pirate, kicking one's knee out, and as he staggered, trying to right himself, Inda slung a swinging block into the other, sending him stumbling to the ground.

Then he stood astride the mage, facing the attackers. A knife, thrown by Fox from the upper deck, thunked into the taller assailant. The one with the smashed knee went down before Inda's hard, fast back stroke.

Inda looked up. The fight was nearly over. He knelt to see if his long-sought prize lived.

Her chest rose and fell beneath the heavy blue robe. Inda looked at the woman's face. Faint lines indicated someone not young, but she wasn't old, either—her skin was too firm for that. Wide mouth, pale now, wind-tousled sand-colored hair not hiding a rising bump behind one ear.

Overhead swung a block. Inda saw what had happened: it had been shaken loose by the ship running on the reef, hitting her on the head.

"We're almost secure," Fox said, and jerked his chin. "Better bind her hands, or she'll be gone as soon as she wakes. Mages don't even need transfer tokens, I was told, but they do make signs along with the words."

"Yes." Inda had experienced instant transfer himself. He felt his pockets, looked askance at the thick, scratchy lengths of leddas-laced hempen rope on the deck around him. He remembered too well what it was like being trussed up and helpless, so he pulled off his scarf. He used that to bind the woman's hands securely behind her, but he ran his fingers around and around inside the binding to make certain it wasn't too tight against the fragile bones of her wrists.

A last look at that face, in which there was no sign of intelligence, no hint of personality. So much at stake here, and the key to it all locked inside that head.

"We'll keep her in my cabin," Inda said. And, "Let's summon *Vixen* and send it back to Bren. It's time for Jeje and Tau to join us."

Chapter Thirty

TAU and the Comet faced one another. How many contests of will had placed them just so, standing on opposite sides of the inlaid table in this beautifully decorated salon that belonged to neither of them?

It no longer mattered—he was leaving.

He was *leaving*. Joy suffused him.

And she saw it. "Just like that?" she said, crossing her arms. "Just like that, stealing out like a thief?"

"No." He laughed. "I might have stolen out like a thief, leaving no word or sign. But I thought I owed you this much: Elgar sent a messenger. Jeje is waiting for me at the Fleet House. Probably impatiently. So I waited for you in order to say good-bye."

The Comet daubed her eyes with the lace at her wrist. Her feelings surprised her. She knew she was not in love anymore than he was. They had been too guarded for that. But there was regret. And tenderness. "We shared so much," she said. "And you dare to turn your back as if none of it mattered?"

"Everything matters," Tau answered. His smile lingered at the corners of his eyes. "Yet my life is not here. You knew that."

"Your life is where you live it." She struggled with her emotions, fury at the sheer waste gaining control. "And so you dash away to your stupid ships and then what? Die under a Venn's ax? You are on the verge of greatness here, Angel."

Angel. Not even his name, though she knew it. "No," he retorted. "I am merely an adjunct to your greatness."

She struggled again, and then grinned, however reluctantly.

"I've been the setting to your jewel," he said. "And it's been fun. I don't regret a moment, even though, as it turned out, I learned little of use. I've even crossed the stage. Always wanted to try it. So I discovered that while I'm decorative, so are all the other players. Again, we serve as your setting."

"You could be great," she said slowly. "Not as a singer. But when you speak."

"Maybe after years of training." He opened his hands. "It's possible. And maybe not. Inevitably there will come someone younger, with the training I need already mastered, and most of all with the determination I lack."

"That might be in ten years. Twenty. Thirty! You will never not be beautiful, even in old age. What a stupid, purposeless waste! *Why?*" She heard her own voice rising toward shrillness, and choked off the word.

While she composed her breathing he gazed beyond her toward the sea. The view from the window was magnificent, though in the recent months he'd hardly glanced out of it. Once he'd spent time at this window, longing for the sea. Then, gradually, the people here absorbed him into their lives. Masked lives, all. It was a world of art and artifice, and he'd enjoyed it, but it wasn't until Jeje's messenger reached him that he discovered how much he'd been yearning for release.

He said, "I can't answer your question. I may never be able to answer it." He spoke not to her, but to that glistening blue sea on the horizon. "Once I killed a woman and enjoyed the killing. Another time I saved one who did not want to be saved. Both times I thought I was right. The one I saved set fire to a ship full of pirates so that they burned to death. Who knows? Maybe the one I killed might have changed and lived to make restitution." He laughed softly. "Though I have my doubts. No, the problem there is not that I killed her so much as that I enjoyed the act."

She stared. He had talked amusingly about some of his experiences, but nothing, ever, about his time with pirates. What little she had learned was through listening to gossip about the doings of the infamous Elgar the Fox. In truth, it was difficult to believe that her decorative Angel had sailed with so sinister a figure, and yet she knew he had.

"The third, I dreamed of killing every night, but in the end I let her go," his dreamy voice went on. "I don't know, might never know, if she lived or died."

Abruptly he stopped. His expression was the acute one she distrusted: he had reached some inward decision, and once again he'd hidden away the moment of resolve, and its motivation. He said, "As for greatness, you're in command of a very small kingdom here." He lifted his hand, sweeping it over the house, and the stage down on the Riverside Road, where the people of rank disported themselves. "But if you truly want greatness, why do you not accept Lael of Colend's invitation to perform in Alsayas? Are you afraid you will not measure up?"

She flushed but did not deny his accusation, because she knew it was true.

He said, "So you've used the old Colendi poets to reach your present place. In a sense you've mastered them. So either rule here and dread someone else coming along who knows the old greats or use the experience you've gained to make new ones. You've the wit and the brains. All you really need is the inspiration, and you might find it in the world's most sophisticated court. Why not take the risk?" He grinned. "Think of me and my Venn ax when you make your bow to King Lael."

She drew a deep breath. "Maybe. Maybe. But what about you? I cannot believe all your wit and will is going to be spent on brawling with the Venn in the strait."

Tau thought of the fine clothes in his room, all left there to be given away. They were the snake skin he was now shedding. "No," he said. "Inda Elgar needs me, and while I'm needed, I have purpose. I guess it's as simple—and as profound—as that."

She said, "I need you."

"No, you want me." His smile was rueful. "More, you want me to need you. I'm sorry, bright star, but though we can direct the will, it is impossible to govern the heart."

He held out his hands. She laid hers in his. He bent to kiss her on both cheeks, and on her forehead; she flung her arms round his neck and claimed his lips with hers, a last, passionate, fiery kiss that left them breathless.

But then he let go.

Jeje almost missed him in the busy crowd along the main street outside the Fleet House, where she waited with her gear bag. Tau had dressed again in his sailing clothes—the black velvet and the ruffles and lace were gone. His hair was tied in the sailor's queue again, no longer braided and set with gems. His expression was pensive, though when he saw her he smiled.

She knew he was twenty-five, two and a half years older than she. Why did he all of a sudden seem much older? There was no line in his face.

"Ready?" he asked. "Or rather, is your mighty force ready? I know you've been panting to get back on board since the day we first landed."

Jeje dismissed this deflection with the ease of a year's intimacy in daily conversation. "Hard to leave her?"

Tau said wryly, "Why would you think that?"

"Because she's the Comet, because she's the most beautiful thing to walk the ground, because all the gossip is about how the only person beautiful enough for her is you—and the only one beautiful enough for you is her, so of course you were together." Her voice roughened. "And apparently at least two people are writing plays about you two."

"Just as well you and I are leaving then, isn't it?" he retorted, light enough, as he hitched his gear back over his shoulder. A surprisingly thin bag, considering how many fabulous clothes she'd seen him in over recent months.

They dodged around an oblivious vendor singing out

about her berry tarts. Jeje almost collided with a couple of flushed sailors smelling of ale who rolled toward the Fleet House; Tau's long steps lengthened and she scrambled after him. "Wait up."

He slowed. "Sorry."

She eyed him. He had on his golden coin smile, benign but about as human as metal. He was shutting out some emotion. She wished she had her blades in hand, and he his—they'd always talked more freely up there on the roof, while throwing one another around. "What's the matter? Don't like the idea of being a character in a play?" She grinned. "I think I'd like that."

"Would you really like to see some fatuous semblance of yourself, a distortion of your worst traits, because those are what people inevitably remember? Or think the most entertaining?" he said over his shoulder, his voice, usually so mellow, almost sharp.

Jeje exclaimed, "You do miss her!"

"I do not."

He sidestepped swiftly as a pony cart trotted by, too fast for the crowded street. The aroma of hot pies wafted behind—a delivery. Jeje toiled behind him, then said, "I'm sorry, didn't mean to pry." And at a quick, inscrutable glance from him, she let out an exasperated breath and exclaimed, "Is everyone else ugly to you, is that it? You gorgeous people are on another plane, like a mountain, and all the rest of us are bugs who cannot look so high?"

Tau's angry flush made her regret the words, pent-up as they'd been. Pent-up, but still taking her by surprise.

And he saw her bemusement, followed by regret, then embarrassment. Her smooth brown cheeks reddened, the long dimples that usually only deepened when she flashed her sudden wide and impish grin tightened in a wince.

"Sorry," she said again, in a reflective voice. "I don't know where that came from. Usually I don't think half a heartbeat about looks." She dusted her summer tunic with its worn and serviceable sash. "As is obvious."

The turnoff down to the harbor was ten steps away, and not far beyond waited Jeje's beloved *Vixen* to take them away from here, and back to Inda and the fleet. But Tau stopped, right there in the middle of the street—discommoding approaching traffic.

She stopped as well, observing how people whose paths they'd just blocked looked into his face and then away, or mumbled something, or smiled that sheepish smile that seems reserved for extraordinary beauty. Jeje flushed again as she looked up uncertainly.

Tau had not spoken because he'd been watching her, reading her expression as easily as he read a play. Her straight black brows quirked doubtfully, and he intuited she was wondering if he looked at her and saw only ugliness.

So how to explain this curious ache behind his ribs? He said, "Jeje." And then faltered, unsure how to go on. It was when the pucker of doubt altered into the lowered eyes of hurt that he forced himself to speak, trying for an easy tone. "There is a piece of gossip from Colend about King Lael Lirendi. They say that as soon as he inherited his throne he invited the most beautiful women in court to stay over the winter, after the season. And then, when spring came around, everyone came back and discovered that he was bored."

Jeje snorted. "Kings—"

"Kings nothing. Maybe that was the wrong example. When I look in the mirror I see only me. When I look at Comet, I can appreciate the artfulness of her style, the grace of her movements, but I don't want to possess them any more than you want to possess a chair you think well-carved. There is more to beauty than the appearance of it."

And you are beautiful, he thought, taking himself by surprise, but he did not say it. How sickening it would be to see her flush and become self-conscious, to misunderstand, worst of all to take more meaning than he meant.

Jeje snorted. Tau was giving her the same lesson her grandmother had so long ago when she was small. But she'd asked for it. So she turned the stupid subject off with a joke. "Glad you don't look at the rest of us and see hoptoads and barnacles. Well, Inda should be pleased with us. We did good work here. Everyone is promised a berth—the traders are glad to get 'em. And they'll gain experience,

and maybe win others to the cause, when the call comes."
She remembered Thess' pride as they toasted one another
at the Lower Deck. All the others. "Yes, my mighty force is
ready."

"Then let us get on board the *Vixen* before they cast off
without us," he said, and they both left the subject—the
true subject as well as the superficial one—behind them.

Chapter Thirty-one

"GOOD morning."

"Good morning." Inda sat down on a stool to face his prisoner.

She lay in his hammock, swinging with the ship's rhythm. She looked, and was, uncomfortable with her hands tied behind her.

"Do you feel any better?" he asked. "Is there anything we can get you?"

"I can see out of my right eye again," she replied.

"Good."

She was surprised: he looked and sounded sincere.

"If you want more lister-steep, Gillor said she has plenty." They spoke in Sartoran. He liked her exotic accent.

"Where are we?" she asked.

"Making slow progress," he said. "The winds hauled 'round enough to send us south. We'll sight land in a day or two. If your scout ships don't spot us first."

"And then?" she asked, scrunching over to ease her arms, and wincing as her headache crashed.

Inda grimaced. He loathed the situation, felt his own joints tweak in memory at the sight of her shifting and scrunching in a failed effort to find a more comfortable position.

He lifted his hands. "And then we try to find out what we need to know." He hesitated, then asked, watching her face, "There is a rumor that you cannot take kinthus."

"True." She smiled, a crooked smile that brought a long dimple in one cheek. "I am told it is a painless death."

He sensed question underlying her words, one he couldn't answer.

During the past years he'd witnessed bloody interrogations and executions by Gaffer Walic. If Boruin and Majarian had lived, he would have presided over an execution, for he would not have set them adrift to perpetrate their evil again. He had been tortured himself, by someone who thought himself the hero and rescuer of a conquered kingdom. All those had been enemies in the personal sense as well as in the larger view. There was no hatred in this woman's face, no rage, no cruelty, only a steady wariness, and, more subtly, the lines of private grief. People she knew had died in the mutiny aboard the Venn scout—whatever the cause—and more had died when he captured the scout.

He needed the magic in her head, but he could not bring himself to do anything, or even threaten anything. Though she would not talk, he would not change his orders to Gillor and Fibi, who traded off as the dag's jailers: "Keep her as comfortable as you can, but don't let her loose or she'll transfer."

He left and climbed up to sit on the yard, where the clean, cold winter wind smoothed away the tremors of memory.

The next time he came back, he found her sitting up, looking scruffy and tired. Though Gillor and Fibi did their best, there wasn't much of a chance to bathe with one's hands tied.

Fibi was feeding her; as he entered he interrupted a broken conversation in Dock Talk and Venn. They turned his way.

He said to Fibi, "Did you ask her?"

The Delf stuck out her lower lip. "Parole for why, says her."

The woman's eyes were an unremarkable greenish-brown, the faint lines around them suggesting that she viewed the world through the sunlight of humor, though there was no trace of humor in her expression now. Just that steady, questioning gaze, the sad quirk at the corners of her mouth.

"I do not betray my people," the woman stated in Sartoran.

"They are betraying us," he retorted. "Or I wouldn't be here. You wouldn't be here."

Her gaze lifted to the stern windows and beyond.

Inda left.

A week later, he came, as usual, early in the morning. This time they were alone.

"We're landing in a cove," he said. "The Fleet Guild will want to talk to you." She stared back at him, eyes steady, brows faintly puckered. Exasperation, anger, self-accusation forced words that he hadn't meant to say: "That's because the Brennish harbor is full of your damned soul-eating packs of invaders."

It was wrong, it wasn't what he meant. He retreated to the weather deck, where cold wind failed to cool his hot face.

Fibi appeared at his shoulder. "Talks the Iascan, that one."

Inda frowned down at her. "What?"

"I say, her talks the Iascan from me. Wants to learn it."

A brief spark of laughter arced through Inda's mind at the notion of the Venn woman speaking Delf-accented Iascan. But it was too soon gone. "Why?"

Fibi grinned. "To you her will talk. When it is right. Her cried, at first. Pipple died in mutiny. I think—I think her maybe talk about that mutiny." Fibi turned away.

Inda caught her arm, though he knew that Delfs did not like being handled. The arm was thin, solid with stringy muscle; Fibi stilled but did not pull away. She gave him her blank blue gaze.

"What has she said?"

"Nossink to be used. Or I tell you." Fibi frowned at his hand on her arm.

Inda let her go. She swarmed up to the top, and moments later heard her raucous crow voice squawking at a pair of younger hands for slack lines.

They eased into the appointed cove, whose single virtue was that the marshland beyond it was uninhabitable. This meeting place had been set by the Fleet Guild, via the *Vixen*, which followed the trysail in, carrying the Guild officials. Through gently drifting snow Inda could see them all on deck, looking stiff and ill-balanced against the rocking of the ship. He glanced impatiently past them, searching for Tau and Jeje, relaxing when he spotted golden hair gleaming in the pale sunlight and next to him, Jeje's short, boyish form and narrow, brown face. Inda grinned, restraining the urge to wave to show how happy he was to see them.

Fox anchored the *Death,* the captured Venn scout ship anchored on its lee, while *Cocodu* stayed farther out, its profile being far less distinctive; the schooners moved to take up their positions, standing off and on in the strait to watch for any Venn who might be searching for their missing scout.

The *Vixen* drifted up on their lee, neat as a swan, Tau and Jeje crowding forward with the grinning Fisher brothers.

When the bundled officials came aboard, Inda was surprised to see a new face, a tall, thin man with an acute gaze and serious demeanor. Old, grizzled Chim and tall, stout, unflappable Perran he already knew; he watched their closed, tight expressions when the new man spoke to them.

Inda said, "The Venn scout is yours. I suggest you rebuild that prow and put it to work."

Chim said, "Prisoners on board?"

"Prisoners? No. We put 'em over the side in the middle of the strait. Probably still making their way north. Only one we kept is the dag."

It had been Inda's intention to turn the prisoner over to Chim, saying, in effect, "This is your war, too. I'm doing the fighting so you get the information." But he said nothing as he followed the visitors into his cabin.

Fibi had done her best by the prisoner, preserving her dignity as much as possible. Her hair had been sponged with water from the purified bucket and combed out and rebraided, and her robe brushed off and straightened to cover her toes.

"She speaks Sartoran," Inda said.

Perran cleared her throat, her usual calm disturbed at the discovery of a small woman about her own age lying there with her hands tied behind her, and not some tall, muscular, ice-eyed, pale-haired Venn warrior. "What is your name?"

The woman regarded them all, then said—to Inda—"I am Sea Dag Jazsha Signi Sofar."

She said the name carefully, at first with a tentative air; Inda heard fear, and then resolve.

The serious man whispered to Chim, flicking a look Inda's way that was a signal flag of danger.

Chim rubbed his hands together and addressed Signi in careful Sartoran, very different from his usual haphazard speech patterns. "We need you to tell us how many ships your fleet has, and where they are. What's Durasnir planning?"

"No talk," she said. "I swore an oath. I must keep it."

Chim's gaze shifted to Inda, then flicked toward the door. Inda was glad to get outside; he heard the new man speaking to the prisoner in the cabin, though he couldn't make out the words.

Chim still spoke in Sartoran. "They won't get anywhere just talking. Not if you haven't."

"No," Inda said, watching Chim's gaze go up to the furled sails, out to the rocky coast with its long, pale birds' nests built into water-carved shelves, then to the quiet cove and its leaping fish. Anywhere but at Inda.

Chim fingered the braids in his grizzled beard, then said, "They'll expect you to do it."

"Do what?" Though Inda thought he knew; the situation was not without a weird kind of hilarity.

"Get the information. Since everyone knows you can't use white kinthus against Venn. We don't know how to do it else," Chim said, thumbing his chest and angling his head over his shoulder. "Perran and me. It stands to reason you Marlovans would be experts at that."

Torture. Rage spiked. Inda drew a breath—then remembered his own thoughts previous to Chim's climbing on deck. He laughed instead, a strangled, helpless sort of laugh.

The old captain squinted up at him in uneasy surprise.

"I was going to say it was your responsibility," Inda admitted. "Yes, Marlovans fight, but against worthy foes. Torture has no honor." He rubbed his scar as memory wrenched his mind from the present to his sweat-sodden bunk in Wafri's castle. Then he forced the memory away, as he'd gotten used to doing—as he suspected he would have to do his entire life. "Marlovans don't take prisoners, as a rule. Kill outright, generally, or take hostages of high ranking people, with a lot of rules. Our old royal family are hostages on their own land—" He glanced Fox's way, then closed his mouth.

Chim sighed. "Then this spy here will take her to the king's prison, and turn her over to those there." He looked guilty. "We at Fleet knew we had spies, but we thought we'd identified 'em all. That long-nosed rodent down there, I thought he was only a chart maker. But when we set up this journey, he popped into Fleet and produced a sved-order today, quick as that. Saying he has to be part of any parley." Chim made a spitting motion over his shoulder. "So the king and the crown princess know pretty much all our business—and don't blame Prince Kavna. He's been trying to protect us, but he has to obey his father, see? And if we refuse, we stand to lose our charter, maybe more."

Inda thought of the sad-eyed, patient woman spirited away to a hidden cell like Wafri's—or worse—and what would inevitably happen there, where the scruples of those with merely a semblance of conscience could not be disturbed.

And he said, "I won't."

"What?" Chim squinted at him with an expression not unlike hope.

"I won't lose anything if I refuse to hand her over. I'm a pirate, aren't I? And she's my prisoner. Aboard my ship. So they issue another warrant against me. I'm leaving. Taking this Venn mage with me. There isn't going to be any torture."

Chim narrowed his eyes. "We've got 'em, you know. Them gold things. We have 'em in a rucksack, on *Vixen*. We didn't want Longnose to see and ask. That much stayed secret, seeing as Perran and me, well, we dealt with Angel ourselves. Your boy Angel knows what to do."

Inda uttered a soft laugh: no need to ask who "Angel" was. "Can you get me a fleet? Assuming your king doesn't decide I'm an outlaw after all, over this torture business."

Chim fingered the braids in his beard, then said, "Half by next tidal flood, all the ones 't Jeje trained. Rest, the ones 't Perran and me been courting, and Prince Kavna on your behalf, if we send messengers. You could have a fleet by, say, next year. Might be longer, with the new rules about travel, and the vagaries of wind and weather."

Inda flicked his hands up in agreement. "Any word on what the Venn war fleet is doing? All we've seen are a few raiders on patrol."

Chim shrugged. "Nothing. Why we asked her. With us stuck in harbor, or hugging the coast, no fishing boats even get a glimpse of 'em. If anyone gets too close to the north shore I hear tell they take 'em, and no one knows what happens. Kavna says everyone thinks they went east to chase you, out Fire Islands' way. But we don't know."

Inda opened a hand. "We haven't seen a single warship. I've been hugging the north coast, and you'd think we would have spotted one on patrol if nothing else, but we haven't. All we've seen in months is a handful of scouts. Including hers, and we only got it because of a mutiny already in progress." He indicated the cabin, where Sea Dag Signi lay tied up. "Maybe they're sailing out in the middle waters, sending the raiders to either side?"

Chim hesitated, then looked away again, at long-winged seabirds circling high in the air, almost obscured by the falling snow. Then he said in a low voice, returning to his accustomed dialect, "The Venn have begun raids against yer land. Idayago, mostly. Quick raids, fleets o' three to six. Burning harbors, ships. Anything bigger than a smack." He cleared his throat, then watched a pair of birds dive down

toward one of the distant nests. "Angel has all the details—
what little we know. He can also tell you what he learned
from that spy about your homeland."

"Spy?"

Chim's low, raspy voice, his many glances over his shoulder, reminded Inda of the old childhood song about the
piece of wool that was pulled from a tree that caused the
tree to fall, which set off a flood, which wiped out a town—

"Year ago, autumn. Some fellow nosing around, asking
not only for Elgar the Fox—we have a harbor full of spies
asking that kind o' question, the Venn being first—but he
out and said yer name, what is it, Indrevet Ala-Grubber?
Anyway, I tried to chase him off, but he came back. That
time he ran athwart the hawse of our old Captain Wenald,
him't spent eight years chained to a galley by pirates—
same pirates hired by the Venn—and he was near killt before your Angel saved him. Said later the jumble o' speech
from the spy was your Iascan."

Inda felt that zing of alert again. His palms were wet, his
heartbeat hammering. "And?"

"Softly, softly, now. That one down there beside young
one-arm is another king's spy, unless I miss me guess." He
indicated the *Vixen,* riding the green waves a coin toss to
the lee. One of the brothers was watching birds through a
glass. The other brother swept the ocean beyond the cove.
A man stood between them, gaze on Inda's ship. "Angel
told me the spy said something about king's orders—he
was a, what was it, a Runner? Something, and he was to
find ye."

Inda drew a breath. "King's orders."

"This Vee-dritt bein' sent last spring by this king—I remembered the name, as it happens, on account it is so close
to me wife's, which is Vyadrit, strange, that, about names—"

Inda did not hear the man's low-voiced discursion into
naming customs. He recognized the name Vedrid. The Sierlaef's boy, back when the king's heir was an academy
horsetail and Inda a scrub. Inda and his fellow Tveis had
known all their names, if only to avoid them, especially
Nallan.

So the Sierlaef had to be king now—Aldren-Harvaldar,

in Marlovan. The hope he'd begun to feel—and hated himself for feeling—had gone, leaving questions. *Why would the Sierlaef send a spy or assassin against me? Or is it the Harskialdna on behalf of his nephew?*

But would the uncle still be Harskialdna, or had the heir gotten his way and made Buck Marlo-Vayir his Harskialdna? But why would Buck—

He felt his mind spinning into uncertainty, and made an effort to shove it back behind the old wall. Speculation was useless. Not enough information.

Chim had stopped talking and was eyeing Inda again.

Inda said, "And so?"

The older man sighed. "And so what Perran feared all along is probably going to come to pass: an embargo will kill the kingdom's trade if we don't obey the new orders. Nearly all the kingdom works either for the river trade comin' up from the south, or else the sea trade. If the threats get worse, the king will take the Fleet for his own, for defense. Only reason he hasn't squashed us is the Venn wouldn't let him have a war fleet. Said they would protect us, that was the treaty ten years ago. So, see, the king pretends he doesn't know about us, but if he needs our fleet, he orders it took over, and puts this young lord who's courtin' the crown princess in charge. If we refuse, we lose our charter—"

"I'll have the prisoner shifted aboard our transport."

The voice behind caused them to turn.

Longnose—Inda never did learn his name—might have been an honest man by his own lights, but Inda never left him enough time to prove it.

It had been a mistake to bring the dag here. But Inda did not have to compound the error. "Off my ship," he said, and gestured to Fox, who straightened up from lounging against the rail far forward. Fox sauntered aft, hand on a knife hilt as Inda said, "See these people off my ship. We are setting sail."

Fox did not speak, nor did his slow saunter alter, but somehow every line of his body, from slanted narrow green eyes to the ring of his boot heels, exuded menace.

Longnose flushed, glared at Fox, then back at Inda. "May I ask where you are bound?" he asked in Dock Talk.

"To scout the east," Inda said.

Longnose gave him a look of comprehension. "Where the Venn happen to be looking for you?"

"I'm scouting for pirates." Inda opened his hands wide. "There are always plenty of pirates."

Chapter Thirty-two

AS the boats rowed away from the *Death* after the captains' conference, Eflis leaned on her oars and glanced back at Sparrow in the bow. "Not saying anything to Dasta. Might get the wind up, like. But that Elgar sure is a strange one."

Sparrow didn't pause in her stroke. "Strange? What do you mean, strange in looks, in manner? Not his plans, surely."

"Oh, not his looks. Right ordinary—until you catch him laughing, and then he's, oh, he's sun-bright, brighter than Tau. Gets that way when he talks plans, too."

"Well, his plans make sense," Sparrow admitted. She would never actually say it out loud, but she'd been impressed by Inda Elgar. On first meeting she'd thought there was more of the lying, that that tall redhead Fox was really Inda. Especially after rumor was whispered around the fleet that Elgar the Fox'd been caught spying in Ymar, and tortured—then not only escaped but set fire to half a city in retaliation. She could see that sarcastic Fox doing all that, maybe with short Inda following, until you actually spent time with Inda, heard him talk, heard him laugh. You didn't notice anyone else, then—he suddenly became the sort of leader one could follow, if one was to follow anyone.

Eflis shrugged. "I like this new plan. Raiding the raiders!

Ought to be fun. But Inda's as short as a Delf. Dasta and Tcholan were much more dashing Elgar the Foxes at the Fire Islands. So tall, and those black duds."

Inda himself had explained the ruse. Sparrow had been inclined to anger until Eflis laughed so hard she knocked over her glass of wine. She thought it great fun having been fooled, and she'd made Inda promise that at least once she'd get to wear the black outfit. When he said, "Of course! Didn't Gillor wear it a few times on the island reconnaissances?" and Gillor responded, "Mine is in the gig. Happy to share," Sparrow's perspective changed: instead of seeing herself and Eflis as having been duped, she perceived that they had been accepted into Elgar's inner ring.

Eflis said, "I can see how it happened. That Fox looks about as sinister as Mad Marshig o' the Brotherhood used to wish he looked. And Majarian did, the stinking shit. But Inda doesn't even try. Dresses like an old dockhand."

Sparrow said, "Practical, is all."

Eflis picked up her oars again, and put some back into her stroke, sending the skiff bucketing over the little waves. Then she stopped again. "As for looks, yee-hoo, Tau is even prettier than I remembered when he was Coco's toy."

Sparrow snorted. Eflis did have a roving eye, but as long as it didn't light on other women, it was fine with her. "And doesn't he just know it."

Eflis rounded her eyes. "You seen him prinking and prancing?"

"No, but he's got about as much heart as a gold coin. If you want cold, arrogant males, for pref, give me Fox. Not in my cabin, but on my deck, fighting off all comers. Huh!"

Eflis chuckled as she flexed her arms. "*How* sore I was after he put us through that first drill. And I thought we were so tight!" She smacked a bicep. "Look at us now!"

"How about let's feel it," Sparrow retorted, "or we're gonna sit on this water all night."

Their laughter drifted over the water as they took oar again, and sped for *Sable*.

Neither Fox nor Tau paid the departing captains any heed.

Tau strolled on deck and breathed deeply of the ocean air: salt, kelp, fish, but no whiff of land. How good it was to be back at sea!

Yet he was restless. Was that because they were heading in the direction of home after all these years?

Inda had said to the captains just now, "Venn raiders are using Idayago as target practice. Shall we go practice on them?"

Jeje had cheered loudest of all. The urge to find Jeje and talk was so instant, so automatic, Tau had to laugh at himself. Of course she wasn't here. There she was, slanting away on her *Vixen* again. And happy to be there.

He did not miss the Comet, or his perfumed life amid Bren's aristocrats and those who kept them entertained. What he missed were the morning talks with Jeje during drill. He felt as thought one eye was missing, or part of his mind; he badly wanted to discuss the astonishing change in Inda, who somewhere, somehow, had learned to laugh. It was such an open laugh, a rushing chuckle that began deep in his chest and sounded so free, often bringing tears that Inda just shook away. Inda talked no more than he ever had, but somewhere, somehow he'd laid aside, or lost, the ability to hide his emotions—

Fox clapped his hands to summon the off-watch for yet another of the endless training workouts. With a sense of relief Tau ran to the forecastle and reached for a weapon.

Down below, Signi listened to the running feet, as she'd listened for carefully counted days.

She lay back, staring out the stern windows at the sea. Elgar the Fox had had the hammock turned, just so she could look out the window. She had only mentioned it to Fibi the Delf as a test of language, more than as a test of persons—or at least so she had thought.

Yes. The time had come to examine the truths in her own mind.

It was true that she was a failure. Chief Sea Dag Valda had entrusted her with the most important task in the world—to get to Sartor with the Venn secret of navigation—and she had failed.

She had failed because though most human beings could

not lie to her without betraying the lies—few were aware that bodies often spoke more truly than lips—she could not descry all Dag Erkric's safeguards. No, call them traps. And so her attempted peaceful mutiny ended in blood and death. And shortly thereafter the very safeguard that Valda had meant to protect her had betrayed her: they were isolated and alone, and thus ripe to fall into the hands of none other than Elgar the Fox.

That discovery had been almost as sharp a shock as had that stunning blow from the wooden block. Except Elgar the Fox had proved over the succeeding days to be nothing like what people said. Nothing at all. She had discovered the truth of Count Wafri's plot by careful listening and putting together of clues when she had been scouting the likeliest ship to request. She knew that Elgar the Fox had destroyed Limros Palace in escaping; she knew he intended to make war on her people. She did not expect him to have such compassionate eyes, a body so eloquent with old hurt. Such scars in one so young! He had to be ten or twelve years younger than she.

He would not give her to the Brennish people to be put to the question.

He asked women to tend her, and to treat her with respect.

And he couldn't bring himself to harm her, though she had long heard of the many deaths at his hands or at his command.

What did he see in her own face?

The cabin door opened, and she composed herself as best she could; she had reviewed the facts. It was now time to acknowledge the new path that the truths revealed.

Inda entered his cabin.

He knew it was ridiculous to leave his prisoner here, forcing himself onto the already crowded mates' area. He sensed that they felt uncomfortable with him there, though he could not imagine why—he was careful to take no more space than anyone else. How could he, with only two changes of clothes? But every time he thought about putting Dag Signi down into the hold away from light and air his mind flinched from the idea.

She lay, as before, in his hammock. He studied her faint, crooked smile, the shadow of the dimple in her cheek.

"We run away from Bren folk," she observed. In Iascan. Her accent was strongly Venn, not Delf. "Why?"

"Because the Brens wanted to keep you, and force me to stay. I think your Venn are going to attack my homeland, and I intend to fight them."

Her brow furrowed as she sorted his words. And she said, finally, "If I give parole."

Inda's head jerked up. Had he heard that right? "Parole?"

She nodded once, a firm nod. "If you attack north side of strait, my people there, parole ends."

She'd practiced that, he sensed. "We are not attacking the north side," he said slowly and clearly. "I was only there to find you. And to chart. But we will be attacking your people who are raiding on the Idayago side."

"You burn people on ships?"

He flushed with guilt and made a warding gesture as he looked away. Then he said, "I'll burn their ships so they can't use 'em, but nobody on them. We won't let 'em land on Idayago, but they can use their longboats and go north with my goodwill."

She nodded. "It is good. I stay."

He tipped his head a little, studying her. "Why?"

She gave a rueful smile. "It hurts."

His entire body was expressive of relief as he flicked his fingers to the knife he wore along his forearm. He pulled the long knife out, but kept the point away from her, his gaze at her elbow, his attitude patient and unthreatening. He was waiting to cut her bonds!

She obligingly scrunched to one side, the hammock jiggling warningly, as he sawed the silk binding her wrists.

"I'll send Fibi down," he said. And did, moving up to the captain's deck, where he stood watching the drill on the forecastle, his mind struggling to comprehend what the mage's parole might mean.

When Signi appeared on deck, she was considerably cleaner, her sandy hair severely pulled back into a short braid, and the grubby blue robe gone, no doubt drying below after a couple of dunks in one of the ensorcelled buckets. He recognized the shirt, green-dyed wool jacket, and sailor's trousers from Gillor's seabag. The two women were about the same height, though this Venn mage was a little more spare than Gillor.

Her movements were peculiarly fluid as she rubbed slowly at her wrists in gentle circles. Though the season was winter the low northern sun was warm on deck, and many went barefoot. The prisoner did also, and Inda could see that she was used to it. Her feet were brown and as tough as his own.

She moved soundlessly, unobtrusively, stopping near the mainmast. Inda suspected her post aboard Venn ships was there. She watched the drill forward, pursing her lips when Fox threw Tau to the deck, gold hair flashing. Grunt, scramble, and the two jumped up, breathing hard, Fox laughing; the old competition was back, but some of the bitter sting had vanished.

It was then that the rest of the crew noticed that they had been joined. Surprise, even shock, riffled through them all at the sight of the mage on deck, her hands free.

Fox raised his knife in ironic salute. Tau said something that Inda could not hear, as the wind came from behind him. The prisoner met his gaze then looked away, her face relaxing a fraction only when she spotted Fibi. She brought her hands up, palms together—a gesture Fibi mirrored with a brisk and graceless clap.

Inda felt a tingling prod over his ribs—his vest pocket. He remembered the new golden scroll-case. It wasn't a round scroll-shape like the Venn one he'd seen in Wafri's hands. Apparently Sartoran ones were square, flat cases that better fit the style of clothes aristocrats wore.

Inda moved aft and opened the case. There was a tiny paper from Jeje, in her round, uneven hand—

The lookout yelled, "Six sail, hull down, lee-bow!"

And on the paper: *6 sail hull up. Venn.*

Hull up: the entire ship visible, hull down: only the masts.

Inda moved to the binnacle, laying his hand on the gold cases there, each paired to one on another of his ships. He got that same magical tingle-poke from two; the third tingled as he touched it, and when he opened them, bits of paper showed variations of the same news.

His first experiment was a disappointment.

"They're worthless," he exclaimed in disgust. And as Gillor stepped close, head cocked in question, "Use the signal flags. I want this as we practiced: we'll maneuver upwind of them. Two to each warship, the scouts to keep circling and keep up the fire-arrows until they strike their flag and go over the side." The Venn had battle flags like most military ships, Inda had discovered, which were used to signal intent to attack, neutrality, or surrender.

Pirates had no such custom, though some mimed military action at whim, but who would believe their signals?

The Venn masts appeared, and soon they were hull up.

The exquisitely beautiful tall-masted square-sail ships were designed for deep waters, which Inda's smaller fore-and-aft ships were not. But the Venn square sails could not sail into the eye of the wind nearly as closely as Inda's fleet. That was their single weakness, he had watched it again and again over the last year, and he would use it against them now.

"And after they go over the side?"

"Drive 'em north. I don't want them landing on the south shore. North, it's none of our affair. And burn the ships after we loot 'em."

"Prisoner?" Gillor's dark-fringed eyes were wide with interest.

"Gave parole. But when their masts heave up on the horizon put her below, in the purser's cabin. Lum can shift his flour barrels somewhere else for storage. Bar it but let her free inside, with a lamp. I don't want to risk the Venn spotting her—this raider pack could be a search for the scout—and she doesn't need to see her own people fought against."

Gillor nodded, then strode forward, issuing orders to the flag hands and to Fox, who listened, head slightly bent. For a moment he observed the two: the woman gesturing, her attitude evocative of intensity and appeal—it was her watch, and she wanted to command—the man listening, remote and intense before the lift of the hand that turned the ship over to her. He moved to the weapons box and took up position with one of the newer defense teams.

With Gillor Inda had relaxed his rule about not sleeping with crew because he enjoyed her laughing abandon, and because she showed him no favor over Tcholan or a couple of the other hands. Her gaze had strayed most often toward Fox—not that that got her anywhere. Like Tau he never slept with crew. Now Gillor's mind was on the attack. *If she carries this one,* Inda thought, *she's got the next ship we capture.*

Ship. Mage.

Signi's expression was intent, inscrutable. Her body poised, evocative of deference and question. How did she do that? He had never seen anyone move like she did. She stood so quietly, without any unnecessary motion, yet it was impossible to look away.

But needs drew his attention; she, sensing his attention elsewhere, began to watch him.

On the deck of his ship he wore authority naturally, as comfortably as he exhibited his strength and the resilience of youth. How beautiful he was! Emotions clear to see as a stream in spring, yet as complex as the knotwork tapestries at home.

Signi let her gaze stray to the two young men on the forecastle, the redheaded one watching the last of his drill crew turning to new tasks, the golden-haired one at a halyard. Those two were startlingly alike, both hiding their natures in similar fashion, the one with trained habit, the other with trained grace.

She was so intent on her observations she was surprised to discover Gillor at her shoulder.

"Come," Gillor said. "They're hull down on the horizon. We need to lock you below."

Interest—joy—doused.

But Signi had given her word. The path lay before her. She had chosen it. She must walk it, and accept what it would bring.

She did feel better when Gillor brought her a lamp, water, and a biscuit she'd stuffed with cheese before she barred the cabin door.

*   *   *

And it was Gillor who let her out just as dawn began to lift the darkness from sky and sea.

Inda leaned on the rail despite a cold, wet wind that smelled of imminent snow, watching the last of the Venn ships slip below the green waves, billows of smoke drifting toward the sky.

The long barges were filled with Venn, all heading north. Through the glass Inda could see mostly yellow heads and broad backs, the oars dipping and rising, as the small craft harried them northward.

He turned, sparks of pain lancing through his temple, his bad wrist, one knee. New wounds or old, he didn't care; he wanted only sleep.

The door to his cabin was ajar. He slipped inside and leaned on the table, frowning down at one of the charts, when he became aware of Signi's scent. It reminded him of roses right before they bloom.

A quiet step beside him. She was carrying a candle, the flame a golden flicker over her face.

"You did not kill them."

"No."

"Why?" She poured a little wax on the table and then set the candle into it. Inda watched her fingers: short, capable, blunt-nailed. There were red welts on her wrists, evidence of silent, futile struggle at some point during her long incarceration. He glanced at his own wrists and was startled to see his barbed wrist guards there. He fumbled them off, feeling uneasy, though he was too tired to figure out why.

"They will seek you." She used Sartoran verbs when Iascan failed her.

"They already seek me," he retorted. "They have for over a year. The 'seek' has probably became a hunt since I took you."

She looked up, her pupils enormous. "They might not know where I am."

"Oh, I suspect they know. Your Venn spies in Bren Harbor would have winnowed out the news by now, if not from

Chim's Longnose, certainly from some other rat. And though I lied and said I was going east, it's inevitable these will report I've gone west. Though it may be a week or two before they reach the north shore—oh, yes! I'm thinking of our own communication times. The sea dags on the ships must have transferred at the beginning of our attack and reported before tucking up in bed for the night." He threw down the golden case onto the table, where it clattered, sending the candle flame dancing, then streaming. "I see what I missed before. It's the positioning that makes communication with other warships possible. I have to keep my ships in line of sight, or how do we identify our positions? We might as well use the flags. You Venn have some method of marking position without landmarks."

She made no answer, yet her lack of denial was, in itself, an answer.

Weak blue light glowed in the stern windows. The candle flame touched with tiny golden sparks of light the contours of her arms, the fine hairs drifting around her face, having escaped her braid. The flame erased lines, making her curiously ageless, both young and old.

"They will try to kill you," she repeated, with that steady gaze.

"And I will fight back," Inda replied, sweeping a hand over the chart; his fleet had reached the eastern end of Idayago.

He frowned down at the coastline as though words of import had been written there. It kept his hands busy, it kept his gaze away from the dip in her shirt that exposed the little hollow in her neck, and the vein beating there, counterpoint to her beating heart. She was alive, she was Venn. They were all alive, Iascan, Venn, Bren, Delf, pirate—alive, with busy hearts and minds and hands, desires, aspirations, fears, hatreds. It was so easy to make them dead; it was his only skill.

He dug the heels of his hands into his eyes, trying to press back the throbbing in his temple, the swoop and soar of strong emotion that he could barely control, and sometimes could not control since his escape from Wafri.

Her voice came again, closer. "Who is he?"

Surprise brought down his hands, banished the flood of remorse. "Who?"

"He who walks at your shoulder. The man so like Venn and Marlovan. How do you say in Yaskani? Spirit-being?"

Shock struck him cold. "Ghost?"

"He is there. Sometimes a shadow. Sometimes less than shadow. I see him now, so very clear. He looks at me." Her eyes focused at a point above and beyond Inda's shoulder.

The hairs prickled on Inda's neck, and he stepped back as he turned, hands up in a defensive block, but he saw nothing. He dropped his hands and uttered a semblance of a laugh.

The woman did not laugh. She gazed and gazed, then said, "He is distinctest one ever I see."

"Blond? Hair long like mine? Tall?" Because Inda strongly suspected who it was.

"Yes," she said, her gaze focused steadily on the air beyond his shoulder.

"His name is—was—is Dun, that's all I know," Inda said, shaking his head in wonder.

Her brows lifted. "You see him, then?"

"No. But I . . . think once I have. Ramis showed me, or tried to. And since then, once or twice I had a sense of someone there." Disbelief had been banished when he stood with Ramis on the deck of the *Knife* and watched the spirit-shades flow in and out of time on Ghost Island.

"Your friend? Brother? Kin?" She shifted her attention from his shoulder at last, met his gaze, then dropped hers. Her posture changed subtly and he struggled against the urge to stare at her body the way she had been staring over his shoulder.

He swallowed. "None of those. Friend, maybe. Crew. He was on my first ship, when I was first sent to sea."

For a time they stood there on either side of the table, both looking down at the candle, which had burned halfway to the table in a puddle of beeswax, but by now the light coming in had strengthened, revealing the bruised look of exhaustion and old pain under his eyes, and the desperate attempt to comprehend—to grasp the truth—narrowing hers.

He brought his hand down on the weak little flame, snuffing it, and shook his head. "Never mind."

She brushed her forefinger across the back of his hand. Her lips parted as if she would speak, but then she left.

He watched her glide, so graceful, smooth, quiet, and cradled his hand where her touch had burned.

Chapter Thirty-three

THUNDER was rare in early spring, but when it occurred it roared across the sky like a charge of heavy cavalry. Blue-white lightning flared in the windows as Hadand followed the little Runner along one of the upper corridors in Iasca Leror's royal castle, past the former Harskialdna's rooms, which were now used for storage.

Evred so rarely broke his impossibly busy schedule she couldn't imagine what he wanted her for. The weather certainly suited a terrible emergency of some sort, except his note had said, *If you are not busy,* and next to it he'd drawn the Old Sartoran sun glyph, which had become a private signal for amusement.

As they stopped near what had been Ndara-Harandviar's rooms—now belonging to Barend, though he'd spent less than a month in them all told—the Runner-in-training called over his shoulder, "He said he'd meet you here, Hadand-Gunvaer. I have to take all these down to the guard side, and I daren't cut across the big court." He waved a sheaf of sealed orders, then sent a glance at the window where a greenish flash, bright and fierce, made them step back.

Five paces away was a familiar cubby with an arrow slit, bricked in overhead the century before, from which Hadand had watched Inda and Evred during their first year in the academy. How long ago that seemed!

Evred's step brought her attention around, and she smiled to see him smiling. He'd gotten thin over the past year, he was all bone and muscle, which made him look older than his twenty-two years. But he would not abate his terrible work schedule a jot, for either meals or needed sleep. "There's time enough when I'm dead, or we have peace, whichever comes first," he said once, and she did not ask again.

"Thought you'd enjoy it," he said. "If not, don't feel constraint."

Oh. He meant the new scrubs' first callover. She and Evred had agreed before their coronation that it would save money to disband the Tvei training, but a general outcry at Convocation had made it clear that the innovation had become a tradition. Younger brothers wanted to come. Expected to come.

And so, this year the scrubs were made up of Ains and Tveis—first brothers and second brothers, all ten or eleven years old—who stood about, looking absurdly small and skinny in their shapeless gray tunics, as rain beat down on them. The thunder was already passing; some of the boys hopped from puddle to puddle—they were wet anyway—and others gawked at the skyline. The rest stood in awkward clumps, until the new Master, Anred Lassad, strode in and shouted, "Line up!"

Three ragged lines of nine formed up and Lassad faced them, taking his time to examine each rain-washed countenance. Up above, he, in turn, was examined by the royal pair. Lassad had become a stocky, snub-nosed man with terrible scars.

"He knows every dirty trick boys can invent," Evred said, smiling.

Hadand bit her lip. "I can never forget what he did to Inda. Worse, to Cama's eye."

"He can't forget either," Evred replied. "You do not know his record. Those fire scars are from his holding an outpost almost single-handedly against one of the pirate attacks on Parayid Harbor. He was barely horsetail age then." He paused, saw Hadand's unexpressed misgivings, and said, "Every act of bravery since, every time he volun-

teered for desperate missions, has been an attempt to get
our scrub years out of his memory, and it never really
works."

"Did he tell you that?"

"No. But I can see it—hear it in his words—so plainly.
He knows the rules, he knows the traditions, he knows how
boys will get around both," Evred stated.

The callover proceeded below, and when the boys were
sent to arrange their bunk spaces and to enjoy the rest of
the day in freedom, Evred observed, "When it came to it I
was reluctant to end the Tvei training. I'm glad the Convocation insisted."

She remained silent, knowing it was his own inner voice
he answered.

"It is the academy that saved my own life, I am convinced," he went on, as they walked back to their own wing.
They spoke in Sartoran, which had become habit. "My
academy mates are my strongest allies in the kingdom."

"And every fifty years there's some sort of war," she observed.

Did he hear? No, his gaze was distant as he paused, his
hand on the latch of the door to the study, "I finally read
my uncle's papers."

She thought of the Harskialdna's rigorously tidy office
down in the guardroom, protected by Algara-Vayir Runners at sword point after that terrible day. Later the boxes
and stacks of papers that Evred had insisted it was his obligation to go through had sat untouched for at least a year.

"And?"

He led the way to his father's study, where he met with
the council, with Barend when he was home and not overseeing the defense on the coast, and with the guard command. He crossed the great rug worked in Montrei-Vayir
crimson and gold to his own study. It was warm, for he
spent long watches there. The furnishings were those from
the old schoolroom, the smell one of summer herbs
worked into the beeswax candles on the table and the
mantelpiece.

A shaft of light lanced with brilliant suddenness through
the window, striking the rug into a splash of glory.

Evred stood before the window, hands clasped behind him. The stance, so like his father's, seemed eerie to Hadand, and she felt uneasy, as if time's river had plunged her over a waterfall, and they were suddenly old.

But then he turned, and smiled, and he was young again, and so was she—young, and her palms moist and her senses alert to his voice, his movements, his every change of mood. "My uncle had become some kind of monster in my mind, but his papers revealed no monster. The academy was very well run, as was the Guard. I had to replace Brath because of proximity to my uncle—he reminded too many people of the past, but I gave him one of the new castles along the Idayagan coast to run. Twenty-five years of service did not make for a dishonorable retirement."

Hadand opened her hand. Of course Evred would think of that.

"But in those papers I saw Uncle Anderle's long plans. His idea had been to bind the Tveis to him, so that they would follow him when it was time to go to war. He was afraid of my father's plans to strike from the sea in order to save our land; he thought ships clumsy, ill-suited for war."

"Did he or did he not betray our first attempts at a fleet?"

"I cannot find evidence that he did, but I think his scorn might have done the business. About everything that mattered to him he was secretive. His communications were all numbered and dated, checked off with different colors when received and executed, all of it in code. The things he considered negligible he talked about more freely, and I suspect that there were those who listened for mention of ships and knew what to do with the information when they heard it."

"What about the attacks against my family?"

"Nothing. Nothing whatever, not even secret codes."

"Could mean anything."

"Except that map was in his hand. I know it now, his handwriting. He made that map himself, just as that pirate turned chart maker said to Barend."

"Then he might've had other secrets not even committed to code."

"Yes. And we might never know. Either that or we will find out suddenly, at the worst time, like poor Barend did with that damned map." Evred sighed, touched a stack of papers, then turned. He wore a fine woolen tunic in Montrei-Vayir crimson, tied with a gold sash, because he'd been interviewing counselors and trade people. On other days, like his uncle, he had gotten into the habit of wearing his old gray coat and cavalry boots, riding trousers stuffed in them even though he seldom had time to ride. He said, looking away, "Back to the war. And the academy."

She knew then what was on his mind, and her insides hollowed out and filled with snow. *A weed with no water will die,* she reminded herself. But then came the answering thought that she had tried so hard to bury: *To him my love is a weed.* And for the first time in her life she did not endeavor to smooth his difficulties for him.

He looked out the window at a last spattering of hail, then at the fire. "One thing I learned is that continuity is important. Especially now that times are so uneasy, we must convey a semblance of continuity, with a line in place." A quick glance at her for her usual swift comprehension.

It was petty, it was painful, but she stood there in silence.

"Heirs," he said, a little desperately. "I know we're young for that—we married five years before people usually marry—and we're ten years before most even think about a family. But, well, with the kingdom in such trouble . . ."

She had a freedom from fear she never would have had as Aldren's queen. What's more, she was valued for her mind, her training, her good sense—but the human heart cannot be schooled to logic. As her mother had warned, there had been closed doors on the king's side of the royal residence, and laughter, and sometimes men's voices singing to the beat of drums.

And so she waited.

And he went on appealing to her reason, because it would never occur to him to appeal to her heart. "Not someday, the way we could afford to in peace. But as soon as we can," he said, the voice she knew so well husky with embarrassment. "Life. Being so uncertain."

Embarrassed he was, but also concerned, for all at once she'd stilled in a way he hadn't seen for a very long time, and had hoped never to see again, her mouth compressed to a line of pain.

Here it was at last, she was thinking, the question she had yearned for for so very long. But what a mockery. He was asking permission to come to her bed, not in desire but in intent. And he would be fair instead of tender, careful instead of abandoned, scrupulous instead of passionate.

For a heartbeat she burned with rage, and struggled against the impulse to grip her knives and strike. Against whom? The uncomprehending Evred waiting for an answer?

It wasn't his fault he would never want her! It was no one's fault. It just was.

The thorned rose.

So that's what Mother meant. The thorns prick my heart, but I cannot forget the blossoms, or all I am left with are the thorns.

There was only one answer for a queen whose duty was guardianship of a kingdom.

"Very well, Evred," she said. And with an attempt at rational briskness, "Shall I chew gerda, then, to make myself fertile? Or would you rather name a day and time and we clasp hands and see if the Birth Spell cooperates?"

Evred had never, in all their years together, heard her speak so sharply. He looked into her face, uneasy. "What do you want, Hadand?" He held out his hands. "I had thought—but we can try whatever way you like. You have only to say, the decision is yours."

Already she was angry with herself; she dashed her fingers over her eyes. He would always be fair and considerate. She probably would not have had that with Aldren, even if the passion had come.

Roses. Weeds. She knew she would take whatever proximity she could get, that her weed of a love wanted to thrive, and would stubbornly persist, with only the faintest touch of sun, the tiniest drop of water, because that was the way she was made. "I will consult the healer, and find out if gerda works faster steeped and drunk, or added to food," she stated firmly.

It was with some relief that Evred watched her go, though he was puzzled, and concerned by her tears. Not that he had much time for such considerations. The crushing weight of embargo, increasing debt—his responsibilities never ended, the boys chomping away in the mess below were testament to that—and the prospect of invasion kept him awake nights, making and remaking plans.

And so, as news filtered southward of repeated sea attacks against the marauding Venn, claiming that once again the mysterious Elgar the Fox was in command, Evred sent Nightingale Toraca bearing one of the lockets. He would try one more time to contact Inda—and if that failed he would put away his old life as Inda obviously had his own.

While Nightingale rode north through melting snow, as trees grew fuzzy with green buds and birds swooped down from the north and began to look for their old nests, in the sea north of Idayago Inda's fleet played hide-and-seek with Durasnir's raiders through the rough-water, befogged strait.

There was no other shipping in the strait, so predators on both sides had the waters to themselves; both sides used small craft for scouting, difficult to see. The Venn had magical communication, but Inda's fleet had learned to sail in a long line, each large ship hull down from the others, and thus there was never a fleet nicking the skyline for the Venn to spot.

Winter's steady eastern winds started shifting uneasily to the south and back again for longer times, warming over land, as the sun strengthened its course over the lower hemisphere.

Four, five, six sea battles along Idayago's coast Inda's fleet fought, the winter winds at their backs shooting them at the enemy. Each time they attacked during full daylight, using their tighter maneuverability to surround the Venn raiders, firing arrows into the sails until there were too many small fires to put out, until the survivors leaped over the sides to paddle their way north. The victories did not come without cost: the Venn fought hard, in one battle sinking three of Inda's new allies, including Halliff's *Sea-King*. The Venn did not take prisoners, but put everyone on the ship they captured to death before burning it.

Everyone else sustained vast damage to sails, masts, and yards, which had to be repaired with care as they did not know when they could next get supplies. They never landed in Idayago, not knowing what kind of reception awaited them. Inda would not permit them to fight Marlovans.

The battles gave Inda a taste of Venn tactics. They also gave his individual commanders a chance to test their own ideas. And always Jeje in the *Vixen* stitched her way between them; during the most recent battle Inda realized he was no longer signaling her. She always seemed to know when he wanted to shift from ship to ship, and even where he'd want to go next.

His prisoner remained silent on deck, looking pained when she saw the lazy smoke rising skyward from the burning ships. But she said nothing, for she always saw survivors paddling northward. He even gave her a glass so that she might always look for herself, a gesture that strengthened the light, a mere gleam, on her lonely chosen path.

And strengthened the bloom of new emotion in her heart.

Inda often stood on the captain's deck, frowning as he swept the seas through his glass.

The Venn surely knew by now that he was attacking their raiders. So why had someone not come to find Signi? Did they believe she was dead? Or was there another reason, relating to why her scout ship had been alone in the first place?

The fact that he never again saw a raider pack separated

like Signi's had been added to his conviction that he had not made his capture by stealth and cleverness so much as by total accident—through a set of circumstances outside of his comprehension.

And it was only through accident that she had lived. He speculated on what value she might hold to the Venn. Perhaps they changed all their spells, so that Signi no longer knew the current ones, much like sides in a conflict change codes and signals after the capture of a captain.

He watched Signi when she walked the deck—he watched how she tried to be unobtrusive, with those quiet, smooth movements, the soundless step. But she couldn't be. Even the way she placed her feet was compelling, almost like a dance.

The woman did not talk, except to Fibi, and a little to Gillor. She kept her space neat, she was self-effacing, interfering with no one. They had given her the purser's cabin, so, to the wardroom's unspoken relief, Inda moved back into his own cabin, where his occasional nightmares and incoherent shouts—about which no one told him—no longer could startle anyone out of their sleep.

And so they fought their way westward.

After the last sea battle, they smelled the change of season on the wind, which no longer drove out of the east with the sting of ice. Inda and his fleet raced west, passing at last from Idayago to the peninsula of Olara, called The Prick by most sailors. Their goal was to make it to the peninsula's tip, generally known as the Nob, before the winds swung around to the southwest in their teeth. When the summer west winds began to blow, Inda spoke of spending the season fighting raiders down the west coast. They could then pass through the Narrows after harvest time and winter at Pirate Island. They could be at Freeport Harbor by next summer, to see what Dhalshev had raised for them there.

Fox said nothing about their proximity to Iasca Leror. He and Inda had shared an undeclared truce on the subject ever since Fox's rescue in Ymar, when they'd talked during their long journey, Inda telling him the story of his life. It had been a relief for Inda to talk at last. Fox knew the academy's place in a Marlovan's life, and asked no awkward questions. His freely expressed invective—his contempt for the Sierlaef and the Harskialdna—made Inda laugh.

It was good to hear him laugh again.

As for the new plan, Fox did not care. One plan was as good as another. And the rest of the fleet agreed.

Chapter Thirty-four

D^{AWN.}
A storm moved out of the south under a sky
streaked with spectacular layers of cloud: high, white-
crystal feathers drifting out of the east; the storm layer
tumbling in cold, wet, gray boulders toward the north. With
first light came a brief lull in the storm.

The lookout stared westward in shock.

"Deck! Lights west off the bow! Venn warships!"

Those not busy with tasks ran forward, and yes, there between bands of rain was a string of lights, in exact formation. And as everyone on deck waited, the only sounds the
plap-plap of raindrops off rigging and sails and blocks, the
creak of wood, the cry came, "It's Venn—three, maybe
four. Can't see beyond that. Got pockets o' rain out there!"

Save for one or two covert glares of distrust in the direction of Inda's prisoner, everyone watched Inda.

Warships—in the west. Maybe they'd taken the Nob—

No speculation. Inda needed facts.

Inda said, "Signal *Vixen* and *Rippler*. I want to know how
many and where they're headed."

He was vaguely aware of Signi vanishing below as he
dashed into his cabin and snapped out the chart of the Nob.

Fox ran into Inda's cabin, tousled from sleep, his eyes
wide and manic in the lamplight. "Want me to go below
and strangle the truth out of your dag spy?"

"Strangle what out of her?" Tau asked, right behind him. "I don't think she knows anything military. Though I've tried for days to find out. She won't talk to me."

Inda smiled at Tau's rueful expression. It was rare indeed that the candlepower of Tau's looks could not loosen a female tongue. Inda had watched him court Signi over the past week. Or rather, he'd watched Tau try to speak to her, always with the same result: she was polite but elusive.

Fox's face tightened with disdain. "You wouldn't even know what to ask, brickhead."

Tau sighed. "How was I to know it mattered to you what Iascan king that poor sod Vedrid served, or who his army commander is?"

Fox opened his mouth, but Inda raised a hand. "Peace. That was a year ago. And even if we knew who serves Aldren-Harvaldar as Harskialdna, it no longer matters. We're not landing, and they can't field a fleet, which is why we're here in the first place."

Tau and Fox both knew that it did matter—which silenced them on the subject. Fox moved to the stern windows to glare out to sea; Tau made a gesture of apology to Inda.

Just as lightning flared. A moment later thunder crashed, diminishing to the roar of rain on the deck over their heads. No one would be able to see an arm's length in that—friend or foe.

Tau faced Inda. "If you had told me more, perhaps I would have been able to find out more."

"I know that," Inda said, now truly impatient. "It's over. Past is past. We have the Nob nigh, and some sort of Venn fleet. I've got to know what they're doing out there."

Fox said over his shoulder, "You really believe your Venn dag hasn't been sending messages by magic?"

Inda said, "She gave her parole."

There was no reply to be made to that, at least nothing of use. After a time Fox left without speaking, and Tau said, "Anything I can do?"

"Make certain no one harasses her. I'm going to grab some sleep while I can."

It seemed he'd scarcely shut his eyes when a hand shook

his shoulder. Pilvig shrilled in excitement, "It's a *long* string of lights, *Vixen* reported."

"What? What?" Inda didn't pause to ask, but ran up to the deck, his breath streaming away northward.

Fox was there, his eyes marked with tiredness. He handed Inda the glass, and Inda peered into the blue darkness that was already swallowing the east under the on-coming clouds of another storm. In the west a sultry red ball sank below the horizon.

There to the south lay the line of the Olaran peninsula, ending abruptly at the Nob; its line was already blending into the gathering darkness. Beyond it, spaced with precision across the northwest, clear in the sharp, clean air, stretched a line of twinkling lights, moving with the current. Though Inda could not see where that line ended, he had a sense that it stretched far to the west. At least nine, maybe more. They'd sailed right into a fleet maneuver.

"They'll have the wind by tomorrow, if not tonight," Fox said. "Look at the clouds."

"They've spotted us!" Mutt yelled from above. "They're hauling over—flanking us."

The fleet tacked in beautiful formation, towers of square sail billowing as they prepared to give chase.

Inda knew they'd seen one another at the same time. "Helm up," he said. "Signal for all ships to ready the lights-out ruse."

He stayed on deck, watching his fleet bear up and head south ahead of that vast fleet. The Venn now had studding sails extended to the sides, making formidable towers of sail; they were tacking against the wind, which his own tri-angular fore-and-aft sails loved.

Inda's fleet sailed toward the land, pushed by the shift-ing winds. Then, when the next band of rain hit, obscuring everything, one by one Inda's fleet doused their lights, hauled over and sped on the wind, lightless and quiet, back to the north—using the bad weather to obscure them as they slipped between the pursuing Venn ships.

At midnight Inda returned to his cabin to get some rest. He emerged again just before dawn, and stood at the rail of his dark ship—no lights anywhere—one hand warding rain from his face, the other pressing the glass to his eye as he watched the graceful prow of the last Venn ship plunge southward. It was maybe twenty-five ship-lengths away, though the glass brought it uncomfortably close. Lights all along the Venn ship outlined its splendid form as its crew tended the towering sails, square all save the spanker aft of the mizzenmast. Lookouts at the masthead, barely visible in the reflected light of their glowglobes, seemed to be watching eastward, from which direction Inda's fleet had sailed the day before. There was no sign of awareness from the Venn, but Inda felt his heart thumping.

"I tried to count them," Fox said, a vague silhouette next to him. "Bearing up into the wind has slowed them to a crawl. They tacked and tacked all night. That and the rain made counting difficult, but I think there are more than twenty."

"A Battlegroup," Inda said as rain roared abruptly, the drops splashing nearly up to knee height, and once again the Venn were obscured. "A Battlegroup protecting the raiders, maybe? Or are they going to take the Nob, despite the Marlovans holding everything below the peninsula?"

Fox gave the back of his hand to the distant ships.

The rain lifted for a few moments, and Inda pressed his eye to the glass, impatiently wiped at steam, then peered again. When the elegantly arched row of stern windows had dwindled to a vague shape against the distant headland of Olara, Inda dropped below to get a meal.

He was halfway through his second biscuit with honey butter when Jug came scrambling down into the wardroom, yelling, "It's a trap! It's a trap!"

Inda choked down his food, started away—then lunged back and took the rest of his bread, cramming it down as fast as he could chew as he dashed up on deck.

The wind had gone cold again, a fretful wind from the south, but from the look of the sky, the smell of the air, it could shift east again.

Fox held out his glass.

"Trap?" Inda asked.

"Maybe. But they were already out here," Fox said. "North by west."

Inda gazed northward into the murky gloom and there

saw the faint gleam of lights aloft on two ships, all with the distinctive curved-swan prow of the Venn. He could barely make out a third in the distance. They were all spaced closed together, like the teeth of a comb—

A second line of 'em, coming down to press them against the Battlegroup in the south hard up against Olara! Whatever their original purpose had been, they clearly intended a trap now.

A quiet, accented female voice: "How many be there?"

Fox's lazy drawl did not mask the sharp consonants of anger. "Thinking your parole is inconvenient?"

Everyone stared at Signi standing motionless next to Inda. The woman put her palms together, then opened them, a gesture of peace. As much as he distrusted her, Fox was distracted by the way she moved—never awkward or careless, yet never with the busy artfulness intended to draw attention. She bent her head—a small move curiously dignified—and then walked away, her bare feet leaving ovals on the wet deck. Almost a dance, yet too subdued, too formal for that.

The rustle and tapping of rain worked down the sails to the deck as a new band of clouds slid overhead.

Inda lifted his voice above the roar, "Those cursed gold things might have a use after all! If Jeje still has hers."

When Fox shook his head, Inda pulled him down by his shoulder and shouted in his ear. They couldn't use them for position or navigation but with this strong southern wind and *Vixen*'s unbeatable speed, how about for limited scouting?

Fox flicked his hand open.

Inda cupped his hands around his mouth. "Pilvig! Signal tack in succession, due west, straight out to sea. No lights." Then he dashed down below to find the case that paired with Jeje's and write a note. *Count Venn ships.*

They watched him put it into the case, shut it, say the words that Tau had taught him so carefully. They watched Inda open it again, to see the paper gone.

Inda's fleet headed straight out to sea, in the direction of the Delfin Islands and the unknown lands directly beyond; the swells here were higher, undiminished by the proxim-

ity to land. But somewhere two currents came together, the
southern flow meeting the waters that streamed down
from the north and curved east into the strait, pushed by
that southern current. If the enemy found that intersection
before they did, the currents alone would carry them, no
matter what direction the winds.

Next morning everyone stood on deck, intent on wind,
sky, and water. Rain squalls slanting in the distance obscured the horizon, but at least so far, they had evaded the
two Battlegroups trying to close on them from the north
and south.

Dawn was a gray-blue smear in the east when Jug
screamed from the masthead, "West by southwest—more
Venn!"

A *third* Battlegroup?

The band of rain passed, revealing the oncoming line of
Venn. As the great ships flashed their sails, changing direction for pursuit, Inda gave the command to tack to the
southeast, in hopes of slanting past them. The oncoming
ships would be fast, with the wind hitting them squarely on
the beam.

Jeje's *Vixen* appeared not long after, racing ahead of the
lead three Venn warships, their mighty prows lunging
through the water, sending gray sprays of white to either
side.

The *Vixen* dashed up on the lee.

Jeje did not wait. Inda felt the tingle of magic, opened
the case. The paper was scrawled with *27 north—27 new
ones in west*.

He glanced up at the sails, then slipped quietly into his
cabin. As expected, he found Signi waiting. She sat at the
table, hands clasped tightly. The words that galloped
through his mind vanished when she said, "How many?"

"Aside from the twenty-seven holding the south, there
are the twenty-seven that came out of the north yesterday,
and now a new twenty-seven racing with the wind out of
the southwest."

She stood, pressing her hands together. "Twenty-seven
constitutes a . . . what you would call a Battlegroup." The

lamp swinging back and forth flickered tiny dots of fire from left to right in her huge black pupils.

"I know that," Inda said. "Durasnir's *entire fleet*—the warships, not the coast raiders—is out here, they're not in the east at all! Signi, this is the invasion fleet we're seeing, isn't it? On maneuvers?"

She gave a long sigh. She was dressed in her blue robe again; she had not worn it since the day she gave parole. She seemed more remote.

He stood across from her, the table between them. His gaze met hers. They each felt the impact, physical as well as mental. She heard her own heartbeat over the sound of his breathing; she tried not to look at the neck of his shirt open, the neglected laces hanging loose, the gleam of rain on his chest, as she said, "Yes. It is to be invasion fleet."

"What can you tell me?"

She lifted her eyes. Tears gleamed along the lower lids; her throat worked as she struggled for words.

Inda looked away from her tears, and became aware of the crowd gathering in the cabin door. "Everyone out." He kicked the door shut, his gaze back on the Venn sea dag.

She resumed her place on the bench, her movements neat as always, but she trembled all over.

Inda sat adjacent, trying not to look threatening—like a jailer. Or worse, a torturer. He didn't know where to put his hands, so he dropped them on his knees. "Go ahead," he said, trying not to sound as tense as he was.

"I am go to Sartor. It was plot—" She groped, then switched to Sartoran. "I was to tell the queen, and only the queen, the secrets of our navigation. To help the south. You must see, that though we sea dags made vows to our kingdom, there are a very few of us who were chosen to study the older magics. Far more powerful. I am one. But before we begin such study, we make vows to the world itself, following the Golden Path—" She passed trembling fingers over her face. "I do not know where to begin!"

"With what concerns us now. We can fill in the holes later."

From above came shouts. Inda felt a change in the heel of the ship, and knew that the wind was veering around to the east. That meant the Venn would not have to make much effort to intercept them.

"I believe you must know. Prince Rajnir wants this land, your land, your warriors. The prince has the gold, and the ships, and the Hilda—the army."

Inda opened a hand. "I saw them war gaming in Ymar."

"The Dag Erkric has the will. To do anything to succeed." She paused, studying Inda. She felt heat and light, but warded it with all her strength. "You are seeing practice maneuvers of the fleet—all eighty-one. When the summer winds shift into west they will come. Two Battlegroups to bring over men and army. Their attached raiders protect them. The third Battlegroup, it—"

"—will go down south to attack our coast, right? To divide our forces?"

Neither of them noticed that "our."

She bent her head in acquiescence, and though Inda would swear she hadn't moved anything but her head, her body was evocative of sorrow, of grief.

Inda thumped his fists on his knees. "All right. And you were going to Sartor, what, to warn them? Is that why we found your ship alone? But why do you go against your people?"

She whispered, low and unhappy, "Hyarl Durasnir, he is commanded by the prince to extend the Venn empire here in the south where the sun is warmer and harvests are more abundant. There are those of us who think—who thought—invasion must end, but the king needs land, needs food, and the prince wishes to be the heir again. There are vast problems at home."

Inda rubbed a scar. "I think I want to know about those problems, but not now. So you disagree, and turned against Rajnir?"

"No. We would have obeyed. And sought to limit the taking of life." She made a curious gesture, then turned her small hand over, palm up. Fingers toward Inda, a gesture of appeal. "But there is a greater threat. The Dag has the will, I said. But worse. In secret, trying new kinds of magic, to use in war. There is evidence he would deal with Norsunder. He seeks to find a way to ensorcell minds, so that he can suborn your Marlovans. Make them ride east and conquer Sartor. He wants the entire continent for the Venn."

Inda cursed under his breath, then said, "He'd loose *Norsunder* against us?"

"By magic. He said if he can have the rift you once saw, he will push anyone through that Norsunder wants. And so our Chief Sea Dag ordered me to take my scout ship to Sartor. I tried. We were discovered by some of the crew, and they killed my friends." She shook her head. "It is no matter to you. But you must know this." She raised her hands, her arms and shoulders tight with warning. "If they know I live, and they must, they are chasing me as well as chasing you. They will think you can get navigation secrets from me——and the plans."

Inda's mind ran swiftly. Now it all began to make sense: the empty strait, the orders to all the trade kingdoms to stay close to the land—to regulate themselves, in effect, while Durasnir's elite war fleet concentrated everything on this attack. "I need to know what you can do. I mean right now."

"Navigate, only I dare not use our signs, for they would know our position instantly. They will have wards raised against me using our . . . our methods."

Inda waved a hand. "You can explain all that later. Can you do anything about your ships on our heels?"

She turned her face upward, as though reading something of import on the bulkheads. Then she sighed. "*We* do not use the . . . the black magic, is how it is called in Sartoran. It sends magic out of the world, you see. The candle goes out, for it takes great force to use. Our magic is called light for it must balance—the candle burns. And so there is little I can do."

"So you can't do something like change the wind."

"Oh, I could, but the land would pay a terrible cost for at least a season to come. We dare not disturb the patterns of wind." Then her face changed, her eyes rounding with discovery. "But I can make moisture, for that rises and then falls back into the sea again . . ."

With that she rose swiftly, opened the cabin door, and slipped past those lurking outside. If she even noticed them she made no sign, but gave a quick glance over the bow at the lead Venn ship, which was perhaps twice arrow range, then she ducked down to the waist, her robes belling behind her.

Inda left the cabin as well and walked up onto the deck where he could study the Venn. With his glass he could make out individual sailors on the deck, though not yet the details of faces. He knew the Venn had to be watching his deck. He knew without asking that if Dag Signi was identified, Prince Rajnir's ships would have orders to destroy her, and the vessel she was on.

Fox stood on the captain's deck, watching everyone and everything through narrowed eyes—ready to relay the first command, and the hands divided their attention between Fox and the approaching Venn warship.

Tau had fetched an old cloak with the idea of throwing it over the dag to disguise her from those Venn watchers, but when he reached the companionway and looked down into the waist, he stopped, the bundle clutched in his arms. Below him, Signi began weaving back and forth, eyes closed, voice soft as she began a long singsong chant. Tau and the rest of the crew felt peculiar, as if thunder threatened, as if the insides of their skulls were brushed by hundreds of butterfly wings.

They were amazed to see moisture rise from the waters in curls and puffs, like smoke, like steam. The eddies of vapor swirled together, forming into thin clouds of white softness, which molded into drifting fingers of mist. From the distance they could hear the faint blat of a horn; Inda beckoned to Fox, and mindful of how sound carries, said in a low voice, "Hard over as soon as we lose sight of 'em."

Fox gestured to Fibi, whose hoarse squawk, damped to a hoarse whisper, commanded the sail teams.

Jeje rode on their lee. Inda bent over the rail, and Jeje ran out to the *Vixen*'s pointed bow. Vapor began to obscure her face, not five arm's lengths below him. "Set every sail you have—I want your best speed ever. Go down our line hard over. Make noise for them to follow. Then get away, and meet us east, under Olara. We're heading for Lindeth."

Jeje grinned. The *Vixen* slid away. The jib sails being set blurred into the thickening swirls of white.

From that fog presently came the clatter of buckets on the *Vixen*'s deck, blocks clacking together, and one of Jeje's crew shouting, "Bear up! Bear up!" The sounds diminished northward.

All the while Signi kept casting her spells, until a faint glow seemed to shimmer about her, and she swayed, weak-kneed from effort.

Gillor appeared and helped the mage down the hatch, as around them the mist thickened to fog.

The magic worked. Inda expelled his breath, then drew it in again, a pure, deep breath of extraordinarily heady pleasure. It was akin to that first spring day when the ice is breaking up and one's footing is unsteady. There might be slips, even a fall, but the smell of living green on the air, the warm wind on winter-numb flesh, fills the world with promise. Winter's thaw makes the world new and right again.

Inda's voice was breathless with husky laughter. "Cut straight east."

Fox sent him a sharp look. He thought he had seen the full range of Inda's moods—he had certainly seen more than anyone else—but never this one. "Won't that brings us toward the land?"

Inda laughed again, his eyes wide and manic, his cheeks flushed. "Let's talk," he said.

The two retreated to Inda's cabin.

Inda shut the door, setting his back against it. He smiled, the old smile of the boy of ten. "I'm going home."

Fox's mouth whitened. "You're a damned fool."

Inda laughed again, an unsteady laugh. He shut his eyes, holding his breath. Fox waited in silence.

"Listen," Inda said at last. And told Fox what Signi had said.

Fox heard him out without interruption, then said, "I take it you believe her, that you don't think it's an elaborate ruse."

"Why? To what end? That scout ship full of dead people
ought to have signaled something out of the ordinary to
you, as it did to me. Those weren't foreigners, that was
Venn fighting Venn."

Fox sighed. "So what? You'll go back to the royal city,
tell your war king that there's an invasion coming, and he'll
reward you with a royal execution, satisfying your notion
of 'honor' all around? What form do you think your portion of this honor will take—your back against a wall, or
the criminal's flogging at the post?"

"Fox."

"What do you think happened to Barend?"

"We don't know. Why are you making an argument?
Didn't you tell me about that last letter the Venn king
wrote all those years ago—you quoted it, when we were
sitting on that cliff, watching the Oneli on their war games
that day. Did not the Venn king promise when they did invade, they would come after your family first?"

Fox's lip curled. "As if my mother and sister couldn't
chase off any Venn marauders."

Inda saw it then: Fox did not question Inda's intent, but
his safety. His emotions rolled again, but this time he caught
hold mid-dive. "If you think I'd lose my ass again, then
come with me. Don't you want to see home? I do. I've been
smelling home ever since we were within a day of the Nob.
I kept my promise for nine years. Now I have a reason to go
home. A good enough reason to maybe get me a hearing."

"Inda! There. Is. No. Justice." Fox smacked the table flat-
handed on each word, then straightened up and crossed his
arms. "Forget what I said before, I was half joking. But
half wasn't. It's far more likely your turning up all these
years later will make you into an embarrassing political
problem for Aldren-Harvaldar, if not for his uncle—who
probably controls the kingdom through him. And whatever they say during the day—after all, you are the son of
a prince—your very first night you'll personally experience
the Montrei-Vayir method of solving problems, as old
Savarend did when he crossed the hawse of Anderle-
Harskialdna's ancestor: a knife in the night. It's neat, it's
fast, it's quiet. And it's final."

Inda snorted. "What, did you think I meant to ride up to the throne on a hired horse and throw down my knitted hat as a war banner? Maybe I talk to no one but Barend, if I can find him. If not I send a message, scout the territory. I don't know." Inda looked troubled, then admitted in a rush, "Once I wanted the academy to line up—the Guard—everyone on parade, so the king himself could clear my name. Now I just want, oh, to hear about home."

"So you don't think you're going to walk right back into your old place and take up life as if nothing ever happened, except for everyone cheering madly?" Fox's tone was light, but Inda knew by now when Fox was upset and when he was angry. The two might look and sound the same, but Inda had learned to descry the difference.

Inda flung his arms out. "As what? Surely my brother's got another Randael trained—he's had more time with the new one than he ever had with me. And all the Tveis are long gone home, and yes, I'm sure I'm forgotten. I have no expectations whatsoever. I want to deliver my message, then I'll cut straight south. Meet you at Parayid. How's that?" At Fox's gesture of disgust, "You don't want to come? You're not curious about your own home?"

"No." Fox's voice was so soft Inda almost didn't hear it. "I have no curiosity whatsoever."

Fox's forehead had tightened with anger, but his long mouth was white-lipped with pain, and for once the challenging derision was all gone. "I don't care if Aldren Montrei-Vayir is bad, good, or indifferent as king," Fox said. "The only surety is that nothing has changed for my family, because there is no justice for the Montredavan-Ans." He glared at Inda, listening so patiently, and thought, *if I had half the wit of my ancestors I would have seen a way to grasp events by the throat and force them to my will. As my forefathers did. As you have done, without ever realizing what it is you do.* He shook his head to dispel thoughts he would never utter. "Maybe someday. But not now."

Inda flicked his fingers up toward the captain's deck. "Then it's simple. Take command of my fleet."

Fox crossed his arms, sardonic again. "But then it becomes my fleet."

Inda opened his hands. "Nothing finite is infinite, as m
mother used to say. I will give you one of these gold thing
When I've delivered my message, I send a message where
to meet me, and either you will be there or you won't."

The corners of Fox's mouth deepened. His eyes wer
wide, steady, bright as spring leaves in the lamplight. "Wa
here," he said, and left, shutting the cabin door firmly be
hind him.

Inda stared at the cabin door. *It's a shame*, he thought
Fox—sardonic, deadly, cynical—would not go home to
drunken sot of a father squatting in his tower. *A mistake t
think he doesn't care. He does. He knows he does. And can
abide it.*

There was no time to consider it further; Fox was back
"Hold out your hand."

Inda did, and Fox dropped the two rings onto his palm.

"Won't you need these?" Inda asked.

"I can see my fleet," Fox retorted.

A measure of safety. "Thanks," Inda said.

Signi had made it about five steps before she crumpled i
a silent faint.

Gillor caught her, carried her to her alcove, laid her i
the hammock, and then sat there beside her, as the ship sli
away steadily to safety in the thick magical fog.

Presently Signi's eyes opened, moved from side to side
and Gillor said, "I take it they couldn't fight your fog?"

"Not the sea dags," Signi whispered, her smile pensive
"The spell will strengthen as they try to break it, whic
they will eventually discover. Few know how to break suc
a spell. The Dag Erkric, who could break it, will be with th
prince on the north coast. It ought to mire them a day an
a night, at the least."

Gillor sprang up, batted through the canvas door that the
had hung for her when she ceased being a prisoner—it let i
more air than the old wooden one. Gillor returned wit
water, which Signi downed gratefully. Color came back int
her face, and she sat up. "Ah, so much better. Thank you."

"So they will know that was you."

"Oh, yes."

"What does it mean for us?"

Signi told Gillor what she had told Inda. Gillor listened, nodded, then said, "Lie quiet. I'll bring you something from the galley." She paused at the door, smiling over her shoulder. "I take it magic-making is something like fighting a night-long battle?"

"That much magic is. It is not so much the making of the vapor but the spell that binds attempts to dispel it into making more."

Signi lay watching the lamplight on the wood above her, permitting her mind to range back, back, over a lifetime of decisions. She would not think about the future, except to discover, step by step, what Ydrasal's path demanded.

The door batted aside, and the delicious smell of fresh fish and rice balls wafted in. Signi sat up. Gillor sat on the tiny storage chest as Signi wolfed down the food. When Signi looked up, feeling very much recovered, she saw the woman studying her, head tilted to the side.

"What do you look for?" she asked.

"For the future," Gillor said. Her Sartoran was accented in a way Signi could not trace. She smiled. "It seems that our commander has decided to beach himself. He's putting on his prince hat again, and going home to tell them what you told us about the invasion. If they don't kill him first."

"Ah," Signi said.

Water slapped the sides of the ship, the wood creaked. The smell of mulled wine wafted through the gently swaying canvas door. From the hold came the sounds of a reed pipe and soft singing, the quick triplets of Sartoran folk music, weaving in and out of minor keys into major.

Signi turned her attention back to Gillor, to meet those steady dark eyes. She felt the hairs along the backs of her arms lift.

"And?"

"And now you have saved us," Gillor said. "And you are in as much danger from the Venn as we."

Signi felt her palms go damp. "You tell me what I know. Why is this?"

"Because you don't know, though you should, that while he was in the galley, Fibi and I and a couple of the others unfolded the old bed from under the stern windows."

Signi's nerves prickled with fire sparks.

"Right now he is alone there, in the cabin—and I don't think he's even noticed the bed. Yet." Pause, sigh, then a last try. "He's going home after we don't know how many years. But what he asks after is you: *is she recovered? Does she need anything?* Dag Signi, go to him."

Signi licked her lips. So the attraction was perceivable, at least to some. "It is not right."

"Was not right. Though that is a matter of debate. When you've been a pirate, you learn that 'right' varies not only from person to person, but from moment to moment. Sudden death can do that." Gillor laughed. "He is kind, and passionate, and if you are kind and passionate back, good!"

"He might not want me. He is much young."

To that Gillor made a rude noise, and so Signi, her heart beating fast, rose, and washed her face in clear water, and then trod barefoot, lightly, to the cabin door. No one was about; she knocked, and heard his voice: "Enter."

She laid her hand on the latch and walked in, to find him sitting alone at the table before his charts—and yes, behind him spread a luxurious bed, fit for a pirate king.

She turned her attention to the papers on the table, and then to the man who had made them. His gaze was not the gaze of the commander working out his plans, it was the gaze of a young man overwhelmed in the whirlpools of emotional turmoil.

Ydrasal . . .

She touched his warm hand and felt the shock of desire that kindled inside her. And him.

They did not have to speak at all.

The sun was setting when they woke, mellow golden light slanting from the west through the stern windows as they sailed under the long Olaran peninsula toward Lindeth Harbor. Inda studied her features: the curve of her brows, the crease in her eyelids, a strand of sandy hair lying stuck to her cheek from the aftermath of passion. Wonder seized him, and on impulse he kissed her.

The ardent steadiness in her gaze rekindled his own fire, burning all thought to cinders as his hands drifted over her warm skin. This time love was slow, languorous, deliberate, spiraling hard down into a white fire as intense as before.

At last they lay side by side again, the rosy slants of fading light painting over their flesh, each listening to the other's breathing.

She said, "What would you do?"

"Do?" he asked, lazily twining a finger through her hair, which was unexpectedly fine.

"When war threat is done. When you have freedom."

Inda lay back and permitted his mind to wheel the sublime currents high above all the troubles of the world, and he smiled, and said, "I would go home. I wish I could show you Tenthen Castle. It—"

He looked down, and flushed, and she thought in anguish how very young he was.

Her gaze was so steady and intense he wondered what was going on in her mind, and then a terrible thought occurred. "Is that damned ghost still here? Watching, um, us?" Embarrassment and disgust cramped his middle.

Signi raised her head a little more, brow puckered as she focused into the air above Inda. Then her face changed, and she sat up in the broad bed, paying no attention to the falling of the sheet away from her breasts; she raised her hands, cupped them and held them out as she spoke in Venn.

It was too quick for him to follow. "Were you *talking* to the ghost? What did you say?"

Her mouth curved in a sad smile. "I said: *Bide and be welcome. If you can feel joy, it is mine to give and yours to share.* He is young like you, far too young. How much love did he get to share before he was taken out of life?"

Inda's annoyance vanished as he contemplated for the first time a generosity that transcended petty human emotion, and embraced not just the body and mind but the spirit.

His eyelids prickled as he looked into her face lit by the ruddy gold of the setting sun, the faint lines of laughter and sorrow carved around eyes and mouth, her steady green-brown eyes; he heard again the benevolence in her voice as she offered to share joy with a dead spirit who was denied the warmth of living flesh, and he felt a strange hollow behind his ribs. The world had changed. No. *He* had changed; quick as that, he thought, I am in love.

Chapter Thirty-five

ONE bell past sunrise Nightingale Toraca met his local eyes and ears upstairs in a new inn high on the Nob's ridge, so new it smelled sharply of fresh-planed wood. The young Runner shook raindrops off her hair, sat down and began weaving hemp and leddas together into rope as she spoke. "Harbormaster says that the Venn are all sailing north. The battle must have been out to sea. There were at least eighteen of 'em! Two blue-skiffs went out far as they dared, and our cliff lookouts, they all reported in with the same sighting: when the great fog cleared, the Venn were retreating to the north."

"Then . . . there was a sea battle?" Nightingale asked.

She shrugged. "That's what they say."

"So they saw arrow flames, burning ships?"

"No, rain was too hard. But what else could there be, if all the Venn go north, except a retreat?"

Nightingale signified agreement, but reserved doubts. In his experience, civilians mistook skirmishes for major battles, and clashes with no result as definitive.

On the other hand these were sea folk, and he knew nothing about the sea and ships. He frowned, considering how to word his new report. The harbor city had been tense for two days of intermittent storms as reports came in, first of a sighting of a long line of Venn ships from the cliff-top lookouts, then from the daring fisher craft who plied the seas below the tip of the peninsula, their sides and sails painted blue to help hide them from the Venn. They had not only corroborated the sighting of Venn warships, they had brought the news of Elgar the Fox's black pirate ship sailing straight into battle.

Then nothing, nothing, nothing, as the blue-painted craft ventured farther out. And at last came report of a mysterious smoke—no, a fog—spreading out across the ocean in a long white worm of a line, a fog that did not dissipate even in the rains.

And here was the latest news.

"So if there was a battle, Elgar the Fox must have won," Nightingale said.

"Yes, and speaking of him, the black ship that Elgar the Fox commands has been sighted, right at dawn, heading east."

"Inland. Toward Lindeth?" Nightingale asked, astonished.

"They will welcome him with joy—he drove off all those ships—the blue-skiffs swear it was more like thirty of 'em out there. Maybe even more!" the Runner replied, grinning in triumph. She looked around, then said, "I had better get to the shop before they notice how long I've been gone. Mistress Lagit doesn't hate Marlovans, but she is nosy."

"Then you must get back at once," he agreed.

Nightingale watched her go. The one good thing about a city being rebuilt was that they needed workers, and not everyone knew everyone else. He'd been able, over the past year, to place young Runners-in-training to observe for the king in every harbor along the coast. They all had other jobs, so no one knew they were Marlovan Runners.

He sighed, thinking of the long journey ahead of him, riding to visit all his Runners once he found out the new orders. If there were any new orders. The Venn, driven north!

He remembered his last report, the grim news that the lines of Venn had been sighted, and everyone in the Nob was arming, preparing for yet another attack on the harbor. Now, for once, he could write the king some good news. A short message via the locket, and his fastest riders with a more detailed report. It had been far too long.

*   *   *

On the plains half a morning's ride from the royal city, Evred-Harvaldar was galloping west, two outriders behind him, pennons streaming. He rode without a helm, his outward intention to watch the first war game of the season, his inward intention to escape his anger at the impending attack on the Nob, an attack he was helpless to do anything about.

He considered throwing away the lockets altogether. What was the good of faraway news you could do absolutely nothing about before it was too late? But he did not. Instead, he spent as much time as possible at his desk to speed the watches and then decided on this ride.

His father had written in his private papers, *The boys must never know, but to watch them is to earn a rare laugh. So like pups they are! But my father was right about one thing, if few others: do not go often, or the effect of your presence is lessened.*

Evred had left his chain mail behind, and his gauntlets and the helm that marked him as the king, as well as all but two of the royal entourage, so in practice he would be invisible, though he remembered well that royal invisibility was merely a matter of degree of royal notice.

The air smelled wet, like new grass, a clean smell that lifted his heart, and cleared from it, for a time, the tensions of council and Horsebutt Tya-Vayir's new, arrogant demands. The fifteen-year-old boys nicknamed ponies riding the camp perimeter straightened up when they spied the banner, and already Evred was repressing laughter. How strange, to find himself in this older body now, when memory threw him so readily back to his scrub days and how they had watched anxiously for the king. At the memory of his father a pang of grief smote him, but these were easier to bear now.

Headmaster Gand was there, overseeing the setting up of camp, and oh, how Evred remembered all the chores, the horse pickets, the cooking, the tent-rigs! Boys were busy everywhere, new-shorn scrubs running about until they were aware of him, then sedulously going about their business, every line of their small bodies indicative of self-consciousness.

Evred rode along the campsite, caught Gand's eye, saw the deepened corners of the old dragoon's tough mouth—not a smile, never that, but Evred recognized humor just the same, and fractionally lifted a hand. Officially there was no notice from king to headmaster, but Evred knew the boys would speculate on the meaning of his visit faster than he could ride by. Just as he had as a scrub the rare times his father had visited.

It was good to see order, to see things as they had been—it boded well for the future. Unless that was mere wish being taken for truth.

Tap. The locket!

Evred rode by, but he no longer saw the horsetails busy with the horses or the pigtails at their chores.

He finished his circuit, and then started back, the outriders behind him; with one hand he fetched out the locket and flicked it open, his fingers catching the little paper before the wind could whip it away.

With one hand he unrolled it, read it, read it again.

The sea battle scarcely registered: what drove residual anger entirely out of his mind and set his heart to drumming were the words *I. ship sighted sailing twd. L.H.*

Evred looked up, his emotions fierce, but just as fiercely he quashed them.

Inda's ship was sailing toward Lindeth Harbor—two weeks' ride from the Nob. Much, much farther from here. Inda might land, but he would be gone again before any message could reach him.

Too many disappointments made Evred wary, almost angry at that sudden surge of unreasoning hope, and so he did his best to dismiss conjecture—and his own reaction. He would keep himself busy. It wasn't as if he did not have plenty to do.

                          *   *   *

Inda stood on the deck of the *Death*. He'd signaled *All captains*, and so they lined the lee rail, Iasca Leror behind them in the east, obscured by bands of rain from the passing storm.

They were silent after Signi's unexpected announcement: "Do not go into the harbor."

Fox sent her a fast glance, eloquent in its distrust. Signi's face was troubled.

Gillor said, "Why not? Is all that stuff about kings and assassins true, then?"

"It is not the Marlovan king. We—the Venn—have watchers there. They will know this vessel."

Inda said, "Do they have magic communications?"

Signi turned her face toward him, relieved he wasn't angry with her, though she could sense in their quick, inadvertent movements and shuffles the angry reactions from the crew. "Yes and no. It is not what you think. The observers write reports. It is a mage-prentice job to transfer to a hidden place, then travel along and collect their reports. Then transfer back to Ymar, or wherever the Dag commands."

"So, what, the Venn have spies among us?"

Gillor's eyes flicked at the "us." Even though the conversation was in Sartoran-laced Dock Talk, it was clear that their commander had already made the inward shift back to his homeland.

"Yes."

"How good, how recent, is the news?"

Signi looked very uncomfortable. She said in a slow, reluctant undertone, "It is good. I know much of events in this land, for we have had watchers there since the fall of Idayago."

Inda turned up his thumb. "All right, then, the harbor is out. We'll land somewhere along the coast to the south."

"I'm going with you," Jeje stated. "If you're going to face some king, then you'll need someone to watch your back o' nights."

I'm going with you. Tau had never felt so exquisite a pain. He did not delve for reasons, just spoke, once again—

as aboard the flagship, before the Brotherhood attack so long ago—hearing his own voice as something entirely outside of himself. "And I," his voice said, "will watch it of days."

Inda gave him a distracted glance. "I appreciate the offer, but do you understand? I'm going inland—to the royal city—not just to Lindeth Harbor."

Fox smiled mockingly, but said nothing.

"Wherever you go." Jeje crossed her arms. "Because you need looking after."

Everyone on deck laughed, but she just stood there glowering.

"I won't argue," Inda said. "Since *Death* can't drop us at Lindeth, we'll take the *Vixen* down the coast and land at some inlet where the Venn don't have spies."

"And we can continue down south, lead any pursuit away," Fox said. "I don't believe the entire Venn fleet is conveniently running north because of a fog bank."

"I'm sure they don't want to be late to their invasion," Dasta said.

There was a mild laugh at this, but the humor did not last long. Everyone imagined the huge fleet traveling north to load up with the Venn invasion force, to return as soon as they had the western wind they'd need to drive those loaded, heavy ships back across the strait.

Tcholan said, "We'll probably see raider packs, is my guess. Soon's they figure out—or nosers tell 'em—which way we went. They'll want to stop us if they can." And turned up a hand in agreement.

Inda slung his dunnage up over his shoulder.

"Well, then." Fox was unsmiling.

Inda faced him. For a moment they stood there, wind fingering their hair and clothing, Fox defiant in pose. There was nothing really to say. The two had spent most of the night before over the charts, drinking mulled wine as Inda rambled on about what he would do next in this or that contingency, and Fox listened but said little.

Now the fleet captains stood against the lee rail, watching. They and the *Death*'s crew seemed to expect at least words, if not a gesture, the way their eyes tracked between the old leader and the new. The crew had accepted the change of command with typical seagoing practicality. Fox had commanded single ships, and had run weapons drills; they respected his fists and his sharp tongue as well as his skill.

It wasn't the change of command so much as how it was done that seemed so strange. The old pirates found a peaceful transfer of power difficult to believe. Inda's people expected nothing else, but did not like to see Inda going off again.

"We'll be back," Inda said finally. "We're only carrying the news. We still have the Venn fleet to fight."

Fox opened a hand. It could have meant anything.

And so Inda led the way over the side, followed by the others, Tau last, Fox laughing silently at how some of the women watched Tau depart, their faces sober, though Tau did not look back.

Then the Fisher brothers sheeted the *Vixen*'s long curved sail home. It filled with wind and the privateers watched their old commander carried to the southeast, the lovely little craft slanting as it picked up speed. On the *Death*'s foremasthead, Mutt clung to the shrouds, his eyes blurred with tears.

From the captain's deck Fox watched the *Vixen* dwindle into a sliver against the land, and then he raised his hand. "Let's give our Venn friends ashore something to spy on and report to the chief snakes, shall we?"

The captains returned to their ships.

And so, guided by Fibi's squawk, the *Death* raised every sail that could draw wind, tacking coastward under the black-and-gold fox banner.

As for those on the *Vixen,* the wind soon brought them the scents of land, familiar scents that evoked in Jeje, Tau, and Inda so many childhood memories. They watched the shoreline grow as Loos slanted them southward, tacking against the currents.

"What we can do is this," Inda finally said. "Jeje, you can

keep your gold thing. I've got its mate with the others." He shook his gear bag, from which came the muted clatter of gold cases. "If I need the *Vixen*, I can signal you."

She shook her head. "I said I'm coming, and that means on land."

Inda grimaced. "I appreciate the offer, but trusty as you are in battle you can't really ward a whole army. If Aldren-Harvaldar wants me dead, he has an entire kingdom to see to it."

"Evred-Harvaldar," Signi said softly.

Inda almost didn't hear her. "You were wonderful in Bren, and I wouldn't ask—" He had been talking to Jeje, whose arms were crossed, her face stubborn. He turned sharply on Signi. "What did you say?"

Signi stepped back, startled by this unfamiliar voice, the intensity of his gaze. "You did not know? The king is named Evred. The second son of Tlennen-Harvaldar. It is so for at least a year."

"Evred," Inda repeated, the words, *Why didn't you tell me?* forming in his throat, but the name was a mere name to Signi. To Tau. To Jeje.

He let out a long sigh, then dug his palm heels into his eyes. They knew that gesture. But when he looked up he was smiling, a smile they had so rarely seen, a smile of unshadowed joy as his entire being filled with sunlight.

"I take it this news alters our plans?" Tau asked.

"Yes. And no," Inda said, turning that smile toward the land. "It doesn't change the news we carry to the king." Then he faced them again, the happiness breaking into laughter. "But it does change how we get it to him."

Sherwood Smith

Inda

"A powerful beginning to a very promising series by a writer who is making her bid to be a major fantasist. By the time I finished, I was so captured by this book that it lingered for days afterward. I had lived inside these characters, inside this world, and I was unwilling to let go of it. That, I think, is the mark of a major work of fiction…you owe it to yourself to read *Inda*." -Orson Scott Card

INDA

0-7564-0422-2

New in Paperback!

THE FOX

0-7564-0483-3

Now Available in Hardcover

THE KING'S SHIELD

0-7564-0500-7

To Order Call: 1-800-788-6262

www.dawboks.com

Patrick Rothfuss
THE NAME OF THE WIND
The Kingkiller Chronicle: Day One

"It is a rare and great pleasure to come on some-body writing not only with the kind of accuracy of language that seems to me absolutely essential to fantasy-making, but with real music in the words as well.... Oh, joy!"   —Ursula K. Le Guin

"Amazon.com's Best of the Year...So Far Pick for 2007: Full of music, magic, love, and loss, Patrick Rothfuss's vivid and engaging debut fantasy knocked our socks off."   —Amazon.com

"One of the best stories told in any medium in a decade. Shelve it beside *The Lord of the Rings* ...and look forward to the day when it's mentioned in the same breath, perhaps as first among equals."   —*The Onion*

"[Rothfuss is] the great new fantasy writer we've been waiting for, and this is an astonishing book."   —Orson Scott Card

0-7564-0474-1

To Order Call: 1-800-788-6262
www.dawbooks.com

DAW 111

The Novels of

Tad Williams

To Order Call: 1-800-788-6262
www.dawbooks.com

DAW 102

Kristen Britain

The **GREEN RIDER** series

"Wonderfully captivating...a truly enjoyable read." —Terry Goodkind

"A fresh, well-organized fantasy debut, with a spirited heroine and a reliable supporting cast." —*Kirkus*

"The author's skill at world building and her feel for dramatic storytelling make this first-rate fantasy a good choice." —*Library Journal*

"Britain keeps the excitement high from beginning to end, balancing epic magical battles with the humor and camaraderie of Karigan and her fellow Riders." —*Publishers Weekly*

GREEN RIDER   0-88677-858-1
FIRST RIDER'S CALL   0-7564-0209-3
and now available in hardcover:
THE HIGH KING'S TOMB 0-7564-0209-3

To Order Call: 1-800-788-6262
www.dawbooks.com